BRANCHES OF THE BROKEN WORLD

THE SKYREND PROPHECY BOOK ONE
JOSHUA J. WHITE

BERSERKER BOOKS

Stay Connected with Joshua J. White

Before you begin...

If you're drawn to myth, mystery, and stories that echo long after the final page,
I invite you to join me on the journey ahead.

This world — and the ones that follow — are part of something much larger. By
joining my mailing list, you'll get early access to new books, hidden lore, exclusive
behind-the-scenes notes, and the occasional dispatch from the quiet woods where
I write.

Sign up here: www.JoshuaJWhiteBooks.com/TheSkyrendProphecy

No noise. No spam. Just stories worth sharing!

— Joshua J. White

Author & Founder, Berserker Books

CONTENTS

PROLOGUE

The black-iron shears hung heavy in Skuld's palm. Cold metal kissed her skin as she clutched the forbidden tool, the weight of it crushing against her bones like the burden of what she was about to do. Frost crept along the curved blades, leaving delicate white patterns that cracked and reformed with each trembling breath she took. The other Norns stood in silence beside her, their bone-white masks gleaming in the half-light beneath Yggdrasil's canopy.

"The threads grow too tangled," she whispered, her voice muffled behind her own mask's frozen lips. "The Allfather binds us still."

Verdandi pressed a hand to Skuld's shoulder, fingers digging into the fur-lined cloak with unexpected strength. "You speak of severing fate itself. Once cut, these threads can never be rewoven." Firelight glinted in the narrow eyeholes of her mask—a face frozen in a permanent laugh that masked the grim set of her true mouth beneath.

Above them, Yggdrasil's branches creaked against the void. The World Tree stretched across realities, its limbs heavy with stars and realms. Skuld could feel its roots beneath her feet, pulsing with ancient blood that flowed through channels older than gods. Here, at the nexus of its three greatest roots, they had built their circle of runestones. Nine stones for nine realms, each carved with sigils that glowed with a sickly blue light.

"I've seen what comes," Skuld said, tracing the edge of the shears with her thumb. A bead of blood welled where the blade bit her skin. "I've watched it unravel a thousand times. The gods grow cruel in their certainty. Fate has made them monstrous."

The third Norn, Urd, stood at the edge of their stone circle. Unlike her sisters, her mask showed a face locked in cold contemplation. The eldest. The wisest. The most dangerous.

"The price will be terrible," Urd said. Her fingers worked through the strands of her weaving, nimble despite her age. Fate-threads shimmered between her hands, woven into patterns so complex that looking directly at them made Skuld's eyes water. "Realms will break. The Tree will scream."

"And what becomes of us?" Verdandi asked, her voice thin against the wind that howled through Yggdrasil's branches. "Fate made us tend its loom."

Skuld looked up at the tangle of stars and branches above. Souls traveled those paths, the dead and the living, the gods and their servants, all bound by weaves set in motion at the dawn of time. Her sisters had spent eternity maintaining these patterns, but Skuld—whose domain was what-must-be—had seen the corruption festering at the pattern's end.

"We become broken things," she answered. "But broken things may yet be free."

Urd sighed, a sound like winter settling into ancient bones. "Then let us begin. The Allfather's ravens circle closer each night."

The three Norns formed a triangle around the runestones. From inside her robes, Skuld drew forth a skein of thread woven from starlight and shadow. It pulsed between her fingers, warm and alive. The fate-thread of Yggdrasil itself—painstakingly unraveled from the great loom over centuries while the gods waged their petty wars.

Verdandi knelt and pressed her palms against the frozen earth. "I call upon what-is-becoming," she intoned. The ground beneath her fingers cracked open, revealing glowing roots that writhed like serpents. They curled around her wrists, binding her to the ritual.

Urd raised her ancient hands to the sky. "I summon what-has-been." The stars above them shifted, constellations bleeding into fresh forms that no mortal had ever witnessed. The eldest Norn's body trembled as memories of creation itself flowed through her.

Skuld stepped forward, the iron shears extended before her. "I embrace what-must-not-be."

She plunged the shears into the center of their circle. The metal struck stone with a sound like a dying god's final breath. Blue fire erupted from the impact, crawling up the blades and over her hands. Skuld gasped as the fire burned cold instead of hot, freezing her flesh where it touched.

"With these shears forged in Muspelheim's heart and cooled in Niflheim's depths," she chanted, "I sever the root that binds fate to form."

The world held its breath. Yggdrasil's branches ceased their eternal swaying. In the silence, Skuld could hear the heartbeats of her sisters, the distant howls of wolves that pursued the sun, and beneath it all, the quiet humming of the threads that bound reality together.

She opened the shears wide. The fate-thread of Yggdrasil lay across the blades, pulsing with the light of countless souls.

"Sister, wait." Verdandi's voice cracked. "There must be another way."

Urd shook her head, the movement barely perceptible. "There is not. I have searched every thread. Every possibility." Her ancient voice dropped to a whisper. "Cut it, Skuld. Cut it now, before my courage fails."

Skuld's fingers tightened around the handles of the shears. Frost crept up her arms, locking her joints with icy fire. One cut. One moment. The end of eternity's chains.

"I free us all," she whispered and closed the blades.

The thread parted with a sound too small for such a catastrophe—a quiet snip that belied the cataclysm it unleashed. For a heartbeat, nothing changed.

Then Yggdrasil screamed.

The sound came from within the very fabric of existence. It tore through Skuld's body, vibrating in her bones and blood. She fell to her knees, the shears tumbling from nerveless fingers. The World Tree convulsed above them, its mighty limbs thrashing against the cosmos.

"What have we done?" Verdandi cried, her mask cracking down the middle, splitting the frozen laugh into jagged halves.

The ground beneath them buckled. Roots burst from the soil, whipping through the air like wounded serpents. One massive root—thicker than a mountain's base—tore free from the earth entirely. It rose like a leviathan, dark soil raining from its writhing form. At its tip, Skuld saw a gaping wound where they had severed its connection to fate. Golden sap poured from the injury, each drop burning with the light of a fallen star as it splashed against the ground.

Urd crawled toward her sisters, her ancient body moving with sudden, desperate strength. "The fragments," she gasped. "We must—"

Her words vanished as a shockwave exploded outward from the Tree. It caught the three Norns and hurled them across the clearing. Skuld slammed against a stone, the impact driving the breath from her lungs. Through blurred vision, she saw the runestones uprooted, spinning through the air like leaves in a tempest.

The sky above split open. Through the rent in reality, Skuld glimpsed other realms—Midgard, Asgard, Jotunheim—all convulsing as Yggdrasil's pain transferred across branches and roots. Flames erupted across the gap, fire unlike any she had seen before. It burned with shadow instead of light, consuming the edges of reality itself.

"The anchors," she croaked, forcing herself to her feet. Blood streamed from beneath her cracked mask. "We must reach the anchors before the Tree falls completely."

Verdandi staggered to her side, clutching her shattered arm to her chest. "The roots separate. Already, they had forgotten what they once were."

Above them, branches thick as mountains splintered. The sound was deafening—wood older than time itself breaking apart, each crack sending shockwaves across the cosmos. Stars fell like rain as sections of Yggdrasil collapsed inward, crushing entire worlds beneath their weight.

Urd had not risen. The eldest Norn lay where she had fallen, her ancient eyes fixed on the catastrophe above. "The fragments will seek vessels," she murmured. "The tree will try to remember itself."

Skuld knelt beside her. "Sister—"

"No." Urd gripped Skuld's wrist with surprising strength. "Listen closely. The roots still live, though severed. Five anchors where they plunge deepest into the realms. Find them. Bind them. Before the void claims what remains."

A massive branch crashed to the ground nearby, the impact throwing them into the air once more. Skuld rolled across frozen earth, coming to rest at the edge of a newly formed chasm. Heat billowed from its depths—the fires of creation exposed as reality tore itself apart.

When she looked back, Urd was gone. Where the eldest Norn had lain, only her mask remained, split perfectly down the middle.

"Verdandi!" Skuld screamed against the roar of destruction. "Sister!"

Through the chaos, she glimpsed Verdandi limping toward the wounded root. The middle sister's hands glowed with fading power as she pressed them against the severed end, trying to stem the flow of golden sap. It was futile—like trying to hold back the tide with cupped hands.

The root gave a final, violent shudder. With a sound that would haunt Skuld until the end of her days, it tore completely free of Yggdrasil's trunk. Verdandi, still clinging to its surface, vanished as the massive root plummeted through layers of reality.

Skuld stood alone amidst the ruins of all they had tended. The shears lay at her feet, their blades now dull and ordinary. She picked them up, feeling their weight—so much lighter now that they had fulfilled their purpose.

"Five anchors," she whispered, clutching the tools of destruction against her chest. "Five Wardens to find them."

Above her, Yggdrasil continued to fracture, its mighty form breaking into segments that fell across the nine realms like dying stars. The Tree that had bound all worlds together was coming undone, and with it, the fate of gods and mortals alike.

Skuld removed her mask and cast it into the abyss. Her face, exposed to the chaos of unbound reality, felt the sting of possibilities never meant to exist. She had cut the thread. She would bear witness to what followed.

The final root gave way beneath her feet, and Skuld fell with it, plummeting toward an uncertain destiny in worlds that would never be the same.

***

Asvarr's axe cleaved through shield and shoulder in a single strike. Blood sprayed across his face, hot and metallic on his tongue. He roared, the sound tearing from deep in his chest, primal and savage. The raid had gone sour. What should have been a simple pillage of the coastal settlement had turned into a bloodbath when they discovered the village harbored twice the warriors they'd expected.

His berserker rage narrowed the world to blood and steel, and flesh. The faces of his enemies blurred into targets, their screams mere background to the thundering of his heart. Asvarr spun, blocking a sword thrust with his axe haft before driving his shield's metal rim into his attacker's throat. The man dropped, hands clutching the crushed windpipe.

"Back to the boats!" Hakon bellowed from somewhere behind him. "They've flanked us at the ridge!"

Asvarr ignored the command. Three more village defenders rushed him, their spears leveled at his chest. He knocked the first aside, caught the second just below the blade with his bare hand, and wrenched it from the wielder's grip. The third spear grazed his side, tearing through leather and skin. Pain flared, bright and clarifying.

Hakon's meaty hand clamped onto his shoulder. "Are you deaf and mad? I said retreat!"

Asvarr whirled, snarling into the bearded face of his raid-leader. "Since when do wolves run from sheep?"

"Since the sheep outnumber us three to one and have reinforcements coming from the south." Hakon's bushy eyebrows drew together, emphasizing the fresh gash across his forehead. "Your death-wish can wait for another day."

They stood on a bluff overlooking the small farming village. Smoke billowed from burning thatch roofs, and the screams of the wounded mingled with the clash of iron. Below, Asvarr's fellow raiders were already disengaging, backing toward the shoreline where their longships waited. The tide of battle had clearly turned.

Asvarr spat a mouthful of blood onto the trampled grass. "Fine."

He turned to follow Hakon down the hillside when a strange vibration shuddered through the ground beneath his feet. The sensation crawled up his legs, into his spine, and settled behind his eyes with an uncomfortable pressure. He staggered, suddenly dizzy.

"What trickery is this?" He pressed his palm against his temple, where a high-pitched ringing had begun.

Hakon hadn't noticed, already halfway down the slope. The village defenders hesitated in their pursuit, confused by the raiders' sudden retreat. None of them seemed affected by the strange tremor.

Then Asvarr felt it again—stronger this time. The ground bucked like a wounded beast. Cracks split the earth in jagged lines, radiating outward from where he stood. The high keening in his head grew louder until he could barely think through the noise.

He looked up.

The sky tore open.

It happened in stages, like watching ice fracture under too much weight. First, a single hairline crack appeared in the clear blue expanse—a dark line that should not exist. Then, as if some massive hand pulled from the other side, the crack widened. The edges frayed into tendrils of shadow that writhed like living things.

"Hakon!" Asvarr shouted, but his voice sounded thin and distant to his own ears.

The raid-leader glanced back, his expression changing from annoyance to shock as he saw what was happening above them. Across the battlefield, all fighting ceased as warriors on both sides stared upward, weapons forgotten in limp hands.

Fire erupted from the tear—not the orange-red flames of earthly fire, but something stranger. It burned with shadow instead of light, consuming the sky as it spread. The flames twisted into impossible shapes before collapsing inward, only to explode outward again with greater force.

"Ragnarök," someone whispered nearby, and Asvarr heard the terror in that single word. The end of all things.

A sound followed that defied description—the scream of something too vast to comprehend. It pierced through Asvarr's skull like a white-hot blade, dropping him to his knees. Blood trickled from his ears.

Through watering eyes, he saw a massive shape plummeting through the tear in reality. It resembled an enormous root, thick as a mountain and long enough to span horizons. Golden fluid gushed from its wounded end, each drop burning like liquid starlight as it fell toward the earth.

"Run!" Hakon bellowed, snapping some warriors from their stupor.

Too late.

The first droplet of golden sap struck the ground near the village. The impact released a shockwave that tore through everything in its path. Trees uprooted. Buildings collapsed. The force of the shockwave tossed bodies—both raiders and villagers—through the air like dolls a petulant child discards.

Asvarr dug his fingers into the soil, clinging to the earth as the blast wave reached him. It lifted him regardless, spinning him through a chaos of debris and screaming men. His back slammed against something solid—a boulder or tree trunk—driving the air from his lungs in an explosive gasp.

More impacts followed. Each droplet of sap created another eruption of force, another ripple of destruction across the land. Through the cacophony, Asvarr thought he heard voices speaking in a language that made his teeth ache—ancient words never meant for mortal ears.

He crawled forward on his belly, vision blurred by blood and sweat. His axe was gone. His shield too. Every breath sent knives of pain through his chest where ribs had cracked.

A severed hand lay in the dirt before him, still clutching a knife. Asvarr didn't recognize the rune-marked band on the wrist. He pried the blade free, needing to feel some weapon in his grasp.

The burning sky cast everything in an unnatural light. Shadows stretched and contracted in impossible ways. The air itself felt wrong against his skin, too thick and somehow charged with a power that raised the hair on his arms.

Asvarr staggered to his feet, swaying as waves of dizziness threatened to topple him. Only then did he see the true devastation. Where the coastal village had stood, now gaped a massive crater. At its center lay the fallen root, partially buried in scorched earth. It dwarfed everything—larger than any tree Asvarr had ever seen, large enough to make mountains seem like anthills in comparison.

Golden sap still pulsed from its wounded end, pooling in the crater. The liquid moved with purpose, forming patterns that burned themselves into Asvarr's mind. He couldn't look away, though his eyes watered from the brilliance.

Someone grabbed his arm. Hakon, his face half-covered in blood, beard singed away on one side.

"We need to go," the raid-leader growled, his voice hoarse. "Now."

Asvarr shook his head, unable to tear his gaze from the root. "What is it?"

"Nothing good." Hakon tugged harder. "Something only the gods should witness. We shouldn't be here."

"The gods..." Asvarr whispered. A memory surfaced—stories told around winter hearths. Yggdrasil, the World Tree that connects all realms. Its roots ran deep through reality itself.

As if responding to his thoughts, the golden sap surged. A tendril separated from the main pool and snaked across the blasted ground—straight toward Asvarr. Hakon cursed and released his grip, backing away in terror.

Asvarr stood transfixed as the glowing liquid approached. He should run. Every instinct screamed for flight. Yet he remained, watching with horrified fascination as the sap reached his boots.

It rose like a serpent, hovering before his face. In its golden depths, he glimpsed visions—a masked woman with shears, three ancient roots pulsing beneath worlds, a crown forged of splinters. Then the tendril lunged.

The sap struck his chest, burning through leather and flesh. Asvarr screamed as liquid fire coursed through his veins. He clawed at his chest, trying to dig out the burning intrusion, but the sap had already vanished beneath his skin. Where it had entered, a rune now glowed—one he'd never seen before, complex and shifting even as he watched.

He fell to his knees, body convulsing. The world flickered around him, sometimes showing the devastated landscape, other times revealing glimpses of strange realms where mountains floated in space and oceans of flame lapped at shores of ice.

"Asvarr!" Hakon's voice came as if from underwater, distorted and faint.

The berserker grabbed handfuls of dirt, focusing on the physical sensation to anchor himself against the visions threatening to sweep him away. Gradually, the world steadied. The burning in his veins subsided to a persistent ache.

When he looked up, the tear in the sky had grown. More roots fell through the gap, each plummeting toward distant horizons. The heavens themselves seemed to come apart at the seams.

"Yggdrasil," he rasped, the word tasting of ash and iron on his tongue. "The tree has shattered."

Hakon crouched beside him, eyes wide with superstitious fear. "What did it do to you?"

Asvarr touched the glowing rune on his chest. The light had dimmed, but heat still radiated from the mark. "I don't know."

Around them, the few surviving raiders and villagers were regaining consciousness. Some wept openly. Others stared at the sky with vacant expressions, minds broken by what they'd witnessed. The boundary between enemies had dissolved—they were all simply humans now, cowering beneath a broken heaven.

The ground trembled again. From the fallen root came a low groan, the sound of ancient wood struggling against its own weight. Cracks appeared along its surface, leaking more golden sap.

"We need to leave," Hakon insisted, helping Asvarr to his feet. "Whatever's happening, it's beyond us."

Asvarr nodded, but his gaze remained fixed on the colossal root. Something called to him from deep within its wounded form—a wordless summons that tugged at his very core. The rune on his chest pulsed in response.

"Not beyond me," he murmured, too quietly for Hakon to hear. "Not anymore."

He turned away with effort, following Hakon down the ruined hillside toward the shore where their longships waited. Behind them, the root continued to settle into the earth, digging deep furrows as if seeking to anchor itself once more.

Overhead, the shattered sky bled shadow and fire. The world had changed irrevocably in the space of moments. Gods had fallen. Realms had broken.

And something in Asvarr had awakened—something that burned with the same golden fire as the sap from Yggdrasil's severed root. Something that whispered of destiny unbound from the chains of fate.

He pressed his palm against the rune on his chest, feeling its heat through his tattered tunic. Whatever had marked him carried purpose. Whatever had chosen him would not easily let go.

Asvarr glanced back one last time at the fallen root. It looked almost like a bridge now—a pathway connecting this world to the tear in reality above. A branch of the broken world.

And he knew, with inexplicable certainty, that he would walk that path soon enough.

CHAPTER 1

ASHFALL IN THE NORTH

Asvarr woke to the taste of ash and copper. He choked, spitting blood onto scorched earth, each breath scraping his throat raw. Embers drifted through the air like malevolent fireflies, stinging exposed skin wherever they landed. The sky above hung low and bruised, the color of old wounds.

He pushed himself to his knees, skull throbbing with every heartbeat. Something wet and warm trickled down his temple. Blood. His blood. The rune on his chest burned beneath his shredded tunic, its glow visible even through the fabric.

The village lay in ruins around him. Not the coastal settlement they had raided—this was Hralvik. His home.

"No," he rasped, the single word hardly more than a breath.

Flames still licked at what remained of the longhouse where he had celebrated his first blood-victory feast. The great oak doorposts, carved with his grandfather's saga, had collapsed into charred stumps. Beyond that, the mead hall stood gutted, its roof having fallen in. Bodies lay scattered across the central clearing like discarded toys, some still burning, others eerily still.

***

Asvarr struggled to his feet, swaying as waves of dizziness threatened to topple him again. How long had he been unconscious? Hours? Days? The last thing he remembered was boarding Hakon's ship after the raid—after the sky had torn open and the great root had fallen. They had sailed north, racing the storm that followed, desperate to return home and seek guidance from the elders.

Home. The word landed like a blade in his gut.

A figure lay crumpled near what remained of the well. Asvarr staggered toward it, dreading what he already knew he would find. Torfa, the shield-maid who had taught him to hold an axe before he could properly walk. Her mail shirt had melted in places, fusing with the flesh beneath. Her right arm clutched her sword still, knuckles white even in death, the blade shattered midway down its length.

"Who did this?" Asvarr growled, the question directed at the uncaring sky.

He scanned the ruins for signs of attackers. Rival clans had raided them before, but never with such devastating completeness. There were no enemy bodies among the dead, no signs of combat beyond the desperate last stands. Whatever had happened here hadn't been a battle—it had been a slaughter.

Movement caught his eye. A shape near the smithy's collapsed wall. Asvarr lurched toward it, hope flaring painfully in his chest. Someone else alive.

He found Hakon half-buried under burning timbers, the raid-leader's legs crushed beneath a fallen support beam. Blood bubbled from between the man's cracked lips with each labored breath.

"Hakon!" Asvarr dropped to his knees, frantically pushing debris aside.

Hakon's eyes flickered open, clouded with pain. Recognition dawned slowly. "As...varr?" The sound barely carried above the crackle of flames.

"What happened here? Who attacked us?" Asvarr pressed his palms against a bleeding wound in the man's side, knowing even as he did so that it was futile. Too much blood soaked the ground beneath them.

"Not...attack." Hakon coughed, spraying Asvarr's forearms with red spittle. "The sky...came down. Tree-root...fell."

Asvarr's hand went instinctively to his chest, to the strange rune beneath his tunic. "Like at the raid? Another root?"

Hakon's gaze sharpened momentarily. "Different. Fire and ice...together. The gods..." His words dissolved into wet, gurgling breaths.

"Stay with me," Asvarr commanded, gripping the man's shoulder. "Hakon!"

The raid-leader's right hand shot up with surprising strength, clutching Asvarr's forearm. "Run," he hissed. "Still...hunting."

"Who's hunting? I don't—"

A crack, like splintering ice, cut through the smoky air. Hakon's eyes widened, staring at something beyond Asvarr's shoulder. His grip went slack.

Asvarr whirled, snatching up Hakon's fallen knife. Twenty paces away, where the path led from the village to the forest, stood a figure unlike any he had ever seen.

It resembled a man in shape only. Its body appeared carved from translucent ice, blue veins pulsing beneath the surface. Frost rimmed its joints and crusted its hairless skull. Where eyes should have been, twin flames burned with unnatural intensity. Its right arm ended in a long, serrated blade of ice.

The creature tilted its head, studying Asvarr with cold curiosity. Steam rose where hot ash landed on its frozen skin.

"What in hell's name are you?" Asvarr snarled, rising slowly into a fighter's crouch.

The ice-creature didn't respond. Instead, it raised its blade-arm and carved a symbol in the air—a complex rune that hung suspended, glowing with pale blue light. The mark resembled the one on Asvarr's chest, yet different in ways he couldn't articulate.

The rune beneath Asvarr's tunic flared in response, pain lancing through his torso as if someone had thrust a red-hot poker into his flesh. He doubled over, gasping.

The creature advanced, its movements fluid despite its seemingly solid form. Frost spread across the ground with each step, extinguishing small fires and coating debris in delicate white crystals.

Asvarr retreated, keeping the distance between them. The knife in his hand seemed pathetically inadequate against this thing. He needed time. Space. A real weapon.

His heel struck something solid. Glancing down, he saw Torfa's broken sword. Better than nothing. He dropped the knife and snatched up the blade, its familiar weight offering a minor comfort.

"Come then," he growled, raising the sword. "I'll send you back to whatever frozen hell spawned you."

The ice-creature paused. Its flame-eyes flared brighter. From its chest, a crack appeared, widening until it split the torso halfway down. Within the gap, Asvarr glimpsed a swirling vortex of snow and darkness. The creature thrust its normal arm into this impossible wound and withdrew something that pulsed with faint golden light—a splinter the size of a finger, dripping with the same sap Asvarr had seen pouring from the fallen root.

It wanted the rune on his chest. The realization struck Asvarr with sudden certainty. This thing hunted those marked by the Tree.

The creature lunged with frightening speed. Asvarr barely parried the ice-blade; the impact sent painful vibrations up his arm. The broken sword held, but a web of cracks spread across its surface. It wouldn't survive many more blows.

Asvarr countered, driving the blade toward the creature's midsection. The sword penetrated with surprising ease, sinking half its length into the icy body. No blood flowed from the wound. No sign of pain crossed the feature-less face. The flame-eyes merely regarded him with that same cold interest.

The creature's free hand clamped around Asvarr's wrist, the cold so intense it burned. Frost crawled up his arm, numbing flesh, threatening to reach bone.

Asvarr roared, more in rage than pain. He twisted, using the creature's grip as leverage to swing himself around and drive his boot into its knee. Something cracked. The creature staggered, its hold weakening just enough for Asvarr to wrench free.

He stumbled backward, clutching his frost-burned arm against his chest. The sword remained embedded in the ice-being, useless to him now. Twenty paces to his left stood the armory—or what remained of it. If he could reach it, find a proper weapon...

The creature straightened, seemingly unconcerned with the sword protruding from its torso. It extracted the blade with deliberate slowness, examining the steel as if puzzled by its existence before discarding it. The wound in its chest closed, ice flowing like water before solidifying once more.

Asvarr's options dwindled with each passing heartbeat. The rune on his chest pulsed painfully, as if warning him. Yet beneath the pain lay something else—a strange heat building inside him, unlike anything he'd felt before. It reminded him of battle-rage, but more focused, more deliberate.

The ice-creature carved another rune in the air, more complex than the first. The symbol hung suspended, pulsing with cold light, then shot toward Asvarr like an arrow.

Pure instinct drove him. Asvarr's hand moved without conscious thought, fingers tracing a counter-symbol pulled from some buried memory that wasn't his own. Fire erupted from his palm, golden fire that burned without consuming his flesh. It met the ice-rune midair. The resulting explosion threw him backward, slamming him into the remains of a stone wall.

Through blurred vision, Asvarr saw the creature halt, flame-eyes widening with what might have been surprise. It carved a third rune, faster this time, with jerky movements that betrayed urgency.

Frost exploded outward in a punishing wave. The temperature plummeted. Asvarr's breath clouded before his face, his eyelashes crackling as moisture froze instantly. The golden fire dimmed but didn't extinguish, forming a barrier that kept the worst of the cold at bay.

Behind the ice-creature, a second figure emerged from the forest path. This one burned with a constant flame, its body composed of living fire. Where it stepped, the ground blackened and smoked. Like its frozen counterpart, it possessed no recognizable face—only a vaguely humanoid head with pits of absolute darkness where eyes should be.

The two elemental beings regarded each other across the smoking ruins. Neither moved. Neither made a sound. Yet Asvarr sensed communication passing between them—a silent confrontation heavy with ancient enmity.

The moment broke when both creatures turned toward him simultaneously. The ice-being raised its blade-arm. The fire-entity extended a hand wreathed in dark flame.

Asvarr knew with bone-deep certainty that he could not defeat both. Even one had nearly overwhelmed him. He scrambled backward, seeking an escape route through the ruins of his home.

His foot struck something solid. Looking down, he saw Hakon's war horn, the curved ram's horn bound with bands of silver, miraculously intact amid the destruction. Without thinking, he snatched it up and raised it to his lips.

The sound that emerged when he blew wasn't the rallying cry of raiders. It wasn't a sound any human instrument should produce. It rang with the same resonance as Yggdrasil's scream—a note that vibrated in the bones and blood, that spoke to something older than flesh.

Both creatures recoiled. The ice-being's form cracked in multiple places, tiny fissures spreading across its surface. The fire-entity dimmed, its flames guttering like a candle in a strong wind.

***

Asvarr didn't question the horn's power. He drew another breath and blew again, longer this time, putting all his rage and grief into the sound. The note grew, expanded, and became something physical that rippled outward in visible waves.

The ice-creature shattered. One moment it stood poised to attack; The next, it exploded into thousands of crystalline fragments that fell like deadly hail. The fire-being let out a soundless howl, its form collapsing inward until only a small, intensely bright ember remained. This flickered once, twice, then shot upward into the bruised sky, leaving a trail of smoke behind.

Silence fell across the ruined village. Asvarr lowered the horn, staring at it in disbelief. The silver bands glowed faintly with the same golden light as the rune on his chest, then faded to normal.

He sank to his knees, sudden exhaustion crashing over him like a physical weight. Around him, embers continued to fall, gentle as snow, covering the dead in a blanket of gray ash. His clan. His people. All gone.

Hakon's last words echoed in his mind. Still hunting. There will be more creatures like the ones he'd just faced. More hunters are seeking those marked by Yggdrasil's fall.

Asvarr clutched the war horn to his chest. Grief would come later. Proper mourning for his people would come later. Now, he needed to move. To survive. To understand what had happened to him—what was still happening.

He forced himself to his feet, swaying with exhaustion. The rune on his chest had quieted to a dull throb. He tucked the horn into his belt and turned toward what remained of his family's longhouse. If anything useful had survived the destruction, he would find it there.

As he picked his way through the ruins, a sound stopped him—a faint vibration, more felt than heard. He turned slowly, scanning the devastation for its source.

There, half-buried in ash near the central firepit, something pulsed with golden light. Something that hadn't been there before the creatures attacked. Something that called to the mark on his chest with undeniable urgency.

Asvarr approached cautiously, one hand on Hakon's horn, ready to use its power again if necessary. The glowing object resolved itself into a stone the size of his fist, covered in runes similar to the mark he bore. It hummed with power, warm to the touch when he knelt and brushed away the covering ash.

The moment his fingers contacted the stone, visions flashed behind his eyes—a woman in a cracked mask, falling through darkness; a great tree splintering across the void; five roots plunging into different worlds. And somewhere, through it all, a whispered name: Skyrend.

Asvarr clutched the runestone, its heat intense. He didn't understand what had happened to his world, to his people. But he understood with sudden, perfect clarity that the stone in his hand and the mark on his chest connected him to forces that had shattered reality itself.

***

Those forces had not yet finished with him.

Asvarr trudged through the ruins of his family's longhouse, the runestone clutched against his chest. Familiar things lay broken and burned—his father's carved chair splintered beyond recognition, his mother's loom reduced to charred sticks and ash-covered thread. The roof had partially collapsed, letting in weak gray light that did little to dispel the gloom.

He kicked aside a fallen beam, sending embers spiraling upward. His throat tightened at the sight of a small wooden toy—a horse he'd carved for his sister's youngest boy. The child himself lay several paces away, small body curled as if merely sleeping. Asvarr's jaw clenched until his teeth creaked. Later. He would bury them all later.

The stone in his hands pulsed again, more insistently. Its glow intensified, casting golden shadows across the debris. The runes etched into its surface shifted before his eyes, rearranging themselves into new patterns. Asvarr had studied runes since boyhood—every warrior knew the basics needed for protection sigils and weapon-blessings. These were nothing like those simple marks. They flowed like water, complex beyond anything human hands could carve.

He made his way toward the hearth—the heart of any Norse home. Though flames no longer danced in the stone-lined pit, heat radiated from it still. Unnatural heat. Too intense for mere coals.

As he approached, the runestone's vibrations grew violent enough to make his hands shake. He knelt beside the hearth, pushing aside collapsed cookware and scorched hearthstones. The glow beneath matched the stone in his hand.

"What are you?" he muttered, scraping away ash with his boot.

Something much larger than his handheld stone lay embedded in the packed earth beneath his hearth. The corner that protruded gleamed like polished bone, inscribed with the same fluid runes that adorned the smaller fragment. Asvarr dug with his bare hands, ignoring the heat that scorched his palms. Blood and soot mingled beneath his fingernails as he excavated the object.

A runestone. No—a runestone slab. Rectangular and massive, it stretched the length of his forearm and was twice as wide. Despite its size, when Asvarr finally wrenched it free, it weighed almost nothing.

The larger stone sang—there was no other word for the high, simple note that vibrated from its core. The smaller stone answered, its tone harmonizing perfectly. Together, they created a chord that made Asvarr's bones ache with recognition, though he'd never heard such a sound before.

He brought the stones together. They snapped into alignment with such force that Asvarr nearly dropped them. The smaller stone melded into the larger, becoming a single piece. The seam where they joined flashed with brilliant light, then vanished completely.

Warmth flowed up Asvarr's arms, pleasant at first, then intense enough to make him gasp. The rune on his chest flared in response. Images flooded his mind: a mask splitting down the middle; three women standing before a tree vaster than mountains; roots tearing free from ancient soil; golden sap flowing like blood from severed limbs.

The vision shifted. He saw himself standing before a branch that pierced the earth like a spear, dripping golden ichor. Shadows moved within the liquid—forms not quite human, not quite beast. They reached for him with limbs of darkness and flame.

Asvarr dropped the stone with a curse. It clattered against the hearthstones, still glowing, still humming. His hands trembled. The mark on his chest pulsed in time with his racing heart.

"Speaks to you, does it?"

Asvarr whirled, snatching a charred piece of firewood as a makeshift weapon. An old woman stood in the doorway—or what remained of it. Her face was a web of wrinkles around eyes sharp as raven feathers. White hair hung loose, past her shoulders, decorated with small bones and wooden beads. She leaned on a staff topped with a crystalline stone that caught the dim light.

"Who are you?" Asvarr demanded, not lowering his improvised club. "How did you survive?"

The crone tilted her head, studying him with unnerving intensity. "I wasn't here when the sky fell. Just returned from the high caves." She tapped her staff against the ground. "I am Æsa, völva of the northern fjords."

Asvarr's grip tightened. A völva—a seeress. Their kind were respected and feared in equal measure; their prophecies rarely welcome news.

"What do you know of this?" He gestured at the runestone with his chin, unwilling to touch it again.

Æsa approached with a shuffling gait, her staff clicking against debris. Age had bent her spine, but nothing about her movements suggested frailty.

"A fragment of the World Tree," she said, crouching beside the stone with surprising agility. "Yggdrasil sheds its pieces across the realms. This one found you." Her weathered finger traced a rune without quite touching the surface. "Or perhaps you found it."

Asvarr snorted. "Riddles won't help me understand why my people lie dead."

"No riddles, berserker." Æsa fixed him with those raven-dark eyes. "The Tree has shattered. The nine realms come undone. When branches break, splinters fly." She waved a gnarled hand at the surrounding destruction. "Some splinters cut deep."

"I saw it happen," Asvarr admitted, slowly lowering his makeshift weapon. "During our raid south. A root tore through the sky. It fell where we fought." His hand went to his chest. "It marked me."

Interest sharpened the old woman's gaze. "Show me."

Asvarr hesitated, then pulled aside his tunic. The rune glowed faintly against his skin, its lines shifting subtly even as they watched.

Æsa sucked in a breath. Her hand reached toward the mark, stopping just short of contact. "Grímmark," she whispered. "The god-etching."

"What does it mean?"

"It means Yggdrasil has chosen you, boy." She straightened, suddenly looking less frail. "The old gods crafted five such marks before time began. Five sigils for five wardens to stand watch over the roots of creation."

The runestone pulsed, its glow intensifying at her words. Asvarr glanced between it and the völva, suspicion warring with a desperate need for answers.

"Why me? I'm a warrior, not a warden of anything."

"The Tree chooses based on threads we cannot see." Æsa prodded the runestone with her staff. "This is just the beginning. Where the great root fell, more will be revealed."

"The root fell leagues from here," Asvarr said. "How did this stone end up beneath my hearth?"

"You carried its essence home in your blood." Her finger pointed at his chest. "The mark draws fragments to itself—seeking to become whole again."

The sound of footsteps crunching through debris outside made them both tense. Asvarr raised his makeshift club again, positioning himself between the old woman and the doorway.

A group of men appeared in the shattered entrance—survivors from neighboring steadings by their garb. Their beards were streaked with soot and blood. Most clutched weapons, though one supported another who could barely stand.

"Asvarr Hrolfdansson," called the tallest, a broad-shouldered man Asvarr recognized as Bjorn from the eastern shore. "We saw the golden light. What happens here?"

"Bjorn." Asvarr nodded cautiously. "My village is destroyed. My people slaughtered. I know little more than that."

The men exchanged glances. One spat on the ground. "Three steadings lie in ruins along the coast. The sky tore open and rained fire and ice."

"Same as what struck during our raid," Asvarr said, glancing at the runestone. Its glow had dimmed, though it still hummed faintly.

"Creatures followed," said the wounded man, his voice tight with pain. "Made of frost and flame. They hunted through the night. Killed any who crossed their path."

Bjorn stepped forward, his hand resting on his sword hilt. "The jarl's son reached us before he died. Said a berserker, returned from the southern raid, carrying doom on his chest." His eyes narrowed. "Said that doom marked the bearer with a burning rune."

The air in the ruined longhouse grew heavy. Asvarr felt the accusation settle around him like a physical weight.

"I brought no doom here, Bjorn. I fought the frost-walker and its fire-kin. Drove them off with Hakon's horn."

"Convenient that you alone survived," called a voice from the back of the group.

Æsa thumped her staff hard against the floor. "Fools. The doom was already upon us when the Tree shattered. This man bears the mark of a Warden." Her voice carried surprising strength. "Without him, worse will follow."

Bjorn snorted. "We trust no völva here, crone. Your kind speaks with forked tongues."

"Then trust your eyes," she snapped. She stooped to pick up the runestone. Before Asvarr could stop her, she thrust it toward the men. Its glow flared brilliantly, bathing the ruined interior in golden light. The wounded man cried out, covering his eyes. Others stepped back, hands raised defensively.

"This is a fragment of Yggdrasil itself," Æsa declared. "The bearer of the Grímmark must take it to where the great root fell."

Bjorn recovered first, his weathered face hard with suspicion. "And why would we allow that? His kind brought destruction to our shores."

"Because if he doesn't," the völva said, "what fell from the sky will seem a gentle rain compared to what comes next."

Asvarr took the stone from Æsa's hands. The moment his fingers touched it, the rune on his chest flared hot enough to make him wince. The runestone's hum deepened to a resonant thrum that filled the longhouse.

"I don't understand what's happening," he said, addressing Bjorn directly. "But I've lost everything too. My clan lies dead around us. I'll find answers where the root fell—and vengeance against whatever caused this."

The wounded man suddenly straightened, eyes wide. "The mark," he gasped, pointing at Asvarr's chest, where the glow was visible through his tunic. "I saw it before, carved in ice on the creature's arm."

Silence fell. Everyone watched Asvarr. Hands tightened on weapons.

"He's one of them," someone whispered.

"No." Asvarr stood his ground. "These marks were stolen from the Tree by the creatures that attacked us. That's why they hunt those who bear the true signs."

He did not know if his words were true, but they felt right as he spoke them. The runestone's vibrations intensified, almost approving.

Bjorn studied him for a long moment. "Three of our best warriors will accompany you south," he finally said. "If you're telling the truth, you'll welcome the aid. If not..." His hand moved meaningfully to his sword.

"I'll go alone," Asvarr countered. "Your men are needed here. More creatures may come."

"All the more reason you shouldn't travel unguarded," Bjorn insisted.

Æsa's staff struck the ground again. "He walks with Yggdrasil's mark. He needs no guard." Her dark eyes fixed on Asvarr. "But he needs guidance. I will accompany him."

Asvarr opened his mouth to refuse, then closed it. The völva knew more about his situation than anyone. And something in her gaze suggested she knew more than she had revealed.

"Fine," he said. "The seeress comes with me. The rest of you, rebuild. Burn your dead. Strengthen your defenses."

Grudging nods met his words. The men withdrew, though suspicion remained etched in their features.

"We leave at dawn," Asvarr told Æsa.

She shook her head. "We leave now. The creatures you fought will return with reinforcements. The mark on your chest blazes like a beacon to them."

Asvarr glanced down at the runestone, its surface still shifting with symbols he couldn't decipher. "I need supplies. Weapons."

"Take what you must, quickly." Æsa moved toward the doorway with surprising speed. "Meet me at the standing stones east of the village. Bring the runestone and the war-horn."

She vanished before he could respond, leaving him alone in the ruins of his home. The runestone pulsed in his hands, almost eagerly.

Asvarr tucked it into his belt, wrapping it in a scrap of leather to dim its glow. He retrieved what he could find—a short axe with a cracked handle but sound blade, a hunting knife, a half-empty waterskin. A partially burned satchel held a fire striker and a handful of dried meat that had somehow survived the destruction.

He paused at Hakon's body. The raid-leader's eyes stared sightlessly at the broken roof. Asvarr knelt and closed them.

"I'll find answers, old friend. And vengeance."

The war horn still hung at Hakon's belt. Asvarr removed it carefully, slinging it over his shoulder. He would return to burn the dead properly, but for now, he could only leave them beneath the open sky.

At the village edge, he turned back one last time. Smoke still rose from multiple points. Bodies lay where they had fallen. The remnants of everything he'd known.

The runestone vibrated against his hip, urging him onward. The mark on his chest throbbed in time with his heartbeat. Whatever destiny had chosen for him, it would not wait for grief.

Asvarr set his face toward the standing stones and the völva who waited there. The answers he sought lay south, where the great root had plunged from the shattered sky. Where shadows moved in golden sap like half-remembered nightmares. Where his path as Warden—whatever that meant—would truly begin.

CHAPTER 2
THE BRANCH THAT BLED

D awn broke reluctantly over the eastern fjords, pale light struggling through a sky choked with ash. Asvarr trudged up the steep incline, boots sliding on frost-slick rock. Each breath burned in his lungs. They had traveled through the night, following deer paths and forgotten trails that Æsa somehow knew by heart despite her age.

The runestone in his belt throbbed like a second heartbeat. Its warmth had intensified over the hours, growing almost unbearable against his hip. Twice, he had to wrap it in additional layers of leather to avoid burning himself.

"How much farther, crone?" He paused atop a granite outcropping, squinting at the völva who scrambled over rocks with the nimbleness of a mountain goat. Her white hair whipped in the biting wind, strands of bone and wood clicking together.

"We'll know when we arrive." Æsa didn't slow her pace. "The branch calls to your mark. Feel it tugging?"

Asvarr grunted. The völva spoke truth; something pulled at him, urging him southward and up. The Grímmark on his chest pulsed with each step, drawing him onward like a lodestone to iron. He'd tried ignoring it once, heading east instead. The pain had driven him to his knees within twenty paces, only easing when he resumed their original direction.

They crested the ridge as watery sunlight spilled across the valley below. Asvarr halted, breath catching in his throat.

A branch larger than the tallest pine had plunged from the heavens into the mountainside. Half-buried in shattered rock, it stretched like a fallen titan across the landscape, its tip disappearing into a distant lake. Bark the color of old bronze wrapped its girth, twisted and gnarled in patterns too complex to follow. Smaller branches—each thicker than a man's waist—jutted at impossible angles, some pointed skyward as if reaching for their lost trunk, others embedded deep in earth.

"Yggdrasil," Æsa breathed beside him. "Witness, berserker. Few mortal eyes have seen the World Tree's flesh."

***

It wasn't the branch's size that stole Asvarr's voice, nor its uncanny angles. It was the glow. Golden light pulsed from a ragged wound at its thickest point, where it had broken from the greater Tree. Sap flowed from the injury, viscous and radiant as the setting sun, pooling in a crater of its own making at the branch's base.

"It bleeds," Asvarr whispered, the words torn from him, unbidden.

"Life-ichor," Æsa nodded. "The Tree's blood flows with memory and power." Her gnarled fingers clutched her staff tighter. "What we seek lies below, where the sap gathers."

The wind shifted, carrying a sound unlike anything Asvarr had heard before—a low, resonant hum that vibrated through bone and sinew. The branch was singing; he realized. A song of pain and remembrance, so primal that it needed no words to convey its loss.

"We can't go down there." Asvarr gestured toward the base of the branch where movement caught his eye. Dark shapes skittered around the golden pool—too distant to describe, but their jerky, insectile motions raised the hair on his arms. "We're not alone."

"The branch draws many seekers." Æsa pointed her staff toward a narrow game trail that wound down the ridge. "Some wish to heal it. Others to feed on its wound."

They descended carefully, using a scrub brush for handholds where the trail crumbled beneath their feet. With each step downward, the branch's song grew louder. The rune on Asvarr's chest thrummed in harmony, warm and insistent against his skin.

Halfway down, Asvarr unslipped the war horn from his shoulder, keeping it ready. The dark figures continued their strange dance around the golden pool, many more than he'd first thought. He counted at least a dozen silhouettes, their movements becoming more frenzied as he watched.

"What are they?" he whispered.

Æsa squinted into the distance. "Shadow-drinkers," she said, revulsion twisting her features. "The broken Tree leaks memory into the realms. Those who drink the sap without bearing a mark become... changed."

"Changed how?"

She didn't answer immediately, studying the creatures with narrowed eyes. "They forget themselves. Become hollow. Only the hunger remains."

The trail leveled out into a frost-covered meadow. Beyond it lay a stretch of forest—pine, ash, and birch—dead or dying near the branch, their needles and leaves turned to rust and bone. The sap's glow reflected off this skeletal canopy, casting long, distorted shadows.

"We'll circle through the trees," Asvarr decided, drawing his axe. "Approach from downwind."

Æsa laid a restraining hand on his arm. "First, we must know what hunts us." Her eyes, unnervingly sharp in her wrinkled face, fixed on his. "Call the rune-sight."

"The what?"

"The mark grants visions. Look through its eye, not your own."

Asvarr frowned. "How?"

"Will it so." She thumped her staff against the frozen ground. "The mark chose you. Command it."

Asvarr closed his eyes, feeling foolish. The Grímmark pulsed against his chest, steady as a heartbeat. He focused on that sensation, imagining the strange rune flaring brighter, extending its influence outward like tendrils of power.

Heat flooded his veins. When he opened his eyes, the world had changed.

Colors bled away, replaced by shades of gold and shadow. The forest transformed into a lattice of light—threads of energy that connected tree to earth to sky in complex patterns. The branch dominated his vision, no longer solid wood but a river of golden fire, so brilliant it should have blinded him. The wound at its center poured forth fragmented images that scattered like embers on the wind—broken memories of worlds he couldn't comprehend.

And the creatures...

Asvarr recoiled, stumbling backward. The shadow-drinkers were human once—he could see the fading outlines of their original forms. But where life should have flowed, only emptiness remained, outlined in tattered remnants of gold. They crowded around the sap-pool like starving dogs, dipping withered limbs into the radiance, absorbing it through skin turned translucent and gray. With each draught, their forms grew more distorted, more wrong. Some had elongated beyond human proportions; others had merged, sharing limbs and torsos in blasphemous configurations.

"End it," he gasped, pressing the heels of his hands against his eyes. The vision retreated, colors and solidity returning to the world. His stomach lurched. "What were they?"

"Men and women who drank what they could not hold." Æsa's expression held grim satisfaction at his reaction. "Memory-starved. The sap contains fragments of Yggdrasil's knowledge. Without a mark to filter it, the power consumes them from within."

Asvarr gripped his axe tighter, knuckles whitening around the worn handle. "Can they be killed?"

"They're already dead in all ways that matter." She gestured toward the lower slope. "We must reach the heart-wound before the shadow-drinkers consume too much. Each draught strengthens them, harder to overcome."

They skirted the meadow's edge, keeping to the trees' shadow. The creatures remained fixated on the golden pool, oblivious to anything beyond their desperate consumption. Closer now, Asvarr saw details that his vision had mercifully obscured—skin stretched paper-thin over twisted bone; faces half-melted into shoulder and chest; fingers elongated into talons that scraped against bark and stone.

The branch's song changed as they approached, its tone lifting from a mournful dirge to something almost questioning. Asvarr's rune responded, sending pulses of warmth down his arm and into his fingers. The runestone at his belt grew hot enough to sear through its wrappings.

Æsa pointed to a tumble of rocks that would provide cover within thirty paces of the heart-wound. "There. We'll observe from behind the stones."

"Observe what? We need that sap, don't we?" Asvarr nodded toward the pool. "Those things stand in our way."

"Patience, berserker." The völva's eyes gleamed. "Watch first. The branch has noticed us."

They reached the rocks without incident, crouching behind weather-worn granite streaked with lichen. From this distance, the sap's glow bathed everything in golden luminescence. The air itself seemed to shimmer, disturbed by currents of power that rippled outward from the wound.

The shadow-drinkers had organized themselves into a rough circle around the pool. Some crawled on all fours; others stood upright, though their limbs bent at impossible angles. One—taller than the rest, with a torso split vertically to reveal a hollow cavity filled with golden light—raised withered arms. A sound escaped it, half-scream and half-song, mimicking the branch's own resonance.

The others responded, their voices a cacophony of broken notes. They swayed in unison, movements becoming more synchronized with each passing moment. The tall one stepped into the pool of sap, the golden liquid rising to its knees. It dipped cupped hands into the radiance and drank deeply.

Change swept over it immediately. Its split torso sealed partially shut. The golden light within intensified, shining through translucent skin. When it raised its face—a smooth, blank oval with only the suggestion of features—Asvarr felt its gaze land on their hiding place with terrible precision.

"It sees us," he hissed.

"Not us." Æsa pointed to his chest. "The mark calls to the branch. The drinkers sense that call."

The tall shadow-drinker stepped from the pool, golden sap dripping from its limbs. It raised one elongated arm and pointed directly at their position. The others turned as one, their not-quite-faces oriented toward the tumbled rocks.

"So much for observation." Asvarr hefted his axe, sizing up the distance to the pool. "I'll hold them off. You get what we came for."

Æsa clutched his arm again. "The sap is not our goal, fool. It's the branch itself." Her voice dropped to an urgent whisper. "A fragment of prophecy lies embedded in its heart. That's what we seek."

The shadow-drinkers moved, abandoning the pool to converge on their hiding spot. Their gait varied—some loped on mismatched limbs, others flowed like liquid across the rocky ground—but all possessed unnatural speed.

Asvarr raised Hakon's war horn to his lips. The sound that burst forth when he blew carried the same resonance as before—a note that vibrated at frequencies beyond human hearing. Several shadow-drinkers stumbled, their unsteady forms rippling like disturbed water. The tall one merely paused, cocking its featureless head as if listening.

"The horn weakens them," Asvarr said, preparing to sound another blast.

"Save your breath," Æsa warned. "These are not elemental hunters. Different prey requires different weapons."

She fumbled within her robes, producing a small pouch. From it, she drew a handful of what looked like iron filings mixed with dried herbs. Murmuring words in a language Asvarr didn't recognize, she cast the mixture toward the approaching creatures. The particles hung suspended in air for a heartbeat, then ignited with cold, blue fire that spread outward in a semicircle.

Three shadow-drinkers caught in the expanding arc of fire shrieked, their twisted forms convulsing as blue flames consumed them from within. They collapsed into piles of ash that scattered on the wind. The others halted, wary now.

"Blood-iron and yew ash," Æsa explained, already preparing another handful. "Burns the memory-starved to their hollow core."

Asvarr slipped the horn back over his shoulder and readied his axe. "How much of that do you have?"

"Not enough." She nodded toward the pool. "The prophecy fragment, berserker. While they hesitate. Cut it from the heart-wound."

The tall shadow-drinker recovered first, gesturing to the others with elongated fingers. They spread out, attempting to flank the rocks. Several dropped to all fours, slithering between boulders with serpentine grace.

"Go!" Æsa threw another handful of her mixture, creating a second wall of blue fire between them and the creatures. "I'll hold them! The mark will guide you to what we seek!"

***

Cursing under his breath, Asvarr broke cover and sprinted toward the golden pool. The branch's song intensified with each step, vibrating through his bones. The Grímmark flared hot enough to sear his skin, its light visible through his tunic.

Two shadow-drinkers intercepted him, skittering across his path with disjointed movements. Asvarr didn't slow. He swung his axe in a wide arc, catching the first across what might have been a shoulder. With minimal resistance, the blade went through the creature, as if it were made of fog and shadow instead of flesh. It made no sound, simply collapsing in on itself, its form dissolving into wispy darkness.

The second leapt at him, elongated fingers grasping for his throat. Asvarr ducked, using his momentum to drive his shoulder into the creature's midsection. It weighed almost nothing. The impact sent it tumbling away, giving him time to close the remaining distance to the heart-wound.

Up close, the branch's scale became even more apparent. Its circumference stretched wider than ten men standing with arms outstretched. The wound itself gaped like a vast mouth, golden sap oozing from shattered wood in thick rivulets. The song emanated from within this opening, from something deeper inside.

The Grímmark guided him, pulsing in a specific rhythm that drew his attention to a particular spot within the wound. There, partially embedded in splintered wood, a fragment of something gleamed. Silvery-white, catching the light in facets like a crystal.

Asvarr reached for it without thinking. The moment his fingers brushed its surface, visions exploded behind his eyes.

A völva carving a rune into his flesh with a blade of ice and fire—

A root twisting upward through soil and stone, seeking the touch of sun—

A masked woman removing her disguise to reveal nothing beneath—

A crown of shattered branches, bleeding sap onto the brow of a kneeling figure—

The prophecy fragment burned cold against his palm. He wrenched it free from the wood with a grunt of effort. The branch's song changed instantly, rising to a piercing keen that drove daggers of pain into his skull. The sap surged, gushing from the wound in a torrent of liquid gold.

"Æsa!" he shouted, turning back toward the rocks. "I have it!"

The völva stood atop a boulder, surrounded by a blue fire that spiraled upward like a protective cage. Shadow-drinkers circled her position, testing the flames with outstretched limbs, only to recoil as the fire consumed whatever it touched. The tall one directed their movements, keeping its distance.

Asvarr took a step toward her, then froze as the ground beneath his feet trembled. The golden pool rippled, its surface disturbed by something moving below. He stumbled backward just as the sap erupted—

Shapes emerged from the molten gold. Humanoid, but not human, they rose silently from the pool, their forms fashioned entirely of animated sap. Eyes like burning coals fixed on Asvarr and the fragment clutched in his fist. They moved with liquid grace, flowing rather than walking across the rocky ground.

"Echoes!" Æsa's voice carried across the distance. "Memory-born! They guard the fragment!"

Asvarr counted five of the sap-beings, each taller than a man, their golden bodies flowing and reshaping with every movement. Unlike the shadow-drinkers, whose very appearance inspired revulsion, these creatures possessed an eerie beauty—perfect but empty, like statues given momentary life.

The closest echo reached for him with fingers that elongated as he watched, stretching impossible distances. Asvarr swept his axe through the extended limb. The blade passed harmlessly through; the severed portion simply flowing back into the main body.

The echo tilted its head, regarding him with those burning-coal eyes. Then, in a voice like wood creaking beneath significant weight, it spoke:

"Grímmark-bearer. Surrender what is not yours to take."

Asvarr tightened his grip on the prophecy fragment, its icy fire burning against his palm. The echo's words hung in the air between them, resonant and unnatural.

"This isn't yours either," he growled, backing away slowly. "The Tree fell. Its pieces scattered. I bear the mark."

The echo's featureless face rippled, mouth forming and dissolving in the golden surface. "The fragment contains truth not meant for mortal flesh. Return it to the sap. We will keep its memory until the Tree grows anew."

The other echoes spread out, surrounding Asvarr in a half-circle of living gold. Their movements flowed with uncanny precision, limbs stretching and reforming as they advanced. Behind them, more shapes rose from the sap pool—darker figures whose forms seemed less stable, more threatening.

"Asvarr!" Æsa's voice cut through the branch's endless song. "Do not listen! They are memory-ghosts, nothing more! The fragment is ours by right of the mark!"

The völva still stood atop her boulder, maintaining her circle of blue fire against the pressing shadow-drinkers. The tall one had moved closer, testing the flames with extended fingers that blackened and crumbled wherever they touched the magical barrier.

The nearest echo lunged forward, its arm becoming a golden whip that lashed toward the fragment. Asvarr dodged, the fluid limb missing him by a hair's breadth. Where it struck the ground, stone hissed and bubbled, partially dissolving.

"The sap burns!" he shouted to Æsa. "My axe passes through them!"

"The horn!" she called back. "Sound it through the fragment's touch!"

Asvarr fumbled for Hakon's war horn with his free hand, never taking his eyes off the advancing echoes. The closest one attacked again, both arms extending into golden tendrils that whipped toward him from opposite directions. He threw himself backward, landing hard on frosted stone as the sap-limbs crossed where he had stood.

Rolling to his feet, he raised the horn to his lips, pressing the prophecy fragment against its silver-bound edge. The moment the two touched, energy surged through both—icy fire from the fragment into the horn, setting the silver bands alight with ice-blue flame.

He blew a single, powerful note.

The sound that erupted bore little resemblance to any horn call Asvarr had ever heard. It tore through the air like a physical force, visible as rippling waves of blue-white energy that expanded outward in concentric rings. Where these waves struck the echoes, their golden forms, shuddered and destabilized, losing cohesion momentarily.

The branch itself responded, its mournful song shifting into a higher register that grated against Asvarr's eardrums. The wound at its core pulsed brighter, sap flowing faster.

"Again!" Æsa commanded, her voice barely audible above the cacophony of competing sounds.

Asvarr drew another breath and blew a second, longer note. This time the horn's call formed a spiraling column of force that shot skyward before cascading down in a shower of ice-blue sparks. Wherever these sparks touched golden sap—whether echo or pool—the viscous substance hardened instantly into crystalline formations that glittered like frozen amber.

Two echoes caught in the shower froze mid-movement, their fluid bodies transforming into golden statues. The others retreated, flowing back toward the safety of the pool. Behind them, the darker shapes sank beneath the sap's surface, leaving only ripples to mark their passing.

Asvarr didn't wait for them to regroup. He sprinted toward Æsa, prophecy fragment clutched tightly in one hand, horn in the other. The blue fire surrounding the völva flickered and waned, her reserves of power clearly fading.

"We need to leave," he panted, reaching her side. The shadow-drinkers pressed closer, sensing the weakening barrier. "Now."

Æsa nodded, her wrinkled face drawn with exhaustion. "The path behind the stones. It leads to higher ground." She pointed with her staff toward a narrow trail barely visible among tumbled rocks. "They'll follow the fragment's light. We'll need to mask it."

The tall shadow-drinker chose that moment to make its move. It launched itself at the failing fire barrier, its elongated body absorbing the blue flames rather than burning. Golden light from its hollow torso dimmed as it consumed the magical fire, drawing the power into itself.

Asvarr reacted without thinking. He swept Æsa into his arms, the old woman weighing no more than a child, and leaped from the boulder. They landed hard, his knees protesting the impact, but he kept his footing and ran for the hidden path.

Behind them, the shadow-drinkers howled—a sound like wind through broken teeth. The echoes had regrouped as well, flowing across the rocky ground with liquid grace, their golden forms gleaming in the weak sunlight.

"Give me the fragment," Æsa gasped as Asvarr set her down once they reached the path. "I can hide its light."

He pressed the silvery shard into her palm. The moment it left his grasp, the visions that had flickered at the edges of his consciousness retreated. Æsa pulled a square of dark cloth from within her robes and wrapped the fragment tightly, murmuring words under her breath. The cloth came alive in her hands, its edges sealing seamlessly until no trace of the prophecy shard remained visible.

"Quickly now." She tucked the wrapped fragment into her robes and gestured up the path with her staff. "The binding will hold for a time, but they'll still sense its presence."

They climbed swiftly, Asvarr surprised by the völva's nimbleness despite her apparent exhaustion. The path wound between massive boulders, eventually opening onto a wind-swept ridge high above the branch. From this vantage point, Asvarr could see the full scale of the fallen fragment of Yggdrasil—a colossal limb stretching for leagues across the landscape, its smaller branches radiating outward like the skeleton of some enormous beast.

"Look there," Æsa said, pointing toward the distant lake where the branch's tip disappeared beneath dark waters. "The fragment seeks to root itself anew."

Asvarr squinted against the harsh glare. Sure enough, where the branch entered the lake, the water had frozen in unnatural patterns—crystalline structures that climbed the wood like inverse icicles, anchoring it to the lake bottom.

"Can it grow again? Separated from the Tree?"

"Perhaps." Æsa leaned on her staff, catching her breath. "Yggdrasil exists beyond our understanding of life and death. Its fragments retain memory—purpose. But without guidance, they grow wild. Dangerous."

A commotion below drew their attention. The shadow-drinkers had found the path and begun to ascend, their distorted forms flowing over and around obstacles with unnerving speed. The echoes had not followed, instead returning to their vigil around the sap pool. The tall shadow-drinker led the pursuit, its elongated limbs grasping rock and shrub as it climbed.

"We can't outrun them," Asvarr growled, drawing his axe. "Not across open ground."

"We don't need to." Æsa pointed her staff at a tumble of massive stones perched precariously at the ridge's edge. "Bring those down onto the path. Seal it."

Asvarr studied the stones. "My axe won't move boulders that size."

"The horn will." She nodded toward the war horn still clutched in his hand. "Sound it against the keystone there." She showed a wedge-shaped rock supporting the larger boulders.

Asvarr positioned himself before the stone formation, raising the horn to his lips. Without the prophecy fragment's touch, he wasn't certain the horn would produce the same power as before. Still, nothing else would save them from the pursuing shadow-drinkers.

He concentrated on the Grímmark on his chest, willing its energy into the horn as he had done with the fragment. The rune responded, warmth flooding his veins and flowing down his arm into the ancient instrument. When he blew, the sound emerged as a physical force once more—a battering ram of concentrated sound that struck the keystone with enough power to crack granite.

The wedge-shaped rock shattered. Without its support, the larger boulders shifted, then tumbled with gathering momentum. They crashed down upon the path in a thunderous avalanche, crushing several shadow-drinkers beneath their immense weight. Dust and pulverized stone billowed upward in a choking cloud.

When it cleared, the path had vanished completely beneath tons of fallen rock. On the far side, the remaining shadow-drinkers paced in frustration, unable to follow.

"That won't hold them forever," Æsa said, already moving along the ridge. "They'll find another way up. We must put more distance between us before nightfall."

Asvarr glanced toward the sky, noting the sun's position as it struggled to penetrate the ashen clouds. "Several hours of daylight remain. Where do we go now?"

"North first, to confuse our trail. Then east, toward the high fells." Æsa tapped her staff against the ground, leaving small scorch marks wherever it touched. "I know a place where we'll be safe to examine the fragment properly."

They traveled in silence for a time, following game trails that wound through scrubby vegetation. The wind grew stronger as they climbed higher, carrying the scent of snow and pine. Asvarr's thoughts kept returning to the golden echoes and their strange speech—"truth not meant for mortal flesh"—and the darker shapes he'd glimpsed rising from the sap pool.

"What were those things?" he finally asked. "The echoes called themselves memory-born, but what does that mean?"

Æsa glanced back at him, her dark eyes unreadable. "When Yggdrasil shattered, it didn't merely break physically. The Tree contains all knowledge, all memory of creation. Its wound bleeds remembrance."

"Those weren't memories. They spoke. They thought."

"Memory given form," she corrected. "The sap holds fragments of consciousness—echoes of beings that once walked the nine realms. Gods, giants, elves, and the forgotten races." She gestured toward the distant branch, still visible behind them. "What you saw were their reflections, shaped from the Tree's essence."

"And the darker shapes? The ones that stayed beneath the surface?"

Something flickered across Æsa's face—concern, perhaps even fear. "Those are... different. Older. From before the Tree. Before the gods themselves."

A chill that had nothing to do with the mountain air crawled up Asvarr's spine. "How can anything exist before the Tree? The sagas say Yggdrasil has always been."

"The sagas tell what we could comprehend," Æsa replied, her voice dropping to little more than a whisper. "Some truths are kept hidden for a good reason."

They crested another ridge and descended into a narrow valley. Stunted pines clung to rocky soil, their needles frosted white. In the distance, a plume of smoke rose from what might have been a settlement or isolated steading.

"We'll avoid villages," Æsa said, following his gaze. "The mark draws attention, and not all who seek it wish you well."

"Like the elemental hunters from my village? Ice and fire?"

"Those were merely servants. Fragments themselves, in a way." She pointed toward a rocky overhang that offered some shelter from the wind. "We'll rest there briefly. I must examine what we've taken."

The outcropping formed a shallow cave, its entrance partially concealed by a curtain of hanging lichen. Inside, the temperature rose noticeably, protected from the biting wind. Æsa settled onto a flat stone, producing the wrapped fragment from her robes.

"Stand guard," she instructed, already unwinding the dark cloth. "The binding masks its light, but any with senses attuned to the Tree might still feel its presence."

Asvarr positioned himself at the cave entrance, one hand resting on the war horn, the other gripping his axe. From this vantage point, he could see back along the path they'd traveled and down into the valley below. No sign of pursuit yet, though the sky had darkened further, heavy clouds gathering in the north.

"Storm coming," he observed.

"Not a natural one," Æsa replied, without looking up from her work. "The fragment disturbs the air, the water, the very fabric of the world. Reality protests its removal from the branch."

The cloth came away completely, revealing the prophecy shard in Æsa's wrinkled palm. Even in daylight, it gleamed with inner radiance—silvery-white like moonlight condensed into solid form. Its edges were jagged where it had broken from some larger whole, its surface inscribed with runes so small and intricate they hurt Asvarr's eyes to look upon them directly.

"What does it say?" he asked, turning his attention back to their surroundings.

"Not all prophecy comes as words," Æsa murmured, tracing one gnarled finger above the fragment's surface, careful not to touch it directly. "This piece holds visions—fragments of what may come if certain paths are walked."

The Grímmark on Asvarr's chest throbbed in response to the shard's proximity. He felt the urge to take it from the völva, to press it against his rune, and let the visions flow freely through his mind.

"You saw some already," Æsa continued, as if reading his thoughts. "When you first touched it. Tell me what you witnessed."

Asvarr described the brief, fractured images: the völva carving a rune, the twisting root, the masked woman with nothing beneath, the crown of branches. Æsa listened intently, her expression growing more troubled with each description.

"The fragment shows different faces to different eyes," she said when he finished. "I see other things. Older things." She held the shard up to catch the fading light. "A tree growing from a skull. A wolf with stars caught in its teeth. A woman weaving fate on a loom of bones."

A sound from outside—subtle, almost lost in the wind—caught Asvarr's attention. He raised a hand for silence, straining to hear. There—a soft scraping, like claws on stone.

"We're not alone," he whispered.

Æsa quickly wrapped the fragment again, tucking it away. She rose with surprising agility, staff at the ready. "What approaches?"

Asvarr peered around the lichen curtain. At first, he saw nothing unusual—just rocks, scrub, and the darkening sky. Then, a shadow moved against the hillside, too fluid to be natural. Another joined it, then a third. They flowed across the rocky ground like spilled ink, converging on the cave entrance.

"Shadow-drinkers," he hissed. "They've found us."

"Impossible." Æsa's brow furrowed. "We sealed the path. They couldn't have followed so quickly."

"These are different ones." Asvarr pointed to their unusual movement pattern. Where the shadow-drinkers at the branch had maintained mostly humanoid form, these flowed like liquid shadow, only occasionally rising into vaguely bipedal shapes before collapsing back into amorphous darkness.

"No," Æsa breathed, her face paling. "Those aren't shadow-drinkers. They're darker-born—what you glimpsed beneath the sap. They've tracked the fragment's essence."

The shadows halted some twenty paces from the cave, pooling together into a single mass of undulating darkness. From this merged form, a shape rose—taller than a man, with limbs too numerous and jointed in all the wrong places. A head formed last, elongated and eyeless, with a mouth that split its face from crown to neck.

"What is that thing?" Asvarr demanded, raising his axe.

"Something that should not be," Æsa replied. Her staff glowed faintly, blue fire flickering along its length. "The dark between stars. The void beneath roots. It hungered before the Tree was seeded, before the gods shaped flesh from clay."

The creature took a step forward, its multiple limbs moving in unsettling synchronicity. Wherever its feet—if they could be called feet—touched the ground, frost spread in intricate patterns, beautiful and deadly.

"Gríiiiiimmark," it called, the word stretched and distorted, as if speaking caused it physical pain. "Giiiive what you've stooolen."

Asvarr's rune flared with white-hot intensity. Pain lanced through his chest, driving him to one knee. The mark recognized this thing—and feared it.

"We need to run," he gasped, fighting through the pain to stand again.

"No use," Æsa said grimly. "It will follow wherever we go." She raised her staff, blue fire now engulfing its entire length. "I'll hold it here. You must take the fragment and continue east."

"I'm not leaving you to die, crone."

"Who said anything about dying?" A fierce grin split her wrinkled face. "I've walked this world nine times. The darker-born don't frighten me."

The creature advanced another step. Frost patterns raced up the rocks surrounding the cave entrance, encasing the hanging lichen in delicate ice crystals that shattered at the slightest touch.

"There's a standing stone half a day's journey east," Æsa continued, pressing something into Asvarr's palm—the wrapped fragment. "Carved with the Elder Futhark. Place the fragment against the sowilo rune at sunset. It will show you where to find the next piece of the prophecy."

"I don't understand any of this," Asvarr growled, frustration boiling over. "Why me? Why the mark? What prophecy demands such a sacrifice?"

"The oldest one," Æsa replied. "The one the Norns themselves tried to unmake when they cut the thread of fate." Her dark eyes fixed on his. "Now go. I'll find you when this is finished."

Asvarr hesitated, torn between his warrior's instinct to stand and fight and the knowledge that his weapons had proven useless against such creatures before. The fragment pulsed in his hand, icy fire seeping through its wrappings.

The darker-born creature let out a sound like ice cracking across a frozen lake—a laugh, perhaps, or a challenge. Its mouth stretched wider, revealing nothing but a void within. It raised its many limbs, darkness pooling between them like liquid shadow given weight and mass.

"Listen well, berserker," Æsa said, her voice dropping to a fierce whisper. "The Tree chose you for a reason. The mark seeks five anchors—five fragments embedded in the five great roots that still live. Find them. Bind them. Or what comes next will make Ragnarök seem a gentle summer rain."

She stepped forward, placing herself between Asvarr and the creature. Blue fire cascaded from her staff, forming a wall of flame that separated them from the darker-born. Through the shimmering barrier, Asvarr saw the creature hesitate, its amorphous form rippling with what might have been uncertainty.

"Go!" Æsa commanded, not looking back.

Cursing under his breath, Asvarr turned and ran deeper into the cave. The passage continued farther than he'd expected, twisting through the mountain before eventually opening onto a narrow ledge on the eastern face. Below stretched a forest of ancient pines, their dark canopy undulating in the rising wind. The storm clouds had drawn closer, their undersides bruised and swollen with unnatural energies.

***

From behind came sounds of battle—Æsa's voice raised in guttural chants, the crack and hiss of magical fire, the inhuman shriek of the darker-born. The mountain itself seemed to shudder beneath Asvarr's feet.

He clutched the prophecy fragment, its icy fire now burning through the cloth wrapping, responding to his turmoil. The mark on his chest pulsed in counterpoint, urging him eastward toward the standing stone Æsa had mentioned.

A final, deafening crack split the air, followed by absolute silence. Asvarr turned, staring back toward the cave entrance, knowing he should return to help the völva.

But the Grímmark flared again, pain lancing through his chest with such intensity that he doubled over, gasping. When it subsided, certainty filled him—bone-deep and undeniable. The mark had chosen. The path lay eastward. Æsa had made her choice as well.

Gritting his teeth against regret, Asvarr began to descend the treacherous path toward the forest below. The fragment burned against his palm, forcing its way through the cloth until bare skin touched its crystalline surface.

Visions flooded his mind again—clearer this time, more insistent. A branch piercing stone. A serpent with one eye open. A blade grown from a root. A woman picking up a rune in the snow.

And beneath them all, rising from some great depth, shadows moving with terrible purpose—the darker-born and their kin, gathering for a hunt across broken realms.

Asvarr stumbled, nearly losing his footing on the narrow path. The prophecy fragment had burned completely through its wrapping now, glowing with silver-white intensity in his hand. Its light cast his shadow long and distorted against the mountainside—a shadow that moved just slightly out of sync with his own movements.

He stared at it, understanding crawling up his spine with icy fingers. Not his shadow at all.

Something followed him. Something born of darkness that even the fragment's light could not fully banish.

CHAPTER 3
THE GRÍMMARK RUNE

Asvarr's lungs burned with each ragged breath. The binding cloth scorched his palm where it wrapped the prophecy fragment, its heat penetrating the fabric despite Æsa's warnings. His boots broke through crusted snow, sinking him knee-deep with each lurching step. Blood—his own—speckled the white trail behind him.

The old völva had fallen behind hours ago. Her last words hammered his skull with each heartbeat. *Find the twin stones beyond the frost marsh. The third standing stone. Go!*

Steel-gray clouds churned overhead, swirling directly above him no matter how far he trudged. The storm tracked him as surely as the darker-born creature that had attacked them at the cave.

The fragment pulsed against his palm, matching the erratic rhythm in his chest where the Grímmark throbbed beneath his tunic. Golden light leaked between his fingers like trapped fireflies struggling to escape.

"Enough," he growled, stopping at the base of a wind-carved ridge. The words came out in a cloud of steam that froze in his beard. "Enough running."

A narrow ravine split the ridge, where wind howled between jagged stone formations. At its mouth stood two ancient pines, their trunks twisted toward each other like wrestlers locked in combat. Beyond them, through swirling snow, three dark monoliths punctured the white landscape—standing stones exactly as Æsa had described.

A woman waited there.

Asvarr dropped behind a boulder, muscles tensing. She stood motionless between the central and eastern stones; her form, a black silhouette against the snow. A crimson cloak whipped around her shoulders, its edges fraying in the wind. Even from this distance, he made out the silver beads and small bones woven into her dark braids.

Another völva. Younger than Æsa.

The prophecy fragment lurched in his hand—yanking toward her like iron to lodestone. The Grímmark flared in response, sending ribbons of molten pain across his chest that made him bite back a shout.

"Twice-marked man." Her voice sliced through the distance, cutting cleanly through the howling wind without seeming to rise in volume. "I see you hiding."

Asvarr gripped his axe but stayed low. "Where's Æsa?"

"The old crow walks shadow-paths now." The völva raised her hands, displaying skin stained black to the wrists. "I am Brenna, frost-speaker's daughter. Three days I've waited in this place."

"How'd you know I'd come here?"

Her laugh cracked like breaking ice. "Sky bleeds memory. Roots scream your name." She pointed directly at the cloth-wrapped fragment. "And *that* calls to those with ears to hear the dead."

His legs trembled as he stood. He'd slept only in nightmare-filled snatches since fleeing the bleeding branch. Hunger clawed at his stomach. The fragment's heat had blistered his palm despite the binding cloth, the pain shooting up his arm to join the deep ache of the Grímmark.

"What do you want with me?" he called, taking one tentative step toward the stones.

"Want?" She lowered her blackened hands. "The wanting is the root's, not mine. Come forward, Asvarr of the broken hearth. Your mark grows restless."

The way she said his name—like she'd tasted it a thousand times before—prickled the hairs on his neck. Yet the Grímmark urged him forward, its heat intensifying with each step toward the stones.

He approached warily, one hand never leaving his axe. The prophecy fragment pulsed faster against his palm, its rhythm speeding as the distance closed.

The standing stones loomed overhead, each carved with spiraling runes worn by centuries of wind and snow. The central stone stood tallest, its crown split into three jagged points, like a broken crown. A crude bowl had been carved at its base, filled with something dark that steamed in the frigid air.

Asvarr sniffed. "Blood?"

"Iron-water and yew sap." Brenna's eyes flashed—green as spring leaves, jarring against her winter-pale skin. "The blood comes next."

Asvarr gripped his axe tighter. "You'll get none of mine."

"You leaked it already, mark-bearer." Brenna stepped closer, her movement as sudden as a striking viper. Her hand pressed against his chest, directly over the Grímmark. The contact sent lightning coursing through him, dropping him to one knee as his muscles seized.

"You fight your wyrd," she whispered, face inches from his. "The mark knows. It burns hotter the more you deny it."

Asvarr grabbed her wrist, but couldn't break her grip. The Grímmark blazed beneath her palm, golden light streaming through his tunic's weave, illuminating both their faces in pulsing radiance.

"What must I do?" he grunted through locked teeth.

"The fragment joins with the mark. The rune completes itself." She drew a bone-handled knife from her cloak with her free hand, its blade blackened like her skin. "I carve what remains unfinished."

Asvarr wrenched backward, breaking her contact. Instantly, the Grímmark's burning subsided to a throb. "You mean to cut into me."

"I mean to save your life." She gestured to the stone. "Three days, I've watched golden fire leak from your chest while you sleep. The mark seeks its true form. Without it, you burn hollow from within."

The knowledge of his dreams startled him. He hadn't told Æsa how each night since the Tree fell, he'd woken to find gold light smoldering in his furs, seeping from the mark.

"How do you know what happens when I sleep?"

"The stones showed me your coming." Brenna touched the tallest monolith. "This rock watched stars before men first walked. It remembers when Yggdrasil was a sapling. Now it remembers *you*."

The stone hummed at her touch, a vibration Asvarr felt through the soles of his boots. The carved runes glimmered with the same golden light as his mark.

"Give me the fragment," she commanded, extending her blackened palm.

Asvarr hesitated, mouth dry. The fragment pulsed violently against his palm, its heat penetrating to bone. "What happens if I refuse?"

"The mark spreads until it devours you whole. The fragment burns until it reaches marrow." Brenna's eyes softened briefly. "Æsa knew. She guided you here to me because my hands do what hers could not."

"Why you specifically?"

"I am Brenna Flame-Carver." She raised her blackened hands. "This stain comes from working with the Tree's blood. Æsa read signs. I write them into flesh."

The fragment gave a violent pulse that buckled his knees. Golden light blazed through the binding cloth, illuminating the bones of his hand from within. Pain lanced up his arm toward his heart.

"It has waited too long," Brenna urged. "Choose now before it chooses for you."

Asvarr locked eyes with her. "If I give you this—if I let you cut me—what becomes of me after?"

"You become what you already are," she answered simply. "Skyrend's Flame."

The name hit him like a warhammer blow. The same whisper he'd heard from the smaller runestone in his destroyed village. The words that had haunted his dreams.

With a grimace, he extended his blistered palm, offering the fragment. Brenna took it, unwrapping the binding cloth with quick, practiced movements. The fragment blazed between her blackened fingers, casting long shadows across the snow.

She placed it in the carved basin. The mixture bubbled and hissed as the fragment sank into it.

"Remove your tunic," she commanded, raising the bone-knife.

Wind cut like shards of glass against Asvarr's exposed torso as he complied. The Grímmark had grown since the Tree's fall—no longer a simple rune but an intricate, half-formed pattern of interlocking lines centered over his heart. Golden light pulsed from its edges, veins of brightness spreading outward across his chest.

Brenna circled him once, studying the mark. "The Tree chose well. Your heart has strength enough to bear this burden."

She dipped her knife into the basin where the fragment dissolved. When she withdrew the blade, it gleamed with golden liquid that clung to the metal, neither dripping nor freezing in the bitter air.

"This will burn," she warned, stepping forward. "Fight it, and it will burn hotter."

Asvarr planted his feet wide in the snow, hands clenched. "Do what must be done."

Brenna pressed her left hand flat against his chest, directly over the Grímmark. Golden sparks cascaded down his torso. With her right hand, she pressed the knife to his skin just below the existing mark and cut deep.

Pain transcended anything Asvarr had known—battle wounds, broken bones, burning timber fallen across his legs as a child. His vision collapsed to a pinpoint as the blade carved somehow deeper, into memory and spirit. His scream shattered against the standing stones as Brenna worked, her face set in fierce concentration, her knife never hesitating.

Images flashed through his mind with each cut: the great tree burning, roots tearing free from the soil, a sky split by lightning, nine realms spinning through the void. He saw himself standing before a throne of twisted branches, saw his hands grasping fire that took solid form, saw shadows circling while he burned with golden flame.

The prophecy spoke directly into his skull: *Five roots torn free. Five anchors lost. Five wardens to find them. Five crowns to bear them.*

"I make you whole," Brenna muttered, her words barely penetrating the roaring in his ears. "I write your wyrd into your flesh."

The knife traced a final line. The Grímmark flared like a captive sun breaking free, golden light erupting from Asvarr's chest in a silent explosion. For one terrible moment, his consciousness fragmented, scattering across nine realms—he saw through countless eyes: wolves stalking frozen forests, eagles riding thermal currents, serpents coiling in lightless depths.

Then, with a thunderclap of inrushing air, his awareness slammed back into his body. He collapsed to his knees, gasping, skin steaming despite the freezing air. The pain receded, replaced by a vibration that synchronized with his heartbeat.

Brenna knelt before him, her face gleaming with sweat despite the cold. The basin at the standing stone's base had emptied, its contents transferred to the completed rune on Asvarr's chest. The mark no longer leaked light. It had settled into a fixed pattern—interlocking lines forming a shape reminiscent of both tree and flame.

"It is done," Brenna rasped, her voice strained. "You are bound to your path."

***

Asvarr tried to speak, his throat raw from screaming. "What... what happens now?"

"You are the first Warden awakened." Brenna traced a finger along the edge of his completed mark. "Skyrend's Flame. The one who finds the first anchor and binds the broken root."

"Is that what Æsa's prophecy said?"

"The oldest prophecy." Grief hollowed Brenna's features. "Written before the Tree, before gods. You must fulfill it before the roots die completely."

She helped him stand. The Grímmark no longer burned but hummed with power. Asvarr felt it spreading through him, changing him in ways his mind struggled to grasp.

"Listen," Brenna urged, watching his face. "Can you hear it?"

Asvarr stood still. Beneath the howling wind, beneath the crunch of snow and the creak of frozen earth, a distant song reached him—mournful and ancient. "The Root," he whispered. "It calls northward."

"Beyond the frost marsh lies the crevasse where the first Root fell. Your mark guides you now."

She retrieved a leather pack and wrapped bundle from beside the stone. "Æsa prepared these for your journey. Food, water, fire-steel. And this."

She unwrapped the bundle, revealing a sword unlike any Asvarr had seen. The blade gleamed with a dull bronze hue, its crossguard formed from twisted metal resembling gnarled roots. Runes lined its fuller, similar to those now completed on his chest.

"Æsa died protecting this sword," Brenna said. "Forged in the Third Age, when the Tree first sickened. It drinks the blood of shadow-born."

Asvarr took the weapon. It balanced perfectly in his hand; the grip fitting his palm as if made for him alone. "Æsa truly fell then?"

"Her flesh has. Her knowing lives in you now." Brenna pressed her fingers to his chest. "The Grímmark carries more than pain. It carries memory. In time, you will find what she knew within yourself."

His fingers tightened around the sword's hilt. "And you? What part do you play in this prophecy?"

Brenna's smile held no warmth. "I am the carver of paths. I have marked four others as I've marked you. When the time comes, your paths will cross."

She stepped back, drawing her crimson cloak tight. "Go north, Skyrend's Flame. The Root guides you. Trust the mark." Her voice dropped to a murmur. "And beware the Ashfather."

"Ashfather?" The unfamiliar name raised hackles on Asvarr's neck.

The completed Grímmark thrummed at the name, sending a single pulse of warning through his body. Suddenly, the wind rose to a howling gale, whipping snow between them in a white wall. Brenna's form blurred.

"He hunts the marked ones!" she called over the storm. "He wears a god's face, but he is the Tree's oldest enemy!"

The blizzard intensified to a solid sheet of white. Asvarr raised his arm against the assault, shouting Brenna's name. When the wind subsided moments later, he stood alone among the standing stones.

Only the completed Grímmark, his new sword, and the pack of supplies proved she had existed at all. That, and the pull he felt deep within—a compass needle of golden heat pointing northward, where the Root awaited its Warden.

Asvarr turned his face toward the frozen waste beyond the stones. The Grímmark pulsed once, firmly, as if approving his resolve. The first step of his unwanted destiny had been carved into his flesh. The next would be carved in the ice and shadows of the North.

Asvarr trudged northward, each step driving him deeper into the frozen wilderness. The weight of the bronze sword pulled at his back where he'd strapped it, a constant reminder of Æsa's sacrifice. His chest no longer burned, but the Grímmark hummed with contained power, guiding him like a lodestone toward the fallen Root.

By sunset, the standing stones vanished behind him, swallowed by distance and swirling snow. Twilight bled purple across the eastern sky while the west burned crimson. The air carried the scent of a coming storm—metallic and sharp, laced with something else he couldn't name.

He paused atop a frozen ridge. Far below, a vast expanse of white stretched toward distant mountains—the frost marsh Brenna had mentioned. A thousand dark shapes dotted its surface, twisted trees frozen in grotesque postures, their limbs reaching skyward like drowning men's arms.

The bronze sword vibrated against his back. Asvarr drew it, the metal gleaming dully in the fading light. Runes etched along its fuller pulsed once, then twice, responding to something he couldn't see.

"What do you sense?" he murmured to the blade.

The sword's vibration intensified. The runes brightened from dull bronze to living gold, matching the pattern on his chest. Through the grip, he felt a warning—vague but urgent.

Movement caught his eye. At the frost marsh's edge, shadows shifted unnaturally, flowing against the wind. His grip tightened on the sword.

"Five roots torn free," he whispered, recalling the prophecy's words. "Five anchors lost."

The Grímmark thrummed in response, as if confirming his memory. With it came a faint, whisper-voice he recognized as Æsa's, though the old völva was dead: *The shadows seek the marked ones. They know what you carry.*

Asvarr's heart pounded against his ribs. Something had changed when Brenna completed the rune. Fragments of Æsa's knowing had transferred to him, locked within the mark itself. He could access them—faintly, like remembering a half-forgotten dream.

He descended the ridge, each step calculated. The marsh stretched before him, a necessary crossing on his path north. No detour was possible if he wanted to reach the Root before the next full moon. Brenna had made that timeline clear, though she hadn't explained why.

The frozen surface cracked beneath his boots, ice crystallized over the sucking bog. Dead trees loomed, their bark blackened as if burned. No birds called. No small creatures rustled the frozen undergrowth. The silence pressed against his eardrums like physical pressure.

The sword's vibration grew stronger the deeper he pushed into the marsh. Its warning traveled up his arm, raising the hairs on the back of his neck. The shadows he'd glimpsed from the ridge had now vanished, yet he felt them watching, tracking his passage.

Something crunched beneath his boot. Asvarr looked down.

Bones. Human bones, cracked and gnawed, scattered across the ice. Ahead lay more—dozens, perhaps hundreds — of skeletons frozen into the marsh, partially exposed where the wind had scoured away snow. Their eye sockets stared upward, jaws locked in silent screams.

The Grímmark pulsed once, hard. Asvarr dropped to a crouch, sword extended.

"Who died here?" he breathed.

Æsa's knowledge stirred in his blood: *The shadow-father's first harvest. Those who tried to reach the Root unprepared.*

A movement twenty paces ahead—a shadow flowing across bone and ice like oil on water, gathering substance with each passing moment. It rose, coalescing into a man-shape that flickered and wavered at its edges.

"Marked one," the shadow-shape hissed. Its voice crackled like burning parchment. "The Ashfather sends greetings."

Asvarr raised the bronze sword, its golden runes illuminating the gathering darkness. "What are you?"

"Memory-thief. Soulskinner. Ash-born." The shape's features sharpened—a gaunt face, hollow eyes that reflected nothing. "Names matter little. What matters is the message."

"Speak it then."

The creature smiled, revealing teeth like shards of obsidian. "The Ashfather offers mercy. Surrender the mark willingly, and your death comes quick."

Asvarr's knuckles whitened around the sword hilt. "Who is this Ashfather?"

"The one who wore a god's face before gods existed." The shadow-shape rippled, growing taller, broader. "The one who will wear the Tree's crown when the last root dies."

Asvarr stepped backward, ice cracking beneath his boot. The bog shifted, threatening to swallow him. "Tell your master I refuse his offer."

"Then you choose the harder path." The shadow-thing's arms extended, elongating into writhing tendrils that reached for Asvarr's chest, for the Grímmark glowing beneath his tunic. "The slow unmaking. The memory-death."

***

Asvarr swung the bronze sword in a wide arc. Where the blade met shadow, golden light flared. The creature shrieked, its body sizzling where the metal touched it. It recoiled, form shimmering at the edges.

"Æsa-forged," it hissed, backing away. "Root-touched metal."

Asvarr advanced, emboldened by the creature's fear. The sword felt alive in his hands, eager for the fight. The Grímmark pulsed in time with his racing heart, feeding strength into his limbs.

The shadow-thing darted sideways, inhumanly fast. Its tendrils lashed out, no longer aiming for his chest but for the sword itself. One wrapped around Asvarr's wrist, cold as a tomb-stone, sapping warmth from his flesh. His fingers numbed instantly.

Asvarr roared, channeling rage into motion. He drove the sword's point directly into the creature's center mass. Golden light exploded from the impact, blinding in its intensity. The shadow-thing's form disintegrated, collapsing into oily smoke that dispersed on the wind, leaving only a lingering scream that echoed across the marsh.

Frost crept up Asvarr's arm from where the tendril had touched him, skin blackening with cold-burn. The pain hit a heartbeat later, sharp enough to drive him to his knees. The bronze sword clattered onto the ice beside him.

"Poison," he gasped. "Shadow-poison."

The Grímmark flared in response. Golden light spread from his chest down his arm, fighting the advancing frost. Where light touched blackened flesh, the frost receded, though slowly, grudgingly.

Asvarr forced himself to breathe. In, out. In, out. The magic of the mark worked through him, burning away the shadow's taint. When he could move his fingers again, he retrieved the sword, its runes now dimmed to their normal bronze hue.

He looked across the marsh. Where one shadow-thing had appeared, others would follow. The bones of failed travelers testified to their numbers and their patience.

"Show me a path," he whispered to the Grímmark. "Safe passage through this death-place."

The mark pulsed once, then twice. A faint golden glow spread outward from his chest, illuminating a narrow trail through the frozen bog—solid ground hidden beneath treacherous ice and snow. Following the mark's guidance, Asvarr began picking his way forward, careful to step only where the light showed safe passage.

Night fell completely, wrapping the marsh in blackness. The only light came from the Grímmark's glow, revealing just a few feet of the path ahead. Beyond that perimeter, shadows gathered, watching. Occasionally, red eyes blinked in the darkness, appearing and vanishing too quickly to target.

Asvarr walked for hours, muscles burning with exertion. The mark's guidance never faltered, though the route twisted and doubled back on itself many times, following hidden safe ground that only the Tree's memory could identify.

Midnight approached when the mark's glow suddenly intensified, drawing Asvarr's attention to a dark shape ahead, half-buried in the marsh. Unlike the twisted trees, this object had purpose in its form—a standing stone similar to those where he'd met Brenna, but this one had fallen, lying at an angle in the frozen muck.

The Grímmark pulled him toward it. Asvarr approached cautiously, bronze sword ready. The fallen monolith bore runes different from those at the ritual site—sharper, more angular, carved deeper into the stone. They did not glow or respond to his presence.

At the stone's base, partially exposed, lay a cloth bundle. The fabric had once been white, now stained brown with old blood. The Grímmark urged Asvarr forward, its pull unmistakable.

He knelt, probing the bundle with his sword tip. Nothing moved or reacted. With careful fingers, he unwrapped the stained fabric.

Inside lay a horn, a musical instrument. Carved from pale wood or bone, its surface bore intricate knotwork patterns that spiraled toward the tip. Small runes, identical to those now completed on his chest, followed the spiral pattern.

The moment his fingers touched it, visions exploded behind his eyes:

A warrior in bronze armor, horn raised to his lips, standing before a circle of standing stones. Golden light blazing from his chest as he sounds a note that splits the heavens.

Five hooded figures gathered around a table of black stone, their faces hidden in shadow. A map scratched into the surface, five X marks scattered across its face.

The great Tree itself, roots torn from the earth, massive trunk splitting. Between the splintering halves, a face—inhuman, ancient, hungry—emerging from within the bark.

The visions broke. Asvarr found himself on his knees, clutching the horn, gasping for breath. The Grímmark burned brighter than ever, recognizing the object he held.

"What are you?" he whispered to the horn.

***

No words came, but knowledge flickered at the edges of his mind—the horn had belonged to the previous Warden, the one who came before, when the Tree first sickened. A summoner of Root-power, a caller of allies.

With trembling hands, Asvarr tucked the horn into his belt. As he rose, the surrounding shadows stirred, agitated by his discovery. Red eyes appeared in greater numbers, blinking from the darkness between dead trees.

"They come!" Æsa's whisper-voice urged in his mind. "Run, Warden!"

Asvarr bolted, following the golden path laid out by the Grímmark. Behind him, shadow-shapes detached from the darkness, flowing across the marsh in pursuit. Their hissing voices called his name, promising suffering, unmaking, memory-death.

The path curved sharply eastward, away from his northern goal. Asvarr hesitated only a moment before following it. The Grímmark would not lead him astray.

The marsh thinned. Trees grew sparser, the ground more solid beneath his feet. Ahead, a ridge of stone rose from the flat landscape, a natural wall thirty feet high. At its base, a dark opening gaped—a cave or tunnel.

The golden path led directly to it. Asvarr sprinted the final distance, shadow-things closing from behind. He felt their icy breath on his neck, heard their clawed feet scrabbling on the ice.

He reached the cave entrance and stumbled inside. Darkness swallowed him. The Grímmark's light revealed rough stone walls covered in ancient markings—handprints in red ochre, spiral patterns that matched those on the horn, stick-figure hunting scenes from an age before memory.

The shadows hesitated at the threshold. Their forms roiled and twisted, unable or unwilling to cross.

"Warded ground," one hissed. "Old magic."

"Marked one," called another, its voice honeyed with false promise. "The horn brings only death. It failed its last bearer. It will fail you too."

Asvarr backed deeper into the cave, sword raised. "Your master fears it, or you wouldn't care that I found it."

The shadow-things conferred in sibilant whispers. Finally, the largest addressed him again:

"The Ashfather remembers you, Asvarr Hjalmarsson. When your father died on his blade, he begged mercy for his son."

Ice formed in Asvarr's veins. "My father died raiding eastern shores. Fell to a farmer's spear."

The shadow laughed, the sound like breaking glass. "Memories lie. Especially those planted by the Ashfather himself."

The Grímmark flared, burning away the cold doubt trying to take root in Asvarr's heart. The mark knew truth from lies, even when his mind could not.

"Begone," Asvarr commanded, raising the bronze sword. Its runes ignited, golden light spilling onto the cave floor. "Tell your master I'm coming for his head, whatever face it wears."

The shadow-things retreated, dissolving into the marsh darkness. Their whispers lingered long after their forms vanished: *The Ashfather comes. The Ashfather comes.*

When silence returned, Asvarr sagged against the cave wall, exhaustion claiming him. The sword's runes dimmed. The Grímmark's light subsided to a gentle pulse that matched his slowing heartbeat.

He examined the horn more carefully in the mark's glow. Its age was impossible to determine—the material neither weathered nor worn despite obvious antiquity. The runes spelled out no words he recognized, yet their meaning stirred at the edges of his consciousness, knowledge waiting to surface.

"Why did you guide me here?" he asked the Grímmark. "The Root lies northward."

Æsa's whispered knowledge provided no answer. The mark had its own purpose, its own memory, older than any völva's wisdom.

Asvarr moved deeper into the cave, following the passage as it wound into the earth. The Grímmark's light revealed more ancient paintings—figures gathered around a great tree, hands raised in supplication or warning. Nine circles connected by lines, representing the realms. A crowned figure holding fire in one hand, roots in the other.

The passage opened into a chamber where water dripped from stalactites into a clear pool. The liquid caught the Grímmark's light, reflecting it in golden ripples across the walls. At the pool's center stood a stone platform that rose just above the water's surface.

Compelled by instinct he didn't understand, Asvarr waded into the knee-deep water. The cold bit through his leggings, but the mark's warmth sustained him. He climbed onto the platform, water streaming from his boots.

In the platform's center, a circular depression waited—perfectly sized for the base of the horn.

Asvarr removed the instrument from his belt. The Grímmark pulsed urgently, driving him forward. He placed the horn into the depression, where it fit perfectly, locking into place with a soft click.

The platform rumbled beneath his feet. Ancient mechanisms ground to life somewhere deep below. The pool's water vibrated, forming patterns on its surface—runes and symbols that shifted too quickly to read.

Asvarr felt the Grímmark respond, its completed pattern resonating with the horn and water. Something was awakening in him.

The horn began to glow with the same golden light as his mark. The runes carved into its surface brightened one by one, spiraling from base to tip until the entire instrument blazed.

He heard a voice, immensely older than Æsa's and beyond understanding, speaking directly to his thoughts.

First Warden awakened. Root-Singer recognized. The summoning begins.

The words burned themselves into Asvarr's memory. The ground shook more violently. Water sloshed against the platform's edges. From deep within the cave came a sound of massive weight shifting, stone grinding against stone.

The horn levitated from its depression, rising to hover before Asvarr's face. It rotated slowly in the air, the glowing spiral of runes hypnotic in its movement.

Take what is yours, Root-Singer. The first token of five. Bind what was broken.

Asvarr reached out. His fingers closed around the horn. The moment he touched it, knowledge flooded him—how to use it, when to call, what notes would summon aid or unleash destruction. This was the first Warden's tool, created when Yggdrasil first showed signs of sickness, long before the catastrophic breaking.

The horn settled into his grip, its light subsiding to a gentle glow that matched the Grímmark's pulse. The cave stilled. The water calmed.

Asvarr turned toward the passage that had brought him here. The path ahead became clear—to the fallen Root and the scattered anchors beyond, across nine realms. The horn would help him reach them and would help him gather the other Wardens when the time came.

"The first token of five," he murmured, securing the horn to his belt.

As if in response, both the horn and Grímmark pulsed once in perfect synchronization. For the first time since the Tree fell, Asvarr felt purpose replacing confusion, determination overcoming reluctance.

He waded back through the pool, water swirling around his legs. At the chamber's exit, he paused, looking back at the platform and the ancient paintings surrounding it. Generations of knowledge waited here, preserved for him to find at exactly this moment.

The shadow-things would still hunt him. The Ashfather, whoever or whatever it was, wanted him dead. The fallen Root awaited, its anchor needing to be bound.

Asvarr gripped the horn with renewed resolve. Skyrend's Flame, the shadow had named him. Root-Singer, the ancient voice called him. Names of power and purpose, carved into his flesh and destiny.

He would earn them both.

CHAPTER 4

OATHS UNDER HOLLOW SKY

Asvarr emerged from the warded cave at dawn. Frost rimmed his beard, and his breath clouded before him in the bitter morning air. The marsh lay quiet under new-fallen snow, with no sign of the shadow-things that had pursued him through the night. Above, the sky stretched empty—a pale, washed-out blue without a cloud or bird. The emptiness made his skin crawl. Even during winter storms, the northern skies had never felt so... abandoned.

The horn hung heavy at his belt, its weight a constant reminder of his new purpose. The Grímmark pulsed steadily beneath his tunic, urging him northward again. Every heartbeat pulled him closer to the fallen Root.

Asvarr shouldered the pack Brenna had given him, adjusted the bronze sword on his back, and began picking his way across the frozen marsh. The Grímmark's glow created a faint, golden path visible only to his eyes, showing safe passage through treacherous ice.

By midday, the marsh thinned. Solid ground replaced the frozen bog. Pine forests crowded the horizon, their dark branches heavy with snow. The Grímmark's pull strengthened with each passing mile.

The first corpses appeared at the forest's edge—warriors like himself, frozen in postures of flight or battle. Their flesh had blackened with cold that went beyond winter's touch. Shadow-poison. The same frost that had crept up his own arm before, the Grímmark burned it away.

Asvarr knelt beside the nearest body, a broad-shouldered man whose fingers still clutched a shattered axe. His clan markings were unfamiliar—southern, perhaps from the fjord settlements beyond the great ridge. No ravens had touched the body. No wolves had stripped the flesh. Even in death, something about these shadow-poisoned corpses repelled nature itself.

"You sought the Root, too," Asvarr murmured, closing the man's frost-clouded eyes. "What drew you here? The same dreams that plague me?"

The dead man offered no answers. Asvarr moved on, following the Grímmark's guidance into the pine forest. More bodies waited among the trees—dozens, perhaps hundreds. Some wore armor he recognized from coastal settlements. Others dressed in unfamiliar skins and furs from inland tribes. All had died fighting something that left no wounds except the creeping shadow-frost.

The trees thinned, revealing a vast clearing a half-mile across. At its center gaped a wound in the earth—a chasm fifty paces wide that cut through forest and stone alike. Something sheared the edges clean, as if a god's blade had sliced open the world itself.

From within the chasm rose the Root.

Massive beyond comprehension, thicker than the greatest mead-hall, it protruded from the earth at an angle. Its surface gleamed bronze-gold in the weak sunlight, bark patterns spiraling in complex whorls no human mind could fully grasp. The exposed portion stretched upward nearly five hundred feet before disappearing into a torn wound in the sky itself—a ragged hole in reality through which distant stars glimmered despite the daylight.

The Grímmark blazed against Asvarr's chest, recognizing its counterpart. His legs carried him forward without conscious thought, drawn by the pull between mark and Root.

He stopped at the chasm's edge. Far below, darkness waited—a fall with no visible bottom. The Root emerged from that darkness, its true length impossible to gauge. Along its vast circumference, thousands of smaller tendrils branched outward like normal tree roots, some thicker than a man's waist, others fine as hairs. Many had been severed, leaking golden sap that pooled and crystallized among the rocks below.

Corpses surrounded the chasm—more dead seekers who had reached this place only to fall to shadow-poison. Their bodies formed concentric rings around the Root, as if they had fought their way forward in waves.

Movement caught Asvarr's eye. Among the dead, a figure stirred—a woman, barely more than a girl, propped against a boulder thirty paces from the chasm's edge. Blood matted her pale hair, and shadow-frost crept up her left arm toward her heart. She clutched a broken spear with her good hand.

Asvarr approached cautiously, bronze sword drawn. "Who still lives here?"

The girl's eyes snapped open—blue as glacier ice, bright with fever or madness. "Another lamb for slaughter?" Her voice cracked from thirst. "The shadows will take you, too."

"The shadows tried. They failed." Asvarr knelt beside her, keeping his sword ready. "What's your name?"

"Hildr." She coughed, blood speckling her chapped lips. "Shield-maiden of Ormvik."

"You're far from home, shield-maiden." Asvarr studied the creeping frost on her arm. Already, it had reached her shoulder, blackening the flesh. "What brought you to the Root?"

"Dreams." Hildr's eyes drifted toward the massive Root. "Every night for a moon-turn. The Tree called. Showed me this place." Her gaze sharpened, focusing on Asvarr's chest where the Grímmark pulsed beneath his tunic. "You bear a mark."

"Yes."

"The others who came... some had marks too. Different patterns." She swallowed with difficulty. "The shadows took them first. Dragged them, screaming, into the chasm."

Asvarr's blood chilled. "Others with marks? How many?"

"Six... maybe seven. They came alone or in small bands." Hildr's breathing grew labored as the shadow-frost crept higher. "One had a mark like fire across his back. Another wore hers on her face like a web of silver. The shadow-king spoke to them before killing them."

"Shadow-king?"

"He guards the Root." Hildr pointed with her good hand toward the chasm. "Tall as three men. Wears a crown of roots and bones. His touch brings this." She glanced at her blackened arm. "Only those with true marks can reach the anchor, he said. The others were false-marked. Pretenders."

The Grímmark pulsed, recognizing truth in her words. Asvarr remembered what Brenna had said—she had marked four others like him. If some of those she mentioned had been killed here...

"How long since the shadow-king last appeared?" he asked.

"Two days. He comes when new seekers arrive." Hildr coughed again, more blood speckling her lips. "He'll smell your mark soon enough."

Asvarr reached for his waterskin. "Here, drink. I can—"

"No." Hildr pushed his hand away. "The frost reaches my heart. Nothing stops it now." Her ice-blue eyes locked onto his. "But I would not die for nothing. Take my oath before I go."

"What oath can I take from you, shield-maiden?"

"The oath of my clan." With visible effort, Hildr straightened against the boulder. "If you survive this place—if you bind the Root as the dreams foretold—you will return to Ormvik. Tell them how Hildr Iron-Heart died facing the shadow-king. Tell them I did not run when others fled."

Asvarr recognized the request for what it was. In their culture, how one died mattered as much as how one lived. To die forgotten was to be erased from the great saga. Hildr wanted her end remembered, her courage witnessed.

"I swear by my mark and blood," Asvarr said formally, drawing his knife and slicing his palm. "If I survive, Ormvik will know of Hildr Iron-Heart's stand at the Root."

Relief flooded the girl's face. She reached out with her good hand, pressing bloody fingers against Asvarr's wound, sealing the oath in the old way. "The shadow-king speaks before he kills," she whispered. "He told the false-marked that his master comes once three Wardens fall. The Ashfather will wear the Tree's crown."

The Grímmark flared in warning. "When does he emerge from the chasm?"

"With the sunset. He brings shadow-born with him." Hildr's voice weakened. The frost climbed her neck, crystallizing along her jaw. "One more thing, marked one. The Root... it hides something." Her words came slower, labored, between frozen breaths. "Something deeper than the shadow-king. Something that sings."

Asvarr leaned closer. "What does it sing of?"

"The end of gods," Hildr whispered. "And the beginning of something worse."

Her eyes clouded as the frost reached them. Her body stiffened, the blackened flesh creaking faintly as water crystallized within. In moments, she looked no different from the other corpses surrounding the chasm—another dead seeker, frozen in her final words.

Asvarr closed her eyes with gentle fingers and said, "Rest well, Hildr Iron-Heart."

***

He stood, studying the chasm with new wariness. Sunset approached—perhaps three hours remained before the shadow-king emerged from the depths. Too little time to formulate a proper plan, but retreat felt impossible with the Grímmark pulling him toward the Root with increasing urgency.

Asvarr circled the chasm, examining the dead, seeking anything useful. Most carried common weapons—axes, short swords, and spears. None had made a mark on their shadowy opponent. Among the bodies, he found six with partial runes burned into their flesh—the false-marked Hildr had mentioned. Their incomplete patterns differed from his Grímmark, cruder and misshapen.

Self-marked, Asvarr realized. Desperate souls who had carved Yggdrasil's runes into their own bodies, hoping to claim power over the fallen Root. The shadow-king had punished their presumption.

Near the chasm's northernmost edge, Asvarr discovered a body unlike the others—an old man in tattered gray robes, his white beard frozen with blood. No shadow-frost marked him. Instead, a single wound pierced his chest, the surrounding flesh scorched black. In his dead fingers, he clutched a leather-bound book sealed with iron clasps.

Asvarr pried the tome from the old man's rigid grasp. The cover bore no title, only a complex knot-pattern stamped into the age-darkened leather. The iron clasps resisted his attempts to open them, growing warm, then painfully hot against his fingers.

The Grímmark pulsed once, hard. Golden light spread from Asvarr's chest, down his arms to his fingertips. The clasps cooled immediately, clicking open at his touch.

Inside, pages of vellum covered in dense script met his eyes. The language was unfamiliar—older than any he had seen, though certain characters resembled runes he recognized. Illustrations filled the margins—detailed drawings of Yggdrasil, its roots, and figures that might be Wardens or gods.

One page bore an illustration of a crowned shadow-figure rising from a chasm identical to the one before him. Opposite it stood a marked warrior, hands raised in what might be defense or supplication. Between them, a spiral of runes connected warrior to shadow.

The Grímmark throbbed in recognition. Some knowledge within the mark recognized this book, these illustrations. Asvarr felt understanding just beyond his grasp—tantalizing fragments of memory that belonged to the mark's previous bearer, perhaps, or to the Root itself.

He tucked the book into his pack. Whatever secrets it held would have to wait. The sun hung low on the horizon, stretching its shadow long across the frozen ground. The time for preparation had ended.

Asvarr checked his weapons one last time—bronze sword, iron knife, Hakon's horn at his belt, alongside the ancient horn from the warded cave. The Grímmark pulsed steadily beneath his tunic, stronger than ever this close to the Root.

He approached the chasm's edge. Looking down into that perfect darkness, Asvarr felt vertigo grip him, a deep dizziness, as if reality itself thinned near the Root.

"I am here," he called into the void. "Warden of the mark. Root-Singer. Skyrend's Flame."

His voice echoed strangely, bouncing back distorted and multiplied, as if many voices answered from below. The air temperature plummeted. Frost formed on Asvarr's eyelashes and beard in an instant.

From the chasm depths rose a sound—stone grinding against stone, massive weight shifting in darkness. A fetid odor wafted upward, the stench of ancient decay preserved in ice.

The shadow-king emerged.

It rose from the chasm with terrible grace, enormous hands gripping the Root itself as handholds. Its form wavered between solid and mist, a towering humanoid shape twelve feet tall with limbs too long and thin for its broad torso. Atop its shoulders, a crown of twisted roots and yellowed bones, beneath which swirled shadow deeper than night. Two pinpricks of crimson light served as eyes, floating in that darkness.

It pulled itself onto solid ground with fluid motions and stood to its full height. The crown of roots brushed pine branches thirty feet overhead.

"Little Warden," the shadow-king's voice grated like glaciers calving. "I smell the Flame-Carver's mark upon you. True-etched, not self-carved like these fools." It gestured dismissively at the corpses surrounding the chasm.

Asvarr kept his bronze sword raised, though the weapon suddenly felt inadequate against this entity. "I've come for the Root's anchor."

"Many come. All feed the hunger below." The shadow-king moved with unsettling speed, circling Asvarr like a predator assessing prey. "The mark burns bright within you, little flame. The first Warden awakened." Its crown of roots twisted, reconfiguring into a mockery of a thoughtful expression. "But one is not enough."

"Enough for what?"

"To matter." The shadow-king stopped circling. "My master comes when three Wardens fall. Already, I have taken two false-marked who thought themselves worthy. Soon he will send others to test you—true-marked but weak, unworthy of their etching."

Asvarr's mind raced. The shadow-king served the Ashfather, clearly, but spoke of other true-marked individuals—the very ones Brenna claimed to have carved.

"Hildr mentioned a song from within the Root," Asvarr said, shifting to keep the creature in view. "What sings beneath your feet, shadow-king?"

The crimson eyes flared with something like amusement. "The anchor dreams. It remembers when it was whole, when the Tree stood unbroken." The shadow-king's voice lowered to a rumble. "It remembers you, little Warden, though you have never stood here before."

"How could it remember me?"

"Time pools around the Root like sap. Past, present, future—all one substance here." The shadow-king's crown twisted again, bones clicking against each other. "In one flow of time, you bind the anchor and awaken the Root. In another, I drag your soul, screaming, into the void. The anchor remembers both."

The Grímmark burned against Asvarr's chest, responding to the creature's words. He felt the Root calling to him with a deep resonance in his blood and bone.

"Enough talk," Asvarr growled, tightening his grip on the bronze sword. "Stand aside, or face me."

The shadow-king laughed, the sound like breaking ice. "Brave little flame. Your sword might harm my servants, but I am not shadow-born. I am the shadow that births." It spread impossibly long arms. "Still, formalities must be observed. Defend yourself, Warden of the mark."

It attacked with blinding speed, covering the distance between them in a single bound. Clawed hands raked where Asvarr's head had been a heartbeat before. He rolled sideways, bronze sword slicing through the creature's midsection.

The blade passed through shadow without resistance. The shadow-king's form flowed around the metal like smoke, reforming instantly.

"First lesson," it hissed, "I am no creature of flesh."

Asvarr retreated, mind racing. If the bronze sword couldn't harm it, what would? The horn at his belt pulsed with the same rhythm as the Grímmark. Acting on instinct, he grabbed it with his free hand.

The shadow-king lunged again. This time, Asvarr stood his ground, raising the horn to his lips. He blew a single, pure note that came from the knowledge locked within the Grímmark.

Sound rippled outward, visible as golden waves in the air. Where they struck the shadow-king, its form solidified momentarily, darkness becoming tangible flesh and bone.

Asvarr swung the bronze sword through that brief solidity. The blade bit deep, drawing ichor black as night. The shadow-king shrieked, the sound shattering ice from nearby trees.

"Second lesson," Asvarr countered, "I am no common warrior."

The shadow-king's form rippled with fury. It retreated several paces, crimson eyes flaring. "The Horn of Binding," it snarled. "Where did you find what was hidden?"

Asvarr advanced, horn ready for another blast. "The mark guided me."

"The mark." The shadow-king's voice dripped with contempt. "A leash the Tree uses to control its puppets. Do you even know what you are, little Warden? What becoming a Root-Singer will cost you?"

"I know my path." Asvarr raised the bronze sword. "Step aside, or face your unmaking."

The crimson eyes narrowed to slits. "You know nothing of unmaking."

The shadow-king's form expanded, growing to twice its already enormous size. Darkness poured from it like liquid night, flowing across the ground toward the surrounding corpses. Where shadow touched dead flesh, the bodies stirred, rising on frost-stiffened limbs, eyes glowing with the same crimson light as their master.

"Third lesson," the shadow-king growled as its undead servants shuffled forward. "I never fight alone."

Asvarr found himself surrounded by a dozen corpse-warriors, each bearing the weapons they had died clutching. Hildr herself rose among them, broken spear raised in a mockery of her final defiance.

"Your oath to her means nothing now," the shadow-king laughed. "She serves me in death, as all Rootseekers do."

Rage burned through Asvarr's veins. The desecration of honored dead violated everything sacred in their culture. The Grímmark flared in response to his fury, golden light cutting through his tunic.

"Her oath is witnessed," Asvarr snarled. "Her name is remembered. You have no power over that."

He raised the horn again and blew a different note—deeper, more resonant. This sound didn't spread outward but downward, vibrating through soil and stone toward the Root itself.

The massive Root trembled. Golden sap welled from its countless wounds, dripping onto the ground where corpse-warriors stood. Where sap touched shadow-animated flesh, the crimson light in dead eyes flickered and died. Bodies collapsed like puppets with cut strings.

The shadow-king roared in frustration. "You dare turn the Root against me? I AM ITS GUARDIAN!"

"You're its jailer," Asvarr countered, advancing as the corpse-warriors fell. "And your prisoner has answered my call."

The shadow-king's form wavered, uncertainty replacing rage. It glanced toward the chasm, toward the Root. Something was changing—the air vibrated with tension, reality bending around the massive Root as it responded to the horn's call.

For the first time, fear showed in those crimson eyes.

The Root trembled, sap flowing more freely from its countless wounds. Tendrils of golden light spread through the frozen ground, forming a network of glowing veins that converged where Asvarr stood. The shadow-king backed away, crimson eyes darting between Asvarr and the massive Root.

"You understand nothing of what you awaken," the shadow-king hissed.

Asvarr advanced, bronze sword in one hand, horn in the other. The golden light from the ground bathed him from below, merging with the Grímmark's glow that poured from his chest. For the first time since finding the mark, he felt power rather than pain flowing through it.

"I understand enough," he said. "You fear it."

The shadow-king's form wavered, edges bleeding into the gathering darkness as twilight deepened. "The Tree broke for reason, Warden. Its wholeness threatened, worse than its shattering."

"More Ashfather lies."

"Ask the Root yourself." The shadow-king gestured toward the chasm. "It remembers why it chose to fall."

The words struck Asvarr like a physical blow. Chose to fall? Everything he'd learned from Brenna and Æsa implied the Tree's shattering was a catastrophe, something to be undone. The idea that Yggdrasil might have broken itself deliberately churned his gut with doubt.

The Grímmark pulsed, steadying him. Whatever truth existed, the shadow-king twisted it to serve the Ashfather's purpose.

"Enough words," Asvarr growled. "Face me, or flee."

The shadow-king's crown of roots reconfigured, forming a grotesque approximation of a smile. "I need neither fight nor flee, little flame."

It raised elongated arms skyward. The twilight sky darkened further, stars vanishing as if swallowed by the encroaching void. From the chasm around the Root came a chittering sound—thousands of slight movements in the darkness below.

The shadow-born emerged, pouring from the depths like a dark tide. Small, twisted creatures with too many limbs and too few features swarmed up the chasm walls. Each stood no higher than Asvarr's knee, but their numbers made the ground itself appear to flow and shift.

"My children hunger," the shadow-king intoned. "The Root has denied them sustenance for too long."

***

The creatures surged forward. Asvarr swung his bronze sword in a wide arc, the blade shearing through the first wave. Where it touched them, shadow-born dissolved into an oily mist that dissipated on the wind. Yet for each one destroyed, ten more scrambled forward.

Asvarr retreated, boots slipping on frozen ground. The Grímmark burned beneath his tunic, its glow intensifying with each shadow-creature he killed. The horn at his belt pulsed in counterpoint, urging him toward the Root.

The shadow-king watched from a distance, its crown tilted in what might have been amusement. "Run to the Root if you wish, Warden. Its touch brings revelation. And madness."

A shadow-born leapt at Asvarr's face, claws extended. He ducked, the creature sailing over his head to land among its kin. Another latched onto his leg, needle-teeth sinking through leather into flesh. Asvarr roared, driving his sword through its center. It dissolved with a shriek, but the wound burned with shadow-poison.

Scores more shadow-born advanced. Asvarr knew he couldn't fight them all. The horn in his hand offered his only chance.

He raised it to his lips and blew three short notes in succession. The sound sliced through the twilight air, carrying power he barely comprehended. Where the notes touched shadow-born, the creatures froze mid-motion.

Asvarr used the moment to sprint toward the chasm's edge, toward the Root itself. Behind him, the shadow-king shrieked commands in a language that scraped against Asvarr's mind like flint on steel. The frozen shadow-born shuddered, beginning to move again.

At the chasm's edge, Asvarr hesitated only a heartbeat before jumping. He landed on the Root's massive surface twenty feet below, boots sliding on bark smoother than any earthly tree. The diagonal angle of the Root formed a natural pathway downward into darkness and upward toward the tear in the sky.

Instinct pulled him downward, toward the Root's source deep in the chasm. The Grímmark throbbed with recognition, directing him along a specific path. Bark patterns beneath his feet reconfigured as he moved, forming steps and handholds where none had existed before.

Above, shadow-born poured over the chasm edge in pursuit. They moved differently on the Root, their forms stretching and flowing along its surface like liquid shadow. The shadow-king watched from the edge, making no move to follow.

"The anchor awaits below, Warden," it called after him. "With it, the knowledge that will break you."

Asvarr ignored the taunt, descending deeper into the chasm. Light from the Grímmark illuminated his way, revealing the true vastness of the Root. What had appeared enormous from above proved more massive still beneath the surface. The Root widened as he descended, sprawling into a network of smaller branches that lined the chasm walls.

Between these branches, embedded in stone, gleamed objects unlike any earthly material—crystal formations that pulsed with internal light, metal veins that sang faintly when he passed, strange growths that might have been fungi or might have been eyes, tracking his movement.

The shadow-born followed, their numbers growing. They maintained distance, herding rather than attacking. Driving him downward toward something they feared to approach directly.

Asvarr paused on a wide section of the Root, catching his breath. Far below, at the limits of the Grímmark's light, he glimpsed his destination—a chamber formed where the Root penetrated solid bedrock. Golden light spilled from the opening, brighter than the mark's glow.

"What waits for me down there?" he murmured.

The Grímmark pulsed, offering no answers, only urgency. Something within that chamber called to the mark, drawing it as a lodestone draws iron.

Shadow-born chittered above, creeping closer. Asvarr continued his descent, following bark-steps that formed beneath his feet. The Root guided him, accommodating his passage while denying easy travel to the pursuing creatures.

The chamber entrance loomed closer—an arched opening thirty feet high where the Root had punched through solid stone. Golden sap coated the walls, hardened to amber. Within this amber, Asvarr glimpsed frozen figures—men and women who had reached this place before him, caught mid-motion in transparent resin.

Their faces showed no fear or pain, only wonder. Many reached toward the chamber beyond, fingers outstretched toward something Asvarr couldn't yet see.

The shadow-born stopped their pursuit at the amber threshold, crowding the Root but advancing no further. Their reluctance only strengthened Asvarr's resolve. He stepped through the archway, bronze sword ready, horn clutched tight in his off-hand.

The chamber beyond stole his breath.

Perfectly circular and hollowed from solid stone, its walls, floor, and ceiling coated with amber sap that glowed with inner light. The Root continued through the chamber floor, plunging deeper into the earth. At its center rose a formation unlike anything Asvarr had seen—a swirling column of golden light that pulsed with the same rhythm as the Grímmark on his chest.

This was the anchor.

Unlike the crude word suggested, this anchor resembled no human tool. It existed as light given form, a spiraling column of pure energy that connected the Root to the stone beneath. Runes orbited it like moons circling a planet, each symbol flaring bright then dimming in complex patterns.

"Flame-bearer," a voice spoke directly into Asvarr's mind. "You have come at last."

The voice came from everywhere and nowhere, resonating with the same timbre as the Grímmark's pulse. Ancient beyond comprehension, yet somehow familiar, as if he'd heard it in dreams throughout his life.

"Who speaks?" Asvarr demanded, turning full circle, sword raised.

"I am Root and Stone. Memory and Rebirth." The voice carried neither gender nor age. "I am the First Anchor, torn from wholeness when fate-threads severed."

The Grímmark flared beneath Asvarr's tunic, responding to the anchor's words. Knowledge flooded his mind—fragments of memory not his own, glimpses of the world before the breaking. Great tree-cities sprawling across mountainsides. Ships sailing between stars on bark-hulls. Beings neither god nor mortal, walking paths of light between realms.

Asvarr staggered under the mental onslaught, dropping to one knee. "Stop," he gasped. "Too much."

The flow of images ceased. "Forgiveness, Flame-bearer. Your vessel remains unaccustomed to Tree-memory."

"What do you want from me?" Asvarr pushed himself upright, grip tightening on sword and horn.

"Want is a mortal concept." The voice rippled through the amber walls. "I exist. You exist. Our existences intertwine through the mark you bear."

"The Grímmark."

"A name given by small minds to a greater purpose." A pulse of something like amusement. "The mark connects you to all five anchors. Through it, we may be bound once more, if you prove worthy."

Asvarr approached the spiraling column of light cautiously. The orbiting runes adjusted their paths to accommodate his presence, flowing around him like fish around a stone in a stream.

"How do I bind you?" he asked.

"Through oath and blood. Through memory and sacrifice." The anchor's voice deepened. "Are you prepared to pay such price, Flame-bearer?"

Before Asvarr could answer, shadow seeped through the amber archway, pure darkness flowing like water. It coalesced into the towering form of the shadow-king, its crimson eyes brighter in the golden chamber.

"He knows nothing of the price," the shadow-king snarled. "Tell him, Anchor. Tell him what creating a Warden truly costs."

The anchor's light dimmed slightly. "The shadow-jailer speaks partially true. The binding requires sacrifice."

"What sacrifice?" Asvarr demanded.

"Memory for memory. Pain for pain." The anchor's voice carried neither threat nor reassurance. "What was sundered cannot be mended without cost."

The shadow-king laughed, the sound scraping against Asvarr's spine. "Tell him the full truth, Root-fragment. Tell him what becomes of Wardens who complete their task."

Silence filled the chamber. The Grímmark pulsed once, hard enough to make Asvarr wince.

"The binding consumes," the anchor finally admitted. "With each Root bound, less remains of what you were. By the fifth binding, little of your former self will survive."

Icy dread settled in Asvarr's gut. "I become something else?"

"You become more." The anchor's light intensified. "And less. Human limits fall away. Human connections fade. This is the price of power needed to rebind what broke."

The shadow-king circled the chamber's perimeter, crown-roots scraping the ceiling. "The Ashfather offers another path. Serve him, and remain yourself. Fight him, bind the Roots, and lose everything you are."

Asvarr's mind raced. Everything he'd learned pointed toward the necessity of binding the Roots, of restoring what had broken. Yet, if the price were his very self...

"Why should I believe either of you?" he challenged.

"Seek truth within," the anchor replied. "The mark holds memory older than both of us."

Asvarr closed his eyes, focusing on the Grímmark's pulse. Its rhythm synchronized with his heartbeat, with the anchor's light, and with the horn in his hand. They formed a circuit of power and purpose older than human understanding.

He saw himself as he might become—transformed by each binding, growing less human with each Root joined. By the final anchor, little would remain of Asvarr the raider, the clan-member, the man. Something greater and more terrible would stand in his place.

Yet in that vision, the Tree stood whole again. The broken realms healed. Life flourished where shadow had consumed.

Asvarr opened his eyes. "If I refuse, what then?"

"The anchors fade," the shadow-king answered quickly. "The Tree's memory dies. The Ashfather claims what remains and builds something new from the ashes. Something without the flaws of the old order."

"And all who live now?"

The shadow-king's crown twisted. "Change demands sacrifice."

Asvarr understood then—the Ashfather sought destruction. A cleansing of all nine realms to build something serving his vision alone.

"I will bind you," Asvarr told the anchor, ignoring the shadow-king's hiss of anger. "Tell me what must be done."

The anchor's light surged. "Blood and oath. Horn and blade. Strike at my heart while sounding the binding call."

The shadow-king lunged forward. "Fool! You doom yourself to unmaking!"

Asvarr sidestepped the attack, bronze sword slicing through the shadow-king's extended arm. The creature howled as the limb dissolved into mist. The sword hummed in Asvarr's grip, drinking shadow like thirsty soil drinks rain.

"I swore to return Hildr's tale to her people," Asvarr snarled. "That oath alone demands I stop you."

He raised the horn to his lips. The binding call came to him unbidden, three notes followed by three more in descending harmony. The sound vibrated through the chamber, through stone and amber and Root alike.

The shadow-king shrieked, its form distorting as the notes struck it. "The Ashfather will hunt you through nine realms for this defiance!"

"Let him come." Asvarr advanced on the anchor, bronze sword extended. "I'll be waiting."

With the horn's call still echoing through the chamber, he plunged the sword into the heart of the spiraling light. Golden energy surged up the blade, through his arm, into the Grímmark on his chest. Pain beyond mortal understanding coursed through Asvarr's body, purifying fire that scoured him to the bone.

The anchor's voice thundered in his mind: "BLOOD AND OATH. BINDING BEGUN."

Images flooded Asvarr's consciousness—memories not his own, knowledge of ages long past. He saw the Tree in its glory and its breaking. Saw the Norns who cut the threads of fate. Saw the shadow that had waited for that moment, patient beyond time.

"REMEMBER," the anchor commanded. "CARRY WHAT WAS LOST."

The shadow-king howled, its form unraveling like smoke in a strong wind. "This is not over, Warden! The Ashfather comes!"

Asvarr barely heard the threat through the roaring in his ears. The binding consumed him, filling every cell with golden fire. The chamber pulsed around him, amber walls liquefying, flowing inward to join with the anchor's light.

With a sound like the world taking a breath, the anchor collapsed inward, drawing sword, horn, and Asvarr himself into its center. For one eternal moment, he existed everywhere at once—seeing through countless eyes across nine realms, feeling every joy and sorrow of living things, touching the edges of understanding vast enough to break mortal minds.

Then, reality reasserted itself. Asvarr found himself kneeling on solid stone, his sword driven point-first into the ground before him. The horn hung silently at his belt. Around him, the chamber had transformed—amber walls now solid stone inscribed with runes that matched the Grímmark on his chest.

The anchor's spiraling light had vanished. In its place stood a sapling no taller than Asvarr himself—a perfect miniature of Yggdrasil, roots extending into the greater Root below, branches reaching toward the distant surface.

"First binding complete," a voice whispered in his mind—the anchor, transformed yet still present. "Four remain."

Asvarr staggered to his feet. His body felt simultaneously lighter and heavier, as if he'd shed some portion of himself while gaining something weightier in exchange. Knowledge pressed against the edges of his thoughts—more than any human mind was meant to contain, yet somehow accommodated by the Grímmark's power.

He knew now what he had not before—where the remaining anchors waited, scattered across realms. Knew the locations of other Wardens, though their faces remained shadowed. Knew the Ashfather's name, though speaking it aloud would shatter stone and boil water.

Most importantly, he knew what waited if he failed—the unmaking of all things, followed by a remaking under shadow's rule.

The sapling trembled, its tiny branches reaching toward him. Without conscious thought, Asvarr placed his palm against its trunk. Connection flowed between them—acknowledgment, purpose, determination.

"I'll find the others," he promised. "I'll bind what broke."

In response, a single leaf unfurled at the sapling's crown—green and vital despite the darkness surrounding it. A promise of renewal, of life continuing despite shadow's encroachment.

***

Asvarr retrieved his sword, the bronze blade now inscribed with runes matching those on the chamber walls. The weapon had transformed during the binding, becoming an extension of his purpose rather than mere metal.

He turned toward the archway, now plain stone without amber coating. The shadow-born had vanished with their master, but Asvarr knew the respite would prove temporary. The Ashfather would send other servants, more dangerous than the shadow-king.

As he began the climb back toward the surface, Asvarr felt the weight of his oath to Hildr alongside this newer, greater purpose. Returning to tell her tale would require a journey eastward to Ormvik, while the second anchor pulled him toward distant mountains in the west. The paths diverged, yet both demanded fulfillment.

Two oaths, equally binding. Two paths, equally necessary.

The answer came from the new knowledge within him. Time flowed differently near the anchor points—what might take months elsewhere could pass in days within the Root's influence. He could honor Hildr's oath and still reach the second anchor before its light faded beyond recovery.

First, he needed to emerge from this chasm, from this place of death and revelation. The climb upward felt simultaneously harder and easier than the descent—harder because his body ached from the binding, easier because the Root now recognized him, forming more substantial paths beneath his feet.

As he neared the surface, light greeted him, the golden-green radiance of the aurora dancing across the night sky. The tear in reality remained, stars visible through its ragged edges. Yet, something had changed in the heavens. The emptiness he'd felt earlier had diminished, replaced by a sense of watchful presence.

The Tree was waking. The first binding had stirred something long dormant.

Asvarr pulled himself over the chasm's edge, standing once more on solid ground beneath the hollow sky. The corpses surrounding the chasm had changed—shadow-frost melting from their flesh, leaving only ordinary death behind. Birds circled overhead, nature reclaiming what the shadow-king's presence had previously repelled.

Among the dead, Hildr's body remained as he'd left it. Asvarr knelt beside her, gently closing eyes now clear of frost.

"Your oath stands," he told her. "I'll bring your tale to Ormvik before seeking the second anchor."

From the belt of a nearby corpse, he took a small ax head, its handle long since broken away. Using this and stones gathered from the chasm edge, he built a small cairn over Hildr's body. It wasn't a proper funeral pyre as tradition demanded, although it was better than leaving her exposed to the elements.

When the task was complete, Asvarr stood beneath the aurora-lit sky, feeling its weight upon him. The burden of the first binding settled into his bones, into his blood, changing him in ways both subtle and profound. He was still Asvarr, still human, but something more stirred within him now—ancient purpose awakened through the Grímmark and the anchor's power.

Four more bindings awaited. Four more transformations. Would anything of himself remain by the end? The question hung in his mind as he turned eastward, toward distant Ormvik and the oath that bound him to the dead.

CHAPTER 5

FROSTBOUND KNOTS

Three days into the eastern journey toward Ormvik, the world changed around Asvarr. First came the trees—twisted pines whose bark spiraled in patterns matching the Grímmark on his chest. Then the snow itself, hardening into crystalline formations that resembled runes when viewed from certain angles. By the fourth dawn, even the clouds overhead arranged themselves in whorls and knots that mirrored the Root's ancient patterns.

Asvarr paused atop a windswept ridge, his breath clouding before him in the bitter morning air. The land stretched white and silent in every direction, the rising sun casting long, blue shadows across virgin snow. No tracks marred the pristine surface—no wolf prints, no rabbit trails, no bird impressions where they might have landed to rest. The emptiness raised hackles on the back of his neck.

The Grímmark pulsed beneath his tunic, attuned to his unease. Since binding the first anchor, the mark had changed—no longer burning with contained power but resonating like a struck bell whenever danger or significant magic approached. The bronze sword at his back and the horn at his belt vibrated with the same frequency, all three artifacts linked through the binding.

Eastward lay Ormvik, two days' hard travel if the weather held. The old trading settlement huddled against the sea cliffs where fishing was good, and raiders seldom bothered with its meager wealth. Hildr's clan deserved word of her courageous end. An oath made in blood demanded fulfillment.

Yet westward, beyond sight but never beyond awareness, the second anchor called. The binding had revealed its location—deep within the Rimefrost Mountains, where ice remained solid even in summer heat. Each passing day weakened its connection to the greater Tree, to the sapling growing from the first anchor's binding.

Asvarr rubbed his chest where the Grímmark lay. The first binding had changed more than just the mark's nature. Memories flooded his mind at unexpected moments—glimpses of worlds and times beyond human experience. The smell of roasting fish might trigger visions of great citadels among the stars. A hawk's cry could unmask the layers of reality, showing nine realms stacked atop each other like pancakes on a platter.

He forced himself forward, boots crunching through knee-deep snow. The descent from the ridge proved treacherous, ice concealed beneath powdery drifts. Twice he slipped, once catching himself on an exposed tree root, once tumbling twenty feet before a snowbank broke his fall.

The lands flattened into a vast, white meadow where summer would bring wildflowers and grass tall enough to hide a mounted warrior. Now, only snow reigned, sculpted by wind into waves and ridges that resembled a frozen sea. At the meadow's center, something disrupted the perfect whiteness—a dark speck that resolved into a crude shelter as Asvarr approached.

His hand moved instinctively to the bronze sword. The Grímmark remained silent, detecting no immediate threat. Still, caution had kept him alive when shadow-things hunted him across the marsh. He circled the shelter, studying it from every angle before approaching directly.

Simple but effective, the structure comprised branches lashed together with strips of hide; the frame draped with animal skins—wolf, bear, and something with scales he didn't recognize. A small fire pit sat before the entrance, cold ashes dusted with fresh snow. No tracks led toward or away from the shelter, as if its occupant had vanished into the air itself.

"Hello the shelter," Asvarr called, sword half-drawn. "I seek only passage through these lands."

Silence answered. Wind whistled across the meadow, driving fresh snow against the shelter's walls. After counting slowly to thirty, Asvarr approached and pulled aside the hide flap that served as a door.

Inside, a single figure sat cross-legged on a bear pelt. Ancient beyond reckoning, the man's skin had the color and texture of tanned leather, stretched taut over prominent bones. White hair hung in beaded braids to his waist. Eyes closed, hands resting palm-up on his knees, he showed no reaction to Asvarr's entrance.

"Old father," Asvarr said, sheathing his sword. "Forgive my intrusion. I thought the shelter was abandoned."

The old man's eyes remained closed. "The sky speaks your name, mark-bearer." His voice creaked like frozen branches in the wind. "The ice remembers your steps before you take them."

The Grímmark pulsed once, sharp and questioning. Asvarr's hand moved to his chest, pressing against the sudden warmth. "You know what I carry."

"I know what carries you." The old man's eyes opened—pale blue irises floating in milky white, blind yet somehow seeing. "Sit. The journey wears on your bones."

Asvarr hesitated only a moment before lowering himself onto a deerskin opposite the elder. The shelter's interior smelled of herbs and old smoke, with undercurrents of something metallic and strange. Small bundles of dried plants hung from the branch framework, alongside intricate knotwork patterns woven from sinew and bone.

The old man reached beside him, producing a clay pot and two rough cups. With precise movements, despite his apparent blindness, he poured steaming liquid into both. "Frost-root tea," he explained, offering one cup. "Clears the mind when Tree-memories crowd too thickly."

The knowledge that this stranger understood the binding's effects unnerved Asvarr more than any threat of violence. He accepted the cup cautiously, studying the dark liquid within. "Who are you, old father?"

"Thorvald Knotmaker, once." The elder sipped his tea. "Now just the knots remain, and little of Thorvald." He gestured to the complex patterns hanging around them. "Each holds what the mind cannot. Memories too large for skull-space."

Asvarr sipped the tea, expecting bitterness but finding instead a complex sweetness followed by a numbing cold that spread from tongue to chest. The chaotic flood of Tree-memories that had plagued him for days suddenly calmed, organizing themselves into manageable currents rather than overwhelming rapids.

"You've walked this path," Asvarr realized, studying the old man with new understanding. "You bear a mark."

Thorvald set down his cup and pulled aside his ragged tunic. Across his chest sprawled a pattern similar to the Grímmark but different in crucial ways—the lines more jagged, the overall shape resembling a frozen lightning bolt rather than a flame-tree hybrid.

"The Frostmark," the old man said. "Third binding of seven in my time."

"Seven?" Asvarr's pulse quickened. "The völva told me five anchors fell when fate-threads broke."

"Five now. Seven before." Thorvald's blind eyes fixed on him with uncomfortable precision. "The Tree sheds different limbs, each breaking. Grows anew in different patterns with each rebirth."

The implications staggered Asvarr. "This has happened before? The Tree has fallen and been restored?"

"Three cycles I've witnessed. More before my time." Thorvald re-wrapped his tunic, concealing the Frostmark. "The Ashfather grows more cunning each breaking. Plants his seeds deeper in the void between worlds."

Asvarr set down his cup, mind racing. "Why do you wait here in the wilderness? If you understand what happens, why not help restore the Tree?"

"My binding days passed with the last cycle." Sadness creased Thorvald's weathered face. "The Frostmark fades. Its power sustains my years, but cannot bind another anchor."

A chill ran through Asvarr unrelated to the winter air. The old man had survived the previous cycle of breakings—how many centuries ago? What price had such longevity demanded?

"The second anchor," Asvarr said. "It waits in the western mountains."

"The Root of Rimefrost. Yes." Thorvald nodded. "Strong still, but weakening. The ice-crown must be claimed before the thaw."

"I've sworn an oath to bring word of a shield-maiden's death to Ormvik," Asvarr explained. "Only then can I turn westward."

"Oaths bind tighter than fate." Thorvald reached for a small leather pouch hanging among his knot-patterns. "But time slips along different paths near the breaking."

From the pouch, he withdrew an object that pulsed with inner light—a small stone disk etched with spiraling runes. Frost formed and melted continuously across its surface, creating an ever-changing landscape of miniature mountains and valleys.

"The Timeknot," Thorvald said, holding it toward Asvarr. "Creation of my binding days. It opens pathways through winter's grip, shortcuts through the folds of world-flesh."

Asvarr stared at the disk, mesmerized by its shifting patterns. "A magical token?"

"A tool. No more." The old man pressed it into Asvarr's palm. "Place it at a crossroads under moonlight. Speak your destination while blood touches stone. The paths will bend for one bearing a living mark."

The disk felt impossibly cold against Asvarr's skin, a cold that somehow burned without causing pain. The Grímmark responded with a steady pulse, recognizing kindred magic.

"Why help me?" Asvarr asked. "You don't know my purpose."

"The mark knows, even if you don't yet." Thorvald's blind eyes tracked something invisible in the air between them. "Your Grímmark burns cleaner than most. Less pride in its fire, more duty in its heat."

Asvarr closed his fingers around the Timeknot, its cold fire spreading up his arm. "If this worked for you, why didn't you bind all seven anchors in your cycle?"

Pain flashed across Thorvald's ancient face. "The bindings change us, young flame. By my third, little remained of the man who had begun the journey. I feared what I would become by the seventh." He turned his face away. "Others completed what I abandoned. They paid prices I was too cowardly to bear."

The admission hung in the shelter's close air. Asvarr remembered the anchor's warning—with each binding, less would remain of his former self. By the fifth, little of Asvarr would survive within the Warden's flesh.

"And this cycle?" he asked. "The Tree breaks differently, you said. Only five anchors now."

"Five roots torn free," Thorvald recited, words matching the prophecy-vision Asvarr had experienced during his first binding. "Five anchors lost. Five wardens to find them. Five crowns to bear them."

"The crowns—" Asvarr began.

A violent pulse from the Grímmark cut him short. Both the bronze sword at his back and the horn at his belt vibrated in warning. Outside, the temperature plummeted so rapidly that frost formed instantly across the shelter's entrance flap.

Thorvald tilted his head, listening to something beyond human hearing. "They've found me," he whispered. "The frost-walkers come."

"What creatures?" Asvarr's hand moved to his sword hilt.

"The Ashfather's hunger made flesh." Thorvald reached for a staff leaning against the shelter wall, its length carved with protective runes. "They seek fading marks to devour, hoping to prevent the next binding."

Asvarr pulled aside the entrance flap. The meadow had transformed in mere moments—no longer pristine white but etched with intricate frost patterns that spread visibly across the snow's surface. The patterns formed runes and symbols of power, corrupted versions of those that orbited the first anchor. At the meadow's edge, tall figures approached—humanoid but wrong in proportion and movement. Their bodies appeared constructed from frost and shadow, limbs too long and thin, torsos emaciated beyond survival.

"How many do you see?" Thorvald asked, gathering small objects from around the shelter and placing them in a pouch at his belt.

"Seven," Asvarr counted, studying their approach. "Moving like hunters who've caught a scent."

"They smell the Frostmark's fading power." Thorvald joined him at the entrance, blind eyes somehow tracking the distant figures. "And your Grímmark burns like a beacon to them, young flame."

"We fight, then."

"You fight. I fade." Thorvald pressed his staff into Asvarr's free hand. "This journey belongs to the new cycle, not the old. Take my staff. It drinks frost as your sword drinks shadow."

"You can't just—"

"Three cycles I've witnessed, mark-bearer. Hundreds of winters watching the same war fought with different weapons." Thorvald's voice held the finality of an avalanche. "My time ends. Yours continues."

Before Asvarr could protest further, Thorvald clasped his wrist. The touch sent ice-fire racing up his arm to the Grímmark, which flared in response. Knowledge transferred between them, understanding born of centuries of observing the eternal conflict between Tree and Shadow.

Asvarr gasped as images filled his mind: seven anchors bound during the last breaking, seven Wardens transformed by their sacrifice, the Tree restored to life before being broken again when the Ashfather found new methods of attack. He saw Thorvald, young and strong, claiming the Frostmark through trial and blood. Saw him binding the third anchor—deep beneath a frozen sea. Saw him turning away from the fourth, fearing what he might become if he continued.

"The knots," Thorvald whispered, releasing Asvarr's wrist. "Take the knots with you."

With trembling hands, the ancient Warden unpinned several knotwork patterns from the shelter walls, pressing them into Asvarr's pack. "Each contains the memory the Tree needs. Knowledge the shadow tried to steal."

The frost-walkers drew closer, moving with unnatural speed across the patterned meadow. Snow crunched beneath their feet—or what might have been feet, appendages that changed shape with each step, leaving crystalline prints that expanded into elaborate frost-runes.

"Go," Thorvald commanded. "Northeast through the stone-teeth ridge. The frost-walkers will follow my mark's scent."

"They'll kill you," Asvarr protested.

"Nothing dies that the Tree remembers." Thorvald smiled, revealing teeth worn to nubs by centuries of use. "My memory lives in the knots now. And soon, in you."

The ancient Warden stepped past Asvarr into the open meadow. Frost patterns surged toward him, drawn by the Frostmark's fading power. The approaching creatures paused, their eyeless faces turning in unison toward the greater prize of a full Warden, even a faded one.

"Remember the ice-crown," Thorvald called over his shoulder. "Second binding reveals what the first conceals. Trust the mark, not the mind."

Without waiting for a response, the old man strode directly toward the frost-walkers. The creatures resumed their advance, gangly limbs propelling them with inhuman speed.

Asvarr shouldered his pack, now heavier with Thorvald's knot-patterns. Every instinct demanded he stand with the old Warden, fight alongside him against the Ashfather's servants. But deeper knowledge—Tree-wisdom flowing from the Grímmark—confirmed Thorvald's strategy. The frost-walkers would pursue the older mark first, drawn by its vulnerability. A diversion that might cost the ancient Warden his life but would secure Asvarr's escape.

With bitter resignation, Asvarr ducked out of the shelter's back, cutting a small opening through the hides with his knife. The Grímmark guided him northeast, as Thorvald had directed, toward a distant ridgeline that resembled teeth against the sky.

He'd covered fifty paces when the screaming began, something high - pitched and inhuman. Asvarr glanced back. Brilliant blue light pulsed from the meadow's center, illuminating the shelter from within like a paper lantern. The frost-walkers surrounded it, their elongated forms silhouetted against the radiance. The frost patterns across the snow shifted, flowing toward the shelter, drawn by whatever power Thorvald had unleashed.

***

Asvarr forced himself to continue, each step heavy, knowing that he had abandoned a fellow Warden to face death alone. Yet, the weight of the knot-patterns in his pack reminded him of his larger duty—to carry forward what might otherwise be lost, to bind what had broken.

The blue light behind him intensified, casting his shadow long across the snow. A concussive boom shook the ground beneath his feet, staggering him mid-stride. When he regained balance and looked back, the shelter and surrounding meadow had transformed into a field of ice sculptures—perfect replicas of the frost-walkers caught in various poses of attack, frozen solid by whatever final magic Thorvald had unleashed.

Of the ancient Warden himself, no sign remained.

The Grímmark pulsed once—recognition, respect, remembrance.

Asvarr resumed his journey toward the ridge, the Timeknot a cold presence in his pocket, Thorvald's staff gripped tight in his hand. The knowledge that cycles of breaking and binding had occurred before—that the Tree had fallen and risen multiple times throughout the ages—changed everything and nothing. His path remained the same: honor his blood-oath to Hildr, then seek the second anchor in the western mountains.

***

But now he understood the true weight of the Warden's burden. The knowledge that the war between Tree and Shadow might never truly end—only enter new phases with each breaking.

The ridge grew closer, stone teeth reaching toward cloud-heavy skies. Beyond them lay Ormvik and his sworn duty. Beyond that, the ice-crown Thorvald had mentioned awaited in the Rimefrost Mountains.

The Grímmark hummed beneath his tunic, reminding him of power and purpose. Five anchors. Five bindings. Five transformations that would leave little of Asvarr by the journey's end.

He strode forward, snow crunching beneath his boots, the dead Warden's staff marking his path with rune-shapes in the virgin white. The frost-bound knots in his pack held centuries of memory, waiting to be unraveled, their patterns revealing truths the Ashfather had tried to bury beneath shadow and ice.

The stone-teeth ridge loomed against the darkening sky, jagged formations thrusting upward like the broken fangs of some buried titan. Asvarr pressed onward, legs burning with exertion. Behind him, the blue glow from Thorvald's final stand had faded, leaving only the deepening twilight and the occasional mournful cry of wind through the rocks.

He stumbled on a hidden stone, nearly pitching headfirst into a snowdrift. The weight of Thorvald's knot-patterns dragged at his pack, physical reminders of worlds now lost, cycles now forgotten. The Timeknot sat cold and heavy in his pocket, its frost patterns shifting continuously against his thigh.

The Grímmark remained silent, detecting no immediate threats in the wasteland. Yet, alertness prickled along Asvarr's spine. Something else tracked him, a presence less tangible than frost walkers. The land itself seemed to watch, stone-teeth casting long shadows that stretched toward him like grasping fingers.

Night fell as he reached the ridge's base. Wind howled between stone pillars, driving needle-sharp crystals of ice against exposed skin. The temperature plummeted with unnatural speed. No natural shelter presented itself among the barren rocks.

Asvarr propped Thorvald's staff against a boulder and used it to anchor the hide cape he'd taken from the old Warden's shelter, creating a small windbreak. Beneath it, he cleared snow to bare rock and used gathered tinder to spark a small fire. The flames danced blue-green, responding to some element in the wood or perhaps to the Grímmark's proximity.

He opened his pack and removed the knot-patterns Thorvald had pressed upon him. Six distinct designs, each woven from sinew, bone fragments, and various fibers. They pulsed faintly in the firelight, each emanating a subtle warmth unlike the bitter cold of the Timeknot.

The smallest pattern—an intricate spiral of fine white thread with tiny vertebrae threaded along its curves—drew his attention first. When his fingers brushed its surface, memory flooded his mind.

A vast cavern, lit by luminescent fungi. Nine figures in bone masks dancing around a sapling with golden bark. Blood dripping from their palms onto its roots. The sapling growing, branches stretching toward a stone ceiling that parts to accommodate them.

Asvarr jerked his hand away, gasping. The memory—Thorvald's memory—had felt as real as his own experiences. He'd smelled the damp earth of the cavern, felt the rhythm of the dance in his feet, tasted copper-salt blood on his tongue.

After a steadying breath, he touched the second pattern—a square grid formed from dark sinew with amber beads marking certain intersections. Fresh memory erupted:

Standing waist-deep in a frozen sea, ice forming and re-forming around his legs. A massive spike of Root, visible beneath the translucent surface, pulsed with golden light. Hands marred by the Frostmark pressed against the ice. Cracking. Splitting. Water rushing up, transforming into liquid light that flooded lungs and veins.

The binding of Thorvald's second anchor. Asvarr felt the old Warden's fear, determination, and the first hints of transformation as something inhuman grew within a mortal frame.

One by one, he touched the remaining patterns, absorbing glimpses of Thorvald's long life—centuries of wandering between breaking cycles, observing, recording, preserving what the shadows sought to erase. Knowledge of star-paths and Root-songs, of binding-magic and protection-runes. Fragments of a language older than humanity, spoken by entities neither god nor mortal who tended Yggdrasil before the Nine Realms existed.

By the time he touched the final pattern—an asymmetrical web incorporating falcon feathers and wolf teeth—his mind throbbed with alien memories. The Grímmark burned hot beneath his tunic, processing this influx of knowledge, storing what his human brain could not contain.

The fire burned low, reduced to glowing embers. Asvarr wrapped the patterns carefully and returned them to his pack. Too much knowledge to absorb in one sitting. The accumulated wisdom of centuries would take time to integrate, to understand.

He tossed another handful of twigs onto the embers, watching blue-green flames leap upward. In their light, a shadow moved where no shadow should exist—a man-shaped darkness cast against stone, though nothing stood between fire and rock to create it.

The Grímmark flared in warning. Asvarr's hand moved to the bronze sword at his back.

"Grímmark-bearer," the shadow spoke, its voice dry leaves scraping stone. "The old one's death-light guided me to you."

"What manner of creature addresses me?" Asvarr kept his voice steady despite the cold dread pooling in his gut.

The shadow rippled, assuming a more defined form—a gaunt human silhouette with elongated fingers and no clear facial features. "I am neither creature nor man. I am memory given form, echo given purpose."

"Speak plainly, or face my blade."

"Your blade passes through memory as wind through mist." The shadow shifted, one arm extending impossibly to point northward beyond the ridge. "I bring warning, Warden. One marked by your Flame-Carver walks toward doom."

Another Warden? Asvarr straightened, alert. "Who?"

"The weaver of roots, the singer of stone. She bears the Jordmark upon her brow." The shadow's form wavered like heat-ripples. "Even now, she freezes, trapped in ice that slows but cannot stop her heart."

The Grímmark pulsed, recognizing truth in the shadow's words. Asvarr recalled what Brenna had told him—she had marked four others besides himself. If the Ashfather hunted Wardens, this Jordmark-bearer might already be in his grasp.

"Where can I find her?" Asvarr demanded.

"Beyond the stone-teeth, where ice remembers faces." The shadow faded, edges dissolving into the darkness. "Seek the frozen woman. Free what slumbers."

"Wait!" Asvarr stepped forward, hand outstretched. "Who sent you with this warning?"

The shadow paused, its form solidifying briefly. "One who watches from the spaces between worlds. One who gains nothing from your failure and everything from your success." A sound like distant laughter rippled through the air. "One who remembers what the Ashfather tries to make all forget."

With those cryptic words, the shadow collapsed into itself, shrinking to a dark spot that winked out like a snuffed candle. The fire flared once, unnaturally bright, then returned to normal orange-yellow flames. Whatever magic had infused the wood had burned away.

Asvarr stood motionless, sword half-drawn, mind racing. A trapped Warden lay beyond the ridge—one of Brenna's marked ones. If the shadow spoke truth, she faced slow death by freezing, her heart preserved by the mark's power but unable to free herself.

He looked eastward, toward distant Ormvik, where his oath to Hildr pulled him. Then, northward, beyond the stone-teeth where this unknown Warden supposedly lay trapped. Two duties, two directions, both claiming precedence.

The Grímmark offered no guidance, remaining silent beneath his tunic. This choice belonged to Asvarr alone, not to the greater power that worked through him.

He sank down beside the fire, withdrawing the Timeknot from his pocket. The disk pulsed with inner frost, patterns evolving across its surface as if mapping unknown territories. Thorvald had said it could bend paths, create shortcuts through "the folds of world-flesh." If true, perhaps he could fulfill both obligations.

First, he needed to verify the shadow's claims. A fellow Warden in peril took precedence over delivering death-news, no matter how sacred the oath. Hildr's clan had waited this long; they could wait another day while he investigated what lay beyond the ridge.

Asvarr doused the fire and dismantled his makeshift shelter. Sleep would have to wait. He gathered his pack, secured the staff across his back alongside the bronze sword, and began climbing the stone-teeth ridge under stars cold and distant as forgotten gods.

The ascent proved treacherous in the darkness. Loose stones shifted beneath his boots, sending miniature avalanches of pebbles skittering into the void. Twice, he lost his footing, saved only by desperate grabs at protruding rocks. The ridge grew steeper, forcing him to scramble on hands and knees up near-vertical faces slick with ice.

At the summit, wind threatened to tear him from his precarious perch. Asvarr pressed his body flat against the stone, fingers digging into narrow crevices. Through watering eyes, he surveyed what lay beyond.

A vast, bowl-shaped valley spread below, its floor a perfect circle of ice so smooth it reflected starlight like a mirror. Surrounding this circle stood thousands of ice formations—humanoid shapes frozen in various postures of motion or rest. Even from this height, Asvarr recognized them as ice sculptures of people—men, women, children, warriors, craftspeople, all captured in perfect detail.

"Where ice remembers faces," he muttered, recalling the shadow's words.

A faint, golden glow emanated from the valley's center, pulsing with a familiar rhythm. The Grímmark responded immediately, flaring beneath Asvarr's tunic, recognizing kindred power. Another mark lay below, active but constrained.

He began the descent, picking his path carefully down the ridge's northern face. The going proved easier than the ascent—less steep, with more secure handholds. By the time his boots crunched onto level ground at the valley's edge, pre-dawn light brushed the eastern horizon.

Up close, the ice sculptures proved even more unnerving. Each captured a single moment with uncanny precision—a woman mid-laugh, a child reaching for something unseen, a warrior drawing a bow. Their expressions ranged from joy to terror, ordinary human emotions frozen for eternity. No natural ice formation could achieve such detail. Magic had crafted these likenesses, or perhaps something more sinister.

Asvarr moved among them cautiously, bronze sword drawn. The Grímmark guided him, its pulse growing stronger as he approached the valley center. The sculptures stood in concentric rings, densely packed near the outer edges but growing sparse toward the middle, as if whatever had created them had worked from outside inward.

At the innermost ring, he stopped cold.

A final sculpture stood alone—a woman encased in transparent ice that glowed faintly from within. Unlike the others, this was no mere likeness. A real person remained imprisoned, suspended in the moment of her freezing.

Tall and strongly built, she wore leather armor reinforced with metal plates over vital areas. Dark hair hung in complex braids, adorned with small metal beads. Her hands extended outward, as if pushing against her icy prison. Upon her forehead, partially visible beneath ice-rimed bangs, a mark glowed golden-green—intricate, interlocking lines forming a pattern similar to Asvarr's Grímmark but unique in its configuration.

The Jordmark.

Her eyes remained open behind the ice—amber irises fixed in a determined glare. Though her body appeared completely frozen, those eyes tracked Asvarr's movement, confirming the shadow's claim. She lived still, held in suspension by the Jordmark's power, even as ice claimed her flesh.

Asvarr approached cautiously, searching for any sign of a trap. The ice surrounding her appeared seamless, at least a foot thick on all sides. No obvious mechanism or magic circle suggested how she had become entrapped or how she might be freed.

He pressed his palm against the ice. Cold bit into his skin, deeper than a natural winter chill, reaching for bone and blood. The Grímmark flared in response, golden light spreading down his arm to combat the unnatural frost.

Inside her prison, the woman's eyes widened. Her mark pulsed brighter, synchronizing with Asvarr's Grímmark. Communication without words passed between them—recognition, warning, urgency.

"I'll free you," Asvarr promised, drawing back his hand. "Hold fast, Jordmark-bearer."

He studied the ice surrounding her, searching for weaknesses. The bronze sword might chip away at it, but the process would take hours, perhaps days. Thorvald's staff offered another option—the old Warden had claimed it "drinks frost." Asvarr removed it from his back, studying the runes carved along its length.

The patterns matched none he recognized, yet the Grímmark provided understanding. Frost-drinking magic required activation—blood freely given to empower the runes.

Asvarr drew his knife across his palm, reopening the wound made days earlier when swearing an oath to Hildr. Blood welled, dark against his skin. He smeared it along the staff's runes, watching as the wood absorbed the offering. The carved symbols began to glow blue-white, frost forming and evaporating along their lengths in a continuous cycle.

He pressed the staff's base against the ice prison. Frost patterns spread outward from the point of contact, covering the transparent surface with intricate crystalline networks. The ice groaned, deep cracking sounds emanating from its core.

The woman inside shifted slightly—the first movement Asvarr had seen from her. Her golden-green mark blazed brighter, working in concert with the staff's magic and Asvarr's Grímmark.

Encouraged, Asvarr pushed harder, willing the staff to drink deeper. The runes flared blinding white. Frost rushed from ice to staff, traveling up its length toward Asvarr's hands. Cold burned his fingers, threatening frostbite, but he maintained his grip.

With a sound like a frozen lake breaking in a spring thaw, the ice surrounding the woman split. Cracks propagated outward from the staff's point of contact, spreading across the entire surface in web-like patterns. Chunks broke free, crashing to the ground and shattering.

The woman collapsed forward as her prison disintegrated, muscles stiff from prolonged immobility. Asvarr caught her before she hit the ground, staff clattering aside. Her body radiated cold that penetrated his clothing, but the Jordmark on her brow pulsed with life-giving warmth.

"Breathe," he urged, supporting her weight. "You're free."

Her first breath came as a painful gasp, followed by violent coughing that racked her entire frame. Ice crystals flew from her lips, sparkling in the growing dawn light. She clutched at Asvarr's arms, fingers digging into muscle with desperate strength.

"How long?" she rasped, voice cracking from disuse.

"I don't know," Asvarr admitted. "I found you only moments ago, guided by a shadow-messenger."

The woman's amber eyes narrowed, focusing properly on him for the first time. Her gaze fixed on his chest, where the Grímmark lay hidden beneath clothing. "You bear a mark," she stated. "The flame-pattern. First Warden."

"Asvarr," he offered. "The Flame-Carver named me Skyrend's Flame."

"Brynja." She straightened, still leaning heavily against him but reclaiming some independence. "Brenna carved the Jordmark three weeks past. Called me Earth-Healer."

The Grímmark hummed in recognition of this second title, this second Warden. Asvarr helped Brynja to a boulder free of ice, where she sat with painful slowness, limbs protesting each movement.

"The ice sculptures," Asvarr gestured at the thousands of frozen figures surrounding them. "What created them?"

Brynja's face darkened. "I did."

The simple claim hung in the cold air between them. Asvarr waited, giving her space to continue when ready.

***

"The Jordmark showed me the second anchor's location," she explained, rubbing circulation back into her arms. "I journeyed here, following its call. But something waited—a creature of living frost." Her eyes turned toward the eastern ridge. "It offered knowledge for 'one small service.' I refused. It attacked."

She held up her hands, displaying palms marked with strange crystalline patterns—frost that had penetrated skin and remained embedded despite her mark's heat.

"The mark protected me, but the creature's touch froze something within." A shadow crossed her face. "I fought back. The Jordmark responded with power I couldn't control. Everyone in the valley—travelers, hunters, a small settlement on the western edge—frozen in an instant. Then, the creature trapped me in ice, feeding on the mark's power while I watched, unable to move or die."

Asvarr absorbed her words, understanding now why the ice sculptures captured such lifelike detail. They were life, transformed by uncontrolled magic.

"These people," he gestured to the frozen figures. "Can they be restored?"

"I don't know." Brynja's voice cracked. "The Jordmark offers no answers. Only more power do I fear using."

Asvarr helped her stand, supporting her weight as she tested weakened legs. "We need to leave this place. The creature that trapped you may return."

"I can't abandon them," Brynja protested, gesturing at the ice sculptures. "This happened because of me."

"And you'll help no one by being recaptured." Asvarr's tone brooked no argument. "We go now. Recover your strength, then return if possible."

Reluctantly, Brynja nodded. She took a halting step, then another, each movement growing smoother as the Jordmark fought the lingering effects of her imprisonment.

Asvarr retrieved Thorvald's staff, noting that the runes no longer glowed. Freeing Brynja fully depleted whatever power the blood-offering had activated. He secured it across his back alongside the bronze sword and guided the second Warden toward the valley's edge.

"The mark speaks of anchors," Brynja said as they walked. "Five roots needing binding. You've found one already?"

"Yes." Asvarr described his journey—the bleeding branch, Brenna's carving, the marsh crossing, the shadow-king, and the first binding. He mentioned Thorvald only briefly, the memory of the old Warden's sacrifice still raw.

Brynja listened in silence, her amber eyes calculating. When he finished, she stopped walking, turning to face him directly.

"The binding changed you," she stated. "I see it in your eyes, in how the Grímmark pulses beneath your clothing. What price did you pay, First Warden?"

Asvarr met her gaze. "Memory for memory. Part of what I was for is part of what the Tree needs."

"And by the fifth binding?"

"Little will remain of who I am now."

Brynja absorbed this, her face unreadable. The Jordmark on her brow pulsed once, responding to some unspoken thought. "And you accepted this willingly?"

"I chose to bind what was broken." Asvarr started walking again. "Would you have chosen differently?"

Brynja fell into step beside him, her movements growing stronger with each passing minute. "I don't know. The mark guides, but doesn't command. We still choose our paths."

They reached the valley's edge as full dawn broke across the eastern ridge. Golden light spilled over the stone-teeth, illuminating the thousands of ice sculptures in the valley below. From this vantage point, Asvarr realized they formed a pattern visible only from above—a vast spiral radiating outward from where

Brynja had been imprisoned, each frozen figure a point in an enormous rune carved across the landscape.

The Jordmark-bearer followed his gaze, understanding dawning in her eyes. "The frost creature," she whispered. "It used my power to create this. But why? What purpose does this pattern serve?"

Asvarr recalled the knot-patterns in his pack, the accumulated knowledge of centuries they contained. One memory surfaced—Thorvald standing before a similar pattern formed in desert sand, rather than frozen figures.

"A summoning circle," he said grimly. "Drawing power from life transformed rather than life sacrificed. Cleverly disguised as random victims of wild magic."

"Summoning what?" Brynja demanded.

"I don't know." Asvarr turned away from the sight. "But we should be far from here before night falls again. The Timeknot may help us."

He withdrew the frost-patterned disk from his pocket, explaining Thorvald's instructions. Brynja eyed it skeptically but offered no objection as they continued toward a natural crossroads where two game trails intersected at the forest's edge.

Behind them, the valley of frozen faces reflected morning light, thousands of eyes staring skyward in mute appeal. The pattern they formed pulsed once with power drawn from sunrise striking ice at precise angles, then faded to dormancy—waiting for moonrise to complete what dawn had begun.

CHAPTER 6
THE FLAME THAT WALKS

Asvarr crouched at the valley's edge, the icy wind tearing at his face as he studied the frozen plain below. The summoning circle of ice-trapped villagers gleamed in the weak morning light, their silent faces caught in expressions of horror and disbelief. Beside him, Brynja's breath fogged the air; her amber eyes narrowed as she traced the intricate patterns.

"This wasn't my doing alone," she said, her voice tight with suppressed rage. The Jordmark on her forehead pulsed faintly in response to her emotions. "The frost creature guided my power, twisted it."

Asvarr's fingers unconsciously touched the Grímmark on his chest. Since binding the first anchor, the rune no longer burned with restrained power—instead, it hummed with a deep resonance that vibrated through his bones. "Can they be saved?"

"I don't know." Brynja's metal-beaded braids clinked softly as she shook her head. "My power flows from the earth, not ice. Whatever this creature planned—"

A flash of movement at the circle's center cut her words short. Asvarr squinted, the Grímmark sending tendrils of heat down his arms.

"There," he hissed, pointing toward a tall figure walking among the frozen victims.

The creature moved with unnatural fluidity, its body composed of rippling flame contained within a vaguely human shape. Where its feet touched the ice, steam rose in thin spirals that twisted into runes before dissolving. The villagers' ice prisons reflected its glow, casting fractured light across the entire valley.

"Fire-wight," Brynja whispered, her hand instinctively reaching for the bone-handled knife at her belt. "More dangerous than the frost-walkers. It's drawing power from the circle."

Asvarr unsheathed his bronze sword, the runes along its blade responding to his touch with a golden gleam. "We need to understand what it's doing before we confront it."

"Planning, Flame-Bearer?" Her voice carried a note of surprise. "I thought berserkers charged first and questioned the corpses later."

"I was that man before the Tree fell." Asvarr felt the weight of Thorvald's memories pressing against his mind. "Now I carry too many lives to waste my own recklessly."

The fire-wight paused at the circle's center, raising its arms. Flames leapt from its fingertips, connecting to each of the frozen figures in thin, burning lines. A complex web of fire spread across the ice, forming a pattern that mirrored the constellation Asvarr had glimpsed in his vision during the first binding.

"The Dragon's Crown," he murmured. "It's completing what the frost creature began."

Brynja's eyes widened. "How would you know that name? It's from the old sky-tongue."

Before he could answer, the web of flame pulsed once, then flashed blindingly bright. The ice didn't melt—instead; it absorbed the fire, transforming from clear crystal to a blue-white luminescence.

"We need to move," Asvarr said, feeling the Grímmark's warning vibration intensify. "Now!"

He grabbed Brynja's arm and pulled her sideways just as a column of flame erupted where they had been crouching. The fire-wight stood at the valley's edge, arms extended toward them, its featureless face rippling with inner heat.

"Skyrend's Flame," it said, its voice crackling like burning wood. "I've waited for you."

Asvarr pushed Brynja behind him, raising his sword. "What are you?"

"I am Cinderheart, last ember of the Second Ragnarök." The creature's form solidified slightly, taking on more distinctly human features—a face with hollows for eyes, a mouth that dripped molten drops when it spoke. "You carry the Tree's mark, but you still have a choice."

"Why have you trapped these people?" Brynja demanded, stepping out from behind Asvarr.

The fire-wight tilted its head, regarding her with empty eye sockets that somehow conveyed amusement. "Earth-Healer. Your power drew the frost creature, and its power drew me. Ancient enemies, united in purpose."

"What purpose?" Asvarr kept his sword leveled, noting how the runes flickered in the creature's presence.

"To break the pattern." Cinderheart gestured to the frozen circle. "They are preserved. When the Great Severing succeeds, they will awaken to a world without the tyranny of the Tree."

Asvarr felt knowledge surfacing from the memories he'd absorbed—fragments of Thorvald's encounters with similar beings. "You serve the Ashfather."

"I serve freedom." The fire-wight's voice dropped to a whisper that somehow carried across the valley. "As could you. The mark you bear can be reshaped to serve a different purpose."

Brynja stepped forward, her Jordmark glowing brighter. "Don't listen. Fire-wights are weavers of lies."

Cinderheart laughed, the sound like logs splitting in a blaze. "The Earth-Healer speaks true about my kind, but she doesn't understand what the Tree demands of you." It extended a flaming hand toward Asvarr. "Come. Let me show you the memory the Tree hides."

Asvarr hesitated, the sword heavy in his grip. Knowledge from Thorvald warned against trusting the creature, but something else—a question that had gnawed at him since the binding—pushed him forward.

"Asvarr, don't," Brynja warned, grabbing his sleeve.

He shook her off. "I need to know what I'm becoming."

"Wise choice," Cinderheart said as Asvarr approached. "Your predecessor thought the same, before the end."

The mention of a predecessor froze Asvarr mid-step. "What do you know of him?"

"Thorvald Knotmaker? More than the Tree allowed him to remember." The fire-wight circled Asvarr slowly, leaving scorched footprints in the snow. "Ask yourself why the Knotmaker lived alone, half-mad with fragmented memories."

A memory flashed through Asvarr's mind—Thorvald's gnarled hands weaving complex patterns, tears tracking down his weathered face as he whispered names of people long dead. The old Warden had bound three anchors, each taking more of his humanity.

"The Tree consumes," Cinderheart continued, now standing so close that Asvarr felt his skin tighten from the heat. "With each binding, you become less yourself and more its vessel."

"I already know this," Asvarr growled, tightening his grip on the sword.

"But do you know what remains when the final binding is complete?" The fire-wight's voice lowered. "Nothing of the man you were. Only the Tree's will, wearing your flesh like a glove."

Brynja shouted something from the edge of the valley, but her words were lost as Cinderheart suddenly lunged forward, pressing its burning hand against the Grímmark.

Pain exploded through Asvarr's chest. He staggered backward, slashing with his sword, but the bronze blade passed through the creature's form without resistance. The Grímmark burned with cold fire; the runes writhing beneath Cinderheart's touch.

"See the truth," the fire-wight hissed.

Images flooded Asvarr's mind—Thorvald standing before a great tree, no longer blind but young and strong. Four others stood with him, each bearing a different mark. Then, pain as the final anchor bound to them. Their screams as something emerged from the Tree, something vast and hungry that devoured their identities, leaving empty vessels behind.

Asvarr fell to his knees, gasping. The vision fragmented as Brynja's voice cut through his consciousness.

"—sword won't work! Use the horn!"

Blinking away the afterimages, Asvarr fumbled for Hakon's war horn at his belt. Cinderheart stepped back, its form flickering with what might have been concern.

"The vision I showed you is truth," it said quickly. "Join us instead. The Ashfather offers freedom from the cycle."

Asvarr raised the horn to his lips, remembering how it had driven back the shadow-king. The bronze instrument felt warm against his mouth, responding to his intention. But before he could blow, Cinderheart gestured sharply.

The frozen figures in the valley shifted, ice cracking around them as they turned as one to face Asvarr. Their eyes glowed with inner fire, mouths opening in silent screams.

"They will die if you use the Warden's call," Cinderheart warned. "Their bodies are fragile, held together only by my will."

Asvarr lowered the horn, conflict tearing through him. "Release them."

"After you hear my offer." The fire-wight's form stabilized, becoming more definitively human-shaped. "The Ashfather knows what you've seen—a potential future where the Tree becomes something worse than what we fight. He offers another path."

"What path?" Asvarr asked, aware of Brynja circling behind the creature, her Jordmark glowing brighter.

"Balance. The Tree must be bound and never allowed to fully awaken." Cinderheart's voice grew passionate, flames leaping higher from its form. "We need Wardens who understand the danger—who will maintain the balance rather than complete the cycle."

The words resonated uncomfortably with the vision he'd seen. What if the Tree was using him for a purpose darker than he understood?

"And the people?" Asvarr gestured to the frozen villagers.

"They remain as they are. A small price for the world's safety."

Brynja had reached a position directly opposite Asvarr, her hand out-stretched toward the ground. He caught her eye, understanding her intent. The Jordmark gave her power over earth—even frozen earth.

"How do I know you speak the truth?" Asvarr asked, deliberately adjusting his stance to keep Cinderheart's attention.

"You bore witness to Thorvald's memories," the fire-wight replied. "Did you see happiness in his isolation? Did you see purpose in his endless knot-weaving? He discovered too late what fate awaits Wardens."

As it spoke, Brynja pressed her palm against the frozen ground. The Jord-mark flared green-gold, and a tremor ran through the earth beneath them.

Cinderheart whirled toward her, sensing the disturbance. "Fool girl! You'll destroy them all!"

The ground split beneath the fire-wight's feet, a jagged crevice opening to swallow it. Cinderheart howled, flames shooting upward as it fell. Asvarr seized the moment, raising the horn to his lips and blowing a single, powerful note.

The sound that emerged was nothing like the horn's normal tone. It rang with the resonance of the Root itself, harmonizing with the humming of his Grímmark. Golden light spiraled from the horn's mouth, encircling Cinderheart as it struggled to climb from the crevice.

"You don't understand what you're doing!" the fire-wight screamed, its flames dimming as the horn's power contained it. "The cycle must be broken!"

Asvarr approached the edge of the crevice, horn still raised. "The frozen people—how do we free them?"

"Only my flame sustains them now," Cinderheart snarled, its form com-pressing under the horn's influence. "Kill me, and they shatter."

Brynja joined Asvarr at the crevice's edge, her expression grim. "It lies. I sense life in them still—faint, but present."

"You understand nothing of fire's nature," the creature hissed at her, then turned its hollow gaze to Asvarr. "But he does. The Grímmark knows flame's truth."

Asvarr lowered the horn, studying the trapped fire-wight. "If I release you, will you free them?"

"Asvarr, no!" Brynja grabbed his arm. "It serves the Ashfather!"

"I serve myself," Cinderheart corrected, flames dimming further. "And yes, Flame-Bearer, I would free them—in exchange for your ear alone. There are truths meant only for the Fire Warden."

Brynja's grip tightened. "Don't trust it."

Asvarr looked from her to the fire-wight, then to the frozen villagers still locked in their icy prisons. The weight of decision pressed on him, complicated by the vision Cinderheart had forced upon him. What if the Tree was using him for purposes he didn't understand? What if the Ashfather, despite his methods, sought to prevent something worse?

The Grímmark pulsed on his chest with a steady rhythm that matched his heartbeat. It offered no guidance, only power—how he used that power remained his choice.

"Free them first," he said finally to Cinderheart. "Then I'll hear your words—alone."

The fire-wight's flames flickered higher with what might have been satisfaction. "As you wish, Warden."

Brynja's face hardened. "If you release it—"

"I'm not releasing it," Asvarr cut her off. "But we need those people free."

"And you trust its word?" she demanded.

"No," he said, meeting her amber gaze. "I trust the power I hold over it."

***

He raised the horn again in silent threat. Cinderheart's flames dimmed in response.

"Very well," the fire-wight said. "Stand back."

Asvarr nodded to Brynja, who reluctantly stepped away from the crevice. With a gesture from Cinderheart, threads of flame shot from its body toward the frozen figures. The fire encircled each victim, suffusing the ice with golden light. Slowly, the blue-white luminescence faded from the ice, returning it to clear crystal.

"Now," Cinderheart said, "for the awakening."

With a sharp, twisting motion of its flaming hands, the fire-wight shattered the ice encasing the villagers. Instead of breaking into deadly shards, the ice dissolved into mist that swirled around each person before dissipating. One by one, the victims collapsed to the ground, drawing ragged breaths.

"They live," Brynja whispered, her Jordmark pulsing as she extended her senses toward them. "Weakened, but alive."

Cinderheart looked up at Asvarr from the crevice. "I have fulfilled my part. Now fulfill yours, Flame-Bearer. Send the Earth-Healer to tend the awakened, and hear what I must tell you alone."

Asvarr turned to Brynja, whose face already showed refusal forming. "They need help," he said before she could object. "Your Jordmark can restore their strength."

"And leave you with that?" She gestured to the fire-wight.

"It's trapped and weakened." He held up the horn. "And I have this."

Brynja studied him, conflict clear in her expression. Finally, she nodded once, sharply. "If its flames grow higher, I'm returning—regardless of what secrets it's sharing."

As she descended the slope toward the recovering villagers, Asvarr turned back to Cinderheart. The fire-wight watched him with its hollow eyes, flames now burning a deep blue at their core.

"What truth is so important that only I should hear it?" Asvarr demanded.

Cinderheart's voice dropped to a whisper, forcing Asvarr to lean closer to the crevice.

"The Tree lies, Warden. It has always lied." The fire-wight's flames contracted, concentrating into an intense blue-white core. "What you saw in my vision was not Thorvald's memory—it was your future. But it wasn't the Tree that consumed those Wardens."

"What are you saying?"

"When the five anchors are bound and the five Wardens gathered, something older than the Tree awakens." Cinderheart's voice grew urgent. "The Ashfather doesn't seek to destroy the Tree—he seeks to control what sleeps within it."

The Grímmark pulsed, sending a jolt of pain through Asvarr's chest. He pressed his hand against it, feeling the runes shift beneath his palm.

"The mark you bear," Cinderheart continued, "is changing you, preparing your body to host what comes after. Each binding makes more room inside you, hollowing out what makes you human."

"Why should I believe you?" Asvarr growled, though dread pooled in his stomach.

"You've already felt it. The memories that aren't yours. The knowledge you never learned. The comfort you take in powers that should terrify you." The fire-wight's flames reached toward him. "Let me show you one thing more—something even the Ashfather doesn't know."

Before Asvarr could react, Cinderheart surged upward, faster than flame should move. A burning tendril lashed out, catching his wrist. The bronze sword clattered to the frozen ground as searing pain shot up his arm.

Cinderheart's fire spread across his skin, sinking beneath the surface, flowing toward the Grímmark. Asvarr tried to raise the horn but found his muscles locked, paralyzed as the fire-wight's essence infiltrated his body.

"What you carry is older than gods," Cinderheart whispered, its physical form dissipating as more of its essence flowed into Asvarr. "Older than the Tree. It remembers when stars were born and died."

The Grímmark flared with golden light, fighting the invasion of blue flame. Asvarr felt his chest become a battlefield, two ancient powers warring for dominance. He fell to his knees, a scream locked in his throat as the marks on his chest shifted, forming new patterns.

Through pain-blurred eyes, he saw Brynja running toward him, her mouth open in a shout he couldn't hear. The world had narrowed to the burning agony in his chest and Cinderheart's voice inside his mind.

The Tree, the Ashfather—two sides of the same eternal conflict. But there is a third path.

With the last of his strength, Asvarr pressed the horn to his lips and blew. The sound came out broken and weak, but the bronze instrument responded, sending a pulse of power through him that momentarily separated Cinderheart's essence from his own.

In that instant of clarity, Asvarr drew his knife and slashed it across the Grímmark. Blood welled, red at first, then mixed with golden sap and blue flame. The competing forces hissed and sputtered where they met his blood.

"Blood-right," he gasped, remembering Thorvald's teachings. "My flesh. My choice."

The blue flame retreated from the blood-drawn boundary, coalescing into a small, intense light hovering over the Grímmark. Cinderheart's voice came faintly, as if from a great distance:

"Remember, Flame-Bearer. When the final binding comes—look for the third path."

The blue flame extinguished with a soft pop. Where it had touched his skin, a new rune had formed—smaller than the Grímmark but unmistakably part of it now, altering its meaning in subtle ways Asvarr couldn't yet decipher.

Brynja reached him, her hands immediately going to his wounded chest. "What happened? What did it do to you?"

Asvarr stared at the new mark, knowledge flooding through him—knowledge from somewhere beyond Thorvald's memories, beyond the Tree's influence.

"It marked me," he said, voice hoarse. "With a choice."

***

Asvarr's blood sizzled against the new mark, the coppery scent mingling with burning pine. Brynja knelt beside him, her fingers hovering above the altered Grímmark where gold, red, and blue swirled together in an impossible pattern.

"This changes everything," she whispered, the green glow of her Jordmark casting strange shadows across her face. "The rune has been corrupted."

Asvarr pressed his palm against the wound, feeling the heat pulse beneath his skin. Each heartbeat sent a ripple of sensation through his chest—pain followed by startling clarity, as if his mind stood on a high ridge overlooking a vast landscape previously hidden in fog.

"Not corrupted," he corrected, surprised by the certainty in his voice. "Expanded."

He rose unsteadily, leaning on his sword for support. Down in the valley, the freed villagers huddled together, many still shaking off the effects of their frozen imprisonment. The summoning circle's pattern remained visible in the disturbed snow, an ancient constellation mapped on frozen earth.

"You don't understand what just happened, do you?" Brynja stood, maintaining a distance between them. "Fire-wights consume their victims, hollowing them out from within. Whatever that thing showed you, whatever it said—it was manipulation."

Asvarr touched the new mark again, tracing its shape with his fingertips. The blue flame had burned a smaller rune that intersected with the Grímmark's central node, altering its meaning without erasing what had come before. Knowledge bubbled up from somewhere deeper than memory.

"Kenaz," he said. "The torch rune."

Brynja's eyes narrowed. "That's not Kenaz. It's twisted, inverted."

"Because it's seen from within." Asvarr picked up the horn, its bronze surface warm against his fingers. "Cinderheart showed me—"

The words died in his throat as pain lanced through his skull. He dropped to one knee, vision darkening at the edges. Images flashed through his mind—the Tree burning, roots withering, something ancient stirring beneath it all.

Brynja moved toward him, then hesitated. "Asvarr?"

He raised a hand to ward her off, breathing through clenched teeth until the vision subsided. "I'm fine."

"Liar." She crouched beside him, careful not to touch him. "You're fighting it right now, aren't you? The fire-wight's influence."

Before he could answer, a shout echoed from the valley below. One of the villagers had collapsed, his body convulsing as blue flames flickered across his skin. Then another fell, and another.

"The fire spreads," Brynja hissed, her Jordmark flaring brighter. "Cinderheart isn't gone—just dispersed."

Asvarr staggered to his feet, the movement sending fresh waves of pain through his chest. Understanding crystallized with brutal clarity: Cinderheart had planned this from the beginning. The summoning circle, the frozen villagers, the confrontation—all to ensure multiple hosts when the fire-wight inevitably fragmented.

"We need to contain it," he said, gripping the horn tighter. "Before it fully infects them."

Brynja gestured toward his chest. "It's already infected you."

"Then I'm immune to further corruption." He started down the slope, legs steadier than they should have been. "Help me gather them."

She caught his arm, fingers digging into his flesh. "Asvarr. Think. We don't know what that mark is doing to you. You could be spreading exactly what Cinderheart wants."

He wrenched free. "And if we do nothing, they die."

A woman's scream cut through the frigid air. More villagers had collapsed, blue flames crawling across their bodies like frost patterns. The survivors tried to help their fallen companions, only to recoil as the fire leapt between them.

Asvarr raised the horn to his lips, then hesitated. When he'd used it before, the sound had pushed Cinderheart's essence away from him temporarily. But if the fire-wight's fragments were already inside these people...

"The horn could kill them," he muttered.

Brynja stepped forward, her expression hardening. "Then, we use earth to contain fire."

She knelt, pressing both palms against the frozen ground. The Jordmark on her forehead pulsed, sending ripples of green-gold light through the snow. The earth groaned, then split in a circle around the afflicted villagers. Steam rose from the newly exposed soil as Brynja's power coursed through it.

"What are you doing?" Asvarr demanded.

"Making a boundary." Sweat beaded on her forehead despite the cold; her breaths coming in quick gasps. "Earth absorbs, contains. I can hold the fragments here, but not for long."

The blue flames attacking the villagers seemed to sense the threat. They intensified, burning hotter as they tried to consume their hosts faster. Several villagers screamed, their skin blistering where the fire touched them.

Asvarr looked down at his chest, where the new mark pulsed in time with his heartbeat. If Cinderheart had truly meant to corrupt him, the fire-wight could have done so while he was vulnerable. Instead, it had given him something else—knowledge buried beneath fear.

"The flame isn't trying to consume them," he said slowly, understanding dawning. "It's trying to transform them."

"Into what?" Brynja demanded, her concentration still focused on maintaining the earthen barrier.

"Vessels. For something waiting to be born." Asvarr reached out with his senses, feeling the connection between the blue flames and the altered mark on his chest. They resonated at the same frequency, called to the same purpose.

The knowledge Cinderheart had forced into him surfaced again—fragments of a plan older than the Tree, older than the shadows that opposed it. A third path, hidden from both sides of an eternal conflict.

Asvarr gripped the hilt of his bronze sword, feeling the runes respond to his touch. "I know what to do."

Before Brynja could object, he vaulted over the earthen barrier and landed among the afflicted villagers. The blue flames surged toward him immediately, abandoning their current hosts to reach for the more compatible vessel.

"Yes," Asvarr breathed, raising his marked chest to the fire. "Come to me."

The flames leapt eagerly, drawn to the altered Grímmark like iron to a lode-stone. As they touched his skin, pain seared through him, but differently than before—heat without burning, power without consumption. The kenaz rune in his chest flared blue-white, absorbing the fire-fragments into itself.

Through watering eyes, he saw the villagers collapse, freed from the flames. Their skin remained blistered, but no longer burned. They would live.

The last fragments of Cinderheart's essence swirled around Asvarr's body before sinking beneath his skin, joining the altered mark. Knowledge flooded his mind—star-patterns, root-songs, the taste of worlds long dead. He screamed, dropping to his knees as his body struggled to contain what no human was meant to hold.

Brynja's voice reached him as if from across a vast distance. "Asvarr! Use the sword! Cut it out!"

The bronze blade lay forgotten in the snow beside him. Asvarr reached for it, fingers closing around the hilt. One slash could sever the connection, drive out Cinderheart's essence before it fully merged with him.

But as he raised the weapon, a deeper understanding stopped his hand. The fire-wight hadn't lied—at least, not entirely. The Tree and the Ashfather, eternally opposed, each concealing their true purpose from their pawns. And between them, a third path walked by those who refused both masters.

Asvarr lowered the sword and pressed his palm flat against the mark. Blood welled between his fingers as he spoke words that rose from somewhere beyond memory.

"By blood-right and flame-bond, I accept this knowing."

The burning sensation peaked, then subsided to a warm pulse. The blue fire vanished beneath his skin, fully absorbed by the altered Grímmark. Where the new kenaz rune had burned, the skin sealed into a raised scar—a torch pointing inward toward his heart.

Silence fell across the valley. Even the wind stilled, as if the world held its breath.

Asvarr rose unsteadily, looking down at the spent bodies of the villagers. They breathed shallowly but steadily, the worst of their burns already fading. Whatever the fire-wight had done to them wasn't meant to kill—only to prepare vessels that might serve if the primary host failed.

Brynja approached cautiously, her Jordmark dim with exhaustion. "What did you do?"

"I accepted a gift." Asvarr ran his thumb along the edge of his sword, cutting just deep enough to draw blood. Where the crimson droplets touched the bronze, the runes flared with blue-gold light. "And a burden."

"You're a fool." Her voice trembled with anger and fear. "That thing is still inside you. Using you."

"No." Asvarr wiped the blood from his blade. "I'm using it."

He turned toward her, aware of how he must appear—blood-smeared, wild-eyed, glowing with unnatural light. But his mind felt clearer than it had since the Tree fell. For the first time, he saw beyond the immediate cycle of war between root and shadow.

"The fire-wight showed me truth, Brynja. Not the full truth—creatures like Cinderheart can't help but twist knowledge to their purpose. But enough to see that we've been walking a path laid by forces neither of us understands."

She studied him, wariness written in every line of her body. "And now?"

"Now I walk with open eyes." He sheathed his sword and looked to the northern horizon, where the first anchored root glowed faintly in his perception. "The Tree needs binding. The Ashfather must be stopped. Both remain true."

"But you've changed," she said. It wasn't a question.

Asvarr touched the altered Grímmark, feeling both mark's pulse in unsettling harmony. "Every binding changes us. Every choice reshapes our wyrd. Thorvald knew this—it's why he lived apart, weaving his knots to preserve what fragments of himself remained."

"And what remains of you?" Brynja asked softly.

The question struck deeper than she could have known. Asvarr had felt the Tree's influence growing since the first binding—ancient memories flooding his mind, perspectives that spanned millennia reshaping how he saw the world.

And now, Cinderheart's essence added another layer, another voice whispering knowledge that humans weren't meant to carry.

Yet beneath it all, something remained that was uniquely his—a core of stubborn will that refused to be subsumed.

"Enough," he answered. "Enough to finish what I've begun."

Brynja's expression hardened. "And if I believe you've become a danger? If the Earth-Healer stands against the Flame-Bearer?"

Asvarr met her gaze steadily. "Then we'll discover which mark burns brighter."

The tension between them stretched, neither willing to back down. In the valley below, the villagers stirred, moaning weakly as they regained consciousness.

"We should help them," Asvarr said finally.

Brynja nodded once, sharply. "Yes. But this isn't finished between us." She gestured to his chest. "Whatever path you think you've found, I don't trust it."

"I don't ask for trust," he replied. "Only that you watch me. Closely. And if what remains of me disappears entirely—"

"I'll do what's necessary," she promised, her hand dropping to the bone-handled knife at her belt.

Asvarr nodded, accepting the implicit threat as both a promise and protection. Whatever Cinderheart had begun by marking him, the consequences would unfold in time. For now, the immediate path remained clear: heal these people, resume his journey to the next anchor, continue the bindings despite knowing each would erode more of his humanity.

***

But as he descended into the valley to help the recovering villagers, a new awareness shadowed his thoughts. The flame-mark pulsed with each heartbeat, sending images flickering through his mind—constellations he'd never seen, roots spreading across worlds beyond counting, and something ancient watching from the spaces between.

When the final binding comes—look for the third path.

Cinderheart's final words echoed in his memory. Between Tree and Shadow, between creation and destruction, a third way waited to be walked. Asvarr pressed his hand against his chest, feeling the double pulse of the marks that now defined him.

He had accepted the flame. Now he would have to learn to wield it—or be consumed by what he'd so willingly taken into himself.

CHAPTER 7

BLOOD PRICE OF THE WOLVES

S now bit into Asvarr's face as he crested the ridge. Three days had passed since he'd parted ways with Brynja, the memory of her final warning still raw. She had gone east to warn other settlements about the spreading chaos, while he continued north toward the second anchor, the pull of the Grímmark leaving him little choice in the matter.

He paused at the ridgeline, breathing hard. The valley spread before him like a vast white bowl ringed by jagged black peaks. The morning light caught on something in the center—a stone circle half-buried in snow, with a massive fissure cutting through its heart. Even from this distance, he could sense the wrongness emanating from it.

The marks on his chest pulsed in discordant harmony. Since absorbing Cinderheart's essence, the Grímmark and the flame-rune fought within him, each pulling in slightly different directions. The Tree's mark drew him toward the stone circle, while the flame-mark recoiled from it. The conflict left him nauseated and disoriented.

Asvarr sank to one knee, driving his bronze sword into the frozen ground for support. He pressed his palm against his chest, feeling the raised scars through his tunic. The knowledge gained from Cinderheart whispered caution—there was something in that valley connected to the Ashfather, something that could sense the flame he carried.

A long howl cut through the silence, followed by another, then a chorus that echoed off the mountainsides. Wolves. But the sound raised the hair on Asvarr's neck. These were no ordinary wolves.

He squinted against the glare, spotting movement along the valley floor—gray-white shapes loping through the snow with unnatural speed, converging on the stone circle. Their bodies seemed to shift and stretch as they ran, caught between beast and human form.

"Ulfhednar," Asvarr muttered, the word rising from Thorvald's memories.

The wolf-warriors were legendary berserkers who took on the aspect of wolves, warriors who shared their souls with beast-spirits. But, according to Thorvald's memories, true ulfhednar had disappeared generations ago. What stalked the valley now were something different—transformed by the Tree's blood rather than ancient rites.

The closest wolf-shape stopped, raising its head toward the ridge. Even at this distance, Asvarr could feel its gaze lock onto him. It threw back its head and howled—a sound too structured to be animal, too raw to be human. A warning. A challenge.

Asvarr drew a sharp breath as the beast's howl resonated with the marks on his chest. The flame-rune flared hot, while the Grímmark hummed with recognition. They knew what he was. They were calling to him specifically.

He needed to move. The stone circle contained something connected to the second anchor—he could feel that certainty in his bones. But reaching it meant crossing a valley full of creatures that were neither wolf nor human, but something torn between realms.

Deliberately, he drew the Horn of Binding from his belt. The bronze instrument felt warm despite the frigid air, responding to his intention. He put it to his lips, hesitated, then lowered it again. The horn's call would alert every transformed creature in the valley to his precise location. Better to watch first, to understand what he faced.

Asvarr slid back from the ridgeline and circled west, keeping to the rocky outcroppings for cover. The flame-rune pulsed warnings with each step closer to the valley, while the Grímmark pulled him forward relentlessly. His body felt like a battleground between competing wills.

From a new vantage point behind a wind-carved boulder, he studied the pack more carefully. Seven wolves—no, nine. Their fur shifted between gray and ghostly white, and where the morning light struck them directly, their bodies seemed to blur at the edges, as if struggling to maintain physical form.

As he watched, one of the larger beasts padded to the center of the stone circle. It reared back, its front legs elongating, shoulders widening, muzzle flattening. The transformation shuddered through it until a man stood where the wolf had been—naked despite the cold, his skin marbled with gray patterns that mimicked fur. The man-shape knelt at the fissure's edge, pressing his palms to the frozen ground on either side.

"Root-blood rises," the wolf-man rasped, his voice carrying unnaturally across the snow. "Circle broken. Pack hungers."

The other wolves paced around him, some maintaining pure wolf form, others caught in grotesque mid-transformation—human eyes in lupine faces, clawed hands extending from paw-like wrists. They whined and growled; the sounds forming a discordant counterpoint to the man's words.

Asvarr leaned forward, straining to see what lay in the fissure. A faint golden glow emanated from deep within—the distinctive light of the Tree's sap. His suspicions crystallized: the stone circle had been built over a fragment of Yggdrasil, perhaps a smaller branch or root splinter that had fallen during the Shattering.

The wolf-man plunged his arm into the fissure, his body convulsing as he made contact with whatever lay below. When he withdrew his hand, it dripped with golden sap that steamed in the cold air. He raised the liquid to his lips and drank.

The change was immediate and horrifying. The man's body contorted, bones cracking audibly across the distance as his form expanded. Fur erupted across his skin in patches, his jaw elongated, yet his body remained upright, growing larger than either wolf or man should be. His howl of pain transformed into triumphant laughter.

"The Warden approaches," he called out, turning to face Asvarr's direction with unnerving accuracy. "I smell the Tree's mark on him—and something else. Something burned."

Asvarr ducked behind the boulder, pulse hammering. The creature had sensed him despite the distance, despite his care. The flame-rune burned against his chest, urging flight, while the Grímmark pulled him toward the circle with increasing insistence.

He heard the scrape of claws on stone, the heavy breathing of large predators on the move. They were coming for him. Decision time.

Asvarr gripped the horn in one hand, his sword in the other. The bronze blade glinted in the morning light, the runes along its length pulsing in time with his heartbeat. He could run, try to circle around, and approach from another angle. Or he could meet them head-on, use the horn to challenge creatures born of the Tree's corruption.

A shadow fell across the snow beside him. He looked up to see a wolf-shape perched on the boulder above, larger than any natural wolf, its amber eyes fixed on him with cold intelligence. It hadn't been with the main pack.

"Flame-carrier," it growled, the words formed with difficulty through fanged jaws. "Alpha wants you alive."

Asvarr lunged without thinking, the bronze sword sweeping upward. The blade connected, drawing a line of golden-tinged blood across the creature's chest. It yelped, more in surprise than pain, and leaped backward.

"You carry root-song in metal," it snarled, circling warily. Its wound already closed, the edges knitting together with unnatural speed. "Alpha will feast on your heart. Become more."

Asvarr raised the horn to his lips and blew a short, sharp note. The sound cut through the air like a physical thing, reverberating off the surrounding peaks. The wolf-creature recoiled, its form flickering between wolf and man as the horn's power washed over it.

Below in the valley, howls answered—pained, angry, hungry. The pack had heard. They were coming.

***

The wolf before him shook its head violently, steadying itself. "Horn cannot save you. We are not shadow-born nor fire-born. We are blood-born of the Tree itself."

"What are you?" Asvarr demanded, keeping the sword between them. "What has the Tree's blood done to you?"

"Made us more." The creature's muzzle pulled back in what might have been a smile. "We were warriors once. Oath-sworn to a jarl long dead. When the sky broke and the root fell, we drank what bled from it. Now we are becoming what waits beneath."

"Beneath what?"

"Beneath all." The wolf-thing's body contorted, bones cracking as it rose to stand on two legs, its form swelling until it towered over Asvarr. Fur receded from its face, revealing a man's features distorted by bestial characteristics—elongated jaw, amber eyes, pointed ears. "We are the ulfhednar reborn. And you, Warden, carry what our alpha needs."

Asvarr backed away, nearly slipping on the icy stone. More shapes appeared on the ridgeline behind the transformed warrior—the rest of the pack, racing up from the valley with impossible speed. He was trapped, outnumbered.

The flame-mark burned hotter, responding to his fear. Knowledge bubbled up—fragments of Cinderheart's memories showing these creatures burning, their flesh unable to regenerate from fire's touch. The fire-wight had fought them before.

Asvarr re-sheathed his sword and pressed his palm against his chest, directly over the flame-rune. "Fire-price," he whispered, the words coming from somewhere beyond his own knowledge. "Blood-call."

Heat flared beneath his hand, racing down his arm. The sensation wasn't painful but overwhelming, like plunging into a hot spring after days in the snow. His fingertips tingled, then glowed with blue-white flames that didn't burn his flesh but danced across his skin.

The ulfhednar warrior hesitated, recognizing the fire. "Flame-marked," it growled, backing away. "Alpha didn't say—"

Asvarr lunged forward, sweeping his flame-wreathed hand toward the creature's chest. The fire leapt eagerly from his fingers, latching onto the ulfhednar's fur. Unlike the golden-tinged blood that had healed almost instantly, these blue flames spread rapidly, consuming fur and flesh.

The creature howled, clawing at the spreading fire. "Brothers!" it screamed, its voice more human in pain. "The Warden bears the Ashfather's flame!"

The rest of the pack hesitated at the ridgeline, watching their burning pack mate with wary eyes. The largest among them—the one who had transformed at the stone circle—stepped forward. He remained in his mixed form, nine feet tall with a wolf's head atop a distorted human body covered in patchy fur.

"You smell of both Tree and Shadow, Warden," the alpha called, his voice a guttural rumble. "Explain yourself before we tear you apart."

Asvarr held up his still-burning hand, the flames casting blue light across the snow. "I am Skyrend's Flame," he said, the Grímmark pulsing as he spoke his title. "I seek the second anchor."

The alpha's ears flattened against his skull. "The anchor is ours. The blood it weeps sustains our transformation."

"Transformation into what?"

"The final form." The alpha gestured to his misshapen body. "We are halfway there. With enough of the Tree's blood, we will complete what was begun. Become the true ulfhednar of legend—the devourers-of-gods."

Understanding dawned, drawn from both Thorvald's and Cinderheart's memories. The original ulfhednar had been warriors who channeled wolf spirits, yes, but the most ancient legends spoke of creatures that existed before the gods, predators that stalked the primordial void. The Tree's blood was reawakening something that had lain dormant in these warriors' lineage.

Asvarr let the flames die from his hand, making a show of considering the alpha's words. "I don't seek to take your blood-source," he lied. "I only need to see the anchor to understand what has happened to the Tree."

The alpha tilted his head, considering. Behind him, the pack shifted restlessly, some dropping to all fours, others maintaining their half-transformed state. The burning pack mate had collapsed to the ground, the blue flames consuming him completely, leaving nothing but ash that scattered in the mountain wind.

"You destroyed Fenrick," the alpha observed. "You wield both Tree-power and Flame-power." His misshapen mouth formed a grimace. "You are an abomination, neither one thing nor another. Like us."

"I am still becoming," Asvarr replied, the words feeling right as they left his mouth. "As are you."

The alpha considered this, then nodded slowly. "Come then, Warden. See what we guard. But know this—you leave your weapons here, and at the first sign of interference with our blood-source, the pack will feed on your flesh while you still live."

Asvarr hesitated, weighing his options. The Grímmark pulled him toward the stone circle with almost painful insistence. The second anchor lay near, and his duty as Warden demanded he seek it. But the flame-mark whispered warnings—these creatures were dangerous, unpredictable, caught between old magic and new corruption.

He decided. Slowly, deliberately, he unbuckled his sword belt and laid it on the stone, followed by the Horn of Binding. He kept only his knife, tucked in his boot where the alpha couldn't see it.

"I accept your terms," he said.

The alpha grinned, displaying rows of jagged teeth. "Then follow, Flame-Bearer. See what the Root has spawned in its dying throes."

As they descended toward the valley floor, the pack encircled Asvarr, keeping him boxed in without touching him. They maintained a wary distance from his hands, having seen what happened to their pack mate. The alpha led the way, his massive form leaving deep impressions in the snow.

"We were shield-brothers," the alpha said, without turning his head. "Twelve warriors sworn to Jarl Ulfrik of the Northern Hold. When the sky broke, we were hunting in these mountains. We saw the branch fall, saw it pierce the stone circle—an ancient place of sacrifice."

"You drank its sap," Asvarr said.

"We tasted divinity." The alpha's voice held reverence and bitterness in equal measure. "It changed us, showed us what we truly were beneath human flesh. Our ancestors were something older than men. The blood awakened their legacy."

They reached the stone circle, seven massive monoliths arranged around a central space. The stones bore weathered carvings—wolves devouring human figures, humans transforming into beasts, spiraling patterns that hurt Asvarr's eyes if he looked at them too long. At the center, a jagged fissure split the ground, steam rising from its depths despite the freezing air.

The alpha stopped at the fissure's edge, gesturing for Asvarr to approach. "Look, Warden. See what bleeds here."

Asvarr stepped carefully to the edge and peered down. Twenty feet below, embedded in stone, lay a fragment of Yggdrasil no larger than his forearm. Unlike the massive root he'd encountered before, this was a slender branch, its bark still intact. Golden sap welled from its broken end, collecting in a small pool that glowed with inner light.

The Grímmark burned against his chest, recognizing the fragment as part of the Tree. But it wasn't an anchor point—just a broken piece, rich in the Tree's essence but lacking the concentrated power he'd felt at the first binding. His confusion must have shown on his face.

"This isn't what you seek," the alpha said, watching him closely. "I see the disappointment in your eyes."

"There should be an anchor nearby," Asvarr said, straightening. "A root fragment larger than this, containing—"

"Containing what?" the alpha interrupted, stepping closer. "What power do you seek, Warden?"

Asvarr chose his words carefully. "The Tree is broken. Five anchors were cast across the realms. I've bound one already. The second calls to me from somewhere near, but this isn't it."

The alpha's amber eyes narrowed. "Bound? You seek to bind the Tree's power to yourself?"

"To stabilize it. To prevent further breaking."

The alpha threw back his head and laughed, a sound halfway between human mirth and a wolf's howl. "You think you're saving it? Fool. The Tree's breaking was necessary—it released what was trapped within!"

The pack closed in around them, growling softly. Asvarr tensed, feeling the weight of their collective hunger. They hadn't brought him here to negotiate or share information—this had been a trap from the beginning.

"The anchor you seek lies beneath the stone circle," the alpha said, gesturing to the surrounding ground. "Buried deep. We've been drinking from this small branch, growing stronger, preparing to dig down to the true power. And now you arrive, marked to open the way for us."

Asvarr took a step back, his hand instinctively reaching for the horn that wasn't there. "You need me to access the anchor."

"The blood responds to those who bear the Tree's mark." The alpha's form shifted again, growing larger, more bestial. "We've tried digging, clawing, breaking through the stone. Nothing works. The anchor protects itself."

Around them, the pack transformed as well, bones cracking, bodies distorting as they shifted to their most dangerous forms—neither wolf nor human but monstrous combinations of both.

"I won't help you," Asvarr said, his hand moving subtly toward his boot.

"You misunderstand." The alpha's voice deepened, rumbling from a chest now barrel-sized. "We don't need your cooperation. We only need your mark."

Understanding hit Asvarr like a physical blow. "You want to carve the Grím-mark from my flesh."

The alpha's misshapen mouth stretched into a horrific smile. "Why do you think we're called ulfhednar, Warden? We wear the skins of what we kill. Your skin will give us access to what lies below."

The pack surged forward, their misshapen bodies blocking every escape route. Asvarr whipped the knife from his boot and slashed at the nearest ulfhednar, drawing a line of golden-flecked blood across its muzzle. The creature yelped, but pressed on, its wound already closing.

"Take him alive," the alpha growled. "We need the skin intact."

Asvarr backed toward the fissure, the knife a slight comfort against eight transformed warriors. The Grímmark burned against his chest, pulsing with the proximity to a true anchor buried somewhere beneath them. The flame-rune responded differently, as if it was awakening, spreading heat through his veins.

He reached for that heat, letting it flow into his free hand. Blue flame erupted from his fingertips, spiraling up his arm. The ulfhednar hesitated, remembering what had happened to Fenrick.

"Your fire cannot burn us all before we tear you apart," the alpha said, circling to Asvarr's left. "Surrender, and your death will be quick."

Asvarr thrust the flame toward the nearest wolf-warrior. "I've survived worse than you."

"Have you?" The alpha tilted his massive head. "We are becoming what hunted the gods before time began. Every drop of the Tree's blood brings us closer to our true form."

The pack closed in, coordinating their movements with the precision of long-time shield-brothers. Two lunged from opposite directions, forcing Asvarr to defend against one while the other caught his jacket in its jaws, dragging him off balance.

He slashed backward with his knife, connecting with flesh. The creature released him with a yelp. Asvarr spun, flame hand extended, burning another across its chest. The ulfhednar stumbled back, golden-tinged fur blackening where the blue fire touched it.

"The flames mark him as an enemy," a wolf-warrior snarled. "He serves the Ashfather!"

"I serve no one," Asvarr shouted, backing toward the center of the stone circle. With each step, the Grímmark pulsed stronger, almost painfully.

The alpha watched him retreat, amber eyes calculating. "You move toward the anchor's heart, Warden. Do you feel it calling to you?"

Asvarr's back foot slipped on the edge of the fissure. He glanced down at the branch fragment below, still seeping golden sap. Something about its position nagged at him—it wasn't natural. The branch had been deliberately placed there, perhaps as a lure.

"You've been drinking from the wrong source," he said, a sudden understanding clicking into place. "This isn't just a fragment. It's bait."

The alpha's ears flattened. "What do you mean?"

"The Tree doesn't transform wolves into gods." Asvarr gestured at their misshapen bodies. "Look at yourselves. You're caught between forms, neither one thing nor another."

***

"We are becoming!" one of the ulfhednar snarled, saliva dripping from elongated fangs.

"You're being poisoned." Asvarr channeled more power into his flame-hand, letting the fire spread up his arm to his shoulder. "The Tree protects itself. This branch is tainted—meant to trap those who would steal rather than earn the Tree's power."

Doubt flickered across the alpha's bestial features. "You lie to save your skin."

"The anchor you seek is buried deep," Asvarr continued, an idea forming. "Only a true Warden can access it safely. Without the proper rituals, you'll end up like that." He pointed to one of the smaller ulfhednar whose transformation had gone wrong—spine twisted, limbs disproportionate, eyes bulging from a half-formed skull.

The pack hesitated, several members glancing at their malformed brother. The alpha growled low, a sound that demanded attention.

"He tries to divide us," the leader snarled. "Take him!"

They lunged as one. Asvarr dropped to his knees at the fissure's edge and slammed his flame-hand against the ground. Blue fire raced along the stone circle's perimeter, creating a momentary barrier between him and the pack. With his other hand, he touched the Grímmark through his torn clothing.

"Where are you?" he whispered to the anchor. "Show me."

The response came as a vision of depth. The true anchor lay directly beneath him, buried under layers of stone and frozen earth. The branch in the fissure was connected to it, a tendril sent upward like a plant seeking light.

The blue fire barrier sputtered, already fading. The ulfhednar prowled just beyond it, searching for weakness. The alpha stood directly opposite Asvarr, watching with unnerving intelligence.

"I see you understand now," the alpha said. "The anchor calls to you. But the only way to reach it is through us."

Asvarr gauged the distance to his weapons at the ridge's edge—impossibly far, with the pack between him and freedom. The flame-rune heated painfully as he pushed its power to maintain the barrier. He couldn't keep this up much longer.

The answer came from an unexpected source. The Grímmark pulsed, sending a surge of knowledge through him. The anchor didn't need to be reached physically—it could be called upward. That's what the branch fragment was—the beginning of a summoning that the ulfhednar had interrupted with their contaminating presence.

"You're right," Asvarr said to the alpha. "I can't reach the anchor without dying. But I don't need to."

He sheathed his knife and extended both hands toward the fissure. The blue flames from his right hand merged with golden light emanating from his left, where the Grímmark's power flowed outward. The combined energies spiraled downward, connecting with the branch fragment below.

"What are you doing?" the alpha demanded, taking a step forward.

"Finishing what you started," Asvarr replied through gritted teeth. "You wanted the anchor? I'm bringing it to you."

The ground beneath them trembled. Cracks spread outward from the fissure, widening rapidly. The ulfhednar backed away, whining with uncertainty. Only the alpha held his position, amber eyes fixed on Asvarr.

"Stop this," the alpha commanded. "We can make a bargain!"

"Too late." Asvarr focused his will through both marks, the competing powers finding unexpected harmony in his purpose. "I am the Warden. I speak for the Tree."

***

The fissure erupted. Earth and stone blasted upward as something massive pushed through from below. The ulfhednar scattered, howling in alarm. Golden light flooded the circle, momentarily blinding Asvarr. When his vision cleared, he found himself face-to-face with the anchor.

Unlike the massive root he'd encountered before, this was a thick branch the size of a small tree trunk, its surface carved with intricate runes that pulsed with inner light. It rose fifteen feet into the air, twisted and gnarled, extending smaller branches in all directions like reaching hands. At its center, a hollow contained a swirling mass of golden energy—the heart of the anchor's power.

The ulfhednar circled it warily, drawn by its power yet afraid to approach. The alpha stepped forward, staring at the anchor with naked hunger.

"It comes willingly to us," he growled. "We are worthy."

"No," Asvarr said, rising to his feet. "It comes because I called it. And it's not what you think."

The anchor pulsed, sending a wave of energy outward. The smaller wolf-warriors yelped, backing away as the golden light washed over them. But the alpha stood his ground, chest swelling with what might have been pride.

"I feel its power," the alpha said. "It recognizes us as the true inheritors."

Asvarr saw the trap unfolding exactly as he'd planned. "Then drink from it directly," he urged. "Take the power you deserve."

The alpha approached the anchor, reaching one deformed hand toward the swirling golden energy at its center. Asvarr stepped back, the Grímmark's knowledge warning him to keep his distance.

"Brothers," the alpha called to his pack. "Witness my ascension!"

The ulfhednar gathered closer, their bestial faces reflecting the golden light. Their leader grasped one of the smaller branches, breaking it off with a sharp crack. Golden sap oozed from the wound. Without hesitation, the alpha brought it to his mouth and drank deeply.

For a moment, nothing happened. Then, the alpha's body convulsed, his fur standing on end. He dropped the branch and clutched his throat, a terrible gurgling sound escaping his twisted lips. The transformation that followed wasn't what any of them had expected.

The alpha's form contracted violently. Bones snapped audibly as his limbs reshuffled, fur receding in patches to reveal human skin. He fell to his knees, howling—a sound that transformed midway into a human scream of agony. His pack mates watched in horror as their leader shrank, his massive frame collapsing inward until a naked human man knelt on the frozen ground, trembling and disoriented.

"What... what have you done to me?" the former alpha gasped, his voice now fully human, thin and reedy compared to his previous growl.

"I did nothing," Asvarr replied. "The anchor did. It's not meant to transform—it's meant to restore."

The man looked down at his human hands with growing horror. "No! Change me back! I won't be weak again!"

The pack circled their fallen leader, confusion and fear in their amber eyes. One of the larger wolves snarled at Asvarr, blaming him for their alpha's transformation.

"The true purpose of the anchor is balance," Asvarr explained, addressing the pack. "It doesn't grant power—it restores natural order. You weren't becoming gods. You were becoming abominations."

"Lies!" the former alpha shrieked, lunging for the broken branch he'd dropped. "I'll drink more—I'll change back!"

Before he could reach it, the branch withered, turning gray and lifeless. The anchor pulsed again, and more branches extended downward toward the wolf-warriors. Several backed away, but the smallest of them—the malformed one Asvarr had pointed out earlier—approached cautiously.

To everyone's surprise, the branch gently touched the deformed wolf-warrior's head. Golden light spread through its twisted body, bones cracking as they realigned. The transformation wasn't a full reversion to human form, but a correction—its body becoming that of a true wolf, sleek and powerful, with none of the grotesque half-transformation the ulfhednar had achieved.

The wolf looked down at itself, then back at the anchor. It dipped its head in what might have been gratitude before bounding away across the snow, freed from its torment.

Understanding rippled through the pack. One by one, they approached the anchor, each receiving the touch of a branch. Each transformed—some back to men who fled naked into the snow, others into true wolves that scattered in all directions. Soon, only the former alpha remained, shivering on his knees.

"This isn't what was promised," he said, teeth chattering. "We were meant to become greater!"

"Who promised you that?" Asvarr asked, suspicion forming. "Who told you to drink the sap?"

The man's eyes darted away. "A wanderer. One-eyed, with a raven cloak. He said we had old blood, that the Tree would recognize it."

The description triggered memories from both Thorvald and Cinderheart. "The Ashfather," Asvarr murmured. "He used you."

"He promised power!"

"He led you here as guardians," Asvarr explained. "To keep others away while he prepared his true scheme."

The anchor pulsed again, more insistently. The Grímmark responded, pulling Asvarr toward it. He understood what needed to happen next—the binding. But unlike the first anchor, this one had been corrupted by the ulfhednar's presence. It needed cleansing first.

The man struggled to his feet, hatred burning in his now-human eyes. "I won't remain this way. I'll find him again—demand he restore me!"

"He won't help you," Asvarr said. "You've served your purpose."

With surprising speed, the former alpha lunged at Asvarr, fingers curved like claws. "Then I'll take your mark for myself!"

Asvarr sidestepped, caught the man's arm, and redirected his momentum. The former alpha stumbled, losing his balance at the fissure's edge. For a heartbeat, their eyes met—human staring into human. Then gravity claimed him. His scream echoed as he plummeted into the dark below, ending with a sickening crack.

Silence fell across the stone circle. Asvarr stood alone with the anchor, its golden light pulsing in rhythm with his heartbeat. The Grímmark burned against his chest, demanding completion of the binding ritual. The flame-rune heated in counterpoint, offering neither resistance nor encouragement.

Asvarr approached the anchor, studying its rune-carved surface. Unlike the first anchor, which had been a root drawing power from beneath, this branch reached upward, distributing energy outward. Knowledge flowed from the Grímmark—this anchor represented growth, expansion, and the spreading of influence.

"I understand what you are," he said to the anchor. "Not just a fragment, but a purpose. The roots draw strength from the depths. The branches spread that strength across the realms."

The anchor pulsed in response, a tendril of golden energy reaching toward him. Asvarr removed his gloves and outer garment, exposing the marks on his chest to the freezing air. The Grímmark glowed gold, while the flame-rune burned blue.

"By blood and oath, horn and blade," he recited the binding words. "I accept this burden. I become Warden of two."

He placed both palms against the anchor's surface. Pain shot through him, far more intense than the first binding. Golden energy poured into him through the Grímmark while blue flame spiraled outward from the flame-rune, creating a spiraling pattern of light that surrounded both him and the anchor.

Visions overwhelmed him—forests spreading across barren lands, branches reaching toward distant stars, life flowing outward from a central point to fill emptiness with possibility. He saw countless beings connected by invisible strands of power, their lives intertwined like branches of an infinite tree.

Through the pain came understanding. The first anchor had shown him the depths of creation, the roots that stabilized existence. This anchor revealed connections—how all things related to one another across vast distances.

The binding reached its peak. Asvarr threw back his head and screamed as the anchor's essence surged into him. The competing marks on his chest flared with blinding light, then merged into a new pattern—the Grímmark expanding to incorporate aspects of the flame-rune rather than fighting against it.

When the light faded, the anchor had transformed. Where the massive branch had stood, now grew a sapling, slender and vibrant, its small branches reaching skyward with new buds despite the winter cold. At its base, golden sap had hardened into a disk-shaped amulet marked with the same pattern now emblazoned on Asvarr's chest.

He fell to his knees, exhausted yet filled with new power. His senses had expanded beyond normal perception. He could feel the distant pulse of the first anchor he'd bound, and could sense the remaining three scattered across different realms. Most importantly, he could perceive the connections between them—the pattern they would form when all five were united.

Asvarr picked up the golden amulet, turning it in his trembling hands. This was his token from the second binding—a physical manifestation of the anchor's power that he could carry with him. As his fingers closed around it, knowledge flowed into him: the amulet would guide him to the third anchor, just as the horn had led him to the second.

He tucked the amulet inside his tunic and retrieved his discarded clothing. The temperature was dropping rapidly as the sun descended toward the western peaks. He needed shelter soon. Looking around the stone circle, he spotted his weapons still lying at the ridge's edge.

As he climbed back up to retrieve his sword and horn, Asvarr examined his changed reflection in the polished bronze of the blade. The marks on his chest had indeed merged into a new pattern—the flame-rune now integrated into the

Grímmark's design. His eyes had changed too, flecked with gold where they had been solid gray before.

The second binding had taken more of his humanity, just as he'd been warned. Yet, the knowledge gained felt worth the price. He understood more about the Tree's nature, about the delicate balance between shadow and light, growth and decay.

He sheathed his sword and looked out across the valley, where wolves and men had scattered in all directions. They had been trapped between forms, neither one thing nor the other. He knew the feeling well.

The amulet pulsed against his chest, urging him onward. Adjusting his pack, Asvarr turned eastward to where the Horn of Binding told him the third anchor waited. Two were bound; three remained. With each binding, he changed. What would remain of Asvarr the berserker when the fifth anchor was secured?

He touched the merged marks on his chest, feeling their combined power flowing through him. The answer lay in balance, guiding transformation, and maintaining connection to his core self even as new knowledge and power altered him. The ulfhednar had lost themselves in their quest for power. He wouldn't make the same mistake.

Asvarr descended from the ridge, leaving the stone circle and its sapling behind. In his altered perceptions, he could see threads of golden light connecting him to both bound anchors, stretching across the distance like roots and branches of an immense tree that existed partially in this world and partially beyond it.

For the first time since accepting his role as Warden, he walked with certainty. The merged marks had given him new insight—there was indeed a third path between what the Tree demanded and what the Ashfather plotted. He would find it, step by careful step, binding what needed to be bound while maintaining enough of himself to make the final choice when it came.

The wind shifted, carrying the distant howl of a true wolf. Asvarr smiled. Balance has been restored to this valley. Now he needed to restore it to the broken realms themselves, one anchor at a time.

CHAPTER 8

THE EYE AT ḤVERGELMIR

Asvarr's boots crunched through the thin ice crust as he descended into the shadowed valley. Four days had passed since the binding at the stone circle, four days of trudging eastward through increasingly strange terrain. The land bore the scars of the Shattering—streams flowed uphill against their nature, stone formations twisted into impossible shapes, patches of summer growth erupted amid winter-dead forests.

The golden amulet pressed warm against his chest, its heat intensifying as he approached his destination. The Horn of Binding had guided him to this place—a deep depression in the earth, ringed by ancient pines that bent inward like watchful guardians. At the valley's center lay a pool, its waters black and utterly still despite the wind that stirred the trees.

Asvarr halted at the treeline, studying the pool through altered senses. The second binding had changed his perception. The merged mark on his chest granted him vision beyond mere sight—threads of connection between living things, currents of power flowing beneath reality's surface. What he saw around this pool disturbed him deeply.

The water absorbed all light, refusing any reflection of the gray sky above, even when sunlight broke through the clouds. Worse still were the movements beneath—thick currents circulating with purpose, resembling blood pulsing through a great heart.

"Hvergelmir," he whispered, the name rising from Thorvald's memories. The Well at the Root's Heart. One of three great wells of Norse cosmology, traditionally located in Niflheim, yet somehow now present in Midgard. The Shattering had rearranged much.

The amulet pulsed against his skin, urging him forward. Asvarr drew his bronze sword, its runes glowing faintly in response to the power emanating from the pool. Each step closer sent conflicting sensations through his body—the Grímmark element of his merged mark pulled him eagerly forward as the flame element recoiled, sensing danger.

"You stand at threshold-edge, Warden," a voice called from behind him.

Asvarr spun, blade raised. A figure stood among the trees, wrapped in a cloak of raven feathers. Its face remained hidden in shadow beneath a deep hood.

"Who are you?" Asvarr demanded, the merged mark heating beneath his tunic.

"A witness. A guide, perhaps." The figure's voice resonated with an ageless quality, impossible to assign to any gender. It gestured toward the pool. "You seek the third anchor. It waits below, but access comes at a price."

"What price?"

"Truth." The figure stepped forward, still keeping its face obscured. "Hvergelmir holds memory and the future entwined. Those who look too deeply risk madness."

Asvarr studied the stranger, trying to sense deception. Since the bindings, he'd developed an instinct for lies—they created discordant ripples in the connection-threads he could now perceive. This being spoke truth, or at least truth as it understood it.

"The anchors must be found," Asvarr said. "Whatever the cost."

"Such certainty." The cloaked figure tilted its head. "Two marks merged where once stood only one. Tell me, Warden—do you still serve the Tree alone?"

The question struck uncomfortably close to Asvarr's private doubts. Since absorbing Cinderheart's mark, since binding the second anchor, his purpose had grown more complex. He still sought the anchors, still worked to restore the Tree, yet the meaning behind these actions had shifted.

"I serve what's necessary," he answered carefully. "The Tree, the realms, the balance."

A sound emerged from beneath the hood—something between a laugh and a sigh. "Diplomatic. The Flame-Bearer grows cautious."

Asvarr relaxed his sword arm slightly. "You know my past."

"I know you're becoming." The figure gestured toward the pool again. "Hvergelmir holds the third anchor deep. To reach it, you must pass the Serpent's test."

"What serpent?"

The hooded figure stepped backward into the shadows between the trees. "The Midgard-guardian. The memory-keeper. Look to water, Warden."

Before Asvarr could question further, the stranger vanished, leaving only disturbed air where he had stood. He turned back to the black pool, unease crawling along his spine. The old tales spoke of many serpents—Jörmungandr, the World Serpent; Níðhöggr, who gnawed at Yggdrasil's roots. Which waited for him here?

He approached the water's edge cautiously, sword ready. The pool formed a perfect circle, perhaps thirty paces across, with a surface so still it resembled polished obsidian. No plants grew along its banks, no insects buzzed nearby. Life itself avoided this place.

The amulet grew painfully hot against his skin. Asvarr removed it, holding the golden disk over the black water. It pulsed with light in a steady rhythm, like a heartbeat. Each pulse sent ripples across the pool's surface, despite not touching the water.

Something moved below. A shadow darker than the black water, massive and sinuous, circling the depths. Asvarr tightened his grip on his sword, though instinct told him the blade would provide little protection against whatever dwelled beneath.

"I seek the anchor," he called out, his voice sounding flat and muffled, as if the air itself swallowed sound. "I am Warden of the broken Tree."

The water remained still for several heartbeats. Then, it erupted upward in a column that towered over Asvarr. He stumbled backward, raising his blade defensively. The water column twisted, reshaping itself—a massive, serpentine head formed from the black liquid, initially with closed eyes, its jaws large enough to swallow him whole.

The water-serpent hovered above the pool, liquid constantly flowing through its form, yet maintaining its shape. One eye opened—a real eye, golden-yellow with a vertical slit pupil, embedded in the fluid body.

"*Warden-fragment,*" the serpent spoke, its voice resonating directly in Asvarr's mind rather than through the air. "*You come broken, mixed, and uncertain.*"

Asvarr stood his ground, fighting the instinct to flee. "I come as I am. I seek the third anchor."

The serpent brought its massive head down, its golden eye examining Asvarr at close range. The pupil contracted as it studied him, radiating ancient intelligence.

"*You wear two marks merged as one. Fire and Tree, enemies joined by circumstance.*" The serpent circled above the pool, its liquid body flowing in impossible patterns. "*Show me the bindings you have made, so I may judge worthiness.*"

Asvarr hesitated, then held out the Horn of Binding in one hand and the golden amulet in the other. "The first anchor gave me this horn. The second, this amulet."

The serpent's eye fixed on the artifacts. "*Tokens of commitment. Proof of sacrifice. Yet incomplete.*" It circled closer. "*What fragments remain of the man who first took up this burden? How much has the mark and memories consumed?*"

The question struck deep. Since accepting the Grímmark, since binding the first anchor, Asvarr had felt himself changing—knowledge and memories from outside himself flooding his mind, altering his perspective. After the second binding, these changes had accelerated. He occasionally caught himself thinking with Thorvald's mind, or seeing through Cinderheart's ancient perspective.

"Enough remains," he answered firmly. "I know my purpose."

"*Do you?*" The serpent's eye narrowed. "*Then seek your reflection in Hvergelmir's depths. Truth awaits those brave enough to face it.*"

The water-serpent collapsed suddenly, splashing back into the pool. The surface stilled immediately, returning to its unnatural flatness. Asvarr approached cautiously, sheathing his sword—steel would prove useless against a being of water.

At the edge, he knelt and gazed into the black depths. At first, he saw nothing. Then an image formed—his childhood self, watching his father prepare for a raid. The memory belonged to him, yet he viewed it from the outside, a spectator to his own life.

The image shifted. His first battle, blood-drunk and laughing as his axe found flesh. Then, later memories—discovering his slaughtered clan, receiving the Grímmark, binding the first anchor. Each scene played with perfect detail, yet something felt wrong. His expressions throughout showed calculation where he recalled rage, ambition where grief had overwhelmed him.

"The pool twists truth," he said aloud. "These memories differ from mine."

"*Hvergelmir shows truth beneath perception. The self you hide from yourself.*" The serpent's voice echoed in his mind.

The visions continued, moving beyond memory into possibility. Asvarr saw himself completing the remaining bindings, growing more powerful with each, more distant from humanity. In the final scene, he stood before a fully restored Yggdrasil; the Tree towering above all reality. Then his future self faded, merging with the Tree until Asvarr vanished completely—leaving only a vessel for the Tree's consciousness.

He jerked back from the water's edge, heart pounding. "I refuse that fate. My essence will remain my own."

The water stirred again, the serpent's eye rising to the surface without emerging fully. "*One path among many.*" The eye blinked slowly. "*Would you see others?*"

Despite his fear, curiosity pulled at Asvarr. He leaned forward again, cautiously. "Show me."

This time, the visions revealed a different future. After the fifth binding, he stood against the Tree's full awakening, using the power he'd gained to contain the Tree's consciousness rather than release it. In this future, he existed between human and divine—a guardian between worlds, solitary yet sovereign.

A third vision followed—darker than the first two. He saw himself joining Cinderheart, turning against the Tree, siding with the Ashfather. This version of Asvarr destroyed the anchors instead of binding them, using their power to reshape reality according to the Ashfather's design. The worlds burned and froze by turns as natural law collapsed.

Asvarr pulled back again, shaken. "How can all these paths exist simultaneously?"

"*All true. All false.*" The serpent's eye regarded him dispassionately. "*Hvergelmir shows what feeds its waters—memory, fear, desire, possibility. The pool at the world's root touches all times, all paths. Your task: discern which deserves your steps.*"

Gathering his courage, Asvarr looked into the water once more. This time, he saw others—Brynja, her Jordmark glowing as she faced a wall of flame; the one-eyed wanderer who had misled the ulfhednar; a woman with white-blonde hair and a mark on her throat, unknown to him. Each fought their own battles across different realms.

"Are these the other Wardens?"

"*Paths intertwined with yours.*" The serpent's voice softened slightly. "*Some are allies, some are enemies, some are both. Your choices shape them as theirs shape you.*"

The visions shifted again, showing the anchors themselves—five points of power scattered across the realms. Asvarr saw the pattern they formed create purpose, like a complex runic formation. At the pattern's center, something vast and ancient slumbered, older than both Tree and Shadow.

"What exists at the center?" he whispered. "What sleeps between?"

The serpent's eye widened. "*You perceive more than expected, Warden-fragment. Your question becomes the test itself.*" The water churned violently. "*What waits at pattern-center? Answer determines your worthiness.*"

Asvarr stared into the depths, mind racing. The visions had shown him many possibilities, many truths. The Tree sought awakening. The Ashfather sought control. The bindings could bring salvation or catastrophe, depending on the perspective taken. At the center of it all waited...

Knowledge from Thorvald, Cinderheart, and his own experiences collided in his mind. The answer came with unexpected clarity.

"Choice," he said firmly. "What waits at the center is choice."

The serpent's eye blinked once, slowly. "*Unexpected answer. The Tree and Shadow would both disagree.*"

"Is it correct?"

"*Correctness depends on outcomes yet unrealized.*" The serpent's massive head emerged fully from the water again, looming over Asvarr. "*Yet your answer intrigues me. Perhaps worthiness exists within you.*"

The black water churned, swirling in a vortex that revealed stone steps leading downward into darkness. At the bottom, Asvarr glimpsed a golden glow—the third anchor awaiting him.

"*Descend if you dare, Warden-fragment. The anchor calls to you. Remember this—what you bind changes you as you change it. Each connection diminishes what you were.*"

Asvarr stood at the edge of the vortex, staring down at the revealed stairway. "Will anything of myself remain after the fifth binding?"

"*Self always changes, Warden. Moving like water, never static as stone.*" The serpent's eye watched him with something resembling compassion. "*Yet essence—the core beneath thought and memory—can survive if you fight to preserve it.*"

Asvarr touched the merged mark on his chest, feeling its steady pulse. The two opposing elements—Tree and Flame—had achieved balance within him. Perhaps this offered a pattern for the greater conflict.

"I'll descend," he decided. "First, tell me your name. I want to know who tests me."

The serpent's liquid body coiled above the pool. "*I am Mímisormr, memory-keeper, knowledge-guard. Born of Mimir's wisdom and Jörmungandr's blood.*" The great eye fixed on Asvarr. "*Upon your return—should you return—I will demand payment for the anchor's release.*"

"What payment?"

"Truth from yourself. Memory, most precious." The serpent sank back into the water. *"Prepare your offering, Warden-fragment. I will consume your past to grant your future."*

As Mímisormr vanished beneath the surface, Asvarr squarely faced the stone steps. They spiraled downward into darkness, ancient and worn smooth by countless years of flowing water. The golden light at the bottom pulsed in rhythm with his heartbeat, calling to the merged mark on his chest.

Descent would bring him closer to completing his task, closer to restoring the broken Tree. Yet, the serpent's visions stayed with him—possible futures where he changed beyond recognition, becoming merely a vessel for greater powers. The warning resonated: each binding diminishes what you were.

His hand dropped to the Horn of Binding at his belt, then to the golden amulet around his neck. Two anchors bound, three remaining. What parts of Asvarr would remain when the final binding concluded? Would anything of the warrior from Hralvik survive these transformations?

The answer waited below, alongside the third anchor. Asvarr placed his foot on the first step, the stone cold and slick beneath his boot. The merged mark burned against his chest, pulling him downward with increasing intensity. Whatever truth Mímisormr would extract as payment, whatever changes the third binding would inflict, his path extended forward, never back.

He descended into Hvergelmir's heart, leaving the world above. With each step, water sealed the stairway behind him, eliminating retreat. His journey forward would require confronting what waited in the depths—the anchor, the binding, and the price demanded by the serpent for passage.

The cold intensified with each step downward. Asvarr's breath clouded before him, growing thicker until it hung in the air like fog. The black water sealed the passage above, light diminishing until only the golden glow from below illuminated his path. The stone beneath his boots felt older than the world itself, worn smooth by currents that flowed before the first human walked under the sky.

At the bottom of the stairway, the steps opened onto a circular chamber carved from bedrock. The walls glistened with frozen moisture; the ceiling, lost in the darkness above. In the chamber's center, suspended in mid-air, floated the third anchor.

This anchor took the form of a seed, small enough to fit in Asvarr's palm. It pulsed with golden light, rotating slowly, trailing wisps of energy that swirled like underwater currents. Thin, golden filaments extended from its surface, reaching toward the walls and ceiling, creating a web of light throughout the chamber.

Asvarr approached cautiously, the merged mark on his chest resonating with the seed's pulse. Each beat sent a wave of warmth through him, fighting the chamber's bone-deep chill. As he drew closer, he noticed the seed had a seam running along its circumference, suggesting it could open.

"The heart holds knowledge," a voice whispered from the shadows. "Wisdom-price must be paid."

Asvarr spun, hand dropping to his sword. From an alcove he hadn't noticed, stepped a figure—a woman so ancient her skin resembled cracked parchment stretched over bone. Her eyes stayed shut, the lids sewn with golden thread. White hair hung past her waist, moving slightly though no breeze touched this deep chamber.

"Who are you?" Asvarr asked, voice tight.

"I am Mimir's daughter. Keeper of depths." She moved with surprising grace, circling the suspended seed. "You passed serpent-son's test. Earned right to bind. But binding demands worthy exchange."

Asvarr studied her warily. The old legends spoke of Mimir—the wise giant beheaded during the Aesir-Vanir war, whose preserved head continued to counsel Odin. This woman claimed a blood connection to him, bound to the third anchor as its guardian.

"What exchange does it require?" he asked, though Mímisormr had already hinted at the answer.

The blind woman stopped opposite him, the seed hanging between them. "Memory for memory. Tree-child hungers for experiences it cannot know. To bind it, feed what you treasure most."

"Why this anchor specifically? The others demanded different prices."

"Root draws power from below. Branch shares it above." Her withered fingers gestured to the seed. "Seeds store wisdom for future growth. Different purpose, different price."

The golden light pulsing from the seed intensified as Asvarr moved closer. The merged mark on his chest responded, growing almost painfully hot. He removed his outer garment, exposing the mark to the chamber's frigid air. The contrast of sensations—the burning mark, the freezing atmosphere—created a strange clarity in his mind.

"How do I begin?" he asked.

"Place hands upon seed-heart. Think of memories most precious. Let anchor decide if worthy." The blind woman stepped back, fading partially into shadow. "Choose carefully, Flame-Bearer. What defines you might surprise even yourself."

Asvarr approached the suspended seed, considering what memory to offer. His mind filled with possibilities—his father teaching him to wield an axe, his mother's songs on winter nights, his first raid, the day he earned his place among the warriors of his clan. Yet, none of these felt essential enough to serve as his most precious memory.

The blind woman spoke again, apparently sensing his uncertainty. "Seed seeks core-truth. Memory that shaped path. Without it, you become someone else."

Understanding dawned. The anchor wanted more than just any cherished memory—it wanted a keystone experience, something that had fundamentally defined his path in life. Something that, if removed, would transform who he is.

Asvarr reached out with both hands, palms hovering inches from the seed's golden surface. The merged mark flared, sending ribbons of light that connected to the seed's filaments. In that moment of connection, he knew which memory to offer—the day he chose to become a berserker.

He had been sixteen, standing over his first kill—a rival warrior who had mocked his father's honor. The man's blood had covered Asvarr's hands, and in that moment, he'd made a choice to embrace the rage, to cultivate it rather than suppress it. That decision had shaped everything that followed, defining the warrior he became.

"I offer the birth of my rage," he said aloud. "The moment I chose the berserker's path."

The seed's rotation accelerated, its light intensifying until it illuminated every corner of the chamber. The filaments connecting to Asvarr's mark pulsed with energy, drawing something from him—the memory itself, along with the emotion, the sensation, the taste, smell, and sound of that moment.

Images flashed through his mind—blood on snow, his heartbeat thundering in his ears, the decision crystallizing within him. Then the images began to blur, details fading. He struggled to hold on to them, but they slipped through his mental grasp like water through fingers.

The blind woman's voice reached him through the haze. "Seed accepts offering. Binds to bearer."

The floating seed split along its seam, opening like a golden flower to reveal a swirling vortex of light within. The light erupted outward, enveloping Asvarr, lifting him from the ground. Pain seared through his body as the anchor's essence flowed into him through the merged mark, integrating with the power of the previous two bindings.

Visions overwhelmed him—possibility flooding his consciousness. He saw seeds sprouting in barren soil, life blooming in desolate places, knowledge preserved through catastrophe to flourish again. The anchor embodied potential—the capacity to store wisdom and release it when needed, different from the root's stability or the branch's connection.

The pain peaked, drawing a ragged scream from his throat. Then, abruptly, it subsided. Asvarr found himself on his knees on the chamber floor. The seed had transformed, now a small, golden sapling growing from a crack in the stone, its few leaves glowing softly.

Where its light touched the chamber walls, runes appeared—ancient symbols predating even the Elder Futhark. Asvarr recognized them without knowing how, understanding they contained knowledge from the dawn of creation, preserved here in this underground sanctuary.

The blind woman approached, kneeling before him. "Binding complete. Warden of Three."

Asvarr touched the merged mark on his chest, finding it had changed again. The pattern had expanded, incorporating an additional element that resembled a seed within a spiral. With each binding, the mark grew more complex, just as his understanding deepened.

He tried to recall the memory he'd sacrificed—the moment he'd chosen the berserker's path—but found only a hollow space where it should have been. He remembered that something important had happened when he was sixteen, but the details, the emotions, the significance had vanished. The knowledge that he had once been a berserker remained, but the pivotal moment that led him to that path was gone.

"What exactly did I lose?" he asked, a strange emptiness spreading through him.

"Seed took rage-birth," the blind woman replied. "Foundation stone of a former self. You walk a new path now."

Asvarr's hands trembled as he pulled his tunic back on. Without the memory of choosing rage, who was he? The berserker identity had defined him for so long—his reputation, his fighting style, his approach to problems. Without understanding why he'd chosen that path, could he still follow it?

He rose unsteadily, surveying the transformed chamber. The binding had changed the space just as it had changed him—what was once dark and frozen now glowed with golden light, the walls alive with ancient knowledge.

Something caught his eye near the sapling—a small, golden object resting where the seed had split open. He picked it up, finding a disk similar to the amulet from the second binding but marked with different runes. As his fingers closed around it, knowledge flowed into him—this was his token from the third anchor, a key to wisdom preserved through the ages.

"The remembrance-key," the blind woman explained. "Opens doors to forgotten knowledge. Third token of five."

Asvarr slipped the disk into his pouch alongside the amulet. "How do I leave this place?"

The blind woman pointed to a passage that hadn't been visible before. "Path leads upward. Returns to serpent-son. Final price awaits."

"What final price?"

"Truth for truth. Memory for memory." She touched his forehead with one withered finger. "Mímisormr will take. Then path to the fourth anchor opens."

Asvarr remembered the serpent's words about consuming his past. After sacrificing his rage-birth memory to the seed, what more could be demanded of him? But he had come too far to turn back. Three anchors bound, two remaining. The path forward offered the only option.

"Thank you for your guidance," he said to the blind woman, surprising himself with the courtesy. Without his rage-birth memory, his responses felt different—measured, contemplative.

"When Tree blooms are complete, remember choice," she replied cryptically. "Pattern-center holds what neither Tree nor Shadow expects."

With those enigmatic words, she backed away into the shadows of the chamber and vanished. Asvarr stood alone with the golden sapling, contemplating her warning. It echoed what he had seen in Hvergelmir's visions—something ancient waiting at the center of the anchor pattern, something beyond both Tree and Shadow.

***

He turned toward the newly revealed passage, a sloping tunnel leading upward. As he began the ascent, he felt the hollow space within him where his rage-birth memory had been. The emptiness created room for something else—a clarity of thought, a detachment from the fury that had driven him for so long.

Without conscious decision, his hand went to the flask at his belt—the smaller one filled with mead that he carried for cold nights. He had always drunk deeply before battle, using the liquor to fuel his berserker rage. Now, he uncorked the flask and emptied it onto the stone floor, watching the amber liquid disappear into the cracks.

The gesture felt right, though he couldn't fully explain why. Without the memory of choosing rage, the tools to maintain it seemed pointless. He was becoming someone else with each binding, just as predicted.

The tunnel curved upward, growing lighter as he climbed. He could sense Mímisormr waiting above—the serpent's presence a vast, patient consciousness extending through the water of Hvergelmir. The "truth for truth" exchange still awaited him, one final price before he could continue his quest.

As he neared the tunnel's end, Asvarr paused, gathering his strength. The binding had drained him physically, but losing his rage-birth memory had created a different kind of exhaustion—an identity fatigue that left him uncertain of his own reactions. Who was he becoming? And would anything of the original Asvarr remain by the final binding?

The tunnel opened into a small grotto where a pool of black water gleamed. The surface rippled, and Mímisormr's massive eye rose to regard him.

"*Warden-of-Three returns.*" The serpent's voice resonated directly in Asvarr's mind. "*Changed again. Less familiar to yourself.*"

Asvarr approached the pool's edge. "I've completed the binding. The seed accepted my offering."

"*Seed-heart takes rage-birth. Good choice. Tree has too much rage already.*" The eye blinked slowly. "*Now my price must be paid.*"

"What truth do you seek from me?" Asvarr asked, bracing himself for another sacrifice.

"*I give. You receive.*" The water rippled as more of the serpent's form emerged—the eye and part of its liquid head. "*Memory for memory. Wisdom-balance.*"

Before Asvarr could respond, the serpent lunged forward, pressing its watery forehead against his. Cold, unlike anything he'd experienced, flooded through him, followed by a cascade of images—memories foreign to him.

He saw Yggdrasil from its beginning—a sapling growing from the void between fire and ice. He watched it spread its branches through emerging realms, its roots anchoring reality itself. He witnessed the birth of gods, the creation of lesser beings, and the establishment of order from chaos.

Then came the first breaking—an ancient fracture long before the recent Shattering. The Tree had broken before, many times, each cycle following a pattern of growth, fracture, and renewal. Each time, Wardens arose to bind the anchors. Each time, something waited at the center of the pattern.

The flood of memories continued, showing him fragments of previous Wardens—men and women who had walked this path before him, sacrificing pieces of themselves to bind the Tree. Some had surrendered completely, becoming vessels for the Tree's will. Others had kept enough of themselves to make different choices when the final binding came.

"*Truth balances sacrifice,*" Mímisormr's voice explained as the memories slowed. "*Seed took; I give. Balance maintained.*"

The serpent withdrew, leaving Asvarr gasping on his knees at the pool's edge. His mind reeled with new knowledge, contextualizing his quest within a cycle far older and more complex than he had imagined. The Tree, the Ashfather, the Shattering—all had happened before in various forms. The pattern repeated with variations, each cycle providing another chance for a different outcome.

"Why show me this?" Asvarr managed, his voice hoarse.

"*Truth-seed planted replaces rage-seed removed. New growth possible.*" The great eye studied him with something resembling compassion. "*Final choice approaches, Warden-of-Three. When five anchors are bound, the pattern-center awakens. What emerges depends on Warden's essence—what remains after all bindings.*"

Asvarr struggled to process the implications. "You mean I can influence what happens when the pattern completes? That my choices matter despite the Tree's will?"

"All cycles contain branch-points. Possibilities. This cycle—unusual. Warden bears two marks merged as one. Your mixed nature creates opportunities." The serpent's liquid body rippled with what might have been excitement. *"New outcome possible."*

The revelation struck Asvarr like a physical blow. The conflicting forces within him—the Grímmark and the flame-rune—might serve as an advantage. A chance to break the cycle, to find the third path Cinderheart had mentioned.

"The fourth anchor," he said, finding his focus again. "Where do I find it?"

"Far realm. Ice-death place. Niflheim's heart." The serpent's form sank back into the black water. *"Passage opens at the pool's far side. Step through water-veil. Path awaits."*

As Mímisormr disappeared beneath the surface, the black water at the far side of the pool shimmered, becoming translucent. Through it, Asvarr could see a landscape of ice and mist—Niflheim, realm of primordial cold, where the fourth anchor awaited.

He stood, gathering his strength. The binding had changed him; the serpent's memories had transformed his understanding, but his purpose remained. Find the anchors. Complete the bindings. Reach the pattern-center before it was too late.

Without his rage-birth memory, Asvarr approached problems differently. Where once he might have charged forward without hesitation, he now found himself planning, considering consequences. The berserker was fading, replaced by something more measured, more strategic.

He checked his weapons and supplies, ensuring he was prepared for Niflheim's killing cold. The three tokens—horn, amulet, and remembrance-key—hung at his belt or around his neck, physical reminders of the path he'd already traveled.

At the edge of the shimmering water-veil, Asvarr paused for one final look at Hvergelmir's grotto. Three anchors bound, his identity fragmenting and reforming with each. Who would he be after the fourth? After the fifth? Would anything remain of the warrior from Hralvik?

The answer waited ahead, beyond this place. Asvarr stepped through the water-veil, frost immediately crystallizing on his beard as Niflheim's bitter cold embraced him. The third binding was complete. The fourth path opened before him—a journey to the heart of ice and death.

CHAPTER 9

THE DEAD REMEMBER SONG

Frozen mud cracked beneath Asvarr's boots as he crossed the emptied markets of Ormvik. Wind-scoured stalls lined the square, their awnings flapping like wounded birds in the bitter gale. He pulled his cloak tighter, fingers brushing against the remembrance-key hanging from his belt. The engraved disk hummed against his touch, sending faint pulses of warmth up his arm.

Three days since the binding at Hvergelmir, and still the visions lingered. The nameless, faceless Wardens who had come before—their sacrifices, their transformations, their endings. He no longer dreamed of battles or glory. Those berserker urges had been cut away with his memories at the pool. Now his sleep brought only roots and branches, seeds, and saplings.

"You there! Outlander!"

Asvarr turned toward the voice. A stooped old man with a white beard tucked into his belt waved a gnarled walking stick at him from the doorway of a longhouse. Smoke spiraled from its roof-hole, carrying the scent of roasting meat.

"You're the one they speak of," the old man said. "The one who bears the mark."

Asvarr's hand instinctively moved to his chest, where the merged runes pulsed beneath his tunic.

"I've fulfilled my oath to Hildr Iron-Heart," Asvarr said. "I brought word of her death to her kin. My business in Ormvik is done."

"No. It isn't." The old man thumped his staff against the frozen ground. "You haven't heard the song."

"I have no time for songs." The amulet at his neck pulled westward, toward the mountains where the fourth anchor waited in the frozen wastes of Niflheim. Even now, he could feel its call—a crystalline whisper promising knowledge and power. And another piece of himself stripped away.

"This one you'll make time for." The old man's eyes, filmy with age, fixed on a point beyond Asvarr's shoulder. "This one speaks your name."

Something in the man's voice—a resonance that vibrated in Asvarr's chest where the runes marked him—made him pause.

"Who are you?"

"Egil Rune-Singer." The old man gestured toward the longhouse door. "Come. Drink. Listen. The storm forces travelers to seek shelter tonight, regardless."

Asvarr glanced skyward. Dark clouds massed on the northern horizon, heavy with snow that would make travel impossible. The old man wasn't wrong.

"One night," Asvarr conceded, following Egil into the longhouse.

Warmth enveloped him as he ducked through the low doorway. The hall stretched longer than he expected, its central hearth blazing with fresh-split pine logs. Twenty or more people huddled on benches along the walls, their faces turned toward a lone figure seated at the far end.

A skald, dressed in a patchwork cloak of raven feathers, ran fingers across a wooden harp. The instrument's frame bore intricate carvings—twisting branches that moved in the firelight like living things. The crowd parted as Egil led Asvarr forward.

"Sit," the old man commanded, pointing to a place of honor near the hearth. "Drink."

A horn of mead appeared in Asvarr's hand, passed from someone in the shadows. The liquid inside gleamed gold—the same hue as Yggdrasil's sap. He hesitated, then drank. The taste struck like lightning: bitter, sweet, and foreign all at once. Memories that weren't his flooded his mind: ice fields stretching endlessly beneath three moons, mountains growing from seedlings, oceans boiling away to reveal cities of bone.

He lowered the horn, gasping. "What is this?"

"Memory-mead," Egil said, settling beside him. "From honey gathered where the Root first fell. It helps you hear the deeper song."

The skald raised his head. His face remained in shadow beneath his hood, but Asvarr felt the weight of his gaze.

"Shall I sing of Asvarr Skyrend's Flame, first Warden of the breaking?" The skald's voice carried the cadence of distant thunder.

Murmurs rippled through the gathered crowd. How did this man know his title? Asvarr leaned forward, hand moving to his sword hilt.

"Who told you that name?"

Egil laid a restraining hand on Asvarr's arm. "The dead remember, Warden. The dead remember everything."

The skald struck a single, resonant chord. The flames in the hearth leapt higher, throwing shadows that moved with unnatural purpose across the walls. When he began to sing, his voice filled the hall with harmonies impossible for a single throat:

"Roots torn five-fold from the world-spine, Anchors scattered across the nine realms. The first bound in blood and rage, The second in earth's remembering, The third in wisdom's sacrifice, The fourth in winter's cruel embrace, The fifth in death's final surrender."

Asvarr sat rigid. Each line struck like a hammer on hot metal. This was the binding sequence—something no living soul should know except Brenna Flame-Carver and the Wardens themselves. Yet here sat a skald in a remote village, singing of what had not yet happened.

"How do you know these things?" Asvarr demanded.

The skald continued as if he hadn't spoken:

"Fire-mark and Tree-mark merged as one, Wolf's blood spilled at the stone circle, Memory surrendered at wisdom's pool, The severed cord at winter's heart, Final binding where no light shines."

Asvarr's throat constricted. The pattern of his quest lay exposed in verse—including events yet to come. The merged marks on his chest burned hotter with each line sung.

"Some songs," Egil whispered, "are written before they're lived."

The skald set his harp aside and stood. Firelight caught his face as he pushed back his hood—revealing skin as pale as new snow, with eyes like pooled silver that reflected the flames.

"I died nine days before the Shattering," the skald said. "I walked nine days beyond the veil, hanging from the branches of what was. I returned to sing what will be."

"Impossible," Asvarr breathed.

"You bear the Grímmark and yet doubt impossibility?" The skald approached, movements fluid as water. "Let me see what you've become, Warden."

Before Asvarr could react, the skald laid a cold hand on his chest, directly over the merged marks. Pain lanced through Asvarr's body, ice and fire racing through his veins. Visions flashed behind his eyes—a hall of roots where masked women cut threads of light, a one-eyed figure burning with golden flame, a crown made of fractured branches, and a woman with amber eyes holding a blade that wept sap.

"You've bound three," the skald murmured. "The sap-song grows stronger in you. Yet you still resist its pull."

Asvarr knocked the hand away, drawing his bronze sword in the same motion. The blade hummed with power, golden runes flaring along its length.

"Who are you?" Asvarr growled, pressing the edge against the skald's throat.

The crowd gasped, drawing back. Only Egil remained unmoved, watching with those milky eyes.

"I am Hrafn," the skald answered. "Once called Wind-Walker, now called Death-Singer. I stood before the Tree when it first stirred with sickness. I sang to heal its rot." He smiled, revealing teeth filed to points. "I failed."

Asvarr's sword remained steady, though questions tumbled through his mind. "You sing of things no living man should know."

"Living." Hrafn laughed, a sound like cracking ice. "What is living now, when the worlds unmake themselves? Look at me, Warden. Look with the Tree's eyes that grow within you."

Reluctantly, Asvarr shifted his perception—calling on the anchor-sight that had awakened after the third binding. The world around him changed. The longhouse walls became transparent, showing the swirling energies of the village beyond. The gathered people glowed with life-fire, threads of gold connecting them to the land and to each other.

But Hrafn... Hrafn had no connections. No life-fire burned within him. Where his heart should be, a swirling void pulsed in rhythm with the song still echoing in the hall.

"You're empty," Asvarr whispered.

"I am a vessel," Hrafn corrected. "The Tree needed voices in the world. It chose those already passed beyond to carry its warnings."

Asvarr lowered his sword, horror and fascination warring within him. "You're dead."

"For nine turnings of the seasons." Hrafn returned to his seat, lifting the harp once more. "And in death, I learned the song the Tree sings to itself—the song of what was and what shall be."

"Why show yourself to me?"

"Because you stand at a crossroads, Skyrend's Flame." Hrafn's fingers brushed the harp strings, drawing forth notes that vibrated through Asvarr's bones. "The fourth binding changes all. Ice remembers differently than root or branch, or seed. When you enter Niflheim, you'll face a choice that can break the pattern."

The remembrance-key at Asvarr's belt suddenly grew hot, its runes glowing through the leather pouch that contained it. He pulled it out, finding its surface covered with frost despite the heat of the hall.

"The dead remember," Egil repeated, nodding at the key. "And the dead can open doors long sealed."

Hrafn sang again, softer now:

"Five Wardens marked by fate's design, Five anchors waiting to be bound. But markings lie, and anchors shift, The pattern set is not the last. Listen close to wisdom's warning: What sleeps within the pattern's heart Is neither Tree nor Shadow born, But something from before the worlds."

The flames in the hearth dimmed with the final note, plunging the hall into near darkness. When they rekindled moments later, the skald's seat stood empty. Only the harp remained, its carved branches now still.

Asvarr rounded on Egil. "What trickery is this?"

The old man shrugged. "No trickery. Only truth sung before its time."

"He spoke of something in the pattern's heart." Asvarr gripped the front of Egil's tunic. "What waits there? What am I awakening with each binding?"

The gathered villagers had fallen silent, watching their exchange with wide eyes. Egil merely smiled, revealing gaps where teeth had long ago fallen out.

"The song has already told you more than I could." He gently removed Asvarr's hand. "But I can tell you one thing more. The next binding waits in Niflheim's heart, where the ice remembers every death since the world's beginning. And someone already seeks it—someone who bears a mark like yours but serves another master."

"Another Warden? Who?"

"Not a Warden. A Reaver." Egil's expression darkened. "One who consumes anchors rather than binds them. The Ashfather's champion."

A cold that had nothing to do with the winter night settled in Asvarr's gut. He had felt something watching him since the third binding—a presence just beyond the edge of perception. Now it had a name. Reaver.

"How do you know these things?" Asvarr demanded.

"I was a runecaster before age took my sight." Egil tapped his milky eyes. "Now I see only what the dead show me."

A sudden commotion arose near the longhouse door. People scattered as a massive raven burst through the entrance, its wingspan wider than a man is tall. It circled the hall once before landing on the harp Hrafn had left behind. In its beak, it carried a small leather pouch.

The bird fixed its gaze on Asvarr, eyes gleaming with intelligence far beyond that of a common raven. It dropped the pouch at his feet, then spread its wings and spoke in a voice that matched the skald's:

"When ice consumes you, break the thread. When memory fails, follow the blood."

With a cry that shook dust from the rafters, the raven launched itself upward, vanishing through the smoke-hole in a flurry of black feathers.

Asvarr bent and picked up the pouch. Inside lay a single object—a tooth, yellowed with age, carved with a rune he didn't recognize. The moment his fingers touched it, frost spread across his palm, and a vision flashed through his mind: a fortress of ice at the edge of a frozen lake, its towers reaching toward stars that hung too close to the world.

"Helgrindr," he whispered, the name coming to him unbidden. "The Death-Gate."

Egil nodded. "The entrance to Niflheim, where the fourth anchor awaits. The tooth will guide you—it belonged to Garm, the hound who guards the frozen realm."

Asvarr closed his hand around the tooth. The cold bit into his flesh, but he welcomed the pain. It felt clean compared to the confusion swirling in his mind.

"Why help me?" he asked. "If binding the anchors awakens something dangerous—"

"Who said I was helping you?" Egil's blind eyes somehow found Asvarr's. "Perhaps I serve the pattern, too. Perhaps we all do."

A sudden gust of wind howled through the hall, extinguishing half the torches along the walls. Outside, the storm had arrived, shrieking like a woman in pain.

Asvarr tucked the tooth into his belt pouch alongside the remembrance-key. Whatever waited in Niflheim—Reaver, anchor, or something worse—he would face it. The pattern demanded completion.

"Rest tonight," Egil said, gesturing toward an empty bench along the wall. "Tomorrow, the path to Helgrindr opens. The dead will show you the way."

As the villagers dispersed to their sleeping places, Asvarr remained by the hearth, watching the flames dance. Within their depths, he saw branches growing, intertwining, and forming the face of the skald. The lips moved, singing silently.

And for the first time since the Shattering, Asvarr wondered if binding the anchors had ever been a choice at all, or if he had always been destined to follow this path—like a song written before it was sung.

***

Dawn broke, cold and clear, over Ormvik. The storm had passed, leaving behind a world transformed by ice. Every branch, every eave, glittered with frozen daggers, catching the sun's first light and shattering it into rainbow fragments.

Asvarr stepped outside the longhouse, frost crunching beneath his boots. The carved tooth in his pouch throbbed with a rhythmic pulse against his thigh. Three bindings completed, two remaining. The path to the fourth anchor pulled at him like an iron hook lodged beneath his ribs.

"Awake already, Warden?" Egil shuffled out of the shadows, his blind eyes somehow finding Asvarr unerringly. "The dead never sleep. Why should those marked by the Tree?"

Asvarr touched the merged marks on his chest. Since the skald's song, they burned with renewed vigor, the kenaz rune flaring against the Grímmark in painful counterpoint.

"The song," Asvarr said, his voice rough with exhaustion. "It's still in my head. Circling like a carrion bird."

"Of course it is." Egil tapped his temple with a gnarled finger. "Death-songs root deep. They're meant to be remembered when all else fails."

Last night's visions had chased Asvarr through what little sleep he'd managed—faces of dead Wardens, anchors bleeding golden sap, the Ashfather's burning gaze, and always, at the edge of perception, the whispered warning: *When ice consumes you, break the thread. When memory fails, follow the blood.*

"I need to leave. Now." Asvarr adjusted his sword belt. "If there's a Reaver hunting the anchor—"

"There is." Egil held out a small bundle wrapped in oiled cloth. "Provisions. You'll find no food in Niflheim save memories, and those will hollow you from within if you feast too long."

Asvarr took the bundle. "Why help me? You said yourself you might serve the pattern."

"I serve what must be." Egil's face creased into a mirthless smile. "The skald showed himself to you. That hasn't happened since the last breaking."

A chill that had nothing to do with the morning cold slithered down Asvarr's spine. "The last breaking? You speak as though you've seen this before."

"I was young when the Tree shuddered last. Not a full breaking, just a tremor. The threads held then." Egil raised his face to the sky. "I was there when they called the Wardens and marked them. Five went forth. Three returned. None remained human."

Before Asvarr could question him further, a horn blast split the morning silence—deep, resonant, carrying across the frozen village. People emerged from their homes, faces tight with fear.

"Raiders?" Asvarr's hand moved to his sword.

Egil shook his head. "Worse. The Reaver comes."

The village square filled with armed men and women. Weapons gleamed in the thin morning light—spears, axes, shields painted with protective runes. The villagers formed a defensive ring at the western edge, facing the forest path.

Asvarr pushed through the crowd. From the forest emerged a procession unlike any he'd seen before. Six warriors rode ahead, their armor crafted from blackened bone and iron. Behind them walked a lone figure, tall and imposing, wrapped in a cloak that shimmered like oil on water. The figure's face remained hidden behind a mask carved from what looked like petrified wood, revealing only eyes that reflected the morning light like polished metal.

"The Ashfather's herald," Egil whispered, having somehow kept pace with Asvarr. "The Reaver has many forms. This one speaks with the voice of roots and ruined crowns."

The mounted warriors halted at the village boundary. The masked figure continued forward alone, stopping ten paces from the defensive line. When it spoke, its voice resonated from within the wooden mask like wind through a hollow tree.

"I seek Asvarr of the Grímmark. Skyrend's Flame." The voice held neither gender nor age. "Stand forth, Warden."

Asvarr felt the marks on his chest flare in response, as if recognizing a counterpart—or an enemy. He pushed past the defensive line, ignoring the protests of the villagers.

"I am Asvarr."

The masked figure tilted its head, studying him with those metallic eyes. "Three anchors bound. The Tree grows within you." It raised a gloved hand, pointing at Asvarr's chest. "Yet fire burns alongside. The third path opens."

Asvarr's hand moved instinctively to his sword. "How do you know these things?"

"I am Runveig, Voice of the Ashfather." The figure made a strange gesture with both hands, fingers weaving patterns in the air. "I have come to offer you alliance, not battle."

A murmur ran through the gathered villagers. Egil gripped Asvarr's arm with surprising strength.

"Careful, Warden," he hissed. "The Reaver speaks with honey on its tongue and poison in its heart."

Runveig seemed to glide closer, the strange cloak rippling, though no wind disturbed it. "The old man fears what he cannot understand. The Ashfather does not seek to destroy the anchors. He seeks to redirect their power—to break the endless cycle."

"Lies," Egil spat. "The Ashfather would unmake the Tree and replace it with his own twisted creation."

"And what of the Tree's creation?" Runveig countered. "What slumbers at the pattern's heart? Did your dead skald sing of that, Asvarr of the Grímmark?"

The tooth in Asvarr's pouch burned suddenly hot against his leg. Patterns of frost spread across the ground beneath Runveig's feet, forming runes Asvarr recognized from his visions—symbols of binding and breaking, of paths between worlds.

"You seek the frost anchor," Asvarr said, flexing his hand near the sword hilt. "Why show yourself to me? Why not simply take it?"

Runveig laughed, a sound like cracking ice. "The frost anchor responds only to those bearing the Mark. Like recognizes like." The masked figure extended a hand. "Join us. The Ashfather offers a different path—freedom from the Tree's consumption."

For a heartbeat, Asvarr hesitated. Hrafn's song echoed in his mind—warnings of the Tree consuming his identity with each binding. The kenaz rune on his chest flared hotter, resonating with Runveig's words.

"The Ashfather sent creatures to hunt me," Asvarr said, fingers tightening around his sword hilt. "Your master tried to kill me before I bound the first anchor."

"Tests of worthiness," Runveig replied smoothly. "Those who cannot survive have no place in the world to come."

In the silence that followed, Hrafn's death-song swelled unbidden in Asvarr's mind. No longer just words, but visions—sharp, clear, and painful. He saw himself at the frost anchor, but now the image split into two possible paths: In one, he stood victorious, the anchor bound, his humanity further diminished. In the other, he stood beside Runveig before the anchor, watching as the Reaver drew forth its power without binding it, reshaping it into something new.

The song burned through him like liquid fire. He staggered, clutching his head as more visions flooded his consciousness:

The Ashfather, seated upon a throne of broken branches, nine realms writhing in agony beneath him.

Five Wardens transformed into hollow vessels, their marks glowing as they fed the pattern's heart.

The slumbering entity at the center of it all—neither Tree nor Shadow born—stirring awake, vast and hungry.

The third path, flickering like a flame between Tree and Shadow, offering neither victory nor defeat, but transformation.

"Asvarr!" Egil's voice seemed distant. "The song takes him!"

Runveig moved with impossible speed, catching Asvarr as he fell to his knees. The Reaver's touch sent ice-cold clarity through him, momentarily silencing the song's roar.

"You see now," Runveig whispered, metallic eyes gleaming. "The Tree's song poisons your mind, filling it with memories not your own. With each binding, you become less yourself and more its puppet."

Asvarr wrenched himself away, drawing his bronze sword in a fluid motion. The blade hummed, golden runes flaring along its length as it recognized a threat.

"I've heard two songs," he growled, backing away from Runveig. "The Tree's and the Ashfather's. Both seek to use me. I'll find my own path."

Runveig's posture shifted, a subtle tension replacing the earlier, fluid grace. "The frost anchor calls to both of us, Warden. We will meet again at Helgrindr."

The Reaver turned to leave, cloak swirling. Asvarr recognized the opportunity—with Runveig's back turned, he could strike. End the threat before it grew. The old Asvarr, the berserker, would have attacked without hesitation.

But that memory was gone, sacrificed at Hvergelmir. This Asvarr watched the Reaver depart, calculating the greater threat: Runveig, or what waited at the pattern's heart.

"You let it go," Egil said with a note of surprise.

"The Reaver isn't wrong about everything." Asvarr sheathed his sword. "With each binding, I lose more of myself. The visions show it clearly."

"And yet you continue."

"Would you have me surrender the anchors to the Ashfather?"

Egil's blind eyes seemed to see straight through him. "I would have you question why every Warden before you has failed."

The gathered villagers dispersed slowly, wary eyes tracking the departing Reaver and its bone-armored escort. Many cast suspicious glances at Asvarr, whispering behind raised hands. Word of the confrontation would spread, marking Ormvik as a place caught between powers.

Asvarr touched the horn at his belt, the token from the first binding. "Did any Warden ever bind all five anchors?"

"Once," Egil said. "In the first age of the world. He became the first Ashfather."

The ground seemed to tilt beneath Asvarr's feet. "What? The Ashfather was a Warden?"

"The first to walk the path. The first to see the pattern for what it truly was." Egil's voice dropped to a whisper. "The first to reject both Tree and Shadow and seek the third path. He failed."

Hrafn's song surged again in Asvarr's mind, bringing fresh visions—a man with a mark like his own standing before five bound anchors, transforming as something vast and ancient reached through him into the world. The pain drove Asvarr to his knees.

"Warden!" Egil knelt beside him, pressing something against Asvarr's lips. "Drink. It will quiet the song."

Cold liquid flowed down Asvarr's throat—sharp, bitter, with undertones of pine and iron. Almost immediately, the song's grip lessened. The visions receded like waves pulling back from shore, leaving only scattered images: the ice fortress at Helgrindr, Runveig standing before the frost anchor, a thread of fate stretched to breaking.

"What was that?" Asvarr gasped, wiping his mouth.

"Memory-mead mixed with ironroot. Dampens the connection between you and the anchors you've bound." Egil corked the small flask and pressed it into Asvarr's hand. "Take it. You'll need it when the song grows too strong."

Asvarr tucked the flask into his belt pouch alongside the tooth. "The song—it's the Tree speaking through me, isn't it? Through the marks."

"The Tree, the anchors, the dead Wardens who carried the marks before you—all speaking at once." Egil helped him to his feet. "That's why the Reaver wants you. A Warden who has bound three anchors carries power and knowledge beyond reckoning."

The eastern sky had brightened fully now, casting long shadows across Ormvik's frost-coated buildings. Asvarr felt the pull of the fourth anchor like a physical tether, tugging him northward toward Helgrindr. The visions had shown him the path clearly—a journey through shadow-woods and across a lake of memories to the ice fortress where the frost anchor awaited.

"I need to leave. Now." Asvarr gathered his meager possessions. "The Reaver travels to Helgrindr. If Runveig reaches the anchor first..."

"It can't bind the anchor without the mark," Egil reminded him. "But it can prevent you from completing your task."

"More than that." Asvarr thought of the visions, of Runveig standing before the anchor with hands outstretched. "I think it means to corrupt the anchor, twist it to the Ashfather's purpose without binding it."

Egil nodded grimly. "Then you must reach Helgrindr first. The path opens at the northern stone circle beyond the ridge. The tooth will guide you from there."

"And you?" Asvarr studied the old man's weathered face. "What will you do when I'm gone?"

"Continue serving what must be." Egil smiled, his blind eyes crinkling at the corners. "Perhaps I'll be here when you return. Perhaps I'll be singing with Hrafn in the halls beyond."

Asvarr clasped the old man's forearm in the traditional warrior's grip. "Thank you, Egil Rune-Singer."

"Remember what Hrafn sang: When ice consumes you, break the thread. When memory fails, follow the blood." Egil squeezed Asvarr's arm once, then released him. "Go with speed, Warden. The song follows, whether you wish it or not."

As Asvarr strode toward the northern ridge, the morning sun at his back, he felt the weight of what had been revealed. The Ashfather—once a Warden, like himself. The pattern—older and more dangerous than he'd imagined. The third path—flickering like an uncertain flame between opposing forces.

The tooth pulsed against his leg, guiding him toward Helgrindr where the frost anchor waited. Behind him, he heard the faint strains of Hrafn's song, carried on the cold morning air:

"Five roots torn free from the world-spine, Anchors scattered across the nine rea lms.The fourth in winter's cruel embrace, Guarded by ice that never thaws, Awaits the choice that breaks the chain."

The song burned in his ears, in his blood, in the marks upon his chest. Whether gift or curse, memory or prophecy, he could no longer silence it. The dead remembered, and through their song, so did he—carrying memories of worlds and wars he had never seen, except through visions that weren't his own.

CHAPTER 10

THE HUNT OF BROKEN FATE

Two days into the frozen wastes, and Asvarr could no longer feel his toes. The wind knifed between the layers of his fur-lined cloak, each gust carrying shards of ice that stung his exposed skin like tiny blades. He trudged forward, boots breaking through the crusted snow, guided by the insistent pulse of Garm's tooth against his thigh.

Helgrindr lay another day's journey north, according to the visions. The fourth anchor awaited him there—the frost anchor—suspended in ice older than the world itself. And somewhere ahead, Runveig traveled the same path, seeking to corrupt what Asvarr had come to bind.

He paused atop a ridge, scanning the bleak landscape stretching toward the horizon. Jagged spires of black rock jutted from the endless white like the bones of some colossal, buried beast. The sky hung leaden and low, pressing down on the world. No birds flew here. No animals moved across the snow. Even the wind seemed to carry no scent but that of ancient cold.

Asvarr pulled the flask of memory-mead from his belt and took a careful sip. The bitter liquid burned down his throat, momentarily silencing the song that had plagued him since Ormvik. Hrafn's melodies still echoed in his mind, but distantly now, like thunder beyond the mountains.

The merged marks on his chest throbbed. Three anchors bound. Three pieces of himself sacrificed. The bronze sword at his hip hummed softly, responding to some unseen energy in the air. Asvarr touched its hilt, taking comfort in its familiar weight.

Movement caught his eye—a flicker of shadow against the snow, gone almost before he registered it. He drew his sword in a single, fluid motion, the runes along its length flaring gold. The blade cast no shadow of its own; he realized suddenly. It never had.

"Show yourself," he called, voice swallowed by the vastness.

Nothing answered but the howl of the wind.

Asvarr lowered his blade slightly, scanning the terrain with the anchor-sight that had awakened at Hvergelmir. The world shifted in his perception, snow and rock becoming translucent, energy currents flowing beneath the surface like frozen rivers of light.

There—a disturbance in the patterns. A void moving against the currents, heading north.

He sheathed his sword and pressed forward, following the anomaly. The cold bit deeper with each step, seeping into his bones. His breath crystallized before his face, forming intricate patterns that reminded him of the frost-runes in Thorvald's memories.

The sun began its swift descent toward the horizon, casting long, blue shadows across the snow. Night in these wastes meant certain death. He needed shelter.

Ahead, a dark opening gaped in the base of a towering rock spire. A cave, or perhaps the entrance to a tunnel system running beneath the frozen land. Asvarr approached cautiously, one hand on his sword hilt. The void-shape he'd glimpsed earlier had vanished in this direction.

The entrance narrowed to a tight passage that forced him to turn sideways to squeeze through. Beyond, the space opened into a chamber tall enough that he couldn't see its ceiling in the gloom. Ice coated the walls, forming columns and curtains that caught what little light filtered from outside, transforming it into ghostly blue illumination.

"Beautiful, isn't it?"

The voice came from the shadows. Female, with an edge like crystal striking stone. Asvarr whirled, sword half-drawn, then froze.

A woman stood on a ledge above him. She wore armor of silver scales that caught the blue light, her dark hair pulled back in intricate braids threaded with small metal beads. Wings—actual wings—arched from her back, not feathered like a bird's but composed of shifting patterns of light and shadow. Her face remained in darkness, but her eyes gleamed with an unnatural brightness.

"Who are you?" Asvarr kept his hand on his sword.

"I am Sigrdrífa," she said, voice echoing strangely in the chamber. "Some call me Valkyrie, though that name has lost its meaning since the Shattering."

"Valkyrie?" Asvarr's grip tightened on his weapon. "You collect the dead for Valhalla."

She laughed, a sound like ice breaking over deep water. "Once. Before the halls emptied. Before the gods abandoned their thrones." She moved along the ledge, her wings folding against her back. "Now I serve a different purpose."

"What purpose?"

"The same as you, Warden. I preserve what remains." She gestured to the surrounding chamber. "This place remembers what was before the breaking. It remembers the true order of things."

Asvarr's marks burned beneath his tunic. Something about this woman—this Valkyrie—set them afire. He pulled the cloak tighter, concealing the glow that would now be visible through the fabric.

"You know what I am," he said.

"Skyrend's Flame. Third binding complete. Fourth binding approaching." She tilted her head, studying him. "The mark has grown within you, taking root where your memories once lived. Soon it will flower, and little of Asvarr will remain."

"How do you know these things?"

"I have watched many Wardens walk this path. None completed all five bindings with their soul intact." She descended from the ledge, moving with unnatural grace, her feet barely seeming to touch the ground. "The Ashfather came closest. He bound the fifth anchor with enough of himself remaining to break free of the pattern—though what emerged was neither Warden nor man."

Asvarr thought of Runveig, of the masked figure's words in Ormvik. "You speak as if you've witnessed cycles of breaking before."

"Nine times, I have watched the Tree shatter. Nine times, I have seen Wardens marked and sent forth." Her voice hardened. "Nine times, I have witnessed the pattern complete itself, only to break again when the time of unmaking comes."

She stopped an arm's length from him. This close, he could see her face clearly—angular features framed by those intricate braids, eyes the color of a winter sky, a small scar bisecting her left eyebrow. Beautiful, but in the way of storm clouds or mountain peaks—remote, dangerous, unconcerned with human perception.

"The Reaver moves toward Helgrindr," she said. "It arrived before you, but cannot access the frost anchor without the mark you bear."

"Why tell me this?" Asvarr lowered his hand from his sword. Something told him the gesture was pointless anyway—if she meant him harm, his blade would offer little protection.

"Because you are different." She moved closer, studying him with unnerving intensity. "You bear the flame-rune alongside the Grímmark. Two paths merged within one vessel. This has never happened before."

"Cinderheart," Asvarr murmured. "The fire-wight's mark."

"The third path." Sigrdrífa nodded. "Neither Tree nor Shadow, but something else. Something new."

She reached toward him, hand hovering over his chest where the marks burned beneath his clothing. He felt their heat intensify, responding to her proximity.

"May I?" she asked.

After a moment's hesitation, Asvarr pushed aside his cloak and tunic, revealing the merged marks. The Grímmark pulsed gold, while the flame-rune beside it flickered blue-white. Together, they formed a pattern neither had originally possessed—something that resembled neither tree nor fire but some merger of both.

Sigrdrífa drew in a sharp breath. "The marks speak to each other," she whispered. "They've begun to merge into something new."

"What does it mean?"

"I don't know." She withdrew her hand. "But it means the Reaver will want you intact, not dead. The Ashfather seeks to understand this merger."

A gust of wind howled through the chamber, carrying with it the distant sound of horn calls. Sigrdrífa's head snapped up, her wings flaring wide.

"They've found us," she hissed.

"Who?" Asvarr drew his sword.

"The Hunt of Broken Fate. The Ashfather's trackers." She moved to the chamber's entrance, peering out into the gathering darkness. "They pursue anything that might disrupt the pattern—especially Wardens who show signs of deviation."

The horn calls grew louder. Three distinct tones, echoing across the wastes. Asvarr joined her at the entrance, trying to gauge the distance.

"We can't outrun them," Sigrdrífa said. "Not in the open. Not at night."

"We?" Asvarr raised an eyebrow.

She turned those winter-sky eyes on him. "Your path and mine are briefly aligned, Warden. I wish to see what becomes of this...merger. Whether it truly offers a way to break the eternal cycle."

More horn calls, closer now. Asvarr glimpsed movement on a distant ridge—tall figures mounted on beasts too large to be horses, their shapes distorted by blowing snow.

"How many?" he asked.

"Nine hunters. Always nine." Sigrdrífa's wings folded tight against her back. "They cannot be killed by mortal means. They are fragments of fate given form—echoes of what might have been, twisted into service."

"Then what do we do?"

She reached into a pouch at her belt and withdrew a small object that gleamed silver in the fading light—a knife no longer than her palm, its blade etched with runes that shifted as Asvarr watched.

"I mark you," she said simply.

"Mark me? How?"

"With the chain of shadow. It will mask your presence from the Hunt, but at a cost." Her expression grew solemn. "It binds your fate temporarily to mine.

Where I go, you must follow. What I ask, you must answer. Until we reach Helgrindr, your will and mine are linked."

Asvarr took a step back. "You ask me to surrender my freedom?"

"I ask you to survive the night." She gestured toward the distant riders, now clearly visible against the darkening sky. "Choose quickly, Warden. The Hunt shows no mercy to those who bear the Tree's mark."

His mind raced. He'd surrendered parts of himself with each binding—memories, rage, identity. But his will had remained his own. To give that up, even temporarily...

"I need to reach the frost anchor," he said finally. "If your chain allows that—"

"It will. I have no interest in preventing the binding." Sigrdrífa raised the knife. "But know this: once marked with the chain of shadow, only death or completion of your task will break it."

The horn calls sounded again, much closer. The lead rider crested a hill less than a mile distant, the massive beast beneath him revealed now as something reptilian, with too many legs and a long, serpentine neck.

"Do it," Asvarr said, pushing back his sleeve to expose his forearm.

Sigrdrífa shook her head. "Not there." She pointed to his left eye. "Here."

"My eye?"

"The shadow-chain connects sight to sight. I must mark the eye through which you see fate's patterns."

The riders drew closer, their mounts leaving trails of frost in the air behind them. Asvarr could make out their armor now—black plates overlapping like scales, helms that covered their entire heads with no visible openings for eyes or mouth.

"Do it," he repeated, forcing himself not to flinch as she raised the tiny blade toward his face.

Sigrdrífa's touch was surprisingly gentle as she steadied his head with one hand. With the other, she pressed the knife's tip just below his left eye and drew it in a quick, precise arc that curved from cheekbone to brow.

Pain flared, sharp but brief. Something cold slithered beneath his skin where the blade had passed, and his vision blurred momentarily. When it cleared, a thin line of shadow remained, visible at the edge of his sight like a chain link etched into his flesh.

"It is done," Sigrdrífa whispered. "You are chain-marked."

The change was immediate and disorienting. Asvarr felt her presence in his mind, connecting to his thoughts like a thread pulled taut between their consciousnesses. He knew, without understanding how, that she experienced the same connection.

"We must move," she said, turning away from the cave entrance. "Deeper, through the tunnels. There's another way out that leads toward Helgrindr."

Asvarr found himself following without question, his body responding to her words as if they were his own decision. The shadow-chain tugged gently but insistently, guiding him after her retreating form.

They moved deeper into the cave system; the ice giving way to bare stone as they descended. Phosphorescent fungi grew in patches along the walls, casting an eerie green glow that illuminated their path. The air grew warmer, though not comfortable.

"What did you mean," Asvarr asked as they walked, "when you said I was 'Breachborn'?"

Sigrdrífa glanced back at him, surprise evident in her expression. "I haven't called you that yet."

A chill ran through him that had nothing to do with the surroundings. "In a vision—you called me Breachborn and said others would come to unmake me."

She stopped, wings flexing slightly. "That hasn't happened yet. But it will." Her eyes narrowed. "Your connection to fate grows stronger with each binding. You're beginning to see fragments of what may come."

"Or what has already happened in previous cycles?"

"Perhaps both. Time moves differently near the anchors." She continued walking. "Breachborn are rare—those who exist outside the pattern while still bound to it. Those who might change the cycle rather than merely perpetuate it."

Behind them, distantly, horn calls echoed through the tunnels. The Hunt had found the cave entrance.

"They'll track us by your scent," Sigrdrífa said, quickening her pace. "The shadow-chain hides you from sight, but not from smell."

"What are they? Truly?" Asvarr asked, half-running to keep up with her.

"Fragments of discarded fate. When the Norns cut the threads at the Shattering, not all possibilities died. Some persisted as echoes, trapped between what was and what might have been." Her voice dropped lower. "The Ashfather gathered these fragments, gave them form, and purpose. Now they serve as his hunters, tracking any who might threaten the new order he seeks to establish."

They reached a junction where the tunnel split in three directions. Without hesitation, Sigrdrífa chose the rightmost path, leading steeply downward. The shadow-chain tugged at Asvarr's eye, compelling him to follow.

"You knew the Ashfather before," he said, less a question than a statement. "When he was still a Warden."

"I guided him to the fifth anchor." Sigrdrífa's voice held no emotion. "I watched as he made his choice. As he broke the pattern and set us on this endless cycle of breaking and restoring."

"What was his name? Before he became the Ashfather?"

She stopped so abruptly that Asvarr nearly collided with her. "Names have power, especially in places like this where reality thins. Ask me anything else, but not that."

The intensity in her voice made him drop the subject. They continued downward until the tunnel leveled out, opening into a vast underground chamber. Unlike the ice cave above, this space bore signs of deliberate construction—smooth walls carved with intricate patterns, a level floor inlaid with spiraling designs that centered on a dais of black stone.

"What is this place?" Asvarr asked, voice hushed.

"A waypoint. One of nine that circle Helgrindr." Sigrdrífa moved to the central dais. "From here, we can travel without crossing the surface where the Hunt has an advantage."

She pressed her palm against a symbol carved into the black stone—a spear piercing an eye. The design flared with silver light, spreading outward along the spiraling patterns in the floor until the entire chamber glowed.

"Quickly," she urged, extending her hand toward Asvarr. "The path opens only briefly."

The shadow-chain pulled insistently. Asvarr stepped onto the dais and took her offered hand. Her skin felt unnaturally cool against his, but solid and real.

"Close your eyes," she instructed. "The passage can break minds not prepared for it."

He obeyed. Instantly, sensation fled from his body—the cold, the weight of his weapons, even the pressure of Sigrdrífa's hand in his—all vanished. He floated in absolute darkness, anchored only by the shadow-chain's persistent tug below his eye.

Then sound rushed back—a roaring like a waterfall, but deeper, more primal. Light stabbed through his closed eyelids, and his body returned in a shock of sensation. He staggered, would have fallen if not for Sigrdrífa's steadying grip.

***

"You can look now," she said.

Asvarr opened his eyes to an entirely different landscape. They stood on a narrow stone bridge spanning a chasm of impossible depth. Above them, the sky burned with colors no mortal sky should hold—sheets of green and purple light dancing between stars too large and too bright. Ahead, perhaps a mile distant, rose the ice fortress of Helgrindr, its twisted spires gleaming under the alien light.

"The realm-between," Sigrdrífa explained, releasing his hand. "We walk the boundary that separates Midgard from Niflheim. Here, the Hunt cannot follow without abandoning their physical forms."

Asvarr stared at the fortress—their destination. The frost anchor waited within those ice walls, calling to him through the marks on his chest. But something else awaited him there, too. Something the visions and songs had warned about but never fully revealed.

"Runveig is already inside," Sigrdrífa said, confirming his thoughts. "The Reaver cannot bind the anchor, but it can prepare the way for what comes after."

"What comes after?"

She turned those winter-sky eyes on him. "The choice that either continues the cycle or breaks it forever." Her gaze dropped to his chest, where the merged marks glowed visibly through his clothing. "The choice only you can make, Breachborn, because you walk two paths at once."

The shadow-chain between them pulsed, and Asvarr felt her concern leaking through their connection. Her concern for something larger than herself, the fate of the realms, perhaps, or something even more fundamental.

"The Hunt will find another way to reach us," she said, starting across the narrow bridge. "We must reach Helgrindr before they circle around."

Asvarr followed, the shadow-chain guiding his steps behind her. Below them, the chasm breathed darkness and whispers. Above, the impossible sky rained light in curtains of color.

And ahead, the ice fortress waited, housing both the frost anchor and a Reaver who served the Ashfather—a being who had once walked Asvarr's path, bound the anchors as he now sought to do, and emerged as something neither human nor divine.

For the first time since receiving the Grímmark, Asvarr wondered if binding all five anchors was truly his wyrd—or if fate itself had been broken enough that he might forge a different ending.

***

The air changed halfway across the bridge, growing thin and sharp as a blade. Asvarr's lungs burned with each breath. Above, the impossible sky bled colors that should never exist together—green fire dancing with purple shadow, stars pulsing like hearts. He kept his eyes fixed on Sigrdrífa's back, following the rhythm of her wings as they folded and unfurled with each step.

The shadow-chain beneath his eye pulsed in time with his heartbeat, a constant reminder of their binding. Through it, he sensed fragments of the Valkyrie's thoughts—her wariness of what awaited them, her curiosity about his merged marks, her memories of countless Wardens who had walked this path before him.

"How many have reached the frost anchor?" Asvarr asked, voice sounding flat and lifeless in the thin air.

"Seventeen," Sigrdrífa answered, without turning. "Twelve bound it successfully. Five fell to what guards it."

"And those who bound it? What did they become?"

She paused, wings spreading for balance on the narrow bridge. "Less human with each binding. More vessel."

Asvarr's hand moved instinctively to his chest, where the merged marks burned. "The Ashfather was once like me, wasn't he? A Warden marked by flame and tree."

"No." Sigrdrífa turned to face him, her wings catching the alien light. "He bore only the Tree's mark. The flame-rune you carry—this is new. Unprecedented." She studied him with those winter-sky eyes. "It may change everything. Or nothing at all."

The bridge ended at a platform of black ice so clear that Asvarr could see the void beneath his feet, stretching endlessly downward. The ice fortress of Helgrindr rose before them, twisted spires and arches forming a structure that defied natural law. It reminded him of frozen lightning, captured in the moment of striking.

"The Hunt will find another way to reach us," Sigrdrífa said, scanning the empty air around them. "They cannot cross the bridge, but there are other paths between worlds."

"You said they serve the Ashfather," Asvarr replied, drawing his bronze sword. The blade gleamed strangely in the colored light, its runes shifting like living things. "But they hunt Wardens who bear his old mark. Why?"

"The Ashfather fears what he once was." She moved toward the fortress entrance—a jagged archway tall enough for giants. "He remembers the price of binding. He remembers what sleeps at the pattern's heart."

They passed under the arch, entering a vast chamber where pillars of ice rose hundreds of feet to a vaulted ceiling. Every surface reflected the light differently—some absorbing it, some bending it, some splitting it into fractal patterns that danced across the walls. The air hummed with power.

Asvarr felt the frost anchor's pull immediately—a cold hook behind his ribs, tugging him forward. The marks on his chest flared in response, sending tendrils of heat and cold warring through his flesh.

"It's close," he whispered.

Sigrdrífa nodded. "The throne chamber. Through there." She pointed toward a corridor that spiraled upward into the fortress depths.

As they moved deeper, Asvarr noticed patterns carved into the ice walls—runes unlike any he'd seen before, older than the futhark, older perhaps than human memory. They pulsed with faint blue light as he passed, responding to the marks he bore.

"What are these?" he asked, gesturing to the symbols.

"The language of winter," Sigrdrífa replied. "From before the Tree, before the Nine Realms. When ice and fire warred across the void."

The corridor widened into a circular chamber lined with alcoves. In each stood a figure encased in ice—men and women of different ages, their features preserved in perfect detail. Their eyes remained open, staring outward with expressions of shock or revelation.

"Previous seekers," Sigrdrífa explained. "Those who failed the frost anchor's test."

Asvarr approached the nearest figure—a young man with braided hair and a half-formed rune carved into his chest. The ice surrounding him was perfectly clear, without bubbles or flaws. Within it, the man's cloak still appeared to ripple as if caught in an eternal moment of movement.

"They're not dead," Asvarr realized, studying the man's eyes.

"No, death would be kinder." Sigrdrífa touched the ice with one fingertip. "They exist in the moment of failure, aware but unable to move forward or back. Outside time."

Asvarr counted seventeen alcoves. "You said twelve bound the anchor successfully. Where are they?"

"Gone to bind the fifth, or transformed into something beyond recognition." She withdrew her hand from the ice. "Some may still walk the worlds, unrecognizable as the humans they once were."

The shadow-chain tugged at Asvarr, and he followed Sigrdrífa through an archway on the far side of the chamber. Beyond lay a spiraling staircase, carved from a single, massive crystal of ice. It carried them upward through the fortress's heart, past chambers filled with artifacts Asvarr couldn't begin to comprehend—weapons that changed shape as he watched, mirrors that showed impossible landscapes, crystals that sang in voices almost human.

At the top of the stairs, they emerged onto a balcony overlooking a vast, circular chamber. In its center stood a throne of blue-white ice, unoccupied but pulsing with light in rhythm with Asvarr's heartbeat.

And there, suspended above the throne, hung the frost anchor.

Unlike the previous anchors, this one had no physical form Asvarr could define. It existed as a distortion in the air, a spherical void where reality bent around absence. Snowflakes spiraled into it, freezing in perfect patterns before vanishing. The temperature dropped precipitously near it, cold enough that Asvarr's breath crystallized instantly.

"The fourth anchor," Sigrdrífa murmured. "The nail that holds winter to the world's flesh."

Asvarr felt his marks respond, golden light from the Grímmark and blue flame from the kenaz rune shifting beneath his clothing. The remembrance-key at his belt grew hot, while the merged ivory disk from the second binding turned cold enough to burn. The horn from the first binding emitted a low, barely audible tone.

"Where's Runveig?" Asvarr asked, scanning the chamber. "You said the Reaver was already here."

The shadow-chain pulsed a warning an instant before Sigrdrífa stiffened. "Below," she hissed.

From the shadows beneath the balcony emerged a figure in flowing robes that shifted like oil on water. The wooden mask gleamed in the strange light, revealing only those metallic eyes.

"Skyrend's Flame," Runveig's voice echoed unnaturally in the chamber. "You've arrived earlier than expected. And with interesting company."

Sigrdrífa's wings flared wide, her hand moving to a short sword at her belt that Asvarr hadn't noticed before. The blade glinted silver, etched with runes similar to those on the walls.

"Reaver," she said, her voice colder than the surrounding ice. "Still hiding behind that mask?"

"Still collecting broken Wardens, Valkyrie?" Runveig countered. "How many have you guided to their unmaking?"

Asvarr felt the tension flow between them—old hatred, older history. Through the shadow-chain, he sensed Sigrdrífa's fear, buried deep beneath layers of determination.

"The anchor calls to me," Asvarr interrupted, drawing their attention. "I came to bind it."

Runveig's metallic gaze fixed on him. "Of course you did. That's what Wardens do—bind the anchors, reinforce the pattern, feed what waits at its heart." The Reaver moved to the base of the throne, one gloved hand trailing across its arm. "But you could do so much more."

"Don't listen," Sigrdrífa warned. "The Reaver twists truth into lies."

"Do I?" Runveig's mask tilted toward her. "Or do I simply offer alternatives to a fate the Valkyries have enforced for nine cycles of breaking? How many Wardens have you guided to their doom, Sigrdrífa? How many have you chain-marked and led to sacrifice?"

The shadow-chain burned beneath Asvarr's eye. Through it, he felt Sigrdrífa's shame, her regret—emotions so ancient and deep they could drown worlds.

"Enough," Asvarr said, drawing his bronze sword. "I don't care about your ancient quarrels. I came for the anchor."

Runveig laughed, the sound distorted by the wooden mask. "So direct. So determined. I see why the Ashfather finds you interesting." The Reaver gestured toward the distortion floating above the throne. "By all means, approach the frost anchor. See if it accepts you."

Sigrdrífa grabbed Asvarr's arm. "Wait. It's not that simple. The frost anchor requires—"

"Another sacrifice," Asvarr finished. "Another piece of myself."

"More than that," Sigrdrífa said. "The frost anchor demands certainty. It freezes doubt. Those who approach with divided purpose..." She nodded toward the alcoves they'd passed.

Runveig ascended the throne's steps, stopping just short of the distortion. "She speaks the truth, Warden. The frost anchor tests conviction. Those who harbor doubt find themselves trapped between moments, frozen in the instant of decision."

Asvarr studied the Reaver carefully. "Then why haven't you claimed it? You found it first."

"Because I lack what you possess." Runveig pointed to Asvarr's chest. "The mark that responds to the anchor's call. I can commune with it, learn from it, but I cannot bind it."

"Then why are you here?"

"To ensure that the binding takes place correctly." The Reaver moved closer, those metal eyes never leaving Asvarr's face. "Not all bindings are equal, Warden. The anchor can be bound in ways that strengthen the pattern—or weaken it."

Sigrdrífa's hand tightened on Asvarr's arm. "Don't trust the Reaver's guidance. The Ashfather doesn't seek to break the pattern—he seeks to redirect it, to place himself at its center."

The shadow-chain pulsed, sending waves of urgency through Asvarr's mind. He sensed Sigrdrífa's desperation; her fear that he might listen to Runveig.

"What would you have me do?" he asked her.

"Bind the anchor as the others before you—with blood and oath, horn, and blade." She pointed to the distortion. "Let it take what it needs. Become its vessel until the fifth and final binding is complete."

Runveig's mask gleamed as the Reaver circled the throne. "And after the fifth binding? What then, Valkyrie? Tell him what awaits at the pattern's completion."

Sigrdrífa's wings stiffened. Through the shadow-chain, Asvarr felt her reluctance, her struggle against words that demanded to be spoken.

"The pattern consumes its Wardens," she admitted finally. "When all five anchors are bound, they draw together. The Warden becomes the conduit—the bridge between what was and what will be."

"Consumes?" Asvarr repeated.

"All that remains of your original self burns away," Runveig said. "Your identity, your memories, your will—all consumed to feed the pattern's heart. To awaken what sleeps there."

"What sleeps there?" Asvarr demanded, looking between them. "What am I awakening with each binding?"

Neither answered immediately. The chamber filled with silence, broken only by the crystalline sounds of ice shifting around them. Above the throne, the frost anchor continued its strange pulsation, drawing snowflakes into its vortex.

"Something older than gods," Sigrdrífa said finally. "Something that dreamed the Tree into existence."

"Something that's been imprisoned within the pattern since the first world formed," Runveig added. "Something that longs for freedom."

The marks on Asvarr's chest burned hotter, responding to their words. He remembered Hrafn's song: *What sleeps within the pattern's heart is neither Tree nor Shadow born, but something from before the worlds.*

"Then why continue the cycle?" Asvarr asked. "If binding the anchors awakens this entity, why not let them fade? Let the pattern dissolve?"

"Because without the anchors, all reality unravels," Sigrdrífa answered. "The Nine Realms collapse. Everything ends."

"Not ends," Runveig corrected. "Changes. Transforms. Becomes something new."

Asvarr looked at the frost anchor, feeling its pull—the inexorable tug on the marks he bore. Three anchors bound, two remaining. With each binding, he lost more of himself. Became more vessel than man.

"You said my marks were different," he said to Sigrdrífa. "The flame-rune merged with the Grímmark. What does that mean for the binding?"

The Valkyrie's wings shifted uncertainly. "I don't know. The merger is unprecedented."

"It means possibility," Runveig interjected. "It means the potential to bind without surrendering. To complete the pattern without being consumed by it."

From somewhere deep within the fortress came the distant sound of horn calls—three distinct tones echoing through the ice passages.

"The Hunt," Sigrdrífa breathed. "They've found another way through."

"They can't enter the throne chamber," Runveig said. "Not while the anchor remains unbound. However, once it's claimed..." The Reaver trailed off, metal eyes fixing on Asvarr. "You must decide, Warden. Bind the anchor conventionally and continue the cycle—or attempt something new."

Sigrdrífa drew her silver blade. "There's no time. The binding must occur now, before the Hunt arrives."

The shadow-chain pulled painfully, nearly dragging Asvarr toward the throne. He resisted, planting his feet.

"Release me from the chain," he demanded. "I need to make this choice freely."

"I cannot," she replied. "Not until your task is complete."

"You mean not until I'm bound to your purpose." Asvarr raised his bronze sword. "Cut the chain, Valkyrie. Let me choose my own path."

Her winter-sky eyes widened. "You would threaten me? After I saved you from the Hunt?"

"I would be free to make my own choice." He placed the sword's edge against the shadow-chain, feeling it as a physical thing connecting them. "Either release me, or I'll sever it myself."

Panic flashed across her face. "You can't. Only death or completion breaks the chain. Attempting to cut it will destroy your mind."

Runveig moved closer, mask tilting with interest. "The Valkyrie speaks truth, Warden. But there is another way."

"What way?" Asvarr demanded, sword still raised.

"The frost anchor itself," Runveig explained. "It freezes all bindings, all fate. It can sever the shadow-chain without harming you—if approached correctly."

Sigrdrífa's wings flared wide. "Lies! The Reaver seeks to manipulate you into binding the anchor incorrectly."

The horn calls sounded again, closer now. Echoing through the fortress came the heavy tread of many feet, the scrape of weapons against ice.

Asvarr weighed his options, mind racing. The shadow-chain pulled him toward conventional binding, toward continuing the cycle as countless Wardens had before him. But the merged marks on his chest—the third path Cinderheart had spoken of—suggested another possibility.

"What would you have me do?" he asked Runveig.

"Approach the anchor with divided purpose," the Reaver answered immediately. "Do not approach it with the certainty the frost anchor traditionally demands; however you must approach it with the duality your merged marks represent. Stand between paths, between choices."

"That's exactly what traps seekers in the ice!" Sigrdrífa protested. "Those alcoves are filled with those who approached with doubt!"

"They bore single marks," Runveig countered. "None carried the merger that Asvarr bears. None walked the third path."

The Hunt's footsteps grew louder. Time was running out.

Asvarr decided. He sheathed his bronze sword and turned toward the frost anchor.

"I'm binding it," he announced. "But in my own way."

He mounted the throne's steps, feeling the temperature drop with each movement closer to the distortion. The merged marks on his chest blazed through his clothing, gold and blue-white light illuminating the chamber. The remembrance-key, the ivory disk, and the horn all resonated together, creating a harmony of sound and energy that made the ice walls vibrate.

"Asvarr, wait—" Sigrdrífa called, but the shadow-chain had gone slack, no longer pulling him to obey.

He reached the top step, standing directly beneath the frost anchor. The void-like distortion hung just above his head, drawing in snowflakes only to annihilate them. He felt its pull on his consciousness—the demand for certainty, for a singular purpose.

Instead, he embraced duality. The tree and the flame. The pattern and its breaking. Vessel and master.

"The frost remembers," he whispered, reaching upward.

His fingertips touched the edge of the distortion.

Absolute cold engulfed him. Time ceased. The world beyond his skin vanished into white silence.

Within that silence, a voice older than worlds spoke directly into his mind:

"What do you seek, mark-bearer?"

"The anchor," Asvarr answered, his words forming as ice crystals in the void. "I've come to bind it."

"To what purpose? Continuation or dissolution?"

"Neither. Transformation."

The voice paused, considering. *"None have answered thus before. All chose one path or the other."*

"I stand between paths."

"To stand between is to be frozen. Trapped between moments."

"I carry both tree and flame," Asvarr replied. "I am already between."

Another pause, longer this time. Then: *"Show me these marks you bear."*

Asvarr opened his tunic, revealing the merged patterns on his chest. In the absolute stillness of the void, they blazed with impossible intensity—the Grímmark's golden light and the kenaz rune's blue-white flame intertwined into something new.

"Unexpected," the voice whispered. *"A third configuration. A path not foreseen."*

"Will you accept my binding?" Asvarr asked.

"The binding requires sacrifice. What do you offer?"

Asvarr thought of what he'd already surrendered—rage at the pool, memory at the seed, identity at the root. What remained?

"My certainty," he answered finally. "I offer the comfort of knowing my path."

A sound like ice cracking across a frozen lake filled the void. *"Accepted. But know this, mark-bearer: to surrender certainty is to embrace chaos. Your path forward will no longer be clear. Choice will burden every step."*

"I accept that burden."

"Then reach forth and claim what is yours."

The void shifted, contracted, condensed into physical form. In its place hung a crystal of ice unlike any Asvarr had seen—a perfect geometric shape with too many facets to count, each reflecting light differently. At its center, a spark of blue-white energy pulsed like a heart.

Asvarr grasped it with both hands.

Pain exploded through his body—pain beyond anything he'd experienced at the previous bindings. Every nerve crystallized, every thought froze mid-formation. He felt himself splitting, fragmenting like ice under too much pressure.

The shadow-chain beneath his eye shattered first, its link dissolving into frost that fell away from his skin. Next came certainty—the clear vision of his purpose, the straight path ahead—all fracturing into countless possible futures, each equally valid, equally flawed.

When it ended, he stood holding the frost crystal against his chest. The marks had changed again—expanded to incorporate a new pattern that resembled a snowflake overlaid on the merged tree and flame.

"Impossible," Sigrdrífa breathed, her winter-sky eyes wide. "You should be frozen. Trapped."

"Three bindings become four," Runveig intoned from below. "The Warden evolves beyond expectation."

Asvarr descended the steps, the frost crystal now hanging from a chain around his neck alongside his other tokens. His mind felt strangely expanded, filled with possibilities where before had been only linear purpose. The binding had taken his certainty, leaving a forest of branching paths in its place.

"The chain is broken," he said to Sigrdrífa, touching the spot beneath his eye where the shadow-mark had been. "Your hold on me is gone."

The Valkyrie's wings drooped slightly. "So it is. You've done what none before you have managed. You bound the frost anchor while maintaining your will."

The Hunt's footsteps had stopped. The fortress hung in perfect silence around them.

"They sense the binding is complete," Runveig said, moving toward one of the chamber's archways. "They'll withdraw now and report to their master."

"And you?" Asvarr asked the Reaver. "Where do you go?"

"To the fifth anchor," Runveig replied. "To prepare for your arrival. The final binding approaches, Warden. The pattern nears completion."

"Or transformation," Asvarr countered.

Beneath the wooden mask, he sensed Runveig smile. "Perhaps. We shall see which path you ultimately choose."

The Reaver departed, cloak flowing like liquid shadow. Asvarr turned to Sigrdrífa, who stood with her wings half-furled, studying him with unreadable eyes.

"Will you try to stop me?" he asked.

"Could I?" Her lips quirked into something almost resembling a smile. "You've proven more adaptable than any Warden before you. The fifth anchor awaits in Helheim, where death and memory intertwine. I cannot follow you there."

"Then, this is farewell."

Sigrdrífa stepped closer, her hand reaching out to touch the frost crystal at his chest. "When you face the fifth binding, remember this moment—when you chose transformation over continuation. The final anchor will test that choice beyond anything you can imagine."

Through the throne chamber's high windows, the impossible sky had begun to dim, stars fading one by one. The realm-between was closing, its brief alignment ending.

"The bridge will vanish soon," Sigrdrífa warned. "You must return to Midgard before the path closes."

Asvarr nodded, gathering his resolve. Four anchors bound, one remaining. The marks on his chest had expanded again, spreading across his torso in patterns that merged tree, flame, and frost. With each binding, he became less the berserker who had witnessed the Shattering, more the vessel of something larger.

Yet, unlike those who had walked this path before, he retained his will. His ability to choose.

"How do I reach Helheim?" he asked. "Where will I find the fifth anchor?"

"The dead will guide you," Sigrdrífa replied. "They always do."

She stepped back, wings spreading wide. In a burst of shadow and light, she transformed—her body dissolving into a swarm of ravens that circled the chamber once before streaming out through a high window.

Asvarr stood alone in the throne room of Helgrindr, the frost crystal pulsing against his chest. Through it, he sensed countless possible futures branching before him—a forest of paths where before had been a single road.

With the certainty of his purpose gone, Asvarr faced the most difficult challenge yet: true choice. To bind the final anchor as expected, or to seek the third path between Tree and Shadow. To complete the pattern, or to transform it.

And somewhere, in Helheim's cold embrace, the fifth anchor awaited.

CHAPTER 11

THE ROOT BELOW NIFLHEIM

The bridge between realms vanished in a shock of cold air. Asvarr stumbled forward, knee-deep in snow where moments before had been solid stone. Above him, the sky returned to Midgard's familiar gray-blue, the impossible colors of the realm-between fading like a dream upon waking. The frost crystal at his chest pulsed once, twice, then settled into a rhythmic heartbeat against his skin.

Four down. One to go.

His breath fogged in the bitter air as he oriented himself. The mountainous terrain looked different from this side, massive spires of black rock jutting from windswept plains of ice. No trails marked the virgin snow. No landmarks guided his path. The light suggested early morning, though the sun remained hidden behind a veil of clouds.

The marks on his chest itched as they settled into their new configuration. Since binding the frost anchor, they had spread across his torso—no longer confined to a single spot but branching outward like frost patterns on a window. The bronze sword at his hip hummed faintly, runes glowing along its length as if responding to something hidden beneath the snow.

He reached into his pouch, feeling for the tokens of his bindings. The horn, from the first, smooth and ancient. The ivory disk, from the second, warm despite the cold. The remembrance-key from the third, surprisingly heavy. And now, the frost crystal, impossibly cold yet causing no pain. Four pieces of a pattern that demanded completion.

A pattern that might consume him entirely if completed as intended.

"Helheim," he murmured aloud. "The fifth anchor waits in Helheim."

The land of the dead. The realm where those who died of sickness or old age dwelled beneath the roots of Yggdrasil. How was he to reach it while still alive?

The dead will guide you. They always do.

Sigrdrífa's words echoed in his mind as he trudged through the snow, seeking shelter from the biting wind. A ridge of dark stone provided some protection, allowing him to gather his thoughts. He pulled provisions from his pack—dried meat, hard bread, the flask of memory-mead that Egil had given him. The bitter liquid warmed his throat and quieted the echoes of Hrafn's song that still haunted his dreams.

His sacrifice at the frost anchor—certainty—left him adrift in possibilities. No clear path revealed itself, just a forest of potential choices, each as valid as the last. For the first time since receiving the Grímmark, Asvarr faced true freedom... and found it terrifying.

The wind changed direction, carrying a new scent—smoke.

He climbed the ridge, peering over its edge. In the valley below, a ring of seven standing stones surrounded a fire pit where blue flames danced without fuel. A lone figure knelt beside the fire, hooded and cloaked in gray, hands extended toward the heat.

Trap or providence? Asvarr couldn't tell. His marks offered no guidance, no certainty. He had sacrificed that comfort at Helgrindr.

He climbed down from the ridge and approached the stones cautiously, one hand resting on his sword hilt. The blue flames cast an eerie light across the snow, revealing runes carved into each monolith—older symbols than those he knew, their lines more angular and primitive.

The hooded figure didn't move as he approached, remaining focused on the flames. Not until Asvarr stood at the stone circle's edge did the figure speak.

"Four marks where once was one. Four tokens where once was none." The voice belonged to an old woman, cracked with age yet carrying an undertone of iron. "Sit, Warden. The fire burns for you."

Asvarr hesitated, then stepped into the circle. The blue flames leapt higher at his entrance, responding to the marks beneath his clothing.

"Who are you?" he asked, remaining standing.

The woman pulled back her hood, revealing a face lined with countless years. Her hair hung in braids of iron gray, decorated with small bones and beads of amber. One eye gleamed, clear and sharp; the other was a milky orb, blind yet somehow focused on him all the same.

"I am Angrboda," she said. "Once witch-wife of Loki, now keeper of the path to Helheim." She gestured to the space across the fire. "Sit. You seek passage to the land of the dead, and such things cannot be discussed standing."

Asvarr sat cross-legged before the fire, arranging his sword across his knees. The flames warmed him despite the surrounding cold, their heat penetrating deeper than mere flesh.

"You've been waiting for me," he said. Not a question.

"For you or another." Angrboda shrugged, her cloak shifting to reveal glimpses of a dress stitched with thousands of tiny runes. "The pattern must complete itself, one way or another. Four anchors bound, one remaining. The dead root calls for its Warden."

"The Root Below Niflheim," Asvarr murmured. "That's what they call the fifth anchor?"

"The oldest of the five." She nodded. "Buried beneath the frozen realm before humans walked the worlds, before gods fashioned their halls of gold and silver. The dead root remembers what came before."

Asvarr touched the frost crystal hanging at his chest. "At Helgrindr, I learned of something sleeping at the pattern's heart. Something older than gods."

"And that troubles you." Angrboda's good eye narrowed. "As well, it should. The Wardens before you asked no questions. They bound the anchors as directed, became vessels for what slept beyond, and vanished from memory when the pattern completed itself."

"Except the Ashfather."

Angrboda stiffened. "He told you of this?"

"His Reaver did. And the Valkyrie Sigrdrífa confirmed it. The Ashfather was once a Warden like me, the first to bind all five anchors and survive... changed."

The witch-wife's face betrayed nothing, but her fingers moved in small, precise patterns at the edge of her cloak—warding signs, Asvarr realized. Protection against names that held power.

"What does he want?" Asvarr pressed. "Why send the Reaver to guide me through the bindings rather than stop me?"

"The Ashfather seeks what all broken things seek—restoration. But on his terms, not the Tree's." Angrboda leaned forward, her blind eye catching the blue firelight. "Five bindings. Five sacrifices. Five transformations. But the final transformation can be guided, shaped by the choices made before. The Ashfather believes your merged marks offer a way to bind the anchors without awakening what waits at the pattern's heart."

"And what awaits there?"

Angrboda smiled, tight-lipped. "Names have power, Warden. Some should never be spoken aloud. But know this—it dreams the worlds into being. It is the source from which Yggdrasil grew, the wellspring of all that is. The Tree is merely its vision given form."

Cold deeper than the surrounding snow crept up Asvarr's spine. "And binding the anchors awakens it."

"Or change its dreams." The witch-wife gestured to the marks visible at the edge of Asvarr's collar. "Your merged marks suggest another possibility—one the Ashfather fears and covets in equal measure. Not awakening, not containment, but transformation. Dream becoming dreamer, dreamer becoming dream."

Asvarr's head spun with the implications. He reached for the flask of memory-mead, taking a small sip to center himself.

"How do I reach Helheim?" he asked finally. "How do I find the dead root?"

"There are three paths to the land of the dead." Angrboda raised one gnarled finger. "First, through death itself—but the dead cannot bind anchors. The mark fades with the flesh." A second finger rose. "Second, through Gjöll's bridge, guarded by Modgud—but she permits no living soul to cross." The third finger joined the others. "Third, through the forgotten way—the path that existed before bridges, before guardians. The root's own passage."

"And where is this forgotten way?"

Instead of answering, Angrboda reached into the blue flames, her hand unburned by their heat. She withdrew something long and slender—a bone needle, its tip blackened with age.

"The path opens only for those who bear the blood-price of passage," she said. "Living flesh must carry the marks of the dead to walk among them."

Asvarr eyed the needle warily. "What marks?"

"Death-runes. Carved into skin, filled with ash from the bones of the long-dead." She held out her free hand. "Your arm, Warden."

Asvarr hesitated. Every binding had required sacrifice—rage, memory, identity, certainty. What would these death-runes take from him?

"What will I lose this time?" he asked aloud.

Angrboda's mouth twisted in what might have been a smile. "Clever question. The death-runes take nothing themselves—they merely allow passage. But..." She tilted her head, milky eye fixing on him with unsettling accuracy. "The dead root will demand its due when you bind it. And being among the dead changes the living in ways you cannot anticipate."

Asvarr considered his options, though the forest of possibilities that had replaced his certainty offered no clear path. Trust the witch-wife? Find another way? Turn back entirely?

No. The last option tasted like ash in his mouth. Four anchors bound. Four pieces of himself surrendered. He would see this through, whatever the cost.

He extended his left arm, pushing back his sleeve to expose the skin of his forearm.

"Do it."

Angrboda nodded once, then gripped his wrist with surprising strength. The bone needle hovered over his flesh.

"This will hurt," she warned. "The dead do not surrender their marks easily."

The needle pierced his skin. Pain flared, sharper than any blade, burning like poison in his veins. Angrboda worked with practiced precision, carving symbols Asvarr didn't recognize—jagged, hungry shapes that seemed to drink his blood as it welled up around the needle's path.

When she finished the first symbol, she reached into a pouch at her belt and withdrew a pinch of gray powder. She pressed it into the open wound.

Fire erupted beneath Asvarr's skin. He bit back a cry, teeth clenched against the agony. The powder—bone ash, he realized—sank into the wound, turning the carved rune black against his flesh.

"One of nine," Angrboda murmured, moving the needle to a new spot on his arm.

By the fifth rune, sweat poured down Asvarr's face despite the cold. By the eighth, his vision blurred, the world taking on a strange, double aspect—the stone circle in snow-covered Midgard overlaid with glimpses of somewhere else: a misty plain where pale shapes moved with languid grace.

When the ninth rune sank into his flesh, filled with the last of the bone ash, Asvarr's consciousness split entirely. His body remained seated before the blue fire, but his awareness extended elsewhere—down through the frozen earth, through layers of stone and ice, into a realm of perpetual twilight.

Helheim.

"The death-runes connect you to what lies below," Angrboda's voice sounded distant, echoing across the divide between worlds. "Follow their pull when the blue moon rises. They will guide you to the roots passage."

Asvarr forced his fragmented awareness back into his body with an effort of will. The nine black runes on his arm pulsed in time with his heartbeat, each one a window into the land of the dead.

"Blue moon?" he asked, his voice rough.

"Tonight." Angrboda gestured eastward. "When Mani's forgotten child crosses the sky. It appears only when the veils between realms grow thin." She began wrapping his arm in strips of linen, covering the death-runes. "Until then, rest. The passage will demand all your strength."

Asvarr glanced at the sky. The cloud cover had begun to thin, revealing patches of deepening blue as day moved toward evening. How long had he sat in the stone circle? Time felt slippery, unreliable.

"You've guided others to the dead root before," he said as Angrboda finished binding his arm.

She nodded, but volunteered nothing more.

"Did any return?"

The witch-wife's good eye met his. "Three sought the dead root in my memory. One returned changed beyond recognition, one returned missing half his soul, and one did not return at all." She closed her medicine pouch. "The choice that awaits you at the root is not one I can prepare you for, Warden. Each binding reshapes you. Each sacrifice diminishes what you were and expands what you become. But the dead root... it offers both ending and beginning."

"You speak in riddles," Asvarr growled, frustration momentarily overcoming the pain in his arm.

"Because the truth has too, many faces to name plainly." Angrboda gestured to the marks visible at his collar. "Your path is unique. No, Warden before you carried merged marks—the Tree and flame combined. No Warden before you has sought a third path between continuation and dissolution."

"The Ashfather did."

"No." Her voice sharpened. "He sought to direct the pattern toward himself rather than what waited at its heart. Substitution, not transformation. You seek something else entirely—a breaking of the cycle itself."

Asvarr fell silent, digesting her words. The runes on his arm throbbed, sending occasional flashes of that other place across his vision—misty plains, pale figures, distant mountains wreathed in perpetual gloom.

"Why help me?" he asked finally. "What do you gain from my reaching the dead root?"

Angrboda's lips curved in a genuine smile this time, revealing teeth filed to points. "I am Loki's witch-wife, Warden. Chaos and transformation are woven into my nature. Nine worlds locked in cycle after cycle of breaking and restoration grows... tedious." She waved a hand dismissively. "The Ashfather would re-place one dream with another. The Tree would continue the dream un-changed. But you..." Her finger pointed to his chest, where the merged marks pulsed. "You might wake the dreamer entirely. And that, at least, would be interesting to witness."

She rose fluidly, gathering her cloak around her. "Rest now. When the blue moon rises, follow the death-runes' pull. They will guide you to the passage."

"And once I'm in Helheim? How do I find the dead root?"

"The death will find you, Warden. They've waited long for someone who walks between worlds." Angrboda stepped out of the stone circle, her form suddenly indistinct in the gathering dusk. "One last warning—in Helheim, living flesh attracts both attention and hunger. Move quickly, speak to none but those who speak your name first, and never look back when you hear footsteps behind you."

Before Asvarr could respond, she vanished between one blink and the next, leaving him alone with the blue flames and the ache of fresh runes in his flesh.

He settled back, using his pack as a makeshift pillow. The stone circle offered some protection from the wind, and the unnatural flames provided warmth without fuel. He should rest, conserve his strength for what lay ahead.

But sleep proved elusive. Each time he closed his eyes, the death-runes pulled his awareness downward, showing him fragments of that twilight realm: a river of knife-sharp water, fields where pale figures wandered aim-lessly, halls of bone and ice where shadows moved with purpose.

And beneath it all, he sensed the dead root—ancient, patient, hungry for connection. Unlike the previous anchors, this one already knew he was coming. It waited, coiled in darkness beneath Helheim's foundations, the last fragment of the shattered World Tree.

The clouds thinned further as night descended, revealing stars scattered across the black vault of the sky. Asvarr traced familiar constellations—the Wolf, the Spear, the Broken Crown—finding comfort in their unchanging positions despite all that had altered within himself.

Then, at the eastern horizon, a new light appeared. The moon rising—but unlike any moon Asvarr had ever seen. Its surface glowed pale blue, casting an unnatural light across the snow. Mani's forgotten child, Angrboda had called it. The blue moon that appeared only when the veils between worlds grew thin.

The death-runes on his arm flared in response, black lines turning silver-blue in the moonlight. The pain returned tenfold, but with it came clarity. Asvarr saw the path now visible to his altered perception. A trail of blue-silver footprints leading away from the stone circle, toward a distant crevasse in the earth.

The forgotten way. The root's own passage to Helheim.

Asvarr gathered his belongings, checked his weapons, and touched each token hanging at his belt. The horn, the disk, the remembrance-key, the frost crystal. Four anchors bound. Four sacrifices made. Four transformations undergone.

One remained.

He stepped out of the stone circle, following the spectral footprints only he could see. Behind him, the blue flames died suddenly, plunging the standing stones into darkness. Before him, the path glowed with unearthly light, guiding him toward the edge of the living world and beyond.

The Root Below Niflheim awaited, and with it, the final binding.

***

The crevasse gaped like a wound in the frozen earth. Asvarr stood at its edge, peering into darkness so absolute it seemed to swallow even the blue moonlight. The spectral footprints he'd followed from the stone circle ended here, vanishing at the precipice.

His death-runes throbbed, sending pulses of awareness downward. Through them, he sensed the path—a narrow ledge spiraling into the depths, invisible to normal sight but clear to his altered perception.

Asvarr took a breath, steeling himself. All journeys had a beginning. This one started with a single step into darkness.

The descent proved treacherous. The ledge barely accommodated his boots, forcing him to press his back against the crevasse wall and inch sideways. The cold intensified with each step downward, a primal cold that sank past flesh into spirit. His breath clouded before him, freezing into crystals that hung briefly in the air before falling into the abyss below.

Three spirals down, the physical world began to blur. The stone beneath his feet grew less solid, more conceptual. The darkness shifted from a mere absence of light to something active, pressing against him with curious tendrils. The line between Midgard and Helheim thinned.

On the seventh spiral, the ledge widened into a small platform. A standing stone waited there, twice Asvarr's height, carved with runes that matched those burned into his arm. The death-marks pulsed in recognition, sending fire through his veins.

Asvarr placed his palm against the stone. Its surface felt neither hot nor cold but somewhere between—the temperature of flesh long divorced from life. The runes flared blue-white beneath his touch, and the stone split down the middle, revealing a passage beyond.

Helheim waited.

He stepped through.

***

The world inverted. What had been a downward spiral became a horizontal passage through misty twilight. The sky—if it could be called that—hung low and colorless, like a perpetual dusk. The ground beneath his feet turned from stone to soil, the texture of ash, yielding slightly with each step.

Asvarr's living flesh felt conspicuous here—too warm, too solid, too *present* in a realm of absence. The death-runes on his arm provided the only heat he felt, pulsing with each heartbeat.

The path led across a plain where pale grasses grew without wind to stir them. In the distance, mountains hunched like sleeping giants, their peaks vanishing into low clouds that never moved. Closer at hand, stands of bone-white trees created skeletal groves where figures drifted aimlessly.

The dead. Hundreds of them—thousands, perhaps. They wandered without purpose, their features indistinct, their forms semi-transparent. Some wore the garb of warriors; others simple farmers' clothes. Many appeared as they had at death—wounds still visible, sicknesses still evident. None paid him any mind. Not yet.

Asvarr remembered Angrboda's warning: *Move quickly, speak to none but those who speak your name first, and never look back when you hear footsteps behind you.*

He kept to the path, eyes forward. The Root Below Niflheim pulled at him, an inescapable gravity centered somewhere ahead in the misty distance. Unlike the previous anchors, this one felt aware—sentient in a way the others had not been. It knew that he had come. It waited.

The path led to a river that flowed with something too viscous to be water. Its surface rippled with reflection, but what Asvarr saw there was memories—fragments of his past playing across the liquid's surface. His childhood in Hralvik. His first raid. The day he received the Grímmark. Each binding that followed.

On the river's far bank stood a figure motionless as stone—a woman wrapped in gray, her face hidden beneath a deep hood. A sword hung at her hip, its blade impossibly long and thin.

Modgud. Guardian of Gjöll's bridge. She who lets none living cross.

But there was no bridge here—only the river of memories flowing between them.

"Warden."

The voice came from behind him.

Asvarr's hand went to his sword hilt, but he caught himself before drawing it. *Speak to none but those who speak your name first.* This voice had called him Warden, not Asvarr. He ignored it, keeping his eyes on the river.

"Warden of four anchors."

Closer now. The voice held a strange echo, as if spoken from the bottom of a well.

"The living do not walk here."

Asvarr felt breath on the back of his neck. Cold breath that carried the scent of grave soil and forgotten names.

Never look back when you hear footsteps behind you.

He kept his gaze fixed on the river, on the far bank where Modgud stood watching. The presence behind him grew stronger, its cold seeping into his bones. Something brushed his shoulder—fingers composed of mist and memory.

"You carry fragments of us."

The death-runes on his arm flared in pain. Through them, he felt the presence feeding, drawing something from his living essence. His vision doubled, the misty twilight realm overlapping with some place darker, older.

Asvarr lurched forward, breaking contact with the entity. Three steps took him to the river's edge. Its surface parted at his approach, forming a narrow causeway across the flow of memories. Impossible by natural law, but nothing here obeyed Midgard's rules.

He strode across before the way could close, feeling the liquid memories lapping at the causeway's edges. They called to him in voices both familiar and strange, promising answers, threatening revelations.

Halfway across, a hand burst from the river—pale, translucent, desperate. It clutched at Asvarr's ankle, pulling with surprising strength. His boot slipped on the liquid surface.

The marks on his chest flared, molten-hot. A pulse of energy radiated outward, breaking the hand's grip. The entity beneath the surface shrieked, a sound like metal tearing, before vanishing back into the flow.

Three more strides brought Asvarr to the far bank. Modgud waited, still as death itself.

"You walk between," she said, without moving. Her voice emerged from the shadows beneath her hood, neither male nor female but something unconcerned with such distinctions. "Neither living nor dead. Neither Tree nor Shadow."

"I seek the Root Below Niflheim," Asvarr replied.

"All seek what lies below." Modgud's hand moved to her sword hilt. "Few deserve to find it."

"I bear the Grímmark. I am Warden of four anchors, bound for the fifth."

"Show me."

Asvarr pulled aside his cloak and tunic, revealing the merged marks that now spread across his chest—tree, flame, and frost patterns intermingling in a configuration that had never existed before his binding journey.

Modgud studied them in silence, her face still hidden in shadow. Then she drew her blade with a sound like time unraveling.

"The Ashfather's Reaver came before you," she said. "Bearing a mask of carved wood and eyes of metal. It sought passage to what lies below, but could not pay the toll."

"What toll?"

"Truth." Modgud raised her impossibly thin blade. "Those who would reach the Root must first pass through me. And to pass through me, you must speak truth, even you do not know."

The sword moved with liquid grace, its edge stopping a hair's breadth from Asvarr's throat. Despite its nearness, he felt no fear—something told him the blade could not harm his physical form, only whatever lay beneath.

"What am I?" he asked.

"A vessel." The sword pressed slightly closer. "A Warden."

"For what purpose?"

"To bind what broke. To wake what sleeps. To continue what was, or change what will be."

The blade began to glow with pale blue light, illuminating Modgud's face beneath the hood—or what passed for a face. Where features should have been, only smooth, blank flesh existed, broken by a single vertical line where a mouth might open.

"Speak truth, Vessel," Modgud commanded. "What sleeps at the pattern's heart?"

Asvarr's mind raced. What did he know? What had his journey revealed? Fragments of understanding collided—Brenna's warnings, Sigrdrífa's revelations, Angrboda's riddles.

"The Dreamer," he said finally, the answer rising from some place beyond conscious thought. "The one who dreams the worlds into being."

"And what happens when the Dreamer wakes?"

"Everything changes. Or everything ends." Asvarr met the blank gaze without flinching. "I don't know which."

"Truth." Modgud's sword withdrew slightly. "Final question. When you stand before the Root, what will you choose—continuation, substitution, or transformation?"

The question struck at the core of his journey. Continuation—the Tree's path, binding the anchors as those before him had done, becoming a vessel for what waited at the pattern's heart. Substitution—the Ashfather's path, redirecting the pattern's power to himself instead of the Dreamer. Transformation—the mysterious third path his merged marks suggested.

"I don't know," Asvarr answered honestly. "I've lost the certainty of my path."

Modgud's blade lowered. "The truest answer of all." The vertical line split, revealing darkness within darkness. "Pass, Warden. The Root awaits below."

The ground beneath Asvarr's feet dissolved. He fell through darkness that felt solid against his skin, like plunging through layers of frozen soil. The death-runes on his arm blazed with cold fire, guiding his descent. The tokens of his previous bindings—horn, disk, key, crystal—grew heavy at his belt, pulling him downward.

He landed in a vast cavern unlike anything he'd seen before. Its ceiling vanished into the darkness above, while its walls curved inward like the inside of a massive bowl. The floor beneath his feet was neither stone nor soil but something organic—the surface of a root larger than any tree should possess.

The Root Below Niflheim.

It stretched across the entire cavern, its ancient bark the color of dried blood, its texture like petrified flesh. Smaller tendrils extended from its mass, reaching toward the walls, the ceiling, winding through the air itself as if grasping for something just beyond reach.

At the cavern's center, the Root swelled into a massive knot the size of a longhouse. There, it pulsed with visible energy, golden sap oozing from cracks in its surface to pool on the floor below. The scent filled the air—sweet, metallic, ancient. The same essence that had marked Asvarr when Yggdrasil first shattered.

But unlike the previous anchors, this Root fragment radiated awareness. It knew he had come. It watched him approach with senses beyond sight.

As he drew nearer to the central knot, the cavern's shadows shifted. Figures emerged from the darkness—spectral yet distinct, more solid than the wandering dead he'd passed on the plain above. Hundreds of them lined his path, watching in silence.

"Previous seekers," a voice spoke from the nearest. The spirit's face held more detail than the others—a man with a beard threaded with gold, eyes the color of amber, a half-formed rune on his cheek. "Those who sought the Root but failed its test."

"And you?" Asvarr asked. "Did you fail as well?"

"I am Jormun, first Warden of the third breaking. I bound four anchors before the Root rejected me." The spirit's hand raised, pointing to the central knot. "It found me unworthy."

"Why?"

"I sought power, not purpose. I came for what the Root could give me, not what I could give it." Jormun's translucent form flickered. "The dead Root is the most alive of all five anchors. It judges. It chooses."

"What will it ask of me?"

"The truth you hide, even from yourself." Jormun's form began to fade. "What you fear most at the journey's end."

The spirit vanished, along with all the others lining the path. Asvarr stood alone before the pulsing knot, its golden sap bubbling from widening cracks.

He approached cautiously, each step vibrating through the living wood beneath his feet. The death-runes on his arm burned cold enough to numb his flesh, while the marks on his chest flared with competing heat. Together, they created a balance, a tension between hot and cold.

At arm's length from the knot, Asvarr stopped. The golden sap had formed a pool at its base, rippling with an inner light. Unlike the sap he'd encountered at the first anchor, this liquid moved with purpose, forming patterns that rose and fell like breathing.

"I am Asvarr," he spoke to the Root. "Warden of four anchors. I've come to bind the fifth."

The sap surged upward, forming a column that twisted into a vaguely humanoid shape. It spoke without mouth or voice, its words appearing directly in Asvarr's mind.

You come marked by Tree and Flame and Frost. You walk the third path. You seek transformation where others sought continuation or substitution.

"I seek to complete what I began," Asvarr replied. "To bind what broke."

To what purpose? That the Dreamer may wake? That you may take its place? That the dream may change?

The golden figure flowed closer, its substance rippling with shifting faces—some he recognized from his journey, others unknown to him.

Four sacrifices made. Rage surrendered at the first binding. Memory given at the second. Identity transformed at the third. Certainty abandoned at the fourth.

The figure circled Asvarr, studying him from all angles.

What remains to be sacrificed? What piece of yourself do you still value above all else?

Asvarr considered the question. What did he still possess that held meaning? Not his rage—that had gone at the first binding. Not his memories of becoming a berserker—surrendered at Hvergelmir. Not his human identity—transformed at the root anchor. Not his certainty of purpose—given up at Helgrindr.

What remained?

The answer came with sudden clarity.

"My free will," he said. "My choice in what I become."

The golden figure paused, its substance rippling with what might have been surprise.

You would surrender the very thing that makes your path unique? The power to choose transformation over continuation or substitution?

"If that's the price of binding the final anchor, yes."

The figure flowed backward, merging once more with the pool of sap at the knot's base.

Then come, Warden. Touch the Root. Complete what broke. But know this—what you surrender may not be what you expect. The dead remember differently than the living.

Asvarr stepped forward, extending his hand toward the Root's surface. The death-runes on his arm flared in warning, sending jolts of cold pain up his spine. The marks on his chest burned hot enough to singe his clothing. His tokens—horn, disk, key, crystal—vibrated at his belt, resonating with the Root's energy.

His palm pressed against the ancient bark.

Connection.

The Root's consciousness flooded into him—vast, ancient, aware in ways that transcended Midgard's understanding of life. It had existed before Yggdrasil, before the nine realms, before gods or humans. It remembered the time when only ice and fire existed, when the void Ginnungagap stretched between them.

***

It remembered the Dreamer.

Asvarr gasped as knowledge poured through him—truths too large for human comprehension. The Dreamer had created Yggdrasil as a vessel for its consciousness, a way to experience the worlds it dreamed into being. The Tree had grown, expanded, connected realms across realities. But the Dreamer had begun to lose itself in the vastness of creation.

The Norns—aspects of the Dreamer's own consciousness—had cut the threads of fate to wake their creator from endless dreaming. They had shattered Yggdrasil, breaking the pattern.

But the breaking had consequences they hadn't foreseen. The Dreamer's consciousness had shattered with the Tree, fragmented across the anchors. Each binding reunited a piece of that fractured awareness, bringing the Dreamer closer to wholeness.

And the Ashfather—the first to bind all five anchors—had attempted to subsume the Dreamer's power rather than restore it. He had failed, but not completely. He had emerged changed, godlike yet broken, trapped between states.

Now, the cycle repeated. Again, the Tree had shattered. Again, Wardens were marked to bind the anchors. Again, the Dreamer's scattered consciousness sought reunification.

But this time, something had changed. The flame-rune merged with the Grímmark offered a new possibility—neither continuation nor substitution, but transformation. A way for the Dreamer to wake without ending the dream or replacing the dreamer.

The choice lay before Asvarr. Three paths. Three possible futures.

Bind the anchor conventionally and continue the cycle, becoming a vessel for the Dreamer's reawakening.

Bind it as the Ashfather had attempted, redirecting the pattern's power to himself.

Or find the third path—transformation—though its outcome remained unknown even to the Root.

Your sacrifice, the Root reminded him. *Your free will. Your choice.*

"I choose—" Asvarr began.

No. You surrender choice itself. That is the sacrifice.

Understanding dawned. To give up his free will didn't mean choosing one path. It meant surrendering the ability to choose altogether.

"Then how is the binding completed?" he asked. "If not through my choice?"

Through truth. Through what you are, not what you decide.

The Root's bark split beneath Asvarr's palm. Golden sap flowed over his hand, his arm, spreading across his body in rivulets that sought the marks on his chest. Where it touched the merged patterns, they flared with painful intensity.

Your true nature will determine the binding's form. Tree or Flame or Frost—or something new born from their merger. The path will choose you, not you the path.

The sap covered Asvarr completely now, a second skin of living gold that pulsed with the Root's heartbeat. It sank into his flesh, his blood, his bones, merging with his essence. Power, unlike anything he'd experienced at the previous bindings, surged through him—raw, unfiltered connection to the pattern itself.

He saw the five anchors simultaneously—root, branch, seed, frost, and death. He perceived the pattern they formed across the Nine Realms, the connections between them pulsing with the Dreamer's fragmented consciousness. With this binding, those fragments would reunite, the pattern would complete, and the Dreamer would—

What? Wake? Transform? Consume him entirely?

The sacrifice of choice meant he would never know what he had chosen until after it manifested.

The Root's awareness pressed deeper, searching for his true nature beneath conscious thought. What was he? Continuation, substitution, or transformation? Which path would his essence choose when choice itself was surrendered?

Pain exploded through Asvarr's body as the binding accelerated, the Root's ancient power flooding every fiber of his being. The death-runes on his arm turned from black to gold, then sank beneath his skin entirely. The marks on his chest expanded, covering him completely in patterns of tree, flame, and frost that swirled together into something new.

With a sound like the world breaking, the binding was completed.

Asvarr fell to his knees on the Root's surface, gasping for breath. Golden light surged from his skin, illuminating the entire cavern in a brief, blinding radiance. When it faded, his body had changed.

The marks no longer showed on his skin. They had moved deeper, becoming a part of his very structure. His flesh felt different, something between fully solid and ephemeral. Through new senses, he perceived the Nine Realms simultaneously—Midgard, Asgard, Jotunheim, Vanaheim, Alfheim, Svartalfheim, Helheim, Niflheim, Muspelheim—all connected by the World Tree's remnants.

And at the pattern's heart, he sensed the Dreamer stirring.

All five anchors bound. The pattern complete. The fragments reunited.

From the Root's knot emerged a final token—a crown woven from ancient wood, golden sap, and something that resembled solidified smoke. It floated before him, waiting to be claimed.

Asvarr reached for it with hands that glowed from within, no longer fully human. The crown settled on his brow, its weight both substantial and immaterial. With its touch came understanding—partial, fragmented, but clearer than before.

The third path had chosen him. Neither continuation nor substitution, but transformation. The Dreamer would wake, but not as it had been. The pattern would complete, but not as before.

He had become the Warden of Five, the bridge between broken and whole, the vessel for what would come next.

Rising to his feet, Asvarr felt the Root Below Niflheim responding to his transformed presence. The cavern shook, ancient dust falling from above. The binding had consequences beyond his understanding, changes rippling outward across all Nine Realms.

A crack appeared in the cavern's ceiling, widening to reveal the twilight sky of Helheim above. Through it, a beam of true sunlight pierced the eternal dusk—impossible by all natural laws, yet happening nonetheless.

The path back to Midgard lay open before him, his transformation granting passage between realms without need for death-runes or forgotten ways.

Asvarr looked down at his changed self once more, wondering what he had become—and what awaited at the pattern's completion. He had surrendered choice itself to bind the final anchor, placing his fate in the hands of his true nature. The third path had claimed him.

Now crowned and transformed, he would face what came next—the awakening of what slept at the pattern's heart, and the fulfillment of the Skyrend Prophecy.

CHAPTER 12
FANGS IN THE FOG

The world shifted around Asvarr in disjointed fragments. He braced against the chill stone of a waypoint chamber, knuckles white as they gripped the edge of a worn stone altar. His chest heaved, lungs burning as if he'd run for days. The fifth binding—and the crown it birthed—had changed him. The way he perceived the realms, not only his flesh.

He saw too much. Everything. All at once.

Motes of light swirled where the chamber walls should end, but instead opened to impossible glimpses: warriors clashing on frost-dusted peaks; a woman with amber eyes cradling a sapling; shadow-hunters racing across a moonlit sea. The weight of five anchors pulled his consciousness in as many directions.

Asvarr squeezed his eyes shut, grinding his teeth until his jaw ached. Beneath his ribs, his heart hammered a frantic rhythm—one, two, three, four, five—the pulse of the bound anchors.

"Control it," he growled to himself. "Chain it, or drown."

The crown sat heavy on his brow, woven of wood and roots, tangled with memory and darkness. He dared not remove it, knowing instinctively that it alone kept him from fragmenting across the Nine Realms. Through sheer force of will, he forced the torrent of perceptions back until he could feel solid stone beneath his knees.

When he finally opened his eyes, the waypoint chamber came into focus: nine black pillars surrounding a central altar, runes carved into each that pulsed with different-colored light. On the stone floor, a spiraling pattern of inlaid silver caught his reflection. The face staring back was both his and not. His features remained, but thin tendrils of gold, like hardened sap, traced paths from his temples down his jawline. The Grímmark no longer stayed confined to his chest—it had spread, the patterns swirling beneath his skin like living ink.

"So, this is what becoming myth feels like," he muttered, voice rougher than before, resonating oddly in the chamber.

Asvarr fumbled at his belt, where the tokens hung in a row: horn, ivory disk, remembrance-key, frost crystal, and now the crown upon his head. Five anchors bound. Five sacrifices made. Five pieces of himself surrendered to the pattern.

Motion caught his eye—something dark shifted in the chamber's corner. He yanked his bronze sword free, the blade singing with all the voices of the bound anchors.

"Show yourself," he commanded, the words carrying the weight of five realms.

Fog curled through cracks in the chamber walls, unnaturally thick and threaded with shadow. It pooled on the stone floor, writhing as though alive. From its depths emerged a figure, man-shaped but wrong—limbs too long, joints moving at impossible angles.

"Warden of Five," it rasped, the sound scraping against Asvarr's ears like bone on stone. "The Ashfather sends his... congratulations."

The fog-being slithered forward, its form billowing and contracting. Eyes formed in the vapor—dozens of them, blinking in unison.

"He did not think you would complete all bindings and yet retain... coherence. Most interesting."

Asvarr leveled his sword at the creature, the blade's edge glowing golden. "I've had my fill of servants and messengers. Tell your master if he wishes to speak, he can come himself."

The fog-being rippled with what might have been laughter.

"He prepares for your meeting even now, Skyrend's Flame. But first, a gift."

It extended a limb that thinned into vapor, depositing a small object on the altar between them. A bone whistle, yellowed with age, curved like a talon.

"For the pattern is complete, but the dreamer still slumbers. To wake, it requires... music."

Asvarr narrowed his eyes. "Why would the Ashfather help wake the dreamer? He seeks to replace it, not serve it."

"Perhaps he sees in you... possibility. A third path, as your flame-mark whispers." The fog-being's many eyes blinked in sequence. "Or perhaps this gift ensures you and the dreamer destroy each other, leaving him to claim what remains."

Asvarr circled the altar, keeping his sword between himself and the creature. The chamber felt wrong now, the runes on the pillars flickering erratically. Something was interfering with the waypoint's magic.

"And if I refuse your gift?"

The fog swirled faster. "Then you have bound five anchors to no purpose. The pattern remains incomplete, the dreamer sleeps on, and the realms continue their slow unraveling." Its form contracted, becoming more distinct, almost human. "You have sacrificed much, Warden. Would you now make those sacrifices meaningless?"

Asvarr tasted metal on his tongue—a warning from the marks, reacting to danger or deceit. Yet, there was truth in the creature's words, too.

"I'll take your gift," he said finally. "But know this—I walk the third path now. Neither Tree nor Shadow will claim what I've become."

The fog-being's mouth split in a too-wide smile. "We shall see, Warden of Five. We shall see."

Asvarr reached for the bone whistle, hesitating just above it. Through his mark-enhanced senses, he saw threads of power woven into the bone—old magic, death-magic, from before the Tree.

As his fingers closed around it, the fog suddenly thickened, billowing outward. The chamber's runes flared brightly, then died, plunging the room into darkness.

"The gift has another purpose," the creature whispered, now sounding as if it spoke from all directions at once. "To bring you where you are needed."

The floor beneath Asvarr dissolved into more fog—thick, choking vapor that filled his lungs and blinded his eyes. He fell, or perhaps the world fell away from him, his sword still clutched in one hand, the bone whistle in the other.

He tumbled through layers of reality, glimpsing fragments of the Nine Realms as he passed through them. A great hall where giants feasted on mountain-sized beasts. A burning plain where shadow-wraiths danced around pillars of black flame. A frozen sea beneath three blood-red moons.

Then, impact—hard, cold earth beneath him. The fog retreated enough for Asvarr to see he had landed in a forest clearing, though like no forest in Midgard. The trees towered hundreds of feet overhead, their trunks wider than longhouses. Their bark gleamed with patterns reminiscent of the runestones, glowing faintly in the dim light. Above, no sky was visible—only more fog, thick and swirling.

Asvarr struggled to his feet, body aching from the fall. The clearing was perfectly circular, as if carved by design. At its center stood a stone table, ancient and worn smooth by time. Carved into its surface was a map—nine interlocking circles, with a tenth at their center.

"The paths between worlds," came a voice, silvery and cold.

Asvarr whirled, raising his sword.

A woman stood at the clearing's edge, or something shaped like a woman. Her skin shimmered with a pearlescent gleam, her hair a cascade of liquid silver. Her eyes held no pupils—only swirling fog captured within human form.

"The Mist-Queen," Asvarr breathed, recognizing her from visions glimpsed during the fifth binding.

She inclined her head, the movement fluid as water. "Once, I had another name, when the worlds were young. Now I am as you see me—guardian of the mist, keeper of paths."

"Where am I?" Asvarr demanded, moving into a defensive stance. The crown on his brow hummed, responding to this realm's strange energies.

"Niflheim's heart," she answered. "Where the first fog was born, where the dreamer first stirred."

"Why am I here?"

The Mist-Queen glided forward, her feet never quite touching the ground. "Because the pattern is complete, but the song is unfinished. Five anchors bound, five sacrifices made, but the dreamer needs a voice." She gestured to the bone whistle still clutched in his hand. "You bear the instrument. Will you play the awakening?"

Asvarr studied the bone whistle more carefully. Small runes, nearly invisible, spiraled along its length. "This is the Ashfather's doing. Why would I help him?"

"The Ashfather did not craft the whistle. It existed before him, before the Tree, shaped from the first being to die in all creation." She moved to the stone table, running translucent fingers over the carved map. "He merely returned what was hidden. The choice to play remains yours."

The fog began swirling faster around the clearing, thickening until the massive trees were barely visible shadows. Within the mist, shapes formed—fanged maws, clawed hands, eyes gleaming with hunger.

"What are those?" Asvarr asked, though he already knew.

"The fog-born," the Mist-Queen replied. "My children, in a manner of speaking. Created from the dreams the sleeping one rejects."

A low growl rippled through the fog, followed by another, then dozens more. The shapes pressed closer, becoming more defined with each passing moment.

"They hunger for what you carry," she continued. "Five anchors' worth of power and memory. If you will not wake the dreamer, they will take your gifts for themselves."

The first of the fog-creatures lunged into the clearing—wolf-shaped but wrong, its legs too many, its fangs dripping vapor instead of saliva. Asvarr's sword sliced through it, the blade singing with five distinct tones. The creature dissolved back into mist, but two more immediately took its place.

"I didn't come here to fight an endless horde," Asvarr shouted, cutting down another beast. "Nor to be manipulated by you or the Ashfather."

"Yet here you stand," the Mist-Queen said, unmoved by the battle unfolding before her. "Warden of Five, at the crossroads of creation. Will you play the awakening and face the dreamer's judgment? Or will you fall here, feeding my children until another Warden rises in some future cycle?"

More fog-beasts poured into the clearing—some like wolves, others resembling bears or lynxes, all twisted with too many limbs or eyes, or mouths. Asvarr fought mechanically, the five anchor marks guiding his movements with memories of battles fought across countless cycles.

"If I play this whistle," he panted between strikes, "what happens to the realms?"

The Mist-Queen's expression changed for the first time, something like surprise crossing her featureless face. "You still care for them? After all they've taken from you?"

"Answer me!"

She gestured broadly. "The dreamer wakes. The cycle either renews or ends, depending on its judgment. The realms either continue in a new pattern or dissolve back into the primordial mist." Her voice softened. "I cannot tell you which. The dreamer's will is its own."

A massive fog-beast, larger than the others, crashed into the clearing. Its form resembled a giant wolf with nine heads, each bearing a different expression—rage, hunger, cunning, fear.

Asvarr knew he couldn't fight them all. Not here, in their domain, where each defeated beast simply reformed from the surrounding mist.

He backed toward the stone table, sword still raised, the bone whistle clutched tight in his left hand. The five tokens at his belt hummed in harmony, resonating with the crown upon his brow.

The ninth head of the great beast spoke, its voice like grinding stone: "The whistle or your life, Warden. Choose."

In that moment, Asvarr saw with perfect clarity. Throughout his journey, he had been pulled between Tree and Shadow, neither fully controlling his fate but both attempting to. The third path—transformation—now lay before him.

He raised the bone whistle to his lips.

"I choose my own path," he declared, "and wake the dreamer on my terms."

With that, he blew a single, piercing note that cut through the fog like lightning through storm clouds.

***

The whistle's note pierced the fabric of the world.

Asvarr felt it ripple through his flesh, through the five marks that now spread across his body. The sound contained no melody, only pure intention—a calling that transcended language. The fog creatures froze mid-lunge, their many eyes widening in unified terror. Even the massive nine-headed wolf retreated, its form dissolving back into the mist.

Only the Mist-Queen remained unmoved, her featureless face watching Asvarr with something approaching curiosity.

"So you have chosen," she said, her voice suddenly distant as the whistle's note continued to resonate through the clearing.

The carved map on the stone table began to glow, each of the nine circles illuminating in sequence. The tenth circle at the center remained dark until the note from the whistle reached its highest pitch—then it blazed with golden light so intense that Asvarr had to shield his eyes.

The ground beneath his feet trembled. The massive trees surrounding the clearing swayed and groaned like living things waking from a deep slumber. Asvarr maintained his stance, refusing to stumble despite the earth's protests.

"What happens now?" he demanded, still gripping his sword.

The Mist-Queen's form wavered, her edges blurring into the surrounding fog. "The dreamer stirs. You summoned it, Warden. Now you must face it."

The golden light from the stone table shot upward in a pillar that tore through the fog ceiling, revealing a starless void above. The light separated into hundreds of golden threads, each seeking a different direction. Five of the threads—thicker and brighter than the others—connected to the five tokens Asvarr carried. The crown on his head grew hot, nearly burning his skin.

"These are the threads of connection," the Mist-Queen explained, her voice fading further with each word. "The pattern by which all realms are bound."

A deep rumbling shook the clearing, and the fog surrounding them retreated like a tide pulled by some unseen force. The forest beyond became visible—endless, gigantic trees spreading in all directions, their bark inscribed with glowing runes that pulsed in rhythm with Asvarr's heartbeat.

In the newly revealed space, something moved as if the forest itself was merely a projection on water, and something vast swam beneath its surface.

Asvarr readied his sword, though instinct told him it would prove useless against what approached. "Show yourself!" he commanded, the words carrying the authority of five anchors.

The air before him shimmered and tore. Through the rift stepped a figure both familiar and impossible—a child no more than eight winters old, with skin like polished amber and eyes that contained galaxies. It wore simple clothing of undyed wool, yet the fabric seemed to shift and change with each movement, revealing glimpses of stars and void beneath.

"Warden of Five," the child spoke, its voice layering over itself in countless echoes. "You have walked all paths to reach this place."

Asvarr held his ground despite the pressure radiating from the being before him—pressure that threatened to unmake his newly transformed body. "Are you the dreamer?"

The child smiled, revealing teeth made of pure light. "I am its voice. Its hand. Its intention given form, that you might comprehend."

"And what does the dreamer want?" Asvarr kept his tone level, fighting against the instinct to kneel before this creature.

"To understand why you have broken the pattern." The child circled him, examining Asvarr from all angles with ancient eyes. "Five anchors bound, yet you remain... yourself. This has never happened before."

"I chose a third path. Transformation, not continuation or substitution."

"Yes." The child nodded, stopping directly before him. "The flame-mark. The sacrifice of certainty. The crown worn by choice. You have done what no Warden has done through nine cycles of breaking and binding."

The golden threads connecting to Asvarr's tokens pulsed brighter, and he felt something pulling at him, something deeper than his physical form. The dreamer was examining his choices, his sacrifices, his very essence.

"The Ashfather believes I will help him replace you," Asvarr said, staring directly into those galaxy-filled eyes. "The Tree expects me to restore the pattern as it was. Neither understands what I've become."

The child's expression grew serious, ancient wisdom shadowing its youthful features. "And what have you become, Asvarr Skyrend's Flame?"

The use of his name—his true name—sent shock waves through his transformed flesh. The marks beneath his skin flared in response.

"Something new," he answered honestly. "Neither servant nor enemy to what sleeps at the pattern's heart. I am Warden of Five, but I will not be used by powers that care nothing for the realms or those who dwell within them."

The child studied him for a long moment, then reached out with one small hand to touch the crown on Asvarr's brow. The contact sent visions cascading through his mind—the birth of stars, the death of gods, the slow unfolding of reality across endless cycles.

"The Ashfather once stood where you stand," the child said softly. "He too sought a third path, but when he gazed upon the dreamer's true form, he chose fear. He chose power. He chose to replace rather than transform."

Asvarr saw it then—the Ashfather's journey through five bindings, his transformation, his final confrontation with the dreamer. Unlike Asvarr, he had sought to consume the dreamer's power, to place himself at the pattern's center.

"And now he waits," Asvarr realized aloud. "Waits for me to either fail or succeed, only to claim what follows."

"Yes." The child withdrew its hand. "This is why he sent the whistle. If you fail, he claims the anchors. If you succeed, he will strike when the dreamer is most vulnerable—during the moment of awakening."

The rumbling beneath their feet intensified. Cracks appeared in the earth, golden light spilling from beneath. The massive trees uprooted themselves, revealing that their trunks extended infinitely downward, merging with the golden light below.

"The dreamer awakens, regardless of choice now," the child said urgently. "The five bindings have set it in motion. You must decide, Warden—will you complete the pattern as it was designed? Will you surrender the five sacrifices and allow the dreamer to consume them? Or will you attempt what the Ashfather could not?"

Asvarr felt the five marks burning beneath his skin, each representing what he had surrendered: rage, memory, identity, certainty, and finally, free will. Yet here he stood, still making choices despite that final sacrifice. He had not given up his will entirely—he had transformed it into something beyond simple choice.

"I will remake the pattern," he declared. "Not as a servant, or as a usurper, but as equals." He placed his sword on the stone table, the blade still humming with the voices of five anchors. "The dreamer seeks experience through the realms. The Tree seeks order. The Ashfather seeks control. I seek balance between them all."

***

The child's galaxy eyes widened. "You would stand as mediator between primordial forces? No mortal has ever—"

"I am no longer merely mortal," Asvarr interrupted, the words coming from a place of absolute truth. "You know this. The dreamer knows this. Five anchors have changed me into something new."

The ground split wide beneath them. The stone table collapsed into the growing chasm, and the golden light erupted upward like a geyser. The child dissolved into particles of light, its form merging with the rising power.

"Then prepare yourself, Warden of Five," the child's voice called out, now coming from everywhere at once. "The dreamer comes to judge your worthiness. If you would remake the pattern, you must first survive its awakening."

The forest disappeared entirely, replaced by an endless sea of golden light. Asvarr floated in its midst, still clutching the bone whistle in one hand. His tokens burned against his skin—horn, ivory disk, remembrance-key, frost crystal, and the crown still on his brow.

From the depths of the golden sea rose a presence so vast that Asvarr's transformed mind could barely comprehend it. Not a shape or form, but It was pure consciousness—ancient beyond measure, curious, and coldly analytical.

The dreamer had no eyes, yet Asvarr felt its gaze upon him, examining every sacrifice, every choice that had led him to this moment.

YOU WISH TO TRANSFORM THE PATTERN. The thought crashed into Asvarr's mind with the force of a mountain falling. *WHY?*

Asvarr faced the presence directly, drawing on the strength of five anchors. "Because the current cycle serves no one. The Tree grows, breaks, and is rebound, while the realms suffer. The pattern needs evolution, not repetition."

AND YOU WOULD GUIDE THIS EVOLUTION? Skepticism colored the dreamer's thoughts, yet also interest. *A MORTAL-BORN CREATURE PRESUMING TO RESHAPE CREATION?*

"I was mortal-born," Asvarr agreed, "but the anchors have changed me. And I have lived nine lifetimes of memories through the bindings. I have seen what works and what fails." He spread his arms wide, letting the golden light flow through him. "I don't seek to control the pattern—only to improve it."

The dreamer's presence drew closer, its attention narrowing to focus solely on Asvarr. The pressure of its regard threatened to unmake him molecule by molecule.

SHOW ME YOUR VISION, WARDEN OF FIVE. SHOW ME WHAT YOU WOULD CREATE.

Asvarr closed his eyes and did something no previous Warden had attempted—he reached out with his transformed consciousness and touched the dreamer's mind directly. Not to control or consume, but to share.

He showed the dreamer his vision of a pattern where Tree and Shadow existed in balance, rather than opposition. Where the realms could evolve without breaking. Where the dreamer itself could experience its creation without cycles of destruction.

The golden sea around him churned violently in response. For endless moments, Asvarr felt himself being unmade and remade, his essence examined down to its most fundamental components.

Then, impossibly, the dreamer responded with understanding, not words or thoughts. Asvarr felt it considering his vision, weighing possibilities against eternities of existence.

INTERESTING. DIFFERENT. DANGEROUS.

"Necessary," Asvarr countered.

The golden light condensed around him, wrapping him in layers of power. The dreamer's attention shifted, suddenly alert to something beyond their interaction.

THE ASHFATHER APPROACHES. HE SENSES MY AWAKENING.

***

Asvarr felt it too—a shadow spreading across the golden sea, a presence of immense power fueled by consumed gods and stolen fate. The Ashfather had waited for this moment, when both Asvarr and the dreamer would be vulnerable.

"Let me face him," Asvarr said. "Test my vision against his."

The dreamer's consideration washed over him, and Asvarr sensed it making a decision unlike any in previous cycles.

VERY WELL, WARDEN OF FIVE. SHOW ME THE STRENGTH OF YOUR THIRD PATH.

The golden sea parted, revealing a rift in reality through which Asvarr could see a familiar figure approaching—tall, one-eyed, bearing a spear of shadow and wearing a crown of broken branches. The Ashfather, coming to claim what he believed was rightfully his.

The dreamer's power flowed into Asvarr's transformed body, filling him with strength beyond anything he had known. The five tokens blazed with renewed purpose, and the marks beneath his skin aligned into a unified pattern—neither Tree nor Shadow, but something entirely new.

"I accept your test," Asvarr declared, rising to meet the approaching shadow. The bone whistle transformed in his hand, elongating into a staff etched with the combined patterns of all five anchors. His sword flew up from the collapsed table, reforging itself in midair before returning to his grip.

As the Ashfather stepped through the rift between worlds, his single eye widened at the sight of Asvarr transformed. Recognition and hatred flashed across his ancient features.

"So," the Ashfather growled, his voice like grinding mountains, "another Warden thinks to claim my rightful place."

Asvarr leveled his reforged sword at the god-like entity. "No, Ashfather. I come to offer something you never considered—a new pattern of transformation."

The Ashfather's laughter shook the very fabric of the realm as he raised his spear of shadow. "Then let us see whose vision is stronger, Warden of Five. Let us see who truly deserves to stand at the pattern's heart."

Behind Asvarr, the dreamer watched with ancient curiosity. Before him, the Ashfather prepared for battle, his form swelling with stolen power. And within him, five anchors hummed in perfect harmony, ready for the true test of the third path.

CHAPTER 13

THE SPEAR-MARKED STRANGER

Golden light faded from Asvarr's vision as reality reassembled itself around him. The sea of the dreamer's consciousness receded, leaving him sprawled on frost-crusted grass. His lungs burned with each breath, and the crown upon his brow felt heavier than a mountain. The staff that had been the bone whistle lay beside him, its runes pulsing weakly in the dim light.

Above him stretched a bruised sky, wounds of purple and crimson gashing the fading daylight. He pushed himself up on trembling arms, his transformed body aching in ways he couldn't have imagined before the bindings. The five marks beneath his skin churned like living things, redistributing themselves across his flesh.

"I'm... back in Midgard," he rasped, tasting blood on his tongue.

Frost crackled under his palm as he forced himself to stand. The confrontation with the Ashfather—had it happened? Or had the dreamer merely shown him what was to come? His memory fragmented, pieces of the encounter sliding away like ice on a warming pond.

A raven's harsh call pulled his attention upward. Three black shapes circled overhead, their wings catching the last copper light of day. One peeled away, swooping low over a ridge to the north. A sign, or simple animal behavior? After five bindings, Asvarr no longer believed in coincidence.

He gathered his transformed sword and staff, their weight reassuring despite his confusion. The five tokens at his belt hummed with subdued power—the horn, ivory disk, remembrance-key, frost crystal, and the crown he now wore. Together, they anchored him to this reality when his transformed consciousness threatened to drift into others.

Asvarr surveyed his surroundings. He stood in a clearing atop a hill, surrounded by wind-sculpted pines heavy with snow. In the valley below, smoke rose from what might be a settlement. The land felt familiar yet wrong—Midgard, but changed by his absence or by his perception.

"How long was I gone?" he wondered aloud, troubled by how the light clung to the horizon as if reluctant to fade.

Movement caught his eye—a figure emerging from the treeline, walking with the measured pace of one who knows exactly where they're going. Tall and broad-shouldered, wearing a weather-beaten blue cloak that flapped against leather-armored legs. The stranger's face remained shadowed by a deep hood, but Asvarr noticed the spear clutched in one gloved hand—a simple weapon with a worn ash shaft and an iron head that gleamed unnaturally in the fading light.

Asvarr's marks flared in warning. He raised his sword, the blade singing with the voices of five anchors.

"Show yourself," he commanded, his voice carrying more power than it once had. "Friend or enemy, I'd see your face."

The hooded figure paused, then planted the spear butt in the snow. "Both and neither, Warden of Five." The voice was deep, resonant, with the cadence of one who chooses each word with deliberate care. "I come as witness, guide, and warning—though which you need most remains to be seen."

The stranger pushed back his hood, revealing a weathered face framed by silver-streaked dark hair and a beard shot through with gray. A leather patch covered his right eye, while the left fixed on Asvarr with unnerving intensity—gray as winter sky and just as cold.

"You," Asvarr breathed, recognition flooding his transformed senses. "The Ashfather."

A smile ghosted across the man's face. "I have worn many names across many cycles. Ashfather is what your kind calls me now." He leaned on his spear. "Though once, I answered to Warden."

Asvarr tightened his grip on his sword. "We fought. In the dreamer's realm."

"Did we?" The one-eyed man tilted his head. "Or was that a vision of what may come?" His single eye narrowed. "Time flows differently where the dreamer slumbers. What you experienced may be memory, prophecy, or something between."

"You sent the fog-being with the whistle," Asvarr said, circling slowly to maintain distance between them. "You manipulated events to wake the dreamer when it would be vulnerable."

The Ashfather's expression remained impassive. "And you blew the whistle despite knowing this. Interesting choice."

Asvarr felt the five anchors pulling at him, urging both attack and caution. The marks beneath his skin mapped connections between himself and this stranger—links of power, purpose, and shared fate.

"Why are you here?" Asvarr demanded. "If our battle is yet to come, why show yourself now?"

The Ashfather stabbed his spear into the frozen ground, where it stood upright, quivering slightly. A gesture of temporary peace.

"Because unlike the Tree, I offer choices." He spread his hands. "I have watched you, Skyrend's Flame. Through nine cycles of breaking and binding, no Warden has done what you have achieved—five anchors bound while maintaining your self."

"The third path," Asvarr said. "Transformation instead of continuation or substitution."

"Yes." The Ashfather's eye glinted with something like approval. "The path I once sought and failed to walk."

Snow began to fall between them, fat flakes that caught the last light like falling embers. The Ashfather reached out, catching one on his palm where it melted instantly.

"The dreamer stirs, Warden of Five. Soon it will fully wake, and the pattern will be remade." His voice dropped lower. "But who shall direct this remaking? The Tree, which seeks only endless repetition? The dreamer, which cares nothing for the realms it created? Or those who have walked the worlds and know their true value?"

Asvarr realized with sudden clarity that this was no ordinary encounter. The Ashfather—his enemy, his predecessor—had come to offer an alliance.

"You would have me join you," Asvarr said, disbelief coloring his words. "After sending creatures to hunt me, after manipulating my journey at every turn."

"I tested your worthiness," the Ashfather corrected. "As I was tested before you. The worthy survive. The worthy transform." He gestured at Asvarr's changed form. "Look at what you've become. No longer human, no longer bound by mortal limitations. You've sacrificed rage, memory, identity, certainty, and will—yet here you stand, still yourself despite it all."

A sharp pain lanced through Asvarr's temple, and fragments of memory crystallized—the child-form of the dreamer warning him of the Ashfather's deception.

"And what do you offer?" Asvarr asked, deliberately relaxing his stance while keeping his guard raised. "If I joined you, what then?"

The Ashfather's face came alive with sudden intensity. "A seat beside me at the pattern's heart. Together, we could reshape the Nine Realms as they should be—realms where mortals aren't playthings of capricious gods and ancient trees. Where strength and wisdom determine fate, not the whims of powers that care nothing for those they rule."

The offer resonated with something deep within Asvarr—the part of him that had raged against the unfairness of fate, that had questioned why good people died while monsters thrived. For a moment, he could see the appeal of the Ashfather's vision.

Then the crown on his brow grew cold, and clarity returned. This was the same temptation the Ashfather had succumbed to—the lure of control rather than balance.

"And the dreamer?" Asvarr asked. "What becomes of it in your vision?"

The Ashfather's expression hardened. "It sleeps again, permanently this time. Its power divided between us, its consciousness... repurposed."

"Consumed, you mean." Asvarr adjusted his grip on his sword. "You would have us become gods."

"We already are." The Ashfather gestured at the marks visible on Asvarr's skin. "What mortal bears five anchor-marks and lives? What mortal walks between realms as easily as crossing a threshold? The Tree has made us into something beyond humanity, Warden. I simply propose we use this gift to its fullest potential."

A raven cawed overhead, joined by its companions. The three birds circled lower, their black shapes stark against the darkening sky. The Ashfather glanced up, a flicker of annoyance crossing his features.

"We are watched," he said. "The Tree sends its spies."

"Or the dreamer does," Asvarr countered, remembering the child's galaxy eyes.

The Ashfather reclaimed his spear with a fluid motion. "Consider my offer, Warden of Five. When the dreamer fully wakes, three paths will lie before you—serve the Tree, serve yourself, or stand with me to create something better than both." He tapped the spear butt against the frozen ground. "I will await your answer at Ymir's Cradle, where the first Root fell."

"And if I choose against you?" Asvarr asked.

The Ashfather's smile held no warmth. "Then we shall meet as enemies, and only one shall stand when the dreamer renders judgment." He turned, cloak swirling around him. "Choose wisely, Warden. The future of nine realms rests on your decision."

Before Asvarr could respond, the Ashfather struck the ground with his spear. The impact sent a shockwave of power rippling outward, momentarily blinding Asvarr with its intensity. When his vision cleared, the one-eyed stranger was gone, leaving only a spear-shaped mark burned into the frost.

The ravens descended, landing in a semicircle around the mark. Their black eyes fixed on Asvarr with unnatural intelligence.

"I know you're not ordinary birds," Asvarr said, addressing them directly. "Speak your piece or leave me to my thoughts."

The largest raven cocked its head, then opened its beak. What emerged was not a bird's call but a woman's voice, distant yet clear.

"Warden of Five," it said, the sound emanating from somewhere beyond the bird itself. "The Spear-Marked One speaks honeyed lies. He would use you as he has used others across nine cycles of breaking."

Asvarr lowered himself to one knee, bringing himself closer to the ravens' level. "And who sends you to warn me? The Tree? The dreamer?"

The second raven spoke, its voice masculine and aged. "We serve the balance, Warden. We are the Memory-Keepers, those who remember what was before the first breaking."

"We have watched you," added the third, its voice childlike and eerie. "Five anchors bound, five sacrifices made, yet you remain. No Warden has achieved this before."

The first raven hopped forward. "The Ashfather offers power and control. The Tree offers restoration and repetition. But there is another path—the one you have already begun to walk."

"Transformation," Asvarr said. "A new pattern, neither continuation nor substitution."

"Yes." All three ravens spoke in unison, their voices layering into a harmonic chord. "But to complete this path, you must understand the Five Anchors and what truly binds them."

The largest raven fluttered onto a nearby rock, its eyes fixed on Asvarr. "Seek the Norn-stone in the valley below. There dwells one who walked with the first Warden, before the Ashfather claimed that title."

"She will show you truths hidden by both Tree and Shadow," added the second raven.

"But beware," the third finished, "for knowledge brings its own price. Are you prepared to pay it, Warden of Five?"

Asvarr studied the three birds, sensing more to them than mere messengers. "Who are you really?"

The ravens exchanged glances, then the largest responded: "We are what remains of the First Wardens—those who bound the original anchors before the Tree grew to connect the realms."

"How is that possible?" Asvarr asked, disbelief mingling with curiosity. "The Tree has existed since the beginning of the worlds."

"Has it?" The ravens' voices merged again. "Or is that merely what the Tree wishes you to believe?"

Before Asvarr could question further, the birds launched into flight, circling once overhead before winging toward the smoke rising from the valley.

Asvarr stood watching them until they disappeared into the gathering dusk. Two encounters, two warnings, two offers of guidance—the Ashfather with his talk of power and control, the ravens with their cryptic mention of an original Warden who preceded even the Ashfather.

The marks beneath his skin pulled him toward the valley, while the crown on his brow grew colder in the direction the Ashfather had indicated. Conflicting paths, exactly as the dreamer had shown him.

Asvarr placed his transformed sword in its sheath and gripped the staff that had been the bone whistle. The valley first, he decided. If the ravens spoke true, knowledge awaited him there—knowledge that might clarify his path forward.

As he began his descent, the spear-mark in the frost glowed faintly behind him. Asvarr felt its presence like an eye on his back, the Ashfather's silent reminder that time grew short, the dreamer stirred, and a decision must soon be made.

The rune-patterns beneath his skin shifted again, forming a new configuration across his chest and arms. No longer the Grímmark alone, nor even the merged patterns of his journey, but something evolving still—Asvarr's own mark, shaped by his choices rather than fate's design.

He touched the crown on his brow, feeling the connection to all five anchors humming through it. "Five roots torn free. Five anchors lost. Five wardens to find them. Five crowns to bear them." The prophecy Brenna had carved into his chest alongside the Grímmark now seemed both fulfilled and incomplete.

A new question formed in his mind as he entered the forest path leading to the valley: What if the prophecy didn't end with the finding and binding? What if that was merely the beginning?

The thought accompanied him as shadows lengthened and the distant smoke beckoned him forward, toward whatever revelations—or deceptions—awaited in the village below.

***

Shadows deepened between the frost-rimed pines as Asvarr descended the winding path toward the valley. The village lights flickered below—scattered pinpricks spread across the valley floor like fallen stars. His transformed senses registered each light as a distinct signature of heat and life, some brighter than others, some barely there at all.

The marks beneath his skin pulsed in rhythm with his steps, responding to hidden patterns in the land itself. Here, in Midgard, Asvarr felt rooted in physical reality. The cold air burned his lungs. The crunch of frozen undergrowth echoed in his ears. This remained the land of his birth, though his perception of it had changed.

He paused at a bend in the path, surveying the valley more carefully. What he had taken for a village revealed itself as something stranger—stone structures arranged in concentric rings, each housing a single light. At the center stood a larger building, dome-shaped and gleaming like polished bone in the fading twilight.

"The Norn-stone," he murmured, understanding that the entire site—not just a single rock—bore the name.

Movement flashed at the edge of his enhanced vision. Three black shapes—the ravens—circled the central dome before settling on its peak. Watching. Waiting. Beckoning.

Asvarr continued downward, his staff tapping rhythmically against the frozen earth. As he neared the first ring of structures, details emerged from the gathering darkness. Each building was a perfect circle, constructed of interlocking stones without mortar. Runes carved into their outer surfaces glowed with subdued power—angular and primitive patterns unlike those Asvarr had encountered on his journey.

No smoke rose from any of the structures despite the lights within. No sounds of habitation disturbed the winter silence. Asvarr's unease grew with each step deeper into the stone circles. He had visited many strange places since receiving the Grímmark, but this place carried a different weight—ancient beyond reckoning, yet somehow alive with watchful purpose.

He reached the innermost ring, finding a narrow path leading to the central dome. Before he could approach, a figure emerged from the nearest circular house—tall and gaunt, wrapped in layers of undyed wool and leather. The stranger's face remained hidden beneath a deep hood adorned with small bones and wooden beads that clacked together with each movement.

"Five marks upon the flesh," the figure said, voice rasping like dry leaves. "Five anchors bound to will. Five tokens carried. Yet still yourself." A hand emerged from the robes—skin pale as milk stretched over bones that seemed too delicate for a human frame. "Remarkable."

Asvarr kept his distance, hand resting on his sword hilt. "I seek the one who walked with the first Warden. The ravens sent me."

The hooded figure tilted their head, bones clacking. "Huginn, Muninn, and Gunnlöð. The rememberers." A wheeze that might have been a laugh escaped the hood. "Always meddling, those three. Always pushing pieces across the board."

"Are you the one I seek?" Asvarr asked directly.

"I am she who remembers the first breaking, when the Tree was young and the dreamer first stirred." The figure pulled back her hood, revealing a face ancient beyond measure—skin translucent and mapped with blue veins, eyes milky with cataracts yet somehow still seeing. White hair hung in thin strands adorned with more small bones and wooden talismans. "I am Gunnhild, Last-Watcher,

Dream-Singer. And you are Asvarr, who once called himself berserker but now bears the title Warden of Five."

The name struck Asvarr with physical force, reverberating through the marks on his skin. "How do you know me?"

Gunnhild smiled, revealing teeth worn down to stubs. "I know all who bear the marks, across all cycles of breaking and binding. I watched the Ashfather when he was merely Gautr, the spear-wielder. I watched the seven before him. I will watch those who come after, if any do." She gestured toward the central dome. "Come. The Norn-stone awakens for your presence. It has waited long to reveal its secrets."

Asvarr followed, keeping a careful distance. The dome loomed larger as they approached—curved segments of yellowed bone fitted together with impossible precision. No door or entrance was visible on its smooth surface.

"The Tree lies," Gunnhild said abruptly, her voice suddenly stronger. "The Ashfather lies. Even the dreamer, in its way, lies. All to maintain the cycle, to keep the wheels turning as they have for eons."

"What cycle?" Asvarr asked, though part of him already knew.

"Death and rebirth. Sleep and awakening." Gunnhild stopped before the bone dome, placing one gnarled hand against its surface. "The Tree arrived later, Warden. It exists as another manifestation of the pattern, just like the Ashfather, just like you."

The bone beneath her palm began to glow, lines of soft golden light spreading outward in spiraling patterns. The entire dome hummed with energy that resonated with the marks on Asvarr's skin.

"The dreamer came before the Tree," Gunnhild continued. "The void preceded the dreamer. And within the void, the first pattern formed—by chance, by the random collision of forces without name or purpose."

The spiraling lines connected, forming a door-shaped archway that sank inward, revealing a passage into the dome's interior. A cool blue light spilled from within, carrying the scent of ice and ancient stone.

"The original Wardens perceived the pattern naturally and worked to preserve it when the void threatened to reclaim all. Their binding of the anchors came through understanding." Her cataract eyes fixed on Asvarr. "Would you learn what they knew, Warden of Five? Would you see the truth that both Tree and Ashfather hide from you?"

Asvarr hesitated at the threshold. "You speak of the First Wardens as if you knew them personally. How is that possible?"

Gunnhild's thin lips curled into a smile. "Who says I didn't? Time flows differently for those who step outside the pattern."

She disappeared into the blue light, leaving Asvarr alone at the entrance. The five tokens at his belt vibrated with increasing intensity, resonating with whatever lay within. The crown on his brow grew warm, then cold, then warm again—conflicting energies battling within it.

Asvarr made his decision. Staff in one hand, the other resting on his sword hilt, he entered the bone dome.

***

Inside, the space expanded beyond what should have been possible. The domed ceiling arched high overhead, its inner surface etched with constellations unlike any in Midgard's sky. At the center stood a stone unlike any Asvarr had seen—a perfect cube of material that absorbed light rather than reflected it, hovering several feet above a circular pool of liquid too still to be water.

Gunnhild waited beside the floating stone, her frail form dwarfed by its massive presence. "The Norn-stone," she said simply. "Older than the Nine Realms. Older than the Tree. Perhaps older than the dreamer itself."

"What is it?" Asvarr approached cautiously, the five marks beneath his skin pulling him forward while his instincts urged retreat.

"A fragment of the original pattern," Gunnhild answered. "The template from which all else grew." She gestured to the stone with one bony hand. "Touch it, Warden. See what your predecessors saw."

Asvarr circled the pool, studying the hovering cube from all angles. No runes marked its surface, no seams or joints interrupted its perfect geometry. Yet it hummed with power he felt in his bones, in the core of his transformed being.

"What will I see?" he asked, removing his gauntlet and extending his hand toward the stone.

"The truth," Gunnhild said. "And the cost of knowing it."

Asvarr's fingers connected with the stone's surface.

***

The world dissolved around him.

He floated in a primordial void, untouched by consciousness or intention. Within this emptiness, threads of possibility flickered like distant lightning—connections forming, breaking, reforming in endless combinations.

Then, from this chaos of potential, a pattern emerged. Simple at first—a mere lattice of connections—then increasingly complex as it folded upon itself, creating depth, dimension, structure. Asvarr recognized it immediately: the same pattern that now lived beneath his skin, the merged mark of five anchors bound.

This is the beginning, came a voice—something fundamental and ancient. *The first pattern, born of void.*

The pattern expanded, grew, encompassed more of the emptiness. As it did, it gained substance, becoming less abstract, more physical. Structures formed within it—the seeds of what would become matter, energy, time, space.

The dreamer awakened within the pattern, the voice continued. *It emerged from the pattern itself as the first consciousness.*

Asvarr witnessed the dreamer's birth—awareness itself coalescing within the growing pattern. He saw it explore, expand, experiment. Creating, destroying, learning.

The dreamer shaped the pattern while the pattern shaped the dreamer. Together, they grew the first Tree—the concept from which Yggdrasil later came. A structure to organize reality, to connect disparate elements across the growing expanse.

The vision shifted, showing the first Tree—a conceptual framework. Within its branches, the first realms formed—primitive versions of the Nine Realms Asvarr knew.

Then came the first breaking. The voice grew somber. *The dreamer, curious about its creation, reached too deeply into the pattern. Reality shuddered. The Tree splintered. The realms began to dissolve back into the void.*

Asvarr watched as cracks spread through the proto-Tree, threatening everything that had formed. Then he saw them—the First Wardens. Collections of consciousness and intent that moved through the breaking pattern, gathering its fragments, reinforcing connections, preventing total collapse.

They saved the pattern at great cost, the voice explained. *Binding themselves to its core structures—what you now call anchors—to prevent another breaking. For eons, they maintained the balance, allowing the pattern to heal, to grow anew.*

The pattern reformed, evolved, became more complex. The Tree regrew in a new configuration. The dreamer withdrew, chastened by the near-destruction, into a quiescent state at the pattern's heart.

Eventually, things changed, the voice continued. *The First Wardens tired. The memory of breaking faded. New entities arose within the pattern—beings you would recognize as gods, though they existed merely as advanced expressions of the pattern itself. Among them, those who would become the Aesir and Vanir.*

Asvarr saw these proto-gods exploring the reformed realms, claiming domains, establishing hierarchies. Among them strode a familiar figure—tall, two-eyed then, carrying a spear.

Gautr, who would become the Allfather, who would become the Ashfather, the voice identified. *Clever, curious, ambitious. He discovered the anchors and the fading First Wardens. He learned of the pattern and its potential. He coveted what they had preserved.*

The vision showed Gautr confronting one of the First Wardens—a battle of wills, of competing intentions for the pattern's future. Gautr emerged victorious, taking the Warden's place at one of the anchors.

One by one, Gautr replaced the First Wardens with beings of his choosing—extensions of his will. He restructured the Tree into Yggdrasil as you know it. He positioned himself as Allfather, as supreme architect of reality.

The familiar nine-realm structure of Yggdrasil formed in the vision. The dreamer remained asleep at its heart, unaware of the changes wrought in its absence.

The pattern remembers its original form, the voice said. *It strains against alterations, against constraints. And so, inevitably, another breaking came.*

Asvarr watched as three figures—the Norns—cut a thread that unraveled reality. Yggdrasil shattered. The realms fractured. The cycle Asvarr knew began.

Nine times has Yggdrasil broken. Nine times has it been restored. Each time, the Ashfather has manipulated events, positioned his chosen Wardens, maintained his control over the pattern while appearing to serve it.

The vision blurred through nine cycles of breaking and restoration, too fast for Asvarr to follow in detail. Yet one constant remained—the one-eyed figure, sometimes in shadows, sometimes in light, always directing events from behind cosmic curtains.

Until you, Asvarr Skyrend's Flame. The voice grew stronger. *You have bound five anchors yet maintained your self. You walk the third path of transformation. You might return the pattern to its original purpose.*

The vision cleared, showing Asvarr as he now was—transformed by five bindings, yet still himself. Connected to the pattern in ways no Warden had been since the First.

The Ashfather fears you, the voice said. *The Tree misunderstands you. The dreamer stirs for you. The moment approaches when everything must change or everything must end. The choice will be yours.*

The vision collapsed, reality rushing back with physical force. Asvarr staggered backward from the Norn-stone, gasping for breath, his mind reeling from revelations too vast to immediately comprehend.

Gunnhild watched him, her ancient face impassive. "Now you know," she said simply.

"The Ashfather—" Asvarr began, struggling to organize his thoughts. "He's been manipulating everything. The Tree, the breaking, the Wardens. All to maintain his control of the pattern."

"Yes." Gunnhild nodded. "For eons beyond counting. He plays Tree against dreamer, gods against mortals, Warden against Warden. All while positioning himself as necessary, as savior, as the only constant in a breaking cosmos."

"And the ravens?" Asvarr asked, remembering their strange words.

"The last echoes of the First Wardens," Gunnhild confirmed. "Their original consciousness has mostly faded, yet enough remains to recognize the pattern's corruption. Enough to guide someone who might restore balance."

Asvarr touched the crown on his brow, feeling the connections to all five anchors humming through it. "What must I do?"

"Something unprecedented." Gunnhild approached, her frail form suddenly radiating purpose. "Confront the Ashfather as his equal. Wake the dreamer for transformation, rather than restoration or replacement. Remind the pattern of its original purpose—connection, possibility, growth."

She touched Asvarr's chest where the five marks now formed a unified whole. "You carry everything necessary—five anchors bound by choice rather than compulsion. Free will surrendered yet paradoxically preserved. The third path made manifest."

A tremendous cracking sound split the air outside the dome. The bone walls shuddered. Dust and fragments rained from the domed ceiling.

"He comes," Gunnhild said, urgency replacing her previous calm. "The Ashfather senses your awakening. He will prevent you from acting freely now that you know the truth."

"Ymir's Cradle," Asvarr recalled. "He said he would wait for me there."

"A trap." Gunnhild's voice hardened. "He planned to ambush you there, weakened and ignorant. Now you come as equal, with knowledge he has hidden for nine cycles of breaking."

Another crack resonated through the dome, closer this time. The Norn-stone pulsed, its dark surface flickering with internal light.

"Take this," Gunnhild pressed something into Asvarr's palm—a small disk of bone etched with a rune he didn't recognize. "When the moment comes—when you stand before both dreamer and Ashfather—break it. The First Wardens will do what they can."

"You're coming with me?" Asvarr asked, pocketing the bone disk.

Gunnhild's thin lips curved in a sad smile. "My time ends here, Warden of Five. I have kept the memory since the first breaking. Now it lives in you." She placed her palm against the Norn-stone. "Go. The passage behind the stone leads to Ymir's Cradle. Confront your predecessor with the truth you now carry."

The floating cube rotated, revealing an opening in the floor beneath it that pulsed with the same blue light that filled the dome.

"The Ashfather will try to convince you his path serves best," Gunnhild called as Asvarr approached the passage. "He will offer power, knowledge, control. Remember what you have seen. Remember the pattern's true purpose."

A final, devastating crack split the air. The bone dome's entrance shattered inward, admitting a blast of winter air and a tall figure silhouetted against the night sky. The Ashfather had arrived, spear in hand, his single eye blazing with cold fire.

"Go!" Gunnhild commanded, raising her arms toward the Norn-stone, which flared blindingly bright in response.

Asvarr leapt into the passage as chaos erupted behind him. The Ashfather's roar of rage pursued him into the blue light, followed by Gunnhild's defiant laughter. Then silence, as the passage sealed itself above him.

He fell through blue radiance, the five marks beneath his skin burning with renewed purpose. In his pocket, the bone disk pulsed with subtle power. In his mind, the revelations of the Norn-stone expanded, connections forming, understanding deepening.

The time for hesitation had passed. The third path—transformation—lay before him. And at its end waited both dreamer and Ashfather, the future of nine realms hanging in the balance.

CHAPTER 14

TRIAL BY MIRROR-RAIN

Blue light faded to darkness as Asvarr fell through the passage beneath the Norn-stone. His stomach lurched with the sensation of plummeting without end, yet his body felt weightless, suspended between moments. The five marks burned beneath his skin, their unified pattern pulsing in time with his racing heart. Each pulse illuminated the narrow tunnel in brief flashes of golden light.

Then impact—a jarring collision with solid ground that drove the air from his lungs and sent his transformed staff skittering across frost-covered stone. Asvarr gasped, dragging in a breath that tasted of iron and ancient ice. He pushed himself to his feet, retrieving the staff and scanning his surroundings.

He stood within a vast cavern hollowed from blue-black ice, its ceiling lost in shadow high above. At its center yawned a massive crater—perfectly circular, its edges smooth as if carved by a giant's blade. From this depression rose what could only be the first Root that had fallen during the Shattering: a colossal trunk of wood wider than ten longhouses, its bark the color of old blood, spiraling upward until it disappeared into the cavern's darkness.

"Ymir's Cradle," Asvarr murmured, his voice echoing strangely in the frozen chamber. The name made sense now—this place where the first fragment of Yggdrasil had fallen, creating a bowl in the earth like the skull-cradle of the first giant from the ancient sagas.

The air hummed with power, making the fine hairs on Asvarr's arms stand on end. The five tokens at his belt resonated in response, each vibrating with a different tone that together formed an unsettling chord. From the crown upon his brow came a heat that matched the chill of the cavern around him, creating a balance point of perfect clarity.

Asvarr approached the Root cautiously. Unlike the anchors he had bound throughout his journey, this massive fragment lay dormant, its surface dull and lifeless. No golden sap flowed from its severed end. No runes glowed upon its bark. Yet Asvarr sensed its importance—this was where it had begun, the first breaking that had set all else in motion.

"So you came," said a voice from behind him.

Asvarr whirled, drawing his sword in a fluid motion. The blade sang with the voices of five anchors as it cleared its sheath.

The Ashfather stood at the edge of the crater, leaning on his spear. His one eye gleamed in the darkness, reflecting the light from Asvarr's marks.

"Despite Gunnhild's interference," the Ashfather continued, his deep voice resonating throughout the chamber. "The Last-Watcher always did meddle in affairs beyond her understanding."

"She told me the truth," Asvarr said, keeping his blade leveled at the one-eyed figure. "About you. About the First Wardens. About the pattern."

"Did she?" The Ashfather's mouth twisted in what might have been a smile. "And what truth was that, I wonder? That I was once like you? That I bound the anchors and faced the dreamer?" He straightened from his casual pose. "Did she tell you what awaited me? What awaits you, should you continue on this path?"

"You chose fear," Asvarr said. "You chose power. You remade everything to serve your vision."

The Ashfather's eye narrowed. "You speak of choices as if they were simple. As if the weight of nine realms doesn't hang upon them." He struck the ground with his spear, the sound cracking through the cavern like breaking ice. "I chose survival, Warden. I chose order. I chose to protect the pattern from the chaos of its original form."

"You chose control," Asvarr corrected. "You remade everything to serve your vision."

"And what would you have done?" The Ashfather circled the edge of the crater, his blue cloak dragging across the frost. "Standing where I stood, seeing what I saw? The dreamer cares nothing for the worlds it created. The pattern tends toward dissolution. The void waits to reclaim all." Each step brought him closer to Asvarr. "Someone must direct. Someone must decide. Someone must bear the burden of maintaining what would otherwise crumble."

Asvarr held his ground, feeling the truth in the Ashfather's words even as he rejected the conclusion. "And for that, you destroyed the First Wardens? You remade the Tree to serve your purposes? You manipulated nine cycles of breaking and binding?"

"I did what was necessary." The Ashfather stopped his advance, planting his spear in the frost. "As you must do now."

The marks beneath Asvarr's skin flared with heat, responding to the proximity of their predecessor. Through his enhanced senses, Asvarr perceived the connections between them—mirrors of each other, one ancient and twisted by eons of control, one new and still evolving.

"The dreamer wakes," the Ashfather said softly. "Even now, it stirs beneath the pattern, questioning, reaching. It remembers the First Wardens. It remembers its original purpose." His voice dropped lower. "And it will destroy everything we know if given the chance."

Before Asvarr could respond, a tremor shook the cavern. Cracks spider-webbed across the ice ceiling. From these fissures fell the first droplets—perfect spheres of liquid that caught the light from Asvarr's marks, reflecting it back a hundredfold.

"The mirror-rain begins," the Ashfather said, looking upward. "The boundary between what is and what might be grows thin." He fixed his single eye on Asvarr. "Your final trial comes, Warden of Five. The dreamer tests you as it once tested me."

The droplets multiplied, falling in increasing numbers until they formed shimmering curtains of liquid light. Each sphere remained perfect as it descended, never breaking upon impact but bouncing once before rolling across the frost.

Where they touched Asvarr's boots, he felt a strange resonance, as if the droplets recognized something in him.

"What is this?" Asvarr asked, watching as the mirror-rain gathered in pools at the crater's edge.

"Possibility made manifest," the Ashfather answered. "The dreamer's way of showing you your paths." He stepped back, melting into the shadows between falling light. "I will await your choice, Warden of Five. When the mirror-rain has shown you what might be, we will speak again."

He vanished into darkness, leaving Asvarr alone in the center of the growing storm. The mirror-rain fell harder now, the droplets larger, each containing fleeting images Asvarr could almost recognize—faces, places, moments yet to come or perhaps never to exist.

One sphere rolled to a stop at Asvarr's feet, larger than the others. Within its perfect surface, he saw his own face reflected—but changed, older, marked by lines of care and authority. This version of himself wore a crown of wood and gold, and behind him stretched a Tree unlike any Asvarr had seen, its branches spanning worlds.

Asvarr knelt and touched the sphere. It burst at his contact, releasing memory and sensation. He gasped as foreign knowledge flooded his mind—the experience of a lifetime unmistakably his yet utterly unfamiliar.

He saw himself as he might become—King of Midgard, Warden of Yggdrasil, protector of the restored pattern. The Tree flourished under his guidance, the realms prospered, the breaking healed. At his side stood Brynja, now his queen, and children who bore the mark of the Warden in their blood.

Yet beneath this vision of order ran a darker current. The dreamer slept, bound once more to eternal slumber by Asvarr's will. The original pattern remained forgotten, replaced by the structure the Ashfather had created. And though Asvarr ruled with wisdom and compassion, he ruled nonetheless—deciding the fates of countless beings across nine realms, just as the Ashfather had done before him.

The vision faded, leaving Asvarr shaken. He rose to his feet as another large sphere rolled toward him, this one gleaming with a different light. Within it, he saw another possible self—gaunt, his eyes burning with inner fire, his skin covered entirely in marks that crawled and shifted like living things.

With trembling fingers, he touched this sphere as well.

A different path unfolded—Asvarr merging completely with the five anchors, surrendering his humanity to become something beyond mortal comprehension. In this future, he stood as guardian of the pattern itself, existing between realms, beyond time. The Tree and dreamer both acknowledged him as equal, a third power in the cosmic balance.

Power flowed through him, limitless and intoxicating. He could reshape reality with a thought, travel between worlds in an instant, know the minds of gods and mortals alike. Yet he stood apart from all, alone in his transcendence, watching the lives of those he had once called kin from an unchanging distance.

This vision too faded, leaving an aftertaste of bitter loneliness. Asvarr stepped back, only to encounter a third sphere that rolled deliberately into his path. This one showed yet another version of himself—his body transformed into a hollow vessel with empty eyes, his chest carved open to reveal a seedling Tree growing within.

Reluctantly, Asvarr touched it.

The third path revealed itself—complete surrender to the Tree. Asvarr sacrificed everything he was, becoming merely a vessel for Yggdrasil's rebirth. His consciousness dissolved into the greater mind of the Tree, his body transformed into the anchor point from which a new World Tree would grow.

In this future, the cycle continued unbroken. The pattern reset to its beginning, the dreamer slumbered on, the Ashfather waited in shadows for the next breaking. Asvarr became a footnote in cosmic history, remembered only as another Warden who served his purpose and vanished into the Tree's endless hunger.

Asvarr jerked his hand back as if burned, but it was too late—the vision had already burned itself into his mind. Three possible futures, three versions of himself, each representing a different choice, a different path.

The mirror-rain fell heavier still, droplets merging into streams that flowed toward the crater's center where the Root rose. Asvarr followed their path, drawn by an instinct he couldn't name. The streams converged at the Root's base, forming a pool that reflected everything and nothing—a mirror to possibility itself.

***

In its depths, Asvarr saw a fourth path—hazy, uncertain, difficult to discern. A version of himself that was neither king nor god nor vessel, but something else entirely. Before he could focus on this image, the surface of the pool rippled violently.

From its center rose a figure—Asvarr himself, or a perfect reflection of him, down to the five marks beneath his skin and the crown upon his brow. The mirror-self stepped from the pool onto the frost, water streaming from its form yet leaving it perfectly dry. It drew an exact copy of Asvarr's sword, the blade singing with the same five-toned voice.

"Who are you?" Asvarr demanded, raising his own weapon.

The mirror-self smiled with Asvarr's face, but the expression held a cold emptiness. "I am what you become if you choose rage instead of mercy," it said with Asvarr's voice. "I am what waits if you forget what makes you mortal."

It attacked without warning, sword flashing in the light of the falling mirror-rain. Asvarr barely raised his blade in time to block the strike, the impact jarring his arm to the shoulder. The mirror-self fought with all of Asvarr's skill, all his strength, all his knowledge of the five anchors—with a cold precision Asvarr himself had never possessed.

"The dreamer tests you," the mirror-self said as they circled each other. "It shows you what lies down each path. What you become. What you lose." It lunged again, scoring a shallow cut across Asvarr's forearm. "I am the shadow of your pride, the echo of your ambition."

Asvarr parried the next strike and countered, his blade passing through the mirror-self's shoulder without resistance, as if cutting mist. The wound closed instantly, mirror-rain flowing into it and sealing it without a scar.

"You cannot defeat me through force," the mirror-self said, attacking again with mechanical efficiency. "I am every battle you've fought, every kill you've made, every moment of berserker rage you've embraced."

Asvarr retreated, trying to create distance between them. The five marks burned beneath his skin, responding to his danger, but their power seemed useless against this opponent born from his own potential.

"Then why fight me at all?" Asvarr asked, blocking another flurry of strikes. "If you can't be killed, what's the purpose?"

The mirror-self paused, sword held at ready. "To show you what awaits. To prepare you for the choice to come." It gestured at the three pools formed by the spheres Asvarr had touched. "King. God. Vessel. Three paths. Three futures. Three versions of Asvarr Skyrend's Flame."

"And you? Which path creates you?"

"All of them," the mirror-self answered. "In each, you sacrifice something essential. In each, you lose some part of what makes you human." It lowered its sword. "The dreamer remembers being mortal once, in the first pattern. It values what mortality brings—choice, change, love, grief. The qualities eternity cannot provide."

The mirror-rain slowed, individual droplets hovering in the air around them, each containing a fragment of possibility. The mirror-self stepped closer, its features shifting subtly to show older, harder versions of Asvarr's face.

"The Ashfather chose power and control. He forgot compassion. He forgot connection. He forgot what it meant to live within the pattern rather than above it." The mirror-self raised a hand, touching Asvarr's chest where the five marks formed their unified pattern. "Will you make the same mistake?"

"I want balance," Asvarr said. "I want to restore what was lost."

"Do you?" The mirror-self's eyes bored into his. "Or do you want to remake everything according to your vision? To correct what you see as flaws in the pattern? To decide what lives and what dies, what grows and what fades, across nine realms?"

The accusation struck deep, touching a truth Asvarr had hidden even from himself—the desire to fix, to improve, to direct. The same impulse that had driven the Ashfather down his path eons ago.

"What should I choose, then?" Asvarr asked, lowering his sword. "If all paths lead to corruption, what hope exists?"

The mirror-self smiled again, but this time the expression held genuine warmth. "The fourth path. The one you glimpsed in the pool. The one the dreamer hopes for but cannot create alone."

"What is it?"

"That," said the mirror-self, "you must discover for yourself."

It dissolved into streams of mirror-rain that flowed back toward the central pool. The suspended droplets fell all at once, creating a thunderous impact that echoed throughout the cavern. The crater rumbled, the Root trembled, and the pool at its base began to glow with golden light.

From behind Asvarr came slow, measured applause. He turned to find the Ashfather standing at the crater's edge once more, his single eye gleaming with reflected gold.

***

"Impressive," the Ashfather said. "You lasted longer against yourself than I did, when I stood where you stand."

"What happens now?" Asvarr asked, sheathing his sword.

"Now?" The Ashfather gestured toward the glowing pool. "Now the dreamer fully wakes. Now you make your choice." He stepped forward, extending a hand. "Join me, Warden of Five. Together, we can guide the pattern rather than destroy it. We can improve what exists rather than risk everything on an uncertain transformation."

The bone disk in Asvarr's pocket burned hot against his thigh, reminding him of Gunnhild's final gift. The five marks beneath his skin pulsed in counterpoint to the Ashfather's presence, rejecting his offer even as Asvarr considered it.

"And if I refuse?" Asvarr asked, hand dropping to the disk through his clothing.

The Ashfather's face hardened. "Then we finish what began in the dreamer's realm. We fight, as we were always meant to fight, for the right to decide what comes next." His voice dropped to a dangerous whisper. "And only one of us walks away."

The pool's glow intensified, golden light spilling up the sides of the massive Root. The dreamer stirred, its consciousness reaching toward the surface of reality. The moment of choice approached—join the Ashfather and maintain the current order, or oppose him and risk everything on the promise of transformation.

Asvarr's fingers closed around the bone disk, feeling its inscribed rune through the fabric. The fourth path—uncertain, undefined, yet somehow right—beckoned from the depths of his mind. His five sacrifices—rage, memory, identity, certainty, and will—had prepared him for this moment, stripping away everything except the core of who he truly was.

He made his decision.

Asvarr pulled the bone disk from his pocket, its etched rune pulsing with amber light. The carving twisted and writhed under his touch, ancient power awakening at the contact with his transformed flesh. Five marks, five anchors, five sacrifices—and now a sixth choice that would define all that came before.

"I refuse both offers," Asvarr said, his voice steady despite the tremor in his chest. "I'll walk the fourth path."

The Ashfather's single eye widened, genuine surprise crossing his weathered features. "There is no fourth path, Warden. Only continuation, substitution, or surrender."

"You're wrong." Asvarr held up the bone disk, its light growing brighter. "The First Wardens knew another way—before you hunted them down and stole their places."

The Ashfather's face darkened, his grip tightening on his spear. "The First Wardens were idealists who nearly let the pattern collapse. I saved reality when they would have let it crumble in the name of freedom and choice."

"Perhaps you feared what they represented." Asvarr stepped toward the glowing pool at the Root's base. "A balance you couldn't control. A pattern that evolved beyond your design."

"Enough!" The Ashfather struck the ground with his spear. The ice cavern trembled, and shards of frost rained from the ceiling. "Nine cycles I've maintained order. Nine cycles I've shouldered the burden alone. If you will join me, then the dreamer must choose between us."

He lunged forward, spear aimed at Asvarr's heart. With reflexes honed by five bindings, Asvarr sidestepped, his transformed sword singing from its sheath. The weapons clashed with a sound like thunder, sending ripples through the mirror-rain still falling around them.

"You fight well," the Ashfather growled, pressing his attack with inhuman speed. "Better than the others who came before you. Yet you remain young, untested against one who has lived eons."

Asvarr parried blow after blow, his sword arm burning with the strain. Each impact sent jolts of pain through his transformed body, as if the Ashfather's spear struck at the very anchors bound within him. He retreated toward the pool, sensing a connection between its golden light and the marks spreading beneath his skin.

"The others surrendered to the Tree," Asvarr gasped, blocking a vicious thrust. "They never reached this point. They never learned the truth of what you did."

"And what difference would it have made?" The Ashfather circled, his single eye gleaming with cold fire. "The pattern requires structure. Direction. Purpose. Without it, chaos reigns."

Asvarr feinted left, then rolled right, coming up beside the glowing pool. Golden light lapped at his boots, singing of ancient memories, primordial forces, a time before gods and trees and wardens.

"Structure, yes," Asvarr agreed, touching the bone disk to his brow where the crown sat. "Your structure. Your direction. Your purpose."

The Ashfather hesitated, recognition flashing across his face. "That disk—where did you get it?"

"Gunnhild gave it to me. A gift from the First Wardens." Asvarr smiled grimly. "They've survived beyond your knowledge."

Fear entered the Ashfather's eye—the first genuine fear Asvarr had seen in the ancient being. He lunged with renewed vigor, his spear a blur of motion.

"Give me the disk, and I will spare you," the Ashfather hissed. "You can still leave this place alive, Warden of Five."

"We can both survive this day," Asvarr countered, meeting the attack with his sword. "You never understood this truth."

The golden pool surged higher, reaching Asvarr's knees. Within its depths, the dreamer stirred, consciousness rising from timeless slumber to witness the confrontation above. The five tokens at Asvarr's belt resonated in greeting, each singing a different note that together formed a harmony both eerily familiar and utterly alien.

The Ashfather struck again, his spear slipping past Asvarr's guard to score a line of fire across his ribs. Blood welled, golden rather than red, sizzling where it touched the pool below.

"Your blood awakens it," the Ashfather said, his voice tinged with alarm. "Stop this foolishness now, before it fully wakes!"

Asvarr stumbled, one knee dropping into the golden pool. Immediately, visions crashed through his mind—the dreamer's memories, stretching back to the void before creation. He saw the first pattern form, the first consciousness emerge, the first breaking and all that followed. He saw the Ashfather—then Gautr—as he had been: young, curious, ambitious, fearful of the pattern's inherent chaos.

Understanding bloomed. The Ashfather sought certainty in a universe built on randomness. Control in a reality built on chance and change. He had remade the Tree, hunted the First Wardens, manipulated nine cycles of breaking and binding, all to impose order on what he perceived as dangerous disorder.

Asvarr looked up, meeting the Ashfather's gaze. "I see you now, Gautr. I understand your fear."

The Ashfather flinched at the use of his original name. "Then you know why I must prevail. Why I cannot allow the dreamer to remember its first purpose."

"And what was that purpose?" Asvarr asked, though he had begun to sense the answer rippling through the golden pool.

"To experience. To evolve. To become." The Ashfather's voice dropped to a whisper. "Without boundaries. Without end. Without certainty."

Asvarr nodded, pieces falling into place. "Evolution frightens you. It defies prediction. It resists direction."

"It leads to chaos!" The Ashfather shouted, his composure cracking. "I have seen it! When the First Wardens guided the pattern, each realm splintered into thousands. Each being chose its own path. The pattern frayed at the edges, reality itself began to unwind!"

"Perhaps it transformed into something beyond our current understanding," Asvarr suggested, rising to his feet despite the pain lancing through his side. "Something your perspective couldn't comprehend."

The Ashfather roared, leaping forward with his spear aimed at Asvarr's heart. In that moment, Asvarr saw his opening—the fear that drove the ancient being, the terror of uncertainty that had corrupted his original purpose.

Instead of dodging, Asvarr dropped his sword. It splashed into the golden pool and sank from sight. He spread his arms wide, leaving himself vulnerable to the attack.

"What are you doing?" the Ashfather demanded, halting his spear mere inches from Asvarr's chest.

"Choosing uncertainty," Asvarr replied. "Choosing vulnerability. Trusting the pattern itself rather than imposing control."

The golden pool surged higher, reaching Asvarr's waist. The five marks beneath his skin blazed with answering light, casting his shadow tall against the cavern walls.

"You fool," the Ashfather whispered. "You'll doom us all."

"Perhaps." Asvarr snapped the bone disk between his fingers. "Or perhaps I'll free us."

The disk shattered with a sound like the breaking of nine worlds. From its fragments erupted blinding light—white, blue, green, red, gold—that spiraled upward in five distinct streams. The streams coalesced into figures standing in a circle around the pool—the First Wardens, or what remained of their consciousness, given temporary form.

They existed unlike any beings Asvarr had encountered—shifting constantly, never settling on a single appearance, yet somehow conveying both ancient wisdom and vibrant youth.

"Gautr," said one, its voice like wind through ancient branches. "Long has it been since we stood as equals."

The Ashfather lowered his spear, his single eye fixed on the apparitions. "You faded. You surrendered to the void."

"We withdrew," corrected another, whose form rippled like water reflecting starlight. "When you chose control over connection. When you remade the Tree to serve your vision alone."

"We waited," added a third, burning with internal flame. "For one who would bind five anchors yet remain whole. One who would walk the third path yet seek the fourth."

"And now," said the fourth, whose body seemed composed of living crystal, "the dreamer wakes. The pattern remembers. The moment of choice returns."

The fifth and final First Warden, a being of shadow and void, turned to Asvarr. "You have come far, Bearer of Five Marks. Farther than any since Gautr himself. What would you ask of us?"

Asvarr felt the golden pool rising higher, reaching his chest now. The dreamer's consciousness brushed against his transformed mind, curious, questioning, remembering.

"I ask for nothing," Asvarr said. "I offer instead. My five sacrifices. My five bindings. My five tokens. Given freely, without demand for power or control in return."

The five First Wardens exchanged glances, their shifting forms momentarily synchronizing into a pattern Asvarr recognized—the same unified mark that now spread beneath his skin.

"And what would you have the dreamer do with your offerings?" asked the Warden of wind.

Asvarr took a deep breath, feeling the weight of nine realms hanging on his words. "Awaken. Remember. Evolve according to its own nature."

The First Wardens nodded in unison. "And what of the Tree?" asked the Warden of water. "What of Yggdrasil as it now exists?"

"It can remain," Asvarr said, conscious of the Ashfather's intense gaze. "Reshaped to serve connection rather than restriction. To allow growth rather than enforce stasis."

"And what of him?" The Warden of fire pointed at the Ashfather. "The one who hunted us. Who remade the pattern to serve his fear."

Asvarr met the Ashfather's eye. "He too can remain. As guardian, as memory-keeper, as reminder of the dangers when fear drives purpose." He extended a hand toward his ancient predecessor. "He need carry this burden alone no longer."

For a long moment, silence filled the cavern. The mirror-rain had stopped, leaving only the golden light of the pool illuminating the ice walls. Then, with a sound like distant thunder, the Ashfather laughed.

"You offer mercy?" he asked incredulously. "After all I've done? After nine cycles of manipulation and control?"

"I offer understanding," Asvarr corrected. "And the chance to grow beyond what fear made you."

The five First Wardens turned toward the Ashfather, their forms solidifying into more recognizable shapes—those they had worn when Gautr first encountered them, eons ago.

"What say you, Spear-Wielder?" asked the Warden of crystal. "Will you step aside and allow the pattern its original freedom? Or must we banish you to the void between realms?"

The Ashfather looked from the Wardens to Asvarr, his weathered face unreadable. Then, with deliberate care, he planted his spear in the ice beside the pool.

"I chose as best I could," he said, his voice heavy with the weight of countless ages. "I maintained what would have shattered. I preserved what would have dissolved."

"You did," agreed the Warden of void. "And now another choice comes. To cling to your vision, or to allow transformation."

The Ashfather stepped forward, placing one hand atop his spear. "If I refuse?"

"Then we battle here, at the brink of awakening," said the Warden of wind. "And regardless of who prevails, the pattern suffers."

The golden pool had reached Asvarr's shoulders now, its warmth spreading through his transformed flesh. The dreamer's consciousness pressed more insistently against his mind, eager to rise, to wake, to remember.

"Decide, Gautr," Asvarr urged. "The dreamer wakes regardless. Will it find us as enemies or allies?"

The Ashfather closed his eye, his face contorting with inner struggle. When he opened it again, something had changed—a spark of what he had once been, before fear twisted his purpose.

"I will stand aside," he said finally. "I will allow the waking. Yet I will remain, to witness what comes of this course."

"As will we all," said the five First Wardens in unison.

They extended their hands toward Asvarr, five streams of elemental power converging on his transformed body. The golden pool surged upward, engulfing him completely, and for a moment he knew perfect unity with the dreamer's awakening mind.

The ice cavern dissolved around them. The massive Root pulsed with renewed life. The five tokens at Asvarr's belt melted into his flesh, becoming permanent aspects of his transformed self. The crown upon his brow flared with blinding light, then settled into a steady glow.

When Asvarr's vision cleared, he stood upon a vast plain unlike any he had known. Above stretched a sky filled with countless stars arranged in patterns he recognized—the nine realms, seen from outside, connected by branches of light.

Beneath his feet, soil stirred with the first seeds of a new Tree—or perhaps the oldest Tree, remembering its original form.

***

The Ashfather stood nearby, changed by his surrender. His eye patch had fallen away, revealing a second eye reborn—silver where the first was gold. His spear had transformed into a staff of living wood. He looked younger, unburdened by eons of solitary vigilance.

"What happens now?" he asked, voice stripped of its former authority.

"Evolution," Asvarr replied, feeling the dreamer's consciousness flowing through the soil beneath them, through the starlight above, through his own transformed flesh. "The pattern remembers itself. The Tree regrows according to its original nature. The realms reconnect freely."

"And us?" The former Ashfather gestured to include himself, Asvarr, and the five First Wardens who now stood in a loose circle around them.

"We guide gently," Asvarr said, understanding flowing into him from the awakening dreamer. "We protect carefully. We nurture patiently."

The ground trembled beneath them. From the soil erupted the first shoot of the reborn Tree—gold and silver intertwined, pulsing with the dreamer's awakened consciousness. It grew with impossible speed, stretching toward the star-filled sky, branches unfurling in patterns both familiar and utterly new.

Asvarr felt himself changing once more, the five marks reshaping themselves across his flesh. The unified pattern expanded, incorporating aspects of the dreamer's reawakened purpose. He remained himself—Asvarr Skyrend's Flame, once berserker, now Warden of Five—yet also became something more: a bridge between old and new, memory and possibility, structure and freedom.

"The fourth path," he whispered, understanding at last what the mirror-self had meant. Transformation that preserved the essential while allowing evolution of the whole.

A hand settled on his shoulder. He turned to find the First Warden of void standing beside him, its form now permanently stabilized into a shape reminiscent of a human woman, though her eyes contained galaxies.

"The breaking ends," she said. "The waking begins. The pattern remembers. The Tree grows anew."

"And the nine realms?" Asvarr asked.

"They will change," said the former Ashfather, coming to stand on Asvarr's other side. "Some gradually, some swiftly. The barriers between them will thin. Possibilities will multiply. Choices will expand." He sighed, a sound of both regret and relief. "Chaos will increase."

"Creative chaos," corrected the First Warden. "The chaos of growth and discovery. The chaos from which the pattern first emerged."

The reborn Tree towered above them now, its branches weaving through the starlight, reconnecting the nine realms in configurations never seen under the Ashfather's rule. Asvarr sensed minds awakening across the worlds—mortal and divine alike—as the dreamer's consciousness touched them through the new connections.

"They will need guidance," Asvarr said, watching as light and shadow played through the Tree's canopy. "Understanding. Protection."

"Yes," agreed the former Ashfather. "I believe they will."

"Then let us begin," said the First Warden of void, gesturing toward the horizon where a golden dawn had begun to break. "The dreamer wakes. The pattern evolves. The Wardens watch."

Together, the seven of them—Asvarr, the former Ashfather, and the five First Wardens—walked toward the rising light. Behind them, the reborn Tree continued to grow, its roots and branches extending throughout reality, restoring ancient connections while forging entirely new ones.

Asvarr felt the weight of his five sacrifices—rage, memory, identity, certainty, and will—transform from burden into strength. He had surrendered them, yes, but received them back transmuted, purified of fear and hunger for control. The crown upon his brow now sat lightly, a reminder of responsibility rather than authority.

The fourth path stretched before him, uncertain yet promising, dangerous yet vital. A path of balance between chaos and order, freedom and structure, evolution and preservation. A path no Warden had walked before, yet one the pattern had always intended.

As the golden dawn washed over him, Asvarr smiled. The breaking had ended. The waking had begun. And whatever came next would unfold according to its own nature—witnessed, guided, and embraced with open eyes.

CHAPTER 15

THE NORN THAT REWRITES

The old forest breathed around Asvarr, exhaling mist that clung to his skin in icy beads. Three days had passed since his confrontation with the Ashfather at Ymir's Cradle, and the weight of that encounter hung on him like a physical burden. His chest ached where the merged mark of tree and flame spread its tendrils across his skin—a constant reminder of the choice he'd made to walk the fourth path.

Frost crackled beneath his boots as he followed the serpentine trail that wound between ancient pines. Their bark twisted into faces that seemed to track his movement, branches creaking in a wind that didn't touch the forest floor. The bronze sword at his hip thrummed faintly, resonating with something hidden among the trees.

"The mark pulls west," he muttered, pressing his palm against his chest where the rune pulsed hot against his skin. The five tokens he'd gathered—horn, amulet, remembrance-key, frost crystal, and crown—clinked gently at his belt, each one catching the meager sunlight that filtered through the canopy.

A raven's harsh cry broke the stillness. Asvarr looked up to see it circling overhead, its wings dark against the pearl-white sky.

"Still watching," he said, recognition flashing. One of the First Wardens, keeping tabs on him. Their interest in his journey had grown since Ymir's Cradle, when he'd broken the cycle of the pattern. Freedom came with scrutiny.

The trail widened suddenly, opening into a clearing dominated by an enormous loom. Taller than three men, it stood askew, its framework of bone-white wood tipped at a precarious angle. Threads of gold, silver, and midnight-black hung from it in a tangled web, some severed and others stretched taut across the clearing like trip lines.

And there, kneeling among the wreckage of broken threads, was a woman. Or something woman-shaped.

She wore a bone-white mask split down the middle, one half smoothed to featureless perfection, the other carved with intricate spirals that seemed to move when Asvarr shifted his focus. Her robes pooled around her like liquid shadow, and her hands—too long, fingers tapering to needle-fine points—worked frantically with thread that spilled from a wound in her side.

"Fate-cutter," she whispered without looking up. "Thread-breaker." Her voice rasped like wind through dry leaves. "Come to gloat over what you've done?"

Asvarr's hand found the hilt of his sword, but he didn't draw it. The mark on his chest burned in recognition.

"I seek no quarrel," he said, measuring his distance to her. "I follow the path the mark shows me."

The figure's laugh cut through the clearing, sharp as a blade. "Path? There are no paths anymore, Warden. Only fragments." She held up a length of severed golden thread. "Do you know what this is? This was a king's life. And this—" She lifted a silver strand. "A mother's joy. Both cut before their time because of what you and the Ashfather did to the pattern."

Asvarr took another step forward, squinting as golden light leaked from between the seams of her mask.

"You're a Norn," he said, remembering Gunnhild's tales. "You weave the fates of men and gods."

"I was a Norn." The masked figure tilted her head, golden light spilling from her eye-slits. "Now I am broken. Skuld, youngest sister, keeper of what-will-be. Or what would have been, before you shattered the loom with your meddling."

Asvarr tensed, the merged mark on his chest pulsing in warning. "I only sought to bind what was broken."

"And in doing so, broke something greater." Skuld stood in a fluid motion that sent threads scattering. She was taller than she'd first appeared, her limbs elongating as she rose. "Do you know what happens when fate's threads are cut without pattern? Chaos bleeds through. Lives end or change without design. The web that connects all beings frays."

Skuld gestured toward the forest beyond the clearing. "Out there, a child who should have been king burns with fever. A village that was meant to stand for centuries drowns beneath a wave born of your actions. A woman destined for greatness now sits empty-eyed, her purpose forgotten."

Her voice cracked with something Asvarr hadn't expected to hear from such a being—grief.

"I did what had to be done," Asvarr said, though doubt wove through his certainty like dark thread through gold. "The cycle of breaking and binding had to end."

"End?" Skuld's laughter scraped the air. "Nothing ends. The pattern transforms. You didn't break the cycle—you only changed its shape." She pointed a needle-finger at him. "The Ashfather thought the same, nine cycles ago. Now look at what you've both wrought."

The trees around them groaned, their bark splitting to reveal glowing golden sap that dripped like tears. The ground trembled.

"What's happening?" Asvarr demanded, drawing his sword. The bronze blade glowed with answering light to the sap that flowed from the trees.

"Reality adjusts," Skuld said simply. "The pattern seeks balance, even now." She fixed her masked face on Asvarr. "You wear five marks of five anchors. You've done what none before you managed. And yet you understand nothing of what awaits you."

She turned back to her tangled threads, fingers working with impossible speed.

"I understand more than you think," Asvarr said, the knowledge gleaned from five bindings flowing through him. "I've seen the dreamer at the pattern's heart. I've walked with the First Wardens."

"And yet you still came here, to me," Skuld replied, not looking up from her work. "Why?"

The question caught him unprepared. Why had the mark led him here, to this broken Norn and her shattered loom?

"I..." he began, then stopped, noticing the threads Skuld wove were forming a shape—his shape, with the five marks spreading across the chest.

"Tell me, Skyrend's Flame, what do you most desire now that you've bound all five anchors?" She continued working, her needle-fingers puncturing the image she'd created. "To return home? To rule? To forget?"

Asvarr stared at the image of himself woven in golden thread. "To understand," he said finally, the answer surprising even him. "To know if what I've done was right."

Skuld went still. The golden light behind her mask dimmed.

"Understanding," she echoed. "That's the most dangerous desire of all." She stood again, approaching him with a gliding motion that left no footprints in the frost. From within her robes, she withdrew a pair of shears forged from black iron, their edges gleaming with impossible sharpness.

"What if I told you I could grant that desire?" Skuld asked, her voice dropping to a whisper. "What if I could show you the consequences of your choices, the lives changed by your actions? The true cost of walking the fourth path?"

The shears opened with a sound like winter wind.

"At what price?" Asvarr asked, feeling the mark on his chest pulse in warning.

"Only a memory," Skuld said. "One small memory, to pay for many more. Cut from you with these shears, woven into the pattern I rebuild."

Asvarr studied her, remembering Mímisormr's demand at Hvergelmir when he'd surrendered his most precious memory. The Norn's offer felt similar—and similarly dangerous.

"Which memory?" he asked, his voice guarded.

"The moment you chose to take the fourth path," she replied. "The pivotal decision that brought us here."

Asvarr's breath caught. That memory defined everything he'd become. Without it, would he still be the same Warden? The same man?

"And in return?"

"I'll show you what you've truly done," Skuld said. "The pattern as it now exists, with all its frayed edges and broken connections. The truth no one else can show you."

She extended the shears, handle first.

"You cut the thread yourself," she said. "From your mind to my loom. Then I'll show you what you need to see."

Asvarr stared at the black iron shears. They pulsed with power older than the Grímmark, older perhaps than the Tree itself. The raven circled lower overhead, its caw a warning he couldn't interpret.

He thought of all he'd sacrificed already—rage, memory, identity, certainty, free will—each binding taking something vital from him. What was one more memory, measured against understanding?

His fingers closed around the cold iron handle, accepting Skuld's offer and whatever consequences might follow.

***

Cold iron bit into Asvarr's palm as he gripped the shears. Their weight surprised him—heavier than their size suggested, as if they contained the burden of countless severed threads. The forest around him had gone silent, the raven overhead falling still.

"The memory sits here," Skuld said, reaching out to touch Asvarr's temple with a needle-finger that pricked his skin. A single drop of blood beaded at the point of contact. "Feel for it, Warden. The moment when you chose your own path at Ymir's Cradle."

Asvarr closed his eyes, the shears trembling in his hand. The moment flooded back to him—standing before the golden pool in Ymir's Cradle, the Ashfather's spear aimed at his heart, the choice laid bare before him. The terror and exhilaration of forging a new path, of trusting his instincts against the weight of nine cycles.

"I have it," he murmured.

"Then cut," Skuld commanded. "Before doubt stays your hand."

Asvarr raised the shears to his temple, their edges gleaming in the filtered light. His arm tensed—

A harsh cry split the air. The raven plummeted from above, transforming mid-dive into a humanoid figure that landed between Asvarr and the broken Norn. It wore a cloak of feathers that billowed around a form blending man and bird.

"Stop," the figure warned, its voice a grating caw. "She deceives you, Warden."

Skuld hissed, her robes billowing outward like wings. "First Warden, you have no authority here. This concerns only the fate-weaver and the pattern-breaker."

"I claim authority where the pattern's balance faces threat." The raven-cloaked figure turned to Asvarr. "She seeks to eliminate your truth, your essential memory."

Asvarr lowered the shears slightly, his temple stinging where the drop of blood slid down his face. "Explain."

The raven-figure gestured to the shattered loom. "Skuld caused the Shattering. Those shears you hold? They cut the thread of Yggdrasil itself."

Skuld lunged forward, needle-fingers extended like claws. "Silence, feather-thief! You know nothing of necessity!"

The raven-figure sidestepped her attack with unnatural grace. "I witnessed your attempt to unmake creation. Now you aim to erase this Warden's vital choice."

Asvarr stepped back, the shears suddenly burning against his palm. "Tell me the truth," he demanded, eyes fixed on Skuld's mask.

The Norn went still, her posture rigid with fury or perhaps shame. The golden light behind her mask flickered like a flame in wind.

"The dream had to end," she finally said, her voice dropping to a whisper. "Nine cycles we watched the pattern form and break and reform. Nine cycles of suffering and struggle, all feeding that thing at the center, the dreamer who dreams while consuming all."

She turned to face Asvarr fully. "We intended to wake it. My sisters and I. To force an ending, to break the cycle of endless consumption."

"By cutting fate's thread," Asvarr said.

"By cutting the thread that kept the dreamer sleeping." Skuld's fingers worked in the air as if weaving invisible patterns. "We failed. The Tree shattered, yes, the dreamer merely stirred. And my sisters..." Her voice broke. "Verdandi fell with the branches. Urd scattered with the leaves. I alone remain, trapped between past certainties and a chaotic future."

The raven-figure made a sound like grinding stones. "And now you would steal this Warden's memory of choice. The very memory that sets him apart from all who came before. Why?"

Skuld's shoulders sagged. "Because the pattern changes into something I cannot read. Because without certainties, what purpose do I serve? A fate-weaver with no fate to weave."

Understanding dawned on Asvarr like ice breaking on a winter lake. "You fear this change," he said. "You fear what I've done."

"I fear losing control," Skuld admitted, the words dragged from her. "Nine cycles I've watched, woven, and waited. Nine cycles of knowing every thread's direction. Then you..." She jabbed a finger toward him. "You severed your thread from the pattern and rewove it according to your will."

Asvarr studied the shears in his hand, recognizing them as Skuld's desperate grasp at preserving the familiar order, the predictable pattern.

"Show me," he said suddenly.

Skuld tilted her head, the mask's eye-slits narrowing. "Show you what?"

"The loom before the Shattering. And after. I want to see what truly changed." Asvarr slid the shears into his belt, keeping them. "Show me everything—with my memory intact."

The raven-figure nodded approvingly. "The Warden grows wiser."

Skuld stared at him for a long moment, then turned toward the massive broken loom. "Very well. Truth awaits you, though you may crave forgetfulness after witnessing it."

She approached the tangled mass of threads, her needle-fingers dancing across the golden, silver, and black strands. They began to glow, to straighten, to weave themselves back together in patterns so complex they made Asvarr's eyes water.

"Behold the pattern as it was," Skuld intoned.

The threads formed an intricate tapestry in the air—a perfect circle divided into nine sections, each representing one of the realms. At the center, a void space pulsed with dark energy. The threads connecting the sections to the center pulled taut, drawing energy inward like a spider drawing prey.

"The dreamer consumed the realms," Asvarr murmured, understanding settling in his bones. "It drained them while pretending to protect."

"Yes," the raven-figure said. "Each cycle increased its hold."

Skuld's fingers twitched, and the pattern shifted. The threads loosened, some snapping completely. The nine sections drifted apart, their rigid alignment fading. The center darkened, then glowed with a different light—golden rather than black.

"And now?" Asvarr asked.

"Now the pattern evolves," Skuld said bitterly. "The dreamer shares its power. The realms exist for themselves." She turned her masked face to Asvarr. "Your choice at Ymir's Cradle caused this disruption. You offered yourself freely, without surrender or combat."

The raven-figure stepped forward. "The fourth path—beyond continuation, substitution, or transformation. Something entirely new."

"What should I call it?" Asvarr asked, the question barely audible.

"Freedom," the raven-figure replied. "You broke free from the pattern, and through that action, liberated the pattern itself."

Skuld made a sound like tearing silk. "And left me purposeless, a fate-weaver in a world where fate unravels."

The threads collapsed, falling to the forest floor in a tangle of gold, silver, and black. Skuld dropped to her knees among them, fingers working frantically to gather them up.

Asvarr approached her, careful to avoid stepping on the threads. "You can find purpose again," he said. "The same freedom awaits you."

"Freedom for what?" Skuld demanded, her voice cracking. "To wander aimlessly? To fade into memory? To watch the worlds spin in chaos?"

"Freedom to create," Asvarr said. He knelt beside her, his hand finding hers amid the tangled threads. Her needle-fingers pricked his palm, drawing blood that fell onto the golden strands. "Freedom to weave anew."

The threads where his blood fell began to glow, to move of their own accord. They twisted together, forming a small, intricate pattern unlike anything in the previous tapestry.

"What happens here?" Skuld whispered, masked face bent low over the glowing threads.

"A beginning," the raven-figure said. "The Warden shows you his discovery—a self-determined path."

Skuld stared at the tiny pattern forming beneath her fingers. For the first time, Asvarr sensed something beyond bitterness in her—a fragile, tentative wonder.

"I could weave anything," she murmured. "Possibilities instead of certainties. Potential futures instead of fixed fates."

"Yes," Asvarr said. "I learned this truth at Ymir's Cradle. We shape the pattern together, through choice." He stood, feeling the mark on his chest pulse with renewed purpose. "Will you join this work, Skuld? Will you help create a pattern no one has seen before?"

The Norn remained silent for a long moment, her needle-fingers hovering over the glowing threads. Finally, she reached up and removed her mask.

Beneath it lay a swirling cosmos—stars and nebulae and dark spaces between, all contained within the rough shape of a human visage. Eyes formed from twin supernovas fixed on Asvarr with burning intensity.

"I will weave," she said, her voice resonating from everywhere and nowhere at once. "I shall become something beyond Skuld the Norn. I will forge my own identity."

She picked up a strand of golden thread, tying it around Asvarr's wrist in an intricate knot.

"A gift," she said. "I once called such things fate-bonds. Now I name this a promise-thread. Follow where it leads to find those walking similar paths. Find others transforming themselves through freedom."

The thread sank beneath Asvarr's skin, leaving a delicate golden pattern around his wrist like a braided band.

"Thank you," he said. The mark on his chest tingled in recognition of this new bond.

The raven-figure stepped forward. "The pattern calls you elsewhere, Warden. Your work here reaches completion."

Asvarr nodded, feeling a tug from the mark—westward, toward mountains just visible through the trees. He started to leave, then paused, his hand going to the black iron shears tucked in his belt.

"Keep them," Skuld said, reading his intention. "They sever more than memory and fate. The time may come when you need them."

With a nod of acceptance, Asvarr turned and followed the pull of his mark toward the western mountains, leaving behind a Norn transforming herself entirely—and taking with him both the weight of black iron shears and the gleam of a golden promise-thread pulling him toward unwritten futures.

CHAPTER 16

THE MIDSONG TREE

The western mountains loomed before Asvarr, their jagged peaks cutting into the twilight sky like broken teeth. Three days he had traveled since leaving the shattered Norn, following both the persistent tug of his mark and the gentle warmth of Skuld's promise-thread around his wrist. His breath plumed in the chill air as he climbed a narrow game trail that switchbacked up the mountainside.

A haunting melody drifted on the wind—faint, almost imperceptible. Asvarr paused, head tilted. The sound vanished, then returned stronger, a sequence of notes that made his skin prickle. The mark on his chest resonated in response, humming with a sympathetic vibration that spread warmth through his tired muscles.

"The Tree," he murmured, certain of its source.

He quickened his pace, clambering over a rain-slick boulder that blocked the path. The five tokens at his belt clinked together, each one glowing faintly in the fading light. The black iron shears hung heavy at his side, their weight a constant reminder of Skuld's desperate attempt to cling to the old pattern.

The melody grew stronger as he climbed, weaving through the wind and mist with increasing clarity. It changed with each gust—rising, falling, transforming. No steady rhythm governed it, only wild, unpredictable shifts that reminded Asvarr of the ancient songs his mother once hummed while working—music from before the gods.

Cresting a ridge, Asvarr found himself on a broad plateau split by a narrow ravine. The land here defied sense. To his left stretched a summer meadow, tall grasses swaying beneath a shower of golden light that fell from nowhere. To his right spread a frozen stretch of tundra, ice crystals glittering under a localized flurry of snow. Ahead, where the music originated, autumn reigned—the trees sporting brilliant crimson and amber leaves despite the season.

He crossed into the autumn section, leaves crunching beneath his boots. Here the melody wrapped around him, vibrating through his bones. The bronze sword at his hip thrummed in answer to the song, its runes glowing gold.

The ravine widened into a sheltered valley. There, in a perfect circle of bare earth, grew a slender sapling—no taller than Asvarr himself, with silver-white bark and leaves that shifted between all seasonal colors. It swayed without wind, and from it came the otherworldly music.

"The Midsong Tree," Asvarr whispered, remembering fragments of knowledge from his bindings. A rare offspring of Yggdrasil, born where fragments of the great Tree fell to earth.

As he approached, the sapling's song changed pitch. The ground beneath his feet transformed—frost giving way to soft moss, then to cracked clay, then to rich black soil. The air warmed, then chilled, then filled with the scent of rain though no clouds gathered above.

"I've never seen anything like you," Asvarr said, addressing the Tree directly. The mark on his chest pulsed as if in greeting.

The sapling trembled, its leaves rustling. A single branch extended toward him, impossibly lengthening until it hovered before his face. At its tip, a bud formed, swelled, and burst open to reveal a perfect miniature apple, golden-skinned and gleaming.

"For me?" Asvarr reached for it, hesitating as memories of shadow-drinkers and ulfhednar flashed through his mind. Those who consumed the Tree's essence without bearing a mark suffered terrible fates.

The sapling's melody intensified, focused on a single, pure note that resonated with the mark on Asvarr's chest. An invitation, a recognition—Warden to Tree.

His fingers closed around the fruit. It came away easily, warm against his palm. The promise-thread around his wrist glowed in response, its golden light matching the apple's sheen.

"What will you show me?" he asked, studying the perfect fruit. Five tiny seeds were visible through its translucent skin, arranged in a pattern that matched his five bound anchors.

The bronze sword at his hip shuddered, its warning clear. Whatever visions the fruit contained would change him further, perhaps irrevocably. Yet the mark drew him forward, recognizing a truth he needed to see.

Asvarr bit into the apple.

Golden sap flooded his mouth, sweet and sharp and ancient. The world blurred, shifted, dissolved—

***

—and he stood on a vast plain beneath a sky of infinite stars. Before him rose Yggdrasil in its full glory, branches extending beyond sight, roots plunging into depths unfathomable. The Tree dwarfed mountains, spanned oceans, brushed against distant stars.

"Magnificent," he breathed, understanding now what had been lost in the Shattering.

"It will never be this way again," said a voice beside him.

Asvarr turned to find a child standing there—the same child-form the dreamer had taken at Ymir's Cradle, with amber skin and eyes containing galaxies.

"Why show me this, then?" Asvarr asked. "If it can't be restored?"

"To understand what comes next, you must see what came before." The child pointed upward, toward Yggdrasil's crown where countless worlds hung like fruit among the branches. "This was the first pattern, before the Ashfather, before the Norns, before the cycles of breaking and binding."

The vision shifted. Yggdrasil withered, branches cracking, roots tearing free. The golden sap that had flowed through it darkened, thickened.

"The first breaking," the child explained. "When the dreamer withdrew."

"Why did it withdraw?"

The child's eyes flashed with distant galaxies. "The dreamer slept too long. In sleep, it dreamed of gods who became real, who then sought to cage the dreamer for power. The withdrawal was... self-preservation."

The withered Yggdrasil collapsed, its massive trunk shattering. From the wreckage rose a new growth—smaller, misshapen, with nine distinct branches.

"The Ashfather's reconstruction," the child said. "He found the dreamer's essence scattered across the broken roots and shaped it to his will. Nine realms to rule, nine cycles to feed upon, nine chances to become a god himself."

Asvarr watched as this new Tree grew, broke, and reformed eight more times—each cycle slightly different, each ending with the Ashfather consuming a Warden and reshaping the pattern.

"Until you," the child said. "The first to walk the fourth path."

The vision shifted again. Asvarr saw himself standing in the golden pool at Ymir's Cradle, making his choice. Then he saw what followed—the pattern transforming, the dreamer stirring, the Ashfather retreating to gather his strength.

"What happens now?" Asvarr asked, his voice barely audible against the vastness of the vision.

"Now the song changes." The child pointed to where a tiny sapling grew from the remains of the ninth breaking—the Midsong Tree, singing its strange melody to a changed world. "The old pattern fades. The new has yet to form fully."

"And the dreamer?"

"Awakening, slowly. Neither captive nor captor. Watching, waiting to see what you will do next." The child's gaze fixed on Asvarr with uncomfortable intensity. "You've freed it from the pattern, Warden. What would you have it do with that freedom?"

Before Asvarr could answer, the vision warped. The starry plain, the child, the broken and reformed Yggdrasil—all swirled together, collapsing into a single point of golden light that streaked toward him, striking his mark with searing heat—

—and he gasped, stumbling backward from the Midsong Tree. The half-eaten apple fell from his fingers, dissolving into golden mist before it touched the ground. The sapling's song had changed, becoming complex, multilayered, urgent.

***

"Warden-kin," spoke a voice from the edge of the clearing. "Step away from the songbearer."

Asvarr whirled, drawing his bronze sword in a fluid motion. Three figures stood at the clearing's edge—two women and a man, each bearing marks similar to his own. The taller woman's forehead bore the Jordmark, its lines glowing green-gold against her brown skin. The second woman's throat displayed a mark like frozen lightning—the Frostmark Thorvald had once borne. The man's shoulders carried twin spirals of silver light—a mark Asvarr didn't recognize.

"Who are you?" he demanded, sword held ready though his mark recognized them as kin.

The tall woman stepped forward, amber eyes fixed on his face. "I am Brynja Hrafndottir, Earth-Healer, bearer of the Jordmark." She gestured to her companions. "This is Svala Storm-Speaker, bearer of the Frostmark, and Leif World-Walker, bearer of the Skymark."

Asvarr's throat tightened. Other Wardens—just as Brenna had promised when she carved the Grímmark into his flesh. Just as the promise-thread had guided him to find.

"Asvarr," he said simply. "Skyrend's Flame."

Brynja's eyes narrowed. "We know who you are, Flame-Bearer. Word of your choices spreads through the broken realms. The question is whether you understand what you've done—and what comes next."

The Midsong Tree's song intensified, its melody splitting into five distinct parts that wove together in complex harmony. The ground beneath them shifted, the circle of seasons expanding, changing. Summer heat blazed to Asvarr's left, while winter's bite sharpened to his right. The autumn leaves above the Tree burned brighter, and spring flowers erupted at its base.

"The song grows stronger," Svala said, her voice crackling like ice breaking on a frozen lake. "It senses all five marks in one place."

"Five?" Asvarr glanced between the three newcomers and himself. "There are only four of us."

Leif smiled, the Skymark on his shoulders pulsing with silver light. "The fifth comes. The Deathmark-bearer approaches from the shadow road."

As if summoned by his words, a patch of darkness formed at the edge of the clearing. It solidified into a hooded figure who stepped into the light, throwing back their cowl to reveal a face half-beautiful, half-skull—the left side that of a young woman with olive skin and dark eyes, the right a bleached skull with an empty socket. Around her neck hung a mark of ash-gray, shaped like a key.

"Yara Death-Walker," she introduced herself, voice melodic despite her appearance. "The Tree's song called me from Helheim's gates."

The Midsong Tree shuddered, its branches extending toward all five Wardens. The song reached a crescendo that made the air itself vibrate with power.

"The Tree summons all Wardens," Brynja said, stepping closer to Asvarr. Her expression held distrust and curiosity in equal measure. "It sings of broken patterns and coming war."

"What war?" Asvarr asked, though dread coiled in his stomach. He already knew.

"The Ashfather gathers his forces," Yara said, her skull-side grinning eerily in the fading light. "He seeks to reclaim what he lost when you freed the dreamer—control of the pattern, dominion over the nine realms."

"He cannot allow the new growth to take root," Leif added, the Skymark on his shoulders flaring. "If the Midsong Tree flourishes, his power diminishes further."

Asvarr looked at the slender sapling, its impossible song changing the very fabric of reality around it. Such power in such a fragile form—exactly what the Ashfather would seek to destroy or control.

"Why gather us here?" he asked. "What can five Wardens do that the dreamer cannot?"

"The dreamer awakens slowly," Svala replied, frost forming around her feet as she spoke. "It needs guardians until it fully stirs. The Tree knows this, so it sings us together—the first gathering of all Wardens since the first breaking."

"And it offers a choice," Brynja said, her eyes locked on Asvarr's. "Stand together against what comes, or scatter and face the Ashfather's vengeance alone."

The Midsong Tree's song shifted again, dropping to a low, ominous hum that made the earth tremble. Wind whipped around the clearing, carrying the scent of ash and iron.

"He comes," Yara whispered, her living eye widening. "The Ashfather approaches with shadow and flame."

Asvarr tightened his grip on the bronze sword, the five tokens at his belt burning with sudden heat. The mark on his chest blazed, recognizing the approach of its ancient enemy.

"I've met him twice and walked away," Asvarr said. "I don't fear him."

"You should," Leif cautioned. "This time he brings the Hunt of Broken Fate—nine shadow-warriors born from discarded possibilities. And he comes for all of us, not just you, Flame-Bearer."

The sky darkened overhead, clouds gathering unnaturally fast. Lightning split the heavens, revealing momentary silhouettes of mounted figures approaching across the distant ridge.

Brynja drew a curved blade from her hip, its edge glowing with the same green-gold light as her Jordmark. "Choose quickly, Asvarr Skyrend's-Flame. Do we stand together as the Tree sings us to do? Or do you walk your fourth path alone?"

The promise-thread around Asvarr's wrist burned, reminding him of Skuld's words: "Where it leads, you will find those who walk similar paths." He looked at the four Wardens surrounding him, each marked by the Tree, each changed by their bindings. Different paths, different sacrifices, yet all drawn here by the Midsong Tree's song.

Thunder cracked above them as the Hunt of Broken Fate drew nearer, and Asvarr made his choice.

***

Asvarr stepped forward, his decision crystallizing like frost on iron. "We stand together."

The words fell from his mouth with the weight of an oath. The promise-thread at his wrist flared golden, sending warmth through his arm and into his chest where the Grímmark resonated in agreement.

"Five Wardens against nine Hunters," Brynja said, a grim smile spreading across her face. She moved to his side, her curved blade gleaming with verdant light. "The Tree chose well."

The sky darkened further, clouds churning overhead like a sea in storm. Lightning branched across the heavens, briefly illuminating the riders cresting the ridge—nine figures astride beasts with too many legs and eyes that glowed like burning coals.

"Form the circle," Svala commanded, frost crackling under her feet as she took position to Asvarr's right. The Frostmark at her throat pulsed with blue-white light, sending tendrils of cold mist spiraling around her shoulders. "Protect the Midsong Tree at all costs."

Leif and Yara moved into place, completing the circle around the singing sapling. The World-Walker's Skymark cast silver reflections across the clearing as it brightened. The Death-Walker's skull face gleamed in the strange light, her Deathmark emitting ashen gray smoke that curled around her fingers.

"They want the Tree," Leif warned, eyes fixed on the approaching Hunt. "Its song and what it represents—growth beyond the Ashfather's control."

Asvarr drew his bronze sword, its ancient runes glowing gold to match his mark. "They'll face five Wardens ready to defend it."

The Midsong Tree's melody shifted, gaining urgency and structure. The notes coalesced into a rhythm that matched Asvarr's heartbeat, then expanded to include four other pulses—the hearts of the Wardens surrounding it. The ground beneath them hardened, the circle of bare earth transforming into a platform of root-carved stone.

"The Tree prepares," Yara murmured, her half-skull face grinning with anticipation. "It remembers how to fight."

Thunder cracked overhead, and the first of the Hunt appeared at the clearing's edge. A rider wrapped in shadow, mounted on a six-legged beast with antlers sprouting from its elongated skull. The rider carried a spear of black ice that dripped with venom that sizzled where it struck the ground.

"Arjunskar, First Hunter," Svala named it, raising her hands as frost gathered between her palms. "Favors poison and fear."

More riders emerged from the storm-dark forest—eight shapes of nightmare and twisted possibility, each distinct in its horror. One rode a beast of flame and smoke, another a mount of twisted bone and sinew. Their weapons varied from serrated blades to barbed whips to bare hands that flickered between flesh and shadow.

The lead Hunter dismounted, its form shifting like smoke caught in wind. When it settled, Asvarr recognized the false likeness of a Valkyrie—similar to Sigrdrífa yet wrong, like a reflection in troubled water.

"Wardens," the Hunter spoke, its voice a discordant harmony of broken oaths and forgotten promises. "The Ashfather extends mercy. Surrender the sapling, and you may keep your marks."

Brynja spat on the ground. "Tell your master we've seen his mercy in nine cycles of manipulation. We stand with the Tree."

The false Valkyrie tilted its head, smoke curling from its eye sockets. "You misunderstand. This lacks negotiation. This merely offers courtesy before slaughter."

Asvarr felt the tokens at his belt heating, responding to the proximity of ancient enemies. The black iron shears from Skuld hung heavy at his hip, their purpose still unclear yet their presence reassuring.

"Where is he?" Asvarr demanded. "Where is your master?"

A cold laugh escaped the Hunter. "He watches. As he always has. As he always will."

Without warning, the Hunter lunged forward, black ice spear aimed at Asvarr's heart. Brynja's curved blade intercepted it with a sound like breaking glass, green-gold sparks flying from the contact.

The circle erupted into chaos.

Hunters charged from all directions, their mounts shrieking with voices that tore at the mind. Asvarr's sword met shadow-steel with a ring that echoed across the clearing. He parried a strike meant to sever his sword arm, then riposted, driving his blade into the formless center of a Hunter that wore a stag's skull for a face.

The creature wailed, dark essence pouring from the wound like oil from a punctured lamp. It retreated, only for another to take its place—this one wielding twin daggers crafted from what looked like fossilized lightning.

Beside him, Brynja fought with fluid grace, her curved blade leaving trails of green light as it sliced through the air. The ground responded to her movements, rising in sudden spikes to impale the legs of charging mounts or dropping away to create traps beneath the Hunters' feet.

"Earth-Healer," Asvarr called to her between strikes. "Can you shield the Tree?"

"Working on it," she grunted, driving her blade into the earth. The ground rippled outward from the point of contact, then rose around the Midsong Tree in a dome of intertwined roots and stone.

On the far side of the clearing, Svala stood surrounded by three Hunters, her hands weaving complex patterns in the air. The temperature plummeted around her, frost coating her skin until she gleamed like a statue carved from winter itself. With a shout, she released whatever power she'd gathered, and the air crystalized, freezing the nearest Hunter solid.

Leif moved like quicksilver, the Skymark on his shoulders allowing him to step between spaces, appearing beside one Hunter only to vanish and reappear behind another. His weapons were twin rods of metal that lengthened and shortened according to need, striking with uncanny precision.

Yara's fighting style proved most disturbing. The Death-Walker seemed to flicker between solidity and shadow, taking wounds that should have been fatal only to have the injuries close with gray smoke. Her weapon was a slender bone knife that left wounds which refused to heal, sending cracks through the Hunters' very essence.

Asvarr parried another strike, then ducked beneath a barbed whip that whistled past his ear. The mark on his chest burned hotter with each exchange, feeding power into his limbs, sharpening his senses. He felt connected to the other Wardens through the Tree's song, anticipating their movements, complementing their attacks.

The Hunt, for all its dreadful power, fought as individuals. The Wardens, despite having just met, fought as one.

"They're pulling back," Leif called as the Hunters broke contact, retreating to a loose semicircle beyond the clearing's edge.

Asvarr caught his breath, noting with satisfaction that three of the nine Hunters now bore serious wounds—one frozen solid, one leaking essence from a bronze sword strike, and one with gray cracks spreading from where Yara's knife had struck its core.

"This was just the first test," Brynja warned, blood trickling from a cut above her eye. "They wanted to assess our strength."

"And our unity," Yara added, her living eye gleaming with fierce joy. "They expected us to fight separately, to be overwhelmed."

The Midsong Tree's song shifted again, becoming a martial anthem that pulsed through the stone beneath their feet. Its branches swayed, lengthened, hardened—taking on aspects of weapons and shields.

"The Tree communes with us," Svala said, frost still coating her hands and forearms. "It offers its strength if we'll accept it."

One branch extended toward Asvarr, a bud forming at its tip. Unlike the golden apple from before, this one opened to reveal a small flame dancing at its center—a perfect match to the fire-rune within his Grímmark.

Similar offerings extended to the others—earth for Brynja, ice for Svala, a mote of silver light for Leif, a shadow-wisp for Yara.

"What does it ask in return?" Asvarr questioned, eyeing the flame warily.

"A binding," Leif answered. "Temporary, yet profound. We become its vessels in battle."

Brynja touched the earth-mote, which dissolved into her skin, sending green-gold patterns racing up her arm to join with her Jordmark. Her eyes took on the same glow. "The Tree knows we cannot hold against all nine Hunters alone. It offers its power through us."

Asvarr hesitated, remembering every binding's cost. "Will we remain ourselves?"

"The Tree wants to empower us, never consume us," Svala said, already reaching for her ice-mote. "Unlike the anchors, this binding leaves us intact. We channel its power, nothing more."

The Hunters regrouped, their leader gesturing in complex patterns that sent ripples of distortion through the air. The storm intensified overhead, lightning striking closer to the clearing with each flash.

"Decide quickly, Flame-Bearer," Yara urged, her half-skull face even more pronounced in the storm light. "They summon reinforcements."

Asvarr eyed the flame hovering before him. The Tree had shown him visions of truth; it had summoned the five Wardens to protect it; it had offered its power freely. The Ashfather, by contrast, had manipulated nine cycles of breaking and binding for his own gain.

The choice was clear.

Asvarr reached for the flame.

Heat surged through his palm, racing up his arm to merge with the Grímmark. Fire erupted across his chest, spreading along the mark's patterns without burning his flesh. The bronze sword in his hand flared golden, its runes shifting to incorporate new symbols—the Tree's gift.

Around him, the other Wardens accepted their motes. Svala became a figure of living frost, her skin translucent as ice with blue-white light shining from within. Leif's Skymark expanded across his entire body, covering him in silver constellation patterns that shifted like stars wheeling across the night. Yara's transformation proved most dramatic—her half-skull face acquired ghostly flesh on the other side, making her whole in a way that transcended life and death.

Brynja, last to complete her binding, slammed her fist into the ground. The earth around the clearing erupted in a forest of stone spikes, forcing the Hunters to retreat further.

"Now we fight as the Tree's champions," she declared, her voice carrying a resonance that hadn't been there before. "Now we show the Ashfather that his cycle of control has ended."

The lead Hunter shrieked in rage, a sound that shattered nearby trees and sent splinters flying like arrows. The Hunt charged again, this time moving in coordinated patterns that suggested a single controlling will behind their actions.

"The Ashfather directs them now," Leif warned, silver light trailing from his fingers as he readied his stance.

Asvarr felt the flame within his mark surge in response to the threat. Knowledge flowed into him—how to channel the Tree's fire, how to work in concert with the other Wardens, how to target the Hunters' weaknesses.

"Together," he called to the others, raising his blazing sword.

The Hunt crashed against them like a tide of shadows and nightmares. This time, the battle moved beyond physical combat into something stranger. The Hunters shape-shifted mid-attack, becoming living weapons, becoming fears and doubts, becoming reflections of paths untaken.

Asvarr found himself fighting a shadow-self—the berserker he might have remained had he never received the Grímmark. It fought with raw fury and savage strength, wielding an axe that cut through the air with deadly precision.

"You abandoned your true strength," the shadow-Asvarr growled, its voice a dark echo of his own. "You could have ruled with blood and steel, feared by all."

Asvarr answered with his sword, driving the bronze blade through the shadow's guard. "I found strength beyond fear."

The shadow howled as golden fire spread from the wound, consuming it from within. It collapsed into wisps of darkness that dissipated in the wind.

Across the clearing, his fellow Wardens faced similar phantoms—shadows of choices unmade, lives unlived. The Midsong Tree's song provided a counterpoint to these illusions, its melody cutting through lies with simple truth.

The tide turned. Two more Hunters fell—one to Svala's ice, another to Yara's death-blade. The remaining four gathered around their leader, merging into a towering form that loomed over the clearing like a storm cloud given flesh. It carried a spear of shadow and lightning that crackled with malevolent energy.

"The Ashfather's avatar," Brynja shouted in warning. "He speaks through them now!"

The amalgamated Hunter opened a mouth filled with starless void. "Wardens," it spoke with the voice of mountains grinding against one another. "You protect a lie. The Tree's song promises freedom while delivering chaos. I offered order. I offered certainty."

"You created a cage," Asvarr responded, the Tree's fire lending strength to his words. "Nine cycles of consumption hidden beneath protection."

"And what do you offer, Flame-Bearer? You who walked the fourth path? Your freedom fails. The pattern needs guidance for survival."

"The pattern will grow through change," Asvarr challenged. "It will flourish beyond your control."

The avatar laughed, the sound causing fissures in the very air. "Change brings death, Warden. I forbid it."

It struck with its spear, aiming at the Midsong Tree itself. The weapon tore through Brynja's stone shield as if it were parchment, hurtling toward the slender sapling with unstoppable force.

Asvarr moved without thought, driven by instinct and the Tree's fire in his veins. He threw himself into the spear's path, sword raised to deflect the blow.

Shadow-steel met bronze with a sound like worlds colliding. The impact drove Asvarr to his knees, his arms straining against the enormous pressure. The bronze sword cracked, a single fissure running from hilt to tip.

"Fool," the avatar hissed. "You cannot stop what comes."

The other Wardens converged on Asvarr's position, adding their power to his defense. Brynja's earth, Svala's ice, Leif's sky-light, Yara's death-shadow—all flowed into the bronze sword, sealing its crack with multicolored light.

"We stand together," Asvarr gritted through clenched teeth. "As the Tree sings, so we act."

With a final surge of strength, he pushed back against the spear, forcing it upward. The movement created an opening that the other Wardens exploited, each striking the avatar with their empowered weapons.

The amalgamated Hunter screamed, its form fracturing under the combined assault. Lightning struck the clearing in a blinding flash, and when Asvarr's vision cleared, the Hunters had vanished. Only scorch marks remained where they had stood.

Silence fell over the clearing, broken only by the Wardens' labored breathing and the Midsong Tree's gentle song—now a melody of triumph and gratitude.

"They've retreated," Leif confirmed, the silver light of his Skymark dimming to a soft glow. "For now."

Brynja knelt beside Asvarr, examining the bronze sword that had saved the Tree. "Look," she said, pointing to where the crack had been. A line of golden sap now ran the length of the blade, hardening into an inlay that strengthened it. "The Tree has marked your weapon as it marked you."

Asvarr stood, feeling the fire of the Tree's binding gradually receding from his limbs. The Grímmark on his chest settled into a new configuration, incorporating aspects of the temporary power he'd channeled.

"The Ashfather will return," he said, sheathing the transformed sword. "He will bring greater force."

"And we'll be ready," Svala replied, frost still clinging to her eyelashes. "This was merely the opening skirmish in a greater war."

The Midsong Tree's branches swayed, its melody shifting to a questioning cadence. One branch extended toward Asvarr again, this time bearing a small, perfectly formed leaf glowing with inner light.

"Another vision?" he asked, reaching for it.

"A revelation," Yara answered, her form slowly returning to its half-living, half-dead appearance as the Tree's power faded. "The Tree reveals the path forward only to those who have proven themselves in its defense."

Asvarr plucked the leaf, which dissolved into golden light that flowed into his eyes. A map formed in his mind—showing connections between realms rather than physical terrain. He saw the five anchors he had bound, saw how they linked to form a pattern, and saw what lay at the pattern's center: a void waiting to be filled.

"All Realms will die unless the Root is healed," he murmured, understanding flowing through him. "The Ashfather seeks to fill the void at the pattern's center with himself, to become the new dreamer. If he succeeds..."

"The cycle begins again, with him at its heart," Brynja finished, reading the knowledge in his eyes. "Complete control, complete consumption."

Asvarr looked at his fellow Wardens, these strangers bound to him through the Tree's song and their shared marks. "We must prevent this. We must heal the Root another way."

The Midsong Tree's song rose again, five distinct melodies weaving together in perfect harmony. Each note corresponded to a Warden, each phrase to a path they might walk. Together, they formed a music of possibility—a future yet unwoven.

"The Tree guides us," Leif said, his Skymark glimmering with renewed purpose. "Five Wardens, five paths, meeting at the pattern's center."

"Then we each have our tasks," Brynja concluded. She extended her hand to the center of their circle, palm up. "I, Brynja Earth-Healer, will walk the path of renewal."

Svala placed her hand atop Brynja's. "I, Svala Storm-Speaker, will walk the path of cleansing."

Leif added his hand to the stack. "I, Leif World-Walker, will walk the path of connection."

Yara completed the circle with her half-flesh, half-bone hand. "I, Yara Death-Walker, will walk the path of transition."

All eyes turned to Asvarr. The weight of nine cycles pressed on him, along with the knowledge of what his choice at Ymir's Cradle had set in motion. He placed his hand atop theirs, feeling the resonance between their marks.

"I, Asvarr Skyrend's Flame, will walk the path of transformation."

The Midsong Tree's song surged in five-part harmony. A burst of golden light exploded outward from the sapling, washing over the Wardens and binding their oath in power stronger than blood or iron.

When the light faded, each Warden bore a small mark on their palm where their hands had touched—a simplified version of the Midsong Tree, a promise of alliance and shared purpose.

The war for Yggdrasil's future had truly begun.

CHAPTER 17

BLACK SNOW AT GÁLGVIÐR

Asvarr trudged through knee-deep snow that whispered with each step. Seven days had passed since the battle at the Midsong Tree, since he and the other Wardens had sworn their oath and parted ways. The small mark on his palm—a simplified Tree etched in gold—pulsed with gentle warmth, the only comfort in the bitter cold of the mountain pass.

The wind sliced through his furs, carrying flakes of black snow that stung his exposed skin. He raised a hand to shield his eyes, squinting at the shadowed forest that sprawled across the valley below. Gálgviðr, the Gallows-Wood, where ancient execution-trees grew from the bones of the condemned. The mark on his chest had pulled him here, insistent and unyielding, though he couldn't fathom why.

His breath clouded before him, crisp white against the strange darkness falling from above. The black snow had begun three days earlier—ordinary flakes that turned to ash upon landing. They left smears of charcoal on his skin and furs, marking him like a coal miner emerging from the depths.

"Warden walks a lonely road," croaked a voice from nearby.

Asvarr whirled, bronze sword clearing its sheath in a single motion. The blade's golden sap inlay caught what little light penetrated the storm, casting an amber glow across the snow.

A raven perched on a gnarled branch protruding from the snowdrift, larger than any bird he'd seen before. Its feathers gleamed with an oily iridescence, and its eyes held an intelligence that made Asvarr's skin crawl.

"World-Walker?" Asvarr asked, wondering if this was Leif in transformed state. The raven cocked its head, considering.

"No kin to the Sky-Marked one," it replied, voice grating like stone on metal. "Huginn, I am called. Memory-Keeper, Thought-Bringer." The raven's beak clacked three times. "Or was, before the breaking."

Asvarr lowered his sword slightly, eyes narrowed. "You serve the Ashfather."

The raven's wings fluttered, sending up a small cloud of black snow. "Served, past-tense, Flame-Bearer. Now I watch, I remember, I survive." Its head tilted at an impossible angle. "Like you must do, in the upside-down forest."

"Upside-down forest?" Asvarr furrowed his brow, looking again toward the valley.

"Gálgviðr grows from clouds, roots in sky, branches below," the raven explained, hopping closer along the branch. "Where the executed hang upside-down, where Odin hung for nine days to gain wisdom of runes." Its eyes glinted. "Where you must go to find what you seek."

Asvarr's grip tightened on his sword hilt. "And what do I seek?"

"The path of transformation requires a guide," Huginn said, evading the question. "One who walks Gálgviðr's paths and knows its secrets." The raven's eyes flickered to something beyond Asvarr's shoulder. "She comes now."

Asvarr turned, keeping the raven in his peripheral vision. A figure approached through the swirling black snow—a woman wrapped in layers of gray and white furs that made her shape indistinct. Her face remained hidden behind a mask carved from pale wood, painted with spirals of blue and black. She carried a staff topped with a crystal that glowed with cold blue light.

"Skyrend's Flame," she said, her voice clear despite the mask and howling wind. "The forest calls you, and I am sent to guide."

"Who are you?" Asvarr demanded, sword still ready.

"Yrsa Ninevane," she replied, planting her staff in the snow. The crystal flared brighter, pushing back the darkness. "I walk between worlds and times. I have awaited you since before your binding, Asvarr Flame-Bearer."

The raven flapped its wings, rising into the air. "Trust, mistrust, matters little," it croaked. "The path forward lies only through Gálgviðr." With that, it ascended into the black snowfall and vanished.

Asvarr studied the masked woman, searching for any sign of deception. The mark on his chest remained calm.

"How do you know who I am?" he asked.

"I know all Wardens," Yrsa replied simply. "I watched the first breaking when the Tree shattered. I guided the Ashfather when he still carried his true name. I witnessed eight cycles of rebinding until you chose the fourth path." She stepped closer, and Asvarr caught the scent of herbs and iron clinging to her furs. "Now I come to guide you through Gálgviðr, if you will accept."

"Why should I trust you?"

Yrsa extended her hand, pulling back her fur sleeve to reveal a mark similar to Asvarr's Tree-mark—though hers appeared faded, ancient, almost scarred into her flesh rather than burned.

"I bear the mark of the first Midsong Tree," she said. "The sapling that grew after the original breaking, before the Ashfather twisted it to his design." Her hand lowered. "The current Tree recognizes me as kin, though distant. It sent you here knowing I would meet you."

Asvarr sheathed his sword slowly, his instincts at war with necessity. He needed guidance, and his mark had led him to this place for a reason.

"What awaits in Gálgviðr?" he asked.

"Knowledge." Yrsa turned, gesturing for him to follow. "The forest has existed since before the first Tree, before the gods. It grows from the clouds down, defying ordinary laws. Within its branches, you'll find what you need for the path of transformation."

They descended the mountain path together, the black snow falling heavier around them. Asvarr noticed that where the flakes touched Yrsa's mask, they turned to ordinary water droplets, leaving no stain.

"The snow comes from the Ashfather's forges," she explained, noting his observation. "He burns memories to forge weapons against the new pattern. The ash carries fragments of forgotten lives."

As they approached the valley floor, the true nature of Gálgviðr became apparent. What Asvarr had taken for a forest in the distance was something far stranger. Above the valley hung enormous, roiling clouds, darker than storm clouds, nearly solid in appearance. From these clouds grew massive trunks—trees that descended from the sky rather than rising from the earth. Their branches spread downward, creating a canopy that barely cleared the valley floor in some places.

"Gálgviðr," Yrsa said, pausing at the edge of this impossible woodland. "The Gallows-Wood, where the barrier between worlds thins and knowledge hangs ripe for plucking." She turned to Asvarr, the painted spirals on her mask seeming to move in the crystal's blue light. "Once we enter, trust nothing your eyes tell you. The forest plays with perception, creates illusions from memory and desire."

"What am I looking for?" Asvarr asked, eyeing the downward-growing trees with unease.

"You seek Yrsa Ninevane, who has walked this realm long before the Shattering," she replied cryptically. "The woman who can tell you what the transformation truly means."

Asvarr frowned. "I thought you were Yrsa Ninevane."

Her laugh came soft and melodic behind the mask. "I am a guide to Yrsa, nothing more. The forest fragments visitors, creates echoes and guides from their own minds." She tapped her mask. "This protects me from the worst effects. Without it, I would be lost among the mirrors."

Before Asvarr could question further, she strode forward beneath the first of the hanging trees. He followed, hand resting on his sword hilt, every sense alert. The moment they passed beneath the outermost branches, the world changed.

***

The constant sound of wind died abruptly, replaced by an unsettling silence. The temperature rose, the bitter cold giving way to a humid warmth that made sweat bead on Asvarr's forehead. Most disorienting of all, the black snow continued to fall, but now it drifted upward from the ground toward the roots above.

"Don't look up for too long," Yrsa warned. "Those who stare at the roots become lost."

Asvarr quickly lowered his gaze, focusing instead on the forest floor. What he had taken for earth was a strange, yielding surface—like walking on tightly woven branches. Beneath, glimpsed through small gaps, he saw stars.

"We walk on the canopy of a forest that grows upward from another world," Yrsa explained, noticing his confusion. "Gálgviðr exists between realms, a bridge and a barrier."

They traveled deeper into the inverted woodland, following a path that seemed to form just ahead of their footsteps and vanish behind them. The hanging trees grew more massive the further they went, their downward-reaching branches thick as a man's torso. Leaves of silver and gold fluttered in a breeze Asvarr couldn't feel, their undersides glowing with faint phosphorescence.

"The forest acknowledges you," Yrsa commented, pointing to the glowing leaves. "It recognizes the marks you bear."

As if in response, the Grímmark on Asvarr's chest pulsed with warmth. The promise-thread around his wrist glowed golden, illuminating their path through the strange woods. The black snow continued its upward drift, occasionally swirling into patterns that almost resembled faces before dispersing again.

"There are eyes upon us," Asvarr murmured, the sensation of being watched prickling along his spine.

"Always," Yrsa agreed. "Gálgviðr has many guardians—some friendly, others less so." She paused, staff raised. "Speak your true name when asked, and offer no violence unless struck first. The forest allows visitors but punishes trespassers harshly."

They rounded a massive trunk hanging from the clouds above, and Asvarr froze. Before them stood a clearing where nine bodies hung upside-down from branches, their ankles bound, arms dangling toward the ground. Their faces were obscured by long hair, and they swayed gently though there was no wind.

"The Nine," Yrsa said softly. "Sacrifices to knowledge. Do not approach them."

Too late, Asvarr realized one of the hanging figures had turned its head toward them. Hair parted to reveal a face identical to his own, eyes milky white, lips moving in silent speech.

"What is this?" he demanded, hand flying to his sword.

"Your fear given form," Yrsa replied, placing a restraining hand on his arm. "The forest tests all who enter. It shows what might be, what once was, what you fear becoming." She pulled him away from the clearing. "Do not engage with the visions. They gain power through attention."

They pressed onward, the path winding deeper into Gálgviðr. The upside-down trees grew closer together, their hanging branches forming tunnels and corridors that shifted subtly when Asvarr looked away. Twice they reached dead ends that hadn't existed moments before, forcing them to backtrack and find new routes.

"The forest resists," Yrsa muttered after their third detour. "Something works against us."

"The Ashfather?" Asvarr suggested, thinking of the raven.

"Perhaps," she conceded. "Or perhaps the forest itself tests your resolve." She stopped abruptly, head tilted as if listening. "This way. Quickly."

She led him through a narrow gap between two massive trunks, emerging into another clearing. This one contained a pool of water that defied understanding—it hung suspended in the air, a perfect circle of liquid. Within its depths, Asvarr glimpsed movement: figures walking, fighting, living lives that seemed both familiar and foreign.

"What is this place?" he asked, approaching the hovering pool cautiously.

"The Well of Echoes," Yrsa explained, staying close beside him. "It shows fragments of other cycles, other paths." She gestured to the water. "Look, but do not touch. The water pulls."

Asvarr peered into the pool. The scenes shifted rapidly—he saw himself as a king, crowned in iron and blood; as a berserker, lost to rage and battle-fury; as an old man, surrounded by family; as a corpse, impaled on the Ashfather's spear. Each image lasted only moments before dissolving into the next.

"Possibilities," Yrsa murmured. "Paths untaken, choices unmade."

A new image formed in the water—Asvarr standing with the other Wardens at the Midsong Tree, their hands joined as they were now. But in this vision, a sixth figure stood among them, hooded and shadowed.

"Who is that?" he asked, pointing to the mysterious figure.

Yrsa stiffened beside him. "One who walks between. The true enemy."

Before she could elaborate, the pool's surface rippled violently. The water surged upward, defying gravity completely, forming into a humanoid shape that hovered above the now-empty basin. It had no features save for a mouth, which opened to reveal teeth of ice.

"Asvarr Skyrend's Flame," it spoke, voice bubbling and wet. "Your presence unbalances Gálgviðr. The forest rejects transformation."

Asvarr drew his sword, the golden sap inlay glowing bright in the dim forest. "Who are you?"

"Mímir's Echo," the water-being replied. "Guardian of forgotten wisdom, keeper of severed heads." It flowed closer, its liquid form constantly shifting. "You seek Yrsa Ninevane, who knows the truth of transformation's path."

"Yes," Asvarr confirmed, sensing no immediate threat despite the creature's unsettling appearance.

The water-being turned toward Yrsa. "And you, guide? What do you seek?"

"Passage," she replied, her masked face revealing nothing. "Safe conduct for the Warden to the heart of Gálgviðr."

Mímir's Echo made a sound like distant waves crashing. "Lies. You seek to reclaim what was taken. You hunt your stolen name."

Yrsa's grip tightened on her staff, the crystal flaring brighter. "My purposes are my own, Guardian. Will you grant passage or must we force our way?"

The water-being's mouth stretched into a grotesque smile. "Violence in Gál-gviðr brings only sorrow, mask-wearer." It turned back to Asvarr. "I will grant passage on one condition, Flame-Bearer. Answer truly: what would you sacrifice to walk the path of transformation to its end?"

Asvarr felt the weight of the question in his bones. He had already sacrificed much to bind the anchors—rage, memory, identity, certainty, free will. What more could transformation demand?

"Whatever is necessary," he answered finally, "except my purpose. I will transform to save the pattern, to prevent the Ashfather's dominion, to free the dreamer fully—but I will not abandon those goals, no matter the cost."

Mímir's Echo regarded him silently for long moments, its watery form rippling with unreadable emotion. Then it nodded, a single sharp movement that sent droplets flying.

"Acceptable," it pronounced. "Follow the black snow's ascent to the heart of the forest. There you will find what you seek." It began to collapse back into the basin, its form dissolving. "Beware, Flame-Bearer. Transformation walks hand in hand with destruction. What emerges may bear your name but will not be you."

With those ominous words, the guardian melted entirely back into the pool, which now appeared as ordinary water once more.

Yrsa turned to Asvarr, her masked face impossible to read. "The way is open now. We should hurry before the forest changes its mind."

"Did it speak truth?" Asvarr asked, sheathing his sword. "About transformation destroying what I am?"

"All significant change destroys what came before," she replied. "A caterpillar dies to make way for the butterfly. A seed breaks to allow the tree to grow." She tapped the mask's painted spirals. "The question is whether what emerges serves your purpose, as you told the guardian."

She turned away, following a stream of black snow that flowed upward toward the cloudy ceiling of the forest. Asvarr hesitated only briefly before following, his mind troubled by Mímir's Echo's warning and the mystery of his guide's true purpose in Gálgviðr.

The path grew steeper, the forest floor beginning to slope upward at an angle that should have made walking impossible. Yet their footing remained sure, as if gravity itself bent to the forest's will. The upside-down trees thinned, revealing more of the star-filled void beneath the branch-woven ground.

"We approach the heart," Yrsa called back to him. "Beyond lies the true Gálgviðr, where Yrsa Ninevane dwells."

The ground before them suddenly dropped away completely, revealing a vast open space beneath the clouds. Suspended in this void hung an enormous tree—the inverse of all others they had seen. It grew upward from some unseen ground below, its branches reaching toward the cloudy ceiling, its highest boughs just brushing the veil between worlds.

And there, perched among those upper branches, Asvarr spotted a small structure—a cabin built around the trunk itself, light glowing from its windows.

"There," Yrsa pointed with her staff. "The dwelling of Yrsa Ninevane, who has walked this realm long before the Shattering."

"How do we reach it?" Asvarr asked, seeing no path across the void.

In answer, Yrsa removed her mask. Beneath it was a swirling vortex of stars and darkness, similar to what Asvarr had seen when Skuld revealed her true nature.

"Now," she said, her voice unchanged despite her inhuman visage, "we fly."

Asvarr recoiled instinctively, his hand flying to his sword hilt. The guide's face—a swirling cosmos of stars and void—pulsed with cold light, casting strange shadows across the forest floor.

"What are you?" he demanded, the bronze sword half-drawn.

"A fragment," the cosmic-faced guide replied, her voice unchanged despite her transformed visage. "A splinter of what once was Yrsa Ninevane, created to guide worthy seekers."

She extended her hand, the stars within her face-void spinning faster. "We must hurry. The forest grows restless."

As if confirming her words, the ground beneath Asvarr's feet trembled. Cracks appeared in the branch-woven surface, revealing glimpses of the star-filled void below. The upside-down trees swayed violently, their hanging branches thrashing like the limbs of drowning men.

"How do we fly?" Asvarr asked, eyeing the distant cabin perched in the uppermost branches of the normal tree.

"Through transformation," the guide answered, grasping his forearm with surprising strength. "The mark you bear allows passage between states."

Before Asvarr could protest, the guide pressed her star-filled face close to his. From the void poured tendrils of darkness studded with pinpricks of light, wrapping around his arms and chest. The mark beneath his tunic flared hot, responding to the cosmic touch.

A sensation like falling and flying simultaneously overtook him. His body felt simultaneously heavy as stone and weightless as smoke. The world lurched sideways, colors bleeding together, sounds stretching and compressing.

Then they were airborne.

The void below rushed past as they soared across the impossible space between the inverted forest and the lone upright tree. Asvarr's stomach clenched with vertigo, his mind struggling to process the experience. He wasn't physically flying—his body remained solid—yet the laws of nature bent around him, allowing movement through air as easily as through water.

"The forest permits temporary transformation," the guide explained, her cosmic face rippling with what might have been amusement. "You walk the path of transformation, after all. Consider this practice."

They landed on a wide branch near the cabin. The guide released Asvarr's arm, and the weightless sensation vanished immediately. He staggered, dropping to one knee on the rough bark as his body readjusted to normal physics.

"That was..." Words failed him.

"Uncomfortable the first time," the guide finished, replacing her wooden mask over her cosmic face. The painted spirals seemed to move more rapidly now, pulsing with inner light. "The true Yrsa waits within. I go no further."

The cabin built around the massive trunk looked ancient yet well-maintained. Its walls were constructed from silvered wood that gleamed in the strange

half-light of Gálgviðr. Windows of clouded glass glowed with warm amber light.
The door bore a complex pattern of interlocking circles that shifted subtly as
Asvarr watched.

"Will you wait?" he asked the guide, uncertain if he would need assistance
returning.

"I cannot. My purpose ends at delivery." She gestured toward the door with her
staff. "The forest knows you now. When your business concludes, you may depart
without escort."

With that, she stepped backward off the branch. Instead of falling, she simply
dissolved into motes of starlight that scattered and vanished among the black
snow still drifting upward from below.

***

Asvarr stood alone on the branch, the cabin door before him. The mark on his
chest pulsed in time with his heartbeat, growing warmer with each step he took
toward the entrance. The promise-thread around his wrist glowed brighter too,
as if responding to proximity to something significant.

He raised his fist to knock, but the door swung inward before his knuckles
made contact.

Inside sat a woman. She appeared young yet ancient simultaneously—her face
unlined, her eyes deep-set and knowing, her silver-white hair flowing past her
shoulders in intricate braids adorned with small bones and crystal beads. She
wore simple garments of deep blue, embroidered with silver threads that formed
patterns similar to the painted spirals on the guide's mask.

"Asvarr Skyrend's Flame," she said, her voice melodic yet weighted with authority. "The Warden who walks the path of transformation. Enter and be welcomed in Gálgviðr."

He stepped across the threshold, ducking slightly beneath the low doorframe.
The cabin's interior was larger than its exterior suggested—impossible angles and
extended spaces that defied ordinary geometry. Shelves lined the walls, packed

with books, scrolls, stones carved with unfamiliar runes, and jars containing substances that glowed with inner light.

In the center stood a table of dark wood polished to a mirror finish. Its surface displayed what appeared to be a map, though the landmasses and boundaries shifted subtly whenever Asvarr looked away.

"You are Yrsa Ninevane," he said, the words a statement rather than a question.

"I am," she confirmed, gesturing for him to sit opposite her. "I have walked this realm since before the first breaking, when the primordial Tree first shattered."

Asvarr remained standing, studying her carefully. "Your guide claimed the same."

A smile touched Yrsa's lips. "My fragment speaks truly. She is me, yet separate—a splinter of consciousness created to navigate Gálgviðr safely." She tapped the table's surface. "Please, sit. We have much to discuss and little time. The Ashfather moves against all Wardens now."

Reluctantly, Asvarr took the offered seat. The bronze sword he kept unsheathed, resting across his knees. The golden sap inlay glowed faintly in the cabin's warm light.

"The Tree-marked sword," Yrsa observed. "The Midsong Tree continues to grow in power, I see." Her gaze shifted to the promise-thread around his wrist. "And Skuld's gift. The youngest Norn finally learned to weave possibilities instead of certainties. Progress, after so many cycles."

"You know much about me," Asvarr said, unease creeping up his spine.

"I know all Wardens," Yrsa replied simply. "I watched the Ashfather bind the first anchors nine cycles ago. I witnessed his transformation from seeker to tyrant." Her eyes reflected pinpricks of starlight, reminiscent of her fragment's cosmic face. "And now I watch you walk the fourth path, the path of transformation, which may finally break the cycle."

"That's why I've come," Asvarr said. "To understand what transformation truly means."

Yrsa nodded, her bone-adorned braids clicking softly. "Then I will show you."

She passed her hand over the table's surface. The shifting map vanished, replaced by an image of Yggdrasil in its full glory—branches extending throughout nine distinct realms, roots plunging into depths unfathomable. As Asvarr watched, the Tree shattered, its fragments scattering across reality.

"The first breaking," Yrsa explained, "when the dreamer withdrew its consciousness from the pattern. The Norns cut the thread, hoping to wake it fully."

The image shifted, showing a tall figure gathering fragments of the shattered Tree, binding them into a new pattern—a smaller, more controlled version of Yggdrasil with nine distinct branches.

"The first Warden, who became the Ashfather," Yrsa continued. "He bound the anchors out of necessity at first—to prevent total collapse of the realms. But with each binding, he took more power for himself. By the fifth, he no longer sought to restore, only to control."

The table displayed cycle after cycle—the Tree breaking, a Warden binding the anchors, the Ashfather consuming the Warden's essence, the pattern resetting with the Ashfather gaining greater control each time.

"Nine times this pattern repeated," Yrsa said, her voice solemn. "Nine Wardens consumed, nine opportunities lost."

"Until me," Asvarr murmured, watching the final cycle unfold—his own journey from receiving the Grímmark to binding the fifth anchor.

"Until you chose the fourth path at Ymir's Cradle," Yrsa agreed. "The path of transformation rather than continuation or substitution." Her fingers traced the image of Asvarr standing in the golden pool, neither fighting nor submitting to the pattern. "Do you understand what transformation truly requires?"

The mark on Asvarr's chest burned hot against his skin. "Sacrifice," he answered. "Each binding took something from me—rage, memory, identity, certainty, free will. What more must I give?"

"Everything," Yrsa said simply. "And nothing."

She waved her hand again, and the table showed five distinct paths spreading outward from a central point—each one corresponding to one of the Wardens who had sworn the oath at the Midsong Tree.

"Renewal, cleansing, connection, transition, transformation," she named them. "Five approaches to healing the pattern. The other Wardens walk their paths even now, as you walk yours."

"And what awaits at the end of transformation?" Asvarr demanded, frustration edging his voice.

"The void at the pattern's center," Yrsa replied. "Where the Ashfather seeks to install himself as the new dreamer. Where you must prevent his ascension."

"How?"

Yrsa's eyes glittered with starlight. "By becoming what you already are."

Before Asvarr could demand clarification, she reached across the table and touched his forehead. Images flooded his mind—fractured memories, possible futures, alternate paths. He saw himself as a berserker, as a king, as a god, as a vessel. Each version simultaneously true and false, real and imagined.

"Transformation means accepting all possibilities," Yrsa's voice echoed through his mind. "Becoming the sum of what you were, what you are, and what you might be."

The visions intensified. Asvarr saw the five anchors he had bound, felt their power coursing through him. He witnessed the pattern forming around them, creating a structure that resembled Yggdrasil yet differed in crucial ways. At its center gaped a void—waiting to be filled by either the Ashfather or something else entirely.

"The dreamer left a vacancy," Yrsa explained, her voice distant through the storm of images. "The pattern requires consciousness at its core. The Ashfather seeks to fill that role, to control all realms through domination. You must offer an alternative."

"What alternative?" Asvarr managed, fighting through the overwhelming torrent of visions.

"Freedom," she answered. "The consciousness of all beings, linked yet individual. A pattern that serves many rather than enslaves many to serve one."

The visions subsided. Asvarr found himself gasping, sweat beading on his forehead despite the cabin's comfortable temperature. Yrsa withdrew her hand, studying him with those star-filled eyes.

"Do you understand now?" she asked.

"Partially," he admitted, struggling to organize his thoughts. "The Ashfather wants to become the new dreamer, controlling the pattern from within. I must prevent this by... transforming into something that can offer a different solution."

"Yes," Yrsa confirmed. "The path of transformation ends with you becoming the catalyst, the enabler of a new pattern."

She stood, moving to a cabinet against one wall. From it, she withdrew a small wooden box engraved with spirals similar to those on her fragment's mask. She placed it on the table between them.

"This will aid your transformation when the moment comes," she said, pushing the box toward Asvarr. "Open it only at the pattern's center, when all five Wardens converge."

Asvarr took the box, surprised by its weightlessness. It felt almost insubstantial in his hands, yet undeniably present. "What does it contain?"

"A fragment of the original dreamer's consciousness," Yrsa replied. "Preserved since the first breaking."

Asvarr nearly dropped the box in shock. "How did you obtain this?"

"I was there," she said simply. "Before Yggdrasil, before the realms. I witnessed the dreamer's first withdrawal." A sadness passed across her features. "I failed to prevent the Ashfather's corruption nine cycles ago. I will not fail again."

The implications struck Asvarr like a physical blow. "What are you?"

Yrsa smiled, the expression ancient and knowing. "A witness. A keeper of balance. One who walks between." She gestured to the box. "Guard that with your life, Warden. It contains the seed of a new pattern."

The cabin suddenly darkened, the warm amber light dimming to blood-red. Outside, a wind howled through Gálgviðr's impossible geography, carrying sounds like distant screams.

"He comes," Yrsa said, alarm flashing in her starlight eyes. "The Ashfather senses our meeting. You must leave—now."

"How?" Asvarr asked, rising to his feet, sword ready.

"The same way you arrived." Yrsa moved swiftly to the door, throwing it open to reveal the branch outside now whipping violently in an unnatural wind. The black snow had become a maelstrom, swirling in tight spirals that occasionally formed screaming faces. "Transformation, Asvarr. Remember the feeling."

"Will I see you again?" he asked, securing the weightless box within his tunic.

"When the five paths converge," she promised. "Now go!"

Asvarr stepped out onto the branch, the wind immediately tearing at his clothing and hair. Far below, something massive moved through the void between worlds—a shadow darker than the surrounding darkness, crowned with broken branches and trailing tendrils of frost and flame.

The Ashfather had found him.

***

Asvarr closed his eyes, focusing on the sensation he had experienced during flight. The weightlessness, the simultaneous heaviness, the bending of natural law. The mark on his chest responded, flaring with heat that spread throughout his body.

He leapt from the branch.

For one terrifying moment, he plummeted toward the void below, toward the massive shadow waiting to consume him. Then the transformation took hold. Reality bent around him, and instead of falling, he flew—soaring horizontally across the impossible space toward the inverted forest.

Behind him, a roar of rage shook Gálgviðr to its roots. The shadow lunged upward, massive hands formed of darkness and broken godhood reaching for him. Tendrils of frost and flame lashed out, barely missing his heels as he fled.

Asvarr focused on speed, on distance, on escape. The promise-thread around his wrist blazed with golden light, illuminating his path through the chaotic storm of black snow. The marks on his chest and palm burned in unison, guiding his transformation, maintaining his flight.

He reached the edge of the inverted forest just as a wall of ice erupted from the void below, attempting to block his path. Asvarr twisted midair, using his newfound awareness of transformation to shift his form ever so slightly—becoming partially insubstantial for just long enough to pass through the barrier.

The ice shattered behind him as he rematerialized fully, crashing onto the branch-woven ground of the inverted forest. The impact drove the breath from his lungs, yet he forced himself to his feet, knowing delay meant death.

The path he and the guide had followed had vanished, the forest reshaping itself in response to the Ashfather's rage. Trees that had hung serenely now thrashed violently, their branches becoming barbed weapons that sought to impale any who passed beneath.

Asvarr ran, letting instinct and the mark's guidance direct his steps. The box from Yrsa bounced weightlessly against his chest, somehow undamaged despite his rough landing. His sword remained clutched in his hand, the golden sap inlay glowing bright enough to illuminate several paces ahead.

Behind him, the forest began to collapse. Entire sections of the branch-ground crumbled away, revealing the star-filled void. The clouds from which the inverted trees grew darkened to pitch black, lightning crackling between them in jagged arcs of purple-white.

"WARDEN!" The voice shook the very fabric of Gálgviðr, causing fissures to split the trunks of the hanging trees. "YOU CANNOT ESCAPE WHAT AWAITS!"

Asvarr didn't waste breath responding. He focused solely on survival, on escape, on protecting the precious cargo Yrsa had entrusted to him. The path of transformation demanded he reach the pattern's center alive.

A massive root erupted from the ground before him, blocking his path. Without hesitation, Asvarr leapt, calling upon the transformation aspect of his mark once more. His body partially shifted, becoming light enough to soar over the obstacle in a single bound.

The effort cost him. Pain lanced through his chest as the mark strained against his flesh, the power of transformation taxing his mortal frame. He landed hard, rolling to disperse the impact, then scrambled back to his feet.

Ahead, a faint glow marked what he hoped was the boundary of Gálgviðr. The inverted forest seemed to stretch endlessly before him, yet his mark pulled him forward with increasing urgency, promising escape lay just beyond reach.

The voice came again, closer now. "THE PATTERN REQUIRES CONTROL, WARDEN. IT ALWAYS HAS."

This time, Asvarr shouted back as he ran. "The pattern requires freedom!"

His defiance was answered by a wall of flame that erupted from the void below, cutting across his path. The fire burned black and cold, consuming light rather than creating it.

Asvarr skidded to a halt, searching desperately for another route. The forest continued collapsing around him, the boundary between worlds fracturing under the Ashfather's assault.

In that moment of crisis, the five tokens at his belt flared with sudden brilliance—horn, amulet, remembrance-key, frost crystal, and crown. Each one pulsed with the essence of the anchor it represented, offering power beyond what Asvarr had yet accessed.

Understanding flashed through him. The five anchors he had bound were connected to him still. Their power remained available, waiting to be channeled through their tokens.

Without hesitation, Asvarr grasped the frost crystal. Ice spread from his fingertips, racing across the ground toward the wall of black flame. The two elements collided in a explosion of steam and shadow.

Through the momentary gap, Asvarr charged, drawing on the power of transformation to enhance his speed beyond mortal limits. The wall of flame closed behind him, singeing his cloak but failing to catch him.

The boundary of Gálgviðr appeared ahead—a shimmer in the air where the inverted forest ended and normal reality resumed. Beyond lay the mountain path where he had first encountered Huginn and the guide.

A shadow fell across him. The Ashfather had manifested directly in his path—a towering figure of darkness and broken godhood, crowned with shattered branches, wielding a spear of shadow and lightning.

"THE FRAGMENT," the Ashfather demanded, voice shaking the very fabric of reality. "SURRENDER WHAT YRSA GAVE YOU."

Asvarr drew upon the power of all five tokens simultaneously. Horn, amulet, remembrance-key, frost crystal, and crown—each one blazed with energy that flowed into his mark, into his very being. The transformation accelerated, his form becoming partially translucent, trailing streamers of golden light.

"Never," he answered, his voice resonating with power beyond his mortal frame.

The Ashfather roared and thrust his spear downward. Asvarr did not dodge. Instead, he embraced transformation completely. His physical form dissolved into pure energy, flowing around the spear like water around stone.

For a brief, transcendent moment, Asvarr existed as pure potential The box from Yrsa, containing the dreamer's fragment, remained part of him even in this transformed state.

Then he was through, passing the Ashfather's physical manifestation and rematerializing beyond the boundary of Gálgviðr. The transformation collapsed as he tumbled onto mundane snow, his body solid once more, the strain of his metamorphosis leaving him gasping and trembling.

Behind him, Gálgviðr shuddered. The inverted forest began to fold in upon itself, the boundary sealing to prevent the Ashfather's pursuit. The last thing Asvarr saw before the realm vanished entirely was the towering figure of his enemy, spear raised in impotent rage, crown of broken branches blazing with dark fire.

Then it was gone. Gálgviðr vanished as if it had never existed, leaving only an ordinary mountain slope covered in ordinary snow.

Asvarr lay on his back, chest heaving, every muscle screaming with exhaustion. The box rested against his skin, still weightless yet undeniably present. The promise-thread around his wrist had dimmed to a subdued glow, while the mark on his chest pulsed with lingering pain.

He had escaped with Yrsa's gift—a fragment of the original dreamer's consciousness, supposedly capable of preventing the Ashfather's ascension to godhood. Yet the encounter had revealed the true magnitude of his enemy's power, the true challenge that awaited at the pattern's center.

As black snow continued to fall from the storm-dark sky, Asvarr closed his hand around the box hidden beneath his tunic. The path of transformation had become clearer, yet infinitely more dangerous. The price of freedom would be himself, complete metamorphosis into something beyond human.

He would pay it willingly, if it meant breaking the cycle forever.

CHAPTER 18

CHAINS IN GINNUNGAGAP

P ain jolted Asvarr from darkness. His eyes flew open to meet absolute blackness, disorienting him further. The ache in his shoulders told him his arms were stretched above his head, wrists bound. His boots barely touched what felt like smooth stone beneath, cold seeping through the thin soles.

He tried to take a steady breath, but the air tasted wrong—metallic, ancient, devoid of life. His lungs strained against it, as if each inhalation required twice the effort.

"Where..." His voice died, swallowed by the darkness with unnatural completeness.

Memory returned in fragments. After fleeing Gálgviðr, he had traveled for two days across the mountain range, the black snow growing heavier, obscuring paths and landmarks. Exhaustion had forced him to shelter in a cave that turned out to be more than a simple hollow in the rock. He recalled walking deeper, drawn by faint light, then a sudden blow to the back of his head.

He tested his bonds, wincing as metal cut into his wrists. Chains, not rope. The sound of his movements produced no echo, suggesting an open space around him rather than narrow confines.

The mark on his chest pulsed weakly, its glow visible through his torn tunic. The box Yrsa had given him—the fragment of the dreamer's consciousness—was gone, along with his bronze sword and five tokens. Only the promise-thread remained around his wrist, its golden light dimmed to a faint shimmer.

A whisper drifted from the darkness. "The Flame-Bearer awakens."

Light bloomed ten paces ahead, a cold blue flame in a stone basin that illuminated nothing beyond its immediate vicinity. A figure stood beside it—tall and thin, draped in gray robes with intricate patterns that shifted like living things. The face remained hidden within a deep hood, but Asvarr glimpsed pale hands adorned with tattoos that resembled chains linked across the knuckles and wrists.

"Who are you?" Asvarr demanded, his voice returning, though it sounded dull and lifeless in this place.

"We are the Sundering Loom," the figure replied, the voice feminine and precise. "We severed fate's thread before the Norns, we shattered bonds before the Ashfather claimed them, we broke the pattern while Wardens still slept."

Another light kindled to Asvarr's right, revealing a second robed figure with similar chain tattoos. Then a third to his left, a fourth behind him. With each new flame, more of his surroundings became visible.

He hung from chains that descended from darkness above, suspended over a circular platform of black obsidian. Concentric rings of silver runes spiraled outward from beneath his feet, pulsing faintly with each beat of his heart. Beyond the platform stretched emptiness—an endless void filled with swirling mist that occasionally parted to reveal distant stars and unknowable shapes.

"Ginnungagap," Asvarr breathed, recognition striking him. The primordial void from which all creation had emerged, the gap between fire and ice where the first giant had formed. A place that shouldn't exist in Midgard, that shouldn't be accessible to mortal steps.

The first figure inclined its hooded head. "You know of the Gap-Between-Worlds. Few remember its true nature."

"What do you want from me?" Asvarr asked, tugging against his chains. The metal bit deeper into his flesh, drawing blood that ran down his arms in thin rivulets.

"The Skyrend Prophecy unfolds," a different voice spoke, deeper than the first. "The Flame-Bearer walks the path of transformation. We wish to understand what you have discovered."

More hooded figures emerged from the darkness until nine stood in a perfect circle around the platform. Each held a chain that connected to Asvarr's bindings, forming a web of metal links that glowed with faint runic patterns.

"Asvarr Skyrend's Flame," the first figure addressed him. "You bear five marks of five anchors. You chose the fourth path at Ymir's Cradle. You met with Yrsa Ninevane in Gálgviðr and received a fragment of the dreamer's consciousness." The hooded head tilted. "Tell us—what does transformation truly demand?"

The question mirrored Yrsa's too closely for coincidence. Asvarr tensed, suspicion flaring. "You follow me."

"We observe all who might break or preserve the pattern," a third voice said, this one androgynous and melodic. "The Ashfather seeks control. The Tree seeks renewal. What do you seek, Warden?"

Asvarr weighed his options. These cultists—the Sundering Loom—clearly possessed knowledge of his journey and the pattern's nature. They might hold information crucial to his path. Yet they had taken Yrsa's gift, the fragment that might prevent the Ashfather's ascension.

"I seek freedom," he answered finally. "For the pattern, for the realms, for all beings caught in the cycle of breaking and binding."

A ripple of whispers passed through the circle of hooded figures. The chains connecting them to Asvarr's bonds hummed, vibrating with energy that traveled up the links to his wrists. Pain flared, then numbness, as if the chains were testing his words for truth.

"Freedom," the first figure repeated, tasting the word. "An illusion. The pattern requires structure—harmony through order." She stepped closer, hood still concealing her features. "The Ashfather understood this once, before ambition corrupted him. Nine cycles he has ruled, nine times he has consumed a Warden's essence. Yet the pattern persists."

"You call it harmony," Asvarr countered. "I call it imprisonment."

The figure directly behind him yanked sharply on their chain. Asvarr's body jerked backward, his shoulders screaming in protest.

"You understand nothing of true imprisonment," this new voice hissed, harsh and cold. "We have watched the cycles since the first breaking. We have seen the dreamer's prison, the Ashfather's cage, the Norns' loom. All structures of control."

"Then why chain me?" Asvarr challenged, twisting to glare at his tormentor. "If you oppose control, why bind a Warden seeking to break it?"

Silence fell, the kind that held weight and purpose. The nine figures stood motionless, their chains taut between them.

Finally, the first figure spoke again. "To test your conviction. To verify your purpose." She raised a tattooed hand, palm outward. "The Sundering Loom opposes false freedom, Warden. We broke the original loom of fate because it constrained all possibility to a single thread. We oppose the Ashfather because he shapes the pattern to serve himself alone."

"And the dreamer's fragment?" Asvarr asked. "What have you done with what Yrsa gave me?"

"It lies safe," she answered, gesturing to a small altar beyond the circle. There sat the wooden box, untouched, its spiral engravings catching the cold blue light. "We sought to understand its purpose, yet it remains sealed to our touch. Only the one who walks the path of transformation may open it."

Hope kindled in Asvarr's chest. If they hadn't opened the box, perhaps their claim of testing him held truth. "Release me, and I'll tell you what I know of transformation."

A laugh rippled through the circle, discordant and unnerving. "Words offered under duress hold questionable value," the melodic voice said. "We require demonstration, we desire proof."

The first figure raised both hands, and the chains connecting her to Asvarr's bonds glowed brighter. "Show us transformation, Flame-Bearer. Prove your path leads beyond control."

Instinctively, Asvarr reached for the power he had discovered in Gálgviðr—the ability to shift his form, to become something between solid and energy. The mark on his chest flared, responding to his will, but then dimmed suddenly. A cold sensation spread through his veins, emanating from the chains at his wrists.

"Your bindings come from void-metal," the first figure explained. "They anchor you to physical form, preventing the very transformation we wish to witness." She lowered her hands slightly. "A paradox, yes? To prove your freedom, you must break what constrains you. Yet what constrains you prevents the power that would break it."

Fury rose in Asvarr's throat. "Your test has no solution. You've already decided I'll fail."

"We've decided nothing," she contradicted, her voice softening. "The test remains real, Warden. Nine cycles we've watched, nine Wardens we've tested. All failed. All surrendered to the Ashfather's will or the Tree's demand. None found the true path of transformation."

The void-mist swirled around the platform, momentarily revealing vast distances beyond. Asvarr glimpsed impossible structures suspended in the emptiness—floating islands of rock, twisted spires of crystal, fragments of realms torn from their proper place.

"What is this place truly?" he asked, his anger subsiding into wary curiosity.

"The Gap-Between-Worlds," the deep voice answered. "Where existence frays at its edges, where patterns dissolve into possibility. The Ashfather cannot reach us here. The Tree cannot spread its roots. We alone maintain this sanctuary beyond the pattern's grasp."

The first figure moved closer, close enough that Asvarr could finally glimpse her face within the hood—pale skin with intricate chain tattoos extending across her cheeks and forehead, eyes solid black without pupil or white.

"I am Hild Chain-Singer," she introduced herself, "First Thread of the Sundering Loom. We have watched you since you received the Grímmark, Asvarr Skyrend's Flame. Of all Wardens who have walked the five bindings, you alone refused continuation and substitution. You alone sought transformation."

"And now you imprison me for it," Asvarr said bitterly.

"We test you for it," Hild corrected. "The path of transformation carries terrible risk, Warden. If you succeed, the pattern changes forever. If you fail, the Ashfather claims the dreamer's throne, and the cycle continues with greater tyranny than before."

She gestured, and the chains binding Asvarr's wrists loosened slightly, allowing him to stand more comfortably. "We will release you if you pass our test. We will aid your journey if you prove worthy. We may even join your cause against the Ashfather."

"And if I fail?" Asvarr asked, though he suspected the answer.

"Then we take the dreamer's fragment and hide it beyond reach of both Tree and Shadow," Hild replied without hesitation. "Better the pattern remains broken than falls under absolute control."

The promise-thread around Asvarr's wrist pulsed once, stronger than before. Hild's black eyes flicked toward it, narrowing slightly.

"Skuld's weaving," she murmured. "The youngest Norn learned some wisdom in her breaking, it seems." Her attention returned to Asvarr. "The test is simple in concept, impossible in execution. Transform beyond physical form while bound by chains that prevent transformation."

Asvarr closed his eyes, considering. In Gálgviðr, transformation had come through the mark's power, through his connection to the five anchors. Here, the void-metal chains suppressed that connection, leaving him physically bound and powerless.

Or did they?

He focused inward, feeling the mark on his chest. Its power remained, though muted. The promise-thread still held its golden glow. The five bindings he had undergone—each taking something from him, each granting something in return—had changed him in ways beyond physical.

Rage, memory, identity, certainty, free will—he had sacrificed all these, yet remained Asvarr. The transformations had already occurred within him, regardless of external bindings.

His eyes opened, meeting Hild's black gaze. "True transformation exists beyond physical change."

Her expression remained impassive. "Explain."

"The five bindings already transformed me," Asvarr said, understanding blooming as he spoke. "Each sacrifice changed my essence beyond flesh and bone. The physical transformations I experienced in Gálgviðr merely extended an inner metamorphosis."

A murmur ran through the circle of robed figures. The chains connecting them vibrated slightly, transmitting some communication Asvarr couldn't decipher.

"Words," the harsh voice behind him dismissed. "Clever philosophy to mask weakness."

"Listen," Asvarr insisted. "The fourth path—transformation—transcends physical form. It rises from accepting limitation, from embracing change." He straightened as much as his chains allowed. "These bonds can't contain what I've become. I transformed with each binding sacrifice."

Hild studied him, her black eyes unreadable. "Prove it."

Asvarr closed his eyes again, reaching beyond power toward understanding. The five sacrifices he had made—what had they taught him? What had they left in their wake?

Rage—sacrificed at the first binding. In its place came clarity of purpose.

Memory—sacrificed at the second binding. In its place grew connection to something greater.

Identity—sacrificed at the third binding. In its place emerged fluidity of self.

Certainty—sacrificed at the fourth binding. In its place arose acceptance of ambiguity.

Free will—sacrificed at the fifth binding. In its place flourished harmony with the pattern itself.

The mark on his chest warmed, responding to his realization. The chains at his wrists remained cold and solid, yet they seemed to shift—still containing his physical form while acknowledging his transformed essence.

"I embody my sacrifices," Asvarr said, opening his eyes. "I exist as what remains after the bindings took what I was. Transformation flows from what I've become, from what I continue becoming."

The promise-thread around his wrist flared suddenly, golden light spreading up his arm. The mark on his chest answered with its own glow, creating a network of luminous lines across his skin—a complex pattern incorporating aspects of all five bindings.

Hild stepped back, something like wonder crossing her tattooed features. "The pattern recognizes you," she whispered.

Around the circle, the other eight figures shifted, their chains going slack. The web of metal links connecting them to Asvarr's bonds pulsed once, twice, then dissolved into mist that dissipated in the void-currents of Ginnungagap.

His wrists remained bound, the void-metal cuffs still solid. Yet something fundamental had changed. The chains connected him to the nine figures surrounding him, to the platform beneath, to the Gap-Between-Worlds itself.

"You see beyond physical chains to the bonds of pattern," Hild said, her voice carrying newfound respect. "This begins true transformation."

She gestured, and the platform beneath Asvarr shifted, the obsidian rippling like disturbed water. From its center rose a small pedestal that supported his bronze sword, the five tokens, and Yrsa's box containing the dreamer's fragment.

"You have passed the first trial, Warden," Hild announced. "The Sundering Loom acknowledges your path."

"First trial?" Asvarr repeated, caution tempering his relief. "How many must I face?"

"Three," she answered. "Mind, body, spirit—the trinity of transformation. You have proven your understanding. Now you must demonstrate your capability and then your commitment."

The void-metal cuffs around Asvarr's wrists changed, the chains reforming into elaborate bracers that wrapped around his forearms. They still maintained connection without binding him physically.

"The Chain-Singer's Gift," Hild explained. "Void-metal responds to the wearer's transformation. For most, it constrains. For you, it may enhance."

Asvarr flexed his freed arms, feeling the strange weight of the bracers. "And the second trial?"

Hild turned, gesturing toward the endless void. The mists parted, revealing what appeared to be a pathway of floating stone fragments leading away from the platform.

"Walk the Void-Path," she instructed. "Find what lies at its end. Return with proof of your journey."

"That sounds deceptively simple," Asvarr said, suspicion coloring his voice.

A smile touched Hild's tattooed face. "The Void-Path changes for each traveler, Warden. It manifests the seeker's greatest challenge." Her black eyes fixed on his. "For you, who walks the path of transformation, expect to confront what you most fear becoming."

Asvarr approached the pedestal, reclaiming his bronze sword and the five tokens. He secured them at his belt, feeling their familiar weight settle against his hip. The dreamer's fragment remained in its box, which he tucked safely into his tunic.

"How long do I have?" he asked, eyeing the Void-Path with wary respect.

"Time flows differently in Ginnungagap," Hild replied. "The journey takes as long as it must." She stepped aside, clearing his way to the edge of the platform. "We will await your return, Asvarr Flame-Bearer."

"And if I choose to leave and never return?" he challenged. "If I take the dreamer's fragment and seek another way out of this place?"

The nine figures of the Sundering Loom stood impassive. Finally, Hild spoke again. "No other way exists, Warden. Ginnungagap touches all realms yet exists in none. The only exit lies through understanding." She gestured to the void-metal bracers on his arms. "Besides, our gift ensures your return, willing or otherwise."

Asvarr understood the implicit threat. The bracers connected him to the Sundering Loom, allowing them to track—perhaps even control—his movements through the void.

With no real choice, he turned toward the Void-Path. The floating stones beckoned, each one just close enough to the next for a careful leap. Beyond them, the mists of Ginnungagap swirled, occasionally revealing glimpses of distant realms—mountains, forests, oceans, cities, all disconnected fragments caught in the primordial void.

Asvarr took a deep breath of the metallic, lifeless air. The promise-thread around his wrist pulsed reassuringly, while the mark on his chest settled into a steady glow. The void-metal bracers felt cold against his skin, a constant reminder of his tenuous freedom.

With one final glance at the circle of robed figures, Asvarr stepped onto the first stone of the Void-Path.

***

The world lurched around him. The platform with the Sundering Loom vanished, swallowed by mist. The stone beneath his feet trembled, then stabilized. Ahead stretched the pathway, now transformed into a winding trail of broken fragments that led toward a distant light.

Asvarr squared his shoulders and began his journey into the Gap-Between-Worlds, toward whatever trial awaited at the path's end.

The obsidian stones shifted beneath his feet as he stepped onto the Void-Path, each one floating momentarily before settling under his weight. Cold certainty gripped his wrists where the void-metal bracers clung, their runes pulsing silver against his skin. Ginnungagap stretched endlessly beyond the floating path—world fragments spinning in slow arcs, star clusters burning in impossible colors, light rivers flowing into nothingness.

"The path reveals what you fear to face," Hild's voice echoed behind him. "Walk it true or fall forever."

The endless expanse of Ginnungagap vanished the moment his foot touched the third stone. In its place appeared a frozen wasteland he recognized immediately—the northern tundra where he'd bound the first anchor. Distorted. Wrong. Voices groaned from the ice beneath his feet.

A figure approached from the white emptiness. His former self—wild-eyed, axe bloodied, muscles tensed with berserker rage. The version who never took the Warden's path.

"You abandoned your strength," his reflection growled, voice thick with contempt. "Traded rage for weakness."

His hand moved to his sword hilt, then stopped. The void-metal bracers hummed against his skin, their runes brightening. This was no physical foe to fight.

"I traded rage for clarity," he said, letting his hand fall from the sword. "There is no weakness in seeing truly."

The berserker version lunged with axe swinging toward his neck. He stood motionless, watching the blade pass through him without impact. The phantom howled in frustration, its form dissolving into fragments that scattered across the ice.

Forest replaced the frozen landscape—the same where he'd encountered the broken Norn, Skuld. She stood before him, wrapped in chains of her own making, her shattered loom rebuilt and working furiously.

"Fool," she hissed. "You think breaking patterns creates freedom? It creates void—and void must be filled. Either by you or by him."

The threads of her loom whipped toward him like serpents. He raised his arm, the void-metal bracer intercepting the golden strands. They wrapped around the metal, pulling tight.

"Patterns will always form," he said. "What matters is who shapes them, and to what purpose."

The threads froze, crystallized, and shattered. Skuld's form melted like snow in sunlight.

A third stride brought a third transformation. Muspelheim's forge materialized around him, the place where he'd bound the fourth anchor. Five figures knelt in chains before him—Brynja, Svala, Leif, Yara, and himself. Empty vessels with hollow eyes, their marks glowing white-hot on their flesh.

The Ashfather loomed over them, wearing his face. "This is transformation's end," the false Ashfather said. "You become what you fight. The pattern demands a center—a controller."

Heat from the forge rose through his feet as molten metal glow reflected in the void-metal bracers. The sensation sparked memory—the flame-rune Cinderheart had pressed into his flesh, the seed of the third path.

"No." He stood taller. "Control breeds rebellion. Destruction breeds chaos. The center I seek holds neither."

"Then what?" The false Ashfather's form flickered. "What does your transformation create?"

His fingers touched the merged marks on his chest. "Balance. Choice. The freedom to grow into what we might become rather than what we're told to be."

The volcanic chamber cracked open beneath them, and the vision dissolved.

Stone after stone, vision after vision, he continued forward. Himself as vessel for the Tree. Himself as tyrant king. Himself cast into eternal void. Each time, he moved through the spectral futures without engaging their false choices.

The final stone loomed ahead—larger than the others, carved with unfamiliar runes. Perfect blackness enveloped him as he stepped onto it, leaving him alone except for a small, glowing ember floating at eye level.

The ember spoke with the voice of the dreamer's child-form: "The second trial ends. Will you take the ember of becoming?"

He studied the tiny spark. Despite its insignificance, unmistakable power pulsed within. The void-metal bracers grew warm against his skin, their purpose suddenly clear.

"What must I surrender to hold it?" he asked.

"Nothing you haven't already given," the voice replied. "The ember is transformation itself—the space between what was and what might be."

He cupped his hands beneath the ember. It drifted down, hovering above his palms without touching. The void-metal bracers shifted, reshaping themselves into intricate meshwork cages around his forearms, creating space where the ember could rest.

"I accept it," he said.

The ember expanded, flaring golden-white before shrinking to a pinpoint that sank into his left bracer. The metal absorbed it, runes flowing like liquid across the surface before settling into new patterns.

The darkness dissolved. The Sundering Loom's circle surrounded him again, nine hooded figures watching in silence. Hild approached, her chain tattoos glowing with the same light as his bracers.

***

"Two trials passed," she said. "The trial of understanding and the trial of confrontation. One remains—the trial of creation."

Her gesture indicated the center of the circle where a stone table had emerged from the obsidian floor. Five objects lay upon it: a horn carved from bone, an ivory disk etched with spirals, a crystal key, a snowflake preserved in amber, and a crown woven from root and shadow. His five tokens, arranged in a perfect circle.

"Your final trial," Hild said. "From these fragments of your journey, forge something new. Show us transformation's true form."

The other eight members moved to encircle the table, their hoods pulled back to reveal faces marked with chain tattoos like Hild's, though each pattern was unique. One was old, withered; another barely more than a child. Their combined gaze weighed on him like stone.

"How?" he asked. "These tokens are bound to the anchors. They're mine only to carry."

"They are precisely yours to reshape," the youngest member said, voice surprisingly deep. "The anchors gave them form, but your sacrifices gave them meaning."

The five tokens drew his gaze as he approached the table. Each represented a binding, a sacrifice, a transformation. The horn from the root of blood and rage. The ivory disk from the branch of earth and memory. The crystal key from the seed of wisdom and identity. The preserved snowflake from the frost of winter and certainty. The crown from the shadow of death and free will.

Warmth emanated from the first token, the horn, as his fingers brushed its surface. It vibrated with a familiar resonance. The void-metal bracer on his left arm pulsed in response, the ember within flaring.

Understanding bloomed within him. These weren't simple tokens—they were keys to different aspects of the pattern itself. Each binding had connected him to a fundamental element of reality: blood, earth, knowledge, time, and death. Together, they formed...

"A map," he whispered. "They're a map to the pattern's heart."

His hands arranged the tokens in a new configuration, a spiraling pattern that felt right beneath his touch. Light bloomed between the objects as the final piece, the crown, settled into place. Golden threads connected them in an intricate web.

The void-metal bracers resonated, drawing the light inward. Where the threads intersected, a small seedling appeared, no taller than his thumb. Its roots were crystalline, its trunk ivory-white, its branches like frozen breath, its leaves shadow-dark, and its single bud blood-red.

"The seed of transformation," Hild breathed, her voice filled with wonder. "The first new growth since the breaking."

His hand reached for it, then hesitated. "What will it become?"

"That depends on where it's planted," the oldest member said. "And by whose hand."

Inner light pulsed through the seedling, sending echoes through the surrounding void. Distant fragments of worlds seemed to turn toward it like flowers tracking the sun.

"The Ashfather will sense this," Hild warned. "Already his servants search the void for you. We can shelter you no longer."

The seedling felt both weightless and impossibly heavy in his grip, as though it contained worlds within. The moment his fingers closed around it, it melted into his palm, sinking beneath his skin. A new mark appeared there—a spiraling tree symbol unlike the anchors' patterns.

"The third trial is passed," Hild announced. "Truly, you walk the path of transformation."

The void trembled around them. Shadows gathered beyond the circle's edge, taking the form of nine mounted hunters with featureless helmets.

"The Hunt of Broken Fate," he said, recognizing the Ashfather's servants.

"Your path leads beyond them," Hild said quickly. "We will create an opening, but you must find your own way through." She clasped her hands together, and the chain tattoos on her face began to glow, spreading outward to link with the patterns of the other eight.

"Before I go," he said, "tell me who you truly are. You're not cultists or dreamers—you're something else entirely."

Black eyes reflected the golden light of her chains as Hild answered. "We are what remains of the first pattern—the original weavers who came before the Dreamer, before the Tree, before the breaking. We are what the Ashfather tried to replace."

"Then why test me? Why not stop him yourselves?"

"Because we cannot shape what comes next," the youngest member said. "We can only witness and guide. The future belongs to those who can transform."

The void beyond their circle cracked open, revealing a swirling tunnel of light and darkness. The Hunters spurred their mounts forward, shadow-spears leveled.

"Go," Hild commanded. "Find the other Wardens. The seed you carry must be planted where all five paths converge."

Bronze steel sang with the memory of five anchors as he drew his sword. "And if the Ashfather reaches the center first?"

"Then all becomes void," Hild said simply. "And the pattern ends forever."

Golden light chains pushed back the advancing Hunters as the circle of the Sundering Loom expanded outward. The swirling tunnel beckoned as he turned and ran toward it, guided by the void-metal bracers pulling him forward.

The seedling's presence pulsed beneath his skin with possibility as he leapt into the vortex. This was more than the fragment the dreamer had given him—this was something new, a potential future taking root in the present.

Ginnungagap collapsed behind him as the void fell away. Through darkness he spun, toward whatever world awaited.

CHAPTER 19

THE STAR-TWINED RUNE

Darkness gave way to blinding light as Asvarr tumbled from the void-path. His back slammed against cold stone, knocking the breath from his lungs. The ceiling above—or what should have been ceiling—stretched away into starless black. His void-metal bracers hummed against his wrists, their runes pulsing faintly in the darkness.

He sat up slowly, muscles protesting every movement. His cell measured perhaps five paces across, three wide. Walls of rough-hewn gray stone surrounded him on three sides. The fourth stood open to a circular chamber lit by a strange phosphorescence that emanated from carved symbols on the floor. Nine other cells identical to his ringed the central space.

"Returned from between-spaces," a voice whispered from the cell to his right. "Marked by chain-singers. Carrying seed-of-change."

Asvarr's hand went to his sword hilt. Gone. The familiar weight of his five tokens missing as well. Only the void-metal bracers remained, along with his clothing—and the transformation seed hidden beneath his palm.

"Who speaks?" he demanded, pressing against the dividing wall.

A thin, pale face appeared at the narrow gap between stones. One eye gleamed silver, the other milky-white. "Hoenir speaks. Watches. Waits. They will come for you when the stars align."

Asvarr touched the spot on his chest where his merged marks still burned beneath his tunic. The Grímmark and flame-rune remained, thrumming with borrowed power from the five anchors. Whatever cell this was, it could not separate him from what he had become.

"Where am I?" he asked, peering into the central chamber.

"The Sundering Loom calls it Ginnungagap's Heart," Hoenir replied. "The place-between. Where stars are born and patterns formed. Look up, Warden. See your wyrd written above."

Asvarr tilted his head back. What he'd first taken for featureless blackness now revealed itself as something more extraordinary. Pinpricks of light dotted the darkness overhead, arranged in complex, shifting patterns. Stars—or what resembled stars—pulsed and moved with deliberate purpose, tracing luminous paths across the void.

"Star-runes," Hoenir whispered reverently. "The oldest writing. Before Tree, before Dreamer, before breaking."

The star-patterns shifted, forming a rune Asvarr recognized from his visions—the transformation mark now hidden beneath his palm.

"Who brought me here?" he asked, voice low.

Hoenir's single good eye blinked rapidly. "The Cult of the Pattern. They who serve neither Tree nor Shadow. They who read the star-runes and prepare for what comes after the In-Between."

Footsteps echoed across the central chamber. Three figures approached, clad in gray robes adorned with silver thread that caught the phosphorescent light. Their faces remained hidden within deep hoods.

"Back away," Asvarr hissed to Hoenir. "Speak of nothing we shared."

The pale face disappeared from the gap as Asvarr moved to the front of his cell. He stood tall, shoulders squared, refusing to show the exhaustion that pulled at him like leaden weights.

One of the robed figures stepped forward, lifting slender hands to push back their hood. A woman's face emerged—sharp-featured with skin the color of burnished copper and eyes of startling violet. Silver tattoos marked her temples and forehead in patterns that mimicked the star-runes overhead.

"I am Svana Sky-Reader," she said, voice melodic yet firm. "First Voice of the Star-Twined Circle. You stand in the Observatory, Warden of Five."

"Your hospitality lacks warmth," Asvarr replied, gesturing to the stone cell.

The corners of Svana's mouth turned upward slightly. "For your protection, not our convenience. The void-paths you traveled tore reality around you. Your body needed time to solidify properly in our realm."

The second figure lowered their hood, revealing an elderly man with a silver beard that reached his waist. Deep-set eyes the same violet as Svana's studied Asvarr with analytical precision.

"The breaking accelerates," the old man said. "The pattern unravels faster than even the star-runes foretold. You carry something new within you." His gaze dropped to Asvarr's palm where the seed-mark remained hidden. "Something that changes everything."

Asvarr flexed his hand, feeling the mark pulse in response. "Return my possessions, and we can speak of what I carry."

The third figure removed their hood—a youth with a shaved head marked by the same silver tattoos as the others. "Your weapons and tokens rest in the Alignment Chamber. They draw power from the star-field above. Power you will need when you face what comes."

Svana approached the cell entrance, stopping just beyond arm's reach. "You must understand, Asvarr Flame-Bearer. We have waited five cycles of breaking for what you represent. The Sundering Loom guided you through the void-path to us for a purpose."

Asvarr felt his merged marks heat beneath his tunic. "And what purpose might that be?"

"To show you what the Ashfather seeks," the old man said. "And why your transformation seed must reach the pattern's center before he does."

Svana gestured to the open cell entrance. The barrier Asvarr had assumed was there—some invisible force field or magical boundary—apparently didn't exist. He had been unconfined the entire time.

"Will you walk with us to the Alignment Chamber? We have little time before the stars show the path to the anchor point beneath the roots of Svartálfr."

Asvarr stepped cautiously through the opening. The central chamber's floor glowed beneath his feet, phosphorescent symbols spiraling outward. Above, the star-field rotated slowly, runes forming and dissolving in complex sequences.

"Who are you people?" he asked, looking between the three robed figures. "You're not part of the Sundering Loom."

The youth with the shaved head smiled. "We are their inheritors. They read the void; we read the stars. They preserve what was; we prepare for what comes."

The old man nodded. "For thousands of years, we've watched the breakings and reformings. The Ashfather's manipulations. The Tree's consumption. The dreamer's sleep. Always the same pattern, slightly different each time, yet leading to the same end."

"Until you," Svana added, her violet eyes fixed on Asvarr. "The first to walk the third path. The first to carry transformation rather than restoration or destruction."

They led him through a curved passage that spiraled downward. With each step, the star-field above remained visible, as though the ceiling were transparent from any angle. The stars shifted, alignments changing subtly as they descended.

"The Observatory was built when the first pattern formed," the old man explained. "Before the realms separated. Before Yggdrasil grew from the dreamer's vision. Here, we've recorded every cycle, every breaking, every reformation."

The passage opened into a vast circular chamber. Nine pedestals arranged in a ring dominated the center, each bearing a different object. Asvarr recognized his sword and five tokens immediately. The remaining pedestals held crystal spheres that reflected the star-field above in miniature.

"The Alignment Chamber," Svana said. "Where star-runes become earthly guidance."

Asvarr approached his sword, hand outstretched. The bronze blade thrummed with familiar energy, eager to rejoin with him. Before he could grasp it, the star-field above pulsed dramatically. Constellations shifted, forming new patterns. The chamber dimmed, then brightened as the light concentrated into a single beam that struck the center of the ring.

Where the light touched the floor, a map formed—mountains, forests, rivers, all rendered in glowing silver. A single point pulsed golden at the heart of a mountain range.

"The anchor point reveals itself," the youth whispered, awe in his voice.

The old man's expression darkened. "Too soon. The alignment wasn't due for another day."

"Something accelerates the pattern's unraveling," Svana said. She turned to Asvarr. "Take your possessions quickly. The path to Svartálfr has opened, but others will see this sign as well."

Asvarr grabbed his sword, feeling the bronze blade resonate with his marks. He gathered his five tokens, each humming with power drawn from the star-field. As he touched the final token—the crown from the fifth binding—a vision flashed through his mind.

The Ashfather stood before an archway carved from black stone. Nine hunters waited behind him, mounted on shadow-steeds. Beyond the arch, darkness pulsed with ancient heartbeat. The Ashfather raised his spear, its tip glowing with stolen power. "The way to Svartálfr opens," he said. "And with it, the fourth anchor point."

Asvarr gasped, the vision breaking as suddenly as it had come. "The Ashfather already moves toward the anchor. He knows where it lies."

Svana's face paled beneath her copper skin. "How is this possible? The star-runes only just revealed the location."

"He has other means," Asvarr said, securing his tokens to his belt. "Other powers drawn from previous cycles."

The youth moved to one of the crystal spheres, placing his palms against its surface. The miniature stars within swirled at his touch. "There's a faster path. Dangerous, but direct. Through the star-well beneath the Observatory."

The old man shook his head. "No one has traveled the star-well in three cycles. The paths have grown unstable since the last breaking."

"We have no choice," Svana said firmly. She approached Asvarr. "You must reach the anchor point before the Ashfather. Your transformation seed is the key to changing the cycle, but only if it bonds with all five anchors."

Asvarr felt the mark on his palm burn. "What exactly is the anchor point? I've bound all five anchors already."

The three exchanged glances before the old man spoke. "What you bound were fragments—echoes of the true anchors. The real anchor points exist where the original pattern touches our reality. Places where one might... reshape the pattern itself."

"The Ashfather knows this," Svana added. "It's how he's controlled the cycle for so long. By reaching each anchor point after a Warden has done the binding work, claiming the pattern-power for himself."

Asvarr looked at the glowing map, the golden pulse marking the anchor point beneath Svartálfr. "And if I reach this anchor point first?"

"Your transformation seed can take root there," the youth said. "Creating a new connection that the Ashfather cannot corrupt."

"But I need the other Wardens," Asvarr said. "The seed must be planted where all five paths converge."

Svana's violet eyes fixed on his. "The anchor points are where those paths naturally meet. The Ashfather has kept this secret for nine cycles, ensuring no five Wardens ever discovered the truth together."

The star-field above pulsed again, constellations aligning into a rune Asvarr recognized from his vision of the pattern's heart. The beam of light intensified, the map growing more detailed.

"Time grows short," the old man said. "The star-well awaits."

They led him to the chamber's edge where the floor opened into a circular shaft. Unlike the black void of Ginnungagap, this well glowed with silver-blue light. Star-runes lined its sides, flowing like water down its seemingly bottomless depth.

"The star-well connects directly to the roots of Svartálfr," Svana explained. "Follow the Grímmark's pull once you enter. Let your transformation seed guide you to the anchor point."

Asvarr peered into the well. "Will you accompany me?"

The youth shook his head. "Our role is to read and record. To witness and remember. The action must be yours alone."

"The other Wardens," Asvarr said. "How will they find the anchor point?"

"The star-runes call to all who bear the marks," the old man said. "Trust that the pattern, even broken, seeks to heal itself."

Svana stepped forward, pressing something into Asvarr's hand—a small silver disk etched with a star-rune. "When you reach the anchor point, place this at its center. It will help your transformation seed take root."

The star-field above pulsed a third time, more urgently. The beam of light narrowed, focused directly above the well.

"Now," Svana urged. "The alignment reaches its peak."

Asvarr secured his sword and tokens, the silver disk tight in his grip. The void-metal bracers hummed against his wrists, resonating with the star-runes that lined the well. The mark on his palm—the transformation seed—burned with anticipation.

"What exactly will I find at the anchor point?" he asked.

The three Star-Readers spoke in unison, their voices blending in eerie harmony: "The truth of what the Tree was meant to be."

With that cryptic answer hanging in the air, Asvarr stepped into the star-well. Gravity shifted. The silver-blue light enveloped him. Star-runes flowed around him like a living river, carrying him downward with increasing speed.

***

The Observatory vanished above him as he plunged toward the roots of Svartálfr—and the fourth anchor point that waited in darkness below.

Silver-blue light enveloped Asvarr as he plummeted through the star-well. Wind tore at his clothing, his hair, yet he felt strangely weightless. Star-runes flowed around him like liquid light, twisting into patterns that burned into his vision before dissolving. The void-metal bracers grew hot against his wrists, their runes pulsing in rhythm with the mark on his palm.

The walls of the well flashed past, narrowing and expanding in impossible ways. Passages branched off at irregular intervals—dark tunnels that led to unknown destinations. Asvarr focused on the pull of his marks, letting them guide him through the dizzying descent.

A shadow crossed below him—something moving through the star-well depths. He glimpsed jagged claws, a sinuous body twisting through the silver-blue light. The transformation seed in his palm flared with warning heat.

"Guardian," he whispered to himself, remembering Svana's warnings about the dangers of the star-well. They hadn't mentioned what kind.

The creature circled back, its full form becoming visible. A massive serpent with scales that absorbed light rather than reflected it. Eyes like burning coals tracked his descent. It opened jaws lined with crystalline teeth that gleamed with the same light as the star-runes.

Asvarr drew his bronze sword. The blade sang in the strange atmosphere, its runes flaring with memories of the five anchors. The serpent's eyes fixed on the weapon, its movement hesitating.

The creature lunged upward with blinding speed. Asvarr twisted in the zero-gravity environment, the void-metal bracers somehow allowing him to control his movement. The serpent's jaws snapped shut on empty air as he spun aside, bringing his blade down across its flank.

The bronze edge bit into shadow-scales. The creature shrieked—a sound like crystal shattering—and whipped its tail toward him. The blow caught him in the chest, sending him tumbling through the well.

Asvarr fought to regain control, the void-metal bracers flaring as he stabilized himself. The serpent circled again, more cautiously this time. Its wound leaked darkness that dissipated in the silver-blue light.

"I seek the anchor beneath Svartálfr," Asvarr called out, uncertain if the creature could understand. "I am Warden of Five, marked by the Tree."

The serpent paused, coal-red eyes narrowing. It circled closer, tongue flicking out to taste the air around him. Asvarr held his ground, sword ready but not threatening.

"Warden," the serpent hissed, its voice a grinding of stone on crystal. "Five times marked. Five times bound. Yet you carry something new. Something unwritten."

Asvarr opened his palm, showing the spiral mark of the transformation seed. "I walk the third path."

The serpent's head drew back, eyes widening. "The forbidden way. The path-between." It circled him once more, but with curiosity rather than hunger. "The Ashfather seeks to close this path. His hunters ride the void-winds below."

Cold dread spread through Asvarr's chest. "How close are they to the anchor?"

"Hours, perhaps. They follow old roads beneath the mountains." The serpent's tongue flicked out again. "I am Níðhöggr, guardian of the deep ways. I test those who would walk the star-paths."

"Then let me pass," Asvarr said. "Time grows short."

Níðhöggr's coal-red eyes studied him. "Payment first. The star-well demands balance."

Asvarr tensed. "I've already sacrificed at each binding. I have nothing left to give."

"Nothing?" The serpent's crystalline teeth gleamed. "You carry tokens of power. Fragments of the anchors. One would suffice."

The five tokens at his belt hummed with energy drawn from the star-field. Each represented a sacrifice, a binding, a transformation. To surrender even one might unbalance everything he'd worked toward.

"I need them all," he said firmly. "There must be another way."

Níðhöggr's tail lashed, sending ripples through the star-runes flowing around them. "Then knowledge. Give me knowledge I do not possess, and I shall show you the swift-path to the anchor."

Asvarr's mind raced. What could he know that an ancient guardian would not? Then he remembered the transformation seed, the revelation from the Sundering Loom.

"The true purpose of the pattern," he said. "The original weave before the Tree or the Dreamer. Before the breaking."

Níðhöggr stilled, entire body frozen in the silver-blue light. "Speak."

"The pattern was never meant to be controlled, by Tree or Shadow or gods. It was meant to be balance—constant transformation and growth. The dreamer didn't create it; the dreamer emerged from it." Asvarr touched the mark on his chest where the Grímmark and flame-rune had merged. "And the seed I carry can restore what was lost."

The serpent's coal-red eyes flickered with inner fire. "Truth," it whispered. "Long-forgotten truth." It coiled its massive body, creating a spiraling tunnel in the star-well. "Follow my path. It leads directly to the deepest roots where the anchor waits."

Asvarr sheathed his sword and tucked the silver disk Svana had given him securely against his chest. The void-metal bracers cooled, their energy redirecting to guide him.

"The hunters will sense you when you reach the bottom," Níðhöggr warned. "Be swift, Warden of Five. The anchor chamber opens only to those who bear the marks."

With that, the serpent shot downward through the well, its body carving a clear path through the flowing star-runes. Asvarr followed, allowing the current to accelerate his descent.

The tunnel plunged through darkness, light, darkness again. Temperature fluctuated wildly—freezing cold giving way to scorching heat, then back again. Pressure built in his ears until he thought his skull might crack.

Then—impact. Asvarr crashed into solid ground, momentum driving him to his knees. Cold stone pressed against his palms as he gasped for breath. The void-metal bracers pulsed against his wrists, adapting to the new environment.

**

He raised his head, taking in his surroundings. A massive cavern spread around him, illuminated by veins of luminescent crystal that ran through the black stone walls. Above, the star-well he'd fallen through appeared as nothing more than a pinprick of silver-blue light, impossibly distant.

The cavern floor was smooth obsidian, reflecting the crystal light like still water. At its center stood a single column of black stone, etched with runes that shifted and moved across its surface.

"The anchor," Asvarr breathed, pushing himself to his feet.

His boots made no sound on the obsidian floor as he approached the column. The mark on his palm burned, responding to the ancient power that pulsed from the stone. His five tokens hummed at his belt, each resonating with the energy that filled the chamber.

Nine tunnels opened into the cavern at regular intervals around its perimeter. Through one, distant torchlight flickered. Voices echoed—the Ashfather's hunters drawing near.

Asvarr quickened his pace, reaching the central column. Up close, he saw the runes more clearly—patterns he recognized from the star-field above, from the Sundering Loom's chains, from the transformation seed in his palm. The original language of the pattern, written in stone.

He placed his hand against the column. The stone vibrated with living energy that traveled up his arm and into his chest. His marks flared beneath his tunic, the Grímmark and flame-rune merging more fully in response to the anchor's power.

The column's surface shifted beneath his touch, runes realigning to form a doorway-shaped seam. Asvarr pressed harder, willing the passage to open. The transformation seed in his palm burned against the stone.

Nothing happened.

The voices from the tunnel grew louder. Torchlight strengthened, casting long shadows across the obsidian floor.

Asvarr pulled the silver disk from his tunic—Svana's gift. Star-runes etched on its surface pulsed in sync with those on the column. Understanding dawned. He pressed the disk into the center of the doorway seam.

The disk melted into the stone. Runes flared golden, then faded back to silver. With a grinding sound, the doorway split open, revealing a chamber within the column itself.

Asvarr slipped inside just as the first of the hunters emerged from the tunnel. The doorway sealed behind him, cutting off their shouts of alarm.

The chamber was barely large enough for him to stand upright. Its walls, floor, and ceiling were covered in star-runes that glowed with inner light. At the center floated a small object—a perfectly formed crystal sphere no larger than his fist, within which swirled galaxies in miniature.

The true anchor.

Asvarr's five tokens pulled away from his belt of their own accord, circling the crystal sphere in a slow orbit. The transformation seed in his palm throbbed painfully, responding to the power concentrated in this tiny cosmos.

The sphere pulsed once, twice. A voice spoke directly into his mind.

"Warden of Five. Bearer of the Third Path. What do you seek at the heart of the pattern?"

Asvarr swallowed, mouth suddenly dry. "Understanding," he answered honestly. "Of what the Tree was meant to be. Of what I'm meant to do."

The sphere expanded slightly, galaxies swirling faster within.

"The Tree was meant to be vessel, not master. Conduit, not controller. The dreamer dreamed it as connection between all things, not as prison or throne."

Images flooded Asvarr's mind—the original pattern, a web of connections without center or periphery. Every point equal to every other, yet uniquely positioned. The Tree as it first grew, a living bridge between realms rather than their axis and ruler.

"What you seek to do has been attempted before. Eight times the pattern has been reformed. Eight times the Ashfather has twisted it to his purpose. This ninth cycle must end differently if balance is to be restored."

Pounding shook the column from outside. The Ashfather's hunters trying to break through.

"How?" Asvarr asked urgently. "How do I ensure this time is different?"

The crystal sphere pulsed again, drawing his five tokens closer to its surface.

"Plant your seed where the five paths truly meet—not here, not at any single anchor point, but at the crossroads of all anchors. Only there can transformation take root."

"And where is this crossroads?"

The sphere contracted suddenly, pulling the five tokens against its surface. They melded with the crystal, disappearing into its swirling depths. The transformation seed in Asvarr's palm flared with searing pain.

"Your tokens will guide you when all five Wardens stand together. Each holds a fragment of the map. But beware—the Ashfather knows this too. It is why he has hunted Wardens since the first breaking."

The column shook more violently. Cracks appeared in the chamber walls, star-runes flickering as their patterns were disrupted.

"Take what I offer. Go quickly."

The crystal sphere shot toward Asvarr, striking him in the chest before he could react. It passed through tunic and flesh without resistance, merging with his Grímmark and flame-rune. The mark expanded across his torso, incorporating new patterns—star-constellations intertwined with tree branches and flame tendrils.

Knowledge exploded behind his eyes—star-maps, hidden pathways, ancient secrets of the pattern's functioning. Too much to comprehend at once. His mind threatened to fracture under the flood of information.

The chamber walls collapsed inward. Asvarr threw up his arms instinctively, the void-metal bracers flaring with protective energy. The star-runes from the walls flowed toward him, coating his skin like living tattoos before sinking beneath the surface.

He heard the Ashfather's hunters shouting, felt the column giving way around him. The transformation seed in his palm burned hotter than ever, responding to the anchor's power now housed within his flesh.

As the chamber disintegrated, Asvarr glimpsed a tall figure beyond the hunters—one-eyed, crowned with twisted branches, radiating cold fury. The Ashfather himself, arrived too late to claim the anchor's power.

Their eyes met for a single heartbeat. The Ashfather raised his spear, its tip glowing with stolen energy from anchors past.

In that moment, the star-runes covering Asvarr's body activated. Reality tore around him. The collapsing chamber, the hunters, the Ashfather—all fell away as he was hurled through pathways between worlds.

His last thought before consciousness faded was of the other Wardens. Brynja, Svala, Leif, Yara. He needed to find them. To gather them at the crossroads of anchors.

Before the Ashfather found a way to stop what had already been set in motion.

CHAPTER 20

THE OATH THAT BINDS

Fire scorched Asvarr's lungs as he crashed through burning air. The star-paths had spat him out like a stone from a sling, hurling him into a realm of choking heat and ash. He rolled instinctively, shoulder striking black stone as he fought for purchase on the uneven terrain.

Around him spread a barren landscape of shattered obsidian and pools of liquid fire. The air wavered with heat, distorting the silhouettes of jagged mountains in the distance. Beneath his palms, the ground pulsed with a steady, living heartbeat.

Muspelheim. The realm of primordial fire.

He staggered to his feet, coughing out ash that coated his throat. The transformation seed in his palm throbbed painfully, responding to this raw, elemental domain. His marks burned beneath his tunic, the star-patterns newly acquired from the anchor point shifting restlessly across his skin like living constellations.

His five tokens were gone—consumed by the crystal sphere in the anchor chamber. Yet somehow he could still feel their essence, incorporated into the expanding mark that now covered most of his torso. The void-metal bracers remained, their surface inscribed with new runes that glowed molten-red in the firelight.

A geyser of flame erupted from a nearby fissure, shooting skyward with a roar that shook the ground. Asvarr shielded his face, skin blistering from the heat. He needed shelter, a direction, a purpose in this realm of constant destruction.

The marks on his chest pulsed in unison, tugging him toward the distant mountains. There—a presence. Someone different from the Ashfather. Someone who resonated with the transformation seed.

Another Warden.

He picked his way across the obsidian field, boots crunching on sharp fragments. Each step jarred his bones, reminding him of the battle with Níðhöggr and his narrow escape from the Ashfather's hunters. His body ached, while the marks granted him strength beyond normal endurance.

A shadow appeared on the horizon—a figure approaching through the heat-haze. Tall, broad-shouldered, moving with deliberate purpose. As the distance closed, Asvarr recognized the gleam of metal. Armor, weapons. A warrior.

His hand went to his sword hilt before remembering the bronze blade had been with his tokens. Gone now, merged with the crystal sphere and absorbed into his marks. He stood weaponless in a hostile realm.

The figure drew closer. A woman, taller even than Asvarr, with skin the color of burnished copper and hair pulled back in warrior braids threaded with iron beads. Intricate tattoos covered her exposed arms—battle-runes rather than decorative patterns. A curved blade hung at her hip, its surface etched with symbols that matched the green-gold mark on her forehead.

"Jordmark," Asvarr whispered. The Earth-Healer. Brynja.

She stopped twenty paces away, hand resting casually on her weapon. Her amber eyes narrowed as she studied him, taking in the void-metal bracers, the marks visible at his collar, the spiral pattern on his palm.

"So," she said, voice like gravel over steel, "Skyrend's Flame walks the fire realm. The Muspel-dwellers speak of a star-birth in the shattered lands. That was you?"

Asvarr straightened, meeting her gaze. "The star-paths brought me here. I've found the fourth anchor point. The true anchor, beyond what we bound before."

Brynja's expression remained impassive, but her fingers tightened on her blade hilt. "You speak in riddles, flame-bearer. Last I saw you was at the Midsong Tree, making oaths with four other Wardens. Now you appear in my territory, marked differently, speaking of things beyond our agreement."

"Things have changed," Asvarr said, taking a careful step forward. "I've learned the truth about the Tree, about the anchors, about the Ashfather's deception across nine cycles of breaking."

A tremor ran through the ground beneath them. Brynja shifted her stance, feet planted like roots seeking soil. The Jordmark on her forehead pulsed with green-gold light.

"Truth comes with a price," she said. "What did you sacrifice for these revelations?"

"My tokens. All five, consumed by the anchor point." He opened his palm, showing the spiral mark. "In exchange, I received this—a transformation seed meant to be planted at the crossroads of all anchors."

Brynja's eyes widened slightly—the first crack in her stoic demeanor. "The crossroads. The Ashfather spoke of such a place when he came to me three days past."

Cold dread washed through Asvarr despite the oppressive heat. "The Ashfather sought you out? What did he want?"

Her laugh held no humor. "The same thing you want, I suspect. Alliance. Knowledge. Power." She drew her curved blade in a single fluid motion. "He offered me rulership of two realms if I would betray the other Wardens. What do you offer that compares to that?"

The blade gleamed green-gold in the firelight, an extension of the Jordmark's power. Asvarr raised his empty hands slowly.

"I offer truth, nothing less. The Ashfather seeks to control the pattern, as he has done for nine cycles. The Tree aims to consume it entirely. I walk the third path—transformation through balance."

"Pretty words," Brynja said, advancing a step. "I've heard pretty words before, from gods and monsters alike. Show me your truth, flame-bearer. Make me believe."

The void-metal bracers heated against Asvarr's wrists. The transformation seed in his palm burned, responding to the challenge. Without his tokens or sword, he had only one way to demonstrate his purpose.

He closed his eyes, reaching inward to the knowledge transferred from the crystal sphere. Star-maps unfurled in his mind, pathways and connections revealed in cosmic patterns. He found what he sought—the personal thread that bound Brynja to her path, the memory that had set her upon it.

His eyes opened, glowing with inner light that reflected the star-patterns now visible beneath his skin. When he spoke, his voice carried echoes of the anchor's power.

"Your father was Hrafn Iron-Hand, jarl of the eastern shores. He taught you to fight when your brothers refused to train a shield-maiden. On your sixteenth winter, raiders came from the sea. Your father died defending the harbor. Your brothers fled. You alone stood against the tide, earning your mark when you called the earth itself to swallow the raiders' ships."

Brynja's blade faltered. "How could you know this?"

"The anchor showed me," Asvarr said, the glow fading from his eyes. "Showed me all our paths, woven together. The Ashfather wants vessels—empty shells to channel his will after he takes the pattern's center."

Her blade lowered an inch. "And what do you want?"

"To find the crossroads where all five paths meet. To plant the transformation seed where it can grow into something new—a balance that serves life itself." He extended his hand, palm up, the spiral mark clearly visible. "I need your help. All five Wardens must stand together for this to work."

A fissure cracked open between them, venting superheated steam that distorted the air. Brynja stared at him through the haze, amber eyes calculating, measuring.

"The Ashfather spoke of the crossroads too," she said finally. "Said only he knew its location. Said the other Wardens would lead me astray."

"He deceives you," Asvarr said. "The true anchor revealed that each Warden carries a fragment of the map within their token. Together, they form the path to the crossroads."

"My token remains with me," Brynja said, touching a pouch at her belt with her free hand. "Unlike yours."

Hope surged in Asvarr's chest. "Then you still hold a piece of the puzzle. The tokens I carried merged with the anchor's power, becoming part of my marks. Together with yours, we might decipher part of the map."

She studied him a moment longer, then sheathed her blade in a single smooth motion. "Words are wind, flame-bearer. Actions have weight." She reached into the pouch, withdrawing a disk of polished amber striated with gold. Her token from binding the earth anchor. "Show me what you've learned."

Asvarr approached cautiously. The ground shuddered again, more violently this time. In the distance, a mountain peak crumbled, sending cascades of molten stone down its slopes.

"This realm grows unstable," Brynja said, glancing at the distant destruction. "The fire-wights say the breaking accelerates. Reality thins between worlds."

"All the more reason to find the crossroads quickly," Asvarr replied, stopping an arm's length from her. "May I?"

She nodded once, extending the amber disk on her palm. Asvarr reached out with his marked hand, the transformation seed nearly touching the token. Power leapt between them—golden light from the disk, spiral energy from his palm. The void-metal bracers resonated, amplifying the connection.

Visions flashed through his mind, too fast to comprehend fully. Mountains of ice. Rivers of flame. Forests growing upside-down from clouds. A vast plain where nine roads converged beneath a sky of shifting colors.

The crossroads.

He gasped, pulling his hand back as the connection broke. "I saw it. Just for a moment."

Brynja's amber eyes were wide, her stoic mask fallen away. "Those mountains at the edge of the vision. I know them. The Frost-Spine range along Niflheim's border."

"You've been to Niflheim?"

"I walk between realms as you walk between trees," she said, tucking the token back into her pouch. "Earth connects all things, if you know how to listen."

A massive tremor shook the ground, lasting longer than the previous ones. Cracks spread across the obsidian field, venting gouts of flame and sulfurous gas.

"This realm rejects us," Brynja said, steadying herself. "Two Wardens in one place strains the pattern when it's already unraveling."

Asvarr looked toward the distant mountains. "We need to find the others. Svala, Leif, Yara. All five tokens must come together."

"Svala hunts in Niflheim's wastes," Brynja said. "Her token might respond to the crossroads' pull if it truly lies near the Frost-Spine."

Another violent tremor. A chasm opened fifty paces away, swallowing a swathe of obsidian plain into molten depths.

Brynja grasped Asvarr's forearm, her grip iron-strong. "I'll take you to the border crossing. From there, we track the Storm-Speaker."

"You trust me now?" Asvarr asked, surprised by her sudden decision.

Her expression hardened again. "I trust the breaking of the realms more than any Warden's words. If the pattern truly unravels as you claim, we have little time for doubt."

She turned, heading toward a narrow path that wound between two flame-geysers. Asvarr followed, the transformation seed thrumming in harmony with the void-metal bracers. Each step felt purposeful, directed, as if the path itself recognized their intent.

"The fire-wights whisper of the Ashfather's movements," Brynja said as they walked. "He gathers his hunters at the void-gates, setting guards on passage points between realms. He knows what we attempt."

"All the more reason to move quickly," Asvarr replied, ducking as a spray of cinders whipped past his face. "What made you reject his offer? Rulership of two realms would tempt many."

Brynja's pace never faltered, but her voice dropped lower. "My father taught me that power without purpose cuts the wielder first, like a blade with no hilt." She glanced sideways at him. "And I saw the emptiness behind his eye. Whatever the Ashfather once was, he has become a vessel for something older, colder. Something hungry."

They reached the base of a steep incline where obsidian gave way to black basalt. The air shimmered with more than heat here—a boundary between realities, thinning with each tremor that shook the realm.

Brynja stopped, withdrawing her token again. "The crossing lies just ahead. Earth to ice, fire to frost. A dangerous transition even in stable times." She studied Asvarr with those amber eyes. "Before we cross, flame-bearer, I require something from you."

Asvarr tensed. "What?"

"An oath," she said simply. "Bound by blood and mark. That you walk the path you claim, that your transformation serves life through balance. That when the moment comes to plant your seed at the crossroads, you will remember those who stood with you."

The void-metal bracers cooled against his wrists, as if affirming the rightness of this request. The transformation seed pulsed once, decisively.

"Blood-oath," Asvarr said, understanding the gravity of what she asked. In the old ways, such bonds transcended death itself. "You would tie your wyrd to mine?"

"Five Wardens, five paths, one crossroads," Brynja said. "If we stand together against both Tree and Shadow, our purpose must be bound as one."

She drew her curved blade, its edge glinting in the firelight. "Your choice, flame-bearer. Oath or solitude. Trust or division. The Ashfather separates. Will you unite?"

Heat rippled around them as another tremor shook the realm of fire. Beyond the shimmering barrier ahead lay frost and darkness—Niflheim's eternal winter. Between these extremes, Asvarr faced his decision.

Extending his marked hand, palm up, he met Brynja's amber gaze. "I will take your oath, Earth-Healer. And offer mine in return."

***

Blood welled from Asvarr's palm where Brynja's curved blade had sliced across his marked flesh. The cut burned far beyond ordinary pain—a searing connection to something primal. He watched as his blood mixed with hers in the shallow obsidian bowl between them, golden energy from the transformation seed spiraling through the crimson liquid.

"By blood and mark, by oath and intent," Brynja intoned, her voice carrying the weight of ancient ritual. "I, Brynja Hrafndottir, Earth-Healer and bearer of the Jordmark, bind my wyrd to yours."

The fire geysers surrounding them fell silent. Even Muspelheim itself seemed to hold its breath as the oath took form. Brynja dipped her finger in their mingled blood and traced a pattern across Asvarr's brow—a downward-pointing triangle bisected by a vertical line.

"Strength to stand against Shadow," she said, completing the mark.

Asvarr mirrored her movements, drawing the same symbol on her forehead in blood, just below her glowing Jordmark.

"Wisdom to resist the Tree's consumption," he replied, the words coming to him unbidden.

The blood marks flared with golden-green light. Power surged through Asvarr's chest as the void-metal bracers resonated with the magic of binding. His marks shifted beneath his tunic, branches and flames and star-patterns realigning to accommodate this new connection.

Brynja gasped as the oath took hold, her amber eyes widening. "I feel your anchor. The marks. The pattern."

"And I sense your earth-bond," Asvarr said, suddenly aware of deep connections running through the stone beneath them, extending outward through the realms like roots of a vast tree.

She took the bowl and poured their blood onto the obsidian between them. The liquid hissed, burning into the stone rather than evaporating. A rune formed, something new, combining elements of both his and hers.

"The oath stands," Brynja said, rising to her feet. "Come. The passage to Niflheim waits for no Warden."

Asvarr followed her up the steep incline toward the shimmering barrier. Each step took them further from Muspelheim's oppressive heat. The air grew strangely thin, caught between elemental extremes.

The blood mark on his forehead pulsed in rhythm with his own heartbeat. Through it, he sensed Brynja's emotions—determination foremost, underlaid with caution, curiosity, and something deeper. A yearning to fulfill a purpose greater than herself.

"The oath binding creates a tether," she explained, noting his surprise. "Temporary awareness of each other's strongest feelings. Useful when walking between hostile realms."

They reached the barrier—a vertical shimmer in the air where heat distortions met crystalline frost patterns. Brynja extended her hand, palm forward, the amber token glowing against her skin.

***

"The crossing requires both tokens," she said. "Mine opens the way. Your seed must recognize the path."

Asvarr placed his marked palm beside hers, the transformation seed radiating spiral energy. Where their hands nearly touched, the barrier thinned, ice crystals forming in impossible geometric patterns.

"When we cross," Brynja warned, "the cold will strike like a hammer. Brace yourself and follow close. Niflheim rejects fire-marked flesh."

She stepped forward into the barrier, which parted around her like water. Asvarr followed immediately, keeping his palm aligned with hers.

The world inverted. Heat vanished. Cold beyond comprehension slammed into him, driving the air from his lungs. His skin contracted painfully as frost rimed his eyebrows and beard. The transformation seed in his palm flared desperately, fighting against Niflheim's elemental rejection.

Brynja grasped his wrist, her Jordmark glowing as she pulled him through the barrier's final layer. They stumbled onto a plain of blue-white ice, wind howling around them like a living entity. The sky above hung low and gray, pressing down with palpable weight.

"Breathe," Brynja commanded, placing her hand on his chest. Warmth spread from her touch, pushing back against the killing cold. "Let the oath-bond balance the elements."

Asvarr dragged frozen air into his lungs, feeling it burn all the way down. The marks beneath his tunic heated, creating a pocket of survivable temperature around his core. The blood symbol on his forehead throbbed, channeling some of Brynja's earth-bond resilience.

"The Frost-Spine," she said, pointing toward jagged mountains barely visible through swirling snow. "Svala hunts those slopes. The Storm-Speaker thrives in Niflheim's heart."

Muspelheim's fire realm disappeared behind them, the barrier between worlds now just a faint heat shimmer nearly lost in the driving snow. Asvarr turned full circle, taking in the vast ice plain stretching in all directions. The transformation seed in his palm pulsed with recognition—this realm contained another fragment of the path to the crossroads.

"The Hunter approaches," Brynja said suddenly, her head tilting as if listening to the wind.

Asvarr strained his senses, seeing nothing but snow and ice. Then—movement. A shadow racing across the plain toward them, moving impossibly fast over the broken terrain. The void-metal bracers cooled against his wrists, responding to this new threat.

"Ashfather's servant?" he asked, instinctively reaching for a sword that wasn't there.

"Worse," Brynja replied, drawing her curved blade. "Hrimthursar. Frost giant. They serve none but their own hunger."

The shadow resolved into a massive figure twice the height of a man, blue-skinned and frost-rimed, charging across the ice with a spear of sharpened glacier-ice clutched in one enormous fist. Behind it came others—five, six, more emerging from the blizzard like nightmare apparitions.

"We can't fight so many," Asvarr said, scanning for escape routes across the featureless plain.

"We don't need to fight," Brynja replied. She sheathed her blade and knelt, pressing both palms against the ice. "We just need to change the battlefield."

The Jordmark on her forehead blazed with green-gold light. The ice beneath them groaned, then cracked in a perfect circle around their position. Frost giants faltered as the ground shifted beneath their feet.

"What are you doing?" Asvarr asked, struggling to maintain balance as the ice platform they stood upon separated from the surrounding plain.

"Creating transport," Brynja grunted, sweat freezing on her forehead despite the effort heating her skin. "The earth remembers older shapes. Older paths."

The circular ice platform rose from the plain, lifting them ten feet, twenty, thirty above the grasping hands of the frost giants. Then it began to move, sliding across the ice like a ship over water, accelerating toward the distant mountains.

Frost giants howled in rage, hurling spears of ice that fell short as Brynja's makeshift sled gathered speed. The lead giant bellowed something in a language of cracking ice and rumbling avalanches.

"They say we trespass," Brynja translated, maintaining her connection to the moving platform. "They claim we carry fire into the realm of eternal frost. They smell the Ashfather's mark on us."

"The Ashfather has been here," Asvarr realized. "Recently."

"Three days past, if the giants speak truth," Brynja confirmed. "Seeking the Storm-Speaker before us."

Cold wind whipped past as their ice platform glided across the plain, leaving the giants behind. Snowflakes stung Asvarr's face, accumulating on his shoulders and in his beard. The transformation seed in his palm pulsed weakly, struggling against Niflheim's hostile elements.

Through the oath-bond, he sensed Brynja's strain. Maintaining their transport while simultaneously shielding them from the worst of the cold taxed even her considerable power.

"I can help," he said, placing his marked palm against the ice beside her hands. "The seed draws power from all elements, even opposing ones."

He focused on the transformation seed, willing it to adapt rather than resist. The spiral pattern shifted, incorporating crystalline elements reminiscent of Niflheim's eternal frost. Power flowed from his palm into the ice platform, reinforcing Brynja's control.

"Earth and fire," she murmured, surprise evident in her voice. "Working together despite their opposition. The third path indeed."

The mountains grew larger ahead, their jagged peaks piercing the low-hanging clouds. Their platform accelerated, guided by Brynja's will and powered by their combined energies. The blood symbols on their foreheads pulsed in unison, the oath-bond strengthening as they worked in tandem.

A massive crack split the air—thunder in a realm of eternal winter. Lightning flashed among the mountain peaks, illuminating the storm clouds from within.

"Storm-kin," Brynja said. "Svala's domain."

The mountains loomed closer. Valleys and passes appeared between sheer cliffs of ancient ice. Their platform banked, following a narrowing ravine that wound toward the heart of the range.

"The Storm-Speaker won't welcome us," Brynja warned. "She guards her territory jealously. The Frostmark makes her volatile, unpredictable."

"Will she attack?" Asvarr asked, eyeing the lightning that now arced between peaks with increasing frequency.

"She'll test us first," Brynja replied. "Determine if we're worthy of alliance."

The ravine opened into a vast cirque—a bowl-shaped valley ringed by towering peaks. At its center stood a structure unlike anything Asvarr had seen before: a fortress carved from living ice, its towers and walls flowing organically from the frozen ground, glowing with internal blue-white light.

Their platform slowed as they approached, finally settling to a stop a hundred paces from the fortress gates. Brynja released her connection to the ice, exhaling heavily as the strain lifted from her shoulders.

"Storm's Heart," she said, nodding toward the structure. "Svala's domain within Niflheim."

Lightning struck the fortress's highest tower, energy flowing through channels carved into the ice walls. Thunder rolled across the valley, echoing between the peaks.

The massive ice gates swung open. A figure emerged—slender, clad in furs and scaled armor that reflected the fortress's blue-white glow. Frost rimmed her pale hair, which hung in complex braids adorned with silver beads shaped like lightning bolts. The Frostmark on her throat pulsed with cold fire.

Svala Storm-Speaker approached with measured steps, leaving no footprints in the snow. Frost gathered and dispersed around her with each breath, forming complex crystalline patterns in the air. Her eyes—rime-white with pupils of deepest blue—assessed them coldly.

"Earth-Healer," she said, voice like ice cracking over a frozen lake. "You bring fire to my domain." Her gaze locked on Asvarr, narrowing. "Flame-Bearer. Warden of Five. The Ashfather spoke of your coming."

Asvarr tensed. "You've spoken with him?"

"He offered alliance," Svala replied, frost swirling more intensely around her. "Offered knowledge of the anchor points, the true bindings beyond what we've accomplished." Her head tilted slightly. "He said you would come with lies and half-truths."

Brynja stepped forward. "We've sworn blood-oath, Storm-Speaker. Our wyrds are bound." She pointed to the blood symbol on her forehead. "The Earth-Healer stands with the Flame-Bearer on the third path."

Svala's expression remained impassive, but lightning flashed overhead, reflecting in her pale eyes. "Blood-oath is an ancient binding. Desperate measure for desperate times." She circled them slowly, frost patterns trailing in her wake. "What does the third path offer that the Ashfather cannot provide?"

"Truth," Asvarr said simply. "I've found the fourth anchor point, learned what the Ashfather has hidden for nine cycles of breaking." He extended his marked palm. "The transformation seed shows the way to the crossroads where all five paths meet. Each Warden's token contains a fragment of the map."

Svala stopped, eyeing his palm with newfound interest. "Show me."

Thunder rolled across the valley as Asvarr extended his hand toward her. "Your token first. Earned from binding the frost anchor."

Svala reached into her furs, withdrawing a small crystalline snowflake suspended in clear ice. "The Frost-Crown. My token." She held it cautiously toward Asvarr's outstretched palm. "If you speak false, Flame-Bearer, the storm will consume you."

The moment the Frost-Crown neared the transformation seed, power surged between them. Blue-white energy from her token, spiral patterns from his palm. The void-metal bracers resonated, amplifying the connection.

Visions flashed through their minds simultaneously—all three Wardens sharing the same revelation. The crossroads appeared more clearly this time: a vast plain where nine paths converged beneath a sky of shifting colors. At its center stood a dais of white stone, marked with runes from the original pattern.

Svala jerked back, breaking the connection. Her eyes wide, Frostmark blazing on her throat. "The crossroads. It exists." She looked between Asvarr and Brynja. "And the other Wardens? World-Walker and Death-Walker?"

"We must find them," Asvarr said. "All five tokens together will complete the map."

Lightning struck the ground mere paces away, ice vaporizing instantly. Svala's expression hardened as she tucked her token away.

"The Ashfather moves against us even now," she said. "His hunters scour the realms. He knows what we attempt."

"Then you'll join us?" Brynja asked.

Svala's gaze fixed on the blood symbol adorning Brynja's forehead. "The Earth-Healer swore blood-oath." She turned to Asvarr. "What binding will you offer me, Flame-Bearer? What assurance that your path leads to salvation rather than destruction?"

Before Asvarr could respond, a horn blast echoed across the valley—deep, resonant, chilling. Svala whirled toward the ravine they had traversed.

"Frost giants," she hissed. "Many. Too many." Her eyes narrowed as she studied the horizon. "And something else. Something colder. The Hunt of Broken Fate accompanies them."

Brynja drew her curved blade, which gleamed with green-gold light. "The Ashfather sends his servants to prevent our alliance."

"Then he comes too late," Svala said decisively. She extended her arm toward Asvarr, pulling back her sleeve to expose the pale skin of her wrist. Frost swirled around her hand, condensing into a blade of pure ice. She sliced her own flesh in one swift motion, then offered the blade to Asvarr. "Blood-oath, Flame-Bearer. Now, before our enemies arrive."

Asvarr took the ice blade, feeling the transformation seed pulse in anticipation. Through his oath-bond with Brynja, he sensed her approval—and her fear for what approached. The choice lay before him: a second binding, permanent and irrevocable, tying his wyrd to another Warden.

Horn blasts sounded again, closer this time. The Hunt of Broken Fate approached—the Ashfather's most dangerous servants.

Asvarr drew the blade across his wrist, blood welling crimson against his skin. The transformation seed flared with golden light as his blood mingled with Svala's in the snow between them.

CHAPTER 21

FIRES OF SVARTÁLFR REFUGE

Heat engulfed Asvarr as the realm-tear deposited him onto smoking stone. His knees struck basalt, the impact jolting through his bones as he tumbled forward. Dim red light pulsed around him, revealing a vast cavern with stalactites hanging like frozen fire from the distant ceiling. His lungs burned with each breath—air thick with sulfur and metal.

The blood symbols on his forehead tingled sharply, then settled into a steady pulse. Three blood-oaths now bound him to the other Wardens—Brynja, Svala, and Leif. Only Yara remained unbound among the five. The transition from Alfheim's airy heights to this subterranean furnace had scattered them, tearing their physical connection despite the blood-bonds.

Asvarr pushed himself upright, head spinning. The last realm-jump had been violent, forced upon them when the Ashfather's hunters converged from multiple directions. Leif's skymark had torn reality around them, hurling the four Wardens toward the final anchor point in desperation.

"Svartálfr," he whispered, tasting metal on his tongue. The underground realm of dark elves and master smiths. Home to the final true anchor.

The void-metal bracers hummed against his wrists, responding to the concentrated ore in the surrounding stone. Through his marks, he could sense the transformation seed reorienting itself, adapting once more to a new elemental domain. Blood, earth, storm, sky—and now, forge. The fifth element, the final piece.

Something skittered in the shadows beyond the pool of dim light. Multiple somethings—quick and cautious, their movements almost mechanical. Asvarr tensed, reaching for a weapon he no longer possessed. In the confusing tumble between realms, they'd all lost physical items, their bond sustained only through the blood-oaths.

"Flame-Bearer?" a voice called softly from the darkness to his left. "Warden of Five?"

Asvarr turned, the bracers flaring in response to potential threat. A diminutive figure stepped into the red light—barely reaching Asvarr's chest, broad-shouldered and sturdy. Dark, leathery skin stretched over angular features. Eyes like polished black stone reflected the cavern's glow. Silver bands adorned his arms and throat, each etched with intricate runes.

A Svartálfr. A dark elf.

"I am Asvarr, marked by Tree and Flame," he replied, keeping his voice steady despite his disorientation. "Warden of Five, bearer of the transformation seed."

The dark elf inclined his head, silver bands chiming softly as they touched. "Gunnar Ironveil, First-Forge of the Deep Holds." His voice carried the texture of stone grinding on metal, precise and unyielding. "We have awaited your coming for seven generations."

More figures emerged from the shadows—perhaps a dozen Svartálfr, each adorned with similar metal bands, though less ornate than Gunnar's. They carried no visible weapons, but their very presence radiated a controlled power.

"My companions," Asvarr said, turning slowly to scan the cavern. "Three other Wardens crossed with me."

"Scattered through the deep ways," Gunnar replied. "The boundary between realms grows thin and treacherous. Your arrivals tore multiple passages instead of one."

The transformation seed burned in Asvarr's palm, responding to something in the chamber. He opened his hand, revealing the spiral mark that now incorporated elements from all four previous anchors. It glowed with golden-green-blue-silver light, casting strange shadows across the rough stone floor.

Gunnar's black stone eyes widened slightly. "The seed grows close to full form. It nears awakening." He gestured to the others, who formed a protective circle around Asvarr. "Come. We must reach the Forge-Heart before the shaking begins."

"Shaking?" Asvarr asked, falling into step beside the Svartálfr.

"The anchor pulses with increasing frequency," Gunnar explained as they moved through a narrow tunnel connecting to the arrival chamber. "Each pulse triggers tremors throughout the realm. The false-dwellers call it mountain-rage. We know its true name—the Root's Pain."

The tunnel widened into a broader passage, its walls smoothed by countless hands over millennia. Glowing veins of ore ran through the stone like blood vessels, providing dim illumination. Runes had been carved at regular intervals, pulsing faintly with inner light.

"These are warding-signs," Gunnar said, noting Asvarr's attention. "They shield us from detection by the Ashfather's servants. The Root-haters cannot pierce our deepest holds."

The passage curved downward, descending through the living rock. Heat intensified with each step, the air growing thicker, richer with metal and stone-dust. Through the blood-oaths, Asvarr could sense distant echoes of his companions—Brynja's earth-connection growing stronger in this subterranean domain, Svala's storm-energy compressed and agitated, Leif's sky-bond straining against the rock overhead.

"The others," he said. "You know where they are?"

Gunnar nodded, silver bands chiming. "The Earth-Healer arrived in the eastern forges. Storm-Speaker in the crystal caves. Sky-Walker in the upper halls. All move toward the Forge-Heart, guided by our kin."

A deep tremor shook the passage, dislodging stone-dust from the ceiling. The Svartálfr halted momentarily, their expressions unreadable as they placed palms against the tunnel walls.

"The sixth pulse since dawn," Gunnar murmured. "The cycle accelerates."

They continued their descent, passing through broader chambers where other Svartálfr worked at strange mechanisms—wheels of stone and metal turning in complex patterns, collecting energies from the glowing ore veins. None paused in their work as Asvarr's group passed, though many cast quick glances at the human in their midst.

"These are the Pattern-Keepers," Gunnar explained. "They maintain the channels that distribute the Root's energies safely throughout our realm."

"Your people know about the anchor?" Asvarr asked.

Gunnar's expression shifted subtly—the first real emotion he'd displayed. "We were the first guardians, Flame-Bearer. Before Tree, before Dreamer, before Breaking. Our ancestors forged the channels when the Pattern first manifested."

This aligned with what Asvarr had learned from the previous anchors—that the original Pattern predated even Yggdrasil itself. "Then you know what waits at the crossroads of all anchors?"

The Svartálfr leader stopped abruptly, turning to face Asvarr fully. The other dark elves continued ahead, leaving them momentarily alone in the passage.

"We know only fragments of the truth," Gunnar said, voice lowered. "Our oldest records speak of the First Pattern—a web of connection that turned chaotic, then calcified into the Tree. When the Ashfather first appeared nine cycles past, he destroyed many of our histories. What remains tells of a balance point where all paths converge."

Another tremor, stronger this time. Dust and small stones rained from the ceiling as both steadied themselves against the walls.

"The Forge-Heart calls with greater urgency," Gunnar said, resuming their descent. "It senses your seed's readiness."

The passage opened suddenly into a vast chamber that stole Asvarr's breath. Hundreds of feet high and twice as wide, it housed what appeared to be an entire underground city. Structures of stone, metal, and crystal rose in concentric rings around a central pit from which poured molten light. Bridges of hammered metal spanned gaps between districts. Thousands of Svartálfr moved purposefully throughout the space, their silver bands creating a constant soft music as they worked.

"Ironhold," Gunnar said simply. "Last refuge of the true Svartálfr."

Asvarr stared, momentarily overcome. In all his travels, he'd never seen a place of such concentrated purpose, such perfect fusion of natural and crafted beauty. The void-metal bracers hummed with recognition, as if greeting distant kin.

"The false-dwellers who rule the upper reaches know nothing of this place," Gunnar continued, leading Asvarr onto a broad walkway that spiraled down toward the central pit. "They mine blindly, following veins of ore, never understanding the patterns they disrupt."

"False-dwellers?" Asvarr asked.

"Those your people call dwarves," Gunnar replied with subtle distaste. "Surface-dwellers who claim kinship with the deep stone while fearing its heart. They are to us as wolves are to dogs—distant kin who chose domestication over truth."

They descended through the rings of the city, passing workshops where impossibly intricate items were being forged. Svartálfr looked up from their work as Asvarr passed, their black stone eyes reflecting recognition and something like relief.

"They know me," Asvarr observed.

"They know what you carry," Gunnar corrected. "The transformation seed has been foretold since the last Breaking. Each cycle, we wait to see if the Wardens will discover the third path or be consumed by the binary conflict between Tree and Shadow."

The central pit grew larger as they approached, revealing itself as a perfect circle perhaps fifty paces across. What Asvarr had first taken for molten metal was something far stranger—a liquid that shimmered with every color imaginable while simultaneously appearing darker than the deepest shadow. It pulsed with a rhythm like a massive heartbeat, each contraction sending waves of heat throughout the chamber.

"The Forge-Heart," Gunnar said with reverence. "The living pulse of our anchor."

Asvarr felt his marks respond, heat building beneath his tunic as the patterns shifted across his skin. The transformation seed in his palm throbbed painfully, sensing its counterpart below.

"It's alive," he whispered.

"All anchors live," Gunnar replied. "Each with different aspect and purpose. The Blood-Root of Midgard draws strength from sacrifice. The Earth-Branch of Vanaheim from growth and connection. The Wisdom-Seed of Alfheim from knowledge and vision. The Storm-Frost of Niflheim from transformation and preservation."

"And this one?" Asvarr asked, unable to look away from the hypnotic pulsing of the liquid anchor.

"The Forge-Flame," Gunnar said. "Creation through destruction. Breaking to remake. Death into life." He gestured to the liquid. "Raw possibility given form through focused will."

A massive tremor shook the chamber, stronger than any previous. Svartálfr throughout the city braced themselves, many dropping to their knees to press palms against the stone. The liquid in the pit surged upward before settling, its rhythm noticeably faster than before.

"The Root grows impatient," Gunnar said, urgency entering his voice. "The Ashfather approaches the borders of our realm. His hunters seek ways past our wards."

"I need the other Wardens," Asvarr said, feeling the blood-oaths pulse in response to his concern. "All five must stand together at the crossroads."

"They come," Gunnar assured him. "But first you must complete what was begun nine cycles past. You must bind the Forge-Flame to your seed, completing the transformation key."

Before Asvarr could respond, shouts erupted from the upper levels of the city. Svartálfr were pointing toward a distant entrance where figures had appeared—three humans descending rapidly toward the central pit.

"Your companions arrive together," Gunnar said with satisfaction. "The Pattern works through you even now, drawing the pieces to their proper place."

Asvarr squinted against the glare from the pit, recognizing the approaching figures. Brynja moved with firm purpose, her Jordmark glowing against her forehead. Beside her walked Svala, frost gathering and dispersing around her with each step despite the chamber's heat. Leif strode with the peculiar grace of one who belonged to the sky, his Skymark shifting like clouds across his shoulders.

As they drew closer, Asvarr felt the blood-oaths strengthen, warmth spreading from the symbols on his brow. The transformation seed flared in response, its spiral pattern expanding slightly.

"Flame-Bearer," Brynja called, her voice carrying easily across the space. "The dark elves speak truth. This realm contains the final anchor."

"And other presences," Svala added, her ice-white eyes narrowed with suspicion. "The Hunt circles above. They cannot pierce the wards directly, but they gather strength."

"The Ashfather himself leads them," Leif said, brushing silver-streaked hair from his eyes. "I glimpsed him from the upper halls. He wears his full aspect now—one-eyed, spear-wielding, raven-cloaked."

Gunnar's expression darkened. "Then we have little time. The binding must begin before the seventh pulse."

The four Wardens stood together at the edge of the pit, their marks resonating with each other and with the liquid anchor below. Through the blood-oaths, Asvarr could sense their combined unease and determination. Each had sacrificed much to reach this point—had abandoned old paths to walk the third way.

"What must I do?" Asvarr asked, turning to Gunnar.

The Svartálfr leader reached into a pouch at his belt, withdrawing a small hammer of strange metal. Its surface rippled like quicksilver but held its form perfectly. "The binding of the Forge-Flame requires forging," he explained. "You must strike the anchor with the Worldsmith's Hammer, allowing it to reshape your seed into its final form."

Another violent tremor shook the chamber. This time, cracks appeared in some of the outer walkways. Svartálfr throughout the city began moving with greater urgency, some evacuating the outermost rings.

"The Root destabilizes," Gunnar said, pressing the hammer into Asvarr's hand. "It senses the approaching conflict and strains toward completion."

The hammer felt impossibly heavy for its size, as if it contained the weight of mountains compressed into a form barely larger than Asvarr's palm. The void-metal bracers resonated with it, their runes flaring with recognition.

"I've lost my tokens to the previous anchors," Asvarr said, gripping the hammer tightly. "What will this one demand?"

Gunnar's black stone eyes fixed on Asvarr's. "The Forge-Flame requires purpose, Warden of Five. It asks what you intend to create with the power you've gathered. What new Pattern will emerge from your transformation seed?"

The question struck deeper than Asvarr had expected. Throughout his journey, he'd focused on what he opposed—the Ashfather's control, the Tree's consumption—without fully articulating what he sought to create in their place.

"I don't know," he admitted, the truth heavy on his tongue.

"Then that is what the anchor will take," Gunnar said softly. "Your certainty of purpose. You will forge the transformation key without knowing what door it will ultimately open."

A shadow fell across the pit. Looking up, Asvarr saw the distant ceiling of the vast chamber darkening, as if night were falling underground. Whispers spread among the Svartálfr, many abandoning their tasks to watch.

"The Ashfather breaches our outer wards," Gunnar said grimly. "His attention focuses here. The binding must begin now, Flame-Bearer."

Asvarr turned to his blood-bonded companions. "Stand with me," he said. "Your marks must witness the final forging."

The three Wardens nodded, forming a triangle around him at the pit's edge. Their combined marks—earth, storm, and sky—pulsed in rhythm with the liquid anchor below. The blood-oaths strengthened their connection, allowing energies to flow between them.

Asvarr stepped to the very edge of the pit, hammer raised. The transformation seed burned in his palm, eager for completion yet fearful of the sacrifice to come.

Without certainty of purpose, what would guide his actions once the key was forged? What new Pattern would emerge from his transformed seed?

The darkness above deepened. A distant howl echoed through the chamber—the Hunt breaching another ward. Time slipped away with each passing heartbeat.

Asvarr brought the hammer down upon the anchor's surface, striking the liquid Forge-Flame with all his strength.

***

The Worldsmith's Hammer struck the liquid surface with a sound like thunder cracking stone. The Forge-Flame parted around the hammer's head, then closed over it, pulling the tool deeper. Asvarr's arm followed, submerged to the elbow in the impossible substance that burned colder than ice yet hotter than flame.

Pain exploded through his body. The transformation seed in his palm blazed with unbearable intensity, connecting directly to the anchor's essence. Through this connection flowed raw possibility—potential futures, abandoned pasts, paths untaken, all washing through him in a torrent of sensation.

Asvarr's knees buckled. Only the void-metal bracers prevented him from falling fully into the pit, their runes flaring with protective energy. The three blood-oaths pulsed on his forehead, channeling support from the surrounding Wardens. Their combined power steadied him as the Forge-Flame reshaped his seed, forcing it to accept its final evolution.

"Hold fast," Gunnar called from somewhere distant. "The binding reaches its critical moment."

Around them, the vast chamber shuddered. Stone cracked. Metal walkways groaned. The darkness above deepened into absolute void, pressing downward as the Ashfather's influence penetrated deeper into the realm.

Through the chaos of sensation, Asvarr glimpsed fragments of intent—the Ashfather's purpose laid bare. Control. Domination. A Pattern locked in perfect stasis, with himself at its center. Each Breaking had been orchestrated, each Restoration manipulated, all to prevent the emergence of true choice.

The liquid anchor pulled harder, drawing Asvarr's arm deeper. It wanted more than his certainty of purpose—it hungered for his identity itself. The void-metal bracers heated to near-melting, fighting to preserve his physical form as the Forge-Flame sought to unmake him.

"I can't hold it," he gasped, voice barely audible over the roar of power. "It's consuming me."

Brynja stepped forward, her Jordmark blazing. Without hesitation, she thrust her own hand into the liquid anchor beside his. The blood-oath between them flared with renewed strength.

"Earth stands with Flame," she declared, her voice carrying the weight of mountains.

Svala moved next, frost-white hair whipping in currents of energy. Her slender hand joined theirs in the molten liquid, Frostmark pulsing at her throat.

"Storm joins the forging," she called, voice sharp as breaking ice.

Leif completed the circle, his Skymark rippling like clouds across his shoulders as he added his hand to the connection.

"Sky anchors the Pattern," he said, words flowing like wind through leaves.

The four Wardens stood joined by the Forge-Flame, their marks resonating in harmony. The blood-oaths bridged the gaps between their separate powers, creating a unified field of energy that the anchor could reshape without destroying.

***

"What of the fifth?" Asvarr managed through gritted teeth. "Death-Walker remains unbound."

"She comes," Brynja said, eyes fixed on something beyond the physical chamber. "The blood-call has reached her."

The Forge-Flame pulsed, surging upward around their joined hands. The transformation seed in Asvarr's palm split open, revealing a spiraling emptiness at its core—a void waiting to be filled with purpose. This was the true sacrifice demanded by the fifth anchor: the willingness to create without knowing what would emerge.

"Accept the unknown," Gunnar urged from behind them. "Surrender certainty to gain possibility."

Asvarr felt his resistance crumbling. The need to know, to understand, to control the outcome—these were the very impulses that had corrupted the Ashfather across nine cycles. True transformation required openness to change without predetermined end.

He released his grip on the hammer, allowing it to sink fully into the Forge-Flame. The liquid anchor surged in response, flowing up their arms toward the blood-oath marks on Asvarr's forehead. Through the connection, each Warden felt the anchor's hunger, its desire to complete what had begun at the Breaking.

"I surrender certainty," Asvarr whispered, the words torn from his deepest self. "I accept transformation without predetermined purpose."

The chamber disappeared. The four Wardens found themselves suspended in void, surrounded by threads of golden light connecting in intricate patterns. The original Pattern, revealed at last—a living web of relationship rather than a rigid hierarchy.

At the center floated a presence both ancient and newborn. It pulsed with the combined essence of all five anchors. The primary colors of existence—blood red, earth green, wisdom gold, storm white, and forge black—swirled together without mixing, maintaining their distinctness while creating harmony through relationship.

"The true anchor," Brynja breathed.

"The crossroads," Svala added.

"The pattern-heart," Leif whispered.

Asvarr saw it clearly—the point where all paths converged, where transformation could truly take root. The place the Ashfather had hidden for nine cycles, the secret he had murdered to protect. With all five anchors truly bound, the Wardens could access this space directly, planting the transformation seed at reality's core.

The vision collapsed as violently as it had appeared. The Wardens found themselves back in the chamber, hands still joined in the liquid anchor. The Forge-Flame had withdrawn, no longer pulling at them, its hunger temporarily sated.

"It is done," Gunnar said, relief evident in his voice. "The fifth anchor is bound."

Asvarr staggered back from the pit, cradling his transformed arm. From fingers to elbow, his flesh had been reshaped, metallic veins running beneath the skin like rivers of quicksilver. The void-metal bracers had fused with his arm, their runes now part of his very being.

The transformation seed was gone from his palm. In its place lay a perfect miniature of the Pattern they had glimpsed—a three-dimensional web of interconnected points, each glowing with one of the five elemental essences. It rotated slowly above his palm, responding to his thoughts rather than physical movement.

"The forged key," Gunnar said with reverence. "The map to the crossroads made manifest."

"What have I become?" Asvarr asked, staring at his altered flesh.

"What you were always meant to be," Brynja replied, her own hand showing subtle changes where it had touched the Forge-Flame. Thread-like patterns of green energy ran beneath her skin, pulsing with earth's rhythm.

Svala and Leif showed similar transformations—frost crystals embedded in Svala's fingers, living clouds swirling beneath Leif's skin. The fifth anchor had marked them all, binding them more completely to their elemental domains.

A violent tremor shook the chamber, stronger than any before. Huge sections of the ceiling collapsed, crushing outer districts of the Svartálfr city. The darkness above had taken physical form—tendrils of void reaching downward like grasping fingers.

"The Ashfather breaches the inner ward," Gunnar shouted over the cacophony of crumbling stone. "The binding has drawn his full attention."

"We must reach the crossroads," Brynja said urgently. "The key shows the way."

Asvarr focused on the miniature Pattern floating above his palm. Within its intricate web, one point pulsed brighter than the others—a nexus where all elements converged. As he concentrated, the key projected a line of golden light pointing toward the eastern edge of the chamber.

"There," he said, following the direction. "The path opens."

The four Wardens moved swiftly, Gunnar and a handful of Svartálfr following close behind. The city was in chaos around them, dark elves evacuating under falling debris as the chamber's structural integrity failed. The liquid anchor in the central pit roiled violently, sending waves of energy in all directions.

They reached the eastern wall where the light beam from Asvarr's key indicated a blank stone surface. No door or passage was visible, yet the key insisted this was their path forward.

"The crossroads exists in all realms simultaneously," Gunnar explained, touching the smooth stone reverently. "With the key forged, you can access it directly, bypassing the physical barriers between worlds."

"How do we open it?" Svala demanded, frost gathering around her fingers as she prepared to defend against the encroaching darkness.

Asvarr placed his transformed hand against the stone, the key still hovering above his palm. The miniature Pattern aligned with something beyond the wall—a larger version of itself existing in a space between physical realms.

"The blood-oaths," he realized. "They're the final component."

The three Wardens joined their hands to his, their marks pressing against the stone. The blood-oath symbols on Asvarr's forehead flared with power, connecting their separate energies into a unified force.

Stone rippled like water, revealing a passage that hadn't existed moments before. Beyond lay a swirling vortex of pure possibility—the direct path to the crossroads at the pattern's heart.

"You must go now," Gunnar urged, backing away from the opening. "We will seal the chamber behind you, preventing the Ashfather from following this route."

"What about the other Warden?" Leif asked. "Death-Walker remains unbound."

"She will find her own path to the crossroads," Gunnar replied. "The Pattern calls all its pieces to the center when completion nears."

A massive tremor shook the chamber. Half the ceiling gave way, crushing entire sections of the city beneath impossibly heavy stone. The tendrils of darkness plunged deeper, searching hungrily for the Wardens.

"Go!" Gunnar commanded. The remaining Svartálfr formed a protective ring around the opening, their silver bands glowing with magical energy as they prepared a final defense.

Asvarr hesitated only a moment, then stepped into the vortex. Brynja followed immediately, then Svala and Leif. The passage sealed behind them, cutting off the sounds of destruction as the Ashfather's forces breached the final defenses of Ironhold.

The vortex pulled them forward with irresistible force, the physical world dissolving around them. Asvarr felt his consciousness expanding, stretching to encompass realities beyond mortal comprehension. The key in his palm grew brighter, drawing them toward the center of all things.

Through the blood-oaths, Asvarr sensed the others experiencing similar transformations. Their separate identities remained distinct yet connected, forming a greater whole without losing individual essence. This was the Pattern's true nature—unity through relationship rather than through consumption or control.

The vortex thinned, reality resolving around them. They stood in a vast, circular space that existed everywhere and nowhere simultaneously. The ground beneath their feet was perfectly white stone, unmarked except for a central dais carved with the same Pattern that floated above Asvarr's palm.

***

Nine pathways radiated outward from the central point, each disappearing into mist after several hundred paces. Above, the sky (if it could be called that) shifted constantly between colors both familiar and impossible.

"The crossroads," Brynja whispered.

Asvarr moved toward the central dais, drawn by the resonance between the key in his palm and the Pattern carved into the stone. This was the heart of all reality—the point where transformation could truly take root and reshape the multiverse.

As he approached, a figure materialized on the far side of the dais—tall, one-eyed, bearing a spear of shadow. The Ashfather had found another path to the crossroads.

"So," the ancient entity said, voice rumbling with barely contained fury. "The Wardens discover the truth at last."

"We found what you tried to hide for nine cycles," Asvarr replied, the key pulsing defensively above his palm. "The heart of the Pattern. The point of transformation."

The Ashfather's single eye narrowed, focusing on Asvarr's altered arm. "You've bound all five anchors. Impressive. None have managed that feat since I walked the Warden's path ages past."

"We know what you did," Brynja said, stepping forward. "How you corrupted the cycle, prevented true transformation, maintained control across multiple Breakings."

"I preserved order," the Ashfather countered, thumping his spear against the white stone. "Without my guidance, the Pattern would have collapsed into chaos millennia ago."

Svala's frost-white eyes glinted dangerously. "You twisted the Pattern to serve your will, sacrificing countless lives to maintain your dominance."

"The alternative was worse," the Ashfather insisted. "I've seen what lies beyond the Pattern—the formless void that hungered before the first dreaming. Would you risk releasing that upon the realms?"

Asvarr studied their ancient adversary. Through the transformed seed—now key—he could see beyond the Ashfather's physical form. Beneath the one-eyed visage, layer upon layer of stolen power coiled like serpents. Nine previous cycles of Breaking and Restoration had left their mark, each adding to his strength while corrupting his original purpose.

"You were a Warden once," Asvarr said quietly. "You walked the same path we walk now."

Something flickered in the Ashfather's expression—a momentary glimpse of the being he had been before fear corrupted him. "I saved the Pattern the only way I could," he said, voice softer. "You cannot understand what awaits if you proceed."

"Then show us," Asvarr challenged, moving to stand directly before the dais. "If your way is truly best, convince us."

The Ashfather's eye widened slightly, surprised by the offer. For the first time, uncertainty crossed his ancient features. He had expected battle, resistance, the eternal conflict between opposing forces. Asvarr's willingness to listen—to understand—offered a path the Ashfather hadn't considered.

"You would hear my counsel?" he asked suspiciously. "After all I've done to stop you?"

"We seek transformation without predetermined purpose," Asvarr replied, the key hovering steady above his palm. "That includes the possibility that you're right."

The four Wardens stood united before the crossroads dais, facing the being who had manipulated reality for thousands of years. The future of the Pattern hung in balance between them, awaiting the choice that would determine whether the cycle would continue or transform into something new.

In that moment of suspended decision, a fifth pathway flared with sudden light. A figure approached along the illuminated road—slender, half-shrouded in shadow, bearing the final mark. The Death-Walker had arrived at the crossroads.

The circle would be complete at last.

CHAPTER 22
THE IRONSEED MEMORY

The Death-Walker emerged from shadow like a blade unsheathing. Half her face gleamed pale as moonlight, the other half darkened to almost perfect blackness, marked with spiraling patterns that caught what little light existed at the crossroads. Her eyes—one amber bright, one pupilless void—fixed on Asvarr with unsettling intensity.

"Flame-Bearer," she said, voice carrying the distant echo of crumbling stone. "The fifth gate opens."

Asvarr held his ground before the central dais as the final Warden approached. The key hovering above his transformed palm pulsed with five-colored light, completing its resonance as Yara Death-Walker joined their circle. Through his blood-oaths with the others, he felt their mingled wariness and relief at her arrival.

The Ashfather hissed, thumping his shadow-spear against the white stone. "Death comes late, as always."

"Death arrives precisely when needed," Yara replied, showing no fear of the ancient entity. The Deathmark on her throat—a rune like an inverted gateway—gleamed with inner darkness. "The void called. I answered."

She completed their circle before the dais, standing between Leif and Svala. Unlike the others, she showed no sign of physical transformation, as if death remained unchanged by any force, even the anchors themselves.

Asvarr extended his transformed arm toward her, the pattern-key still hovering above his palm. "We need your bond to complete the circle. To plant the seed at the heart of the Pattern."

Yara studied him with her mismatched eyes. "You've bound the five anchors. Walked the third path beyond Tree and Shadow." Her gaze shifted to the blood-oath symbols on his forehead. "Yet you seek more binding still."

"Without all five Wardens united, the transformation will fail," Brynja said, the earth-threads beneath her skin pulsing with urgency. "The Pattern requires completion."

The Ashfather laughed, a sound like grinding glaciers. "Listen to them, Death-Walker. They speak of patterns and transformation without understanding the consequences. I alone have seen what waits beyond the veil."

Yara turned her unsettling gaze toward him. "And what did you see, Old Wolf, that turned you from guardian to jailor?"

Something flickered across the Ashfather's features—pain, memory, perhaps even fear. "Chaos unending. The void-hunger that existed before the first dreaming. The formless dark from which even gods fled."

"He speaks half-truths," Svala snapped, frost crystals forming and dissolving along her transformed fingers. "The void he fears simply represents possibility unrealized."

"Perhaps," Yara acknowledged. "Perhaps so." She stepped closer to Asvarr, examining the key above his palm. "This pattern-key opens the door to transformation, but what guarantee exists that the change brings improvement?"

The question struck at the heart of Asvarr's sacrifice to the fifth anchor. He had surrendered certainty of purpose—accepted that transformation might lead anywhere, that creation without predetermined end required faith in possibility itself.

"None," he admitted. "The void-metal bracers sank into my flesh when I sacrificed certainty for possibility. I forge without knowing the final shape."

Yara nodded, as if his answer confirmed something she already knew. "Then you understand the price of my binding."

She drew a bone-white knife from within her shadowed cloak. Its edge gleamed impossibly sharp, seeming to cut the very air around it. "Death demands the deepest sacrifice, Flame-Bearer. A memory you've never shared, the seed from which your wyrd first sprouted."

Brynja stepped forward, protective instinct flaring through their blood-oath. "He's already given five sacrifices to the anchors. What more can you ask?"

"The Ironseed Memory," Yara replied simply. "The moment that forged his first and truest self. With this sacrifice, transformation becomes possible."

The Ashfather stirred, his single eye narrowing. "Give her nothing. Death consumes everything it touches."

Asvarr felt the weight of the choice before him. The key in his palm vibrated with building energy, the Pattern at the crossroads straining toward completion. Yet Yara demanded the most personal sacrifice yet—beyond rage, beyond identity, beyond certainty. She asked for the foundation of his very self.

"What happens if I refuse?" he asked.

"Then the Pattern remains incomplete," she answered. "The transformation seed withers before taking root. The cycle continues as it has for nine renewals, with Shadow and Tree battling while reality slowly unravels."

The Ashfather raised his spear, shadows gathering around its point. "Choose the known path, Warden. I offer stability. The Tree offers dissolution. These options have always existed."

Asvarr looked to his blood-bonded companions. Brynja's face showed fierce determination, the earth-threads beneath her skin pulsing with the rhythm of mountains. Svala's ice-white eyes reflected both caution and courage, frost gathering at her fingertips. Leif stood with quiet certainty, the clouds beneath his skin shifting like winds preceding change.

"What exactly must I surrender?" Asvarr asked Yara, turning back to the Death-Walker.

She raised the bone-white knife. "The memory of your mother's final moments. The seed from which all your choices have grown."

Shock stole Asvarr's breath. Of all his memories, that one lay buried deepest—a moment of anguish and love so profound he had sealed it away even from himself. How Yara knew of it, he couldn't fathom.

"That memory belongs to me alone," he said, voice tight with sudden emotion.

"Nothing belongs to anyone," Yara replied. "All returns to the void eventually. I merely hasten what time would claim regardless."

The key above Asvarr's palm flared with golden light, responding to the intensity of his emotions. The five-colored energies within it—blood red, earth green, wisdom gold, storm white, and forge black—swirled together, straining toward the Pattern carved into the central dais.

"If I give you this memory," he asked, "what happens to it?"

"It becomes the nourishment for what grows next," Yara said. "The transformation seed requires deep roots. Your memory will feed the new Pattern that emerges."

The Ashfather stepped forward, his massive form radiating ancient power. "Enough games, Death-Walker. You've delivered your ultimatum. The Warden refuses."

"I haven't refused," Asvarr countered, meeting the one-eyed gaze with newfound resolve. "I'm considering the cost."

"The cost exceeds reason," the Ashfather insisted. "I too stood where you stand, ages past. I chose differently, and preserved reality from unmaking."

Through the blood-oaths, Asvarr felt his companions' support—Brynja's steady strength, Svala's fierce clarity, Leif's boundless perspective. They stood with him regardless of his choice, bound by shared purpose while respecting individual autonomy.

He closed his eyes, reaching deep within himself to the memory Yara named. It lay buried beneath layers of pain and purpose, a precious wound never fully healed. His mother's final moments as raiders attacked their village. Her voice, her touch, her sacrifice to save him. The genesis of everything he had become.

"If I surrender this," he asked, opening his eyes to fix them on Yara, "will the transformation succeed?"

"Nothing is certain," she replied. "That is the nature of true creation. Yet without your sacrifice, failure remains assured."

The crossroads waited, nine paths stretching away into infinite possibility. The Pattern carved into the central dais pulsed with potential energy, matching the rhythm of the key above Asvarr's palm. All that had happened—all five bindings, all gathered Wardens, all sacrifices made—led to this moment of choice.

"The ironseed memory," he said finally. "Take it. Complete our circle."

Yara approached with the bone-white knife. The other Wardens gathered closer, forming a protective ring around Asvarr as he faced the Death-Walker.

"Kneel," she commanded.

Asvarr dropped to one knee on the white stone of the crossroads. The Ashfather watched from beyond the circle, his ancient face unreadable save for the intensity of his single eye.

Yara placed her left hand—the shadowed one—against Asvarr's forehead, directly over the blood-oath symbols. The bone-white knife hovered at his temple, its impossible edge catching the shifting light of the crossroads.

"Remember," she whispered.

The memory bloomed in his mind with perfect clarity—his mother's face, once faded by time, now vivid as yesterday. He was six years old again, huddled in the storage pit beneath their longhouse floor as raiders attacked the village. His mother's hands gripping his shoulders, her voice urgent yet loving.

"Live, my little flame," she whispered, using the pet name that only she had ever called him. "Whatever happens, live."

The sound of splintering wood above. Heavy footsteps. His mother's hand pushing him deeper into the darkness as she moved to replace the trapdoor.

"I love—"

The knife moved.

Pain lanced through Asvarr's skull as Yara extracted the memory. He felt it pulling free—the visual images, the sounds, and the emotional core of the moment, the foundation upon which his entire being had been constructed.

***

His mouth opened in a silent scream as the memory tore loose. Yara stepped back, the bone-white knife now glowing with golden light. Hovering above its blade was a small, crystalline seed—the memory given physical form.

"The ironseed memory," she said, holding it reverently. "The moment of separation that created your first self."

Asvarr gasped, clutching his head. Where the memory had been, a void now existed—a blank space he could sense while unable to fill it. His mother's face, her voice, her final words—gone completely, leaving only the knowledge that something precious had once existed there.

Yara approached the central dais, the memory-seed balanced on her knife's edge. "With this sacrifice, I bind myself to your circle, Flame-Bearer."

She pricked her own palm with the knife's tip, then pressed the bleeding wound to Asvarr's forehead beside the other blood-oath symbols. A mark like an inverted gateway burned itself into his skin, completing the circle of five.

The moment the blood-oath took hold, the key above Asvarr's palm blazed with blinding light. All five elemental energies surged together, creating a perfect harmony of opposed forces. The Pattern beneath their feet responded, the carved lines in the white stone glowing with matching radiance.

The Ashfather roared, raising his shadow-spear. "Stop this madness! You cannot comprehend what you unleash!"

Yara placed the memory-seed at the center of the dais. It sank into the white stone as if the solid surface were water, disappearing from view. The Pattern's glow intensified, spreading outward along all nine pathways.

"It begins," she said simply.

The ground beneath them shuddered. The crossroads, existing in all realms simultaneously, resonated with the transformation taking root at its center. Through his blood-oath with Yara, Asvarr felt a new dimension of awareness opening—an understanding of endings and beginnings that transcended linear perception.

"The seed roots," Brynja said, wonder in her voice.

"The pattern shifts," Svala added, her frost-white eyes wide.

"The worlds awaken," Leif whispered.

Asvarr staggered to his feet, the void-metal fused with his arm pulsing with newfound power. The key still hovered above his palm, yet its form had changed—evolving beyond a miniature of the Pattern into something new, still taking shape as the transformation progressed.

The Ashfather charged forward, shadow-spear aimed at the center of the dais where the memory-seed had vanished. "I will end this! Nine cycles I've maintained order! Nine cycles I've prevented the unmaking!"

Yara stepped between him and the dais, her form shifting between solid and shadow. "Your time ends, Old Wolf. The wheel turns."

The other Wardens moved to join her, their transformed flesh glowing with elemental power. Earth, Storm, Sky, and Death stood united before the dais, protecting the vulnerable seed as it took root in reality's heart.

Asvarr raised his transformed arm, the key's light blazing. "We choose trans-formation, Ashfather. We forge a third path beyond control or consumption."

"Fools!" the ancient entity snarled. "You gamble everything for an uncertain future!"

"Yes," Asvarr replied simply. "Such is the price of true creation."

The Ashfather struck with his shadow-spear, its point tearing through the space between them. The five Wardens moved in perfect synchronicity while maintaining their individuality. Each responded according to their nature—Brynja with stubborn defense, Svala with precise counterattack, Leif with fluid evasion, Yara with shadow-stepping anticipation.

Asvarr met the spear with his transformed arm, the void-metal absorbing the shadow energy completely. The key above his palm flared in response, sending a pulse of five-colored light up the spear's shaft toward the Ashfather himself.

The ancient entity howled as the light touched him, peeling away layers of accumulated power built over nine cycles of manipulation. Glimpses of his original form appeared—a Warden like themselves, before fear transformed his purpose to control.

"You cannot win!" the Ashfather shouted, voice cracking with emotion entirely unlike his previous coldness. "The void comes! It always comes!"

"Then we face it together," Asvarr replied. "Through transformation itself."

Light blazed from the center of the Pattern. The memory-seed took root in reality's heart, its crystalline structure spreading through the white stone like veins of quicksilver. The nine pathways extending from the crossroads pulsed with resonant energy, carrying transformation outward into all realms simultaneously.

Asvarr pushed back against the Ashfather's spear, the void-metal in his transformed arm absorbing the shadow energy. The key above his palm continued sending pulses of five-colored light up the weapon's shaft, stripping away layers of accumulated power from the ancient entity.

"This ends now," Asvarr growled, the five blood-oath marks burning on his forehead. "Nine cycles is enough."

The Ashfather snarled, his single eye wide with desperation. More of his true form emerged as the key's light peeled away his acquired power—a tall warrior with braided beard, his face marked with faded runes similar to the ones adorning Asvarr's chest. The shadow-spear in his hand flickered, losing cohesion as its wielder's nature changed.

"You cannot understand," the Ashfather gasped, voice shifting from thunder to something more human. "I've seen what waits beyond the Pattern. I've faced the void-hunger."

"Then show us," Brynja demanded, earth-threads pulsing beneath her skin as she moved to flank him. "Truth, Ashfather. After nine cycles, we deserve truth."

The ancient entity's resistance faltered. The five Wardens surrounded him, each transformed by their anchor bindings, each connected through blood-oaths that formed a unified circle of power. Their combined presence created a space where deception became impossible, where reality itself demanded honesty.

"The void consumes everything," the Ashfather whispered, lowering his faltering spear. "When I stood where you stand—when I bound the five anchors of my cycle—I glimpsed what waited at the Pattern's heart."

The crossroads trembled as memory rippled outward from the center. The white stone beneath their feet became transparent, revealing layers upon layers of previous Patterns—previous attempts at creation, abandoned or collapsed.

"Show us," Asvarr urged, the key above his palm resonating with the Ashfather's words. "Show us what you saw."

Something broke in the ancient entity's expression. Fear, genuine and raw, replaced the mask of control he had worn for nine cycles. With a gesture of surrender, he thrust his hand into the transparent stone, connecting directly with the awakening memory-seed.

Vision engulfed them all.

Darkness. Absolute void. A hunger so vast it defied comprehension. Within it, sparks of potential—fragile and fleeting, devoured before they could take form. This was what existed before the first Pattern, before the first dreaming. Endless possibility trapped in endless destruction.

A spark. Brighter than the others. Taking form, creating boundaries. The first Pattern, the first attempt at stable existence. Growing, evolving, expanding.

Then—failure. The void-hunger finding ways through the Pattern's defenses. Creation collapsing back into primordial chaos.

Again. Another attempt. Another Pattern forming, growing, failing.

Cycle after cycle. Creation and destruction. Pattern and void.

Until the current Pattern emerged. More complex, more resilient. The Tree growing as its organizing principle, bringing structure to chaos. For a time, stability.

But the void-hunger persists always. Waiting at the boundaries. Finding ways to infiltrate. Breaking the Pattern again and again, necessitating renewal while threatening complete dissolution.

The vision faded. The Ashfather stood diminished, his acquired power stripped away to reveal what he had once been—a Warden like themselves, who had made a different choice.

"I preserved what I could," he said quietly. "I controlled the Breaking and the Renewal to maintain the Pattern's structure against the void-hunger. I became the center that holds when all else fails."

Asvarr studied the being who had manipulated reality for nine cycles. In the Ashfather's face, he saw fear born of responsibility, control born of desperation.

"You became the Pattern's jailor," Yara said, her voice carrying neither judgment nor mercy. "Preservation through stasis. Continuation without growth."

"I prevented dissolution," the Ashfather countered. "What alternative existed? Allow the Pattern to evolve freely and risk complete destruction? The void-hunger waits for exactly such vulnerability."

The memory-seed at the center of the crossroads pulsed stronger. The Pattern beneath their feet continued its transformation, ancient structures dissolving while new possibilities formed. The white stone regained its solidity, no longer showing the layers of previous attempts at creation.

"There is another way," Asvarr said, the key hovering steady above his palm. "Transformation beyond control or consumption. Evolution with conscious intent."

The five Wardens moved into position around the central dais, forming a perfect circle with the transforming Pattern at its center. Each represented a fundamental element of existence—Blood, Earth, Wisdom, Storm, Death—connected through their blood-oaths with Asvarr at the fulcrum.

"Balance," Brynja said, placing her transformed hand on the dais. Earth-threads pulsed beneath her skin, connecting with the memory-seed.

"Harmony," Svala added, frost crystals gleaming on her fingers as she joined the connection.

"Unity," Leif said, living clouds swirling beneath his skin as he placed his hand alongside the others.

"Renewal," Yara finished, her half-shadowed hand completing the circle.

Asvarr faced the Ashfather across the dais. "Will you join us? Will you help transform rather than control?"

The ancient entity wavered. For a moment, something like hope flickered in his single eye. Then fear returned, hardening his features.

"I cannot risk it," he said, backing away. "I've seen too much dissolution, too much destruction. The Pattern must be preserved as it was structured."

"Then stand aside," Asvarr said, voice firm but without malice. "Your cycle ends. Ours begins."

The Ashfather's shoulders slumped in defeat. His shadow-spear dissipated entirely, leaving him unarmed and diminished. "You doom all existence," he whispered. "When the void-hunger finds your new Pattern, unprepared and evolving, it will consume everything."

"Perhaps," Asvarr acknowledged. "Or perhaps transformation itself becomes our defense—adaptation rather than rigidity."

The ancient entity turned away, moving toward one of the nine pathways leading from the crossroads. "I have done what I could for nine cycles," he said, voice hollow with exhaustion. "The responsibility passes to you, Wardens of the Fifth Cycle. May your creation survive what mine could not."

He stepped onto the pathway and vanished into mist, leaving the five Wardens alone at the Pattern's heart.

***

The moment the Ashfather departed, the transformation accelerated. The memory-seed at the center of the dais sprouted visibly, sending golden-white tendrils throughout the Pattern's structure. The key above Asvarr's palm changed form again, becoming a miniature tree with five distinct branches, each glowing with one of the elemental colors.

"It's working," Svala breathed, frost crystals forming and dissolving along her transformed arm. "The Pattern transforms rather than merely restoring."

"The Breaking becomes Renewal becomes Creation," Leif added, clouds shifting beneath his skin in complex patterns.

Pain lanced through Asvarr's chest where the merged marks spread across his torso. The void-metal in his transformed arm burned cold then hot, adapting to the changing Pattern. Through the five blood-oaths, he felt the others experiencing similar transformations—their bodies struggling to accommodate the new reality taking shape around them.

"We must complete the planting," Yara said urgently. "The Pattern requires anchoring in all five elements simultaneously, or it will collapse in transition."

Asvarr placed his transformed hand at the center of the dais, directly over the sprouting memory-seed. The key floating above his palm descended, merging with the growing sapling. Five-colored light exploded outward, temporarily blinding all within the crossroads.

When Asvarr's vision cleared, a small tree stood at the center of the dais—no taller than his forearm, yet radiating power beyond anything he had encountered. Its trunk twisted in impossible geometries, its five branches extending in perfect balance. Leaves of shifting color and texture adorned each branch, representing the five elements bound in harmony.

"The new Pattern takes root," Yara said with satisfaction. "Our task completes."

"What happens now?" Brynja asked, studying the small tree with wonder.

"The transformation spreads throughout all realms," Yara replied. "Reality itself evolves according to the principles we've established—balance, harmony, unity, renewal."

"And us?" Svala questioned, examining her frost-transformed flesh. "What becomes of the Wardens when our task concludes?"

The answer came from the tree itself. Its five branches extended toward each Warden in turn, touching their transformed flesh with gentle authority. Where contact occurred, change followed—the elemental alterations receding, returning their bodies to more human form while leaving traces of their binding experiences.

Asvarr watched as the void-metal in his arm liquefied, flowing back into the bracers around his wrist. The spreading marks across his torso contracted, concentrating into a single pattern over his heart—a miniature of the tree at the center of the dais. The five blood-oath symbols on his forehead shifted, merging into a circle of interconnected runes.

"We remain Wardens," Asvarr realized, flexing his now-normal hand. "But our role changes. From defenders to gardeners."

"The Pattern will require tending as it develops," Yara confirmed. "Guidance rather than control."

The crossroads shuddered. The nine pathways glowed with increasing intensity, straining to contain the transformation energy flowing through them. The small tree at the center continued growing, its branches extending while its roots spread throughout the white stone.

"The boundaries thin," Leif warned. "We cannot remain at the crossroads during full transformation. Reality destabilizes around us."

"Where do we go?" Brynja asked. "Back to our separate realms?"

"Together," Asvarr said firmly. "The five Wardens remain united through our blood-oaths. We face whatever comes as one."

Yara pointed to one of the nine pathways, which glowed with golden light distinct from the others. "That path leads to Midgard—to where the first anchor was bound. A cycle completes."

The crossroads trembled more violently. Cracks appeared in the white stone as the tree's roots expanded beneath the surface. The transformation accelerated beyond control, reality itself struggling to adapt to the new Pattern taking form.

"Now," Svala urged. "We must leave or be consumed by the transformation."

The five Wardens moved as one toward the golden pathway. Behind them, the small tree grew taller, its branches reaching upward while its roots delved deeper. The Pattern carved into the dais shifted, evolving into something new yet recognizably balanced.

As they stepped onto the pathway, Asvarr felt the void where his ironseed memory had been—the empty space that once held his mother's final moments. Though the emotional connection remained severed, something new grew in its place—a sense of purpose beyond personal history, identity beyond individual experience.

The golden pathway pulled them forward, the crossroads fading behind as they traveled between realms. Through their blood-oaths, the five Wardens remained connected, sharing strength and awareness as they journeyed toward an uncertain future.

Reality blurred around them. Images flashed past—fragments of the nine realms transforming under the influence of the new Pattern. Mountains shifting shape. Forests growing in impossible directions. Oceans changing color. The very physics of existence rewriting itself according to principles of balance and harmony rather than rigidity and hierarchy.

"The Breaking completes," Yara observed as they traveled. "True transformation begins."

Asvarr felt a question forming in the absence left by his sacrificed memory. "If the Ashfather's fears prove justified—if the void-hunger finds the new Pattern—what then?"

"Then we adapt," Brynja answered, her voice steady with earth's certainty. "We transform again. Evolution becomes our defense."

The pathway narrowed, focusing their journey toward a single point of light ahead. The smell of salt air and pine forest reached them—Midgard waiting beyond the veil between worlds.

"We arrive where you began," Svala said to Asvarr. "The circle closes."

The light expanded, enveloping them completely. For a moment, Asvarr felt suspended between states—belonging to the Pattern yet separate from it, transformed yet still himself, connected to four others yet maintaining his individuality.

This was the balance they had created. This was the transformation they had planted. This was the third path beyond control or consumption.

The light faded. Solid ground formed beneath their feet—a hilltop overlooking a familiar northern fjord. Below, the remnants of Asvarr's village stood outlined against the morning sky, abandoned since the initial Breaking.

***

But something had changed. Amid the ruins, a sapling grew—a miniature version of the tree they had left at the crossroads. Around it, the soil teemed with new life, grasses and flowers spreading outward in a perfect circle of regeneration.

"The first anchor point transforms," Yara said, satisfaction in her voice. "The others will follow. The Pattern evolves in all realms simultaneously."

Asvarr touched the tree-mark over his heart, feeling its connection to the sapling below and to the greater tree at the crossroads. The five blood-oaths pulsed on his forehead, linking him to the four Wardens standing beside him on the hilltop.

The transformation had begun. The Breaking had become Renewal had become Creation. The cycle continued, yet fundamentally changed.

What waited beyond, even the Wardens could not know. The sacrifice of certainty meant embracing possibility in all its forms—both wondrous and terrible. The void-hunger might test their new Pattern as it had tested all others before.

But this time, the Pattern could adapt. This time, existence itself could transform rather than merely resist.

Asvarr looked toward the horizon, where the sky displayed colors never before seen in Midgard—evidence of reality's ongoing evolution. The mark over his heart pulsed in rhythm with the sapling below and the tree at the crossroads.

The Breaking was complete. The true transformation had only just begun.

CHAPTER 23

BATTLE AT THE BLEEDING HOLLOW

B lood pooled beneath Asvarr's boots, the golden sap of the Root mixing with the crimson of his own wounds. The hollow beneath Svartálfr rumbled, stone cracking as the Root trembled with newfound awareness. He braced one hand against the ancient bark, its surface hot and pulsing beneath his palm. His bronze sword felt heavy in his other hand, the blade slick with the black ichorous blood of the cultists who had followed them into the depths.

"They're coming again," Gunnar growled, the dwarf's breath ragged as he pressed a cloth against the gash in his side. "I can hear them in the eastern tunnel."

Asvarr looked down at the Svartálfr craftsman who had guided him through the molten tunnels to this sacred place. Gunnar's weathered face had gone ashen, blood seeping between his fingers despite his efforts to staunch the wound. They had fought their way through three ambushes already, and the Root still wasn't fully awakened.

"How many?" Asvarr asked, his voice echoing in the cavernous space. The ceiling arched high above them, stalactites dripping with golden sap that collected in pools around the massive Root that dominated the chamber's center.

"More than before." Gunnar coughed, spitting blood onto the stone floor. "They've called their Ash-Priest. I heard his chains."

Asvarr's Grímmark burned on his chest, the rune pulsing in time with the Root's own rhythm. He could feel the anchor stirring, responding to his presence, but the binding ritual remained incomplete. The cultists had interrupted at the crucial moment, pouring into the hollow like a tide of shadow and steel.

"We need more time," Asvarr said, glancing toward the Root. The anchor point glowed within the bark, a nexus of golden light that called to him. "I have to finish what we started."

"Time is the one thing we don't have," Gunnar replied, struggling to his feet. He lifted his war hammer, its head inscribed with runes that glowed faintly blue in the dim light. "The Skyrend want to destroy the Root completely."

The name sent a chill through Asvarr's blood. The Skyrend cultists worshipped the breaking, revered the shattering of Yggdrasil as liberation. He had encountered them before, on the surface, their bodies marked with inverted runes carved into their flesh, their eyes hollow with a fervor that transcended reason.

"They serve the Ashfather," Asvarr said, memories of his encounters with the one-eyed wanderer flashing through his mind.

"They serve chaos," Gunnar corrected, limping toward the eastern tunnel entrance. "The Ashfather promises them freedom from the pattern, while he delivers unmaking."

A distant chanting echoed through the tunnels, words in an ancient tongue that made the Grímmark on Asvarr's chest burn with recognition. The language predated human speech, syllables that twisted reality as they were uttered.

"You can't fight them alone," Asvarr said, stepping toward Gunnar. "Your wound will slow you too much."

"I don't plan to fight them, Flame-Bearer." Gunnar smiled grimly, blood in his beard. "I plan to delay them. Long enough for you to complete the binding."

Before Asvarr could protest, a high, piercing note cut through the chamber. Both men turned toward the southern tunnel where a slender figure stood silhouetted against the darkness. She held a carved bone flute to her lips, her form draped in tattered robes emblazoned with broken rune patterns.

"Seidr-witch," Gunnar spat, raising his hammer defensively.

The woman lowered the flute, her face a web of ritual scars forming a fractured tree pattern. "The Hollow awakens," she said, her voice resonating unnaturally. "The Ash-Priest comes to claim what is broken."

"You've arrived too late," Asvarr replied, stepping between her and the Root. "The anchor answers to me now."

The witch's laughter rippled through the chamber, disturbing the pools of golden sap. "Poor Warden, so certain your mark grants you ownership." She raised one arm, revealing fingers tipped with iron claws. "The Root remembers older pacts than yours."

She strode forward with unnatural grace, her feet barely touching the stone floor. From the shadows behind her emerged three figures, their bodies twisted by whatever fell magic the cultists practiced. Their skin stretched taut over elongated limbs, eyes sunken and mouths sewn shut with black thread. Each carried a curved blade of dark metal that drank the light around it.

"Gunnar," Asvarr said quietly, "can you reach the western tunnel?"

"Aye," the dwarf replied, understanding immediately. "The forges lie that way. If I can reach them, I can seal the passages."

"Go," Asvarr said, raising his bronze sword. The runes along its length awakened, glowing with the same golden light as the Root behind him. "I'll hold them here."

Gunnar hesitated only a moment before nodding and backing toward the western tunnel. The Seidr-witch noticed, flicking her wrist toward him. One of her twisted servants leapt with inhuman speed, its blade whistling through the air toward Gunnar's exposed back.

Asvarr moved without thinking, the Grímmark flooding his limbs with power. He intercepted the creature, his bronze sword meeting the dark blade with a sound like a thunderclap. The impact sent shockwaves through his arm, but the runes on his weapon flared, countering whatever foul magic imbued the cultist's weapon.

"Run!" he shouted to Gunnar, who didn't waste the opportunity. The dwarf vanished into the western tunnel, the sound of his limping steps fading quickly.

The witch hissed in frustration. "Kill the Warden," she commanded, and all three twisted servants converged on Asvarr at once.

He spun to meet them, the training from his berserker days returning in a flood of muscle memory. The first creature lunged, its blade sliding past Asvarr's guard to score a line across his ribs. Pain flared, but the Grímmark's power dulled it to a distant burn. He countered, driving his bronze sword through the creature's chest and feeling it shudder as golden light erupted from the wound.

The other two attacked from different angles, forcing Asvarr back toward the Root. One blade caught his shoulder, biting deep, while he parried the other with a desperate swipe. Blood and sweat stung his eyes as he fought, each movement bringing him closer to the massive anchor behind him.

The Seidr-witch observed from a distance, her flute raised once more to her lips. As she played, the air in the chamber thickened, reality bending around the notes. Asvarr felt his limbs growing heavy, as if moving through water.

"Your mark possesses greater potential," she called between notes. "The Ash-father could unlock its full power."

Asvarr ignored her words. He ducked beneath a slash that would have opened his throat, then drove his knee into one attacker's midsection. The creature doubled over, and Asvarr's sword separated its head from its shoulders in a spray of black blood.

The remaining servant circled more cautiously now, its sewn mouth stretching in a silent snarl. The witch's melody changed, becoming more urgent, and the shadows in the chamber deepened, coalescing into half-seen shapes that clawed at Asvarr's legs.

He felt his back press against the Root, its surface thrumming with energy. The Grímmark responded, pulsing painfully as it recognized its counterpart. In that moment of distraction, the last servant lunged, its blade aimed at Asvarr's heart.

The Root moved.

A massive tendril of bark and sap lashed out, intercepting the dark blade. The servant's weapon sank deep into the wood, stuck fast as golden sap oozed around it. Before the creature could retreat, more tendrils erupted from the Root, wrapping around its limbs and torso, crushing with inexorable force. A sound like breaking branches filled the chamber as the servant's twisted form was literally torn apart.

The Seidr-witch's melody faltered, her eyes widening with genuine fear. "The Root awakens," she whispered, backing away. "The Ash-Priest must know."

She turned to flee, but Asvarr was faster. Drawing on the power flowing from the Root through his mark, he crossed the distance between them in an eyeblink, seizing her by the throat. "Tell me why the Skyrend came here," he demanded, his voice rough with exertion.

The witch remained still in his grasp, her scarred lips curving into a smile despite the pressure on her windpipe. "We came to witness," she rasped. "Every Root you bind brings the true unmaking closer. The Ashfather sends his regards, Warden."

Before Asvarr could question her further, she bit down hard on something concealed in her mouth. Bitter almonds scented the air, and her body convulsed once before going limp in his grasp. Her final breath escaped in a hiss that sounded almost like laughter.

Asvarr let her body fall, frustrated at the lost opportunity for answers. The silence in the chamber felt oppressive after the clash of combat, broken only by the subtle creaking of the Root as it settled back into place.

He turned back to the anchor, determination hardening his features. Blood still flowed from his wounds, but he ignored the pain. He had to complete the binding before the Ash-Priest arrived with more cultists. Without Gunnar's guidance, he would have to rely on instinct and the knowledge embedded in his mark.

The Grímmark pulsed as he approached the center of the Root, his steps leaving bloody footprints on the stone floor. The golden light within the bark intensified, recognizing him, opening to him. He placed his palm against the spot where the light was brightest, feeling the bark part beneath his touch, revealing the anchor within.

Unlike the previous anchors he had encountered, this one took the form of a pulsing heart-like structure, veins of golden sap spreading outward through the Root's core. It beat with a steady rhythm, each pulse sending ripples through the chamber.

"By blood and oath, horn and blade," Asvarr intoned the binding words, drawing his bronze sword and laying it across his open palm. "I claim this anchor in the name of renewal."

The words echoed strangely, as if spoken by multiple voices. The Root responded, the heart-anchor quickening its pulse. Asvarr felt the power building, the connection forming—

A thunderous boom shook the chamber, dust and small stones raining from the ceiling. Asvarr stumbled, nearly losing his connection to the anchor. Another boom followed, then another, each impact more violent than the last.

From the eastern tunnel came a procession of hooded figures, their robes emblazoned with the Skyrend emblem – a tree split by lightning. They moved in perfect unison, chanting in that same ancient tongue that set Asvarr's teeth on edge. Behind them, ducking to fit his massive frame through the tunnel, came the source of the thunderous steps.

The Ash-Priest stood nearly twice the height of a normal man, his body a grotesque amalgamation of flesh and wood. Bark grew from his skin in twisted patterns, branches erupting from his shoulders and back to form a crown of thorns above his head. Where his eyes should have been, only hollow sockets remained, filled with swirling ash. Great chains wrapped his torso and limbs, each link inscribed with runes that smoldered with inner fire.

"Warden," the Ash-Priest's voice scraped like stone on stone, echoing throughout the chamber. "The Ashfather sends his blessings."

Asvarr maintained his connection to the anchor, feeling its power flowing into him. "Your blessings hold no value here," he replied, his voice steady despite the dread that filled him at the sight of the monstrous priest.

The Ash-Priest's lipless mouth stretched in what might have been a smile. "The Root awakens, yet remains unclaimed." He raised one massive hand, the chains rattling. "Its memory belongs to us all."

With that, he brought his fist down upon the chamber floor with devastating force. The stone cracked, fissures spreading rapidly toward the Root. The cultists spread out around the chamber, their chanting growing louder, more frenzied.

Asvarr felt the anchor's rhythm faltering as the fissures reached the Root's base. Golden sap bled from new wounds in the bark, pooling on the fractured stone. He had to complete the binding now, or all would be lost.

Drawing on the power already flowing through the Grímmark, Asvarr cut his palm with the edge of his bronze sword. Blood mingled with the golden sap as he pressed his wounded hand deeper into the anchor's core.

"I offer my blood as binding," he continued the ritual, his voice rising above the chanting. "I offer my oath as tether."

The Ash-Priest roared, recognizing what Asvarr attempted. He charged forward, chains whipping around him with unexpected speed for one so massive. The cultists drew curved knives, converging on Asvarr from all sides.

"I offer myself as Warden," Asvarr's voice grew stronger as the connection deepened, the anchor responding to his call. The Grímmark blazed on his chest, so bright now that it shone through his tunic like a second sun.

A knife blade slashed across his back. Another buried itself in his thigh. Asvarr gritted his teeth against the pain, refusing to break the connection. The Ash-Priest was nearly upon him, one massive hand reaching to tear him from the Root.

In that moment of dire need, a new rune formed in Asvarr's mind—a pattern he had never seen before, yet somehow knew intimately. It burned behind his eyes, demanding release. Without conscious thought, he traced it in the air with his bleeding hand, leaving a trail of mingled blood and sap that hung suspended before him.

"I claim this anchor," he shouted, the final words of the binding ritual, "in the name of transformation!"

The rune ignited with blinding light. The chamber itself seemed to hold its breath—and then the ceiling split open with a deafening crack, the stone parting like fabric torn by giant hands. Daylight poured in, shocking after the dimness of the hollow. But it wasn't only light that entered.

The sky itself had split open, mirroring the fissure in the chamber ceiling. Through that impossible tear in reality streamed ribbons of pure golden energy, lashing down like lightning strikes. They smashed into the cultists, scattering them like leaves in a gale. One struck the Ash-Priest squarely in his chest, driving him backward with such force that he crashed into the far wall, chains shattering upon impact.

The hollow trembled, caught between competing forces—the Ash-Priest's destructive power and the Root's awakening strength. Asvarr maintained his connection to the anchor, feeling it latch onto him, binding itself to his essence even as he bound himself to it. The process was nearly complete.

A bellow of rage drew his attention back to the Ash-Priest, who was struggling to his feet, black ichor pouring from wounds in his twisted body. The golden energy had burned away portions of his bark-skin, revealing something else beneath—something ancient and furious.

"This is far from the end, Warden," the priest growled, his voice no longer stone-on-stone but something more human, more dangerous. "Every Root you bind brings us one step closer to the true unmaking. The Ashfather will—"

Another stream of golden energy silenced him, driving him back toward the eastern tunnel. The remaining cultists fled in disarray, their chanting broken, their unity shattered by the unexpected assault from above.

Asvarr felt the binding nearing completion, the anchor's rhythm synchronizing with his own heartbeat. The Grímmark expanded, new patterns forming across his chest as the Root claimed him just as surely as he claimed it. The pain was extraordinary, but so was the power that came with it.

The chamber shook more violently, chunks of stone falling from the damaged ceiling. If Asvarr didn't complete the binding soon, they might be buried alive in the hollow. But where was Gunnar? Had the dwarf succeeded in reaching the forges, or had he fallen to more cultists along the way?

As if summoned by the thought, a horn blast echoed from the western tunnel—the signal they had agreed upon. Gunnar lived, and the forges were ready. Now Asvarr needed only to finish what he had begun, to claim this Root as he had claimed the others before it.

With one final surge of will, he pushed his bleeding hand completely into the heart-anchor, feeling it close around his flesh like a living thing. "The Root is bound," he declared, his voice carrying the weight of ritual. "The anchor is sealed. The Warden stands."

The golden energy streaming from the split sky intensified, bathing the entire chamber in light so bright it burned away all shadow. The Ash-Priest gave one final roar of defiance before retreating with his remaining followers, driven back by the purifying radiance.

As the binding completed, Asvarr felt something fundamentally shift within him. This anchor differed from the others—more primal, more connected to the essence of creation itself. The knowledge it contained flooded his mind, threatening to overwhelm his human consciousness.

He saw visions of the world's forging, of the Tree's growth, of roots spreading through void to create reality itself. He saw the Ashfather as he once was—a Warden like himself, before fear and ambition twisted him. He saw the pattern that connected all things, and his place within it.

When the visions cleared, Asvarr found himself kneeling before the Root, his hand still buried within its core. The golden energy had subsided, though the split in the sky remained, a ragged wound in reality that would take time to heal. Blood pooled around him, both his own and that of the fallen cultists.

Slowly, painfully, he withdrew his hand from the anchor. Where his flesh had merged with the Root, something new had formed—a small, perfect seed resting in his palm, glowing with inner light. The fourth token, the physical manifestation of his bond with this anchor.

The Root itself had changed as well. Where before it had been dormant, now it pulsed with visible life. New shoots sprouted from its surface, tiny leaves unfurling as if in springtime. The golden sap flowed more vigorously, sealing wounds and nourishing growth.

Asvarr tucked the seed token securely into his belt pouch with the others he had gathered on his journey. Each one brought him closer to fulfilling his purpose, though that purpose itself seemed to shift and evolve with every binding.

Heavy footsteps approached from the western tunnel, and Gunnar appeared, leaning heavily on his war hammer. The dwarf's face was paler than before, his wound clearly taking its toll, but his eyes widened at the sight of the transformed Root and the split sky above.

"By the Forge-Father," he breathed, limping toward Asvarr. "You did it."

"At great cost," Asvarr replied, looking down at his blood-soaked clothing and the new patterns formed by the Grímmark on his chest. "The Ash-Priest escaped."

"He'll be back," Gunnar said grimly, surveying the damage to the hollow. "With more followers. The Skyrend never surrender."

Asvarr nodded, retrieving his bronze sword from where it had fallen during the binding. The blade had changed, just as he had—its runes deeper, more complex, glowing with the same inner light as the seed token.

"We need to leave this place," he said, sliding the transformed weapon into its sheath. "The binding is complete, but the hollow stands compromised. And you need healing."

Gunnar waved away the concern, though he couldn't hide his wince of pain. "The forges remain secure. I've opened a path that will take us back to the surface." He looked up at the split sky. "Though you seem to have created a more direct route."

Despite everything, Asvarr felt a smile tug at his lips. "I acted on instinct," he admitted, "the new rune emerged... forcefully."

"Rune-craft follows its own will," Gunnar said knowingly. "Especially when wielded by one marked as you are." He studied Asvarr with new respect. "You've changed, Flame-Bearer. The Root has left its mark on you in many ways."

Asvarr felt it too—a deepening of his connection to the pattern, a shifting of his very essence. Each binding transformed him, made him less human and more... something else. Something without name.

"Four anchors bound," he said quietly, touching the pouch containing the tokens. "One remains."

Gunnar's expression grew somber. "Aye, and it will challenge you beyond all others." He gestured toward the eastern tunnel. "The Ash-Priest goes to report your success to his master. The Ashfather will respond with fury."

"Let him come," Asvarr replied, new determination hardening his voice as he helped Gunnar toward the western tunnel. "I've faced him before. I'll face him again."

As they left the hollow, Asvarr cast one last look at the awakened Root and the torn sky above it. The Grímmark pulsed in response, reminding him of the power he now carried—and the responsibility that came with it.

Whatever the Ashfather planned, whatever "true unmaking" the cultists spoke of, Asvarr would stand against it. He was Warden now, bound to the very fabric of creation. His resolve would remain unshaken.

***

Gunnar collapsed halfway to the surface. His weathered face had gone gray, the hasty bandage around his midsection soaked through with blood. The Svartálfr craftsman had guided them through three winding passages since their escape from the hollow, each tunnel narrower than the last, but the toll of his wounds had finally overcome his stubborn will.

"Leave me," he gasped, slumping against the rough-hewn wall. "Get yourself to the surface, Warden."

Asvarr knelt beside him, examining the wound by the light of phosphorescent fungi that lined the ceiling in uneven clumps. The gash had widened during their flight, and a sickly black discoloration spread outward from the edges. The cultist's blade had carried poison.

"I'll carry you if I must," Asvarr said, sliding an arm beneath Gunnar's shoulders.

The dwarf pushed him away with surprising strength. "Fool. The Skyrend will be regrouping." He coughed, speckling his beard with flecks of blood. "Take the eastern fork ahead. It leads to my kin."

Asvarr hesitated. The fourth token, the seed from the Root, pulsed in his belt pouch with otherworldly warmth. Its power called to him, urging connection with the other tokens he'd gathered. Only one anchor remained unbound, and time grew short. Yet he couldn't abandon the dwarf who had risked everything to help him.

"What poison did the blade carry?" he asked, reaching for his waterskin.

Gunnar's eyes narrowed, lines deepening across his weathered face. "Shadow-ice. From the depths beneath the Forge-Heart. There's no—"

His words cut off as heavy footfalls echoed from the passage behind them. Many feet, moving quickly.

"Go!" Gunnar hissed, fumbling at his belt. He pressed something cold and metallic into Asvarr's palm—a heavy iron key etched with runes. "Third door in the Hall of Embers. My people will aid you."

The footfalls grew louder, accompanied now by the clinking of chains. The Ash-Priest had recovered faster than expected.

Asvarr's Grímmark burned beneath his tunic, the expanded patterns throbbing with warning. He couldn't fight the Ash-Priest again so soon, especially with Gunnar wounded. The binding had left him drained, his own wounds still seeping blood.

"I won't leave you to them," he said, hefting the dwarf despite his protests.

Gunnar's face contorted in pain as Asvarr lifted him. "Stubborn human," he growled, though gratitude flickered in his pain-glazed eyes.

They moved deeper into the tunnel, Asvarr matching his stride to Gunnar's labored breathing. The sound of pursuit grew steadily closer. When they reached the eastern fork Gunnar had mentioned, Asvarr paused. The left passage was wider, lined with carefully fitted stones bearing the craftmarks of Svartálfr masons. The right narrowed quickly, looking more like a natural fissure than a constructed path.

"Which way?" Asvarr asked.

Gunnar's head lolled, consciousness fading. "Left... to the Hall..." His voice trailed into ragged breathing.

Asvarr took three steps into the left passage before faltering. Something felt wrong. The mark on his chest burned with warning, and the seed token in his pouch grew cold rather than warm. He turned back, examined the fork again. There—almost invisible in the dim light—a spray of symbols painted in what looked like dried blood across the archway of the left passage. Skyrend markings.

The cultists had laid a trap.

With a muttered curse, Asvarr adjusted Gunnar's weight and took the right fork instead. The passage narrowed immediately, forcing him to turn sideways to navigate the tightest sections while supporting the dwarf. The sounds of pursuit faded, then returned with angry shouts as the cultists discovered his choice.

The fissure widened abruptly into a roughly circular chamber dominated by a pool of dark water. Steam rose from its surface, carrying the sharp tang of metal and sulfur. No visible exit presented itself.

"Dead end," Asvarr muttered, carefully setting Gunnar down against the wall. The dwarf's breathing had grown more labored, the dark discoloration spreading visibly beneath his skin.

Gunnar's eyes fluttered open, focusing with effort. "Water path," he said, voice barely audible. "Blood... opens the way."

Asvarr understood. Many Svartálfr passages required payment—blood, riddle, or crafted offering. He drew his bronze sword, wincing at the pull of his own wounds, and sliced his palm. Blood welled, mingling with the remnants of golden sap still clinging to his skin. He knelt at the pool's edge and let the mixture drip into the steaming water.

The effect was immediate. The water churned, color shifting from dark to golden as ripples spread outward from where his blood had fallen. The Grímmark pulsed in response, and the seed token in his pouch grew warm once more.

A grinding sound echoed through the chamber as a section of wall slid open behind the pool, revealing a new passage lit by the glow of distant forges.

Shouts from the cultists grew closer. Asvarr retrieved Gunnar, whose eyes had closed again, and waded into the pool. The transformed water felt like liquid fire against his skin, yet left no burns. It rose to his waist at the deepest point before he reached the hidden passage, half-carrying, half-dragging the unconscious dwarf.

As they passed through the opening, the wall slid closed behind them with the sound of stone scraping against stone. The cultists' shouts cut off abruptly.

The new tunnel sloped gently upward, growing warmer with each step. Ribbons of gold and silver ore veined the walls, reflecting the red-orange glow that suffused the air. After several minutes of struggling with Gunnar's weight, Asvarr saw the tunnel open into a vast cavern—the Hall of Embers, he presumed.

Dwarven crafters worked at dozens of forges, hammers rising and falling in complex rhythms that echoed throughout the space. The ceiling arched so high above that it disappeared into shadow, while the floor descended in concentric terraces toward a central pit of molten metal. Walkways of dark stone connected the terraces, crowded with Svartálfr moving with purpose between workstations.

Asvarr's appearance at the tunnel mouth caused an immediate reaction. The nearest dwarves shouted in their guttural tongue, and within moments he found himself surrounded by armed guards with intricately crafted axes and mail that gleamed with runes.

"I bring Gunnar Ironveil," Asvarr said quickly, shifting the unconscious dwarf to show his face. "He's wounded. Shadow-ice poison."

Recognition flickered across the faces of the guards, followed by alarm. Two stepped forward and carefully took Gunnar from Asvarr's arms. Another, wearing a helm adorned with metallic feathers, addressed him in the common tongue.

"How came you here with the First-Forge wounded thus?" The guard's tone carried accusation beneath the question.

"Skyrend cultists," Asvarr replied, too exhausted for anything but directness. "They attacked us at the Bleeding Hollow. The Root is bound, but Gunnar took a poisoned blade in my defense."

The mention of the Root sent a murmur through the gathered dwarves. The helmeted guard studied Asvarr with new intensity, gaze lingering on the blood-soaked patches of his tunic where the expanded Grímmark pulsed visibly.

"You bear the mark," he said, voice lowered. "Gunnar spoke of you. The Flame-Bearer."

Asvarr nodded. "Gunnar gave me this." He held out the iron key. "He said your people would aid me."

The guard's eyes widened at the sight of the key. He barked orders to his companions, who hurried away with Gunnar toward one of the upper terraces. To Asvarr, he made a gesture of respect—right fist pressed to left shoulder.

"I am Thrain, Shield-Captain of the Forge-Hold. Follow me. Our healers will tend your wounds while they work to save Gunnar."

Asvarr matched the dwarf's brisk pace across one of the stone walkways. Svartálfr crafters paused in their work to watch him pass, their expressions a mixture of curiosity and wariness. He stood nearly two heads taller than most of them, a stranger in their sacred domain.

"Will Gunnar survive?" Asvarr asked as they climbed a spiral staircase to an upper level.

Thrain's shoulders tensed. "Shadow-ice is... difficult. The poison comes from the void between worlds. It unmakes rather than kills." He glanced back. "But our forge-healers are skilled. If any can save him, they can."

They passed through a stone archway into a chamber far different from the industrial clamor of the main hall. Here, soft light glowed from crystals embedded in the walls, and the air carried the scent of herbs and heated metal. Several low beds occupied the center of the room, one now holding Gunnar's still form. Dwarven healers in copper-threaded robes worked around him, grinding herbs in mortars and heating small metal implements in a specialized forge.

"Sit," Thrain commanded, indicating another bed. "They will tend you next."

Asvarr obeyed, the adrenaline of battle and escape finally draining from his limbs. The Grímmark's power had sustained him through the binding and flight, but now exhaustion claimed its due. His wounds throbbed with renewed intensity.

While he waited, he removed the seed token from his pouch, examining it in the crystal light. Unlike the tokens from previous bindings—the horn, the ivory disk, the remembrance-key—this one pulsed with visible life. Tiny rootlets emerged from its surface, reaching outward before withdrawing again in rhythmic motion. When he held it in his palm, the Grímmark responded with matching pulses, and knowledge flooded his mind—glimpses of the pattern as seen through the Root's perspective.

A female dwarf with a silver-streaked beard approached, carrying a tray of implements. "Your wounds," she said simply, gesturing for him to remove his tunic.

Asvarr complied, revealing the full extent of the Grímmark. What had begun as a single rune on his chest had expanded into an intricate pattern that spread across his torso from shoulder to waist, incorporating elements from each binding. The newest additions glowed faintly with the same golden light as the seed token.

The healer drew in a sharp breath. "The mark grows," she said, carefully cleaning the gash on his shoulder with a mixture that stung and then numbed the flesh. "With each binding, it claims more."

"You know of the bindings?" Asvarr asked, surprised.

She nodded once, focusing on her work. "Ours is the knowledge of the deeps. We remember what the upper realms forget." Her hands moved with practiced efficiency as she stitched his wounds closed with thread that gleamed metallically. "The Skyrend attacked because they know what comes next."

"The final binding," Asvarr said.

"The awakening," she corrected, applying a salve that smelled of iron and frost to his stitched wounds. "What sleeps will wake. What was forgotten will be remembered."

Before Asvarr could press for clarification, a commotion at Gunnar's bedside drew their attention. The dwarf had regained consciousness, his voice rising in argument with the other healers.

"—must tell him! Before it consumes me!" Gunnar's face contorted with pain as he tried to rise.

The healer attending Asvarr moved quickly to join her colleagues, leaving Asvarr to pull his blood-stiffened tunic back on. He approached Gunnar's bed cautiously, aware of the tension in the room.

Gunnar's gaze fixed on him, clarity returning despite the black lines spreading up his neck toward his face. "Flame-Bearer," he gasped. "They try to silence me, but you must know."

Thrain stepped forward, one hand on his axe. "First-Forge, the shadow-ice speaks through you. Rest and let the healers work."

"No!" Gunnar's voice cracked with effort. "The fifth anchor—it lies within death itself. The Ash-Priest goes there now, to claim it before the Warden can."

A chill passed through Asvarr. "Within death? You mean Helheim?"

Gunnar nodded weakly. "The Door of Souls stands open since the shattering. The Ashfather's servants go to corrupt the anchor before you can bind it." His hand clutched at Asvarr's arm with desperate strength. "Promise me you will not delay. My death buys you time, but little of it."

"You're not dying," Asvarr said firmly, though the spreading blackness beneath Gunnar's skin told a different story.

A bitter smile crossed the dwarf's face. "We forge-folk know the shape of our ending when we see it." He pulled Asvarr closer, voice dropping to a whisper. "The key I gave you—it opens more than doors. When the moment comes, use it to bridge the gap between living and dead."

The lead healer intervened, firmly separating them. "Enough! The poison reaches his mind. He needs rest and treatment."

Gunnar fell back, strength fading, but his eyes remained fixed on Asvarr. "Remember," he mouthed silently.

Thrain guided Asvarr away from the bed. "Come. You need food and proper rest yourself. The journey to Helheim is long, and you are in no condition to attempt it yet."

Asvarr allowed himself to be led from the healing chamber, the seed token a warm presence against his skin where he had tucked it back into its pouch. His mind raced with Gunnar's warning. The fifth anchor within death itself. The Ashfather's servants already moving to claim it. Time slipping away like sand through fingers.

They entered a small chamber dominated by a stone table laden with food and drink. Asvarr ate mechanically, his attention focused inward on the expanded Grímmark and the knowledge it contained. Four anchors bound, their power flowing through him, transforming him with each connection. What would the fifth do? What would he become when all five were joined?

"The First-Forge speaks truly," Thrain said eventually, breaking the silence. "The shadow-ice will claim him before the next forge-lighting."

Asvarr looked up sharply. "There must be something your healers can do."

Thrain's expression remained impassive. "The void unmakes. It cannot be healed, only endured until it completes its purpose." He stroked his beard thoughtfully. "Gunnar Ironveil knew the risk when he guided you to the Bleeding Hollow. He chose his path with open eyes."

"He chose to help me bind the anchor."

"He chose to preserve the pattern," Thrain corrected. "As his ancestors did before him. As mine did. The Svartálfr remember the time before the Tree, Flame-Bearer. We remember the chaos that came when there was no pattern to bind reality."

A memory flashed through Asvarr's mind—a vision granted during the binding. The world before Yggdrasil, formless and wild. The Ashfather as he once was, before fear twisted him. The pattern that connected all things.

"What did Gunnar mean about the key?" he asked, pulling the heavy iron object from his belt.

Thrain's eyes narrowed. "That is no mere key. It is a soul-forge, one of three crafted when the first deeps were mined." He made a gesture Asvarr didn't recognize—warding or reverence, he couldn't tell. "It can bind essence to form, spirit to matter. In the right hands, at the right moment..."

He trailed off, but Asvarr understood. It was a tool for crossing boundaries, for traversing the gap between living and dead. A means to reach Helheim while still drawing breath.

"I need to leave as soon as possible," Asvarr said, rising from the table. His wounds protested, but he ignored them. "The Ash-Priest has a head start."

Thrain nodded grimly. "Rest tonight. Your body needs healing, even if your spirit drives you onward. I will prepare supplies and a guide for tomorrow's first light." He stood, adjusting his feathered helm. "The way to Helheim is treacherous even in the best of times. Since the shattering, the barriers have thinned, and things slip between that should not."

***

After Thrain departed, Asvarr sat alone in the chamber, turning the soul-forge key over in his hands. Its weight felt significant beyond its physical presence, a burden of responsibility more than metal. He placed it beside the pouch containing the four tokens, watching as they reacted to each other's proximity. Faint light pulsed between them, the artifacts recognizing their shared purpose.

The Grímmark burned with sudden intensity, pulling his attention elsewhere. He closed his eyes, letting the sensation guide him. Through the expanded awareness granted by the bindings, he sensed distant movement—the Ash-Priest and his remaining cultists, traveling fast along hidden ways that paralleled the roots of Yggdrasil. They had a two-day lead at least, their path bending toward the frozen wastes where the barriers between Midgard and Helheim had grown thinnest.

Asvarr's eyes snapped open, resolve hardening within him. He could not wait until morning. The Skyrend would reach the Door of Souls first if he delayed, and the fifth anchor would fall to their corruption. All he had accomplished with the previous bindings would mean nothing if the pattern remained broken.

He gathered the tokens and the soul-forge key, securing them inside his tunic where they rested against the Grímmark. Then he moved silently to the chamber door, peering into the corridor beyond. Two guards stood at the far end, their attention directed outward.

Asvarr retreated to the healing chamber's entrance. Through the doorway, he could see Gunnar surrounded by healers, their expressions grave as they worked. The First-Forge had sacrificed himself to ensure the Root's binding. Asvarr would not let that sacrifice be in vain.

Drawing on the power flowing through the Grímmark, he reached for the new rune-knowledge granted by the fourth binding. The pattern formed in his mind—a symbol of passage and transformation. With his blood-crusted fingertip, he traced it on the stone beside the doorway, watching as it sank into the rock like a brand into flesh.

The stone rippled, revealing a passage that hadn't existed moments before, leading upward toward the surface. The rune had bent reality itself, creating a path where none had been.

Asvarr cast one last glance toward Gunnar's distant form, silently promising to complete what they had begun together. Then he slipped into the new passage, the stone sealing behind him as if it had never parted.

The path twisted upward through the living rock, growing colder as it neared the surface. The Grímmark guided him, its power illuminating the way with faint golden light. After what felt like hours of climbing, he emerged onto a snowswept plateau beneath a sky filled with curtains of green and blue light—the aurora that marked the boundaries between realms.

To the north, hardly visible at the horizon's edge, a black spire rose from the ice. The Door of Souls, the passage to Helheim. The final anchor awaited him there, and the Ash-Priest raced to claim it.

Asvarr adjusted his cloak against the bitter cold and began walking, each step carrying him closer to the fifth binding and whatever transformation it would bring. The soul-forge key pulsed against his chest like a second heartbeat, reminding him of its purpose.

Bridge the gap between living and dead. Complete the pattern. Wake what sleeps.

The aurora flared above him, casting its eerie light across the endless snow, illuminating his solitary figure as he set forth on the final leg of his journey. Five anchors to bind the pattern anew. Four secured. One remaining.

The race for Helheim had begun.

CHAPTER 24
VOICES IN THE VERDANT FLAME

F ire spirits danced across Asvarr's fingertips, casting emerald shadows on his face as he huddled against the killing cold. Three days of travel across the frozen wasteland had left his supplies depleted and his strength waning. The Door of Souls loomed closer now, a jagged obsidian spire that pierced the auroral sky, still a day's journey ahead.

The verdant flames he'd conjured from the Root's essence provided meager warmth at best. Unlike natural fire, they consumed nothing, feeding instead on the power channeled through his expanded Grímmark. Each flicker of green fire drained him further, yet he persisted—freezing to death before reaching Helheim's entrance remained the grimmer alternative.

He closed his eyes, focusing on the seed token nestled against his skin beneath layers of frost-stiffened clothing. It pulsed with life, tiny rootlets shifting against his flesh, seeking purchase. The other tokens responded in kind—the horn, the ivory disk, the remembrance-key—each humming with purpose as they drew closer to the final anchor.

"Your blood runs thin, Flame-Bearer."

Asvarr's eyes snapped open. A figure stood at the edge of the verdant light—a woman wrapped in tattered hides, her face obscured by a hood of stitched pelts. She had materialized without warning, and his mark had given no signal of approach.

"Who are you?" he demanded, his hand moving to his bronze sword. The runes etched along its blade flared in response to his touch.

The woman laughed, the sound like ice cracking across a frozen lake. "I am called many things by many tongues. Hel-seer by some. Death's-bride by others." She pulled back her hood, revealing a face half-beautiful, half-decayed—flesh and bone divided perfectly down the center. "You may call me Kára."

Asvarr kept his grip on his sword, though he knew instinctively this was no physical threat he faced. "What do you want?"

"Want?" Kára cocked her head, the motion unnaturally fluid. "I want nothing. I simply am. The question is what do you want, traversing the death-fields with four tokens burning against your heart?"

"The fifth anchor," Asvarr replied, seeing no point in deception. "It lies beyond the Door of Souls."

"Ah." Kára nodded, stepping closer to his verdant fire. The green flames cast her divided face in stark relief, making the contrast between living flesh and exposed bone even more grotesque. "The Root that grows in death's domain. Many have sought it. Few have touched it. None have bound it."

"The Ash-Priest seeks it now."

"Indeed he does." She extended skeletal fingers toward the flames, which coiled around her bones without burning. "The death-touched priest and his followers passed this way two days past. They carry something... unusual. A container of ash and golden sap mixed with blood."

Asvarr's stomach tightened. "For corruption."

"For transformation," Kára said, withdrawing her hand from the flames. "Just as you seek to transform the anchor through your methods, they seek to transform it through theirs. Different paths leading to different ends."

The fire spirits suddenly swirled more vigorously, rising from Asvarr's palm to spiral between them. They took vague humanoid shapes, dancing and twisting as if trying to communicate. One darted close to Asvarr's face, leaving a trail of emerald light that hung suspended in the air.

"They speak to you," Kára observed, her living eye widening with interest. "The fire-born recognize one of their own."

"I'm merely—" Asvarr began, then stopped as voices whispered from the flames, multiple tones overlapping in a dissonant chorus.

Warden of four... bearer of the mark... forge-flame burns within... final binding approaches...

The voices grew louder, more insistent, as the spirits danced more frantically.

The Ash-Priest prepares the vessel... black sap for black purpose... the anchor weakens...

Asvarr struggled to make sense of the fragmented warnings. "What vessel? What black purpose?"

Corruption seeks rebirth... death-tie beyond unmaking... false anchor to draw true power...

"Enough!" Kára commanded, sweeping her arm through the flames. The spirits scattered, their voices fading to whispers. "They speak of matters beyond their knowing. Fire-born see fragments only, reflections of might-be and never-was."

Asvarr closed his hand, extinguishing the verdant flames. In the sudden darkness, Kára's face seemed to glow with its own pale light. "Why have you come?" he asked again. "You evaded my question before."

She smiled, the expression ghastly on her half-rotted face. "The dead take interest in those who walk willingly toward death's door. Especially those who carry pieces of the world's foundation." She gestured toward his chest, where the tokens lay hidden. "I came to offer guidance."

"At what price?"

Her laugh came again, sharper this time. "You learn quickly, Flame-Bearer. Nothing in the borderlands comes freely." She extended her hand, palm up—flesh on one side, bone on the other. "A memory. One that burns brightest in your heart. Give it to me, and I will show you a hidden path to the Door of Souls. One that will let you reach the anchor before the Ash-Priest completes his work."

Asvarr hesitated. He had already sacrificed memories to previous bindings. How many pieces of himself could he lose before ceasing to be who he was? Yet time worked against him. The Ash-Priest's corruption of the final anchor would spell disaster.

"What kind of memory?" he asked cautiously.

"Joy," Kára replied simply. "I collect joys. So few reach these lands untarnished."

Asvarr thought of his life—the battles, the losses, the hardships that had forged him. Moments of joy stood like rare sun-touched islands in a dark sea. To lose even one seemed an impossible price.

"I need to know more about what awaits me," he countered. "The Ash-Priest's plan. The nature of the anchor within Helheim. Information first, then I'll consider your price."

Kára's expression soured, dead muscles pulling taut across exposed bone. "Bargaining with Hel's handmaiden? Bold, Warden. Very bold." She lowered her hand, contemplating him. "Ask three questions. I will answer what I can. Then you decide if my path is worth your brightest joy."

Asvarr nodded, gathering his thoughts. "What exactly is the Ash-Priest planning to do with the anchor?"

"He cannot bind it as you can—he lacks the mark," Kára explained, gesturing to Asvarr's chest where the Grímmark lay hidden. "Instead, he means to graft a piece of his master onto it—the vessel of ash and sap you heard mentioned. This will enslave the anchor, forcing its power to flow into the Ashfather rather than the pattern."

"And if he succeeds?"

"The Ashfather gains dominion over death itself. The cycle of rebirth breaks. Souls remain trapped in Helheim or scattered to the void between worlds." Her living eye fixed on him intently. "Your second question."

Asvarr suppressed a shudder. "What is the nature of the fifth anchor in Helheim? How does it differ from the others I've bound?"

Kára's expression grew solemn. "The anchor in death's realm exists as the first and oldest of them all. When the pattern fractured and Yggdrasil shattered, this anchor remained unchanged. It remembers what the others have forgotten—the original purpose of the pattern and what lies at its heart."

She traced patterns in the frost with her bone fingers. "Unlike the others, it has awareness. Will. It has watched countless cycles of breaking and binding. It chooses its Warden rather than being chosen." Her gaze returned to his face. "Your final question, Flame-Bearer. Choose wisely."

Asvarr weighed his options carefully. So much remained unknown, but he sensed his time with Kára growing short. "What sacrifice will the fifth anchor demand of me? The others each took something—rage, memory, identity, certainty. What will the last one take?"

A slow smile spread across the living half of Kára's face. "The truest question at last." She leaned close, her breath cold against his ear. "It will take everything you have left. And offer everything you've lost in return."

She pulled back, watching his reaction. "Now, my price. Your brightest joy for the hidden path. Do we have agreement?"

Asvarr thought of the few pure moments of joy in his life. His first successful hunt. The pride in his father's eyes when he took his place among the warriors. The feast where Torfa had chosen to sit beside him, her shield touching his as they shared mead and laughter.

Each memory a fragment of who he was, who he had been before the mark and the burden of Warden.

"Show me the path first," he said finally. "Then I'll give you your payment."

Kára's eyes narrowed, but she nodded once. "Stand."

When Asvarr rose, stiff from the cold, she moved behind him and placed her hands on his shoulders—one warm with life, one cold as the grave. Her grip tightened, and she turned him slightly to the east, away from the direct path to the Door of Souls.

"Do you see the twin peaks there, where the aurora pools between them like water?" she asked, her voice close to his ear.

Asvarr squinted against the darkness. In the distance, barely visible in the auroral light, two jagged mountains rose against the horizon. Between them, the shimmering curtains of light seemed to gather and intensify, forming an eerie, shifting pool of color.

"I see them."

"The Ash-Priest travels the direct route, the Corpse Road that winds before the Door. His followers guard it heavily now." Her bone finger extended past his shoulder, tracing the route. "Through the Aurora Gate between those peaks lies a passage through the borderlands. It will bring you directly to the foot of the Door from behind, bypassing the Ash-Priest's watchers."

"The borderlands?" Asvarr questioned. "Between what borders?"

"Between life and death, between being and unmaking." Kára's half-smile pressed against his cheek. "A dangerous path for most, yet for you—one who walks between worlds already—the way opens. Your tokens will guide you, and your mark will shield you—if your will holds firm."

She released him and moved to stand before him once more. "Now, my payment. Your brightest joy."

Asvarr weighed his options one final time. The direct path would cost him days he didn't have. This borderland route might be his only chance to reach the anchor before the Ash-Priest.

"Very well," he said at last. "How do you take it?"

"Give me your hand."

Asvarr extended his right hand. Kára took it in both of hers, pressing his palm between flesh and bone. A cold sensation spread up his arm, followed by a pulling feeling behind his eyes.

"Think of it," she instructed. "Your purest moment of joy. Hold it in your mind's eye."

Asvarr closed his eyes, searching through his memories. Past the battles, past the bindings, past the weight of prophecy and mark. Back to a summer evening long ago, before raiders came, before the world broke. He had climbed the tallest pine near his village, higher than any other child dared. At the top, he'd watched the sunset paint the fjord golden, the distant mountains purple with shadow. For one perfect moment, the world had seemed infinite with possibility, his future unwritten.

A sharp pain lanced through his head. His eyes flew open to see Kára holding something between her fingers—a tiny, glowing ember the color of sunset. His memory, extracted and condensed to its essence.

"Beautiful," she whispered, lifting it to her lips. She inhaled, drawing the ember into herself. The living side of her face flushed with color, eyes brightening momentarily. "Payment accepted, Flame-Bearer."

Asvarr touched his temple, feeling a cold void where the memory had been. He knew intellectually that he'd lost something precious, could sense the outline of its absence, but could no longer recall the specific moment itself. The thought brought an unexpected hollowness to his chest.

"The path will open at dawn," Kára said, seeming more substantial now, more present in the world. "Sleep if you can. Death's realm taxes even the strongest of the living."

She turned to leave, her form already fading at the edges.

"Wait," Asvarr called. "You still haven't explained why you're helping me. What do you gain if I reach the anchor first?"

Kára paused, looking back over her shoulder. For a moment, her decayed half seemed to flicker, revealing glimpses of the whole woman she might once have been.

"I have watched nine cycles of breaking and binding, Warden. Nine times the pattern has fractured, nine times it has been remade—each time growing more rigid, more confined." Her voice carried a weight of ages. "Perhaps this tenth cycle will bring change. Perhaps this time, the binding will liberate rather than constrain."

With that, she dissolved into the darkness, leaving Asvarr alone beneath the aurora-lit sky.

***

He recreated the verdant flames, smaller this time to conserve strength. As the emerald fire flickered between his fingers, voices whispered from the depths once more—fragmented warnings, cryptic prophecies, desperate pleas. Asvarr listened intently, trying to piece together meaning from their disjointed speech.

Five anchors, five sacrifices... the circle nears completion... beware the door behind the door... what's lost may be regained... what's bound may be unleashed...

One voice rose above the others, clearer and more distinct. Unlike the chaotic chorus, this one spoke directly to him, its tone familiar though he couldn't place it.

Asvarr Flame-Bearer, Warden of Four, the fifth binding approaches. What sleeps will wake. What was forgotten will be remembered. The Ashfather seeks to break the cycle through domination. You must break it through transformation.

He leaned closer to the flames. "Who are you?"

I am what remains. I am what endures. I have waited for you through nine cycles of breaking and binding.

A chill passed through him that had nothing to do with the frozen wasteland. "You're the fifth anchor."

I am its voice, a fragment sent to find you. The Ash-Priest's corruption spreads. Time grows short.

"Tell me how to defeat him," Asvarr demanded. "How do I bind you properly?"

Transformation supersedes binding. The old ways end with you, Flame-Bearer. The final sacrifice centers on what you choose to become, beyond what you surrender.

The flames surged suddenly, taking the shape of a female figure wreathed in emerald fire. Her features shifted constantly, indistinct, yet her eyes burned with golden light.

Listen carefully. When you stand before me in Helheim, you will face three paths. One offered by death, one offered by the Ashfather, one offered by memory. Reject all three.

"What should I choose instead?" Asvarr asked, frustration edging his voice.

Forge your own path. This distinguishes you from your predecessors. This explains why you bear four marks where others bore one.

The fiery figure began to fade, the verdant flames diminishing. *Dawn approaches. The Aurora Gate will open soon. We will speak again when you stand before me in the death realm.*

"Wait—"

But the flames collapsed inward, leaving only normal fire in his palm, the voices silenced. Asvarr stared at his hand, wondering if exhaustion had spawned a hallucination, or if he had truly communed with a fragment of the fifth anchor.

He looked eastward, toward the twin peaks Kára had indicated. The aurora between them pulsed more intensely now, colors shifting from green to blue to purple and back again. Dawn approached, the perpetual twilight of these northern reaches growing marginally brighter.

The soul-forge key grew hot against his chest, responding to the changing energies. Asvarr gathered his meager supplies, checking that all four tokens were secure. His wounds from the battle at the Bleeding Hollow had barely begun to heal, and weariness clung to him like a second skin. Yet there was no time for rest, not with the Ash-Priest so close to the final anchor.

As the first true light of dawn touched the horizon, Asvarr saw the aurora between the twin peaks intensify and solidify, forming what appeared to be a shimmering doorway of living light. The Aurora Gate opening, just as Kára had promised.

He took a deep breath of the biting cold air, steeling himself for what lay ahead. Five anchors to bind the pattern anew—four secured, one remaining. Whatever transformation awaited him in Helheim, he would face it. Whatever sacrifice the fifth anchor demanded, he would pay it.

The path to the Aurora Gate lay before him, a bridge between worlds. Asvarr began walking, the verdant flame extinguished but its voices still echoing in his mind.

The final sacrifice centers on what you choose to become, beyond what you surrender.

The Aurora Gate shimmered with every color imaginable as Asvarr stepped through. His skin prickled, nerves alight with the sensation of passing through a living curtain of energy. One moment he stood on frozen ground beneath an arctic sky; the next he plunged into a realm where reality bent like heated metal.

The borderlands stretched before him—a twilight plain where light came from everywhere and nowhere. Stunted trees dotted the landscape, their branches twisted into impossible geometries. The ground beneath his feet felt solid yet yielding, as if he walked upon thinly-frozen water. Above, the sky pulsed with veins of gold and silver that reminded him of the Root.

Asvarr drew a deep breath and immediately regretted it. The air here tasted of metal and ash, with an underlying sweetness that reminded him of rotting fruit. He spat, trying to clear the taste from his mouth.

"I wouldn't breathe too deeply if I were you," a voice called from behind him. "The air of the borderlands carries memories. Some less pleasant than others."

Asvarr spun, his hand instinctively going to his bronze sword. Several paces away stood a figure in a tattered cloak of raven feathers. Its face remained hidden beneath a hood, but Asvarr glimpsed pale hands with too many joints.

"Who are you?" he demanded, wincing at how his voice sounded flat and dull in this place, as if the air swallowed sound.

"A fellow traveler. You may call me Grímur." The figure bowed slightly. "I watch the paths between worlds for those who might pass." It cocked its head, studying Asvarr with unseen eyes. "You carry the mark of the Warden. And something else... the soul-forge key. Interesting combinations."

Asvarr kept his distance, noting the way the ground rippled subtly where the stranger stood, as if struggling to support its weight. "I seek the Door of Souls."

"Many do. Few find it." Grímur gestured with one multi-jointed hand toward a path that wound between several of the twisted trees. "Yet you already walk the right road. Hel-seer Kára has guided you well."

Asvarr's fingers tightened around his sword hilt. "You know Kára?"

"I know all who dwell in the margins." Grímur's voice held a smile though his face remained hidden. "She takes joy; I take purpose. We each collect what sustains us."

A cold dread settled in Asvarr's stomach. "And what purpose would you take from me?"

Grímur laughed, the sound like dry leaves rustling. "None today, Warden. Your purpose burns too bright, too necessary." The figure extended one hand toward the path. "I merely offer guidance. The borderlands shift constantly. What seems a straight path may lead you in circles if you lack proper knowledge."

Asvarr weighed his options. The four tokens pressed warmly against his chest, while the Grímmark pulsed with warning. Yet time worked against him. Every moment spent in deliberation gave the Ash-Priest more opportunity to corrupt the fifth anchor.

"What do you want in exchange for this guidance?" he asked warily.

"A glimpse," Grímur replied. "Let me touch the seed token. I wish to see what the Root has become under your wardenship."

The request sent alarm racing through Asvarr's blood. The tokens remained his most precious possessions, especially the seed from the fourth binding. Yet he needed to reach Helheim quickly, and wandering lost through the borderlands would cost him dearly.

"A touch only," he stipulated, reaching into his tunic to withdraw the seed token. It pulsed in his palm, tiny rootlets extending and retracting in rhythmic motion. "No taking, no damage."

"Agreed." Grímur approached, moving with an unsettling gliding motion. One pale, too-many-jointed hand extended from beneath the ragged cloak.

Instinct screamed at Asvarr to pull back, to protect the token, but he held firm. Grímur's fingertip touched the seed token with surprising gentleness. The moment contact was made, a flare of verdant flame erupted between them, illuminating the space beneath Grímur's hood.

Asvarr glimpsed a face with no features save for a vertical slit where a mouth should be. Within that slit, countless tiny eyes blinked in unison.

Grímur withdrew sharply, the cloak smoldering where the verdant flame had touched it. "Fascinating," he hissed, sounding pained yet pleased. "The Root speaks through you now. It has never done that before, through all the cycles."

Asvarr hastily returned the seed token to its place against his chest. The brief contact had revealed something to him as well—a flash of knowledge, a glimpse behind the veil. Grímur was old, ancient even by the standards of the beings Asvarr had encountered. He had watched cycles upon cycles of breaking and binding, gathering stray purposes from those who wandered lost through the borderlands.

"You've guided others to the Door before," Asvarr said, pieces falling into place. "Other Wardens."

"I guide all who ask," Grímur replied, still rubbing his smoking hand. "Whether they reach their destination depends on what they carry within." He pointed again to the winding path. "Follow this road. Do not stray, no matter what you see or hear. The borderlands test those who pass through."

"And at the end?"

"The Door of Souls awaits, exactly as promised." Grímur bowed once more, lower this time. "May your step be sure, Warden of Four. The fifth binding approaches, and with it, change comes to worlds above and below."

Without another word, Grímur glided backward into the twilight haze, his tattered cloak melding with the shadows until he vanished completely.

Asvarr stood alone on the path, the borderlands stretching eerily around him. With no better option, he began walking, keeping his eyes fixed on the twisted road ahead. The soul-forge key warmed against his chest, responding to this place between life and death.

As he walked, the landscape gradually shifted. The stunted trees gave way to stone formations that resembled figures frozen in various poses of agony or ecstasy. The ground hardened beneath his feet, changing from the yielding almost-ice to cracked obsidian that reflected his image with disturbing distortions.

Voices whispered from the periphery of his vision—fragmentary sounds just beyond comprehension. Occasionally he caught his own name, or mentions of "Warden" and "binding," but nothing coherent enough to engage with. Following Grímur's warning, he kept his gaze forward, ignoring the pull of curiosity.

The path wound between two tall stone spires that leaned toward each other like hooded sentinels. As Asvarr passed between them, the air grew colder, the metallic taste intensifying. Ahead, the path descended into a valley filled with swirling mist.

He paused at the valley's edge, studying the fog below. Unlike natural mist, this moved with purpose, forming half-seen shapes that dissolved before becoming fully defined. The path continued directly through the thickest part.

"Keep to the road," he reminded himself, taking the first step downward.

The moment he entered the mist, the voices grew clearer, more distinct. They spoke with the cadence of flames, reminiscent of the verdant fire spirits, yet deeper and more resonant.

The fifth awaits... the circle nears completion... the Ash-Priest works his corrupt ion... hurry, Warden...

Asvarr quickened his pace, keeping his eyes fixed on the ground before him. The path remained visible despite the thickening fog—a ribbon of black glass cutting through the swirling white.

Your sacrifice approaches... what will you become?... the pattern shifts with your choice... many watchers now...

The mist brushed against his skin with physical presence, leaving behind a residue that tingled and burned. Each breath filled his lungs with the voices, making them resonate within his very flesh. The Grímmark flared in response, spreading warmth throughout his torso.

He stumbled suddenly as a figure materialized directly in his path—Gunnar Ironveil, the dwarf who had guided him to the Bleeding Hollow. His weathered face appeared gaunt, the shadow-ice poison having consumed most of his flesh, leaving him half-corpse.

"You abandoned me," Gunnar accused, his voice carrying the same resonance as the mist voices. "Left me to the unmaking while you sought glory."

Asvarr's step faltered. "You told me to go. The binding—"

"Always the binding," Gunnar snarled. "Always the next anchor. How many must die to feed your ambition, Warden?" The dwarf's form flickered, the shadow-ice visibly consuming more of his remaining flesh. "You'll sacrifice anything, anyone, to complete your quest."

The accusation struck deep, piercing a guilt Asvarr had buried beneath necessity. He had left Gunnar, just as he had left others before. The path of the Warden demanded sacrifice—both his own and others'.

"Gunnar is alive," Asvarr said firmly, though doubt crept through him. "This is a test, a borderland illusion."

The dwarf's laugh twisted into a cough that spattered black ichor onto the glass path. "Am I? The shadow-ice consumes. Perhaps I lived when you fled, but now? Who can say what remains of Gunnar Ironveil in the halls of his ancestors?"

Asvarr closed his eyes briefly, centering himself. Grímur had warned him—do not stray, no matter what you see or hear. When he opened his eyes again, he stepped forward, walking directly through the apparition of Gunnar.

Cold pierced him to the marrow, a soul-deep chill that made him gasp. For one terrible moment, he felt the shadow-ice spreading through his own veins, tasted its bitter corruption on his tongue. Then he passed through, and the sensation faded, leaving only the memory of that killing cold.

The mist grew thicker, and more figures appeared—faces from his past. Warriors who had fallen in battles he survived. Villagers from settlements razed during raids. His mother, face twisted in disappointment. All accused him, all demanded explanation, justification, atonement.

Asvarr pressed on, walking through each apparition, enduring the unique agony each passage inflicted. Some burned, some froze, some filled him with emotions so intense he nearly fell to his knees. Still he kept to the path, one foot before the other, focusing on the warmth of the tokens against his chest.

Gradually, the mist began to thin. The apparitions appeared less frequently, their accusations fading to whispers. The path inclined upward, leading out of the valley toward another pair of leaning stone sentinels.

As Asvarr approached them, a final figure materialized—himself, or rather, a version of himself from some potential future. This doppelgänger stood straighter, power radiating from him in palpable waves. Golden sap flowed through veins visible beneath his skin, and his eyes shone with the same light as the Root. Around his brow sat a crown of interwoven branches, burning with verdant flame.

Unlike the other apparitions, this one didn't speak. It simply watched Asvarr with those golden eyes, its expression neither approving nor condemning. As Asvarr drew level with it, the figure extended one hand, offering something small and glinting.

Despite his wariness, Asvarr found himself stopping. "What is this?"

His double remained silent, hand outstretched, the small object catching the twilight glow. Asvarr looked closer and saw a tiny seed, smaller than the token from the fourth binding, yet somehow more concentrated in its essence.

The knowledge struck him suddenly, intuitively—this was a fragment of his own purpose, condensed and offered back to him. Just as Kára had taken his joy and Grímur collected purposes, the borderlands themselves had extracted something from him during his passage. Now it returned a portion, changed by its passage through this realm.

Asvarr extended his hand, allowing the seed to drop into his palm. The moment it touched his skin, it dissolved, sinking beneath the surface like water into parched earth. Warmth spread up his arm, connecting with the Grímmark and filling a void he hadn't known existed—the hollow left by Kára's extraction of his brightest joy.

The sensation wasn't the return of that specific memory, but rather something new—purpose distilled to its purest form, unencumbered by doubt or fear.

His double nodded once, then dissolved into mist that swirled away on an unfelt breeze.

Asvarr passed between the stone sentinels and emerged onto a plateau overlooking a vast chasm. On the far side rose the Door of Souls—a massive obsidian spire that pierced the twilight sky. Unlike when viewed from Midgard, here in the borderlands it revealed its true form: a doorway large enough for giants to pass through, formed by the split in the spire's base.

Beyond the door lay only darkness, a void so complete it seemed to consume light itself. Helheim waited beyond that threshold.

Between Asvarr and the door stretched a narrow bridge of the same black glass as the path, arching over a chasm filled with swirling mist. As he watched, shapes moved within the fog—the half-formed souls of those neither living nor truly dead, trapped in the borderlands.

Voices rose from the chasm, a cacophony of pleas and threats, promises and warnings. The borderlands' final test, Asvarr realized—crossing while maintaining focus despite the distractions below.

He took a deep breath, centered his mind on the five tokens and the Grímmark, and stepped onto the bridge. The glass felt slick beneath his boots, threatening to send him plunging into the sea of souls below with any misstep.

Halfway across, movement caught his eye. On the far side, emerging from the Door of Souls, came a procession of figures in bone-white robes. At their head walked a tall, gaunt figure bearing a staff topped with a cage containing swirling darkness. The Ash-Priest, returning from Helheim.

Asvarr froze, instinctively dropping to a crouch to avoid detection. The glass bridge offered no cover, but the twilight haziness of the borderlands might conceal him if he remained still. From this distance, he couldn't tell if the Ash-Priest carried anything from the fifth anchor—any sign that he had succeeded in his corruption.

The procession moved with eerie coordination, following a path that skirted the chasm rather than crossing it. They headed toward another passage through the stone sentinels, one Asvarr hadn't noticed before. The Ash-Priest never glanced toward the bridge, his attention fixed on whatever lay inside the cage atop his staff.

Within minutes, the procession vanished into the mists of the borderlands, leaving Asvarr alone on the bridge once more. He rose slowly, uncertainty gnawing at him. Had he arrived too late? Had the Ash-Priest already completed his work at the fifth anchor?

The Grímmark pulsed suddenly, sending a surge of heat through his chest. The verdant flame manifested in his palm unbidden, forming a small figure that danced with urgency.

Hurry, Warden... the seed of corruption planted... but the Root resists... there remains time... the final binding awaits...

Relief flooded through Asvarr, followed immediately by renewed urgency. The Ash-Priest had begun his work but hadn't completed it. The fifth anchor still awaited true binding.

He continued across the bridge with renewed purpose, moving as quickly as he dared on the slick surface. When he finally reached the far side, he stood before the Door of Souls, staring into the absolute darkness beyond the threshold.

The soul-forge key burned against his chest, almost painfully hot. Asvarr withdrew it, holding the iron key before him. Its runes glowed with inner light, responding to the proximity of death's domain.

"Bridge the gap between living and dead," he murmured, remembering Gunnar's words.

He stepped forward and thrust the key into the darkness. For a moment, nothing happened. Then the void rippled, as if the key had pierced a membrane. The darkness parted like curtains drawn aside, revealing a path beyond—a road of pale bone leading downward into a twilight realm.

Helheim opened before him.

Asvarr stood at the threshold between worlds, the borderlands behind him, the realm of death ahead. The four tokens hummed against his chest, sensing the proximity of their fifth counterpart. The Grímmark spread warmth throughout his body, preparing him for whatever sacrifice the final binding would demand.

The words of the fifth anchor's fragment echoed in his mind: *The final sacrifice is not what you surrender, but what you choose to become.*

Whatever awaited him in Helheim—whether transformation or destruction—he would face it. He had come too far, sacrificed too much, to turn back now.

With the soul-forge key clutched in one hand and his bronze sword in the other, Asvarr stepped through the Door of Souls and onto the bone road leading to the heart of Helheim. The void closed behind him, sealing him within death's domain.

The hunt for the fifth anchor had reached its final stage.

CHAPTER 25

THE SKYREND HEIRLOOM

Helheim air filled Asvarr's lungs with the taste of aged iron and bitter herbs. The bone road beneath his feet thrummed with each step, sending vibrations up through his legs like whispered warnings. Mist clung to the ground in patches, swirling around his ankles as if trying to hold him in place.

Ten strides into death's realm, and already the weight of it pressed upon him. The sky—if it could be called such—hung low and colorless, a perpetual twilight state that cast no shadows. The landscape stretched before him, a vast plain of ashen soil where twisted trees grew with no leaves, their branches reaching skyward like the fingers of the drowned seeking air.

The Door of Souls had sealed behind him the moment he crossed the threshold, leaving only smooth obsidian where the entrance had been. The soul-forge key in his hand grew cold and inert, its purpose apparently fulfilled. Asvarr slid it into his belt pouch, its weight a reassurance against what lay ahead.

The Grímmark burned steadily beneath his tunic, its warmth spreading through his chest in pulsing waves that matched his heartbeat. The four tokens—horn, ivory disk, remembrance-key, and seed—resonated with increasing intensity as he followed the bone road deeper into Helheim. Through the bond of the mark, he sensed the fifth anchor pulling him forward, its energy distinct from the others—older, deeper, more aware.

A distant sound caught his attention—drums beating in perfect rhythm, the cadence matching the pulse of his Grímmark. The bone road curved around a stand of gnarled trees, and as Asvarr followed it, he came upon the first inhabitants of Helheim he had encountered.

They stood arranged in concentric circles around a central pit, swaying to the drumbeat. Pale, translucent figures with hollow eyes and gaping mouths, their forms wavering like reflections in disturbed water. The dead, numberless and silent save for the drums that beat from somewhere unseen.

Asvarr gripped his bronze sword, its runes flaring in response to the proximity of so many spirits. He had expected to fight his way through Helheim—to face guardians and obstacles as he had in his quest for the previous anchors. Instead, the dead simply watched him, parting to form a path through their ranks as he approached.

Their mute attention unnerved him more than any attack would have. He moved forward cautiously, keeping his sword ready. The bone road led directly through the gathering, toward the pit at its center. As he passed through the ranks of the dead, Asvarr felt their eyes upon him—with a terrible, hungry hope.

The pit opened before him, a perfect circle carved into the ashen ground. Inside burned a fire unlike any Asvarr had seen before—flames of deep violet and midnight blue that cast no heat yet illuminated the faces of the dead with stark clarity. At the fire's edge stood a woman with her back to him, her form more substantial than the spirits surrounding her.

"Welcome, Warden of Four," she said without turning. Her voice carried both age and youth simultaneously, resonating in Asvarr's bones rather than his ears. "The anchor has awaited you through nine cycles of breaking and binding."

Asvarr halted at the pit's edge, studying her. Unlike the transparent dead, she wore flesh—or the appearance of it. Her hair hung in a single white braid to her waist, adorned with bones and iron beads that clinked softly when she moved. Her clothes seemed crafted from raven feathers and strips of pale hide sewn together with silver thread.

"Who are you?" he asked, voice steady despite the dread that had settled in his stomach.

She turned then, revealing a face that shifted subtly between youth and age, beauty and decay, never settling on one form. Only her eyes remained constant—black as the void beyond the Door of Souls, with pinpricks of light deep within them like distant stars.

"I have been called many names across the cycles," she replied. "To the first breaking, I was Hel-Harrower. To the fifth, Death-Singer. The Ash-Priest named me Helstrom when he passed through." Her mouth curved in a smile that never reached her star-filled eyes. "You may call me Eir."

"You spoke with the Ash-Priest?" The Grímmark flared with heat at the mention of his enemy.

"He came seeking the anchor, as all do when the cycle nears completion." Eir gestured to the violet flames. "He planted his corruption in the fire-heart, yet the root resists. It remembers you from before, Flame-Bearer."

Confusion furrowed Asvarr's brow. "Before? I've never been to Helheim until now."

"Time flows differently in death's domain. The anchor exists in all moments simultaneously—past, present, and what-may-come." She studied him with those void-dark eyes. "Parts of you have stood before me in every cycle, wearing different flesh while carrying the same purpose."

The drums increased tempo, the dead swaying faster to their rhythm. Asvarr fought to make sense of Eir's words, to reconcile them with what he knew of the breaking and his role as Warden.

"I came to bind the fifth anchor," he said, focusing on his purpose. "To complete the pattern and stop the Ashfather."

Eir's expression sharpened. "And what will you give to bind death's anchor, Warden of Four? What sacrifice do you offer to become Warden of Five?"

Before Asvarr could answer, a cold wind swept across the gathering, carrying the scent of frost and iron. The dead stilled their swaying, hollow faces turning toward the northern edge of their circle. Eir's form flickered like a candle in a draft, her features momentarily revealing bone beneath the flesh.

"He comes," she hissed, all pretense of calm abandoned. "The Ash-Priest returns too soon. The corruption spreads faster than I foresaw."

Asvarr spun toward the disturbance. Beyond the outer ring of the dead, a procession approached along the bone road—figures in bone-white robes led by the towering form of the Ash-Priest. In his hand he carried the staff topped with a cage, within which swirled darkness shot through with streaks of golden light. Corruption and anchor essence intermingled.

"The flame-heart," Eir said urgently, grabbing Asvarr's arm with fingers that burned cold through his sleeve. "You must reach it before he completes his working."

She pointed to the violet flames in the pit. "The anchor awaits within. Find the blade grown from the Root itself, and use it to cut away his corruption."

"Blade?" Asvarr questioned, but already the drums had fallen silent, the dead parting to admit the Ash-Priest's procession.

The priest towered over his followers, his twisted form even more grotesque than when Asvarr had faced him in the Bleeding Hollow. The bark-like growths on his skin had spread, consuming most of his visible flesh. Branches erupted from his shoulders and back, forming a crown of thorns around his hollow-socketed face.

"Flame-Bearer," the Ash-Priest's voice grated like stone on metal. "You trespass in death's domain."

Asvarr stepped forward, positioning himself between the priest and the flame-pit. His bronze sword glowed with the combined essence of the four anchors he had already bound, the runes along its length shifting and reshaping themselves.

"I come to bind what belongs to the pattern," Asvarr replied, drawing strength from the Grímmark's heat. "Your corruption ends here."

The Ash-Priest's lipless mouth stretched in what might have been a smile. "Bold words from one who understands so little." He raised the cage-topped staff, the darkness within writhing with greater intensity. "The Ashfather sends his regards. He looks forward to welcoming you among the hollow ones when this is done."

With a gesture from the priest, his followers spread out to encircle the flame-pit, cutting off any retreat. They moved with unnatural coordination, their robes rustling like dead leaves in a graveyard.

Asvarr tensed, ready for the attack that surely came next. Instead, the Ash-Priest plunged his staff into the ashen ground, the cage splitting open upon impact. The corruption contained within—the swirling darkness threaded with stolen golden light—seeped into the earth like spilled oil.

The ground trembled. Fissures spread outward from the staff, glowing with the same corruption that had escaped the cage. The dead scattered, their transparent forms dissipating like mist before a strong wind. Only Eir remained, her shifting face locked in an expression of horror.

"The final binding approaches," the Ash-Priest intoned, his voice rising to fill the twilight air. "Nine cycles broken, nine cycles remade. The tenth shall break the wheel forever."

The fissures reached the edge of the flame-pit, and the violet fire flared in response, twisting away from the encroaching corruption. Asvarr felt the anchor's distress through his Grímmark—a silent scream that resonated through his very bones.

"Get to the flame-heart!" Eir shouted, her form beginning to unravel as the corruption spread. "Find the blade! It is the only way!"

The Ash-Priest turned his hollow gaze upon her. "Silence, guardian. Your watch ends with this cycle." He raised one massive, bark-covered hand, and Eir's form shredded like fabric torn by an unseen force. Her scream lingered in the air long after her physical presence had vanished.

Rage welled in Asvarr's chest, hot and sharp. The Grímmark blazed in response, golden light spilling from beneath his tunic to illuminate the ashen ground around him. The four tokens he carried burned against his skin, urging him toward the flame-pit, toward the anchor that called to him.

With a battle cry that carried all his defiance, Asvarr charged. The bronze sword in his hand sang with power as he cut through the first of the robed figures that moved to intercept him. The blade passed through the cultist as if they were made of smoke, yet they fell screaming, their essence dispersing into the twilight air.

The Ash-Priest's followers converged, their hands extending from beneath white robes to reveal flesh blackened and twisted by corruption. Asvarr fought with the skill born of countless battles and the power granted by four bound anchors. His sword flashed, each strike dissolving another opponent, yet for each one that fell, two more stepped forward.

"The pattern frays, Warden," the Ash-Priest called, still standing by his planted staff. "Even now the Ashfather gathers the threads. A new weaving begins."

Asvarr cut down three more cultists in a single sweeping arc, clearing a path to the flame-pit. The violet fire surged toward him as if in recognition, even as the corruption-filled fissures crept closer to the pit's edge.

Without hesitation, Asvarr leapt into the flames.

***

No heat seared him, no pain engulfed him. Instead, he felt a profound stillness settle over his awareness, as if he had stepped into the eye of a storm. The violet flames surrounded him, shifting to blue and then to emerald green—the same verdant flame he had conjured from the Root's essence.

Within the fire, reality peeled away. Asvarr found himself standing in a vast chamber with walls, floor, and ceiling formed of intertwining roots that pulsed with golden light. At the chamber's center rose a dais upon which rested a sword unlike any he had seen before.

Its blade appeared to have grown organically from the root material, curves and spirals flowing along its length like sap trails in living wood. The crossguard formed two branches that wrapped around to protect the wielder's hand, while the pommel held a perfect sphere of golden amber, within which swirled what looked like a galaxy of tiny stars.

Warden of Four, come to claim the fifth binding. The voice emanated from the sword itself, resonating within Asvarr's mind rather than his ears.

He approached the dais cautiously. "I seek to bind the anchor and complete the pattern."

The anchor chooses its Warden. The sword pulsed with inner light. *Nine cycles have come and gone. Nine Wardens have stood where you stand. None have passed the final test.*

"The Ash-Priest corrupts the anchor even now," Asvarr said, urgency driving him forward. "There's no time for tests."

Time exists differently here, at the heart of death's domain. The sword's light dimmed slightly. *The corruption cannot reach the anchor's core until you make your choice.*

"What choice? What test?" Frustration edged Asvarr's voice. Outside this chamber, beyond the verdant flame, the Ash-Priest worked his dark purpose. Every moment spent in conversation meant more corruption seeping toward the anchor.

The choice between memory and purpose. The test of what you're willing to become.

The sword rose from the dais, hovering in the air before Asvarr. The amber pommel glowed brighter, and within it, the galaxy of stars expanded, filling Asvarr's vision until he stood among them, surrounded by points of light stretching into infinity.

Each star contained a memory—his own and others', fragments of lives lived across nine cycles of breaking and binding. He saw previous Wardens, men and women who had bound four anchors only to falter at the fifth. He witnessed the Ashfather as he once was, a Warden like himself, before fear and ambition twisted him.

The blade grown from the Root itself demands a price, the voice continued, now seeming to come from everywhere around him. *Each memory it holds came at the cost of someone's identity. To wield it is to risk becoming like those before you—empty vessels filled only with the pattern's purpose.*

The stars swirled, converging into a single point of light that resolved into the image of the sword once more. It hovered before Asvarr, both invitation and warning.

What will you give, Warden of Four, to become Warden of Five? What memory feeds your purpose? What will you become when that memory is gone?

Asvarr stared at the weapon, understanding dawning. This was the Skyrend Heirloom—a blade passed from Warden to Warden, each adding their essence to its power, each risking erasure in the process. The fifth anchor demanded the greatest sacrifice because it was the lynchpin of the entire pattern.

The four tokens pressed against his chest, urging him to action. The Grímmark burned with purpose, the expanded pattern spanning his torso in lines of golden fire. Beyond this moment of stillness, beyond the chamber of roots and the verdant flame, the Ash-Priest's corruption spread ever closer to the anchor's heart.

Asvarr reached for the sword, hesitating just before his fingers touched the hilt. "If I give you my memory, what happens to me? To who I am?"

That depends on which memory you choose to surrender, the voice replied. *Choose a trivial recollection, and you remain essentially unchanged—yet the blade gains little power. Choose a memory central to your identity, and both you and the blade transform. Many before you chose power over self. The Ashfather chose power above all else.*

"And became an empty vessel for another's purpose," Asvarr murmured, understanding at last what truly awaited at the pattern's center.

His mind raced through his remaining memories—so many already sacrificed to previous bindings. What defined him now? What shaped his purpose? What could he surrender without becoming like the Ashfather—a shell filled with power alone?

A memory surfaced unbidden: his first raid as a young warrior, the moment he chose to embrace the berserker rage that had defined much of his life. He had stood over a fallen enemy, axe raised for the killing blow, and made a conscious choice to surrender to battle-fury to escape the moral complexity of taking a life with full awareness.

That choice had shaped decades of his existence. It had made him a feared warrior among his people, while distancing him from deeper human connections. It had given him strength in countless battles, even as it cost him the ability to fully engage with his own emotions outside of rage.

It was, perhaps, the most defining memory he still possessed.

"This one," Asvarr said, focusing on the recollection. "My first surrender to the berserker rage. The moment I chose fury over feeling."

The sword trembled in the air before him, the amber pommel glowing brighter. *A worthy sacrifice. It will transform both blade and bearer. Are you prepared for what you might become when rage can no longer shield you?*

Asvarr took a deep breath, steadying himself. "I am."

Then take up the Skyrend Heirloom, and complete the binding.

His fingers closed around the hilt.

Pain exploded through Asvarr's consciousness as the sword's essence connected with his own. The memory he had offered burned bright for one searing moment—every detail crystal clear, every emotion razor-sharp—before it began to fade, drawn into the amber pommel like water into parched earth.

***

As the memory drained from him, Asvarr felt something fundamental shift within his being. The wall that had separated his rage from his deeper emotions crumbled, allowing feelings long suppressed to flood through him. Grief for those lost along his journey. Fear of what awaited at the pattern's center. Hope that his choice might break the cycle that had claimed nine Wardens before him.

The sword changed as well, its blade straightening and sharpening, the root-like curves along its length becoming more pronounced, more intentional. The amber pommel swirled with new light, Asvarr's memory adding to the galaxy of stars within.

Binding accepted, the voice said, now emanating from the sword in his hand. *The fifth anchor acknowledges you, Warden of Five.*

The chamber of roots dissolved around him, reality rushing back with dizzying speed. Asvarr found himself standing in the flame-pit once more, the verdant fire swirling around him without burning. In his hand he held the Skyrend Heirloom, now bonded to him through the sacrifice of his defining memory.

Outside the flames, the Ash-Priest's corruption had nearly reached the pit's edge. The priest himself stood watching, his hollow eye sockets fixed on the fire that had changed from violet to green. His followers had formed a circle, chanting in that ancient language that bent reality itself.

"Too late, Warden," the Ash-Priest called, his voice carrying over the chanting. "The corruption has taken root. The anchor will serve the Ashfather now."

Asvarr raised the Skyrend Heirloom, its blade catching the emerald light of the flames. "We'll see about that."

With a single fluid motion, he brought the blade down on the nearest corruption-filled fissure. The sword cut through the darkness as if it were cloth, the severed corruption withering and fading wherever the blade touched. Golden light spilled from the cut, pure anchor essence freed from contamination.

The Ash-Priest roared in rage, the branches forming his crown bristling with sudden growth. "Stop him!" he commanded, and his followers surged forward, heedless of the verdant flame.

Asvarr stepped out of the pit, the fire parting around him like a cloak being drawn aside. The Skyrend Heirloom hummed in his hand, eager for the battle to come. With the berserker rage gone from his fighting style, Asvarr moved with a new clarity—each strike precise, each defense calculated.

The blade cut through the Ash-Priest's followers with impossible sharpness, severing their physical forms along with the very corruption that animated them. They fell in silence, their white robes collapsing empty to the ashen ground as if they had never contained bodies.

The Ash-Priest raised his staff, darkness gathering at its tip. "The Ashfather will not be denied his due, Flame-Bearer. Nine cycles have ended in his victory. The tenth shall be no different."

Asvarr advanced steadily, cutting through corruption-filled fissures with each step. The freed golden essence flowed back to the flame-pit, strengthening the verdant fire. Through the Grímmark and the five tokens, he felt the anchor responding to his actions, gathering power for the binding to come.

"This cycle ends differently," Asvarr said, raising the Skyrend Heirloom. "The pattern transforms and evolves."

The blade in his hand blazed with emerald light, illuminating the twisted features of the Ash-Priest. In that moment, Asvarr saw past the corruption, past the bark-like growth and hollow eyes, to the man the priest had once been—another Warden, another bearer of the mark, who had chosen differently when standing where Asvarr now stood.

For the first time since beginning his journey as Warden, Asvarr faced his enemy without rage clouding his perception. What he saw filled him with equal parts pity and resolve.

The final confrontation had begun.

The Skyrend Heirloom sang in Asvarr's grip as he advanced on the Ash-Priest. Each step pressed his boot prints into the ashen soil of Helheim, ground that shifted and settled beneath him like disturbed grave dirt. The blade glowed with verdant flame, casting his shadow long and sharp across the battlefield.

"You hold a weapon you cannot comprehend," the Ash-Priest said, his voice like grinding stone. "It devoured those before you. It will devour you as well."

Asvarr said nothing, focusing on the spread of corruption through the fissures in the ground. The blade had a weight beyond the physical, each swing requiring concentration where mindless fury had carried him through countless battles before. The loss of his berserker memory had transformed him—a cold clarity now flowed through his veins in place of battle-rage.

The Ash-Priest raised his staff, darkness boiling around its jagged tip. "The Ashfather awaits our return. When I bring him your hollowed corpse, he will wear your skin as he has worn others before."

A blast of corrupted power erupted from the staff, a torrent of darkness shot through with stolen golden light. Asvarr raised the Skyrend Heirloom instinctively. The blade caught the corruption, splitting it like water breaking against stone. The darkness parted around him, leaving him untouched at the center of destruction.

"Impossible," the Ash-Priest hissed, hollow eye sockets widening. The branches forming his crown bristled with sudden new growth, sharp tips elongating toward Asvarr like spears.

Asvarr recognized the opening and lunged forward, bringing the Heirloom down in a precise arc that severed three of the branch-spears before they could reach him. The wood parted cleanly, the cut surfaces instantly blackening as if burned. The Ash-Priest shrieked, a sound like wind through dead trees, and stumbled backward.

For the first time, Asvarr saw fear in the priest's posture—the hunching of shoulders, the defensive raising of arms. He pressed his advantage, cutting through more corruption-filled fissures as he advanced. Each cut released golden light that flowed back toward the flame-pit, strengthening the anchor against the Ashfather's influence.

"The others failed," the Ash-Priest growled, recovering his composure. "Nine Wardens before you. Nine cycles ended the same. What makes you different?"

Asvarr felt the amber pommel of the Heirloom pulse against his palm, the galaxy of memories within it shimmering with ancient knowledge. "They fought alone. They surrendered to the blade's hunger." He cut through another fissure, freeing more golden essence. "I carry fragments of them all now."

The dead began to return, materializing around the flame-pit as pale, translucent figures. They formed concentric rings once more, watching silently as Warden and priest circled each other in their center. The drums resumed their beating, matching the rhythm of Asvarr's heart and the pulse of the Grímmark beneath his tunic.

The Ash-Priest gestured with his gnarled hand, and four of his remaining followers broke from their circle, rushing Asvarr from different directions. They moved with unnatural coordination, white robes billowing as they closed in.

Asvarr parried the first cultist's attack, driving the Heirloom through his chest. The blade emerged clean on the other side, the robes collapsing empty to the ground. He pivoted smoothly to face the others, the sword guiding his movements as much as he guided it.

Two more cultists fell in quick succession, their corporeal forms unraveling at the Heirloom's touch. The fourth halted, watching his companions dissolve. Fear broke through his devotion, and he turned to flee. Asvarr let him go. There had been enough death in this realm already.

"You show mercy," the Ash-Priest observed. "A weakness your predecessors lacked."

"You confuse clarity with weakness." Asvarr cut through another fissure, watching golden light spiral back to the flame-pit. Only two major corruption channels remained, both running directly beneath the Ash-Priest's feet. "Surrender now. The anchor rejects your corruption."

The priest's lipless mouth stretched in a rictus grin. "The anchor has no choice. The pattern frays. The wheel breaks." He drove his staff deeper into the ashen ground, and the corruption surged with renewed vigor. "You cannot stop what has already begun."

The dead watching from their circles began to change, their transparent forms darkening as corruption seeped into them. Their hollow eyes filled with swirling shadow as they turned toward Asvarr, arms extending with grasping fingers.

The drums faltered, their steady rhythm breaking into irregular, discordant beats. The dead moved forward, closing their circles around Asvarr and the Ash-Priest, cutting off any retreat to the flame-pit.

"The tenth cycle nears completion," the Ash-Priest intoned. "The Ashfather comes."

A cold wind swept through the gathering, carrying the scent of burning worlds and ancient ice. The twilight sky above darkened further, colors leaching away until only void remained. At the northern edge of the gathering, a tear appeared in reality itself—a vertical split that widened to reveal a figure wreathed in shadow and flame.

The Ashfather stepped through.

He stood taller than the Ash-Priest, his form both substantial and ephemeral. A crown of broken branches encircled his head, and where his face should have been, only a single eye burned with golden fire. His cloak seemed woven from shadow itself, moving and shifting around him with a life of its own.

The dead fell prostrate before him, and even the Ash-Priest lowered himself to one knee, head bowed in submission. Only Asvarr remained standing, the Skyrend Heirloom blazing with defiant light in his hand.

"Warden of Five," the Ashfather's voice resonated within Asvarr's skull rather than through his ears, each word a physical pressure against his thoughts. "You have come far to fail now."

Asvarr felt the weight of the Ashfather's presence pressing down upon him, a crushing force that threatened to drive him to his knees. The Grímmark burned in response, spreading warmth through his body to counter the chill emanating from the one-eyed figure.

"I haven't failed yet," Asvarr replied, his voice steady despite the pressure. "The anchor resists your corruption. The fifth binding holds."

The Ashfather moved forward, each step leaving frost crystals in the ashen soil. "I once stood where you stand, bearer of five marks, holder of the blade." His single eye fixed on the Skyrend Heirloom. "I know what it takes from you with each binding. I know the hollow shell that remains when the fifth is complete."

Asvarr retreated a step, maintaining distance between them. "You chose power over self. You surrendered to the blade's hunger instead of mastering it."

"There exists only surrender. The pattern demands it." The Ashfather extended one shadow-wreathed hand. "Give me the blade, and I will show you mercy. Resist, and your essence joins the galaxy of forgotten Wardens within its pommel."

The amber pommel of the Heirloom pulsed against Asvarr's palm, the memories within it swirling with increased urgency. Among them, he felt his own sacrificed memory—the moment he had first embraced berserker rage—shining with a distinctive light. The Heirloom had taken it, yet something of it remained connected to him, a thread of identity that couldn't be completely severed.

Understanding dawned. The blade transformed memories, storing their essence while maintaining connection to their owners. The previous Wardens lived on; they had been preserved. Their failures came from surrendering themselves to its power, allowing it to consume them completely.

"The blade preserves," Asvarr said, raising the Heirloom before him. "It remembers everything you chose to forget."

The Ashfather's single eye narrowed. "Foolish child. The blade preserves only echoes of what is gone." His form seemed to grow larger, shadow and flame extending outward. "As you soon will be."

He lunged forward with impossible speed, shadow-wrapped fingers reaching for Asvarr's throat. Asvarr brought the Heirloom up in a defensive arc that caught the Ashfather's arm, cutting through shadow to strike something solid beneath. Golden light spilled from the wound—pure anchor essence, stolen and corrupted over nine cycles of breaking and binding.

The Ashfather recoiled, his shadow cloak swirling violently. "You dare strike me with my own blade?"

"It belongs to all Wardens, past and present," Asvarr countered. "It was never yours alone."

He advanced, driving the Ashfather back toward the tear in reality. The dead stirred from their prostration, confusion evident in their hollow faces as they watched their master retreat.

The Ash-Priest rose, staff raised to intervene. "Master, let me—"

"Silence," the Ashfather commanded, and the priest froze in place, bark-covered body suddenly rigid. "This confrontation belongs to Wardens now."

Asvarr pressed his advantage, using the Heirloom to sever the two remaining corruption channels in the ground. Golden light erupted from the cuts, flowing back to the flame-pit in streams that formed a protective circle around it. The verdant fire within the pit surged higher, forming a pillar that reached toward the void-dark sky.

"You cannot bind what serves me already," the Ashfather said, retreating another step toward the tear. "The anchor has served me through nine cycles. It will serve me again."

"The anchor chooses its Warden," Asvarr replied, the blade's knowledge flowing through him. "It chose me, as it once chose you before you turned from its purpose."

The Ashfather's shadow cloak lashed out like tentacles, striking at Asvarr from multiple angles. The Heirloom moved with fluid grace, cutting through shadow wherever it touched. Each severed piece dissolved into motes of golden light that joined the streams flowing back to the anchor.

"You steal my rightful power," the Ashfather hissed, his form diminishing as more shadow was cut away. "Centuries of gathered strength, essence drawn from nine breakings."

Asvarr advanced steadily, the Heirloom guiding his movements. "You corrupted what you stole. The anchors serve no single master." He cut through another shadow tendril. "They exist to maintain balance between chaos and order, upholding the pattern."

The Ashfather's single eye blazed brighter. "The blade taught you this?" A harsh laugh escaped him. "It lies. It always lies, filling Wardens' heads with illusions of purpose while consuming their essence."

"The blade preserves," Asvarr insisted. "It holds the truth of nine cycles—the pattern broken and remade, growing more rigid and confined each time." He raised the Heirloom to the level of the Ashfather's burning eye. "Show him."

The amber pommel flared with sudden brilliance, the galaxy of memories within it expanding outward to envelop both Warden and Ashfather in a sphere of light. For a brief moment, Asvarr glimpsed the truth through the Ashfather's eye—the first breaking, the original Warden, the pattern as it was meant to be. A dynamic balance, ever-changing yet fundamentally stable, neither completely ordered nor utterly chaotic.

The vision collapsed as the Ashfather tore himself away, retreating fully to the edge of the tear in reality. His form had diminished further, the crown of broken branches askew, the shadow cloak tattered and trailing golden light from a dozen wounds.

"This is not over, Warden of Five." His voice had lost some of its resonance, now sounding almost human. "The pattern cannot return to its original state. Too much has changed. Too much has been lost."

"Then we create something new," Asvarr replied. "Something transcending the cycles of breaking and binding."

The Ashfather's eye dimmed slightly. "You remain ignorant still." He gestured to the tear behind him. "Beyond the pattern exists only void. Beyond the cycles waits only unmaking. No 'new' can be forged, only variations on what has always been."

He stepped backward into the tear. "Complete your binding, Warden. Take up your place in the cycle. We will meet again when the wheel turns once more."

The tear sealed behind him, reality knitting itself back together. The dead remained still, their hollow eyes fixed on Asvarr as he stood alone at the center of their circles.

The Ash-Priest stirred, bark armor cracking as he moved. "He abandons me," he murmured, voice heavy with disbelief. "After all I have sacrificed."

Asvarr turned toward him, the Heirloom still glowing with verdant light. "Your master fears the truth the blade reveals. He gathers strength in the spaces between worlds, preparing for the next breaking."

The priest raised his staff, the tip glowing weakly with the last of its corrupted power. "Then I shall prepare the way for his return." He brought the staff down hard against the ashen ground, intending to create more corruption fissures.

Nothing happened.

The Ash-Priest stared at his staff in confusion, then understanding dawned in his hollow eye sockets. "The anchor rejects me." He looked up at Asvarr. "Kill me then, Warden. Complete your victory."

Asvarr studied him, seeing the Warden he had once been beneath the corruption—a man who had stood before the fifth anchor, made his choice, and lived with the consequences. Without berserker rage clouding his judgment, Asvarr felt compassion stirring within him.

"I refuse to kill you," he said, lowering the Heirloom. "The blade has witnessed enough death."

The priest's twisted features contorted in rage. "You mock me with mercy? Finish what you started, or I will rise again to serve my master."

"Your master abandoned you," Asvarr replied. "The corruption fades. You face a choice now—remain the Ash-Priest, or remember your former self."

The Heirloom pulsed in Asvarr's hand, the amber pommel glowing softly. Within it, one particular memory shone brighter than the others, something far older than Asvarr's surrendered rage. The original moment when the Ash-Priest had stood before the fifth anchor and made his choice, sacrificing his humanity for power.

"A possibility exists," Asvarr said slowly, raising the blade. "The Heirloom preserves what was surrendered. Perhaps it can restore as well."

The Ash-Priest stared at the glowing amber pommel, recognition flickering in his hollow gaze. "You would return what was taken? After all I have done?"

"The cycle must end somewhere," Asvarr said. "Why not here? Why not now?"

He touched the flat of the blade to the Ash-Priest's bark-covered chest. The amber pommel flared, and a single spark of golden light leapt from it to sink into the priest's twisted form. The bark cracked, light spilling from the fissures as the corruption began to dissolve.

The priest fell to his knees, branches breaking away from his crown, hollow eye sockets filling with something almost human. "I remember," he whispered, voice losing its stone-on-metal quality. "Before the corruption. Before the binding." He looked up at Asvarr with eyes that now held both fear and wonder. "What have you done to me?"

"Given back what was taken," Asvarr answered. "The rest becomes your choice."

The dead stirred around them, their transparent forms growing clearer, more defined. The corruption that had seeped into them faded, leaving them as they had been—witnesses to the cycles of breaking and binding, waiting for release.

Asvarr walked past the kneeling form of the former Ash-Priest, toward the flame-pit at the center of the gathering. The verdant fire still burned brightly, forming a column that reached skyward. Within it, he could sense the fifth anchor, fully awakened now, free of corruption.

The binding called to him, demanding completion. He had sacrificed his berserker rage to claim the Skyrend Heirloom, but the fifth anchor required its own price. What remained for him to give? What final piece of himself would complete the pattern?

The Heirloom hummed in his hand, the galaxy of memories in its pommel swirling with ancient knowledge. Through it, Asvarr understood what the fifth anchor truly required—a sacrifice beyond memory, beyond identity. It wanted choice itself, the surrendering of individual will to the pattern's purpose.

Yet the blade had shown him another possibility. Previous Wardens failed because they surrendered completely, subjugating themselves to the pattern. The anchors desired connection, a harmonious interweaving of their essence with their chosen Warden.

Asvarr stepped into the verdant flame, feeling its cool embrace surround him. The fifth anchor pulsed at the fire's heart, waiting for his decision. He could complete the binding through traditional sacrifice, giving up his will to the pattern, or forge a new connection, creating partnership where masters and servants had existed before.

The Skyrend Heirloom blazed in his hand, illuminating the choice before him. In its light, Asvarr made his decision—one that would change the pattern forever.

CHAPTER 26

THE FALSE GOD'S SHADOW

Golden light pulsed through the chamber of roots, casting Asvarr's shadow in multiples against the curved walls. Each heartbeat brought a new revelation as the fifth binding settled into his flesh, his blood, his bone. The Skyrend Heirloom still hummed in his grip, though its song had changed from the sharp clarity of battle to the deeper resonance of completion.

He had made his choice within the verdant flame, rejecting both surrender and dominance. The fifth anchor had accepted his offering—partnership rather than subjugation, a mutual binding that preserved both anchor and Warden. The transformation had cascaded through him like molten metal being poured into a new mold, breaking and remaking him in ways he had only begun to understand.

The chamber walls pulsed with his heartbeat, the intertwining roots shifting and growing with each breath he took. The chamber existed now as an extension of himself, a physical manifestation of his connection to the five anchors.

"It is done," said a voice from behind him.

Asvarr turned, the movement sending ripples through the golden light. A figure stood at the chamber's entrance—a man in a gray cloak, his face half-hidden beneath a deep hood. His remaining eye gleamed with reflected light, the empty socket where the other should have been covered by a patch of tooled leather.

"Ashfather," Asvarr acknowledged, raising the Heirloom. After their battle in the flame-pit, he had expected the ancient enemy to retreat for longer before confronting him again.

The cloaked figure laughed, a sound oddly warm and human. "Half-right, Warden. I am what remains after the shadow was cut away." He pushed back his hood, revealing a weathered face lined with age yet vibrant with life. Silver-streaked dark hair fell to his shoulders, and a neatly trimmed beard framed his mouth. "I am Gautr, as I was before the corruption."

Asvarr kept the Heirloom ready. The former Ash-Priest had shown similar signs of recovery, yet that transformation had been tentative, fragile. "How did you find this chamber?"

"I built it, long ago." Gautr spread his hands, palms open to show he carried no weapons. "Before the first breaking, when the pattern still sang with its original harmony."

A tremor ran through the chamber, the roots creaking with sudden tension. The Heirloom vibrated in Asvarr's hand, the galaxy of memories within its pommel swirling with agitation.

"The blade remembers me," Gautr said, his single eye fixed on the sword. "It remembers my betrayal, my corruption, my fall."

"Why come here now?" Asvarr asked, his voice steady despite the unease crawling up his spine. The Grímmark burned beneath his tunic, five patterns intertwined where once there had been only one.

"To witness what I could never achieve." Gautr moved deeper into the chamber, running his fingers along the root walls. Where he touched, golden light flickered and dimmed. "Nine cycles I tried to recreate the original harmony. Nine times I gathered the anchors, only to lose myself in the binding."

Asvarr circled, keeping distance between them. The chamber responded to his movements, roots shifting to maintain his path. "You corrupted the pattern. You became its destroyer."

"Fear corrupted me," Gautr corrected, turning to face him fully. "Fear of what lies beyond the pattern, in the void from which all things emerged. I glimpsed it during the first breaking, when the Norns cut the thread of fate." His single eye clouded with memory. "Such hunger in that darkness, such ancient malice."

The roots trembled, sending cascades of golden dust into the air. Asvarr felt the anchors respond, their energy flowing through his Grímmark in waves of heat and cold, growth and decay, creation and unmaking.

"The bindings are complete," he said, watching Gautr closely. "The fifth anchor accepted me. The pattern will hold."

"For how long?" Gautr asked softly. "A hundred years? A thousand? The void hungers always, Warden. The pattern weakens with each cycle." He touched the wall again, and this time the roots withered beneath his fingers, blackening as if burned by frost. "I bought time by corrupting the pattern, forcing it into rigidity where once it flowed. Ugly, yes. Destructive, certainly. Yet necessary."

Anger flared within Asvarr, different from the berserker rage he had sacrificed. This was colder, sharper, born of understanding rather than blind fury. "You corrupted the anchors. You consumed previous Wardens. You turned the pattern into a prison when it should have flourished as a garden."

"I did what was needed." Gautr's voice hardened. "When you have watched worlds die, when you have seen reality itself torn apart by what lurks beyond, then judge me." He gestured to the chamber around them. "This renewal you've achieved—this fifth binding that preserves both anchor and Warden—how long do you think it will last?"

Before Asvarr could answer, a tremor shook the chamber, stronger than before. Cracks appeared in the root ceiling, spilling dust and fragments to the floor. The light dimmed, flickering like a flame in wind.

"It begins already," Gautr said, a hint of satisfaction in his tone. "The pattern you've forged lacks strength. Its flexibility makes it vulnerable. It cannot withstand the pressure from beyond."

Asvarr braced himself against the shaking, one hand pressed to the chamber wall. The roots responded to his touch, warmth flowing into his palm. Through the Grímmark, he sensed the five anchors straining against something vast and cold that pressed against the fabric of reality.

"This chamber exists at the center of the five anchors," Gautr continued, apparently unaffected by the tremors. "From here, you can feel the true state of the pattern. Can you feel it straining? Tearing? The void presses ever closer, drawn by the light of your binding."

Asvarr focused, extending his awareness through the Grímmark. The five anchors pulsed in rhythm with his heart, each one a point of light in the fabric of reality. Between them stretched the pattern, a web of connection and possibility. And beyond that...

Darkness. Vast, ancient, hungry. Pressing against the pattern like water against a cracking dam.

He recoiled, stomach churning. "What is that?"

"The truth I tried to shield you from." Gautr sighed, his shoulders sagging beneath his gray cloak. "The real enemy, Warden. The void-hunger that consumed worlds before Yggdrasil, that will consume all worlds after."

Another tremor rocked the chamber. A large section of the ceiling tore loose, revealing a glimpse of sky—or what should have been sky. Instead, darkness roiled above, shot through with veins of sickly purple light.

"Your binding freed the pattern from my control," Gautr said, watching the hole widen. "It restored the original flow, the dynamic balance the Tree was meant to embody. But that very freedom creates vulnerability. The void-hunger can now reach through where before my corruption held it at bay."

Asvarr raised the Heirloom, its light steadying as he gripped it with renewed determination. "I refuse to corrupt the pattern as you did. Another path must exist."

"It does exist," Gautr agreed, stepping closer. "The Ashfather—the being I became—sought to rule the pattern through force. Yet another approach awaits." He touched his empty eye socket. "I sacrificed much to glimpse it, during moments when my true self surfaced through the corruption."

The chamber shuddered again. More roots tore loose, revealing larger sections of the darkness beyond. The golden light dimmed further, retreating to pool around Asvarr's feet.

"What approach?" Asvarr demanded, struggling to maintain his footing as the chamber floor buckled.

"The path of integration," Gautr replied. "The anchors must be united, beyond mere binding. The pattern must return to wholeness, as it existed in the beginning, before the first breaking."

"How do I achieve that?"

Gautr smiled, a sad expression that didn't reach his eye. "You've already begun. Your binding preserved both anchor and Warden, creating partnership where only master and servant existed before. Now you must extend that partnership to include all five anchors simultaneously."

Asvarr looked down at the Heirloom in his hand. The amber pommel swirled with memories, generations of knowledge gathered through nine cycles of breaking and binding. Within it, he sensed the truth of Gautr's words—the anchors sought unity, had always sought it, though previous Wardens had forced them into separation and subjugation.

"The chamber is collapsing," Gautr said, his voice urgent now. "The void-hunger draws nearer. You must act quickly, Warden, or all will be lost."

Another section of the ceiling tore away, and something reached through—a tendril of darkness that moved with horrible purpose. Where it touched the chamber walls, the roots blackened and crumbled to ash.

Asvarr stepped back, raising the Heirloom. The blade's light cut through the darkness, forcing the tendril to recoil. "Tell me what to do. How do I unite the anchors?"

Gautr moved toward the chamber's center, where the golden light shone brightest. "The Skyrend Heirloom holds the key. It was forged from the essence of the original pattern, before the breaking. Place it here, at the heart of the chamber, and channel the power of all five anchors through it."

Asvarr hesitated, suspicion flaring. "Why should I trust you? Hours ago you tried to kill me as the Ashfather."

"Hours ago corruption still gripped me," Gautr replied, his expression open and earnest. "When you defeated me at the flame-pit, when you showed mercy to my priest, you freed something within me. A fragment of my original self, preserved through nine cycles of darkness."

Another tendril pushed through, then another. The darkness above the chamber seethed with movement, with hunger. The chamber floor cracked, golden light spilling through the fissures like blood from a wound.

"Doubt has no place now," Gautr urged. "The void-hunger senses the weakened pattern. It will devour everything if you don't act now."

Asvarr stepped forward, the Heirloom raised before him. The weight of nine previous failures pressed upon him—nine Wardens who had tried and fallen, nine cycles ending in corruption and rigidity. Could he succeed where all others had failed?

The Grímmark burned on his chest, five patterns intertwined into something new. Through it, he sensed the five anchors reaching for him, for each other, straining toward unity. The Heirloom resonated with their call, the memories within its pommel swirling faster.

"Place the blade at the center," Gautr instructed, stepping back to give him space. "Drive it into the heart of the chamber, and channel your will through it. Unite what was sundered. Heal what was broken."

Asvarr raised the Heirloom, its light blazing against the encroaching darkness. The blade felt right in his hand, an extension of his will rather than a separate entity. With it, he had bound the fifth anchor in partnership rather than domination. With it, he might indeed unite all five into a new whole.

Yet something held him back—a whisper of caution from the Grímmark, a resonance from the anchors themselves. He studied Gautr, seeing the eagerness behind his calm facade, the tension in his shoulders beneath the gray cloak.

"The Heirloom preserves memories," Asvarr said slowly. "It showed me the truth of the first breaking, the original pattern. It showed me your identity before you became the Ashfather."

Gautr nodded, encouragement in his single eye. "Yes, Warden. It holds the truth of all cycles."

"Then why does it warn me against you now?" Asvarr asked quietly.

The eager light in Gautr's eye dimmed, replaced by wariness. "The blade's confusion stems from containing too many memories, too many versions of the truth. Trust what you've seen with your own eyes. Trust what you feel through the Grímmark."

More tendrils pushed through the ceiling. The darkness grew thicker, more substantial, forming shapes that writhed with malevolent purpose. The chamber's light waned further, retreating to a small circle around Asvarr's feet.

Gautr's urgency increased. "Do it now, Warden! Drive the blade into the center before all is lost!"

Asvarr stepped toward the chamber's heart, where golden light still pooled. The Heirloom hummed in his grip, its song shifting between harmonies as if uncertain. The five anchors pulsed through the Grímmark, their energy flowing into him, through him, waiting for direction.

He raised the blade overhead, preparing to drive it into the golden pool.

The Heirloom's song changed abruptly, discordant notes jarring through its melody. The amber pommel flared, and within it, one memory shone brighter than all others—a memory from the first breaking, when Gautr stood where Asvarr now stood, the Heirloom raised above a similar pool of light.

In that memory, Gautr drove the blade down, into the chest of a woman with starlight in her eyes and the mark of the first Warden upon her brow. As she fell, Gautr tore the power from her, absorbing it into himself along with the essence of the blade. The corruption began in that moment, with that betrayal.

Asvarr froze, the Heirloom still raised. "You lied," he said, voice cold with certainty. "You were never the first Warden. You murdered her and stole her power."

Gautr's face hardened, the pretense of earnestness falling away. "The identity of the first Warden means nothing. I saved the pattern when she would have allowed chaos to claim it. I maintained order across nine cycles while the void-hunger pressed ever closer."

"You corrupted everything the pattern was meant to be," Asvarr countered, lowering the Heirloom to point at Gautr's chest. "You turned the anchors into tools of control instead of sources of balance."

"I did what was necessary," Gautr snarled, his hand going to his belt. From beneath his cloak, he drew a curved dagger of black iron, its surface etched with runes that drank the chamber's light. "As I will do now."

He lunged forward, blade aimed at Asvarr's heart. Without the berserker rage that had once guided his reflexes, Asvarr moved with calculated precision, parrying the strike with the Heirloom. The two blades met with a sound like thunder, sending shockwaves through the chamber.

"You need me," Gautr hissed, pressing his attack. "Only I know how to face the void-hunger. Only I have stood against it and survived."

"You merely delayed it," Asvarr replied, countering another strike. "Your corruption weakened the pattern with each cycle. The void calls for balance, harmony, and connection—the opposite of your rigid control."

Gautr laughed, a harsh sound far from his earlier warmth. "What foolish idealism, Warden. Balance? Harmony? Such weakness will see all worlds consumed by the hunger."

The darkness above the chamber thickened, tendrils pushing through in greater numbers. They writhed toward the combatants, drawn by the conflict, by the power of the anchors flowing through Asvarr's Grímmark.

"The true path," Asvarr said, deflecting another attack, "requires dynamic balance between order and chaos, structure and freedom. The pattern flourished before your corruption twisted it with fear."

Gautr's eye narrowed. "Your ignorance astounds me. I've faced the void. I've felt its hunger. Balance crumbles before it. Only unyielding structure survives. Only absolute control endures."

A tendril lashed down between them, forcing them apart. Where it touched the floor, the golden light hissed and steamed, darkness spreading outward in corrosive ripples.

Asvarr retreated to the chamber's edge, the Heirloom blazing in his hand. Through the blade, through the Grímmark, he felt the five anchors calling to him. Their energy flowed through him to reach each other. They sought reunion, a return to their original unified state.

"The anchors know the truth," he said, realization dawning. "They remember what came before the first breaking. They seek to restore what was lost."

Gautr's expression twisted with fury and desperation. "They exist as tools, nothing more. Power sources to be harnessed, directed, controlled." He raised his black dagger, its runes pulsing with sickly light. "As you will be, once I reclaim what belongs to me."

More tendrils poured through the shattered ceiling, drawn by Gautr's rage and Asvarr's power. The chamber groaned, roots creaking as they struggled to maintain its structure against the encroaching void.

Asvarr raised the Heirloom, its light forming a barrier against the darkness. The five anchors pulsed through him, their energy flowing into the blade, strengthening its glow. Within the amber pommel, the galaxy of memories shimmered and swirled, showing him fragments of truth from across nine cycles of breaking and binding.

And there, in the oldest memory, he saw the answer—the true purpose of the Skyrend Heirloom, the real reason it preserved memories. It was forged to reunite, to heal, to restore. The blade preserved memories so nothing would truly be lost.

"The blade heals," Asvarr said, clarity filling him. "It restores. It remembers every fragment."

Gautr lunged again, his black dagger aimed at Asvarr's heart. "Enough philosophy, Warden. Give me the blade, or die here as the void consumes us both."

Asvarr met the attack, the Heirloom singing as it parried the strike. The two weapons clashed, light against darkness, memory against oblivion. In that moment of contact, Asvarr saw the truth behind Gautr's mask—the fear that had driven him for countless ages, the desperate need for control that had twisted him into the Ashfather.

"The shadow still grips you," Asvarr said, holding firm against Gautr's pressure. "Your form has changed, yet corruption remains."

"I embody what I must," Gautr snarled, bearing down with inhuman strength. "What the pattern requires."

The chamber shuddered as more darkness poured through the ceiling. The golden light retreated further, concentrating around the two combatants like the last embers of a dying fire.

Asvarr felt the anchors pulse through him, their message clear now. The chamber couldn't hold much longer. The void-hunger drew nearer with each passing moment. He had to act, had to trust the knowledge flowing through the Grímmark and the Heirloom.

With sudden decision, he stepped back, breaking contact with Gautr's blade. Before the false god could press his advantage, Asvarr drove the Heirloom into the chamber floor, directly into the pool of golden light at its center.

"What are you doing?" Gautr cried, genuine alarm in his voice.

The Heirloom sank to its hilt, the amber pommel flaring with blinding intensity. Through the blade, Asvarr channeled the power of all five anchors—serving as a conduit for their reunion.

Golden light erupted from the point of contact, spreading outward in a wave that drove back the darkness. The chamber walls pulsed, roots growing with renewed vigor, weaving a living barrier against the void-hunger above.

"No!" Gautr lunged forward, black dagger raised to strike at Asvarr's exposed back.

From the pool of light where the Heirloom stood embedded, a figure began to rise—a woman formed of golden energy, with stars in her eyes and the mark of the first Warden upon her brow.

Gautr froze, his single eye wide with shock. "Impossible," he whispered. "I killed you. I consumed your essence."

The golden figure turned toward him, her expression both sorrowful and resolute. "You took my power, Gautr. But the Heirloom preserved my memory, as it has preserved all memories surrendered to it across nine cycles of breaking and binding."

She reached out, her hand passing through Asvarr's shoulder to point at Gautr's chest. "Your corruption began with my murder. Your fall stemmed from that first betrayal. The rigid control, the cycles of breaking and binding, the slow death of the pattern—all grew from that poisoned seed."

Gautr stepped back, his confident facade crumbling. For the first time, Asvarr saw him clearly—an old man twisted by fear and guilt, clinging to power because he knew no other way to face the darkness.

"I saved the pattern," Gautr insisted, though doubt crept into his voice. "I held back the void-hunger for nine cycles."

"You merely delayed it," the golden figure corrected gently. "You weakened the pattern with each cycle, making it more vulnerable, more rigid, less able to adapt."

The chamber trembled again, but the tremor felt different now—transformative rather than destructive. The roots grew, extending upward to weave a new ceiling against the darkness above.

The golden figure turned to Asvarr, her star-filled eyes meeting his. "Warden of Five, you have done what nine before you could not. You have bound the anchors through partnership. Now you must complete what was begun at the first breaking—the renewal of the pattern as it was meant to be."

She gestured to the Heirloom, still embedded in the chamber floor. "The blade remembers. It heals. It restores. Through it, the five anchors can be reunited, their power flowing freely once more."

Asvarr placed his hand on the Heirloom's hilt, feeling the five anchors pulse through it. "What must I do?"

"Channel the anchors' power through the blade," she instructed. "Let them flow according to their nature, as equal partners. Be the conduit, the bridge, the balance point."

Gautr stepped forward, his black dagger still raised. "Her lies will doom us all, Warden. The void-hunger will consume everything through flexibility. Structure alone protects us. Control alone saves us."

"The void-hunger thrives on rigidity," the golden figure countered. "It breaks through the cracks in what cannot bend. True strength comes from flexibility, from adaptation, from balance."

Asvarr looked between them, the false god and the first Warden, Gautr's fear and the golden figure's certainty. Through the Grímmark, through the Heirloom, he felt the truth resonating.

With decision born of clarity rather than rage, he turned his back on Gautr and grasped the Heirloom's hilt with both hands. Through it, he channeled the power of all five anchors, letting their energy flow freely, guided only by his intent to restore balance.

***

Golden light erupted from the blade, spreading throughout the chamber in waves that pushed back the darkness above. The roots grew with renewed vigor, weaving a living ceiling that sealed out the void-hunger's tendrils.

Behind him, Asvarr heard Gautr cry out—in rage or fear or perhaps even relief, he couldn't tell. What mattered was the flow of power through the Heirloom, through the Grímmark, through the chamber itself as the pattern began to heal.

The false god's shadow loomed behind him, blade raised for a final desperate strike. But Asvarr remained focused on the task before him, trusting in the anchors that had accepted him, in the pattern that sought renewal through him.

The choice had been made.

Gautr's black dagger plunged toward Asvarr's back, its runes pulsing with malevolent hunger. At the moment of impact, the chamber exploded with golden light. The blade struck something solid between itself and its target—an invisible barrier forged of memory and anchor-light.

"You cannot stop this, deceiver," the First Warden's golden form declared, her voice resonating through the chamber like the toll of an ancient bell. Her starlit eyes blazed with the combined power of nine cycles of breaking and binding. "The pattern remembers the balance it once held."

Gautr roared in frustration, hammering at the barrier with his dagger. Each strike sent ripples through the golden light but failed to penetrate it. "Fool woman! The void-hunger will consume everything!" Spittle flew from his lips, his composed facade shattered by rage and desperation. "I saved the worlds once! I can save them again!"

Asvarr remained focused on the Heirloom, channeling the power of all five anchors through its embedded blade. The golden light pulsed from the point of connection, spreading through the roots of the chamber in ever-expanding waves. Where the light touched darkness, the void-hunger's tendrils recoiled, hissing with frustration or pain.

The First Warden hovered beside him, her form growing more substantial as the light intensified. "The anchors remember their original unity, Warden of Five. They seek to restore what was sundered at the first breaking."

Through the Heirloom, through the Grímmark spanning his chest, Asvarr felt the five anchors pulse in unison. Each had its own nature—blood, earth, wisdom, storm, death—yet together they formed a harmony beyond their individual powers. They had never been meant to exist separately, only to express different aspects of the same fundamental pattern.

The chamber shuddered as more darkness poured through the fractured ceiling. The golden light pushed against it, creating a stalemate that stressed the very fabric of reality. Asvarr's arms burned with the effort of maintaining the connection, sweat streaming down his face and back.

"You can't maintain this forever," Gautr called, circling to find a weakness in the barrier. His voice had lost some of its commanding power, a hint of pleading creeping in. "The void-hunger is endless. It will outlast your strength, your will, your very soul."

"He speaks from experience," the First Warden observed, her gaze following Gautr's movements. "He tried to stand alone against the void. He relied on rigid control when he should have sought harmony and balance."

Asvarr's muscles trembled with the strain of channeling so much power. The Grímmark burned across his torso, five intertwined patterns pulsing in time with his racing heart. His vision blurred, darkness creeping in around the edges.

"I can't hold this much longer," he gasped, fingers tightening around the Heirloom's hilt. "The anchors are too powerful together."

"Because you still think of them as separate entities," the First Warden said, her golden hand passing through his shoulder in an attempt at reassurance. "They must become one again, as they were in the beginning. You must help them find unity, guide them back to their original state."

"How?" The word came out as a pained whisper, Asvarr's strength faltering.

"Remember what you learned when binding the fifth anchor. Partnership, harmony, balance. The anchors seek to flow together, to become a single pattern again."

Understanding flashed through Asvarr's mind, sharp and clear despite his exhaustion. He had been trying to channel the anchors' power, to direct it according to his will. Instead, he needed to serve as a vessel for their reunion, to allow them to find their own balance through him.

He relaxed his grip on the Heirloom, no longer trying to control the flow of power but simply providing a conduit for it. The burning sensation in his arms eased, replaced by a spreading warmth that flowed through his entire body. The Grímmark's pain transformed to pleasure as the five patterns began to merge, flowing together like streams joining to form a river.

The golden light surged, driving back the darkness with renewed force. The chamber resonated with a deep harmonic tone, the roots singing in response to the united power flowing through them. Gautr stumbled backward, raising his arm to shield his eye from the intensifying brilliance.

"No," he whispered, his voice breaking. "You don't understand what you're doing. The void-hunger will find a way through. It always does."

The First Warden turned toward him, compassion tempering the sternness in her starlit gaze. "Your fear made you its first victim, Gautr. You became what you sought to prevent—a reflection of the void's hunger for control, for consumption."

"I had no choice!" Gautr's voice cracked with the weight of nine cycles of isolation and corruption. "I saw what lay beyond the pattern. I felt its hunger!" His hand tightened around the black dagger, knuckles white with tension. "You would have let it devour everything!"

"I would have trusted the pattern to adapt, to find balance," she corrected gently. "As it was always meant to do."

The unified power of the anchors surged through Asvarr, stronger than anything he had felt before. The Heirloom glowed white-hot, the runes along its blade shifting and flowing like living things. The amber pommel pulsed with the galaxy of memories it contained, each star a fragment of someone who had stood where Asvarr now stood.

Through their eyes, through their experiences, he saw the truth of nine cycles of breaking and binding—the slow corruption of the pattern, the gradual weakening of the barrier between reality and the void-hunger. Gautr's rigid control had delayed the inevitable at the cost of making the pattern less able to adapt, less capable of finding new ways to resist the darkness.

The chamber walls pulsed with golden light, the roots growing more vigorously, weaving together to form an impenetrable ceiling against the pressing void. The floor beneath Asvarr's feet became a mirror of the ceiling, roots bursting upward to embrace those descending from above. The chamber was transforming into a sphere, a perfect enclosure of living wood pulsing with golden light.

"The Pattern-Chamber awakens," the First Warden said, wonder in her voice. "It remembers its original purpose."

Gautr backed away, his face a mask of conflicting emotions—fear, awe, anger, yearning. "You'll destroy everything," he whispered, yet doubt tinged his words. "The pattern cannot stand against the void-hunger without structure, without control."

"The pattern needs balance," Asvarr said, his voice steadier now as the anchors found harmony within him. "Dynamic, adaptive balance. The void feeds on rigidity, on that which cannot bend."

The Heirloom pulsed, drawing Asvarr's attention back to the task at hand. The flow of power through the blade had changed, becoming more focused, more purposeful. The anchors were no longer seeking merely to push back the darkness; they were working to repair the damage done by nine cycles of corruption and control.

Golden light spiraled outward from the Heirloom, forming intricate patterns that resembled the five marks Asvarr had carried—yet different, more primal, more interconnected. These were the original forms of the anchors, before they had been separated and bound to individual Wardens.

"Your marks are fading," Gautr observed, a tinge of satisfaction in his voice. "The anchors abandon you, as they abandoned me."

Asvarr glanced down at his chest, where the Grímmark had spread across his torso. The five intertwined patterns were indeed changing, the golden light within them dimming as their power flowed into the Heirloom. Yet he felt no sense of loss, no diminishment of his connection to the anchors. If anything, the bond grew stronger as the marks faded, becoming internal rather than external, spiritual rather than physical.

"They're not abandoning me," he replied, understanding dawning. "They're becoming part of me, as I am becoming part of them. The marks were never meant to be permanent sigils of control, only temporary guides to connection."

The First Warden nodded, approval in her starlit eyes. "You understand now what nine Wardens before you could not. The anchors seek reunion, harmony, balance—with themselves and with their chosen vessel."

The spiral patterns of golden light converged on the Heirloom, flowing into it like rivers into the sea. The blade thrummed with power, its song changing from the battle-hymn Asvarr knew to something older, gentler, yet no less potent. This was the music of creation itself, of pattern and possibility merging in endless harmony.

Gautr watched the transformation with a mixture of longing and dread. "It won't last," he insisted, though his voice had lost its certainty. "The void-hunger never rests, never relents."

"Then the pattern must learn to adapt, to find new ways of resistance," Asvarr replied, feeling the truth of the words as they left his lips. "Rigidity invites breaking. Flexibility ensures survival."

The chamber completed its transformation into a perfect sphere of living wood, sealed against the darkness beyond. Within this sacred space, reality itself seemed more fluid, more responsive to the harmonized power flowing through the Heirloom. Roots grew and shifted in mesmerizing patterns, golden light pulsing through them like blood through veins.

Asvarr felt a change within himself as well, a shifting of perception that allowed him to see beyond the physical realm into the underlying structure of reality. The pattern revealed itself to him as a living, breathing tapestry of connections, constantly shifting yet fundamentally stable.

And beyond it, pressing against the boundaries of existence, the void-hunger waited—vast, ancient, patient. It had existed before the pattern and would exist after, should the pattern fall. Yet it was no inevitable destroyer, merely the chaos from which order emerged and to which it would eventually return. The cycle of creation and dissolution was itself part of a greater pattern, one that encompassed both void and form.

"I see it now," Asvarr whispered, awe suffusing his voice. "The void is half of the whole. Without chaos, there can be no order, no growth, no change."

The First Warden smiled, her golden form brightening. "Yes. This was the truth Gautr could never accept. The void is fear-made-manifest to those who desire only control, only permanence. Yet it is also the wellspring of all possibility, the source from which new patterns emerge."

Gautr shook his head, clutching his black dagger like a drowning man grasping at floating debris. "Pretty words. Empty philosophy. I've felt its hunger, its hatred for all that exists."

"You felt your own fear reflected back at you," the First Warden countered. "The void mirrors what approaches it. Bring fear, and you find hunger. Bring acceptance, and you find possibility."

The Heirloom's song reached a crescendo, the blade glowing so brightly that Asvarr could no longer look directly at it. The amber pommel expanded, the galaxy of memories within it growing to encompass the entire chamber. Stars whirled around them—each one a fragment of someone who had touched the pattern, whose essence had been preserved within the blade.

Among them, Asvarr recognized his own sacrificed memories—rage, identity, certainty. They had never truly been lost, only transformed, preserved within the greater whole. He sensed the memories of other Wardens as well, men and women who had stood where he now stood, who had tried and failed to restore the pattern to its original harmony.

And there, at the center of the galaxy, a single star burned brighter than all others—the First Warden's essence, preserved through nine cycles of breaking and binding. She had never truly died, only been fragmented, her power stolen by Gautr in his desperate bid to control the pattern.

Now she reclaimed that power, drawing it back from Gautr, from the corrupted cycle he had created. The false god staggered, his single eye widening in shock as golden light poured from his chest, streaming toward the First Warden's outstretched hand.

"No," he gasped, dropping to his knees. "You can't take it. I earned it. I preserved it when you would have squandered it on foolish ideals."

"It was never yours to take," she replied, her voice gentle despite the inexorable pull of her power. "You stole what was freely given to me by the pattern itself. Now it returns to its rightful vessel."

Gautr clutched at his chest as more golden light streamed from him, his form diminishing, shrinking from the towering presence he had been to something smaller, more human. The crown of broken branches that had marked him as the Ashfather crumbled to dust, and his gray cloak hung loose on suddenly frail shoulders.

"What will you do with it?" he asked, his voice barely audible above the Heirloom's song. "Will you become what I became? Will you control, preserve, maintain?"

The First Warden shook her head, gathering the reclaimed power into a sphere between her palms. "I will return it to the pattern, where it belongs. No single vessel should hold such power, Gautr. It was never meant to be controlled, only guided, balanced, harmonized."

She turned to Asvarr, extending the sphere of golden light toward him. "Warden of Five, you have proven worthy where nine before you failed. Will you accept this final trust? Will you return the pattern's power to itself, restoring the balance that was broken at the first shattering?"

Asvarr hesitated, acutely aware of the immense responsibility being offered. The sphere contained the essence of creation itself, the power to shape reality according to his will. With it, he could remake the world as he saw fit, could build a new order from the ashes of the old.

The temptation whispered through him, showing visions of a world remade in his image—a world of balance and harmony, yes, but also a world shaped by his understanding, his perspective. He would become, in essence, what Gautr had been—a god in truth, if gentler and wiser than his predecessor.

Yet the lessons of five bindings echoed in his memory. True strength came from partnership, harmony, balance—never from control, domination, or rigid structure. The pattern needed guidance, perhaps, but never a master.

"I accept the trust," he said, meeting the First Warden's starlit gaze, "but not the power. I will return it to the pattern, as it should be."

He placed his hands on the Heirloom's hilt, channeling his intent through the blade. The sphere of golden light drifted from the First Warden's palms to hover above the embedded sword, pulsing in time with the melody it sang.

"Speak the words of restoration," the First Warden instructed, her form beginning to fade as her task neared completion. "The pattern remembers, even if the worlds have forgotten."

Words rose to Asvarr's lips, words in a language he had never learned yet somehow knew—the original tongue of creation, spoken before the first breaking. "Let what was sundered be made whole. Let what was broken find healing. Let the pattern remember its harmony, its balance, its endless dance of form and void."

The sphere of golden light descended, touching the Heirloom's hilt. For a heartbeat, nothing happened. Then, with a sound like the world taking its first breath, the light exploded outward, engulfing the chamber, the Heirloom, Asvarr, Gautr, and the fading form of the First Warden.

Reality itself seemed to bend and flex, responding to the release of power long constrained. The roots of the chamber sang with joy, growing and shifting in patterns too complex for mortal mind to comprehend. The Heirloom's blade dissolved, transforming into pure light that flowed upward, outward, through the roots and beyond, carrying the restored power of the pattern back to the worlds it had abandoned.

When Asvarr's vision cleared, the Heirloom was gone, leaving only a small sapling growing from the spot where the blade had been embedded. Its trunk twisted in a spiral pattern, leaves gleaming gold and silver in the gentle light that now permeated the chamber.

"The first new growth," a voice said from behind him.

Asvarr turned to find Gautr still kneeling, his form diminished but no longer withering. The black dagger lay beside him, its runes dead and dull, its power exhausted. The false god looked up at Asvarr with eyes—two now, both human, one blue and one brown—that held wonder rather than desperation.

"You did what I could not," Gautr continued, his voice steady despite his weakened state. "You trusted the pattern to find its own balance."

"The pattern trusted me," Asvarr corrected, extending a hand to the fallen god. "As it once trusted you, before fear clouded your judgment."

Gautr stared at the offered hand for a long moment before taking it, allowing Asvarr to help him to his feet. "What happens now? The void-hunger still waits beyond the pattern. The threat remains."

"The pattern adapts," Asvarr replied, feeling the truth of the words resonating through him. The Grímmark had faded entirely from his chest, yet he felt its power still, transformed into something more subtle, more pervasive. "It grows and changes, finding new ways to maintain balance. The void-hunger will always exist, as will the pattern. Each defines the other, each gives the other meaning."

Gautr shook his head, a hint of his old stubbornness returning. "Philosophy again. I dealt in certainties, in structures that endured."

"And they broke under their own rigidity," Asvarr pointed out, gesturing to the sapling. "This will grow differently than what came before. It will adapt to challenges rather than resisting them. That is true strength."

The roots of the chamber pulsed with golden light, a final echo of the power that had flowed through them. The perfect sphere they had formed began to open, sections of the ceiling parting to reveal a sky—no longer filled with roiling darkness but with stars, countless stars stretching into infinity.

"The pattern extends beyond the Tree now," Asvarr said, understanding flowing through him like the anchors' power had moments before. "It's no longer confined to Yggdrasil's branches, no longer limited by the structures we imposed upon it."

Gautr stared upward, wonder and fear mingling in his expression. "Without boundaries, without structure, how will it maintain itself against the void?"

"Through adaptation, through growth, through the endless dance of creation and dissolution." Asvarr placed a hand on the sapling's trunk, feeling life pulsing beneath his fingertips. "The Tree will grow again, differently than before. It will become what it needs to be, not what we demand of it."

The false god turned away, his diminished form casting a long shadow in the golden light. "And what of me? I who betrayed the pattern, who corrupted its flow for nine cycles?"

Asvarr considered the question, feeling the echoes of the pattern's restored power flowing through him. There was no anger in him now, no desire for vengeance or justice. Only understanding, and perhaps a measure of compassion for the fear-driven being who had sacrificed so much in his desperate attempt to preserve what he loved.

"You're part of the pattern too," he said finally. "Your corruption, your control—they happened within the pattern, not outside it. Even your fear has its place in the greater whole."

"So I remain free? After all I've done?" Disbelief colored Gautr's voice.

"Free to find your own place within the renewed pattern," Asvarr clarified. "Free to learn what it means to exist without control, without fear. The void-hunger has no more hold on you, Gautr. The shadow of the false god is lifted."

Gautr's shoulders straightened slightly, his gaze returning to the sapling. "And if I choose to oppose this new growth? To return to the old ways?"

"Then you will fail," Asvarr said simply. "The pattern remembers, Gautr. It will recognize the old corruption and adapt to resist it. You cannot break what bends, cannot control what flows."

The chamber trembled, a gentle vibration that traveled up through the floor and into Asvarr's bones. The roots were shifting, responding to some unseen signal. The sapling glowed brighter, its leaves rustling without wind.

"Time to go," Asvarr said, feeling the chamber's intentions through his connection to the pattern. "This place returns to its original purpose—a nexus between worlds, a point of balance in the greater whole."

Gautr hesitated, his gaze lingering on the sapling. "Where will you go, Warden of Five? Or should I say, Warden of None, now that the anchors have been restored to the pattern?"

Asvarr touched his chest where the Grímmark had been. Though the physical mark had faded, he felt its echo still, a subtle warmth that connected him to the renewed pattern. "I go where the pattern guides me. There's healing to be done, balance to be restored across the Nine Realms."

"And I?" Gautr asked, vulnerability creeping into his voice for the first time. "Where does a fallen god go in a world renewed?"

Asvarr considered the question, seeing a being who had lost his way, who had allowed fear to dictate his choices for countless ages. "You go where you must to find peace, Gautr. The pattern will guide you too, if you let it."

The chamber shuddered again, more insistently this time. The roots began to separate, creating a passage that led outward, away from the central sapling. Golden light spilled through the opening, illuminating a path that seemed to lead everywhere and nowhere simultaneously.

"The way opens," Asvarr said, moving toward the passage. "Will you come?"

Gautr stared at the offered path, conflict evident in his expression. Nine cycles of control and corruption weighed against the uncertain freedom of a renewed pattern. Fear of the void-hunger balanced against the possibility of growth, of change, of redemption.

With visible effort, he straightened his shoulders and took a step forward. "I will see what lies beyond the shadow I cast for so long."

Together, they walked into the golden light, leaving behind the chamber of roots and the sapling that would grow into something new—neither Tree nor Pattern as they had known them, but a synthesis of both, guided by its own nature rather than the will of gods or Wardens.

The false god's shadow fell away, dissolved in the brilliance of possibility. What emerged into the renewed pattern was something simpler, more human, yet perhaps more meaningful for its limitations.

Behind them, the Pattern-Chamber sealed itself once more, returning to its vigil at the center of all things. Within it, the sapling's roots spread, seeking connection with the greater whole. Its first branch unfurled, reaching toward distant stars.

The pattern remembered. The pattern grew. The pattern endured.

CHAPTER 27

SACRIFICE OF THE SILENT

B lood dripped from Gunnar Ironveil's wounded arm as he staggered forward, his breath forming ragged clouds in the frozen air of the forge-hall. The dwarf's eyes, dark as polished obsidian, fixed on the sacred forge ahead—the one place in all Svartálfr where the Root's essence might be saved.

"More haste, Flame-Bearer," he growled, glancing back at Asvarr. "The poison spreads."

Asvarr matched the dwarf's pace, tracking the black tendrils that crawled beneath Gunnar's skin from the gash left by the cultist's blade. The wound pulsed with sickly light that made his Grímmark burn in response. Their footsteps echoed across the vast hall, empty now save for the handful of forge-priests huddled around the central pit.

"You believe this will work?" Asvarr touched the hilt of his bronze sword, its runes glimmering in tune with the forge's heartbeat.

"Belief?" Gunnar laughed, a sound like grinding stone. "The Ashfather walks now. Certainty belongs to fools and the dead. Yet the Root remembers those who serve it."

The forge-priests parted as they approached. Unlike Gunnar, these dwarves wore their beards twisted into complex knots, each plait embedded with shards of gleaming ore. The eldest stepped forward, her face weathered like ancient leather.

"You bring corruption to the sacred forge, Ironveil."

"I bring hope, Ember-Singer," Gunnar replied, dropping painfully to one knee. "The Flame-Bearer has bound four anchors. The fifth calls to him."

The Grimmark flared on Asvarr's chest, sending sharp heat through his veins. The sensation had changed since the fourth binding, resembling molten metal flowing beneath his skin rather than fire.

The Ember-Singer's eyes widened. "The mark speaks truth." She turned toward Asvarr, studying him with ancient eyes. "You remain flesh, mortal still. The fifth binding demands more than blood and oath."

"I've given rage, memory, identity, and certainty," Asvarr said, his voice steady despite the chill seeping into his bones from the forge's unnatural cold. "What sacrifice remains?"

"Life," whispered Gunnar, clutching his wounded arm. Black veins now reached his shoulder. "Mine."

Asvarr grabbed the dwarf's good shoulder. "I refuse to accept this. Another path must exist."

"Many paths exist," Gunnar smiled through gritted teeth. "Few lead where we must go."

The forge-pit at the center of the hall pulsed in rhythm with Gunnar's labored breathing. Unlike the roaring fires of mortal smithies, this sacred forge burned with cold blue flame that consumed stone rather than wood. At its center floated a perfect sphere of golden light—the heart of the Root itself.

"The shadow-ice poison claims me regardless," Gunnar explained, his voice growing weaker. "My death serves the Root or feeds the void. I choose the Root."

The Ember-Singer nodded solemnly. "The offering must be willing. The sacrifice must be witnessed." She drew a knife of strange crystal, its edge so sharp it seemed to cut the air itself. "Do you consent, Ironveil, to give your essence to the Root?"

"I do." Gunnar turned to Asvarr, his face pale but resolute. "When I fade, strike the sphere with your blade. My spirit will forge the connection you seek."

Asvarr's throat tightened. In his journey across the realms, he had surrendered much—memories, certainties, fragments of self given to the anchors he'd bound. This felt different—watching another sacrifice everything while he continued forward.

"This can't—"

"It can," Gunnar interrupted, his voice surprisingly gentle. "This wyrd belongs to me, Flame-Bearer. The forge-smoke showed me this path since your arrival. Death comes for me either way—let it carry meaning."

Around them, the forge-priests began to chant in a language older than the mountains, a tongue that made the very stones of the hall vibrate in response. The Ember-Singer raised her crystal blade.

"Wait," Asvarr said, kneeling beside Gunnar. "Tell me why, at least. Why give yourself for me—for this?"

Gunnar's laugh turned into a wet cough. "The sacrifice serves my people, human, never you alone." He gestured toward the shadows at the edge of the hall where Asvarr now noticed dozens of silent figures watching—dwarven children with wide, frightened eyes. "It serves what follows us. The Ashfather would return everything to void, unmake all creation. The Root..." He drew a shuddering breath. "The Root remembers. It grows. It joins worlds together."

Asvarr saw truth in the dwarf's eyes—the same truth he'd glimpsed in the previous anchors. The Root existed beyond mere power; it embodied connection, restoration, wholeness.

"Your sacrifice will matter," Asvarr promised. He clasped Gunnar's good arm in the warrior's grip, forearm to forearm. "What name shall I carry forward?"

"Gunnar Ironveil serves well enough," the dwarf smiled through his pain. "Though the elders once named me Soulforge."

The Ember-Singer stepped forward, crystal blade gleaming. "The ritual begins."

Gunnar released Asvarr's arm and straightened his back, facing the forge-pit. The shadow-ice poison had reached his neck now, black veins pulsing beneath his beard.

"Forge-Mother, root of worlds, accept this offering freely given," the Ember-Singer intoned, pressing the crystal blade against Gunnar's chest. "Take his spirit to strengthen your own. Bind his essence to your heart."

With a swift motion, she plunged the blade into Gunnar's heart. The dwarf made no sound—only a soft exhalation as his eyes widened in momentary pain, then relaxed into peace. The crystal blade drew no blood; instead, it shimmered with golden light that spread throughout Gunnar's body, replacing the shadow-ice with radiance.

Asvarr watched, transfixed, as the light inside the dwarf grew brighter. Gunnar's form began to dissolve, transforming into motes of golden light that spiraled toward the forge-pit. The sphere at its center pulsed faster, responding to the offered essence.

"Now, Flame-Bearer!" the Ember-Singer commanded. "Strike the sphere with your blade while his spirit joins with the Root!"

Asvarr drew his bronze sword, its runes blazing with accumulated power from the four previous bindings. The weapon felt almost alive in his grip, eager for this moment. He approached the forge-pit, heat and cold washing over him in alternating waves that made his skin prickle.

The golden sphere expanded as Gunnar's essence merged with it, creating swirling patterns that reminded Asvarr of the connections he'd seen in the previous anchors—the vast web that united all living things.

He raised the blade, its edge catching the light of the forge. Through the golden haze, he thought he saw Gunnar's face one last time, smiling with newfound peace.

"For what comes after," Asvarr whispered, and brought the sword down upon the sphere.

Light exploded outward, blinding in its intensity. The Grímmark on Asvarr's chest responded with matching brilliance as connections formed between his essence and the Root's heart. Unlike previous bindings, this one brought no pain—only a profound sense of joining, of separate paths merging into one.

Visions flooded his mind: forests growing from barren stone, rivers carving new paths through ancient mountains, stars shifting in unfamiliar patterns. He saw the nine realms as branches of the same tree, currents in the same river, notes in the same song. Unity through diversity, strength through connection.

When his sight cleared, the forge-pit had transformed. Where the cold blue flame had burned, a small sapling now grew, its trunk formed of intertwined gold and silver, its leaves shimmering with inner light. The forge-priests had fallen to their knees in reverence or shock—even the Ember-Singer stared in wide-eyed wonder.

"Root-heart to tree-form," she whispered. "Nine cycles have passed since we last witnessed this miracle."

Asvarr felt changed as well. The Grímmark no longer burned on his chest; it had spread across his skin in intricate patterns resembling both roots and stars. His bronze sword had transformed, its blade now veined with the same gold-silver alloy as the sapling.

Beyond these physical changes, he sensed something greater within—a connection to ancient wisdom transcending individual consciousness. Gunnar's essence had joined with the Root, and through it, a fragment of the dwarf's knowledge now resided within Asvarr.

He knew what must come next.

"The binding stands complete," Asvarr said, his voice resonating with new power. "The Ashfather gathers his forces. We must protect the sapling until it takes root."

The Ember-Singer nodded grimly. "Our defenses weaken hourly. Cultists press from the upper tunnels, and strange shadows gather at the eastern gates."

"Those gates require my presence," Asvarr decided, sheathing his transformed sword. "The Root has shown me the Ashfather's lieutenant waiting there."

"You would abandon the sapling?" one of the younger priests asked, fear evident in his voice.

"The sapling enjoys greater protection here than anywhere else," Asvarr replied with certainty that came from the Root itself. "Should the Ashfather breach your defenses, safety will exist nowhere." He turned to the Ember-Singer. "Gunnar's sacrifice granted us time. I intend to use it fighting, advancing."

She studied him for a long moment before inclining her head. "What would you have us do, Warden?"

The title caught Asvarr by surprise. He had answered to many names—berserker, Flame-Bearer, Root-Singer—but "Warden" carried weight he hadn't fully understood until now. With the fifth binding, he had become guardian of possibility itself.

"Protect the children," he said, glancing toward the shadow-huddled youngsters who had watched Gunnar's sacrifice in silence. "And prepare for what comes after."

As he walked toward the eastern tunnels, Asvarr felt Gunnar's presence within him—as knowledge and purpose rather than voice or ghost. The dwarf had given everything to protect his people and strengthen the Root. Asvarr would honor that sacrifice by finishing what they had started.

The fifth binding stood complete, yet the true battle merely began. Ahead waited the Ashfather's most trusted servant, the shadow-priest who had hunted Asvarr across three realms. Behind him grew the sapling that might restore what had broken.

And somewhere between them lay Asvarr's own fate, shaped by sacrifices both given and received.

***

The eastern tunnels twisted deeper into Svartálfr, their walls veined with ore that caught the light of Asvarr's torch. Each pulse of the metal matched the rhythm of the sapling behind him—the heartbeat of the fifth binding. He ran his fingers along the wall, feeling heat gather beneath his touch where the Grímmark's power flowed through him.

Voices echoed from ahead, harsh and guttural. Asvarr extinguished his torch with a swift motion, darkness claiming the tunnel. He drew his transformed sword, the gold-silver alloy in its blade giving off a faint luminescence that he willed into dormancy.

The darkness held no terror for him now. Since the binding, his vision had changed, allowing him to perceive the vital energies of living things and the currents of power that flowed through stone. The tunnel walls glowed with a faint amber light through his altered sight, and ahead, five forms burned with sickly purple fire—cultists, their essence corrupted by the Ashfather's touch.

"The Flame-Bearer approaches," one of them whispered, voice like stones grinding together. "I smell his blood."

Asvarr pressed his back against the tunnel wall, weighing his options. The passage narrowed ahead, a natural bottleneck where the cultists had positioned themselves. Breaking through by force would alert others, drawing more enemies than he could face. But Gunnar's knowledge, now merged with his own, suggested another path.

He closed his eyes, reaching through the stone with his expanded senses, feeling for weaknesses in the tunnel's structure. There—a hollow space running parallel to this passage, perhaps a natural cavern or an abandoned mining shaft. With careful pressure from his hand, he channeled the Root's power into the wall. The stone softened beneath his touch, becoming malleable as clay.

The wall parted silently, creating an opening just wide enough for him to squeeze through. Beyond lay a forgotten tunnel, its floor littered with broken mining tools and the bones of small creatures. Asvarr stepped through, willing the stone to reseal behind him. The cultists' voices faded, still unaware of his passage.

This older tunnel followed the same general direction but sloped downward, delving deeper than the main passageway. The air grew colder, carrying the metallic tang of deep water. Asvarr's expanded senses picked up a vast open space ahead—the eastern gate chamber where the Ashfather's lieutenant waited.

The tunnel opened abruptly onto a narrow ledge overlooking an immense cavern. Asvarr dropped to a crouch, surveying the scene below. The chamber housed a subterranean lake, its black surface still as glass, reflecting the golden glow of forge-lanterns that lined the walls. At the far end stood massive doors of dark metal, covered in runes that pulsed with protective magic—the eastern gates.

Before the gates stood a figure that made Asvarr's Grímmark burn in recognition. Taller than any dwarf, yet stooped and twisted, the Ash-Priest moved with the deliberate precision of an insect, its bark-covered limbs clicking against stone.

Behind it, a dozen acolytes arranged obsidian shards in a complex pattern on the cavern floor.

From his vantage point, Asvarr could see the purpose of their work—a summoning circle designed to bypass the gates' defenses from within. The pattern mirrored fragments he'd glimpsed in the visions granted by the fifth binding. They planned to open a path for the Ashfather's forces directly into Svartálfr's heart.

Movement at the water's edge caught his attention. A dwarf child crouched behind a stack of supply crates, watching the cultists with wide, frightened eyes. One of the silent children from the forge-hall, here in the most dangerous place imaginable. The child clutched something to his chest—a hammer marked with the same runes as the gates.

The key to the eastern gates. If the Ash-Priest found the child...

Asvarr tensed, calculating distances. The ledge stood thirty feet above the cavern floor, with the child forty paces from his position and the Ash-Priest twice that distance. Too far to reach without being seen, too close to risk calling out.

The decision was made for him when one of the acolytes turned, freezing as he spotted the child. His cry of discovery echoed through the chamber.

"A watcher! Seize it!"

Asvarr launched himself from the ledge without hesitation, channeling the Root's power to slow his descent. He landed in a crouch between the advancing acolytes and the child, his transformed sword flaring to life in his hand, golden light blazing through the runes etched in its blade.

"Run," he told the child without turning. "Back to the forge-hall."

The dwarf child stood frozen for a heartbeat, then bolted toward a tunnel opening at the chamber's edge. Two acolytes moved to intercept, but Asvarr was faster. His sword cut through the air, trailing streamers of golden light that solidified into barriers, blocking their path.

The Ash-Priest turned slowly, its hollow eye sockets fixing on Asvarr. "Warden," it creaked, the word emerging from a mouth formed of twisted branches.

"You have completed the binding." It tilted its head in an unsettlingly inhuman gesture. "My master felt the shift in the pattern."

"Your master has lost," Asvarr replied, moving to maintain distance between himself and the encircling acolytes. "The fifth anchor is bound. The sapling grows."

"Growth can be stunted. Saplings can be uprooted." The Ash-Priest raised a gnarled hand, bark creaking with the motion. "Did you think binding the anchors was the end? It is merely prologue."

Asvarr felt the truth in those words. The fifth binding represented culmination but also beginning—the anchors secured, but the pattern itself still vulnerable. The sapling needed time to root deeply, to spread its influence through the broken pattern and restore balance.

Time he needed to buy.

"Surrender the rune-hammer," the Ash-Priest demanded. "The gates must open."

"The gates stay sealed," Asvarr countered, shifting his grip on his sword. "Your forces remain outside."

The Ash-Priest's branches rustled—a sound like dry laughter. "Forces? I need no army." It spread its arms wide. "We stand upon the bones of the fallen, Warden. The silent dead of Svartálfr await my call."

The obsidian shards on the floor began to glow with sickly light. The still waters of the lake stirred, ripples spreading outward as something arose from the depths. Skeletal hands broke the surface first, followed by skull-faces with empty eye sockets filled with purple fire—the dead of ancient battles, dwarves who had fallen defending these very gates in ages past.

"The silent serve me now," the Ash-Priest intoned. "As your dwarf friend will soon serve. Did you think sacrifice brought peace? Death is merely transition into my master's embrace."

Cold fury rose in Asvarr's chest. The mention of Gunnar's sacrifice triggered something primal within him—not berserker rage, which he had surrendered long ago, but the focused wrath of the Warden he had become. The marks across his body flared with golden light.

"Gunnar Ironveil serves the Root," Asvarr declared, raising his sword. "As do all the fallen who gave themselves willingly."

Knowledge flooded through him—Gunnar's knowledge of the eastern gates, of the defenses woven into the very stone of this chamber. The dead emerging from the lake moved with unnatural speed, closing the distance with jerky, puppet-like motions. Asvarr didn't retreat. Instead, he drove his transformed blade into the stone floor.

"Root of worlds, heart of patterns, hear your Warden's call," he intoned, words coming from somewhere beyond his own understanding. "The willing dead stand with you still."

Golden light erupted from the sword, racing through the stone in branching patterns that mimicked roots. Where they touched the skeletal figures, the purple fire in their eye sockets flickered, shifted, transformed to amber gold. The dead stumbled, their movements no longer directed by the Ash-Priest's will.

The creature screamed, a sound like trees breaking in a storm. "Impossible! The dead are void-claimed!"

"The dead remember who they were," Asvarr countered, maintaining his focus on the spreading network of golden light. "Those who fell defending these gates died willingly, knowingly. Their sacrifice echoes Gunnar's. They choose the Root."

The skeletal dwarves turned as one, facing the Ash-Priest and its acolytes. The purple fire had fully transformed to amber gold in their eye sockets—the Root's essence flowing through them, guided by Asvarr's will. They advanced on the cultists, bone hands reaching for flesh.

The Ash-Priest backed toward the gates, its bark-covered form trembling with rage. "This changes nothing, Warden! The gates will fall. The sapling will burn. My master comes!"

"Then let him come," Asvarr replied, pulling his sword from the stone. "But he'll find no welcome in Svartálfr."

The dead surged forward, overwhelming the acolytes with relentless advance. Screams echoed through the chamber as flesh met bone. The Ash-Priest raised its hands, shadows gathering around it in a protective cocoon. Before the dead could reach it, the shadows contracted violently, then exploded outward in a wave of force that knocked Asvarr back several steps.

When the shadows cleared, the Ash-Priest was gone—fleeing through some void-path beyond Asvarr's perception. The remaining acolytes fought desperately, but the dead showed no mercy, tearing them apart with methodical precision.

Asvarr leaned on his sword, suddenly exhausted. Channeling the Root's power through the dead had drained him more than he expected. The golden light in the skeletal figures began to fade, their purpose fulfilled. One by one, they collapsed, bones clattering on stone, the amber fire in their eye sockets extinguished.

A small sound drew his attention to the tunnel where the dwarf child had fled. The boy stood there, clutching the rune-hammer to his chest, eyes wide with mixture of fear and wonder.

"You woke them," the child whispered. "The ancient defenders."

Asvarr nodded, sheathing his sword. "They remembered their purpose."

"Will they sleep again now?"

"Yes," Asvarr said, approaching slowly to avoid frightening the child. "Their sacrifice is complete. They can rest."

The boy looked down at the rune-hammer in his hands, then held it out. "The Ember-Singer said to bring this to you if the gates were threatened. She said you would know what to do."

Asvarr took the hammer, feeling power pulse within it. The runes matched those on the gates exactly—a master key to Svartálfr's defenses. With it, he could reinforce the seals or open the way, depending on need.

"What's your name?" he asked the child.

"Thrim," the boy answered. "Son of Jormund, forge-apprentice."

"You were brave to come here, Thrim. The hammer might have fallen into enemy hands without you."

The boy's chest puffed with pride, though fear still lingered in his eyes. "The Ember-Singer said the silent ones would protect me."

Asvarr glanced at the scattered bones. "And they did." He knelt to the child's level. "Can you find your way back to the forge-hall?"

Thrim nodded. "Through the service tunnels. They're too small for the shadow-folk."

"Go then. Tell the Ember-Singer the eastern gates are secure for now, but the Ash-Priest escaped. The Ashfather will try another approach."

As the child disappeared into the tunnel, Asvarr turned back to the massive gates. The rune-hammer grew warm in his hand, resonating with the defenses woven into the metal. He approached, feeling the power that flowed through the ancient barriers—power that would keep the Ashfather's forces at bay a while longer.

Yet something troubled him. The Ash-Priest's words echoed in his mind: "The silent serve me now." If the creature could turn the willing dead against their purpose, what else might it corrupt? The thought of Gunnar's essence, merged with the Root, potentially twisted by the Ashfather's influence sent cold dread through him.

He pressed his palm against the gates, closing his eyes to extend his senses beyond the metal. Outside, shadows gathered like storm clouds, pressing against the barriers. The Ashfather's army—not yet at full strength, but growing hourly. They would find another way in eventually.

The rune-hammer pulsed in his hand, drawing his attention to a small panel beside the gates. Intricate mechanisms lay within, designed to channel power through the defenses. Gunnar's knowledge, now part of Asvarr's consciousness, recognized their purpose. With the hammer, he could create a connection between these gates and the sapling in the forge-hall, strengthening both.

Decision made, Asvarr placed the hammer against the panel. Golden light flowed from the Grímmark into the tool, through it to the gates, and outward through the stone in all directions—a network of power linking to the sapling at the heart of Svartálfr.

"The silent dead have served," he murmured, feeling the connection solidify. "May their sacrifice shield what grows."

The hammer fused with the panel, becoming part of the gate itself. The runes flared briefly, then settled into a steady golden pulse that matched the rhythm of the sapling and the beating of Asvarr's heart.

With the eastern gates secured, Asvarr turned back toward the forge-hall. The Ash-Priest had escaped to report to its master. The Ashfather would soon know exactly what had occurred here—and would redouble his efforts to reach the sapling before it rooted deeply.

The fifth binding was complete, the anchor secured, but the true battle for the pattern's future was only beginning. And somewhere beyond these stone halls, the other Wardens fought their own battles, unaware of what had awakened beneath Svartálfr.

Asvarr touched the expanded Grímmark that now spread across his chest and arms. Through it, he sensed distant echoes—four other marks, four other Wardens who must be gathered if the pattern was to be truly restored.

He had bound five anchors, but his journey had only just begun.

CHAPTER 28

THE BARK THAT SCREAMS

The sapling writhed. Its branches twisted against each other, scraping with a sound like nails on slate. Golden sap wept from knotholes as the smooth silver-gold bark split along invisible seams, revealing dark hollows beneath.

Asvarr pressed his palms against the trembling trunk, feeling the discord pulse through the wood. Three days had passed since the binding, three days of careful nurturing as the sapling stretched toward the cavern ceiling. Then, without warning, it had begun to spasm, convulsing like a beast in pain.

"Something attacks it from within," the Ember-Singer murmured, her weathered hands hovering inches from the bark. "The Root rejects itself."

"Impossible," Asvarr said, though the truth vibrated through his expanded Grímmark. The sapling's pain resonated with his own—a strange doubling sensation, as though he both inflicted and suffered the torment.

"The dead we awakened spoke of corruption." The Ember-Singer's eyes narrowed, reflecting the sapling's golden glow. "The Ash-Priest plants its seeds deep."

Dwarven forge-priests circled the sapling, chanting in rhythmic pulses that matched the Root's heartbeat. Their efforts had kept the worst convulsions at bay, but with each hour, the intervals of calm grew shorter while the spasms intensified.

A sharp crack echoed through the forge-hall as a branch snapped, falling to the stone floor. The broken limb leaked sap that bubbled and hissed, carving shallow channels in the rock.

Thrim, the dwarf child who had carried the rune-hammer, darted forward to examine the fallen branch. "Master Warden! Look at the patterns!"

Asvarr knelt beside the boy. The branch's interior revealed grain unlike any wood he'd seen—concentric rings in shades of amber and crimson, each ring bearing tiny script in a language he couldn't read but somehow understood. Memories, encoded in the wood itself. Lives lived and sacrificed, binding after binding, cycle after cycle.

And among them, a corruption. Dark veins threaded through the golden wood, pulsing with malevolent purpose.

"Poison," he muttered, tracing the veins with his fingertip. Where he touched, the darkness receded, fleeing from the power in his transformed Grímmark. "Something taints the memories within the Root."

"Can you heal it?" Thrim asked, eyes wide with wonder and fear.

Asvarr stood, facing the trembling sapling. The corruption visible in the broken branch must run throughout the entire structure—an infection attacking from within. If left unchecked, it would devour the fifth anchor from the inside out, undoing everything Gunnar had sacrificed to achieve.

"I need to enter the memory-stream," he told the Ember-Singer. "See what the Root sees."

The elderly dwarf straightened her shoulders. "Such communion risks your mind, Warden. The Root holds memories beyond counting—some from realms beyond mortal comprehension."

"The Root accepted my binding," Asvarr countered, rolling his shoulders as the Grímmark tightened across his chest. "Gunnar's sacrifice forged the connection."

"Gunnar gave his essence willingly," she responded. "The Root welcomed him. Yet something within now writhes against that welcome."

Another branch cracked, then another. The dwarven chanting faltered as priests ducked to avoid falling debris. The sapling's golden heartwood gleamed through lengthening splits in the bark, but shadows crawled within that light—twisting, grasping tendrils of something that should not exist within the pattern.

"I must try," Asvarr insisted. "Guide me."

The Ember-Singer studied him for a long moment, then nodded. She gestured to the forge-priests, who widened their circle around the sapling. From a pouch at her belt, she withdrew a handful of metallic dust that glittered with inner fire.

"Ore from the first mountain," she explained, sprinkling the dust in a precise pattern around the sapling's base. "Mined before the first breaking, when the pattern still ran true."

The dust ignited where it touched stone, burning with steady blue flame but consuming nothing. The sapling responded immediately, its convulsions stilling as though soothed by the ancient metal's presence.

"This will calm the exterior manifestation," the Ember-Singer said, "but the corruption continues within. When you touch the heartwood, speak your intent clearly. The Root holds many paths. Without focus, you may wander into memory-streams from which no mortal returns."

Asvarr drew his transformed sword, its gold-veined blade humming with accumulated power from the five bindings. "And if I find the corruption?"

"Excise it if you can. But remember—all that lives within the Root once lived in truth. Even corruption had purpose before it turned."

With the blade held before him, Asvarr approached the stilled sapling. The blue flames circling its base cast eerie shadows across the silver-gold bark. Through widening cracks, he glimpsed the heartwood pulsing with golden light, shadows writhing within its radiance.

"I am Asvarr, Warden of Five, bound to the anchors by blood and oath," he declared, the formal words rising unbidden to his lips. "I seek the corruption that taints your essence."

He pressed the blade's flat against the bark. The sapling shuddered, then went completely still. A seam opened along its trunk, a deliberate parting, revealing a hollow space within, large enough for a man to enter.

"Three hours," the Ember-Singer warned. "Longer, and your mind merges permanently with the memory-stream."

Asvarr nodded, sheathing his sword. The hollow beckoned, golden light pulsing within like a heartbeat. He stepped forward, ducking his head to enter the opening.

Inside, the space expanded beyond what should have been possible. The hollowed trunk contained a vast, spiraling chamber that stretched upward beyond sight and downward into impossible depths. Golden light suffused everything, flowing in currents that carried fragments of memory—faces, voices, landscapes from realms he'd never seen.

The memory-stream.

Asvarr extended his hand, brushing his fingers through a passing current. Images flooded his mind: a woman with silver hair standing atop a mountain peak; a black city burning beneath twin moons; a child curled around a seed large as his head, sobbing as it cracked open. Disconnected fragments from countless lives, preserved within the Root's essence.

He pulled back, forcing himself to focus. He hadn't come to lose himself in ancient memories. The corruption—that was his purpose.

"Show me what poisons you," he commanded, his voice echoing strangely in the spiraling chamber.

The currents shifted, golden light dimming as darker streams coalesced before him. Within the darkness swam images that made his eyes burn: shadows with too many limbs crawling through minds; cities built from still-living flesh; a face he recognized—the Ashfather, younger, with both eyes intact, standing before a throne of twisted bone.

At the darkness's heart writhed a single memory more substantial than the others—a scene playing over and over. The Ash-Priest knelt beside a pool of black water, murmuring words that made the air itself recoil. From the pool rose a viscous tendril that the priest guided to an open wound on his bark-covered forearm. The darkness flowed into the wound, spreading beneath his skin like ink through parchment. When he stood, something else looked out through his hollow eyes—something ancient and hungry.

The priest had become a vessel, willingly accepting corruption to carry it into the heart of the Root.

Asvarr drew his sword, its blade gleaming in the memory-light. "This is the poison-seed," he said, certain of the truth. "Show me how it spreads."

The darkness expanded, tendrils reaching outward to touch other memories. Where darkness met light, corruption spread, tainting golden recollections with shadow. Faces contorted, landscapes withered, voices twisted into screams. The poison rewrote the pattern's memory, turning truth to lie, growth to decay.

And at the center of the spreading corruption—Gunnar.

The dwarf's essence, merged with the Root during his sacrifice, twisted in silent agony as darkness wrapped around his memory. Unlike the other fragments, Gunnar retained coherence, his identity preserved by the nature of his sacrifice. The corruption sought him specifically, trying to subvert the newest and strongest addition to the Root's conscious memory.

Anger kindled in Asvarr's chest, a focused wrath directed at the violation of his friend's sacrifice. He raised his blade, stepping into the dark current.

Instantly, pressure closed around him. The corruption recognized an intruder, coiling tighter around Gunnar's essence. Asvarr pushed forward, using his sword to part the darkness as one might cut through thick vines. Each stroke scattered fragments of corrupted memory, which dissolved into the greater stream.

"Gunnar!" he called, his voice muffled by the oppressive darkness. "Fight it!"

The dwarf's essence flared briefly, golden light pushing back against the shadow. But the darkness surged, smothering the response. Whatever consciousness remained of Gunnar couldn't break free alone.

Asvarr forced himself closer, slicing through tendrils that reached for him with hungry purpose. The corruption shifted tactics, no longer trying to simply block his advance. Instead, dark fingers of memory brushed against his mind, offering images designed to shatter his resolve.

Gunnar's willing sacrifice perverted, used to strengthen the Ashfather's hold...

The other Wardens falling one by one, their marks corrupted by shadow...

The sapling withering, its essence feeding the void between worlds...

Asvarr gritted his teeth, rejecting the visions. "Lies," he snarled, bringing his blade down in a sweeping arc that severed a thick tendril of darkness. "The memory-stream preserves truth."

"*Truth is malleable,*" hissed a voice from the darkness—the Ash-Priest's voice, layered with something older and colder. "*Memory can be rewritten.*"

The darkness contracted suddenly, forming a humanoid shape before him. Though composed of corrupted memory, it moved with purpose, raising arms that elongated into blade-like appendages.

"*You bind anchors only to lose them,*" the shadow-form taunted. "*The dwarf gave himself to strengthen the Root, yet his essence now feeds my master.*"

Asvarr didn't waste breath on debate. He lunged forward, driving his transformed blade through the center of the shadow-form. It shrieked—a sound that rippled through the memory-stream, causing currents to shudder and disperse. The shadow-form dissolved, its substance scattering into the darkness, but Asvarr knew he'd destroyed only a manifestation, not the corruption itself.

He pressed onward, following the thickest tendrils of shadow to where Gunnar's essence struggled against its bonds. With each step, the resistance increased. The memory-stream itself seemed to constrict, golden light dimming as darkness gained supremacy.

"*Mortal minds cannot contain the pattern's truth,*" the disembodied voice continued. "*You will break before the corruption yields.*"

Sharp pain lanced through Asvarr's skull, his expanded Grímmark burning as though branded anew. The memory-stream began to intrude on his own thoughts, corrupted fragments attempting to overwrite his identity. He saw himself through strange eyes—a berserker consumed by rage, a Warden seduced by power, a vessel empty of all but the Root's purpose.

Versions of himself that might have been, had he made different choices.

"I chose my path," he grunted, each word an effort as he forced himself forward. "As did Gunnar."

At last, he reached the heart of the corruption, where Gunnar's essence pulsed feebly within a cocoon of shadow. Up close, he could see the dwarf's memory-form—a golden silhouette that retained Gunnar's shape but transcended physical limitation, radiating purpose and sacrifice.

The darkness squeezed tighter, attempting to extinguish that purpose. From the shadow rose spectral faces—the Ash-Priest, the Ashfather, and others Asvarr didn't recognize, ancient entities with hunger in their eyes.

"*All returns to void,*" they whispered in unison. "*All patterns unravel. All sacrifice feeds the unmaking.*"

Asvarr raised his sword, its golden veins blazing in response to the Root's distress. Before he could strike, a tendril of darkness lashed out, wrapping around his blade-arm with paralyzing cold.

"*The dwarf accepted his end,*" the voices continued. "*Now watch him feed our beginning.*"

The cocoon constricted with sudden violence. Gunnar's essence screamed—a sound unlike anything Asvarr had heard, beyond physical dimension, the cry of a soul being unmade. The sound reverberated through the chamber, echoed by the sapling outside, bark splitting further as corruption spread.

"No!" Asvarr roared. With his free hand, he grasped the tendril restraining him. The expanded Grímmark flared, channeling power through his grip. Where he touched, darkness withered, memories realigning to their uncorrupted state.

Understanding dawned. The corruption couldn't be destroyed with blade alone—it had to be *remembered* correctly, restored to its original purpose.

He dropped his sword, which dissolved into the memory-stream. Reaching out with both hands, he plunged them directly into the shadowy cocoon surrounding Gunnar's essence.

Pain exploded through him, darkness flooding his mind with twisted visions. He fought to maintain focus, concentrating on what he knew to be true—Gunnar's willingness, the dwarf's purpose, the sacrifice's meaning. Through the Grímmark, he pushed that truth into the corrupted memories, forcing them to realign with reality.

"Remember who you are," he commanded, speaking to both Gunnar and the darkness itself. "Remember your purpose."

The cocoon began to unravel, threads of shadow retreating from his touch. Gunnar's essence grew brighter, drawing strength from Asvarr's certainty. The Grímmark spread its influence through the corruption, golden light flowing along the tendrils that had carried darkness, transforming them to their original purpose.

"This changes nothing," the voices insisted, though weaker now. *"The Root writhes against itself. The pattern cannot hold."*

"The pattern evolves," Asvarr countered, pressing his advantage as the darkness receded. "As does memory. As do I."

With a final surge of effort, he grabbed Gunnar's essence, pulling it free from the dissolving cocoon. The dwarf's memory-form solidified, features becoming distinct. His spectral eyes opened, recognition dawning.

"Warden," Gunnar's voice echoed strangely, yet remained unmistakably his. "You should not be here."

"The Root screams," Asvarr explained. "Your sacrifice is being corrupted."

Gunnar nodded, his form growing more substantial as the surrounding darkness retreated. "I feel it. The poison spreads from the oldest memories—the first breaking, when the Ashfather claimed the Tree."

"Can it be stopped?"

"You've already begun the process." Gunnar gestured to where the Grímmark's influence continued to push back corruption, restoring golden light to tainted streams. "But the Root contains more memory than any mortal mind can touch. The darkness will return unless..."

He hesitated, spectral features tightening with concern.

"Unless what?" Asvarr pressed.

"Unless you share your grief," Gunnar said softly. "The corruption feeds on isolation—the belief that sacrifice leads only to void. Your sorrow, freely given, would remind the Root that loss connects rather than divides."

Asvarr stared at the dwarf's ghost-like form, understanding sliding into place. The sapling writhed because it experienced Gunnar's sacrifice as abandonment rather than connection. The corruption exploited that misunderstanding, turning willing sacrifice into forced subjugation.

"How?" he asked simply.

"Remember," Gunnar replied. "Remember everyone you've lost. Every sacrifice that has shaped you. Offer those memories to the Root as bridges to be crossed."

The dwarf's form began to fade, merging once more with the golden stream. "Quickly, Warden. Your time in the memory-stream grows short."

Asvarr closed his eyes, focusing inward. Grief had always been his enemy—a weakness to be conquered through rage or numbed through mead. He had built walls around his losses, refusing to acknowledge the hollow spaces they left within him.

Now, he deliberately dismantled those walls.

The first memory came unbidden—his mother's face, firelight dancing across her features as she sang him to sleep. The song's words had long since faded, but her voice remained, rich and warm as mulled wine. Asvarr had buried this memory beneath layers of rage and mead, fearing the hollow ache it carried.

Now he offered it freely to the memory-stream.

The golden currents surged around him, absorbing the recollection. Where the memory touched corrupted streams, darkness recoiled, tendrils curling away like mist before sunlight. Encouraged, Asvarr delved deeper.

His father, teaching him to hold an axe with fingers still too small to span the haft. The pride in the man's eyes when Asvarr landed his first blow against the practice post. The emptiness of returning home to find his father's shield but never the man himself, lost to a raid no one survived to recount.

Each memory flowed from him into the golden stream, spreading outward to touch the darkness. The corruption fought back, feeding him visions of despair—his father fled, his mother singing to another child while he starved alone. Asvarr recognized these as lies, rejecting them with the stubborn certainty that had carried him through five bindings.

"Memory cannot be undone," he growled, pressing forward through the darkness. "Only forgotten or twisted."

He reached for deeper grief—the faces of his clan, burned into his memory as he'd found them after the Shattering. Men and women he'd grown alongside, children he'd taught to swim in the fjord's icy waters. Gone in an instant when the sky broke and the Root fell.

Their names poured from him, each syllable a link in a chain that bound him to the world even as it reminded him of all he'd lost. The golden streams brightened, memory feeding memory, truth reinforcing truth. The corruption withdrew further, its hold on Gunnar's essence weakening.

Still it wasn't enough. The darkness maintained its core strength, feeding on some grief Asvarr hadn't yet acknowledged.

"What do you hide even from yourself?" Gunnar's voice echoed, his essence glowing brighter as the corruption retreated. "What loss cuts too deep to face?"

Asvarr hesitated, then reached for the wound he'd sealed away most thoroughly—the memory he'd refused to examine even in his darkest moments.

It came in fragments: the raid gone wrong, outnumbered four to one. The retreat called, boats pushing away from shore. His axe rising and falling, blood-slick and heavy in his hands. The spear that should have taken his life deflected at the last instant by a shield thrust between him and death. Torfa, shield-maiden and friend, falling with a blade meant for him buried in her throat.

He'd left her body on that beach, carried away by comrades who wouldn't let him return for her. The rage that followed had consumed him for years, fueling his berserker fury. He'd blamed himself for her death, then buried that blame beneath bloodlust and battle-glory.

This grief he'd never shared—the knowledge that Torfa died because he'd been too slow, too blind to the danger until she paid the price for his mistake.

"I'm sorry," he whispered into the memory-stream. "I should have been faster. Should have seen the blade coming."

The memory flowed from him, raw and ragged. The golden streams pulsed with recognition—Torfa's face appearing briefly in the current, her features set in the fierce determination he remembered. For an instant, Asvarr thought he glimpsed her nod, acceptance in her spectral eyes.

Then the memory was gone, absorbed into the Root's consciousness.

The effect rippled outward explosively. Corrupted streams unraveled, darkness dispersing as golden light reclaimed its dominance. The cocoon surrounding Gunnar's essence dissolved completely, freeing the dwarf's memory-form.

"Well done, Warden," Gunnar's voice resonated with new strength. "The Root remembers itself."

Around them, the memory-chamber shuddered, realigning as corruption fled. The darkness retreated to the furthest reaches of the space, condensing into a humanoid shape that glared at Asvarr with hollow eyes.

"This changes nothing," the shadow-form hissed in the Ash-Priest's voice. "Memory may heal, but the pattern remains vulnerable. The Ashfather comes."

The shape imploded, vanishing into the memory-stream like smoke drawn into a chimney. Asvarr could sense the corruption's essence moving deeper into the Root, beyond his ability to follow.

"You've driven it back, not destroyed it," Gunnar warned, his form beginning to fade as his essence reintegrated with the Root. "The Root remembers its wounds now, but scars remain."

"Will it attack again?" Asvarr asked, feeling fatigue settle into his bones as the memory-work drained his strength.

"The darkness always returns," Gunnar replied, his voice already distant. "But the Root knows its true enemy now. It stands ready."

Gunnar's essence dissolved completely, rejoining the golden streams that flowed through the chamber. Asvarr felt the memory-space beginning to contract around him, pushing him back toward the entrance. His time grew short—the three hours the Ember-Singer had warned about must be nearly exhausted.

He turned toward the opening where he'd entered, now a brilliant slit of light in the chamber wall. Before he could reach it, a new current intercepted him—golden light swirling into a vaguely humanoid shape. Unlike Gunnar or the other memory-fragments he'd encountered, this presence felt ancient beyond measure, its edges blurring into the fabric of the chamber itself.

"Warden," it spoke, voice like wind through barley fields. "The Root acknowledges your sacrifice."

"I sacrificed nothing," Asvarr answered truthfully. "I shared what was already mine."

"The sharing is the sacrifice," the presence replied. "To open wounds long sealed requires courage similar to receiving new ones."

The golden form extended what might have been an arm, offering something that glowed with concentrated light. "Take this," it commanded. "The essence of what you've learned."

Asvarr reached out, accepting the offering. Light flowed into his palm, coalescing into a small object—a seed, translucent as amber, with intricate patterns shifting beneath its surface.

"Plant this in your heart," the presence instructed. "When the Ashfather comes, when choices narrow to void or submission, this will guide your hand."

The light-form dissolved, leaving Asvarr holding the seed as the chamber contracted around him. With no time to question, he pressed the seed against his chest, directly over his heart. It sank into his flesh without pain, a sensation of warmth spreading from the point of contact.

The memory-chamber collapsed, walls and ceiling rushing inward. Asvarr lunged for the exit, crossing the threshold as golden light enveloped him.

He stumbled from the sapling's interior, gasping as though surfacing from deep water. The forge-hall materialized around him—stone floor solid beneath his knees, the Ember-Singer's worried face swimming into focus. The circling forge-priests had ceased their chanting, watching with wide eyes as the sapling's convulsions stilled.

"You return," the Ember-Singer said, her weathered hand steadying his shoulder. "We feared you lost to the memory-stream."

Asvarr shook his head, clearing the last fragments of memory-vision from his sight. "The corruption retreats. Gunnar's essence is freed."

The Ember-Singer studied his face, seeing something that made her eyes widen. "You've changed, Warden."

Before he could ask her meaning, Thrim darted forward, pointing at the sapling with an excited cry. "Look! The bark heals itself!"

Asvarr turned to see the sapling's silver-gold trunk knitting closed, splits sealing as though they'd never existed. The branches that had twisted against each other now straightened, stretching upward with renewed purpose. Where broken limbs had fallen, fresh buds sprouted, unfurling into delicate golden leaves.

"The Root remembers its purpose," Asvarr said, rising unsteadily to his feet. His hand went reflexively to his chest, feeling the seed's warmth pulsing beneath his skin in time with his heartbeat.

The Ember-Singer's gaze followed the motion, her eyes narrowing. "What did you receive in the memory-stream?"

Asvarr hesitated, unsure how to explain. "A seed," he finally answered. "A... fragment of memory, distilled to its essence."

"The Root gives nothing without purpose." The elderly dwarf clasped her hands, metal rings clinking against each other. "What purpose did it name?"

"Guidance," Asvarr replied. "For when the Ashfather comes."

The forge-hall fell silent at the mention of that name. Even the sapling seemed to still, its leaves pausing mid-unfurl. The forge-priests exchanged uneasy glances, hands moving to form protective signs in the air.

"Then come he will," the Ember-Singer said grimly. "And sooner than we hoped."

She turned to the priests, voice hardening with command. "Double the wards on all entrances. Station sentinels at every tunnel junction. Nothing enters Svartálfr without challenge."

As the dwarves hurried to obey, Asvarr felt the seed pulse within his chest—a warning or encouragement, he couldn't tell which. He opened his mouth to question the Ember-Singer further, but a sudden commotion at the forge-hall's entrance interrupted him.

A dwarf guard stumbled in, blood streaming from a gash across his forehead. "Eastern gates breached," he gasped, collapsing to one knee. "The defenses shattered like glass."

Asvarr froze, disbelief coursing through him. "Impossible. I secured those gates myself, bound them to the sapling's power."

"No attack from without," the guard continued, his voice ragged with exhaustion. "Something... opened them from inside. A child's shape, but twisted. Wrong."

Cold dread pooled in Asvarr's stomach. He glanced at the Ember-Singer, seeing his own fear mirrored in her eyes.

"The Ashfather comes," she whispered.

The seed in Asvarr's chest flared with sudden heat, searing his Grímmark from within. Knowledge flooded through him as possibility this time, not memory, paths branching from this moment into futures both bright and dark.

***

The sapling trembled, responding to his alarm. Its branches twisted toward the forge-hall's entrance, leaves shivering as though in a wind only they could feel.

"How long until they reach us?" Asvarr demanded, drawing his sword. The blade had reformed since he'd lost it in the memory-stream, but changed again—its golden veins now pulsed with light that matched the seed's glow beneath his skin.

"Minutes," the guard answered. "No more. They move faster than—" His words cut off in a strangled gasp as he pitched forward, revealing a dart protruding from his back. Dark veins spread from the wound, corruption claiming another victim.

From the shadows behind the fallen guard stepped a figure that made Asvarr's blood run cold. Child-sized but wrong in every proportion, its limbs bent at impossible angles, skin the texture of fresh bark. Where a face should have been, only a vertical slit opened and closed like a wound breathing.

"The Warden stands by the sapling," it spoke, voice high and sweet despite the horror of its form. "Just as the master foresaw."

More shapes emerged from the tunnel entrance—twisted parodies of children, each bearing the same slitted face and bark-like skin. The forge-priests scrambled for weapons, forming a protective circle around the sapling.

"Get behind me," Asvarr told Thrim, pushing the dwarf child toward the relative safety of the priests' circle. To the Ember-Singer, he said, "We can't let them reach the sapling."

"They won't," she replied, drawing a crystal knife from her belt—twin to the one she'd used in Gunnar's sacrifice. "The dead protected the gates. The living will protect the heart."

The seed burning in Asvarr's chest supplied knowledge he hadn't possessed moments before. These weren't simply the Ash-Priest's minions, but vessels—empty forms animated by fragments of the same corruption he'd driven from the memory-stream. Their purpose wasn't destruction but replacement—to steal the sapling's position at the pattern's center.

"They want to plant something else," he realized aloud. "Something that serves the void."

"Then they must fail," the Ember-Singer said simply, readying her knife.

The twisted children attacked as one, moving with the skittering grace of insects. Asvarr met the first with his blade, severing a too-long arm that spurted black ichor instead of blood. The child-thing shrieked—a sound like bark scraping stone—but pressed forward, unconcerned with its wound.

All around the forge-hall, similar battles erupted. Dwarven axes flashed, cutting down the twisted forms only to have them rise again, pulled upright by the corruption that animated them. Conventional weapons slowed them, nothing more.

The Ember-Singer's crystal knife proved more effective, its blade flaring with blue light as she drove it into a child-form's chest. The creature convulsed, bark-skin cracking as the corruption within it burned away. But there were dozens more, and only one knife.

Asvarr fought his way toward the sapling, instinct drawing him to the anchor he'd bound. The child-forms seemed to anticipate his move, swarming thicker in his path. His sword cut a bloody swath, but for each creature he felled, two more took its place.

A high, sweet laugh echoed through the forge-hall—the same voice as the first child-form, but amplified a hundredfold. The sound vibrated in Asvarr's bones, sending spikes of pain through his skull.

"The Root screams," the voice sang. "Listen to its bark splitting, its branches breaking. Listen to its fear."

The sapling trembled violently, leaves falling like golden rain. Another convulsion shook it, bark cracking as internal corruption resumed its assault. Asvarr's connection through the Grímmark let him feel the sapling's distress—the memory-healing he'd performed unraveling under renewed attack.

"What have you done?" he demanded, grabbing the nearest child-form by its throat. The bark-skin felt warm and pulsing beneath his fingers, alive in a way that defied explanation.

The slitted face opened wider, revealing rows of wooden teeth. "Planted our own seeds," it giggled. "While you wandered memory-streams, we seeded the foundation stones. The corruption returns, stronger than before."

Asvarr flung the creature away, understanding crashing over him like ice water. The memory-stream journey had been a diversion—keeping him occupied while the real attack proceeded elsewhere. The child-forms were merely the visible manifestation of corruption that had already taken root throughout Svartálfr.

He fought toward the sapling with renewed desperation, sensing that their only hope lay in the anchor's power. Three forge-priests fell to his right, swarmed under by giggling child-forms. The Ember-Singer stood her ground before the sapling, crystal knife flashing as she dispatched attacker after attacker.

When Asvarr finally reached the sapling, he pressed his palm against its trembling trunk. The connection was immediate—Root to Warden, anchor to binding. Through it, he sensed the full extent of the corruption's spread. It flowed beneath the forge-hall, a network of darkness feeding on the very stone that supported them.

The seed in his chest burned hotter, knowledge crystallizing into certainty. There was only one way to save the anchor now.

"The sapling can't remain here," he told the Ember-Singer. "The foundation is poisoned."

Her eyes widened with understanding and grief. "To move it risks killing it. The Root needs stability, a place to grow deep."

"It needs survival more," Asvarr countered, feeling the seed's guidance pulse through him. "We must take it to higher stone—uncorrupted ground where it can establish new roots."

The Ember-Singer hesitated only momentarily before nodding. "The High Forge. Three levels up, built on the mountain's original stone." She glanced at the battling dwarves, her expression grim. "Few of us will make it."

Asvarr placed both hands on the sapling's trunk, reaching through the Grímmark to connect with the anchor's essence. "Root of worlds, bound by blood and oath, hear your Warden's call. Your foundation crumbles. Accept this journey to safer ground."

The sapling shuddered, then went completely still. For a heartbeat, Asvarr feared rejection—that the anchor would choose death over displacement. Then the trunk began to shrink, branches folding inward as the sapling compressed itself into a more portable form.

Within moments, what had been a twelve-foot sapling condensed into a seedling no larger than Asvarr's hand, its roots drawing up from the stone to twine around themselves. He cradled it carefully, feeling its life pulse against his palm.

"The path to the High Forge," he urged the Ember-Singer. "Quickly."

She barked orders in the dwarven tongue, gathering the surviving forge-priests around them. By unspoken agreement, they formed a protective circle, weapons facing outward as they began to move toward a narrow passage at the forge-hall's far end.

The child-forms howled in unison, recognizing their quarry's escape. They swarmed the dwarven circle, clawing and biting with inhuman strength. One leapt over the defenders, landing directly before Asvarr with slitted face stretched in a grotesque smile.

"The Root is defenseless now," it crooned. "Give us the seedling, Warden. End your struggles."

Asvarr's response was his blade through the creature's chest. It collapsed with a sound like breaking branches, black ichor pooling beneath its twitching form.

The seed burning in Asvarr's chest supplied new knowledge—these child-forms could regenerate from any wound save fire. He turned to the nearest forge-priest.

"Your forge-fire," he commanded. "We need it."

The dwarf reached into a pouch at his belt, producing a small metal cube inscribed with glowing runes. With a twist of his thick fingers, he activated the device. Blue flame erupted from its top, contained but intense.

"Forge-flame," the dwarf explained, holding it before him like a torch. "Burns without wood or oil."

The child-forms recoiled from the blue light, bark-skin cracking at its proximity. Their advance slowed, giving the dwarven circle room to maneuver toward the passage.

Asvarr led the way, cradling the seedling in one hand while his sword cleared their path. The Ember-Singer followed close behind, her crystal knife gleaming with the corruption of those she'd dispatched. With each step toward the passage, the fighting grew fiercer, child-forms throwing themselves at the defenders with suicidal abandon.

"They fear where we go," the Ember-Singer observed, ducking a scythe-like limb that swept toward her head. "The High Forge must remain uncorrupted."

"Then we make our stand there," Asvarr decided, feeling the seedling tremble against his palm. Whether from fear or anticipation, he couldn't tell.

They reached the passage entrance, a narrow tunnel that would force them to proceed in single file. Asvarr turned to the Ember-Singer, making a swift decision.

"Take the seedling," he said, pressing it into her weathered hands. "Get it to the High Forge. I'll hold them here."

She accepted the tiny sapling, cradling it with the same care she might show a newborn. "You stand alone against their horde."

"The Root stands with me," Asvarr replied, feeling the seed in his chest pulse with confirmation. "Go. Quickly."

As the dwarves disappeared into the tunnel, Asvarr turned to face the advancing child-forms. They moved more cautiously now, sensing the change in their prey's demeanor. The seed's heat spread throughout his body, power flowing along the pathways of his expanded Grímmark.

He raised his sword, the blade igniting with golden fire that matched the light now pouring from his eyes and the rune-patterns across his skin.

"Come then," he invited the twisted horde. "Let's see if the Root remembers how to fight."

CHAPTER 29

REBIRTH AT THE RUIN ALTAR

B lood and soot streaked Asvarr's face as he staggered up the final staircase toward the High Forge. Echoes from below told him the child-forms still pursued—their chittering voices bouncing off the stone walls, high-pitched and gleeful. His sword arm hung limp, a deep gash across his shoulder leaking warmth down his back. The blade itself remained intact, golden veins pulsing with diminished light as his strength waned.

He had held them at the forge-hall entrance long enough for the Ember-Singer to escape with the seedling. Then, when the horde threatened to overwhelm him, he had retreated upward, collapsing tunnels behind him as he went. The stone-singing power granted by the seed in his chest had proven useful for more than healing—it could unmake as well as restore.

The stairway opened onto a vast chamber carved from the mountain's peak. Unlike the workmanlike forge-hall below, the High Forge gleamed with ancient grandeur—ceiling lost in shadows, walls inlaid with precious metals that caught the light of massive forge-pits burning with blue flame. The air tasted of metal and mountain wind, cold and clean compared to the corruption-tainted atmosphere below.

The Ember-Singer stood at the chamber's center, surrounded by the surviving forge-priests—fewer than a dozen remained of the thirty who had guarded the sapling. They formed a circle around a stone altar, weathered and cracked with age. Atop it sat the seedling, now slightly larger than when Asvarr had last seen it, tiny gold-silver leaves unfurling in the mountain air.

"Warden," the Ember-Singer called, relief washing over her weathered features. "We feared you lost."

Asvarr limped toward the altar, leaving bloody footprints on smooth stone. "They follow still. I've bought minutes, nothing more."

The elderly dwarf nodded grimly, turning to the forge-priests. "Seal the entry-way behind him. Use the fire-channels."

Two priests hurried to obey, manipulating complex mechanisms set into the wall beside the staircase. Metal plates slid into place, blocking the entrance. Blue flame erupted from channels carved around the doorframe, forming a barrier that would incinerate anything attempting to pass through.

"That will hold them a while," the Ember-Singer said. "Long enough to complete what we've begun."

Only now did Asvarr notice how the altar had been prepared. Ancient runes covered its surface, freshly filled with gold dust that glowed with inner fire. The stone itself had been chiseled to form a shallow basin around the seedling, its weathered cracks sealed with some metallic substance that pulsed like a heartbeat.

"A binding altar," he realized, recognition flowing from the seed in his chest. "You're anchoring it to this place."

"The highest point in Svartálfr, nearest the sky, furthest from corruption," she confirmed. "This altar predates our people in these mountains. The ancestors found it here, recognized its purpose."

Asvarr studied the ancient stone more carefully. Its shape reminded him of patterns he'd glimpsed in the memory-stream—a vessel meant to contain transformation, to focus rebirth. The runes belonged to no language he knew, yet their meaning resonated with his expanded senses: stability, protection, growth.

"The ruin altar," he murmured. "A place of endings and beginnings."

The Ember-Singer's eyes widened. "You know its name?"

Before Asvarr could answer, a thunderous boom shook the chamber. The sealed entrance vibrated, metal plates glowing red-hot as something massive slammed against them from the other side. The blue flame barrier flickered, weakening under the assault.

"They've broken through the lower defenses faster than I thought," Asvarr said, raising his sword despite the pain lancing through his shoulder. "We need to complete the binding."

The Ember-Singer nodded, turning to the altar. "The seedling has already begun to root itself in the altar's stone. The runes draw power from the mountain itself, feeding the anchor's growth." She gestured to the forge-priests, who took positions around the circle, chanting in the ancient dwarven tongue. "But it needs a final catalyst—the essence that connects it to its Warden."

The seed in Asvarr's chest pulsed with understanding. He approached the altar, standing opposite the Ember-Singer with the seedling between them. Its tiny trunk had already thickened, roots visibly burrowing into microscopic cracks in the stone. Golden sap oozed from various points along its bark, filling the basin around it.

Another thunderous impact rocked the chamber. One of the metal plates cracked, a sliver of darkness seeping through like black water.

"Your blood, freely given," the Ember-Singer instructed. "The fifth anchor must recognize its Warden in this new place."

Asvarr drew his knife and sliced across his palm without hesitation. Blood welled up, dark against his skin. He held his hand over the seedling, allowing crimson drops to fall upon its silver-gold leaves. Where blood touched sap, the two fluids spiraled together, forming patterns that matched the expanded Grímmark across his chest.

The seedling shuddered, then grew visibly taller, adding inches even as Asvarr watched. Its trunk thickened, branches extending toward the chamber's distant ceiling. The roots drove deeper into the altar stone, cracking it along ancient seams that had awaited this very purpose.

"The altar stone is breaking," a priest cried in alarm.

"No," the Ember-Singer corrected, wonder in her voice. "It's opening."

The stone split further, each crack filling with golden sap that hardened into amber veins. What had appeared to be damage revealed itself as deliberate design—the altar contained internal chambers that now filled with life, nurturing the sapling's expanding root system.

A third impact hit the sealed entrance, this one accompanied by an inhuman shriek that made Asvarr's teeth vibrate in his skull. The metal plates bulged inward, blue flame sputtering as the barrier weakened.

"Something larger comes," he warned, images of the Ash-Priest and his master flashing through his mind. "Something beyond the child-forms."

The Ember-Singer looked grim. "We must complete the binding before they breach the chamber. The final step requires all of us—a circle of witnesses to anchor memory to place."

The surviving forge-priests formed a tight ring around the altar, linking hands. The Ember-Singer beckoned Asvarr to join them, taking his bloodied hand in her weathered one. The sapling—for it had grown beyond seedling now—pulsed with golden light that matched the rhythm of Asvarr's heartbeat.

"Root of worlds, anchor of pattern," the Ember-Singer began, her voice carrying ritual weight that made the chamber's air thicken. "We bind you to this mountain stone, this ruin altar. Accept our witness, our protection, our service."

The forge-priests took up the chant, their deep voices resonating with the mountain itself. Asvarr felt the seed in his chest respond, heat spreading outward through the pathways of his expanded Grímmark. Words formed on his tongue, drawn from knowledge beyond his own experience.

"I am your Warden, bound through blood and oath," he declared. "From ash you rose, through ruin you persisted. In rebirth you find your strength."

Golden light erupted from the sapling, illuminating the entire chamber. Its branches spread wider, leaves multiplying until they formed a canopy above the altar. Where the light touched stone, metal veins appeared—a network of power radiating outward through the mountain itself.

Another deafening impact hit the entrance, metal plates finally giving way. Through the breach poured a tide of shadow—darker and more substantial than the child-forms, moving with deliberate intelligence. At its forefront stalked a figure that made Asvarr's blood run cold.

The Ash-Priest had changed since their last encounter. Its bark-skin had hardened into armor-like plates, branch-limbs twisted into weapons sharper than steel. The vertical slit that served as its face had widened, revealing rows of teeth formed from splinters. Behind it came the child-forms, crawling over each other in their eagerness to enter.

"The sapling thrives," the Ash-Priest observed, its voice grating like branches scraping stone. "How predictable you remain, Warden. Always seeking higher ground, as though elevation might save you from what rises from below."

"The binding is complete," Asvarr replied, stepping away from the altar to place himself between the enemy and the sapling. "This anchor belongs to the Root now, beyond your corruption."

The Ash-Priest's laugh chilled the air. "Nothing stands beyond corruption. The void touches all eventually." It gestured to the floor beneath their feet. "Even now, our tendrils reach through the mountain's roots. Your elevation merely delayed the inevitable."

A forge-priest screamed as the stone beneath him cracked, black ichor seeping upward. The corruption had followed them even here, working through the mountain's natural fissures to reach its peak.

The Ember-Singer's face hardened with determination. "The binding altar holds its own power, forgotten by your master. It remembers a time before the Ashfather's claiming."

Her words sparked recognition in Asvarr's mind. The seed's knowledge flowed through him, revealing the altar's true purpose—a nexus of renewal. The ancients had built it as a counterbalance to corruption, a place where endings could become beginnings.

"Flame of renewal," he called, raising his sword. The blade ignited with golden fire, matching the light now pouring from his eyes and the expanded Grímmark across his skin. "The Root remembers what the Ashfather forgot."

The Ash-Priest hesitated, something like uncertainty crossing its features. Then it gathered itself, branch-limbs extending into scythe-like blades. "Memory fades. All returns to void."

It lunged forward with unnatural speed, blade-limbs slashing toward Asvarr's throat. He parried with his sword, golden fire meeting shadow with a sound like thunder. The impact drove him back a step, pain flaring through his wounded shoulder.

Around them, forge-priests engaged the child-forms with crystal knives and forge-hammers. Blue flame erupted from channels in the floor, creating barriers that the smaller creatures couldn't cross. But the corruption continued to seep upward through cracks, eating away at the chamber's foundations.

"The altar weakens," the Ember-Singer warned, hurrying to reinforce the runes with fresh gold dust. "Its power divides between anchoring the sapling and fighting the corruption."

Asvarr ducked another slash from the Ash-Priest, countering with a thrust that scored its bark-armor. Black ichor welled from the wound, hissing where it touched stone. He fought with cold precision, bereft of the berserker rage that had once driven him. Each movement calculated, each breath measured.

The seed in his chest burned hotter, knowledge crystallizing into certainty. The altar possessed power beyond mere anchoring—it could channel the Root's essence throughout the mountain, reclaiming corrupted stone. But it needed direction, purpose beyond mechanical binding.

It needed a Warden's will.

"Hold the perimeter," he called to the Ember-Singer. "I must commune with the altar."

She nodded, understanding in her ancient eyes. "We'll buy you time."

Asvarr disengaged from the Ash-Priest with a sweeping slash that forced the creature back. Before it could recover, he dashed toward the altar, sheathing his sword as he ran. The sapling had grown further during the battle, its trunk now thick as his thigh, branches forming a protective dome over the altar stone.

He placed both hands on the altar's edge, feeling the ancient power humming beneath his palms. The stone itself retained memory older than the mountain—knowledge of a time when the pattern flowed uncorrupted through all realms. That memory could reawaken, if properly guided.

"I am the Warden of Five," he murmured, focusing his will through the expanded Grímmark. "By blood and oath, I call upon the altar's purpose—rebirth through ruin, renewal through ending."

The seed in his chest ignited, power flowing outward through his arms into the altar stone. The runes flared brighter, their gold dust melting and running into the cracks like molten sunlight. The sapling shuddered, then extended new roots that broke through the altar's stone, reaching toward the chamber floor.

Where those roots touched, corruption receded. Black ichor dried and crumbled to dust, revealing clean stone beneath. The process spread outward in an expanding circle, reclaiming the High Forge's floor inch by inch.

The Ash-Priest screamed in rage and pain, as though the purification directly wounded its essence. It charged toward the altar, branch-limbs raised to strike.

"Stop him!" the Ember-Singer commanded, and forge-priests moved to intercept, forming a wall of flesh and steel between the creature and Asvarr.

The Ash-Priest carved through them with terrible efficiency, leaving broken bodies in its wake. But their sacrifice bought precious seconds as the altar's purification continued to spread.

Asvarr poured more of himself into the connection, drawing on memories from the Root itself. The ruin altar responded, ancient machinery awakening within its stone. The entire chamber began to hum with power that had slept for ages, waiting for this moment.

The floor split open along geometric lines, revealing channels carved through the mountain's heart. Golden light flooded these channels, carrying purification deeper into Svartálfr. The corruption's advance slowed, then halted as two primal forces met in opposition.

"Warden!" The Ember-Singer's warning came too late.

The Ash-Priest broke through the final defenders, reaching the altar with blade-limbs raised. Asvarr couldn't release the connection to defend himself—interrupting the altar's awakening now would doom them all.

A blade-limb plunged toward his unprotected back.

In that moment, the sapling moved. A branch whipped downward with impossible speed, intercepting the blade before it could reach Asvarr. Where wood met wood, golden sap sprayed outward, burning the Ash-Priest's bark-armor like acid.

The creature recoiled, sizzling holes spreading across its form. The sapling pressed its advantage, more branches lashing out to entangle the priest's limbs. Within seconds, it was completely ensnared, struggling against living bonds that grew tighter with each movement.

"Impossible," the Ash-Priest hissed, its voice losing the harmonics that had given it power. "The sapling has no will of its own."

"The anchor remembers now," Asvarr replied, maintaining his connection to the altar as he turned to face the captured creature. "It remembers what it chose to forget—that trees defend themselves."

The Ash-Priest thrashed against its bonds, bark cracking as the sapling's grip tightened. "My master comes," it wheezed. "This mountain will burn. This realm will fall. All returns to void."

"Perhaps," Asvarr acknowledged. "But not today. Today, the Root reclaims its own."

The sapling's branches squeezed tighter, golden sap flowing down to coat the Ash-Priest's form completely. Where the sap touched, corruption bubbled away, revealing glimpses of what lay beneath—not wood or bark, but flesh. Human flesh.

Understanding dawned in Asvarr's mind. The Ash-Priest had once been a person, consumed and reshaped by corruption. The sap wasn't destroying it, but unmaking the corruption's work, revealing the original being beneath.

The process accelerated, corruption sloughing away in black sheets that dissolved to nothing on the chamber floor. The branch-limbs receded, revealing arms; the bark-armor fell away, exposing a torso covered in ritual scars. Finally, the vertical slit collapsed, reforming into a human face—eyes closed, features slack with unconsciousness.

A man lay at the altar's foot, naked and vulnerable, wholly human again.

The child-forms wailed in unison, their connection to their master suddenly severed. Without direction, they scattered, some fleeing back through the breach, others simply collapsing into piles of inert bark.

The Ember-Singer approached cautiously, nudging the unconscious man with her foot. "The priest returns to his original form," she murmured. "I didn't think such healing possible."

"The altar remembers creation, not just binding," Asvarr replied, knowledge flowing through him from the seed and the altar's ancient memory. "It unmade what corruption had made."

Around them, the chamber continued to transform. Where corruption had seeped through cracks, golden light now flowed, spreading purification throughout the mountain. The sapling had become a young tree, its canopy brushing the chamber's ceiling, roots visibly extending through the altar stone and down into revealed channels.

Asvarr felt the connection shifting. The fifth anchor had bound fully to this place, drawing power from the mountain itself while extending its influence throughout Svartálfr. His role as conduit was ending—the rebirth had begun.

He withdrew his hands from the altar, physical contact no longer necessary. The expanded Grímmark across his chest settled into a steady pulse, synchronized with the tree's swaying branches.

"What happens now?" the Ember-Singer asked, looking from the tree to the unconscious man to the purification spreading through her realm.

Asvarr felt the seed's guidance pulse within his chest, granting clarity about what must come next. His work in Svartálfr was complete—the fifth anchor secured, the immediate threat neutralized. But greater dangers approached.

"The Ashfather will learn what happened here," he said, wiping blood from his sword as he resheathed it. "He'll seek other ways to corrupt the anchors I've bound."

"And you?" The elderly dwarf studied him with knowing eyes.

Asvarr looked up at the sapling—no, the young tree—that represented the completion of his primary quest. Five anchors bound, the pattern beginning to stabilize. Yet the seed's knowledge told him this was merely preparation for what lay ahead.

"I must find the other Wardens," he decided, certainty settling in his bones. "The one who bears the Jordmark, and her fellows. Together we might stand against what comes."

The Ember-Singer nodded slowly. "The tree speaks to you, doesn't it? Through your mark."

"It shows me possibilities," Asvarr corrected. "Paths that might be walked, choices that might be made." He gestured to the transformed chamber around them. "This was one such path—rebirth at the ruin altar, turning ending to beginning."

"And your path leads away from Svartálfr?"

"For now." He looked toward the chamber's far wall, where high windows opened to the sky beyond. "The tree stands secure, anchored to the mountain's heart. My mark calls me elsewhere."

As if in confirmation, the expanded Grímmark pulsed more strongly, sending a pleasant warmth along his left side—eastward, toward realms beyond the mountain. The seed's knowledge translated this sensation: a Warden awaited, bearing the mark of earth, in need of guidance as he had received.

The decision crystallized. With the fifth binding complete and the anchor secure, his duty called him onward—to find those who shared his burden, to prepare for the greater conflict that loomed on the horizon.

The Ember-Singer surveyed Asvarr, her weathered face composed yet troubled. "You felt the mark's pull before. What makes this summons different?"

"Completion." Asvarr touched the expanded Grímmark through his torn tunic. "Five anchors bound, five tokens gathered. The pattern solidifies, but remains vulnerable until all Wardens unite."

The elderly dwarf nodded slowly, fingering the metal rings that adorned her fingers. "Our ancestors spoke of a gathering at the end of cycles. Five Wardens bringing five powers to a convergence point."

Dawn light streamed through the high windows, casting the chamber in gold and amber hues. The unconscious man—formerly the Ash-Priest—groaned softly as two forge-priests bound his wrists with iron shackles. The young tree's branches swayed without wind, leaves rustling with a music only Asvarr could fully interpret.

"You'll need provisions." The Ember-Singer turned from contemplation to practicality. "And that wound requires proper treatment before you journey eastward."

Asvarr rolled his injured shoulder, wincing at the flare of pain. "There's no time. The Jordmark-bearer faces her own trials, unprepared for what hunts her."

"And you'll help her by collapsing on the mountainside?" The Ember-Singer snorted. "Even Wardens require food and healing."

Before Asvarr could argue further, a forge-priest appeared at the chamber entrance, breathing hard from rapid ascent. "Honored Singer! Strangers approach the eastern path—two humans and a sky-child!"

The Ember-Singer's eyes widened. "Armed?"

"The woman carries a curved blade etched with green-gold runes. The man bears twin metal rods that change length at his command."

Asvarr straightened, ignoring the pain shooting through his shoulder. The seed in his chest pulsed with recognition, knowledge flowing into his mind. "The Jordmark-bearer comes to us."

"How?" The Ember-Singer's face creased with suspicion. "Our mountain paths remain secret from outsiders."

"The pattern guides her, as it guided me." Asvarr strode toward the entrance, renewed purpose overshadowing his fatigue. "Let me greet them."

The Ember-Singer hesitated, then nodded to the forge-priest. "Escort the Warden to the Sunlight Gate. Keep weapons ready, but hidden."

The Sunlight Gate lived up to its name—a natural archway in the mountain's eastern face where the dawn illuminated a narrow stone ledge. Asvarr stood within its shadow, watching three figures navigate the treacherous path that wound up the mountainside.

The woman led, moving with fluid confidence despite the precipitous drop beside her. Dark hair braided with metal beads framed a face weathered by travel but still youthful. The Jordmark gleamed on her forehead—a verdant rune that pulsed with earth-energy. She wore leather armor stained with travel dust and what looked like dried blood, a curved blade hanging at her hip.

The man followed, tall and thin with silver-white hair that caught the morning light. Twin metal rods hung crossed at his back, and his shoulders bore the shimmering Skymark—twin spiral runes that occasionally sent sparks into the air. He appeared more wary than his companion, eyes constantly scanning the mountainside for threats.

Behind them floated—rather than walked—a small figure that defied easy description. Neither human nor animal, it resembled a child composed of clouds and lightning, its lower body dissipating into mist. Silver eyes dominated its featureless face, and when those eyes found Asvarr, recognition flashed in their depths.

"Warden of Five," the cloud-child called, voice like distant thunder. "We feel your binding's completion."

The woman's head snapped up, her hand instinctively moving to her blade. When she spotted Asvarr in the gate's shadow, tension visibly flowed from her shoulders. "Flame-Bearer. We've searched for you across three realms."

"Brynja Earth-Healer," Asvarr responded, the name flowing from knowledge granted by the seed. "The pattern told me you would come, though I expected to journey to you."

She climbed the final stretch of path and stepped through the Sunlight Gate, her companions close behind. Now within arm's reach, Asvarr could see exhaustion etched in the lines around her eyes and mouth. Her leather armor bore burn marks and tears that spoke of recent battles.

"We bring warning," she said without preamble. "The Ashfather moves openly now. His forces attack the anchors you've bound, seeking to corrupt or destroy them."

Asvarr's stomach tightened. "The fifth anchor stands secure, but the others—"

"Hold, so far," the silver-haired man interrupted. He offered a short bow. "Leif World-Walker, bearer of the Skymark. We've monitored the anchors through the paths between realms. The Ashfather tests their defenses but hasn't breached them yet."

The cloud-child drifted forward, silvery mist curling around Asvarr's ankles. "I am Svala Storm-Speaker," it—she—announced. "The skies show disturbance patterns. The Ashfather prepares something beyond simple corruption."

Asvarr nodded to each in turn, feeling the expanded Grímmark respond to their presence. Three Wardens together—only one remained unfound. The seed's warmth spread through his chest, confirming the rightness of this gathering.

"Come," he said, gesturing into the mountain. "The dwarves offer shelter, and we have much to discuss."

The forge-priests who had accompanied Asvarr maintained a respectful distance, their initial wariness giving way to awe as they recognized fellow Wardens. One hurried ahead to inform the Ember-Singer of their guests.

As they followed the winding passage back into the mountain's heart, Brynja fell into step beside Asvarr. "You've changed since the visions showed you to me," she observed. "The mark has spread."

"Five bindings change a man." Asvarr touched his chest, where the Grímmark pulsed beneath his skin. "As your own mark changes you."

***

She smiled thinly. "My forehead bears a single rune, while yours covers half your body. You've walked further down this path than any of us."

The passage opened into a smaller chamber adjacent to the High Forge—a meeting room with a stone table and low benches. The Ember-Singer waited with a selection of food and drink arranged before her.

"The mountain welcomes the marked ones," she said formally, offering a shallow bow to the newcomers. "Share bread and mead while we speak of what comes."

They seated themselves around the table, the cloud-child Svala hovering rather than sitting. The simple meal consisted of dense mountain bread, smoked meat, and strong dwarven mead. Asvarr hadn't realized his hunger until the food lay before him. He tore into a chunk of bread while Brynja explained their journey.

"The Jordmark guided me after my binding," she said, running a finger over the verdant rune on her forehead. "I found Leif battling corruption-born creatures in a forest glade. Together we located Svala in the storm-peaks."

"The fifth Warden remains unfound," Leif added, sipping cautiously at the potent mead. "Death-Walker, bearer of the Deathmark. Our visions show only shadows where that one should be."

The Ember-Singer leaned forward, rings glinting in the chamber's lamplight. "Four Wardens together for the first time in nine cycles. The pattern strengthens with your convergence."

"Yet the Ashfather grows stronger too," Svala's misty form rippled with agitation. "The sky-paths show his power gathering like storm clouds before a deluge."

"What does he plan?" Asvarr asked, wiping mead from his beard. "The fifth anchor stands secure, purified through the ruin altar. If the others remain uncorrupted—"

"Corruption isn't his only weapon," Brynja interrupted, her voice tight with urgency. "We found evidence in an ancient archive—records from previous breakings. When corruption fails, the Ashfather turns to direct assault."

Leif nodded grimly. "He gathers an army at the void-edges. Creatures that serve the unmaking. When they strike, they'll target all five anchors simultaneously."

Cold dread pooled in Asvarr's stomach. The seed in his chest pulsed with warning, confirming their words. The fifth anchor might stand secure for now, but no single point could withstand a coordinated attack without its Warden present.

"We must protect what we've bound," he said, setting down his drink. "Return to each anchor point and strengthen its defenses."

Brynja shook her head. "Scattered, we're vulnerable. The pattern requires unity, all five Wardens at the convergence point when the Ashfather strikes."

"Yet the fifth Warden remains unfound." The Ember-Singer's weathered fingers traced patterns on the stone table. "Your circle stands incomplete."

Asvarr closed his eyes, focusing on the seed's guidance. Images flowed through his mind—five points of light connected by golden threads, forming a pattern that strengthened with each connection. One point flickered, uncertain yet drawing nearer.

"Death-Walker approaches," he murmured, opening his eyes. "The mark pulls them toward the pattern's center."

"The center?" Leif's brow furrowed. "We've found no reference to a central anchor point."

"Because it doesn't exist yet." The words came from Asvarr's mouth though the knowledge flowed from the seed. "The five anchors we've bound are fragments of a greater whole. When all five Wardens stand together at the convergence point, a sixth anchor will manifest—the heart of the pattern itself."

Silence fell over the table as the others absorbed this revelation. The Ember-Singer stared at Asvarr with newfound respect, perhaps understanding that he now spoke with knowledge beyond his own experience.

"Where is this convergence point?" Brynja finally asked.

Asvarr felt the seed pulse, directing his attention to the stone table before them. With his knife, he carved five points forming a star pattern, then added a sixth at the center. "Here," he said, tapping the central mark. "Where the first root fell during the Shattering. Where my journey began."

"Midgard," Svala whispered, silver eyes wide. "The forest clearing where the sky broke."

"My clan's lands," Asvarr confirmed, memories of that terrible day flooding back. "The heart of the breaking now becomes the heart of restoration."

Leif studied the carved pattern with a tactician's eye. "If we journey there together, we leave the anchors we've bound undefended."

"They must protect themselves for a time," Asvarr replied, remembering how the sapling had defended him against the Ash-Priest. "Each binding transforms the anchor, grants it awareness. They'll resist corruption long enough for us to complete the pattern."

"And if the Ashfather attacks before we reach the convergence point?" Brynja challenged. "Before the fifth Warden joins us?"

The seed pulsed with certainty, knowledge flowing through Asvarr like a current. "The Ashfather won't strike until all five Wardens gather. He fears the unified pattern more than anything—he'll try to corrupt or kill one of us before we converge."

"Then we protect each other," Svala declared, her misty form brightening with determination. "Four shields around a single flame until the fifth arrives."

The Ember-Singer rose from her seat, the movement drawing all eyes. "While you plan, the day passes. The mountainsinger who healed the Warden's wound reports he may travel safely now."

Asvarr touched his shoulder, surprised to find the pain gone. In the urgency of meeting the other Wardens, he'd forgotten his injury entirely. The mountain dwarves had worked their healing craft while he focused elsewhere.

"We leave at dawn," he decided, looking to each of his fellow Wardens for confirmation. "The path to Midgard follows the sunrise. With the binding completed here, nothing holds us to Svartálfr."

The others nodded agreement, though Brynja's mouth tightened with concern. "Long road lies between here and your homeland, Flame-Bearer. The Ashfather's servants watch the realm-paths."

"Let them watch," Asvarr replied, feeling the certainty of his path for the first time since accepting the Grímmark. "Four Wardens together present a challenge even the Ashfather's hunters will hesitate to engage."

The Ember-Singer touched the knotwork patterns in her beard. "Our loremasters will scour the ancient texts for anything that might aid you. The mountain remembers secrets from the first breaking that may prove useful at the convergence."

As the others discussed practical matters of supplies and routes, Asvarr stepped away from the table and approached a narrow window carved into the chamber's outer wall. Through it, he could see the eastern horizon stretching beyond the mountain range. Somewhere out there, the fifth Warden moved toward them, knowingly or unknowingly drawn by the same pattern that had guided him through five bindings.

And somewhere, the Ashfather watched and waited, planning his final assault against the pattern's restoration.

The seed in Asvarr's chest warmed with purpose. For the first time since waking among the ashes of his village, he glimpsed the full scope of his journey, completing a cycle of renewal that spanned nine previous breakings. The Ashfather had manipulated those cycles, turning restoration into control. This time, the pattern would fulfill its original purpose.

Asvarr touched the expanded Grímmark, feeling each of the five bindings that had transformed him from berserker to Warden. Rage surrendered for clarity. Memory given for connection. Identity dissolved into fluidity. Certainty exchanged for acceptance. Free will offered for harmony.

Each sacrifice had prepared him for what came next—the convergence that would either restore the pattern to its original balance or surrender all realms to void.

"Warden." The Ember-Singer had approached silently, her voice pitched for his ears alone. "There's something else you should know before you depart."

She gestured toward a side passage. "The former Ash-Priest woke during your meeting. He remembers his name."

Asvarr followed her through winding corridors to a small chamber guarded by two forge-priests. Inside, the man sat on a stone bench, iron shackles still binding his wrists. Without corruption warping his form, he appeared ordinary—middle-aged, with graying hair and hollow cheeks. Only his eyes suggested his former nature, holding shadows that shifted when he moved.

"Warden," he acknowledged, voice hoarse but human. "You unmade what the master made of me."

"What do you remember?" Asvarr asked, studying the man who had nearly destroyed the fifth anchor.

"Fragments only." The former priest stared at his hands as though seeing them for the first time. "My name was Halvard. I served in a temple dedicated to the Tree before the breaking. When the sky shattered, something entered me through the wounds in reality—something ancient that wore me like a garment."

"The Ashfather's corruption," the Ember-Singer murmured.

Halvard nodded slowly. "He promised knowledge beyond mortal understanding. I accepted willingly, never recognizing the price."

"And now?" Asvarr pressed. "What remains of that corruption within you?"

"Echoes only." Halvard met Asvarr's gaze directly. "But those echoes whisper still. They tell me the Ashfather prepares his final move. When the fifth Warden joins your circle, he will strike with everything he commands."

"Why tell me this?" Asvarr's hand drifted to his sword hilt, suspicious of lingering deception.

A bleak smile crossed Halvard's face. "Because I remember serving the Tree once. Because the Root's sap burned away enough corruption for me to see what I became." His shackled hands clenched into fists. "And because I know where the Death-Walker hides."

The Ember-Singer drew in a sharp breath. "You've seen the fifth Warden?"

"The Ashfather sought all five marks from the beginning," Halvard explained. "Four he found and tracked. The fifth eluded him until recently."

Asvarr leaned forward, urgency quickening his pulse. "Where?"

"The bone-forest at the edge of Niflheim. A place where death and life blur together." Halvard's voice dropped to a whisper. "She walks the boundary, half in shadow, half in light. The Deathmark allows her passage where others would be consumed."

"She?" The Ember-Singer exchanged a glance with Asvarr.

"Yara Death-Walker. Last of her bloodline." Halvard slumped back against the wall, seeming exhausted by the information he had shared. "The Ashfather sends hunters even now. If they reach her before you do..."

He left the thought unfinished, but Asvarr understood the implications. Without all five Wardens, the convergence would fail. The pattern would remain vulnerable to the Ashfather's final assault.

Asvarr nodded grimly to the Ember-Singer. "Our departure can't wait until dawn. We leave now, heading north toward Niflheim before turning eastward to Midgard."

"I'll inform the others," she agreed, already moving toward the door.

Asvarr turned back to Halvard, studying the man who had been his enemy hours before. "If you've lied to me—"

"I've done enough serving darkness," Halvard interrupted. "Kill me if you must, but find the Death-Walker first."

The former priest's eyes held no deception Asvarr could detect. The seed in his chest pulsed with confirmation—the information aligned with the pattern's guidance.

Four Wardens gathered, one still to find. The convergence point awaiting their arrival. The Ashfather preparing his final assault.

The next phase of his journey crystallized with sudden clarity. No longer a lone Warden binding scattered anchors, but part of something greater—five Wardens united to restore what nine cycles of breaking had distorted.

Asvarr left the chamber without another word, purpose driving him forward. The gathering had begun.

CHAPTER 30

THE SKY CRACKS AGAIN

Frost crunched beneath Asvarr's boots as he crested the ridge overlooking the bone-forest. Four days of hard travel had brought the Wardens to the border between Niflheim and the void-lands, where perpetual twilight cast everything in shades of silver and gray. The trees below deserved their grim name—pale trunks twisted into humanoid shapes, branches like outstretched arms ending in finger-like twigs, roots that coiled above ground like exposed ribs.

The seed in Asvarr's chest pulsed with recognition. Somewhere in that eldritch forest walked the fifth Warden.

"Death-realm trees," Brynja muttered beside him, her breath clouding the frigid air. The Jordmark on her forehead glowed with sullen green light, responding to the unnatural flora below. "They feed on the boundary between living and dead."

"Yara walks among them," Asvarr replied, hand pressed to his expanded Grímmark. "The seed guides me toward the eastern grove."

Leif approached from behind, twin metal rods strapped across his back gleaming in the strange half-light. The Skymark on his shoulders threw occasional sparks that dissipated in the cold. "Svala's returned from scouting. The Ashfather's hunters approach from the north—six void-walkers with hounds."

Asvarr's grip tightened on his sword hilt. "How much time?"

"Hours at most." Leif's expression darkened. "They move faster than natural creatures should."

Svala drifted over the ridge, her misty form barely visible against the twilight sky. "The storm-signs show disruption patterns," she reported, silver eyes narrowed. "The Ashfather himself walks the void-paths, watching, waiting."

Cold dread settled in Asvarr's stomach. With each passing day, the enemy grew bolder, his forces pressing closer. If they failed to reach Yara before the hunters...

"We split up," Asvarr decided, drawing his transformed sword. Golden light flowed along the blade's runes, illuminating their position. "Brynja with me toward the eastern grove. Leif and Svala circle south to cut off the hunters if they approach."

Brynja nodded, unsheathing her curved blade. Green-gold energy flickered along its edge, resonating with her Jordmark. "Four Wardens divided weakens us."

"Four Wardens hunting separately covers more ground," Asvarr countered. "If we find Yara, we'll signal with the Horn of Binding."

Leif and Svala exchanged glances, then nodded agreement. The cloud-child drifted closer, her misty lower body curling around Asvarr's ankles like cool smoke.

"Be wary, Flame-Bearer," she whispered, voice crackling like distant thunder. "The bone-forest distorts perception. Trust your mark more than your eyes."

With that warning, they separated—Leif and Svala gliding down the western slope while Asvarr and Brynja began the treacherous descent toward the eastern grove. The ridge offered no clear path, forcing them to pick their way over frost-slick rocks and patches of treacherous black ice.

"The former priest believed his information," Brynja said after several minutes of careful climbing. Her sure-footed movements reminded Asvarr of mountain goats he'd seen as a child—deliberate, precise, efficient. "Whether the Ashfather allowed him to know truth or fed him lies remains unclear."

"The seed confirms Halvard's words," Asvarr replied, testing his weight on a narrow ledge before committing to it. "Yara walks these woods."

Brynja made a noncommittal sound, her eyes fixed on the bone-forest ahead. "I've bound only one anchor, while you've bound five. The Jordmark shows me fragments—pieces of a larger pattern. You see more clearly."

The observation struck Asvarr as significant. Each Warden perceived different-ly, their marks granting distinct insights. Together, perhaps they would see the full truth that had eluded nine previous cycles.

They reached the forest edge as twilight deepened toward something resem-bling night. Here, the bone-trees grew densely packed, their twisted forms creat-ing a barrier that seemed deliberately designed to repel intruders. Gaps between trunks narrowed to barely shoulder-width, forcing them to proceed single file.

"I'll lead," Asvarr said, raising his sword to illuminate the path. The golden light cast eerie shadows across the bone-white trees, making them appear to shift and reach with wooden fingers.

Brynja followed close behind, her curved blade readied. The forest closed around them like a cage, temperature dropping further with each step. Sound dampened unnaturally, their footsteps absorbed by the dense mist that clung to the gnarled roots.

"This place walks the boundary," Brynja murmured, her voice barely carrying despite their proximity. "Neither fully in Niflheim nor fully in the death-realm."

Asvarr nodded, feeling the truth of her words through the expanded Grím-mark. The bone-forest existed in multiple states simultaneously—a physical manifestation of the liminality that Yara Death-Walker supposedly embodied.

They pressed deeper into the twisted woodland, guided by the seed's pulsing warmth. With each step, Asvarr felt the forest's resistance increase—branches shifted to block their path, roots rose to trip unwary feet. Yet the obstacles parted when his sword's golden light touched them, recognizing the Root's authority if not welcoming its presence.

After what felt like hours, they reached a clearing unlike anything Asvarr had encountered in his travels. Perfect circular, the open space contained a pool of utterly black water that reflected nothing—not the twisted trees surrounding it, not the silver-gray sky above, not even Asvarr and Brynja as they approached its edge.

At the pool's center stood a figure that made the seed in Asvarr's chest flare with recognition.

She balanced on the water's surface as though it were solid ground, one foot placed precisely before the other. Half her body—the right side—appeared solid and human: pale skin, dark hair braided with small bones, eye the color of honey. The left side existed in a state of partial transparency, revealing glimpses of skeleton beneath translucent flesh, eye socket filled with silver light rather than a normal orb.

Around her neck hung a key-shaped mark that pulsed with gentle radiance—the Deathmark.

"Yara Death-Walker," Asvarr called, sheathing his sword to appear less threatening.

The woman paused in whatever ritual dance she performed, both eyes—one human, one silver light—fixing on him with unsettling directness.

"Warden of Five," she replied, voice containing dual tones that overlapped—one living, one echoing as if from great distance. "You bring the living to the death-road."

Brynja stepped forward, lowering her blade. "We come seeking the fifth Warden. The convergence approaches."

Yara tilted her head, the movement unnaturally fluid on her spectral left side. "Convergence requires five willing participants. I have not yet decided my willingness."

Asvarr felt the seed pulse with urgency. Time grew short—both for their mission and before the hunters arrived. He touched the expanded Grímmark, letting its light shine through his tunic.

"The pattern awakens," he said, drawing on knowledge granted by the seed. "Five anchors bound across five realms. The sixth awaits at the convergence point. Without all five Wardens, the pattern remains vulnerable."

"Patterns change," Yara countered, resuming her careful steps across the black pool. "Death teaches patience. Nine cycles have passed without resolution. Perhaps the tenth merely continues the wheel."

Frustration flickered through Asvarr. The woman spoke in riddles while danger approached. Yet the seed counseled caution—Death-Walker walked a different path from the other Wardens, perceived through different eyes.

"What do you seek, Yara?" he asked instead of arguing. "What purpose does the Deathmark serve in your understanding?"

The question seemed to surprise her. She completed another circuit of the pool before answering, each step sending ripples through the black water despite her apparent weightlessness.

"The Deathmark grants passage," she finally replied. "Between states of being, between realms of existence. I walk thresholds that others cannot cross." She gestured to her divided form. "Half in life, half in death. Neither wholly one nor wholly the other."

"And this serves what purpose?" Brynja pressed, impatience edging her voice.

Yara's dual-toned laugh echoed strangely in the clearing. "Purpose assumes destination. Death teaches that the journey itself holds meaning."

Asvarr exchanged a frustrated glance with Brynja. They needed Yara's cooperation, yet she seemed content to speak in philosophical abstractions while the Ashfather's hunters drew ever closer.

The seed warmed suddenly against his heart, offering insight. He took a step toward the black pool, careful not to touch its surface.

"The Deathmark lets you walk between realms," he said slowly, understanding forming. "You've been searching the death-roads for something. Something lost in previous cycles."

Yara went still, both eyes fixed on him with new intensity. "You see more clearly than expected, Flame-Bearer."

"What do you seek?" Asvarr repeated his earlier question, but with deeper meaning.

A shadow passed over Yara's divided face—grief perhaps, or something adjacent to it. "The First Wardens walked the original pattern before the Ashfather's corruption. Their essence scattered across realms when the Tree first shattered. I seek their fragments, hoping to understand what they understood."

"And have you found these fragments?" Brynja asked, her tone softening.

"Pieces only." Yara completed her circuit and finally stepped from the pool onto solid ground. Up close, her divided nature appeared even more pronounced—life and death coexisting in one form, neither canceling the other. "Enough to know the pattern was never meant to be what it became. The Tree grew from something older, something the Ashfather feared."

Asvarr felt the seed pulse in agreement. This aligned with knowledge gained through his bindings—hints of an original pattern corrupted through successive cycles.

"The convergence offers a chance to restore what was lost," he said. "Five Wardens together at the pattern's heart, undoing nine cycles of corruption."

"Or continuing them in different form," Yara countered. "How do you know your path doesn't simply replace the Ashfather's control with another?"

The question struck uncomfortably close to doubts Asvarr had harbored since binding the fifth anchor. The seed warmed against his chest, with the acknowledgment that the question itself held value.

"I don't know with certainty," he admitted. "Each binding changed me, showed me fragments of truth without revealing the whole. But I believe the third path—"

A piercing howl cut through the unnatural silence of the bone-forest, raising the hairs on Asvarr's neck. Brynja spun toward the sound, her curved blade raised defensively.

"Void-hounds," she hissed, the Jordmark flaring brighter on her forehead. "The hunters have found our trail."

Asvarr drew his sword, golden light blazing in the gathering darkness. "We're out of time for philosophy. The Ashfather's servants come for the fifth Warden. Will you stand with us or remain neutral while the pattern unravels?"

Yara studied him for a long moment, her divided face unreadable. Finally, she reached up to touch the key-shaped mark at her throat.

"Death teaches that all paths eventually converge," she said, the Deathmark pulsing under her fingers. "Perhaps this convergence warrants my participation."

Relief flooded through Asvarr, quickly tempered by the sound of another howl—closer now, joined by others. The hunters approached from multiple directions.

"We need to find Leif and Svala," Brynja said, scanning the dense trees surrounding the clearing. "Four Wardens might repel the hunters. Five would ensure victory."

"No time to search," Asvarr replied, reaching for the Horn of Binding secured at his belt. "We signal and make our stand here."

He raised the ancient horn to his lips and blew a single, powerful note that cut through the bone-forest's oppressive silence. The sound carried power gathered through five bindings, resonating with the expanded Grímmark across his chest. Trees trembled as the note passed through them, black mist swirling in agitated patterns.

The howling abruptly ceased, replaced by an ominous silence that pressed against Asvarr's ears like physical weight.

"They know our position now," Brynja muttered, moving to stand back-to-back with him. "Along with everyone else in three realms."

"Good." Asvarr leveled his sword toward the northern edge of the clearing, where shadows deepened unnaturally. "Let them come to us rather than hunting Leif and Svala separately."

Yara stepped beside them, drawing a bone-white knife from her belt. The weapon gleamed with inner light on its left side—the death-side—while remaining ordinary metal on its right.

"Void-walkers cannot be killed by conventional means," she warned, her dual-toned voice oddly calm. "They exist partially outside reality. The Deathmark allows me to touch their essence, but even I can only banish, not destroy."

"Banishment will suffice," Asvarr replied grimly, "if it buys us time to reach the convergence point."

The shadows at the clearing's edge solidified into lurching forms—humanoid figures with elongated limbs and faces obscured by swirling darkness. Behind them padded massive hounds with empty eye sockets and mist leaking from between jagged teeth. The void-walkers carried weapons that seemed to absorb light rather than reflect it—hooks and blades designed to capture rather than kill.

"The Ashfather wants us alive," Brynja observed, green-gold light intensifying around her curved blade. "Easier to corrupt Wardens than kill and start over."

One void-walker stepped forward, its featureless face turning toward Yara. When it spoke, its voice rasped like dead leaves scraping stone.

"Death-Walker," it grated. "Our master extends his invitation once more. Join his gathering rather than the Flame-Bearer's doomed convergence. Walk the void-paths freely, seeking your precious fragments without interference."

Yara's half-human lip curled in distaste. "Your master perverts the death-roads with his corruption. I walk my own path."

The void-walker's shoulders lifted in what might have been a shrug. "Then we take you to him regardless of preference. All five Wardens will kneel before their true master before the cycle completes."

It raised a hand, signaling the other hunters. The void-hounds tensed, mist pouring more thickly from their jaws as they prepared to spring.

Asvarr felt the seed pulse with sudden heat, flowing power through the pathways of his expanded Grímmark. The mark's light blazed through his clothing, responding to imminent threat. Beside him, Brynja's Jordmark and Yara's Deathmark similarly intensified, the three Wardens forming a triangle of radiance against the encroaching void.

The lead void-walker hesitated, darkness swirling more rapidly around its misshapen form. "The marks strengthen in proximity," it observed, voice betraying something like concern. "Take the Flame-Bearer first. The others will falter without his binding-knowledge."

The hounds leapt forward with unnatural speed, covering the clearing in a single bound. Asvarr's sword met the first, golden light slicing through mist-flesh and sending the creature sprawling. Brynja's curved blade caught another mid-leap, shearing through its shadowy form with green-gold energy that caused it to dissolve into scattered darkness.

Yara moved with uncanny grace, her half-spectral form allowing her to sidestep a third hound before plunging her bone knife into the back of its skull. The creature shrieked—a sound like iron scraping slate—and collapsed into swirling mist that dissipated across the black pool.

The remaining hounds circled more cautiously while the void-walkers spread out, cutting off escape routes back into the bone-forest. Asvarr recognized the tactic—they sought to separate the Wardens, neutralizing the apparent strength they gained from proximity.

"Stay together," he commanded, shifting to keep the other two Wardens in his peripheral vision. "Our marks reinforce each other."

The observation proved immediately relevant as a void-walker lunged at Brynja, shadow-hook extending to snare her sword arm. The Jordmark flared, and a barrier of green energy intercepted the attack—an ability Asvarr hadn't seen her demonstrate before. The void-walker recoiled, darkness roiling where the energy had touched it.

"The Earth-Healer learns quickly," it hissed to its companions. "Overwhelm them with numbers."

The remaining hunters attacked as one, void-hounds and walkers converging from all sides. Asvarr raised his sword, golden light forming a dome around the three Wardens as the expanded Grímmark channeled power through the five bindings he'd completed. The nearest void-walker struck the dome and recoiled, its shadow-substance smoking where it contacted the light.

"We can't maintain this defense indefinitely," Brynja warned, her Jordmark pulsing with effort as she contributed to the protective barrier. "And we still need to find Leif and Svala."

"I can open a death-road," Yara offered, the Deathmark glowing at her throat. "A passage between here and elsewhere. But I need time to create an anchor point."

Asvarr nodded grimly. "How much time?"

"Moments only, if you maintain this shield."

"Do it," he commanded, bracing himself as another void-walker tested their barrier. "Brynja and I will hold them off."

Yara knelt at the center of their protective triangle, bone knife drawn across her palm. Silver-white blood—normal on the right side, luminous on the left—dripped onto the ground as she began tracing complex symbols with practiced precision. The Deathmark pulsed in rhythm with her movements, each symbol flaring with pale fire when completed.

Outside their shield, the void-walkers conferred, then adopted a new strategy. Rather than striking directly, they pressed against the barrier from all sides, darkness flowing like water seeking cracks. The golden dome dimmed slightly under the sustained pressure, the void-essence siphoning energy from their defense.

"They're draining us," Brynja grunted, sweat beading on her forehead despite the biting cold. The Jordmark flickered, green light pulsing erratically as she poured more power into their shield.

Asvarr felt the seed burning in his chest, channeling strength through the expanded Grímmark to reinforce their failing barrier. Five bindings had granted him deeper reserves than the others, but even he had limits. Against the concentrated void-essence of six hunters and their hounds, those limits approached rapidly.

A patch of barrier directly before him dimmed dangerously as a void-walker pressed both misshapen hands against it, darkness flowing through its elongated fingers to corrupt the golden light. Asvarr focused on that section, directing power through his sword to shore up the weakening defense.

The effort cost him concentration elsewhere. On the opposite side, another void-walker found a vulnerable spot where Brynja's flagging strength created a weak point. Shadow-substance poured through the gap, forming a tendril that snaked toward Yara's unprotected back.

"Behind you!" Asvarr shouted, unable to intervene without abandoning his own position.

Yara didn't look up from her working, but the completed portion of her death-road symbols flared with sudden intensity. The encroaching shadow-tendril contacted the outer ring of symbols and recoiled as though burned, void-essence sizzling where it touched the pale fire.

"Death recognizes void," Yara commented without pausing her tracing. "Both exist beyond conventional reality, yet remain fundamentally opposed."

The observation sparked realization in Asvarr's mind. The void-walkers possessed unique strengths but corresponding vulnerabilities. Their shadow-substance threatened to overwhelm the Wardens' barrier, yet specific aspects of each mark affected them differently.

"Brynja," he called, "focus your earth-energy on the ground beneath them!"

The Earth-Healer understood immediately. The Jordmark blazed with renewed purpose as she shifted her defense to offense. Green-gold energy flowed from her forehead down her arms and into the earth beneath their feet. The clearing trembled, then heaved upward in precise locations, stone spikes erupting beneath each void-walker's position.

The hunters hissed in unison as solid matter disrupted their semi-corporeal forms, forcing them to abandon their coordinated press against the barrier. The void-hounds scattered, mist pouring more heavily from their jaws as they circled in agitation.

"The death-road opens," Yara announced, completing the final symbol. The entire pattern ignited with pale fire, forming a perfect circle around the three Wardens. "I've anchored it to the northern edge of Midgard—as close to your convergence point as my knowledge allows."

"What about Leif and Svala?" Brynja demanded, maintaining her earthen assault on the regrouping void-walkers.

"The Horn called them," Asvarr replied, though worry gnawed at him. The other two Wardens should have reached them by now, unless they'd encountered troubles of their own. "We can't wait longer. The convergence takes priority."

Yara's half-spectral hand gripped his forearm, her touch both warm and cold simultaneously. "Step into the circle when I complete the key-sign. Do not hesitate or the passage collapses."

Asvarr nodded, then tensed as a new sound cut through the bone-forest's unnatural silence—a high, keening wail that made the void-walkers freeze in apparent recognition.

Above the clearing, the twilight sky rippled with sudden disturbance. Colors shifted from silver-gray to deep crimson, then split along a jagged line that stretched from horizon to horizon. Through the widening gap poured brilliant golden light that struck the clearing with physical force, driving void-walkers and hounds alike to their knees.

"The sky cracks again," Yara whispered, awe in her dual-toned voice. "As it did during the Shattering."

The seed in Asvarr's chest burned with confirmation, knowledge flooding his consciousness. This was no attack but something else—reality itself responding to the gathering of Wardens, the pattern reacting to the approach of convergence.

Through the radiant tear in the sky, two figures descended—one gliding on currents of wind, the other floating on a self-generated cloud.

"Leif and Svala," Brynja breathed, relief evident in her voice.

The void-walkers shrieked in unified dismay, cowering from the golden light that poured through the breach. Their shadow-substance smoked where the radiance touched them, void-essence fundamentally opposed to the pattern's energy.

Leif landed first, the Skymark blazing on his shoulders as he wielded his twin metal rods against the nearest hunter. The weapons extended impossibly, silver light trailing their arc as they shattered the void-walker's form into dissipating mist.

Svala hovered above the clearing, her cloud-child shape more defined within the golden light streaming from the sky-crack. Silver eyes narrowed in concentration as she gestured toward the remaining void-hounds. Lightning erupted from her misty fingertips, striking each creature with unerring precision and reducing them to scattered shadow.

"The pattern protects its own," Leif called, voice carrying easily despite the chaos. The remaining void-walkers retreated toward the bone-forest's edge, their mission unraveling in the face of five Wardens' combined power.

Within her completed circle, Yara traced the final symbol—a key-shape that matched the Deathmark at her throat. Pale fire erupted from the completed pattern, forming a vertical doorway that shimmered with otherworldly light.

"Now!" she commanded. "The death-road opens!"

Asvarr hesitated, looking toward Leif and Svala still engaging the fleeing hunters. "We need all five—"

"They'll follow through the sky-crack," Yara interrupted, already stepping half through the shimmering doorway. "The pattern has provided its own path. Now move, or lose this one!"

Brynja didn't wait for further argument, plunging through the death-road after Yara. Asvarr cast one final glance at the sky-crack, where golden light continued to pour through the widening breach.

The seed pulsed with certainty, guiding his decision. Five Wardens would converge, whether through death-road or sky-crack. The destination mattered more than the path.

Sheathing his sword, Asvarr stepped through Yara's shimmering doorway into blinding whiteness.

***

Blinding whiteness gave way to forest green as Asvarr stumbled through Yara's death-road. The air changed from Niflheim's bone-numbing cold to Midgard's gentler chill, carrying scents of pine and loam. Beneath his boots, familiar soil replaced the bone-forest's petrified ground. He gasped, lungs filling with home-realm air that tasted of autumn leaves and wood smoke.

Brynja stood a few paces ahead, her curved blade still drawn as she scanned their surroundings. Beyond her, Yara knelt at the center of another symbol circle, her divided form even more pronounced in Midgard's natural light—right side solid, left side translucent with glimpses of bone visible beneath spectral flesh.

"We've reached the northern edge of what was once your clan's territory," Yara said, rising from her completed circle. The symbols had burned black into the forest floor, marking the death-road's exit point. "The convergence point lies half a day's journey south."

Asvarr turned slowly, recognition flowing through him as he absorbed the landscape. Ancient pines towered overhead, their upper branches swaying in a wind that barely reached the forest floor. Moss-covered stones formed natural boundaries between clearings. A stream gurgled somewhere nearby, its music achingly familiar.

"The hunting grounds," he murmured, memories surfacing of tracking deer through these woods with his father. "We're in the outer reaches of Hralvik's domain."

The seed in his chest pulsed with confirmation, warmth flowing through the pathways of his expanded Grímmark. They had come full circle—returning to where his journey began, where the first Root had fallen during the Shattering.

"And Leif and Svala?" Brynja asked, sheathing her blade once she'd confirmed they faced no immediate threats. "Will they find us here?"

Yara gestured upward. Through gaps in the pine canopy, the sky showed disturbing similarities to what they'd witnessed in Niflheim—crimson ripples spreading across blue, a fracture forming along the same path as the original Shattering.

"The sky-crack follows the pattern's awakening," she explained, dual-toned voice resonating strangely in Midgard's denser air. "The Five gather, and reality responds. They'll emerge where we need them most."

Asvarr nodded, trusting the Death-Walker's understanding of realm-passages. The seed's warmth spread confidence through him—five Wardens would converge, one way or another.

"We should move south," he decided, orienting himself by the sun's position. "The village ruins lie beyond that ridge. The exact point where the Root first fell."

They set off through the forest, Asvarr leading with easy familiarity despite the years that had passed since he last walked these paths. The woodland had changed since the Shattering—trees growing in strange patterns, clearings appearing where none had existed before, streams redirected by the Root's impact.

Yet beneath these alterations, the essential character of the land remained un-changed. This was still home.

As they traveled, Brynja moved closer to Asvarr, pitching her voice for his ears alone. "The Jordmark shows disturbances ahead. The earth remembers trauma here."

Asvarr nodded grimly. "The Root tore through everything when it fell. My entire village, everyone I knew..." He trailed off, old grief rising despite the changes the five bindings had wrought in him. "This was where it all began."

"And where it may end," Yara added, her divided form gliding soundlessly alongside them. "Cycles often complete where they start."

Something in her tone caught Asvarr's attention. "You've seen this before?"

"Fragments only," she replied, the Deathmark pulsing at her throat. "Death-roads show echoes of previous cycles. Nine times the pattern has almost restored itself. Nine times the Ashfather has corrupted the convergence."

Cold dread pooled in Asvarr's stomach. "And you believe this time will be different because...?"

"Because no previous cycle included a Warden who bound all five anchors before the convergence," Yara answered simply. "Because no previous gathering included one who walks the third path."

The seed warmed in Asvarr's chest, confirmation flowing through him. He had always sensed his journey differed from previous Wardens, though he hadn't un-derstood why until completing the fifth binding. The knowledge gained through each sacrifice had shown him fragments of a larger truth—the pattern had been corrupted long before the first Shattering, its original purpose twisted by the Ashfather's fear.

They crested a ridge, and Asvarr stopped abruptly. Before them spread a valley transformed beyond recognition. Where his village had once stood, a massive crater scarred the earth, its edges softened by years of rainfall and forest encroach-ment. At its center rose the unmistakable form of the first Root—a colossal trunk of twisted wood and bark that had once connected to Yggdrasil before the Shattering.

Unlike when Asvarr had last seen it, the Root now pulsed with golden light. Sap flowed visibly through external channels that traced rune-like patterns across its surface. The surrounding crater had filled partially with clear water, forming a shallow lake that reflected the Root's glow and the disturbed sky above.

"The first anchor responds to your return," Brynja observed, the Jordmark on her forehead pulsing in rhythm with the Root's illumination. "It recognizes its Warden."

Asvarr nodded, feeling the connection through his expanded Grímmark. Of the five anchors he'd bound, this first one had formed the deepest link—his introduction to the pattern, the first time he'd surrendered part of himself to the greater whole.

"All five anchors have awakened," Yara said, her spectral left eye tracking something beyond normal vision. "Across the realms, they pulse in harmony, preparing for convergence."

The seed in Asvarr's chest burned hotter, knowledge flowing through him with increasing urgency. "We need to reach the Root before—"

A thunderous crack split the air as the sky-fracture widened dramatically. The forest fell utterly silent in its aftermath, birds and insects stilled by primal fear. Through the widening breach poured golden light that cast everything in sharp relief, shadows stretching oddly across the crater's edge.

Within that light appeared two figures—Leif and Svala descending from the sky-crack toward the crater's edge where Asvarr and the others stood. The World-Walker and Storm-Speaker had survived the battle in Niflheim, finding their own path to the convergence point.

"The pattern provides," Yara murmured with something like reverence in her dual-toned voice.

Relief flooded through Asvarr as Leif landed lightly on the ridge, the Skymark blazing across his shoulders. Svala hovered nearby, her cloud-child form more substantial in Midgard's air than it had appeared in Niflheim.

"The void-walkers scattered when the sky opened," Leif reported, his silver-white hair gleaming in the golden light. "The pattern itself rejected them."

"The sky-paths show disturbance spreading across all realms," Svala added, silver eyes reflecting the Root's pulsing light. "The Ashfather marshals his remaining forces for one final assault."

Asvarr nodded grimly. "Then we complete the convergence before he arrives." He gestured toward the crater below. "The pattern's center awaits."

The five Wardens descended together toward the lake surrounding the Root. As they approached, Asvarr felt the seed's heat intensify, spreading power through the Grímmark's pathways. Around him, the other Wardens experienced similar reactions—Brynja's Jordmark blazed with green-gold light, Leif's Skymark sent silver sparks crackling across his shoulders, Svala's misty form condensed into more defined shape, and Yara's divided nature balanced into perfect symmetry between life and death.

Five marks, five Wardens, five sacrifices to restore what nine cycles of corruption had twisted.

They reached the lake's edge, clear water lapping gently at the shore. The Root rose from its center like a colossal pillar, golden sap flowing more rapidly as they approached. Asvarr felt his connection to all five anchors strengthen, knowledge crystallizing into certainty about what must happen next.

"We need to form the pattern," he said, the seed's guidance flowing through his words. "Five points surrounding the center where the sixth anchor will manifest."

Without hesitation, the Wardens spread out around the lake's circumference, positioning themselves at equidistant points with the Root at the center. Asvarr took the northernmost position, the expanded Grímmark blazing through his clothing. Brynja stood to the southeast, Leif to the southwest, Svala to the northeast, and Yara to the northwest—forming a perfect pentagram around the crater.

The moment they settled into position, the Root's golden light intensified. Streams of sap flowed down to touch the lake's surface, creating glowing patterns across the water that connected each Warden to the others. The sky-crack widened further, its edges now stretching from horizon to horizon.

"The convergence begins," Yara called, her voice carrying clearly despite the distance. "Each Warden must offer what they've gained through binding!"

Asvarr understood immediately. The five tokens gathered through his bindings pulsed against his chest—the Horn of Binding, the golden amulet, the remembrance-key, the frost crystal, and the crown of roots. Each represented a sacrifice made, a piece of himself surrendered to the pattern.

One by one, the tokens floated free, hovering before him in the golden light. The other Wardens watched with varying degrees of surprise as their own tokens manifested—items Asvarr had never seen before, gathered through their individual journeys.

"Cast them into the center," he commanded, following the seed's guidance. "Complete the pattern with what we've gained through sacrifice."

Asvarr cast his five tokens toward the Root, watching as they spun through the air before disappearing into the golden light surrounding the massive trunk. The other Wardens followed suit, their tokens joining his in the radiance at the crater's center.

The moment the final token vanished, the lake's surface began to roil. Golden light erupted from the water, forming a vertical column that connected the Root to the sky-crack above. The very air vibrated with power as reality reshaped itself around the convergence point.

Within that column of light, something formed—a structure both familiar and alien. Asvarr recognized elements of the five anchors he'd bound, merged and transformed into something new. A sapling took shape, its trunk formed of intertwined gold and silver, branches reaching toward the sky-crack, roots extending into the lake and beyond.

"The sixth anchor manifests," Yara called over the growing tumult, the Death-mark blazing at her throat. "The heart of the pattern itself!"

The sapling grew with impossible speed, rapidly approaching the size of the Root that had spawned it. Unlike the fallen fragment of Yggdrasil, this new growth emerged from the pattern's own essence—growing from within, a manifestation of the original purpose before corruption twisted it.

Asvarr felt the seed in his chest respond to the sapling's emergence, heat flowing through him with almost unbearable intensity. Knowledge poured into his consciousness—the full truth of the pattern, its original form before the Ashfather's fear corrupted it cycle after cycle.

He saw the Tree as a living web of possibilities. A boundless tapestry where all existences are intertwined. The original pattern had never been meant for control but for connection—endless growth and transformation rather than static order.

As this understanding crystallized, a fresh crack echoed across the sky—a new breach tearing open directly above the convergence point. Unlike the golden light of the pattern's awakening, this new rent leaked darkness that swirled with hungry purpose.

"He comes," Leif shouted, the Skymark flaring in warning. "The Ashfather breaches reality directly!"

From the dark tear descended a figure that made the seed burn with recognition. Tall and broad-shouldered, clad in shadow that moved like living cloth, crowned with twisted branches. His single golden eye fixed on the manifesting sapling with undisguised hunger. In one hand he carried a spear of darkness that drank light; in the other, a curved blade that leaked misty essence with each movement.

"Nine cycles I've waited," the Ashfather's voice boomed across the crater, shaking the water's surface with its force. "Nine times I've redirected the convergence. This time, the pattern falls completely."

Shadows extended from his form, reaching toward the golden column where the sixth anchor continued to manifest. Where darkness touched light, reality itself hissed and steamed like water on hot metal.

"The cycle completes," the Ashfather continued, descending until he hovered directly above the forming sapling. "Five Wardens, five sacrifices, five tokens—all necessary components to manifest the sixth anchor. I should thank you for doing the difficult work."

Cold realization struck Asvarr. The Ashfather hadn't tried to prevent the convergence—he'd manipulated events to ensure it happened under specific conditions. Every hunter sent, every corruption planted, every obstacle placed had guided the Wardens precisely where he wanted them.

The seed pulsed with confirmation, knowledge flowing through Asvarr with terrible clarity. In previous cycles, the Ashfather had corrupted the convergence after it began. This time, he sought to claim the sixth anchor at the moment of its birth—absorbing the pattern's heart directly into himself.

"Our sacrifices protect the pattern," Asvarr called out, drawing his transformed sword. Golden light blazed along the blade, matching the expanded Grímmark's radiance. "The third path stands against you!"

The Ashfather's laugh rumbled like distant thunder. "What is sacrifice against void? What is transformation against unmaking? The pattern belongs to whoever claims its heart!"

He plunged downward, spear aimed directly at the manifesting sapling. The other Wardens cried out in unison, their marks flaring with protective power. But distance separated them from the crater's center—too far to intervene physically before the Ashfather struck.

Asvarr acted on instinct driven by the seed's guidance. Raising his sword, he poured his will into the expanded Grímmark, connecting simultaneously to all five anchors he'd bound. Power flooded through him, golden light erupting from his chest and flowing outward toward the other Wardens.

"Five as one!" he shouted, the Grímmark sending streamers of light to connect with each of the other marks. "The pattern protects itself!"

The connections solidified into gleaming threads that linked all five Wardens, forming a pentagram of power around the crater. Where those lines crossed the water, they created a barrier of golden light directly above the manifesting sapling.

The Ashfather's spear struck this barrier with world-shaking force. Power coruscated outward from the impact point, reality itself groaning under the strain. The five Wardens staggered, feeling the blow through their connected marks. Yet the barrier held, the pattern's protection forcing the Ashfather back.

"Impossible," he snarled, shadows swirling more violently around his form. "No previous convergence created such resistance!"

"No previous convergence included five fully awakened Wardens," Yara called back, the Deathmark glowing like a small sun at her throat. "You face the pattern unleashed, not the pattern controlled!"

The Ashfather raised his dark blade, cutting a vertical slash through reality beside him. Through this new breach poured his remaining servants—void-walkers accompanied by twisted creatures Asvarr had never seen before, their forms constantly shifting between states of being.

"Then face destruction instead," the Ashfather commanded. "Tear them apart! Break their connection!"

The creatures streamed toward the Wardens, each targeting a different point of the pentagram. Asvarr raised his sword as three void-walkers rushed his position, their shadow-hooks extended to snare and drag.

"Hold the pattern!" he shouted to the others, golden light blazing from his blade as he met the first attacker. "The sapling nearly manifests!"

The void-walker dissolved into mist where Asvarr's sword struck it, but two more pressed forward, flanking him from opposite sides. He spun to face them, maintaining his position even as he defended himself. The expanded Grímmark burned with effort, channeling power both to his own defense and to maintain the protective barrier around the sapling.

Across the crater, the other Wardens faced similar assaults. Brynja had raised barriers of earth and stone, green-gold energy flowing from the Jordmark to repel void-creatures that scuttled on too many legs. Leif wielded his extending metal rods with blinding speed, silver light trailing their arcs as they shattered shadow-forms into dissipating mist. Svala hovered above the surface, lightning erupting from her fingertips to strike creatures that tried to drag her into the water. Yara stood perfectly still, the Deathmark projecting a field that turned attackers half-transparent before her bone knife banished them from reality entirely.

Despite their individual successes, Asvarr saw the strategy behind the Ashfather's assault. The endless waves of attackers would eventually exhaust them, weakening the pentagram's protective barrier at the crucial moment of the sapling's manifestation.

The seed burned with increasing urgency, knowledge crystallizing into action. He needed to change the pattern of battle—five Wardens fighting separately would eventually fall, but five Wardens acting as one might yet prevail.

Asvarr struck down another void-walker, then raised his sword high. "To me!" he called, his voice carrying power that made all other Wardens turn toward him. "Unite at the northern point!"

Without hesitation, they abandoned their positions, fighting their way through the swarms of attackers toward Asvarr's location. The pentagram's light flickered as they moved but didn't collapse—the connection established between their marks maintained the protective barrier despite their physical relocation.

One by one, they reached him—Brynja first, her curved blade slick with void-essence, then Leif and Svala together in a storm of silver light, and finally Yara, gliding through shadow-forms as though they were mere mist.

"Back to back," Asvarr commanded, the five Wardens forming a circle with shoulders touching. "The pattern flows through all of us now."

The moment they connected physically, their marks flared with blinding intensity. The Grímmark spread its influence to each of them, just as the Jordmark fed strength into the earth beneath their feet, the Skymark cleared the air above them, the Frostmark chilled approaching enemies, and the Deathmark thinned the barrier between life and death around their circle.

Five powers, united and amplified.

The Ashfather roared in frustration, abandoning his direct assault on the sapling to focus on the Wardens themselves. Shadows gathered around him into a spear of pure void-essence that he hurled directly at their circle.

Acting as one, the five Wardens raised their weapons. Five marks blazed with unified purpose, creating a dome of golden light that intercepted the shadow-spear. The impact sent ripples across reality itself, trees at the crater's edge swaying as though in high wind, water churning with sudden currents.

Yet they held, five sacrifices proving stronger than the Ashfather's rage.

Beneath the protective barrier, the sixth anchor completed its manifestation. The sapling had grown to full size, its silver-gold trunk now thick as ten men standing arm to arm, branches extending to touch the sky-crack overhead. Roots spread visibly through the clear water, anchoring deeply into the earth below and extending outward beyond the crater's edge.

"NO!" the Ashfather howled, hurling himself directly at the Wardens' circle. "The pattern is MINE!"

Before he could reach them, the fully manifested tree pulsed with blinding light. Reality shimmered around it as power flowed outward in a concentric wave. This wave passed through the Wardens harmlessly, their marks resonating with its energy. But when it reached the Ashfather, he screamed—a sound of primal agony that shook the very air.

The wave continued outward, dissolving void-walkers and shadow-creatures wherever it touched them. Trees bent before its advance, straightening in its wake as though recognizing a fundamental truth. The sky-crack itself rippled, edges healing inward, golden light fading as the breach mended itself.

At the crater's center, the Tree—for it had become something greater than a mere sapling—stood fully realized. The original pattern restored to its intended form. Branches extended in all directions, not just upward, creating a spherical canopy rather than a hierarchical structure. Roots similarly radiated outward rather than downward, connecting rather than supporting.

The Ashfather fell to the crater's edge, his shadow-cloak dissolving to reveal a more human form beneath—an old man with silver-streaked hair and beard, two eyes now restored where once he'd had only one. His weapons had vanished, along with most of his power.

"The convergence succeeds," Yara murmured, awe in her dual-toned voice. "The pattern awakens as it was meant to be."

The five Wardens' marks pulsed in harmony, resonating with the Tree's stabilizing energies. Asvarr felt the seed in his chest changing, knowledge pouring through him in a steady stream rather than urgent bursts. Understanding settled into certainty—they had succeeded where nine previous cycles had failed. The pattern had been restored to its original purpose.

Brynja pointed toward the crater's center, where the Tree continued to transform the landscape around it. "Look—the sixth anchor strengthens the other five!"

Asvarr followed her gesture, seeing streaks of golden light extending from the Tree in five distinct directions—toward the locations of the five anchors he'd bound across the realms. These connections hummed with power, no longer fragile threads but sturdy bonds that would resist corruption.

"The pattern protects itself now," Leif observed, the Skymark calming to a gentle glow on his shoulders. "Our role changes from wardens to witnesses."

"From defenders to gardeners," Svala agreed, her cloud-form settling into more stable shape. "Tending what grows rather than fighting what breaks."

Yara said nothing, her divided gaze fixed on the fallen Ashfather. Her expression combined pity and wariness—recognizing both the tragic figure he'd become and the danger he still represented.

Asvarr followed her gaze, the seed's knowledge confirming his suspicions. The Ashfather had been stripped of shadow-power but retained his essential nature. Given time and opportunity, he might again seek to control rather than connect.

"What becomes of him?" Brynja asked, her curved blade still drawn as she watched the former god struggle to his knees.

The Ashfather looked up, his face a mask of confusion and loss. "What have you done?" he whispered, voice now merely human rather than world-shaking. "The void still hungers beyond the pattern. Without control, all dissolves into chaos."

"The pattern was never meant for control," Asvarr replied, sheathing his sword as he approached the fallen figure. "Its purpose has always been connection—balance between order and chaos, structure and freedom."

"Balance fails," the Ashfather insisted, desperation edging his voice. "I've seen beyond the pattern, Flame-Bearer. The void consumes everything eventually."

"Perhaps," Asvarr acknowledged, feeling the seed's warm confirmation of his words. "But walls and chains protect nothing in the end. They only delay while stealing meaning from what they claim to preserve."

He knelt before the being who had orchestrated nine cycles of corruption, who had sent hunters and priests to capture or kill him, who had nearly undone everything the Wardens had sacrificed to achieve. Yet Asvarr felt no hatred—the five bindings had burned such emotions from him, leaving clarity in their place.

"Your place in the pattern remains," he told the Ashfather, seeing truth in the seed's knowledge. "Changed, as we all are changed. The sixth anchor requires tenders from all realms, even those who once sought to control it."

The Ashfather stared at him with naked disbelief. "You offer me a place after everything I've done?"

"The pattern offers completion rather than punishment," Asvarr corrected, rising to his feet. "Accept or reject, the choice remains yours. That's the fundamental truth you never understood—the pattern thrives on choice, not control."

He turned away, rejoining the other Wardens who stood watching the Tree's continuing transformation of the landscape. All around the crater, new growth erupted—hybrid forms that combined elements from multiple realms. The boundaries between worlds thinned as the pattern restored connections long severed.

"It begins," Yara said softly, the Deathmark at her throat pulsing with gentle light. "The renewal spreads outward from this point, touching all realms, all beings."

Asvarr nodded, feeling the changes through his expanded Grímmark. The seed's heat had settled into steady warmth, no longer urgent but reassuring. Five anchors bound, five sacrifices made, five Wardens united—all to restore the sixth anchor at the pattern's heart.

Looking toward the crater's center, where the Tree stood fully realized, Asvarr understood what his journey had always been leading toward. This was not the end, but a new beginning—the first step in a new cycle, untainted by the fear and control that had corrupted previous iterations.

Behind them, the Ashfather made his choice.

EPILOGUE

A raven dropped from the snowbound sky, its wings cutting through lazily falling flakes. The bird circled three times above a forest clearing before descending to perch on a gnarled branch. In its beak gleamed something that caught the weak winter sunlight—a carved rune stone no larger than a child's thumb.

When the raven released it, the stone fell through brittle air to land in a snowdrift. There it might have remained, buried beneath winter's steady accumulation, had a figure not been watching from the forest's edge.

Brynja Hrafndottir stepped into the clearing, her breath clouding before her face. The Jordmark on her forehead pulsed with muted green light, responding to the energy emanating from the fallen stone. She moved with fluid grace despite the knee-deep snow, leaving a trail of boot prints that filled almost immediately as fresh flakes swirled in her wake.

The raven observed her approach with a tilted head, its glossy feathers ruffling against the cold. When she stooped to retrieve the stone, the bird gave a throaty croak that echoed unnaturally in the winter stillness.

"Yes, I see it," she told the raven, turning the rune stone between gloved fingers. Its surface bore markings she recognized immediately—the same pattern now permanently etched into her forehead. "Another Warden rises. The cycle begins anew."

The raven bobbed its head once, then launched itself skyward, wings beating powerfully until it disappeared into the gray clouds overhead. Brynja watched it go, her expression unreadable save for the slight tightening at the corners of her eyes.

Four months had passed since the convergence. Four months since five Wardens united to manifest the sixth anchor and restore the pattern to its original purpose. Four months of healing and growth as the Tree expanded its influence across the realms, repairing damage wrought by nine cycles of corruption.

Brynja closed her fingers around the rune stone, feeling its primal energy pulse against her palm. The Jordmark responded with answering warmth, her connection to the earth anchor strengthening. Tendrils of green-gold light traced the veins in her wrist momentarily before fading beneath her skin.

She turned eastward, toward the distant mountains where a plume of smoke marked Asvarr's steading. The Flame-Bearer had chosen to rebuild near the convergence point, establishing a home within sight of the Tree that now dominated the valley. Their paths had diverged after the pattern's restoration, each Warden drawn to different tasks as the realms stabilized. But the marks they bore maintained their connection—five points tied to the central anchor, forever linked through sacrifice and purpose.

Tucking the rune stone into a pouch at her belt, Brynja began the trek toward Asvarr's dwelling. Snow crunched beneath her boots as the wind picked up, driving crystalline flakes horizontally through the trees. She pulled her furred cloak tighter, grateful for its warmth though the Jordmark protected her from the worst of winter's bite.

The forest thinned as she neared the valley's edge, giving way to an overlook that provided her first clear view of what had once been Hralvik. The village remained gone, its foundations buried beneath new growth that defied winter's hold. At the crater's center rose the Tree, its silver-gold trunk gleaming even through the snowfall. Unlike the trees surrounding it, this one retained its leaves despite the season—impossibly vibrant foliage in shades of amber and emerald that shimmered with internal light.

Below the overlook, smoke curled from the chimney of a newly built longhouse. Its construction showed careful craftsmanship, the wood harvested from fallen trees rather than living ones. A fence of stacked stones enclosed a small yard where chickens scratched at the snow, searching for feed scattered earlier.

Beyond the fence stretched cleared fields, now dormant under winter's blanket but marked with furrows that promised spring planting.

Brynja descended the slope toward the steading, noting the protective runes carved into fence posts and door frame. The expanded Grímmark had granted Asvarr knowledge beyond mere fighting skill—magic worked into wood and stone that would turn aside those with ill intent. She felt the gentle pressure of these wards as she approached, the Jordmark allowing her passage where others might find themselves mysteriously redirected.

Before she reached the gate, the longhouse door swung open. Asvarr stepped out, sword belt buckled over simple woolen clothes dyed deep blue. The Grímmark visible at his collar had settled into permanent patterns that spread beneath his garments—a living record of five bindings and the sacrifices they entailed.

"Earth-Healer," he greeted her, genuine pleasure warming his voice. "The marks whispered you were coming."

Brynja allowed herself a small smile. "Flame-Bearer. Your wards grow stronger." She gestured toward the fence posts. "Even Leif commented on their effectiveness when he visited last month."

"The World-Walker comes and goes as he pleases," Asvarr replied, opening the gate for her. "His paths between realms ignore conventional boundaries." He paused, studying her face. "Something's happened."

Brynja extracted the rune stone from her pouch, holding it up between them. "The ravens delivered this. Another Jordmark awakens somewhere in the northern forests."

Asvarr's expression grew serious as he took the stone, turning it in calloused fingers. The runes carved into its surface glowed faintly at his touch, responding to the powerful mark he carried.

"So soon," he murmured. "The pattern moves more quickly this cycle."

"The sixth anchor strengthens the others," Brynja reminded him. "New Wardens will emerge as the pattern expands."

They walked together toward the longhouse, boots leaving parallel tracks in the fresh snow. Within, a fire crackled in the central hearth, filling the single large room with warmth and the scent of burning pine. Simple furnishings lined the walls—a bed piled with furs, a table and bench crafted from split logs, shelves holding dried herbs and preserved foods. Against the far wall stood a rack displaying weapons both practical and ceremonial, crowned by the transformed sword Asvarr had carried through five bindings.

He hung his sword belt beside the door, then poured mead into two carved wooden cups. They sat on opposite sides of the hearth, the fire casting dancing shadows across their faces. For several minutes they drank in companionable silence, each lost in private thought.

"You'll go to them," Asvarr said finally. It wasn't a question.

Brynja nodded. "My path leads north. The Jordmark calls to its own."

"As each mark now calls to awakening bearers." Asvarr stared into the flames, firelight reflecting in his eyes. "Svala travels the storm-paths, seeking those who hear thunder in their dreams. Yara walks the death-roads, gathering those balanced between states."

"And Leif?"

"Moves between all realms, finding those who see doorways where others see walls." Asvarr took a long drink of mead. "The Ashfather's choice created consequences none of us predicted."

The mention of their former enemy sent a ripple of tension through Brynja's shoulders. That final moment at the convergence—when the fallen god had reached toward the restored pattern with trembling hands—remained vivid in her memory. His choice to surrender rather than continue fighting had surprised them all, particularly when the Tree had accepted his essence, integrating rather than destroying the being who had corrupted nine previous cycles.

"His knowledge flows through the pattern now," she said, voicing the thought that had troubled all five Wardens in the months since the convergence. "For good or ill, the Tree holds his memory alongside our sacrifices."

"Balance requires all voices." Asvarr touched his chest where the seed had once burned with urgent purpose, now a permanent part of his expanded mark. "Even those that once sought control rather than connection."

Brynja set down her empty cup, considering her next words carefully. "There are rumors in the northern settlements. Whispers of shadow-walkers moving between twilight and darkness. Some believe the Ashfather rebuilds his forces despite his choice at the convergence."

"Not the Ashfather," Asvarr corrected. "What remains of his essence merged with the pattern, becoming part of the sixth anchor. But void-born creatures still prowl the boundaries between realms. The pattern restores balance, not perfect harmony."

A log shifted in the hearth, sending sparks spiraling upward. Outside, the wind rose to a mournful howl, driving snow against the longhouse walls. Brynja studied Asvarr's face in the flickering light, noting the subtle changes wrought by four months of peace. The constant tension that had marked him during their quest had eased, replaced by a quieter strength. He had built this steading with his own hands, turning from Warden to farmer without apparent regret.

Yet the expanded Grímmark showed clearly at his collar, a reminder that some transformations could never be undone. Five sacrifices had permanently altered him, just as her single binding had changed her. They remained Wardens despite the pattern's restoration, tied to the anchors they had bound through blood and oath.

"The new bearer will need guidance," she said, returning to their original subject. "The Jordmark grants power but offers little understanding of its purpose."

Asvarr nodded. "Take them to the earth anchor first. Let them bind through sacrifice as we did, but with the pattern already restored, perhaps the cost will prove less severe."

"Perhaps." Brynja didn't sound convinced. "Power always demands payment, whether through sacrifice or surrender."

"True enough." Asvarr rose, moving to a small chest beside his bed. From it he withdrew a leather pouch, then returned to the hearth. "When you find them, give them this."

He emptied the pouch into his palm, revealing a small disk of polished amber shot through with gold. Brynja recognized it immediately as his token from binding the earth anchor—the second of five he had gathered during his journey.

"You should keep it," she protested. "The five tokens—"

"Served their purpose at the convergence," he finished. "Now this one will serve a new bearer as they come to understand their mark." He pressed the disk into her hand, closing her fingers around its smooth surface. "The pattern provides what each Warden needs, when they need it most."

Their fingers touched briefly, the Jordmark and Grímmark pulsing in resonance. Through that connection, Brynja glimpsed fragments of Asvarr's thoughts—concern for the new Wardens who would emerge without the desperate circumstances that had driven their own awakening, hope that the restored pattern would guide them toward purpose rather than mere power, determination to maintain what they had sacrificed so much to achieve.

She tucked the amber disk into her pouch alongside the rune stone. "I'll leave at first light. The northern forests grow dangerous in deep winter."

"Stay the night, then," Asvarr offered, gesturing toward the spare furs piled near the wall. "Share a meal before your journey."

Brynja accepted with a nod, setting aside her cloak and boots. As Asvarr prepared a simple dinner of smoked venison and winter vegetables, she found herself studying the longhouse with greater attention. Despite its rough-hewn construction, the dwelling held unmistakable signs of permanence—stores gathered for the long winter, tools hung with care, small comforts accumulated over months rather than days.

After binding the fifth anchor, she had wondered if Asvarr could ever return to anything resembling normal life. The expanded Grímmark had changed him profoundly, granting knowledge and power beyond what the other Wardens possessed. Yet here he was, building a steading and planting fields even as he maintained his connection to the pattern.

They ate in comfortable silence broken occasionally by practical conversation—reports of conditions in distant settlements, observations about the pattern's expansion, news carried by travelers from other realms. When the meal ended, Asvarr banked the fire while Brynja arranged her borrowed furs near the hearth's warmth.

As darkness settled over the longhouse, snow continued to fall outside, coating the world in crystalline white. Brynja lay awake, watching shadows dance across the ceiling beams. The Jordmark pulsed gently at her forehead, resonating with the earth beneath the longhouse. Through it, she sensed the distant presence of the Tree, its roots spreading outward from the convergence point to touch all corners of the realm.

"You feel it too," Asvarr's voice came softly from the darkness. "The pattern stirring."

"Something changes," she agreed, turning toward the sound of his voice. "More than just new Wardens awakening."

"The sixth anchor strengthens, drawing all five aspects into greater harmony." The furs on his bed rustled as he shifted position. "But harmony invites counterpoint. Where pattern expands, void presses against its boundaries."

"The Ashfather warned of this," Brynja recalled. "His fear of what lies beyond the pattern drove him to control rather than connect."

"Fear has power," Asvarr acknowledged. "Yet connection proves stronger than walls in the end. The restored pattern grows through relationship, not confinement."

His words carried the weight of knowledge gained through five bindings—wisdom beyond his years, purchased through sacrifice. Brynja found herself wondering, not for the first time, how much of the original berserker remained beneath the Warden's mantle. How much of herself had changed after just one binding?

"Rest, Earth-Healer," Asvarr's voice gentled. "Your journey begins early."

Brynja closed her eyes, allowing the Jordmark's steady pulse to lull her toward sleep. Yet even as consciousness faded, she felt the rune stone in her pouch vibrate with urgent energy. Somewhere in the northern forests, a new bearer struggled to understand the mark suddenly emblazoned on their forehead. Their awakening heralded the beginning of a new cycle—one shaped by restoration rather than corruption, by connection rather than control.

Her last waking thought was of the raven that had delivered the stone, its knowing eyes and purposeful flight. Ravens had once served the Ashfather as messengers and spies. Now they carried rune stones to those who guarded the pattern, maintaining balance between order and chaos, structure and freedom.

As sleep claimed her, Brynja smiled into the darkness. Her war had only just begun.

***

The girl found the leaf during the first spring thaw, when patches of bare earth emerged from winter's blanket like islands in a white sea. It lay half-buried in mud at the forest's edge, glowing faintly with inner light that caught her eye as she gathered kindling for the evening fire. When she picked it up, the leaf felt warm against her palm despite having lain in snow for unknowable time.

Unlike the brittle brown remains of autumn, this leaf retained vibrant color—gold veined with silver, edges impossibly crisp. Stranger still were the markings etched across its surface—runes unlike any the girl had seen in her twelve winters. They shifted as she tilted the leaf toward the afternoon sun, rearranging themselves into patterns that tugged at her memory.

Kari tucked the curious find into her belt pouch, completing her chore with greater haste than usual. By the time she returned to the settlement, her mind buzzed with questions that demanded answers. Only Grandmother Helga might know what to make of such a discovery.

The settlement of Stjernehavn sprawled across three hills overlooking a deep fjord. Smoke rose from cone-shaped houses built half into the earth for protection against winter storms. People moved with renewed energy as spring approached—mending nets, preparing fields, repairing boats that would soon return to sea. Kari wove between them, acknowledging greetings with distracted nods, her thoughts fixed on the leaf that seemed to pulse against her hip.

She found Grandmother Helga outside her dwelling at the settlement's edge, grinding herbs with practiced motions of mortar and pestle. Age had bent the old woman's spine and whitened her hair, but her eyes remained sharp as winter stars, missing nothing that passed before them.

"You've found something," Helga observed before Kari could speak. The pestle stilled in her gnarled hand. "Something that troubles your spirit."

Kari approached, carefully withdrawing the leaf from her pouch. "In the forest, beneath the melting snow. It glows, Grandmother."

Helga set aside her work, wiping green-stained fingers on her apron before accepting the offering. The moment the leaf touched her palm, she went utterly still, breath catching in her throat. Her eyes widened, darting from the leaf to Kari's face and back again with unusual urgency.

"Inside," she commanded, rising with surprising swiftness for one so bent with age. "Quickly, child."

Kari followed her grandmother into the dim interior of the earth-house. The single room smelled of herbs and smoke, walls lined with shelves holding Helga's treasures—stones with natural holes, bundles of dried plants, carved figures of forgotten gods. A fire burned low in the central hearth, casting dancing shadows across packed-earth floor and timber roof beams.

Helga closed the door firmly, then moved to a wooden chest in the darkest corner. From it she withdrew a bundle wrapped in faded red cloth, handling it with reverence typically reserved for sacred objects. When she unwrapped it, Kari gasped at the sight of a book bound in strange leather, its cover inscribed with runes similar to those on the leaf.

"My mother gave me this," Helga explained, setting the book beside the leaf on her small table. "And her mother before her, stretching back nine generations to when the sky first broke and mended itself."

Kari stared at the book with renewed interest. Few in Stjernehavn could read, and fewer still owned books. That her grandmother had kept such a treasure secret all these years spoke to its importance.

"Open it," Helga urged, pushing the book toward Kari. "If the leaf called to you, the pages may speak as well."

With trembling fingers, Kari lifted the cover. The first page bore a single rune that seemed to shimmer in the firelight. Turning it revealed more pages filled with careful script interspersed with drawings—a massive tree with roots spreading through nine circles, a crown formed of twisted branches, five figures standing in a pattern around a central light.

"I can't read this," she admitted, trailing fingers across unfamiliar symbols.

"You will," Helga said with surprising certainty. She placed the leaf between two blank pages near the book's end. "The marks will teach you, as they taught me when my time came."

Kari looked up sharply. "My time for what?"

Instead of answering directly, Helga pushed aside the neck of her woolen kirtle to reveal a mark on her collarbone—a rune etched into her skin as though carved there, faded with age but still clearly visible. It matched one of the symbols Kari had seen on the leaf.

"Nine cycles ago, the sky broke and roots fell through the breach," Helga said, her voice taking on the rhythm of practiced storytelling. "Five Wardens bound five anchors across five realms, manifesting the sixth at the pattern's heart. Their sacrifices restored what nine previous cycles had corrupted."

She touched the mark on her collarbone. "When I was scarcely older than you, a raven brought me a stone marked with this symbol. The mark transferred to my flesh when I held it, burning like ice and fire together. I became a Warden of the pattern's edge—one of many who maintain the balance between connection and isolation."

Kari stared at her grandmother with dawning comprehension. The tales Helga told—of the Tree that connected worlds, of the Ashfather who sought control, of five heroes who restored the pattern—had always seemed like myths meant to explain winter's bite or summer's bounty. Now she understood them as history, preserved through generations by those who bore marks like the one on Helga's skin.

"And now..." Kari's gaze dropped to the leaf preserved between blank pages. "You think I..."

"The leaf found you," Helga confirmed. "The pattern chooses its own, in ways we cannot predict. The marks will come in their time, whether tomorrow or years hence. The book will prepare you for that day."

A knock interrupted them—three sharp raps against the wooden door. Helga frowned, clearly unaccustomed to visitors seeking her out. She closed the book swiftly, rewrapping it in red cloth before handing it to Kari.

"Hide this beneath your bed furs," she instructed. "Speak of it to no one until I tell you otherwise."

While Kari secreted the book beneath her cloak, Helga moved to answer the door. Outside stood a tall stranger wrapped in a travel-stained cloak, face shadowed by a deep hood. Snow melted from boots that had clearly walked far across difficult terrain.

"I seek Helga Olafsdottir," the stranger said, voice identified as female despite its low register.

"You've found her," Helga replied, stance wary but not fearful. "What business brings you to my door?"

The stranger pushed back her hood, revealing a striking face framed by dark hair braided with metal beads. Most remarkable was the mark on her forehead—a green-gold rune that pulsed with internal light, reminiscent of the leaf's glow.

"I am Brynja Hrafndottir," she said, touching the mark with unconscious familiarity. "Earth-Healer and bearer of the Jordmark. The pattern guided me to Stjernehavn with purpose that becomes clearer now." Her gaze moved past Helga to fix on Kari, who clutched the concealed book tightly against her chest.

"The child," Brynja observed. "She's found something."

Helga stepped protectively into the doorway. "My granddaughter discovered a leaf from the Tree. Nothing more."

"Nothing more?" Brynja's mouth quirked. "A leaf from the sixth anchor travels hundreds of leagues to reach a specific hand, and you call it nothing?" She reached into a pouch at her belt, withdrawing a small object that captured the fading daylight. "Perhaps this too means nothing?"

In her palm lay a disk of polished amber shot through with gold. Runes similar to those on the leaf encircled its edge, pulsing in rhythm with the mark on Brynja's forehead.

Helga's stern expression softened slightly. "You bring a binding token. The first Warden sent you."

"Asvarr Flame-Bearer believes new Wardens require guidance," Brynja confirmed. "The pattern expands, and with it, the need for those who understand sacrifice's purpose. He sends tokens to ease the binding process for those newly marked."

Kari stepped forward, curiosity overcoming caution. "You know the Flame-Bearer? From Grandmother's stories?"

Brynja's gaze shifted to Kari, expression warming. "I stood beside him at the convergence when five Wardens united to manifest the sixth anchor. He bound all five points of the pattern while the rest of us managed only one. His mark spread further with each binding, changing him in ways we're still learning to understand."

Helga studied the Earth-Healer with renewed interest. "You've traveled far, Brynja Hrafndottir. Come inside and share our fire. The evening brings cold winds, and we have much to discuss before morning."

Brynja ducked through the low doorway into the earth-house, removing her cloak to reveal leather armor worn smooth by travel and weather. The Jordmark on her forehead pulsed in the firelight, casting green-gold reflections across packed-earth walls.

While Helga busied herself preparing a simple meal, Kari remained transfixed by their visitor. The Earth-Healer moved with fluid grace that belied her road-weariness, every gesture deliberate as she arranged her belongings against the wall and seated herself by the fire.

"You have questions," Brynja said to Kari, gesturing for the girl to join her near the hearth. "Ask them while your grandmother works. Plain speaking saves time we may lack later."

Kari sat cross-legged opposite the Earth-Healer, the book hidden beneath her cloak momentarily forgotten. "Are all the stories true? The breaking of the sky? The Ashfather? The five sacrifices?"

"True, yes, though incomplete as all stories become in retelling." Brynja stretched her hands toward the fire, revealing calluses and small scars that spoke of battles fought. "Nine cycles of breaking and binding preceded ours. Nine times the pattern nearly restored itself, only to fall to corruption. The tenth succeeded because Asvarr walked the third path—transformation rather than control or surrender."

"And now new marks appear," Kari said, understanding dawning. "New Wardens to maintain what you restored."

Brynja nodded. "The pattern expands, creating need for those who understand its purpose. Some will bear marks like mine—" she touched the Jordmark, "—or like Asvarr's, binding new anchors as they form. Others will carry smaller marks, maintaining balance at the pattern's edges."

"Like Grandmother's," Kari whispered, glancing toward Helga's bent form as she stirred something in a cooking pot.

"Your grandmother served well in her time," Brynja confirmed. "Now age claims her strength, and the pattern seeks new vessels."

Kari's hand moved unconsciously to her belt pouch where the leaf had rested. "You think it chose me."

"I know it did," Brynja said with quiet certainty. "The question remains which mark you'll bear, and what sacrifice it will demand."

Helga returned with wooden bowls filled with fragrant stew. "Enough talk of sacrifice," she scolded, handing one to Brynja. "Let the child eat before you burden her with choices beyond her years."

Brynja accepted the food with a respectful nod. "Age brings wisdom, Elder. I defer to yours in this."

They ate in companionable silence, allowing the hearth-fire's warmth to ease travel-weariness and winter's lingering chill. Outside, darkness claimed Stjernehavn, stars emerging one by one across the clear sky. When the meal ended, Helga took the empty bowls to her washing basin, leaving Kari and Brynja by the fire.

"I leave for the earth anchor at dawn," Brynja said quietly. "Those who hear its call should join me."

Before Kari could respond, a sound cut through the night—a distant horn blast that echoed across the hills with unnatural clarity. Brynja rose in fluid motion, hand moving to the curved blade at her hip.

"What was that?" Kari asked, heart suddenly pounding.

"The Horn of Binding," Brynja replied, expression grave. "Asvarr sounds the warning."

Helga appeared from the shadowed corner, face drawn with concern. "What comes?"

"I can't be certain from so far," Brynja said, gathering her cloak and pack with swift efficiency. "But the horn calls all Wardens to readiness. The pattern faces threat."

She turned to Kari, extending her hand. The amber disk lay on her palm, runes pulsing with increasing urgency. "Your choice comes sooner than expected, child. The mark or the waiting—you must decide now."

Helga stepped between them, protective instinct overriding respect for the Earth-Healer. "She's too young for binding. The mark would consume her."

"Age matters less than purpose," Brynja countered, though her tone held no challenge. "The pattern chooses those ready to serve, regardless of years lived. The amber token eases the binding's cost—a gift from one who bore all five marks."

Another horn blast sounded, closer now, carried on wind that suddenly rose to rattle the door in its frame. Kari felt something shift inside her chest, as though a dormant part of her spirit had awakened at the sound. The book beneath her cloak seemed to warm against her side, reminding her of its presence.

"I'll decide for myself," she said, standing straighter despite the fear coursing through her veins. She withdrew the book, holding it before her like a shield. "Grandmother prepared me for this day, whether she knew it or not."

Brynja's expression registered surprise, followed by dawning understanding as she recognized the book. "A Warden's Chronicle. Few remain since the convergence."

"Nine generations preserved," Helga said, resignation replacing protest. "Waiting for one who could read its marks."

Kari opened the book to where she had placed the leaf. To her astonishment, the blank pages now bore markings—runes flowing across the paper in patterns that somehow, impossibly, she could understand. The knowledge flowed into her mind like spring meltwater into thirsty soil.

"The Tree sings," she whispered, fingers tracing symbols that glowed beneath her touch. "It calls those willing to hear."

Brynja stepped forward, offering the amber disk once more. "Then hear it, Kari of Stjernehavn, and choose your path."

The third horn blast shook the earth-house to its foundations, dust sifting from roof beams as though the world itself trembled. Kari looked from the disk to her grandmother's weathered face, reading acceptance there despite the fear that clouded her eyes.

"I choose to serve," Kari said, setting aside the book to reach for the amber token. "As your blood served before me."

The moment her fingers touched the disk, warmth spread up her arm and across her chest. The runes etched around its edge flared with golden light, lifting from the surface to hover in the air between them. One by one, they aligned into a single, complex pattern that moved with deliberate purpose toward Kari's sternum.

When the rune touched her flesh, fire and ice pulsed through her veins in alternating waves. The earth-house spun around her as knowledge poured into her consciousness—memories not her own, sacrifices made by those who walked the same path, obligations carried by all who bore the mark.

Through the haze of transformation, she heard Brynja speaking urgent words: "The Grímmark chooses her. Asvarr must be told immediately."

Helga's voice answered from what seemed a great distance: "The Flame-Bearer's mark? It will consume her entire!"

"No," Brynja countered. "The third path changes all. What once destroyed now transforms. She walks the Warden's path, but with connection rather than control as guide."

Kari felt the mark spreading across her chest, branches of golden light flowing beneath her skin as it took root in her flesh. Unlike her grandmother's small rune, this mark grew more extensive with each heartbeat, forming patterns that matched illustrations she had seen in the book. The sensation burned fierce yet cleansing, like fever that breaks disease's hold.

When her vision cleared, she found herself kneeling on the packed-earth floor, supported by Brynja's strong hands. The Earth-Healer's face showed a mixture of awe and concern as she studied the mark now visible through Kari's thin woolen shirt.

"The Grímmark grows differently in her," Brynja murmured. "More controlled than Asvarr's was, yet still expansive."

Kari looked down, seeing golden light pulse beneath her clothing in rhythm with her heartbeat. Knowledge settled into her mind like sediment after a storm—clear understanding where confusion had reigned moments before.

"I hear it," she whispered, voice changed by what she had become. "The Tree sings through all nine realms, connecting rather than controlling."

She rose unsteadily to her feet, new strength flowing through limbs that should have been weakened by the mark's claiming. The earth-house seemed smaller now, constrained by walls that separated her from the pattern she could sense pulsing beyond them.

"We must go," she said, certainty driving hesitation from her voice. "The Horn of Binding calls all Wardens to the convergence point. Something stirs in the void beyond the pattern."

Brynja nodded, gathering her remaining belongings with swift efficiency. "The earth anchor lies three days' journey south. From there, we can reach the convergence in another seven, if we travel without rest."

"Too slow," Kari said, the Grímmark pulsing as new knowledge flowed through it. "The Tree provides faster paths for those who bear its mark."

She moved to the earth-house door, pushing it open to reveal night fallen completely over Stjernehavn. Stars glittered overhead in patterns she now recognized as more than mere lights—connections between realms, pathways for those who understood their purpose.

Helga joined them at the doorway, face lined with worry yet proud as she studied her granddaughter. "You leave, then? For how long?"

Kari touched the older woman's cheek with gentle fingers. "Until the threat passes. Then I'll return to teach what I've learned, as you taught those who came before me."

"Take the book," Helga urged, pressing the leather-bound volume into Kari's hands. "Add your chapter to those who came before."

With the chronicle secured in her pack, Kari stepped into the night air. Above, the stars shifted subtly, one pattern brightening to form a path visible only to those who bore the mark. Brynja saw it too, the Jordmark on her forehead pulsing in response.

"The sky-path opens," the Earth-Healer said with quiet awe. "It recognizes you already."

Kari nodded, feeling the Grímmark warm as it connected her to something vast beyond imagining. The anchor points spread across nine realms pulsed in her awareness like heartbeats, the sixth and strongest calling with special urgency from where the convergence had occurred.

The Horn of Binding sounded a fourth time, its call now clear in purpose—five Wardens summoning their successors to council. The new age required new guardians, those who understood connection rather than control. Those willing to sacrifice without being consumed.

Kari turned to Brynja, newfound purpose steadying her voice. "Teach me as we travel. The Grímmark holds knowledge, but I need guidance to use it properly."

The Earth-Healer smiled, a gesture that softened her weather-worn features. "As Asvarr once guided me, I will guide you. The pattern provides what each Warden needs, when they need it most."

Together they stepped onto the path only they could see, the Jordmark and Grímmark pulsing in harmony as they began their journey toward the convergence. Behind them, Helga watched from the doorway of her earth-house, witness to the beginning of a new chapter in the endless cycle of breaking and binding.

Above them, in the star-strewn sky, a raven circled once before winging toward the distant horizon, where a tree unlike any other spread its branches through nine realms, singing a song only the marked could hear.

CLAIM YOUR REWARD

Unlock Exclusive Worlds – Free Prequel + Beta Reader Access!

The adventure doesn't end here. Sign up for Joshua J. White's newsletter to receive a free prequel novella and get early access to upcoming books as a potential beta reader. Dive in now:

www.JoshuaJWhiteBooks.com/TheSkyrendProphecy

ABOUT THE AUTHOR

Joshua J. White resides in Russellville, Arkansas with his wife and four children. He founded Berserker Books as a vessel for stories that transport readers beyond everyday experience, with *The Skyrend Prophecy* marking his debut series.

His writing emerges from a deep appreciation for world-building and mythology, particularly the rich traditions found in Norse culture. Joshua crafts fictional realms where imagination flourishes, unbound by conventional limitations.

The natural landscapes of Arkansas provide both sanctuary and inspiration, where Joshua often explores with his family. These wilderness excursions nurture his creative vision while reinforcing his dream of establishing a homestead where his family can live in closer harmony with the land.

Joshua started Berserker Books with two dreams in mind: to build fantastical worlds on paper and, eventually, to build a homestead where his family can live more harmoniously with the land. Both dreams spring from the same source—a belief that we are meant for more than the constraints of modern existence.

The Skyrend Prophecy represents the first chapter in what Joshua envisions as a meaningful literary journey shared with readers who sense that our human story contains volumes yet to be written—stories penned in bold imagination of undiscovered possibilities.

For readers who have walked through Joshua's pages and felt something stir, he invites them to join him in continuing the story. Readers can receive exclusive prequels, early looks at new books, and opportunities to step deeper into these worlds by signing up here:

www.JoshuaJWhiteBooks.com/TheSkyrendProphecy

BOOKS BY JOSHUA J. WHITE

The Skyrend Prophecy Series

1. Branches of the Broken World (Book 1)

2. The Verdant Gate (Book 2)

3. Children of the Serpent Sky(Book 3)

4. Forge of Storms (Book 4)

5. Harmony's Twilight (Book 5)

Other Series by Joshua J. White:

- Stay tuned for upcoming epic fantasy series set in worlds beyond the Skyrend.

49830080R00312